FOX

ON THE

RHINE

FOX
ON THE
RHINE

DOUGLAS NILES

and

MICHAEL DOBSON

A TOM DOHERTY ASSOCIATES BOOK

NEW YORK

This is a novel of alternate history, in which a historical event is changed, as are the consequences of that event along with it. Historical characters are portrayed in a fictional way; all their actions, words, thoughts, and behavior on or after 12:42 P.M. Berlin time (11:42 A.M. Greenwich mean time) on July 20, 1944, are solely the authors' invention. Furthermore, invented characters in this book are fictitious. Any resemblance to actual persons, living or dead, is purely coincidental. Details of the actual historical event and other background material can be found in the appendixes to this book.

FOX ON THE RHINE

This book is printed on acid-free paper.

A Forge Book
Published by Tom Doherty Associates, LLC
175 Fifth Avenue
New York, NY 10010

www.tor.com

Forge® is a registered trademark of Tom Doherty
Associates, LLC.

Library of Congress Cataloging-in-Publication Data

Niles, Douglas.
    Fox on the Rhine / Douglas Niles & Michael Dobson.—1st ed.
      p. cm.
    "A Tom Doherty Associates book."
    ISBN 0-312-86894-4 (acid-free paper)
    1. World War, 1939–1945—Fiction.   I. Dobson, Michael Singer.
II. Title.
PS3564.I375 F69 2000
813'.54—dc21   00-027675

First edition: June 2000

Printed in the United States of America

0 9 8 7 6 5 4 3 2 1

This book is respectfully dedicated to our fathers,
Donald Niles, Sr., and Odell F. Dobson

CONTENTS

Lieb Vaterland, magst ruhig sein,
Fest steht und treu die Wacht am Rhein!*

—*Die Wacht am Rhein,* 1840
(a patriotic song)

*"Dear fatherland, may you be steady,
stand firm and true and guard the Rhine!"*

PROLOGUE

July 17, 1944

**Livarot–Vimoutiers Road, Normandy, France,
17 July 1944, 1817 hours Greenwich Mean Time (GMT)**

Every day, Field Marshall Erwin Rommel toured the front. The inspections seemed increasingly futile, but remained his duty nonetheless. His duty to the men of his command now overshadowed his duty to those above him, those who had betrayed his men, ignored his plans, hesitated at crucial moments, divided scarce resources, issued ludicrous orders, and enabled the Allies to secure a beachhead on the bloody shores of Normandy. Once he had thought the obstructions came from petty people in the shadow of the führer, but now he knew they came from the führer himself. The Desert Fox knew he could have stopped the Allied invasion, turned the American and British armies back, or at the very least delayed them, but his hands had been tied. And now the Allies were here to stay.

The campaign was futile, but still the battle raged on. Rommel's army fought tenaciously, because of the oath he had taken, the oath his men had taken, the oath to which they all subscribed. He knew the war must be ended, and ended now—he'd even spoken quietly to other officers about how it would be better to live as a British dominion than see Germany ruined. But as long as Adolf Hitler lived, the Fatherland faced a future of inevitable destruction.

The field marshal had exchanged brusque words with Hitler only days before. Rommel had been outraged by the massacre at Oradour-sur-Glade, in which the SS division Das Reich had killed more than six hundred men, women, and children in reprisal for the killing of a German officer in Oradour. But the SS had picked the wrong Oradour—there were two of them. "Such things bring disgrace on the German uniform," he told the führer. "How can you wonder at the strength of the French Resistance when the SS drive every decent Frenchman into joining it?"

Field Marshal von Runstedt, the supreme commander, had appeared shocked at the outburst, though Rommel suspected that Runstedt, like so many of the old aristocracy, was secretly in sympathy with him. Both field marshals had been giving subtle hints about making overtures to the western Allies, but Hitler would have none of it.

"That has nothing to do with you. It is outside your area. Your business is to resist the invasion."

Now the field marshal shook his head in disgust, and to clear the thoughts from it. "What is the matter, Herr Feldmarschall?" asked Captain Lang, riding in the backseat of the staff car.

"Nothing, nothing," the Desert Fox replied irritably. This day they had toured the 276th and 277th Infantry Divisions, which had repulsed a heavy enemy attack the night before. Then he had endured a frustrating meeting with General Sepp Dietrich at the Second SS Armored Corps. They had left the meeting around four o'clock because he was anxious to get back to Army Group B headquarters, where he would attempt to deal with yet another enemy breakthrough on yet another part of the front.

The SS divisions, a separate military structure, were a particular irritation. When Rommel commanded in northern Italy, he had faced continual trouble from General Dietrich. The field marshal had finally ordered the SS units out of Milan, out of his area. They were not honorable soldiers. They did not obey orders. They looted and brutalized in ways that fell outside the pale.

A thunderous concussion rocked the air—another Allied bomb. "They're rather heavy today," observed Lang diffidently.

The field marshal turned to look at him. His famous temper began to boil up; he admired physical courage and stoicism and disliked its obverse. But he calmed at once. "Yes, they are," he replied mildly. For the unchallenged Allied air superiority was one of the obstacles that even the great field marshal's tactical and strategic skills could not overcome. He could not blame Lang for feeling helpless in the face of Allied fighter bombers, the hated Jabos, for he did himself.

He looked out the window as they passed one more burning truck, yellow flames still licking the shreds of canvas cover. In the distance a great plume of black smoke smudged the sky over the main highway. No doubt the pyre marked the death of an entire convoy of his precious vehicles, men, and supplies.

Sergeant Holke, the spotter, binoculars pressed to his eyes, shouted from the back. "They've seen us—two are coming this way."

A different man would have cursed, but the field marshal merely tightened his fists and ordered Corporal Daniel to make haste. The driver pressed the accelerator, and the big staff car surged forward. "There is a crossing ahead, Herr Feldmarschall," called Daniel, without taking his attention from the road.

"Turn off there," said the field marshal. "At least we'll have a little shelter."

If they could only reach the side road in time, they could likely dash away before the speeding aircraft turned to pursue. Twisting in his seat, Rommel looked to the rear, his keen eyes spotting the first of the enemy planes. The aircraft followed the line of the road, coming up very fast behind them, startlingly close to the ground.

He knew they would never make the crossroads.

Tracers flashed and dust rose from the gravel right behind the car. A moment later metal and glass splintered with terrible violence. The field marshal lost consciousness as a punishing blow crushed the socket of his left eye and broke bones in his cheek and skull. He felt nothing as the grievously wounded driver convulsed at the wheel, steering the car violently into a tree.

The vehicle spun back across the road, bounced off a wall, and rolled over to land on its top in the ditch. The field marshal lay on the ground, blood flowing from his eyes, nose, and mouth. Overhead, the second tactical fighter roared in, more guns firing. At the last minute the pilot released a small fragmentation bomb, plunging the deadly missile into the carnage below.

An hour later, a French doctor pronounced the Desert Fox a hopeless case. He was put in a hospital bed to die, while in the rest of Normandy, in Germany, and throughout the world, the greatest of all wars raged upon its relentless course.

OPERATION VALKYRIE

July 20, 1944

Wolfschanze, East Prussia,
20 July 1944, 1132 hours GMT

The sharp-featured Prussian field marshal approached Hitler's headquarters bunker, trailed by several staff officers. The SS *hauptmann* standing guard at the door snapped his arm upward in a salute and shouted as a heavy cement truck rolled by.

"Field Marshal Keitel. Der führer is expecting you. Since they are reinforcing the command bunker, the conference will be held in Minister Speer's barracks."

"Very well," the aristocratic commander replied. His face was etched with deep lines, and black circles darkened the skin around his eyes. Keitel turned to one of his accompanying officers and glanced down at the man's solid briefcase. "Did you bring the information on the Replacement Army?"

Colonel Count Claus Schenk von Stauffenberg instantly tightened his grip on the satchel's handle. He stood stiffly, nearly as tall as the field marshal, and was every bit his equal as an aristocrat if not in military rank. Von Stauffenberg was a soldier who had suffered grievously for the Reich. A black patch covered his left eye, and his sleeve on the same side was pinched shut at the wrist, hanging empty beside his Wehrmacht colonel's tunic. He clasped his large briefcase in his right hand, even though he had lost fingers there to the same explosion that had claimed his arm and his eye. "*Jawohl,*" he replied, indicating the briefcase with a nod. He was sweating for reasons other than the oppressive heat.

The colonel glanced over at the footings for the new large command bunker, a symptom of the Soviet advance. A foreman was yelling at his crew; as always, Wolfschanze, the "Wolf's Lair," was a beehive of construction activity, with new fortifications being thrown up while the war moved closer and closer.

Keitel noticed Stauffenberg looking at the new command bunker. "The tide will yet turn in our direction," the field marshal observed.

Stauffenberg looked at his commander. "Yes, Field Marshal," he replied. "And perhaps sooner than we think." His face was carefully expressionless, giving away nothing of his true thoughts. Only the beads of moisture on his forehead betrayed his tension, and those could easily be explained by the heat. He knew Keitel was still loyal to the führer and would be until the end—which would come sooner than the field marshal could possibly imagine.

Minutes before, Stauffenberg had opened the briefcase and reached inside to crush a glass ampule. The subsequent chemical reaction had activated a fuse. By the colonel's estimate, the bomb in the briefcase would go off in about ten minutes. If all went well, by the end of the day Germany would begin to emerge from the long night of dictatorship and fascism.

Keitel merely nodded, obviously pleased at the patriotic response, as he led his staff toward the barracks. Twice, staff officers offered to carry Stauffenberg's briefcase, but each time he refused the help. The seconds crept slowly by as they approached the Speer Barracks. This was one of the old wooden structures, built before fortifications at the Wolf's Lair were deemed necessary. The building looked like a long one-story lodge in the woods, not at all like a sophisticated field headquarters for the mighty military machine that was the Third Reich.

To von Stauffenberg, the change raised a pragmatic concern. He worried that his bomb might not be sufficient for the job, that the open windows would diffuse the blast and reduce the damage it would cause. He suppressed a grimace. Why had Keitel interrupted him before he could get the second bomb from Haeften? But there was nothing to be done about that now.

Inside the conference room more than a dozen uniformed officers stood about in various states of unease, while an equal number of stenographers scribbled their notes at writing tables placed haphazardly around the perimeter of the conference bunker. A broad map table filled the center of the room, and the short, dark-haired figure of the führer bent over those sheets, his shoulders and arms tight with barely-concealed tension. He looked up, piercing eyes flashing angrily, as Keitel and Stauffenberg entered.

General Adolf Heusinger was clearly trying to complete his briefing without provoking another Hitler outburst. "The attempts to reform Army Group Center are being met with some . . . , er, limited success. Zhukov's armies continue to advance, however. Three days ago some elements of the First Guards Tank Army crossed the Bug River into Poland—although the defenders of Lvov stand heroically firm. In the north, I regret to report, there is a real possibility that Stalin's horde will reach the Baltic. In that case, our armies in Latvia and Estonia will be lost . . . unless . . . or rather, if, they were to make a strategic movement toward the Fatherland—"

"The German army will never withdraw! It will fight and be victorious—or it will die! But it will never retreat." He was sweating for reasons other than the oppressive heat. Hitler's voice rose nearly to a shriek, his eyes fastened on the quivering lieutenant general. "How is it that you cowards in the Wehrmacht can't get that fact through your thick heads? Proceed—but do not mention withdrawal!"

"Jawohl, mein Führer!" Heusinger gulped and mopped his brow, then

continued with the dolorous report, trying unsuccessfully to highlight the rare bits of positive news.

Stauffenberg felt some sympathy for the man, knowing that the task of sugarcoating the news was virtually impossible. In truth, Army Group Center—the greatest concentration of men and matériel ever gathered under German command—had been virtually obliterated by the massive Soviet spring offensive. About the best the hapless Heusinger could do was dangle the hope that the sweeping Soviet advance must surely be carrying the Russian tanks far beyond their bases of supply. Also, he emphasized, the bridgehead across the Bug was still small. Of course, none of the unspoken realities would escape any of the experienced army officers here, but these professional soldiers knew to a man that it was nothing short of suicide to confront the führer with truths he did not wish to hear.

Stauffenberg stepped up to the table as Field Marshal Keitel moved to Hitler's side. The colonel had asked Major von Freyend to find him a place close to Hitler to compensate for his poor hearing, and von Freyend was happy to oblige. Stauffenberg's one good eye never blinked as it appeared to consider every detail on the wide map, with its huge expanse of flags and colored lines, the sweeping horde beneath the hammer and sickle closing onto the heart of the Reich. His heart pounded, and anger and despair writhed together as he observed this graphic depiction of national catastrophe. *So this is the end to which the führer would lead us. Well, today, right here, the madness stops.*

The colonel carefully set his heavy briefcase down underneath the table. Months of stealth, of plotting, of careful recruiting had led to this moment. The explosion would kill most of the people in the barracks, he knew, and not all of them deserved to die, but then so many people had not deserved to die. These deaths, at least, would bring the insanity to an end.

"Herr Oberst—there is a call for you, from Berlin." Stauffenberg turned to see a messenger whispering at his side. "General Fellgiebel said it was urgent." Nodding silently, the crippled officer took one last look at Adolf Hitler, führer of the Third Reich, and smiled his tight smile before following the messenger from the conference hut, moving quickly across the compound toward the communications building, following the cue of his coconspirator. He completely forgot his cap and gunbelt.

He didn't forget his briefcase. It remained exactly where he wanted it, under the table, a few feet from the führer's legs.

Colonel Heinz Brandt moved into the space at the table vacated by Stauffenberg. Brandt, an aide to General Heusinger, was an operations officer on the general staff. He was pondering a disturbing bit of news. Unconfirmed reports from the Balkans had been coming into the OKW headquarters, indicating the possibility of defection by Rumania and Bulgaria. The two nations had never been enthusiastic participants in the epic war against the USSR, and now that the eastern hordes rolled toward them, Brandt's sources indicated that either or both countries might be preparing to change sides.

Yet how could he bring this up to the führer? Brandt's idealism and patriotism had been sorely tried these past months. He still revered his führer, but those bursts of temper were coming more and more frequently. And too often they meant disgrace or disaster to the recipient.

His position at the table was awkward, and he realized that his foot was blocked by Stauffenberg's briefcase. He reached down to move the leather satchel to his right, finding that it was surprisingly heavy. As he started to shove it behind the thick stanchion supporting the table, however, he was possessed by the sudden urge to sneeze. He froze, embarrassed by his awkward stance, tense because of his proximity to Hitler. Struggling to suppress the tickle in his nose—a distraction such as a sneeze, however involuntary, always irritated the führer—Brandt decided that the briefcase could remain where it was. He straightened with careful dignity, ignoring the damnably heavy satchel, relieved that he managed to keep from attracting unwanted attention to himself.

More ominous facts and figures mounted up: the Americans and British continued to reinforce their beachhead in Normandy, which was now six weeks old. The German defenders held their positions with heroic courage, but the *Wehrmacht* commander in the west, Field Marshal Erwin Rommel, had just been critically injured by an Allied air attack. The report sent by his replacement, von Kluge, indicated that his troops were stretched to the breaking point, that the defensive shell must soon crack.

Meanwhile the heavy bombers kept coming, day and night, raining death on Germany's cities and destruction upon the Third Reich's industrial capabilities. Reichsmarschall Hermann Göring's representative reluctantly admitted that the Luftwaffe was horribly depleted, critically short of spare parts, barely able to scrape together enough fighters to harass the thundering fleets of enemy bombers.

Hitler's eyes again flashed. "And the rigging of the jet bombers? How fares that?"

The unfortunate Luftwaffe officer paused awkwardly. Like every other former combat pilot, he undoubtedly realized the potential of the rocket-fast plane designed by Willy Messerschmidt—the Me-262. Certainly it was glaringly obvious to him, and to everyone else in the Luftwaffe, that the short-ranged aircraft would make a magnificent fighter. Still, Hitler felt a passionate need to strike back at the enemy homeland in revenge for the bombing of Germany, and to that end he had insisted that the aircraft be rigged to carry bombs—a task for which the plane was patently unfit. Thus, the development of a premier weapon had been placed indefinitely on hold. Brandt, an army man more familiar with diplomacy than air power, nevertheless felt sympathy for the flying officer who was now forced to confront his ruler's irrationality.

The man would never formulate his reply.

The explosion ripped through the confined space with the deafening power of thunder, a blaze of fiery light and a shockwave that twisted the ground itself. An eruption of smoke and debris choked Brandt, who suddenly found himself lying on his back, staring up at the tattered remnants of the ceiling's crude wooden paneling. Patches of sky showed through the lumber, a fact that struck him as bizarre.

What had happened? The colonel couldn't fully grasp the situation. Looking around, blinking the dust of the explosion from his eyes, he saw Field Marshal Keitel stagger past. The tall man's hair stood on end, and his face was plastered with soot as he knelt beside a shapeless form to Brandt's left. Other officers groaned or cried for help while two stenographers stumbled toward the door, which hung limply by a single hinge.

Idly, with a sense of curious detachment, Colonel Brandt dropped a hand below his own waist, noticing that his legs were gone. He was dying, he realized, though it was a distant thought. The horrific wound didn't seem to hurt, a fact that surprised him. He noticed a leather shred, the same color as the heavy briefcase, fluttering in the ruins of the smoke-filled room.

Then he saw Keitel lurch to his feet, the field marshal's face distorted with a grief so strong that it penetrated even Brandt's mortal haze. Rubbing a hand across the blasted skin of his face, the chief of staff tried unsuccessfully to conceal his profound distress. His jaw stretched tight by emotion, the field marshal's words caught in his throat. He looked down again, as if to deny some madness that afflicted his mind. Finally, haltingly, he spoke.

"*Der führer ist tot,*" Keitel declared, his voice as dull as the echoes of the assassin's bomb.

General Erich Fellgiebel, standing outside the Speer Barracks, spun around in alarm as the sound of the explosion echoed through the Wolf's Lair. For a moment his mind froze in awful, incomprehensible fear. *What have we done?* The question resounded through his mind until he roughly pushed it aside. *We have taken back the Fatherland!*

The older general's mind still churned with the conflict between his military oath and his duty to his country as he saw it. It was a difficult choice, a bitter draught from a cup he'd wished would have passed him by. History might brand him a traitor, an oath breaker, and the thought of his reputation forever stained by betrayal was almost too much to bear. He admired the younger Stauffenberg's stoicism, his aristocratic certainty that his choice was correct, honorable.

He watched the dust cloud trailing Stauffenberg's staff car as the colonel and his driver drove away from the Wolf's Lair without apparent urgency. His coconspirator would board an aircraft for Berlin within a few minutes. Not so long ago he'd thought of the young officer as almost a son. Now, in the end, it seemed as if their roles had reversed. *May God be with him . . . and with the Fatherland.*

Fellgiebel knew that he had his own mission to carry out, but now that the time had come the general's will strangely deserted him. He knew he had only minutes to live.

"Treachery! Murder! Help—bring the surgeon!" The cries came from the destroyed staff building, and several officers stumbled into the sunlight, caked with dust and debris. Was Hitler among them?

Fellgiebel gawked, frozen in place, feeling the pulse pounding in his temples. Had they succeeded? What should he do?

"The führer is slain!" gasped one general, falling to his knees in shock or despair.

In that admission Fellgiebel found his strength and darted through the door of the communications center. Idle couriers stared in surprise as the general pulled open a large case, withdrawing several long hand grenades. Holding the fragmentation bombs in one hand, he drew his pistol with the other. The wide-eyed radio operator lurched to his feet, staring at the general in disbelief, while the two operators spun around at the telephone switchboard.

"Back!" snarled the general, gesturing the men away from the signals equipment. Gun in one hand, grenade in the other, he made a formidable picture of persuasion. Stumbling over chairs, the communications staff scrambled toward the doors.

The general ran to the switchboard and picked up the telephone speaker, barking a series of numbers into the phone. In another moment, the line was answered with a curt *"Was?"*

"Die Brucke ist verbrennt!" barked the panting Fellgiebel, before quickly breaking the connection.

The signal for success—"The bridge is burned!"—would be spread by the conspirators across the Reich, though Fellgiebel now felt a piercing regret at the knowledge that he wouldn't be alive to see the effect of those momentous words. Arming the grenade, he dropped it behind the bank of the telephone switchboard.

Next the general fired four shots from his Walther into the cabinet-size radio, each slug splintering tubes and wiring. Fellgiebel reached out and pitched the huge radio onto its side before firing more shots from his handgun.

He was still shooting as an SS guard burst through the door. Fellgiebel did not look up as the man's Schmeisser erupted, stitching a line of bloody holes up the general's back, knocking him onto the switchboard that would never be used again.

A second later, the grenade behind the telephone switchboard exploded, shredding the panel into lethal shrapnel, simultaneously ripping into the SS guard and tearing away at Fellgiebel's unfeeling corpse.

Belorussia, Soviet Union, 1157 hours GMT

"Die Brucke ist verbrennt!" crackled a voice over the radio. Hauptmann Paul Krueger ignored it—obviously some code phrase that had nothing to do with him. He had other things on his mind as he piloted his Messerschmidt through the clear summer skies.

This morning had started out bad and gotten worse. A pitifully few fighters were all that remained of the once mighty Luftwaffe on the Russian front, and most of those were in a sorry state of repair. Some otherwise flyable machines had been stripped for parts to make a few craft airworthy. Ammunition supplies were low, trained pilots were scarce, and the creeping carpet of Slavs kept advancing, like a race of army ants, or perhaps cockroaches. Kill a hundred, and a thousand more crawl out from under rocks.

That was what his fellow pilots, his officer, and especially his maintenance people kept arguing, until his towering fits of rage shut them up. He could see in their eyes they were afraid of him—and rightly so—but their opinions were secretly unchanged. In his mind, that made them effectively Soviet agents and saboteurs, and he would cheerfully have stood them all up against a wall and shot them dead with his own pistol.

His mechanic, Willi, had approached him, trembling. The anger on Krueger's face was obvious, and when Krueger was angry, no one but Willi would approach him. "Hauptmann—I'm sorry to tell you, but your wingman won't be flying today."

His glare was enough to stop Willi in his tracks. "It's spare parts—like always—I just can't get enough to keep all the planes in the air. The colonel says you're not going up today."

The inner flame rose within Krueger. "Not going up?" he said with deceptive quiet.

"The colonel says . . . not without a wingman . . . ," Willi stammered.

The back of Krueger's hand slashed across the mechanic's face, leaving an angry welt where his ring hit flesh. He turned and strode to his plane. Knowing better than to argue, the young mechanic hurried behind him, starting the preflight ritual. There would be no excuse for Krueger's plane not to fly.

Krueger was still angry about the failure. The colonel, the mechanics—they thought they had a good excuse, but they were wrong. There was no excuse. First, Krueger knew better. He was an engineer, and a damned good one—and an even better fighter pilot. He knew what was possible. And second, he was German. He was a member of the master race, and so were the others in his Gruppe. The thought that any number of Slav bastards or their crummy American-made airplanes could stop the German knights of the skies was simply, finally, absolutely unacceptable. But his fellows were weak. He could see it in their eyes. They were defeatist, and if they did not change their attitude, they should be shot.

The führer himself once said, "If the German people despair, they will deserve no better than they get. If they despair, I will not be sorry for them if God lets them down." He'd written similar statements in *Mein Kampf*, a book Krueger had read so many times he'd virtually memorized it. The German people through their führer had been given a chance to fulfill their destiny, but if they did not grasp it, they were already doomed.

Krueger loved to fly and he loved to kill, and nothing would work out the day's frustrations like some dead and bleeding Slavs. His anger had dissipated as the ground fell away, and finally there was just himself and his machine, alone in the sky and vigilant on the hunt. And it was not long before the hunter found his game.

Banking his Messerschmidt Bf-109G through a lazy circle, he glared at the long column of Soviet T-34 tanks extending almost to the far horizon. He sat up high in the cockpit, unlike most of his fellow pilots, who crouched low in case of a stray bullet or piece of flak. He wanted to see, and he wanted the world to understand that he had no fear, not of anything the Reich's enemies could throw at him.

Nazi artillery fired, and a few bursts of flame, far too few to suit him, illuminated the landscape. In past years, he might have expected to see some Stukas dropping bombs with pinpoint accuracy among the crowded vehicles, but the Stukas were gone, along with most of the rest of the Luftwaffe.

He felt a fiery impulse to strafe the column, to shatter Russian bodies with the machine guns and cannon of his deadly fighter, but it was impractical. Few of his shells would have penetrated the heavy armor of the tanks—and the Soviets' accurate antiaircraft fire would have almost certainly brought him down. Today, with no wingman, it was even more dangerous. Perhaps if he'd come across a file of the soft-skinned trucks or horse-drawn carts the Soviets used to transport men and supplies, he'd have taken the chance to shred the target, especially if there were gasoline trucks to explode in balls of smoky flame. But those vehicles would be far to the rear, under skies that had become the undisputed province of the Red Air Force.

They were overbreeding scum, those Slavs, threatening the purity of the Aryan homeland only by dint of sheer numbers, and their awful winters. Cockroaches, the lot of them. The führer's legions would defeat them, though, and Krueger would carry an avenging torch to purify the land by fire. From his days in the Hitlerjugend, the Hitler Youth, to his earliest commissioning, Krueger

had been the most loyal, the most dedicated of Nazis. When weaker men's faith faltered, Krueger was inspired by thoughts of secret weapons still to be unleashed—though, truth be told, he could not completely believe in them until he himself sat at the controls. He was too much the engineer for that, priding himself on knowing his aircraft inside and out.

Krueger's fighter growled along nearly two thousand meters above the level steppe as he contemplated the column. But the tanks were hardly a new sight. He'd observed nearly as many surrounding Stalingrad during the disastrous winter of '42, and at Kursk, only a year ago—though it seemed now in the distant past—he'd seen an even greater number. Though he'd destroyed many, sending their occupants to hell where they belonged, there were always more.

A flash of movement darted through his peripheral vision, and Krueger's attention immediately focused. Two airplanes flew low, past the front of the T-34 column, toward a clump of woods that lay in the Red Army's path. Flames blasted from the pointed noses of the aircraft, and a series of explosions walked their way into the grove. Abruptly a jet of red fire shot from the treetops. The German tank lurking there—an old Panzer III, to judge from the turret that tumbled across the ground—had been destroyed.

Krueger dipped his 109 into a shallow dive. The telltale flashes confirmed his identification—the Soviet aircraft were American-made Bell P-39 Airacobras. The planes were heavily armored and, though slow in a climb, possessed a 37-mm cannon that fired through the hollow prop shaft and had proved ideal for destroying German tanks. Too, they were very fast at low altitude—he'd need all the speed of his dive to catch them.

But catch them, and kill them, he would. Make them pay, make them die in flames. They had no idea who they were up against, and they would not know until it was far too late for it to matter. He'd killed many, so very many, and he was not done yet.

The descending Messerschmidt accelerated quickly, dropping toward the tail of the trailing Airacobra as the Soviet attack planes continued in their search for enemy armor—so intently that neither pilot noticed the checkered nose of Krueger's aircraft growing larger to the rear. At this rocketing speed the 109 was hard to control, forcing Krueger to wrestle the stick with both hands, fighting the buffeting pressure of the air as the ailerons grew stiff, and he closed the distance rapidly. Finally he dropped his flaps to slow down while he prepared to fire. With an idle tickle of surprise he noted the unusually square shape of the P-39's rudder as it filled his sights.

The 109's cannon also fired through the prop shaft, and it erupted when the Luftwaffe pilot pressed the trigger. His eyes followed the tracers into the right wing of the Airacobra. Immediately the Soviet pilot pulled his machine into a hard turn to the left, skimming a hundred feet above the ground. The

German followed him inexorably, cannon fire hammering across the length of the wing, up the side of the fuselage, and finally into the cockpit.

Armored glass surrounded the pilot, but it couldn't stand up to this kind of punishment. Flashes of flame marked the impact of Krueger's shells, and as the windshield exploded into fragments the Airacobra wobbled through a roll and quickly plunged, upside down, into a marsh. Smoke and water billowed into the air at the moment of impact, but Krueger's Messerschmidt was already pulling away, wheeling and climbing as his unblinking stare covered the expanse of sky.

Steadily gaining altitude, the whine of his engine rising to a shriek, the German ace scanned the horizon until he saw a flash of movement. The second Airacobra had wheeled around, and it too climbed—into the skies over the vast Russian horde. A quick look behind and above showed Krueger that his tail remained free of Soviet fighters, so he turned after the ground attack craft.

The old Daimler-Benz engine cranked out every one of its nearly fifteen hundred horsepower, pistons pounding, spinning the three blades of the propeller and lifting the German fighter through the air. The sound of the motor remained throaty and strong, though a quick check showed Krueger that the temperature began to rise uncomfortably. Yet, even as he soared upward, the Luftwaffe pilot watched with astonishment as the Soviet fighter climbed away. Always before, these stub-winged airplanes had proved easy prey once they tried to gain altitude, but now this machine rose beyond the range of his guns with arrogant ease. Curiously, there was a telltale stream of brown in the 'cobra's exhaust—a sign of water injection, which he had never before seen in a P-39.

Cursing, Krueger pressed his throttle, all but pounding on his control panel in his effort to increase the speed of his desperate pursuit, when the confidence of the Soviet pilot was demonstrated still further. The Airacobra wheeled tightly and dived back toward the Messerschmidt!

Lips clenched over his teeth in a tight smile, Krueger fixed his sights on the diving Bell. The flashing guns on the Soviet fighter winked first, the tracers falling below the 109 as the Luftwaffe pilot steadied his aim. Finally, a few seconds before collision, he pinched off a quick, deadly burst. His shells exploded at the nose of the Airacobra, and flames immediately burst from the fuselage. As the stubby plane screamed into its final dive, Krueger again got a look at that squared, geometrical rudder, noticeably different from the P-39s he'd fought before.

A form tumbled away from the wreck as flames and smoke billowed into the air, and in another second the canopy of a parachute snapped into view. *Bastard thinks he's safe now, does he?* The Messerschmidt curled into a dive, and Krueger watched the Soviet pilot wriggle helplessly as the 109 roared closer. The German snapped off a few rounds from his machine guns, observing with grim satisfaction as the bullets shredded the Russian's jerking body, then left him hanging limply in the harness of his chute.

Flaming tracers of near misses arced past Krueger, and a dim voice in the pilot's brain told him that this was ground fire. Now he pulled back on the stick and the 109 clawed its way upward, away from the annoying antiaircraft into the tenuous safety of the sky. Other specks appeared to the east, buzzing closer like angry hornets. At least two dozen fighters of the Red Air Force swarmed toward Krueger, their pilots undoubtedly bent on vengeance. The German shrugged away the prospect of the unequal match, banking toward the west and leveling his flight, knowing that if he held full throttle he should outrun the heavy Ilyushins—unless they, too, had suddenly gained some magical impetus of speed, he thought sourly.

He recalled an intelligence report he'd read a month or two earlier. Supposedly the Americans had developed an improved version of the P-39, dubbed the P-63 Kingcobra. The more he thought, the more Krueger became convinced he'd faced two of these new models. It was reportedly much speedier than the older machine, and when he remembered the brown exhaust the pilot suspected the American designers had in fact added water injection to the engine. *And when will we get new models?* he thought angrily. More incompetence, more cowardice. *If I were in charge of production, there would be no excuses,* he thought with a grim smile.

Only then did the Luftwaffe pilot look down at the temperature gauge, noting calmly that the needle was creeping toward the red. He veered toward the northwest, toward friendly lines and his airbase. Since he could see or feel no sign that the airplane had been damaged, he suspected that the worn pistons had finally begun to score the cylinders. By the time he crossed into Poland and approached his field, the power plant was gasping and sputtering like a dying man.

Old equipment and not much of that, he thought. Control of the air, he knew, was critical to turning the tide of battle. *We are still Germans. We are still supreme. If we have the will as a people, we cannot be stopped.*

He throttled back as his plane descended toward the dirt landing strip. He could see people waving, the colonel striding angrily over to him to berate him for disobeying orders. But Krueger was not worried. The colonel tended to back off when Krueger was truly angry. And if this time he didn't, well, Krueger had totaled up the numbers. With the two downed aircraft today, he'd scored his 150th kill.

Supreme Headquarters Allied Expeditionary Forces (SHAEF), London, England, 1215 GMT

General Omar Bradley, commander of the United States First Army, nodded to the secretary outside the supreme Allied commander's door. "Go right in, General," she said. "He's ready for you."

Dwight D. Eisenhower, five-star general, put down his half-eaten sandwich and smiled. "Welcome back to England, Brad," he said, standing up and offering his hand.

"Thanks, Ike," Bradley replied. "Sorry to interrupt your lunch. I'm just passing through, though. I go back across the Channel tomorrow."

"I'll be over there soon enough myself," Eisenhower said. "But there's all this to get through first—" he indicated a maze of paper. "I've been in so many meetings lately that my keister is qualified for the Purple Heart."

Bradley laughed and settled into a chair.

"So what's new that isn't already in these reports?" Eisenhower asked. He had often voiced his frustration to Bradley about being shut off from firsthand experience so much of the time; he had to put together his knowledge from other people's accounts to make sense of the myriad reports that piled up before him. And there were few people he trusted as much as Omar Bradley, who had been a classmate of Eisenhower's at West Point.

"We're opening the Cherbourg port tomorrow; all the German demolition damage is just about corrected. That means we'll be able to bring in tanks and troops through a regular port and not through the artificial ports. Monty's got his hands full with German armor but keeps talking about a breakthrough. At least we're getting more troops and more equipment across every day, and that's going very well." Bradley's quiet and calm demeanor was a contrast to the often bombastic and too frequently self-serving or political rhetoric Eisenhower got from his other generals. Especially his two chief prima donnas—Monty, the British field marshal Bernard Montgomery, who had been commander of ground forces in the D-Day landings, and General George Patton, the brilliant but egotistical tank commander who had been sidelined during D-Day in a huge and successful bluff to convince the Germans that the attack would come elsewhere than Normandy.

"We're making progress, Ike. Not as fast as we'd like, of course, but we've rocked the Krauts back on their heels along the whole line. It's a hell of an accomplishment since D-Day."

Eisenhower nodded in grim agreement. The risk and the carnage of the D-Day landings—only six weeks past!—was still fresh in everyone's mind. The situation on the ground in Normandy was much more fluid and dangerous than the Allied command wanted.

"And Operation Cobra?" asked the supreme commander, referring to the military plan for the Allied breakout from the Normandy peninsula into France.

"On track. We'll start the final briefing soon. With luck, Cobra should get us out of those damned hedgerows and heading through France."

"There's a long road ahead of us still," Eisenhower observed.

Bradley nodded. "But we'll win. There's no doubt left, really." Coming from the imperturbable Bradley, the statement was unassailable.

"Did you hear about Rommel?" Eisenhower asked. "Three days ago he got shot up by a British fighter—Canadian, excuse me. We thought he was dead, but he's in the hospital. Pretty badly wounded, by all accounts. Looks like his war is over."

Field Marshal Erwin Rommel, the famous Desert Fox who had fought so brilliantly in North Africa, had commanded the defense of the D-Day beaches, in places nearly driving the Allies back into the sea. In the end it might have been only Hitler's refusal to believe that the Normandy invasion was real that had saved the attack. The führer had refused to allow Rommel to counterattack with his panzer divisions, forcing the German tanks out of action until the Allies had a secure foothold on the shore.

"It's good we don't have to fight him any more in Normandy," Bradley mused.

"Well, I wanted another crack at the son of a bitch!" The voice of George Patton, his characteristically high-pitched squeak, came from the office door as the general strode into the room.

"George," Bradley acknowledged, standing to shake Patton's hand. He noted that even here he wore his twin ivory-handled revolvers in their belt holsters. Despite his voice, the general, in his immaculate tunic and shiny cavalry boots, demanded respect, even from his superior officers. Bradley studied him, wondering where Patton's volatile personality was going to take them today.

"So, Ike, Brad?" Patton said with easy familiarity, though he made no move to join Bradley in sitting down. "When do I get my army?"

Bradley grimaced while Eisenhower chuckled. The supreme commander indicated his field commander. "You want to tell him, Brad?"

"I wouldn't be taking anything for granted if I were you," Bradley snapped. "But yes, we're going to activate Third Army. It looks like you'll take over about the first of August—if you don't make an ass out of yourself before then." Once personally close—Patton had been Bradley's commanding officer—the two had an increasingly tendentious relationship.

For a second the bombastic front fell away and Patton grinned like an enthusiastic child. Then he was serious again. "You won't regret this, either of you. Just turn me loose over there! And I don't care if it's Rommel or Old Scratch himself on the other side!"

Eisenhower nodded, satisfied. "Though now it looks like von Kluge is in charge of the front." He turned back to Bradley. "Does that make any real change in your plans?"

"Not really. Kluge is competent; hell, they all are. But he's going to have to deal with Hitler and all kinds of directives that are going to mess up any smart strategy. The Germans are going to be troublesome all through France, but I don't think they'll be able to do much once we break out all the way, at least until we hit the German border."

"I agree. Sometimes I think Hitler's one of the best military allies we've got. He's tying the hands of his generals in ways we can only dream about." The three men laughed. "So, Brad, you've got your new units in place?"

Bradley stole a look at Patton and wished that the army commander wasn't here, not right now. But he went ahead anyway.

"Just wanted to review the final status of the Nineteenth Armored Division, which I'm activating and shipping over this week. I've got Jack King in command with Henry Wakefield as his executive officer."

"King's aggressive as hell. George, you'll like him. But you're pairing him with Henry Wakefield?" Eisenhower put his hand on his chin. "So, Henry finally got away from training commands, hmm?" The supreme commander himself had been a tank instructor, with Henry Wakefield as a contemporary.

"Yep," replied Bradley, with another glance at the scowling Patton. "You know why he didn't go to Africa or Italy."

Eisenhower nodded. He remembered the pivotal meeting at the Command and General Staff College, where Henry Wakefield and George Patton had butted heads. It was loud and explosive. The doctrinal points were important, though perhaps not as crucial as the two men believed—Patton tended to believe anyone who didn't see the future of armor the way he did was a blind idiot, and Wakefield had his own insights into tank warfare. When Patton became operational commander in North Africa, any chance Wakefield had of getting an armored command of his own evaporated. But now that the Allies had landed in Europe, there was too much need.

"I guess you have in mind that Henry will keep Jack from getting too far ahead of himself," Ike mused.

"That's right," replied Bradley. "And Henry deserves a chance. He's a good man; he just came out on the losing end of a headquarters fight."

Patton couldn't keep quiet. "You ask me, he doesn't belong on a battlefield."

"George, I didn't ask you!"

"Well, I'm—"

Eisenhower cut them off. "Listen, George, let me finish up with Brad. I'll see you at the map in the situation room—ten minutes."

"Yessir!" Patton agreed, once again relaxing into that boyish grin. He turned and stalked out the door, and Bradley could easily imagine the clerks and secretaries scattering out of his path. He turned back to Eisenhower as the supreme commander spoke again.

"Who's Jack got to head up his combat commands?"

"Two colonels, both blooded. Colonel Bob Jackson . . . and Colonel James Pulaski."

Eisenhower's eyebrows raised. Bradley knew he considered Jackson to be a good and stable choice. "Pulaski?"

"I know, Ike. He's a Patton man through and through, and he's a hothead to boot. You know and I know that his Silver Star is partly for luck, but luck isn't such a bad characteristic for a tank leader. And I think this is a good assignment. He'll get along well with King, and with any luck, Wakefield will pound a little sense into his head in the process."

Bradley was familiar with the young officer's being sound. In the North Africa campaign, Pulaski, then a newly-minted major, had led five tanks into what turned out to be a German trap, but then had fought his way out with the loss of only one of his own tanks, while crippling four panzers, and had been awarded the Silver Star. Eisenhower had groused about the stupidity of getting trapped in the first place, but then the handsome young officer had gotten his picture in the paper and become a brief celebrity. Patton liked him, and he'd been made a major.

A minor wound had returned him Stateside for a few months. Then he'd struggled to get back into the war, but Patton's assignment to run the semi-imaginary First U. S. Army Group, the bluff operation to make the Germans believe the invasion was coming into Pas de Calais, had made him unable to support his erstwhile protégé. This was Pulaski's chance to return as a freshly made colonel.

Eisenhower shook his head. "Brad, this is your show. I hope to hell you know what you're doing, mixing fire and gasoline like that."

"If it works, that mixture will get a lot done," Bradley said.

"If it works," emphasized Eisenhower. "So, what other surprises can we expect?"

"With Hitler, who can tell?" replied Bradley.

Templehof Airport, Berlin, Germany, 1340 hours GMT

The speedy twin-engine Heinkel He-111 bomber descended toward the runway from the west, providing its two passengers with a splendid view of the German capital. The plane was far faster than the lumbering Junkers Ju-52 transport plane that had brought the conspirators to their fateful meeting with Hitler. "The capital of a new Germany," Colonel von Stauffenberg shouted over the engines. "A Germany without Hitler, free from its Nazi masters!"

Lieutenant Werner von Haeften, the colonel's aide, was fidgeting in visible agitation. It wasn't done yet, not nearly, and he was still coming to grips with the irrevocable enormity of their action. Although a loyal member of the conspiracy—he had carried the second bomb, in case it had been needed—it was hard for him to grasp that the deed had actually been done. A Germany without the führer was a truly alien concept. He felt as if he'd killed a deity, a national father figure. Was he a parricide or a hero? Or both?

As the bomber taxied to a halt, he followed Stauffenberg to the waiting staff car and settled in the back.

"Bendlerstrasse, and quickly," Stauffenberg commanded the driver. As the staff car raced toward the War Ministry building, he let some of the tension in his face relax.

"Now the difficult work begins," Stauffenberg said with a dangerous smile.

Haeften knew he was being teased for his obvious nervousness. "And what would you call what we have just done?"

"Merely a prelude, my dear Werner," the colonel said. "There is so much more to accomplish, and so little time. Operation Valkyrie must be turned into a reality. General Olbricht has approached General Fromm to put his influence and the power of the Replacement Army behind the coup. The reserve force should have—must have—begun to muster by now. We have a lot of work to do—Himmler needs to be neutralized, and Göring eased into command so that he can negotiate a surrender. We have accomplished the beginning, but our comrades in the conspiracy also have important roles to play."

Haeften had joined the plotters early, in those difficult and dangerous days in which even the attempt to sound out officers to find those who might be sympathetic could easily lead to betrayal, torture, and death. Years of plotting, including two failed attempts on Hitler just this month—and only now coming to fruition. "But the führer is dead!" he said triumphantly.

Stauffenberg smiled. "Finally, after all these years, it seems almost too good to be true. The fuse worked soundlessly, just as our British friends had promised."

Nearly running through the doors of the huge War Ministry building in Bendler- strasse, where Stauffenberg served as chief of staff to General Fromm, the two successful plotters entered Stauffenberg's office. It was crowded with the gath- ering conspirators, men sitting and smoking, or pacing anxiously. Stauffenberg was first struck with the lack of action, the lack of initiative among his fellow conspirators. It gave him an immediate pang of concern.

"Claus—thank God you've made it back!" Olbricht was the first to speak, rising to his feet and clasping the count's hand warmly.

"Success!" cried Stauffenberg. "He's dead! Now, how fares the coup?"

He noticed Beck, then, looking vaguely out of place in his uniform—the uniform he had not worn in six years. The old officer, venerable survivor of the pre-Hitler general staff, who had resigned in protest against Hitler's plans to invade Czechoslovakia, clasped Stauffenberg's hand warmly. Beck's face was flushed, his eyes watering. He was obviously moved, and more than a little disturbed, by the actions of the men in this room.

Gradually the colonel realized that no one had answered his question. "The telephones?" He gestured to the dozen or so instruments in the room, none of which were in use. "Have you put through the calls to Vienna . . . Munich? Has Stulpnagel acted in Paris?"

"We—we wanted to make sure, to hear from you yourself," General Olbricht explained, somewhat sheepishly. Though he outranked the colonel, his manner clearly indicated who the conspirators valued as leader. "The message came—*Die Brucke ist Verbrennt*—but we wanted to make sure it wasn't some kind of trick."

Precious minutes wasted. *Damn it!* Stauffenberg flared with anger. *How can they just sit there like that?* "It's no trick! He's dead, I tell you! Quickly, to the phones—spread the word! Where's Fromm—will he go along with us?"

Again there came that awkward silence. "He—he wouldn't command the Replacement Army to revolt," Olbricht explained again. "I'm afraid we've shuttled him into a closet."

"What about Remer? Has the Ninth Regiment surrounded the Ministry of Propaganda?"

"Oh, yes," Olbricht said, obviously relieved at having good news. "Yes, he is awaiting further orders. And, by the way, I'm ready to initiate command of Operation Valkyrie."

"But surely that operation has already begun?" the count demanded, increasingly frustrated. One could not select one's coup partners, he realized, nor simply court-martial or transfer them if they did not work out. Years of subservience to Hitler had made lapdogs out of many of the generals. He supposed he should not be surprised at their lack of initiative now, when it was needed most.

Olbricht nearly stammered in his eagerness to justify himself. "Of course—well, the orders are prepared, in any event. We weren't sure whether to send them in clear or encode them."

In other words, you have done nothing, he thought, but forced aside his frustration to consider the question. A clear message would be received almost immediately by all units of the Wehrmacht—but also by the many listening posts of the Allies. He recalled the ominous words of Roosevelt—unconditional surrender. Would they take advantage of the chaos to launch attacks? Almost assuredly.

"Send the announcement in code!" he declared, deciding that the extra time required for individual copies, for decoding, would be worth the added security.

Only later would he realize the enormity of his mistake.

Normandy, France, 1345 hours GMT

The sight of the D-Day beaches shocked any potential comment right out of Colonel James Pulaski's vocabulary. As the flat-bottomed tank transport churned toward Utah Beach, he was stunned to silence by the swath of rusting carcasses scattered across the shallows and the flat landscape beyond. Unconsciously he touched the silver crucifix he wore just below his throat, and he wondered at the savagery that had rocked this coast.

Mangled LCTs rested on the shoals, while the burned-out hulks of several tanks settled into the soft sand to form a strange sort of sculpture, as exotic and memorable in its size as Stonehenge, or the heads of Easter Island. Burial details had long since cleared the beaches of the thousands of bodies, but the machinery stood like statuary, or the violent aftermath of giant children's sandbox battles, marking the battlefield's violence and horror. It was a strange and moving memorial.

Around and through this rusting sculpture garden the machinery of war progressed at a pace of steady frenzy. Trucks and tanks rolled from the bellies of high, blocky LSTs, the ships having pulled right up to shore before their bow doors lowered to burp out their gasoline- and diesel-powered cargo. Cranes lifted other cargoes clear, while army engineers drove bulldozers back and forth and military policemen kept a wary eye on the chaos of organization.

Pulaski, six feet tall, blond hair and blue eyes, a handsome officer with the solid build of a natural athlete, wore his new colonel's wings with pride, still not quite able to believe where he was. He put his hands on his hips as he surveyed the scene. "Jesus Christ, what a fight this must have been," he whispered, his voice betraying awe at the wreckage of war still scattered everywhere, though the invasion had occurred nearly six weeks earlier.

"They say it was even worse over there," observed Major General Jack King, pointing east. "At Omaha Beach the First Division almost got pushed back into the channel." General King, new commanding officer of the Nineteenth Armored Division, also wore fresh insignia, his second star gleaming silver. A thin, angular, man with wavy silver hair, uniform crisp and spotless even in a combat zone, he looked almost as if Central Casting had sent him over for the job.

Pulaski realized that General King was as impressed—even awed—as he was. He knew the general had much more combat experience than he, even though Pulaski himself had served with distinction in North Africa, winning a Silver Star for his heroism. Still, it was hard for either man not to react to the scene in front of him.

"Well, they made it ashore—and now here we are to finish the job," announced Pulaski with barely contained anticipation. "I sure hope Hitler's got a few Krauts left!"

"Wouldn't worry about that," the general replied as the two men climbed down the landing ramp and headed toward the already debarked tanks.

"They look ready for anything, don't they?" Pulaski stared with unconcealed pride at the row of M4 Sherman tanks gathered at the base of one of the long causeways that connected this isolated beach to the mainland of Normandy and the rest of France.

These were his tanks, members of the lead company of his combat command. The eighteen humpbacked armored vehicles of Company B, 38th Tank Battalion of the Nineteenth Armored Division had been unloaded from the LST earlier in the day. Their crewmen had been reunited with their tanks, and each had been started and warmed up. Now they simply waited for the command to move off of the beach. The rest of the three battalions in Pulaski's combat command were still aboard the nearby LSTs but were due for debarkation in the next twelve hours.

"When's the rest of the division come in?" inquired Pulaski. He was impatient, ready to drive toward the war immediately.

King looked unconsciously across the still waters of the English Channel. "Tomorrow P.M., supposedly," he replied. "At least, that's when Bob Jackson and his HQ company land. But we want you up to the bivouac tonight." He looked at the younger officer affectionately, an elder to a bright youngster who had the potential to turn into something fine. Pulaski was a little annoyed at the implied patronization—*hell, I'm thirty-three years old*—but General King had a fine combat record, and he was entitled to his opinion. Pulaski might be a trifle unseasoned in his new command role, but the experience would happen soon enough, once they encountered Germans. He could hardly wait.

"Fair enough—just tell me when to go," declared Pulaski. He returned King's look with an unabashed grin, unable to conceal his nervous energy.

"Believe me, when we jump off you'll be leading the way," the general declared. "You know I'm counting on Combat Command A."

The younger officer reached out to pump the general's hand. "And you know how much this command means to me, sir," he said, his voice thickened by gratitude. "I won't let you down."

"Hell, call me Jack—in private, at least. We're going to be working together a lot, you and I," replied King with a wide grin, teeth glistening. "You're going to make a first-rate tank officer. Find the chinks in the German defenses, push through, and open the gaps to crack the enemy into little pieces."

"I've arranged for you to get the first of the division's 76-mm guns," King added, as Pulaski again took in the row of his immaculate Shermans. Four of the tanks were armed with cannons that were significantly longer than the guns on the rest of the stubby vehicles. These big barrels were also distinguished by a hollow flash guard at the terminus of the gun.

"You think it's true what they say about the German tanks—that a 75-mm armor-piercing round will bounce right off the turret?" asked Pulaski skeptically. "We had those same 75s on the Lees in Tunisia, and I've seen their AP rounds punch right through enemy armor."

"That was in '43, and things change. From what I hear, the Panther is damned tough," King replied. He and his colonel had seen the same intelligence reports. "And the Tiger is a real monster, but they don't have too many of them on the front."

The colonel turned to watch as the components of Combat Command A continued to roll off of several ships. He knew a thrill of pride at the thought that he was in charge of a third of the division's firepower—its lead strike force. The combat command included full battalions of tanks and armored infantry in half-tracks, as well as a recon company, assault-gun company, and the eighteen big guns of a self-propelled artillery battalion. All in all, they would move out with more than five hundred vehicles and ten times that many men.

"Whatever you come up against, Ski, I know Combat Command A of the Nineteenth Armored will make a real name for itself."

"Thank you, General. I'll do my best." He touched his new shoulder patch. The Nineteenth Division's insignia was a white star on a badge of crimson.

"I know you will," replied King with a grin.

"Excuse me—General King?" A military policeman approached them through the grassy sand. He saluted casually as he reached the two officers. "I'm to take you up to Carentan tonight. Is your first battalion ready to go?"

King looked at Pulaski, who nodded enthusiastically. "Ready and willing," the colonel replied. "But what about that traffic jam?"

"We take our places at the back," said the MP with a shrug. "Don't worry, sir—we might get up to three or four MPH once we're off the causeway."

"What about the rest of the division?" asked King.

"They'll be met tomorrow, General—you can wait here if you want to or come up to Carentan with the Thirty-eighth."

"Guess I'll hitch a ride, Ski," the general said. "After all, I can't let my junior commanders get the best rooms in the hotel!"

"Sergeant Dawson!" Pulaski called his headquarters sergeant over. Dawson, a sturdy man with an advanced age somewhere in his mid-thirties, trotted over and saluted. He had the bulk of a radiophone slung over his shoulder. "Have you seen any sign of Captain Miller?"

"Eyeing up the causeway, Colonel. He'll be back in a flash."

Miller was the captain of B Company, and he did appear a few minutes later. He had planned ahead, so his company was ready to roll.

The vehicles of the headquarters platoon were nearby. Together with Sergeant Dawson and the MP, King and Pulaski climbed into the nearest half-track. Pulaski's driver—a wiry farm kid from Georgia named Keefer—eased in the clutch. The colonel and Dawson climbed up into the cab while the MP and King chose to ride in the back, seated in the lurching hull. The smells of gasoline exhaust rose around them. It was an honest odor, signifying powerful combustion and capable machinery.

The eighteen tanks and two jeeps of Company B joined, in file, the column of vehicles crawling over the narrow causeway and onto the constricted roads beyond. Broken into small plots by tall, tangled hedgerows, each field was a potential fortress to a defender. This bocage country, as Normandy was often described, had exacted a grim and bloody toll from the American troops who had wrested it from tenacious German defenders. Each hedge was a mound of earth, often six feet or more in height, with a bristling barrier of shrubbery growing from the crest. The bocage was perfect for defensive concealment and hell on maneuver—two grave liabilities for tank operations.

The column passed the shells of houses and barns in the darkness, the ruins looming like ghostly tombs to either side of the road. Often Pulaski had the impression of hedges pressing close to either side of the road, and it seemed in the eerie night that the half-track might have been rumbling down a long, narrow tunnel.

"You're up in the Eight Corps area, General," shouted the MP, speaking over the throaty rumble of the engine. "Under General Bradley's command, First Army."

"That's what I've been told—so show me the way," replied King, shouting in return.

"Say—I hear that before too long Old Blood and Guts hisself might be coming over here to take over a field command!" the MP shouted, trying to make conversation.

"Patton? Goddamn right he is—and then we're heading straight for Berlin!" The general grinned in a sharp line of gleaming straight white teeth, and Pulaski couldn't help but believe him.

The MP proved an enthusiastic escort, pointing out the route, talking about some of the firefights that had pocked the buildings and cratered the ground. Occasionally he brandished a written sheet of orders to the other MPs manning the checkpoints that frequently blocked the way. By the time Company B pulled into the trampled field of their bivouac site, they had come a dozen miles and passed a thousand or more individual proofs of war's fury.

The glow of sunset still brightened the western sky mere hours after Pulaski's landing on the beach at Normandy. As the tank engines died they were replaced by an equally persistent growl, a thunder that rumbled from beyond the horizon to the south. He knew immediately the true import of the sound. It was an artillery barrage—batteries of heavy 155-mm guns steadily pounding the Germans at their front.

"Well, Ski," the general commented, "it sounds like we found the war."

Wehrmacht Hospital, Vesinet, France, 1500 hours GMT

A fly . . . no, two flies . . . they buzzed past his ear to thunk repeatedly, loudly against something hollow and close beside him . . . a lampshade, perhaps. The injured man seized on that sound, clung to it for the proof that he had not yet died, that the darkness might be parting before him.

Rising through that small opening was pain, a pure agony that was utterly marvelous for the fact that it confirmed his vitality. The left side of his face was a mass of broken, burning flesh, and he vaguely recalled that he had been thrown from the car. And before the crash there had been the bullets from the sky, tearing into his body. He remembered that a tree beside the road had exploded, ripped apart by cannon shells. Wounds throbbed in his torso and his leg, his head was racked by a monstrous aching, and through all the sensations the most important thing was that his body was whole, would have at least a chance to heal.

And he would live.

Then the darkness crept upward again. Physical suffering waned, but now his mind was torn by nightmare . . . roaring, whining, lethal aircraft . . . deadly Hurricanes and Typhoons, murderous Spitfires and Thunderbolts flying everywhere, bringing flames and death to his brave men and his magnificent panzers.

The darkness was a river, and he slipped backward . . . back to 1914, to the first time he'd come under fire. His guts ached from remembered food poisoning and still he led a patrol, so tired and so sick he could barely remain in the saddle. Shots rang out of the fog . . . he halted the platoon and went on with three men. The new lieutenant followed a path through a hedge, heard voices, and saw the enemy. Fifteen—no, twenty of them.

His training urged him to bring up the platoon, but instead he attacked, firing rapidly as the enemy survivors scrambled for cover in nearby farmhouses, from where they returned fire. His platoon moved up and he had them ignite bundles of straw, half his men providing covering fire as the others kicked in doors and threw the flaming bundles into the farm buildings. He led them on foot, house by house, until the village was cleared. And he could see the flames, hear the screams, remembered his own pain, and struggled to awake.

Still he lived . . . they could not kill him . . . but like all those who survived he was helpless, frozen in concealment under the glare of daylight. At night he might scuttle across the landscape like a crab, but he would have to seek another hiding hole before dawn brought the lethal aircraft swarming back into the skies. Even now he could hear them droning, fighters and bombers diving from all sides, roaring around his head. . . .

The sounds formed the rhythm of his darkness, the dull hum of skyborne doom. For a time it was North Africa . . . and then it was France . . . and then ultimately it made no difference, for everywhere was the same beneath the naked sky . . . the enemy would find him, kill him, kill his men, his tanks, his Fatherland. Always there was the sound, the nagging buzz . . .

But again the thick curtain parted, and it was not the sound of aircraft. They were merely flies . . . insects, a minor irritant, but they were nearby and they were real . . . as he was real. He almost wished he weren't, for if he was real, he would be forced again to preside over defeat. Defeat for the Fatherland, defeat for his soldiers, defeat for himself. For there was no longer any hope as long as the enemy held the skies.

Voices of men in the room, coming from the space beside his bed.

He held the curtain of consciousness apart with a pure effort of will, embracing the pain through his entire body . . . he could not see, nor gesture, nor even make a sound, but through a great cloud he understood words.

". . . other man would have died—Dr. Schennig says it is so."

"Any man but the Desert Fox . . . you watch, he will be up biting the surgeons by the end of the month!"

"Surely not—he lost so much blood!"

"Bah—it matters not. I tell you he will make it! You should have seen him in Africa, standing tall in his car, racing right along with his tanks while the bombardment fell all around! No, they shan't get him this easily!"

"But the head wound—the bullet went into his temple!"

"And I repeat—he will live . . ."

More words, then, but it was too much to make them out. A *head wound,* he thought. *My brain—my mind . . .* Was that the reason he was having so much trouble organizing his thoughts? A depressing chill settled into him. He would sooner lose an arm, or a leg, or an eye—anything other than accept damage to his intellect. *It's my best weapon,* he thought.

Worry was futile. If he could worry, his mind could not be completely gone. Instead, he yielded to his fatigue; but now when the darkness came there was peace, and he slept.

Ministry of Propaganda, Berlin, Germany, 1915 hours GMT

The Reich minister of propaganda limped across his huge office to surreptitiously pull the curtain aside once more. Outside, in the streets of Berlin, the summer evening was still well lit, long shadows and an enlarging sun the only evidence that night was falling. He could see them: at least a full battalion of Wehrmacht infantry, outfitted with grenades and small arms. They had marched into place a few hours before, coming south from the Brandenburg Gate. At each corner surrounding the huge house a machine gun rested on its squat tripod, dark barrels pointed all too obviously at the doors of the structure.

Irritably he stalked away from the window. In his agitation his crippled leg nearly collapsed beneath him, and he lunged forward to catch himself on the edge of the desk. Furiously he picked up the phone.

"This is Dr. Goebbels! Have you connected me to the Wolfschanze? Idiot—keep on trying! It's imperative that I speak with the führer!"

Slamming down the phone, the Nazi minister stared at the wood-paneled walls of the elegant office. He ignored the lush Persian carpet covering the floor, the gold and silvered plaques adorning the walls. His gaze rested upon a man, the only occupant of the room.

"What does it mean—'The bridge has been burned'?" demanded the chief of propaganda. "Why do they fill the airwaves with such drivel?"

The other man remained silent—it was not a question he could have answered in any event.

"Leave me!" spat Goebbels. "Go find out why those troops are there!"

The other man, taller and younger, stiffened at the tone in the minister of propaganda's voice. "Come, Herr Speer," Goebbels added, his tone modulating to the persuasive purr he reserved for such moments. "I must make some private telephone calls. And we have to communicate with the officer outside the building—find out whose orders he follows!"

"Very well," replied Minister of Armaments Albert Speer, turning and leaving abruptly.

Goebbels spent another fifteen minutes rebuking the telephone operator for his failure to reach the Wolf's Lair when the door to the office opened and a Wehrmacht major entered the room. He halted at rigid attention, fixing the minister with an impassive stare. "I am Major Remer—you wished to see me, Herr Reichsminister?"

"Why have you encircled my residence?"

"I act under the orders of my commander, Major General von Haase. I am to seal off these blocks of the government quarter—no one is allowed to enter or leave."

"But why? You are an officer—you've taken an oath to your Reich!"

"An oath to my führer, Herr Reichsminister. And now he is slain. I can only obey my commander. This quadrant is rife with conspirators!"

The news hit Goebbels like a thunderclap, and he had to clasp the desk for support. "You lie!" he gasped. "The führer is alive—I spoke to him at Wolfschanze this morning!"

The young major was obviously uncomfortable with the subject. His own face showed the strain of grief mingled with disbelief. "He was killed this afternoon—a bomb planted in his headquarters!"

"In that case, you must know that I cannot possibly be implicated!" pleaded Goebbels, whining. "You must release me—allow me to draw in the reins of government!"

At that instant a burst of small arms fire stuttered through the air, coming from the yard beyond the huge house. The minister of propaganda blanched, his eyes going to the Walther in the holster at the major's side. "No . . ." He whispered the word, his eyes darting from the officer to his desk and back again. He would not be captured, tortured, killed by the enemies of the Reich. Better he controlled his own fate, no matter how cruel.

Abruptly Goebbels lunged at the desk, pulling open a drawer with astonishing quickness. Major Remer watched miserably, obviously reluctant to draw his weapon against this man who had been such an icon of the state. "Don't!" he groaned, eyes wide.

Frantically the minister reached inside the desk, scrambling for something with groping fingers. His eyes glowed and his lips were twisted into a crazed sneer—a taut grin of triumph, it must have seemed to the hapless Remer.

"Stop it!" cried the officer, finally drawing his sidearm and leveling the cold steel barrel. He watched Goebbel's hand emerge from the desk drawer, and relaxed slightly when he saw no gun there. "Come with me, Herr Reichsminister. . . ."

Major Remer's words were cut short by the cackle of glee emanating from the quivering Nazi. Goebbels raised a hand and Remer saw that it wasn't empty—the minister held a tiny white object between his fingers. Again the major raised his gun, ineffectually waving it as the man popped the capsule into his mouth.

"No—wait!" cried the soldier, dropping his gun and lunging forward. But Goebbels bit down hard, cracking the capsule. Immediately potassium cyanide filled his mouth, passing almost as quickly into his system through the salivary glands.

Three seconds later he was dead.

SS Command, East Prussia, 2200 hours GMT

Another headquarters lay concealed in the East Prussian woods, though it was not so large or so active a compound as Wolfschanze. Here, too, the swastika hung listlessly, and black-shirted SS guards patrolled with pacing Alsatians. Besides the smaller size, there was another, more subtle difference to this compound—here all the guards wore black. Nowhere could be seen the *feldgrau* tunics of the Wehrmacht, for this was the headquarters of Reichsführer SS Heinrich Himmler.

During the course of the hot afternoon and muggy evening, no sign of undue excitement had stirred around the gray concrete blocks or amid the wide walkways bordered with bright flower beds. Yet within these bombproof shelters, a controlled frenzy drove the officers who manned the radio and telephone centers. Desperately they tried to establish contact with the Wolf's Lair—with Hitler, or at least with some member of his staff. Meanwhile, the reichsführer had brooded in the darkness of his office, consulting star charts and then pacing in agitation, waiting for news as darkness settled over Poland and inched westward to blanket the rest of the continent.

For most of these hours the officers had been able to establish precious few facts—until shortly before midnight a frantic telephone call arrived from the Wolf's Lair. Within minutes, General Gerhardt Fuller entered the reichsführer's office and snapped to attention. His black eyes gleamed beneath the brim of his high, peaked cap—the only sign of the general's rising state of excitement.

"The führer is dead!" he began, without preamble. "Conspirators have moved in Berlin, Munich, and other districts—but there is a lack of coordination in their efforts."

Himmler turned to look at the general. His hands were clasped behind his back. In the dark room, his black uniform made him virtually invisible, except for the metallic glistening of the SS death's-head insignia. As usual, the general's skin crawled as he felt the penetrating eyes of the reichsführer on him. Although Himmler was not a physically prepossessing figure in his wire-rimmed spectacles, there was something about his gaze that put Fuller in mind of a snake facing a rabbit. Fuller could swear that Himmler was not surprised by the earthshaking news.

"Are you certain?" said Himmler in a mild voice.

"Yes, Herr Reichsführer. Hauptmann Braun, a loyal officer of the SS, reached us by ordering a technician to splice into the telephone line at the Wolf's Lair—the switchboard and radios there were destroyed shortly after the assassination. In fact, the man underwent no little risk to get his message out."

"I see," observed Himmler. "Please continue."

"A bomb was planted, apparently by Count von Stauffenberg, Fromm's chief of staff. No one knows who's in command, and everyone is accusing everyone else."

"Yes, I suppose that's to be expected. And the rest of the army?" inquired Himmler, his voice almost prim.

"They are paralyzed. There is no doubt that high-ranking officers stand behind the revolt, but the bulk of the rank and file—and the generals as well—await guidance, orders."

"Of course," murmured the leader of the SS. For a few moments Himmler was silent, and Fuller remained rigid.

The leadership of the state stood vacant, but it would not remain so for long. Of course, with the Reich threatened by looming defeat on all sides, even the prize of the government might seem a hollow trophy. Still, the murderous act meant that right now Himmler was the most powerful man in Nazi Germany. As personal commander of the SS, the reichsführer had the fanatical loyalty of those vast legions—a private army that existed alongside, and even within, the conventionally structured Wehrmacht. Could he use that power to seize control, to arrest this chaos in the early stages?

It was Fuller's job to see that he didn't get that opportunity. The import had been clear to Fuller since those five words had been whispered over the telephone, long before Braun had leaked the news to SS command. The bridge has been burned—the phrase still echoed in his mind. Neutralizing the SS was crucial to a successful coup, and that meant Himmler needed to die. Fuller knew that his own death would follow quickly thereafter. *It is too bad that Stauffenberg couldn't have gotten them both together,* he thought regretfully.

Slowly, with mechanical precision, he drew his automatic and raised it toward the reflective reichsführer.

Himmler blinked, the only expression of his surprise. Two shots thundered in quick succession, resonating in the confined office.

The impact of the bullets hurled General Fuller backward, smashing him into the closed door before he slumped to the floor. His eyes were wide, staring in an expression of astonishment.

"Well done, Colonel Bücher," Himmler observed quietly as a second SS officer emerged from behind a wall partition. The scent of gunpowder followed him as he trained his Luger carefully on the lifeless Fuller. The general's blood looked black in the shadowy room.

The fierce-eyed SS colonel looked at the dead man with a cold, contemptuous stare, allowing himself the shadow of a smile. The dueling scars that had slashed both his cheeks blazed redly, the only sign of his emotions. As Fuller's life ebbed away, his passing was marked only by the sharp degrading smell of his bowels releasing.

"Quickly!" he commanded, throwing open the door. "Get this offal out of here!" SS troops rushed in to drag out the corpse. Bücher was sorry only that he would not have a chance to interrogate him. Soon, he was left in the darkness with Himmler once again. Only a little of the odor of Fuller's death remained in the room, and that was tinged with the smell of gunpowder.

"Herr Reichsführer," the tall, lean officer said, "I must confess that I found it hard to believe you when you said an SS general would turn against you. And is it true—the führer is dead? This is a black day for the Fatherland." Left unstated was the two men's realization that Göring was now destined to become führer—and both men shared the same low opinion of the Luftwaffe head.

"Indeed it is, but from these ashes we will yet come back to life," Himmler said. "I didn't expect the attack against the führer at Wolfschanze; I thought the conspirators would wait until the führer and I were together. Still, I have made plans against this day. Only the SS can save Germany now. And as for you—my special thanks, *General* Bücher."

Before the loyal officer could frame a reply, Himmler absently gestured for the phone, and Bücher hastily handed him the receiver.

"Commence Operation Reichsturm." The SS reichsführer spoke these three words into the telephone, nodded dismissively at Bücher, and sat back in his chair with an expression of pensive satisfaction. Bücher's last image of him was Himmler as a black shadow, even darker than the surrounding night.

OPERATION REICHSTURM

July 21–31, 1944

Rockefeller Center, New York, United States,
21 July 1944, 0655 hours GMT

Chuck Porter crushed his cigarette into the overflowing ashtray and lifted his weary body out of his swivel chair. It was a dull night on the early out of New York, where he was the supervisor of the newsroom, and the minute hand was creeping so slowly toward three o'clock in the morning that he thought it was stuck. It was so boring that he'd spent the last hour doodling variations on the letters "cheAP," which reflected his opinion of the Associated Press pay scale.

It was hard enough making the change from North Carolina to Manhattan culturally without the additional shock of the living expenses. The payoff was supposed to be prestige, but the title wasn't prestige enough to compensate for the lack of money.

Worse, he had recently passed his thirty-fifth birthday. His hair was thinning and his waistline was expanding. He'd never been a handsome man, but he had possessed an intensity and a drive that had stood him well in his years of reporting. He could cover a fire and interview a politician. He was even something of a ladies' man and knew his way around a martini. He'd spent three years in Europe reporting on the German military buildup in the late 1930s, but most of those stories had been spiked.

He was afraid that some of the younger men were starting to think he was over the hill. They didn't listen to his advice, his experience, and his perspective the way he thought they should. He'd long since forgotten how he himself regarded editors in his own salad days. Well, he'd show them. He had his application in for the Paris bureau chief's job, just as soon as Paris was liberated. He wasn't washed up yet. He could even get a smile out of Trish, the secretary.

Earlier that night he'd spent an hour holding forth on the end of the war. One of the new reporters suggested that there might be some surprises to come. "Not a chance," Porter said. "It's a straight grind from here on out. They'll retreat, we'll advance, and between us and the Soviets, Germany's going to end up about a mile wide from border to border."

"No way," an argumentative reporter said. "They'll surrender first."

"You're wrong," Porter said flatly. "Hitler's going to lead the German people over the cliff like a herd of lemmings." He liked the analogy and made a mental note to use it again soon. "They'll fight until the last one is alive.

Hitler's like a god to them. People get fanatical when they're following their god."

But no one was interested in more of his wisdom right now. He was tired of doodling. *When in doubt, check the Teletype,* he thought. A good way to waste some time on a slow news day. He scanned the cavernous newsroom in the Rockefeller Center headquarters—a fluorescent-lit football field stuffed with desks, mostly deserted on the night shift, a few lazy people sipping coffee, chatting, one or two actually typing on their big Underwoods. The clatter of the bank of gray Teletype machines was a constant backdrop.

Then the four-bell "Flash" signal on the Teletype rang. News—real news—was rare on the night shift. Editing filler material and follow-up pieces, that was most of the work. A "Flash"—that signaled breaking news. Get it in, get it edited, get it out to the client papers over the wire.

Porter, already moving, was the first over to the Teletype. The chattering keys printed out the story. His eyes widened as he read, silently willing the slow printer to move faster. A crowd gathered. The only sound was the steady clacking of the machine.

FLASH/BULLETIN
LONDON, 21 JUNE, 0600 GMT
COPY 01 HITLER REPORTED DEAD
DISTRIBUTION: ALL STATIONS

LONDON, 21 JUNE (AP) BY EDWARD REED
THE ASSOCIATED PRESS HAS LEARNED THAT ALLIED RADIO MONITORS HAVE
PICKED UP GERMAN BROADCASTS ANNOUNCING THE DEATH OF ADOLF
HITLER.
        THIS REPORT, SO FAR UNCONFIRMED BY SUPREME ALLIED COMMAND
HEADQUARTERS, IS STILL UNCERTAIN AT THIS TIME.
        GERMAN RADIO BROADCAST AT 0600 HOURS GMT THAT ADOLF HITLER
HAD BEEN ASSASSINATED BY "JEWISH TERRORISTS." HERMANN GÖRING,
LUFTWAFFE HEAD AND HITLER'S DESIGNATED SUCCESSOR, ASKED FOR CALM
BUT DEMANDED REVENGE AGAINST JEWS AND ROOSEVELT, WHOM GÖRING
CALLED "THE JEWS' GREATEST ALLY AND A SUSPECTED JEW HIMSELF."
        GÖRING IS OFFICIALLY THE NEW FÜHRER. "THE VALIANT GERMAN PEO-
PLE MUST REDEDICATE THEMSELVES TO THE ARMED STRUGGLE," GÖRING
SAID, "TO REVENGE THE DEATH OF THE FÜHRER AND ACHIEVE THE OBJEC-
TIVES FOR WHICH HE GAVE HIS LIFE."
        NO COMMENT FROM ALLIED LEADERS IN ENGLAND. A HIGHLY PLACED
SOURCE SAYS THE BRITISH CABINET IS CURRENTLY MEETING.
        A MILITARY SOURCE CAUTIONED NOT TO TAKE THIS REPORT AT FACE

VALUE. "THE WHOLE THING IS UP IN THE AIR," HE SAID. "NO ONE REALLY
KNOWS WHAT'S GOING ON EXCEPT THE GERMANS. AND I'M NOT ENTIRELY
SURE ABOUT THEM."

MORE

AP LON 333548 JF/072044

With the final routing code complete, the Teletype chatter stopped. There
would be more later, but this was enough to go on. There was a brief pause.
This was big enough to shock even the most unflappable reporter.

Porter broke the silence first. "All right, people, let's go! Harry—pull the
Hitler obit and spruce it up. Frank—background on the military situation.
Lambert, Eaker, McCulley—start calling around. Reactions! I want reactions!
Smith—rewrite and get a flash bulletin out now! Go! Go! Go!"

He looked at the other Teletype machines with satisfaction. Nothing on
Reuters or UPI yet, he thought. Even a few minutes of scoop was important.

He watched his troops shift into high gear with satisfaction. The sounds of
furious typing, of reporters pleading for quotes, waking up newsmakers in the
middle of the night, of stories being created out of thin air—suddenly, being supervisor was a good job. "The war will be over inside a month," Porter opined
loudly, his previous certainty forgotten. "Maybe only a week. Göring's a fat incompetent and he'll quickly negotiate surrender terms." No one paid attention
in the heat of the moment, but Porter was sure they all agreed with him.

Yes, I sure love the night shift, Chuck Porter thought with satisfaction as
he picked up the telephone to make the first of many calls.

Southampton, England, 0930 hours GMT

Winston Churchill's resonant voice was flattened by the static hiss of the military radio, but his words were clear.

"It is with a joyous heart that I bring to you good news. At long last, Adolf
Hitler, Führer of the Nazis, is dead. At noon yesterday, a brave group of German officers, sickened and disheartened at the ruin caused by this man, this
tyrant, this cowardly criminal, finally brought him to his just fate by means of
a well-placed bomb.

"Does this mean the final curtain has been brought down on this terrible
conflict? Not yet. For there are still Nazis who will struggle to hold on to their
inevitably declining power, who will struggle to escape their final fate. Perhaps
the brave German officers who slew the tyrant will succeed in ushering in a

new age for their beleaguered nation, or perhaps they will fall, as have so many others, to the Nazi sword.

"But it is certain that if this is not yet the final curtain, it is at least the final act, for our brave forces, now securely placed on the continent of Europe, will continue their march, will continue their fight, will continue their great crusade for victory—"

Brigadier General Henry Wakefield, executive officer of the Nineteenth Armored Division, snapped off the radio. "Goddamn it!" he snarled, grinding out the butt of his cigar. "Why does that son of a bitch have to get killed just as I finally get into the war?" His large hands clenched into fists of frustration.

He picked up his hat and shoved it onto his head. He was a solid man, short and squat and powerful. His hair was mostly gone on top, and what was left was shaved so close as to be virtually invisible. Shoving the remains of his stubbed-out cigar into his mouth, the general strode out of his cramped office. He picked his way through a mob of enlisted clerks who tried manfully to master the maze of paper needed to move an armored division across the English Channel. On the other side of the water, action awaited.

Outside, at the overcrowded Southampton harbor, the raucous chaos of his office was magnified. Sergeants bellowed at heavy, slow-moving machinery, trying to speed them up by sheer force of will, while hapless enlisted men tried to jockey tons of mammoth equipment through cramped spaces and around boxes and crates into the awaiting fleet of battered and ugly landing craft— tanks, the LCTs that would move his division across the choppy Channel into France. A number of the ungainly flat-bottomed boats were already filled with armor and equipment; they had less than twelve hours to go and would need every minute of that time.

Wakefield shoved his way through the mess, his anger radiating before him, melting away any possible obstacle. It wasn't nearly the tangle it appeared to be—indeed, this kind of chaos was inevitable, expected. But suddenly his sense of urgency had been magnified. He had suffered through too many training commands and staff jobs to have his war snatched out from under him at the last minute. Hitler's death wasn't good news, not at all. That bastard should have died when Wakefield blew a personal hole through him, and not a day before. But now that was too late. Another situation O. B. E.—"overtaken by events."

Finally, Wakefield saw the man he was looking for. "Jackson!" he bellowed at a young colonel whose eagle insignia was as fresh as Wakefield's star. Colonel Bob Jackson, slicked-back black hair, sharp face, wide grin, looked up. His uniform was crisp and new, his tall and thin frame made him a contrast in every way—height, weight, age, and coloration—to his division XO. He was the commander of Combat Command B, the second of the armored fists that composed the one-two punch of the Nineteenth Armored.

Jackson handed his red clipboard, filled with a sheaf of papers needing checkmarks and signatures, to a captain standing next to him, who picked up the work without missing a beat, and pushed his way through a cluster of sergeants. "Yes, General?" he said in a laconic southern accent, saluting casually.

"Jackson—I've got to go up to London for a briefing on the Hitler situation."

The young colonel looked at Wakefield, his grin widening. "I guess the Germans figured out we were coming and decided to end it all first, sir. But it would sure put me out if that meant we didn't get into the war, General."

"No Nazi son of a bitch is going to keep me out of this goddamn war," Wakefield growled. "You suffered through too many goddamn training commands with me, and I made us both a promise. We're going to kick some goddamn Kraut bastards back to where they came from before this thing is over." He was personally less sure about that than he wanted to let on, but he was damned if he was going to disappoint Jackson on the eve of the transshipment to the Continent.

Jackson's dark eyes brightened. "Yes, *suh!*" he said with pride and pleasure, his accent becoming even more pronounced.

Wakefield's mouth twisted into a half smile. "Bob, meeting or no meeting, I don't want to see the rest of our division leaving one minute behind schedule. Pulaski and General King and all of CCA are already in position. Getting CCB across, and the rest of the division troops ready—that's now your job. Get them on the boats, get them the hell out of here. Early if possible. I probably won't be back in time to join the trip, but don't let anything stop you or slow you down. Get over there and get moving. I'll catch up. Understand?"

"Yes, *suh,* General, *suh!*" Jackson grinned.

He was a good kid, thought Wakefield. Hadn't yet seen serious action, needed some seasoning, but he had the right stuff. He was smart, hardworking, and aggressive. A new-model tank officer, drilled in the latest ideas and ready for action. Wakefield felt good about having him, though he growled at him a bit about sorting the goddamn mess out a little faster, just to emphasize his seriousness.

"See you in France, General," Jackson said with a final salute as Wakefield turned to go.

"Goddamn right," he growled around his cigar, returning the salute with a quick chop.

Fifteen minutes later the sounds of machinery and yelling so characteristic of a big military move ebbed away as his jeep left the harbor area. Southampton looked just like an American military base except for some of the local buildings. As he passed into the southern English countryside, soon all evidence of the war and the buildup began to fade. The landscape was different, but the farms had the same feel as the one where he grew up. Fifteen kids, of which eight survived past age six; good, honest hard work; a solid life. He'd joined the Army in time for the Big One, World War I, got in at the beginning of armored warfare, then, like so many career officers, languished through the years in the wilderness between the wars. Promotions were few and far between, funding was scarce, and he was lucky to have a job at all during the Great Depression.

And then a chance for action. New respect. A chance at the general's stars he'd coveted for so long. But there were too damn few career officers and too many new soldiers to train, and—for three years—Wakefield had been stuck trying to turn civilians into armored cavalrymen. Important work but not what he wanted, even though he had gone home each night and slept in the same bed as his wife of twenty years. Finally, he'd gotten his call, gotten his ticket to the war, and now he was afraid that everything would be for nothing. "Son of a bitch," he grumbled to himself. Wisely, his driver ignored him. It was easy in the racket of the open car.

London was crowded and twisty as always. The snapping one-star flags that adorned the hood of his jeep didn't count for much; generals were thick on the ground here and you needed two or three stars to be part of the big game. Wakefield didn't care; he wanted to be part of the show—the real war.

SHAEF—Supreme Headquarters Allied Expeditionary Forces—was overcrowded and still expanding. Soon, most of its functions would be transferred to the Continent, moving closer to the action, but the bureaucrats would remain, the acres of Teletypes and the dog robbers and the ass kissers and all the other bastards who turned trees into paper and turned the paper into a blizzard that took up more and more of his time.

"General Wakefield?" said a young lieutenant, saluting briskly. "The briefing will be held in room 101. Please follow me, sir."

The division commanders were all present, except for those who were already on the Continent—like his division commander, General Jack King. Wakefield wondered if they were just as annoyed as he was to be here instead of with their units. The large briefing room had a head table, and standing behind it was the supreme commander, as well as Field Marshal Montgomery, the top Brit, and Omar Bradley, Wakefield's friend and mentor for many years. A few of the generals were clustered around, some legitimately, some just asskissing.

There were some two-stars there, too. With a thin smile, Wakefield noticed his old nemesis, George Patton, sitting out with the division commanders instead of at the head table, where Wakefield was sure he thought he ought to be. Wakefield for a moment couldn't think of that old German word, the word for feeling some pleasure in someone else's misfortune. *Schadenfreude,* he remembered. That was it. He'd had a number of battles with Patton over the years, and lost too damn many of them.

Patton was smart and capable, but he kept assuming that everyone else was therefore a jackass, and that kept getting him into trouble. He'd done a great job commanding in Africa against Rommel, the Desert Fox, but he'd put his foot into his mouth over and over again, from slapping a soldier to making impolitic remarks about the Russian allies. Actually, Wakefield agreed with him about the goddamn Rooskies, but a good officer had to understand how to keep his goddamn mouth shut.

"Gentlemen, please take your seats," announced a colonel. Wakefield grabbed one of the uncomfortable chairs and lowered his bulk into it.

General Dwight Eisenhower began the briefing. "Men, you heard the prime minister's speech and you've read the newspapers. Truth is, we don't have a lot more to add. We believe we know the people who did it. Obviously, we'd like to encourage them to form a new government and surrender unconditionally, but it's not at all sure they'll succeed. Therefore, at this point, we're not looking at any changes in our overall battle plan, except to say we're going to keep our eyes and ears open, and just watch and see. It's possible that there'll be some spot surrenders or a morale drop in the German military that will help us, but it's also possible that the Nazis will be able to keep the lid on. No changes for now in any of your orders."

Then what the hell are we having a meeting for? Wakefield thought. No news, no changes in tactics, just a statement of common sense.

Eisenhower called for questions. Patton was the first to shoot his hand up. "Seems to me that we ought to hit 'em twice as hard while they're confused," he growled. "Why give them the initiative?"

Field Marshal Montgomery leaned forward, his beret tilted rakishly, and smiled at Patton with smug superiority. "And what exactly do you think we're holding back right now?" he sneered. Monty and Patton, in the parlance of politics, "went way back" in personal enmity. Wakefield disliked Montgomery nearly as much as he did Patton, but at least he had some respect for Patton's abilities. He had none for Monty's.

Patton was ready to launch into a chapter-and-verse critique of the current plan along with recommended actions, but Eisenhower smoothly cut him off. "As soon as we make the breakout from the Normandy peninsula, there will be a lot of new possibilities, but they're not on the table quite yet," he said, shutting up both of the ego-driven commanders before their dialogue degenerated into a war of words. "For now, we continue as planned and watch for any changes. Other questions?"

"What about Rommel?" asked another general.

"He's not dead, but he's badly wounded and probably out of the war for good," said Eisenhower. "He was shot up on a strafing run and is in the hospital right now. Field Marshal von Kluge is now in command of the German forces in the west."

"Was he part of the plot?"

"Evidently not, as far as we know. But who knows where his sympathy lies now that Hitler's dead? That's why we're continuing steady on course for now. I think it's going to take a little time for all this to shake out."

Since all the generals were present, Bradley provided a situation update. The foothold in Normandy, secured at such horrific cost on the sixth of June, scant weeks ago, was stable. Allied forces were moving across the Channel steadily, but the Germans were able so far to bottle up the Allies in the Normandy peninsula with their forces, built-in fortifications and obstacles, and the natural terrain, especially the bocage hedgerows that bogged down armor and infantry so effectively. Nevertheless, Bradley was certain that the breakout would be relatively soon. "Operational details will be provided as soon as they have been fully developed. In the meantime, building up Allied forces on the ground remains the number one goal."

Thorough, professional, competent, and modest, Omar Bradley was Wakefield's ideal of the right kind of career military officer. Never a hotshot, but always reliable. That's what won wars in the long run. No one deserved his fourth star the way Bradley did. Perhaps he didn't have all of Eisenhower's renowned diplomatic skills, but he was the officer Wakefield most trusted to get any job done.

After the meeting broke up, most of the generals stayed to chat and—in Wakefield's eyes—kiss up. Grudgingly, he didn't give into his first impulse, which was to bolt the room and head back at top jeep speed to Southampton. He made his way through the knots of people to Bradley's side.

"Henry! Good to see you," Bradley said. "The star looks good on you."

Wakefield smiled. He knew that Bradley's influence was one of the big reasons he got assigned to the Nineteenth with his newly minted star. "Thanks, General," he said.

"Hell, don't thank me," Bradley said with a grin. "I had nothing to do with it. Well deserved and overdue, that's all there was to it."

"If you say so, General," Wakefield said, taking the cigar out of his mouth.

"I do say so, Henry," Bradley said. "And I'll look forward to having you cover my flanks in France."

"My pleasure," Wakefield growled back, unable to keep the smile off his face. It looked like he'd get into the war after all.

Karinhall, North of Berlin, Germany, 2110 hours GMT

The telephone rang in Hauptmann Ernst Schmidt's office shortly past ten o'clock. The Luftwaffe officer lifted the receiver without speaking.

"Ein Gewitter nähert sich," said the caller, his voice taut with suppressed tension. A second later the line went dead.

The code phrase—"A thunderstorm approaches"—sent a surge of adrenaline through Schmidt's veins. For a moment he feared that he would become physically sick, but he roughly forced down the emotion.

Still, his hand trembled as he pulled the Walther P38 automatic from the shelf behind his desk. Smaller than the long-barreled Mauser 7.63 mm he usually carried, the hard-hitting 9 mm was the weapon Schmidt wanted for tonight's task.

Holstering the gun, he rose and stepped through the door of his office into the darkened corridor of Karinhall. The vast home, residence of Reich Minister—now Führer by the will of Adolf Hitler—Hermann Göring, sprawled dark and silent around him. Once these halls had echoed with parties, music, and laughter. The finest French champagne had been served, and the most elegant members of Berlin's nouveau-riche society had admired the priceless artwork hanging on the long walls—pieces stolen for the most part from the wealthy Jews who had since utterly disappeared from German society.

But it had been a long time since the great manor had hosted such a gala. Now most of the elegant guests were frightened to travel, with the ever-present threat of air attack. Others had been called by the war to different endeavors, and more than a few who had once laughed and drunk here were dead.

These thoughts danced like ghosts through Schmidt's mind as he passed through the darkened ballroom, toward the spot of light spilling from the office door that stood slightly ajar. Though he typically approached the minister a dozen times a night with information and requests, the captain unconsciously lightened his step—tonight, he didn't want to be heard.

He paused for a minute, disgust rising in his gorge as he looked at the bloated man fidgeting nervously at his massive desk. Göring swallowed the last gulp of whiskey from a tall tumbler. Most of the bottle on his desk was gone. He was sweating furiously, although the room was not hot.

Slowly, with visible reluctance, the air marshal opened a drawer and looked longingly into the concealed space. Schmidt knew what was going through the man's mind: he needed another injection, and he needed it soon. Göring stared longingly into a desk drawer, where he undoubtedly had a morphine-filled syringe ready to soothe his pain, his fear, his rage.

Schmidt stepped forward, and the air marshal slammed the drawer shut with a guilty gesture. He looked up at the door as the hauptmann pushed it all the way open.

"Mein Führer," he began, but he was startled at the shock and guilt on the man's face. It was as if Göring suddenly expected Hitler himself to walk through the door, alive. He'd been like that since he'd first heard of Hitler's assassination—jumpy, ill at ease, unable to focus.

"What—oh, yes," Göring stammered back, realizing that he was being addressed. For a moment, Schmidt saw the immense man straighten up, and inside the rolls of fat he could see, albeit dimly, the trim Luftwaffe leader who once had been an inspiration for Germany.

And then Göring looked up and noticed the gun in Schmidt's hand. His eyes widened in shock, but not in surprise. One of Göring's immense paws immediately moved beneath the desk, his huge body shifting awkwardly as he reached for the Luger he kept there.

Schmidt stood there for a moment, gathering his thoughts, giving Göring a quick few seconds in which to draw his gun—and seconds to see the contempt, the anger, in the eyes of his erstwhile aide.

Schmidt fired as Göring pulled his arm upward.

The large bullets shot forth in precise cadence. The first one struck the minister's bemedaled chest, forcing him heavily backward as a crimson stain immediately marred the powder-blue uniform. Göring's unused Luger clattered to the floor as another slug struck higher, and the third punctured the rolls of fat ringing his neck, snapping the huge head backward. Other shots continued to hit, still higher, but by this time the obese reich marshal was already dead.

SHAEF, London, England, 22 July 1944, 0907 hours GMT

Die Brucke ist verbrennt. Ein Gewitter nähert sich. Major Reid Sanger stubbed out the butt of his cigarette in the remaining half inch of cold black coffee and scratched his head. Code phrases, obviously, but whose? The first one he knew; British intelligence had provided support to the German coup plotters and instantly intercepted the code message that revealed the death of Adolf Hitler. The second one was a mystery, and he didn't like mysteries. That's why he was in military intelligence, even if other people called it an oxymoron.

Hitler dead. It had sort of an unreal quality to it. Sanger was only a second-generation American, and his parents, among others, had worshiped the German führer when he first rose to power. So had Sanger, as a teenager, until he'd gotten a firsthand look.

It had been the summer of his seventeenth year, and his parents scrimped and saved to give him a summer in his homeland. He'd flown the giant airship *Hindenberg* across the Atlantic Ocean, the majestic swastika on its tail revealing German glory and might to the entire world. His German cousins, a few years older, wore the proud uniform of Hitlerjugend—Hitler Youth. He'd joined in a burst of patriotic fervor, only to have the true nature of the Hitler mystique revealed to him on a night of atrocity and horror in which he'd been a willing participant, to his eternal shame. As the consequences of his actions set in, he turned against the Nazi Party, resigned his membership—to the dismay and disdain of his cousins. Having severed connections to that side of his family, he boarded the *Hindenberg* for the long and now lonely flight home, wracked with guilt and confusion.

The day of the landing, the *Hindenberg* had burst into flames. Most of the passengers escaped, including him, but he would never forget the horror of the inferno that raged around him. He bore scar tissue up his right arm and shoulder, creeping up his neck, divine retribution, he believed, for his actions on that night in Germany.

That trip had altered the destiny of his life forever. At first rated 4-F because of the fire damage, he'd finally managed to worm his way into the military with the aid of a sympathetic doctor. Because of his fluent German, he even managed to get a military intelligence post. He'd had to put up with inevitable suspicion about his background, and even now he suspected that his career was held back and his access limited for fear that he was a deep-background agent. The suspicion pained him, but it was inevitable, so he lived with it, refused to let it hurt him, and put all his energies into the war effort.

Ein Gewitter nähert sich. A thunderstorm approaches. He reviewed the steps in the conspiracy: the assassination of Hitler according to plan. Goebbels: dead, but not a direct target of the conspirators. Interesting. Himmler: attempt failed. Well, it was a long shot to have a deep-cover agent attempt the job. The SS Reichsführer was nearly as well protected as Hitler, possibly more so. And now Göring, dead. That wasn't part of the plan either. The logical conclusion, therefore, was that there were two conspiracies at work: the Stauffenberg group and the "Thunderstorm" group.

So far, so good. Next question: Who is "Thunderstorm" and what are its motives? The possibilities were, first, dissident elements within the initial coup plotters who thought the plan didn't go far enough and wanted to take out others in the Nazi high command. Objection: Now that the carnage is done, there is no reason they should not reveal themselves. It's not as if anyone on our side would disapprove.

Second possibility: A separate conspiracy group, unconnected to Stauffenberg. Objection: Unless they're more Nazi than Hitler, they would have reached out to the Allies . . . or Soviets, possibly . . . for aid. And when Hitler was killed, why not come out to the conspirators?

Third possibility: A coup within a coup . . . someone who either (a) wanted Hitler dead or (b) in the event of Hitler's death wanted to take control of Germany. And that someone would have to be . . . the survivor. Himmler.

The SS. Of course. Thunderstorm had to be Himmler. The Gestapo had either infiltrated the conspiracy, in which case Himmler wanted Hitler dead so he could take over, or Himmler had a little backup plan just in case Hitler got killed so he could pick up the pieces. Göring dead, Goebbels dead—would Speer pose a threat to Himmler's accession? Probably not. *How many divisions does Speer have?* he asked himself, paraphrasing Stalin. And there was Rudolf Hess, of course, still languishing in prison. Unlikely that he would be a ringleader in any countercoup, though it was possible that he might get a later role to play in any plan. Himmler had to be the key.

All right. Himmler has launched a countercoup, starting by killing off his key rivals in a way that attributes their deaths to the Stauffenberg conspiracy. He won't move against the conspirators yet, because he needs them as a threat to help him consolidate power. Afterward, he'll liquidate them all in a series of show trials, blaming them for the excess deaths and making sure no one is left alive to challenge him.

Next move? Mobilize the party faithful and reach out to the German people. The party faithful can be reached by SS and Gestapo easily enough. The people . . . communications! He sat up, knocking over the dregs of coffee and watery cigarette butts. "General Waverly!" he yelled as he pushed his way into the conference room. "We've got to get in touch with the Stauffenberg team—now!"

The general looked up with mild eyes and held up his hand. "Radio program from Berlin has been interrupted. The special announcement from Stauffenberg's team is coming on now."

"No, sir," said Sanger. "I don't think it's going to be Stauffenberg at all."

Broadcast House, Berlin, Germany, 1115 hours GMT

The sound of gunfire echoed in the streets of Berlin as SS General Horst Bücher's car passed the Chancellery building and turned the corner onto the Wilhelmstrasse. SS troops had stormed into the communications building and seized all vital areas. Two Panzer IVs flanked the entrance, and a twin phalanx of riflemen formed a corridor from the curb to the front doors. The newly made general of SS climbed from the car, saluted briskly, and studied the stone edifice of the Reich's central radio facility, Broadcast House. There were fresh scars in the stone, revealing the battle for the soul of the Reich, just as fresh as the new insignia on his black SS uniform.

Horst Bücher was a perfect specimen of the SS ideal, body and soul an emblem of German pride. From his early days in the Hitlerjugend, where he gained distinction by reporting his father, a city government bureaucrat from Mainz, for anti-Nazi sentiments, he was marked for greatness. Strong and rigid, he won a competitive scholarship to Heidelberg University, where he was a championship fencer—the scars on each cheek were evidence of his dueling prowess with the saber—and an honors student in military history. There, his European history professor had proved too understanding of the Bolshevik movement, and besides, he dated back to the Weimar days—the professor, like his father, was dragged away by the Gestapo, never to be seen again.

Bücher's progress through SS ranks was steady; Himmler had seen in him the perfect Aryan looks and build that, strangely, numerous top Nazis did not themselves possess. He'd served with distinction under the noted commando Otto Skorzeny. And now he was a general of the SS, and not just any general—he was Himmler's strong right arm, securing the Reich for the party and the SS. Now he had been charged with tightening Nazi control of the central radio facility.

The martial tones of Wagner blared from an array of speakers on the walls. Bücher knew this was the current broadcast of the station—the network had fallen back on staple fare until instructions were issued concerning the current crisis.

He ignored the troops, dark eyes intent upon the doorway before him. His temporary aide, a full colonel pulled from Himmler's staff, trotted several paces behind as he stalked up the walkway, climbed the steps, and passed through the doors into the tiled hallway. The building was not so grandiose as the Chancellery or the Reichstag, but that only made sense to Bücher. After all, this place was designed to disseminate words, not pictures.

Two guards lay in pools of blood beside the doors to the broadcasting chambers. Bücher was used to the smell of the charnel house, and this time barely noticed the odor. Whether the guards had resisted, or simply failed to comply quickly enough when the SS troops commanded them to stand aside, was moot. It was a well-known principle that once one or two were shot, it had a salutatory effect on the cooperation of others.

Or perhaps it had not, at least in this instance. An officious little producer, sleekly bald and wearing a threadbare but unmistakably expensive suit, appeared from nowhere to block the general's steady advance.

"Apologies, Herr General—but you cannot come in here!" he stammered with remarkable boldness. "The orders of Reichsminister Goebbels himself are required before—"

"This man is to be shot, immediately," Bücher snapped. The fellow's face went slack with an almost comical effect. He gasped noises, unable to articulate anything beyond a gurgling plea. One of the SS sergeants was raising his Schmeisser when the general suddenly recalled the mess he'd passed at the door. No need to take the lesson farther than necessary. "Take him outside, first!" he amended his order.

The sergeant roughly prodded the blubbering producer away, and Bücher stalked into the broadcasting section. Pale, tight-lipped secretaries stared at his scarred face from behind a wooden counter, while a storm trooper rushed forward to indicate the proper booth.

As the Nazi officer burst through the doors a trembling announcer sprang to his feet, gesturing Bücher toward the microphone with frantic obsequiousness.

"Very good," declared the general with a secret smile. There would be no need to shoot anybody else; these civilians were now completely cowed. He settled into the chair provided. "Signal the control booth to prepare for a broadcast—Reichsführer Himmler has a very important announcement. . . ." The clock showed a few minutes past noon.

War Ministry, Berlin, Germany, 1125 hours GMT

Just after noon, Stauffenberg and his coconspirators allowed the phones to rest. All that could be done via mere communication had been done. The coded messages had been sent and were now being decrypted by conspirators all across Europe, in cities of Germany and conquered nations, in various commands of the Wehrmacht. Throughout the Reich bold Germans should be preparing to take action to overthrow the Nazi yoke. Now they could only wait and hope.

Beck settled back in his chair. The old man's eyelids drooped with weariness, and the tension of the day had left him drawn and haggard. It was an exhaustion shared by them all, yet still overshadowed by the great truth: Hitler was dead!

"When do we make the broadcast to the nation?" General Olbricht inquired, as the colonel who was their leader rubbed his three fingers across his face.

"Sometime tomorrow morning, I should guess," Stauffenberg replied. "As soon as all the pieces are in place." The encoding of the coup announcement had taken considerable time, and though it had been sent some hours ago, none of the Wehrmacht units had had time to react. Still, the plotters felt certain that, with the death of Hitler confirmed, the German army would quickly fall into line.

One of the phones rang, and Olbricht lifted the receiver, listening for a minute before hanging up. "That was Stulpnagel—the SS and Gestapo troops in Paris have all been rounded up. They're keeping them under guard at the Hotel Continental," he added wryly.

"Good—together with Munich that gives us a good start on a power base," the one-eyed colonel remarked. That important city, capital of Bavaria, had yielded to the plotters earlier in the evening.

"I wonder what happened at the ministry of Propaganda—how the good Dr. Goebbels got himself killed!" Beck could not suppress his good humor—though the death of the minister of propaganda had not been part of the plan, none of them had greeted the news with anything like dismay.

"If only we can be so lucky with Himmler and the SS leadership," added Olbricht. The conspirators looked at each other with pretended nonchalance, but all of them knew the importance of the question. Himmler, with his legions of Gestapo and Waffen SS troops, presented the greatest obstacle to the plot. Since he had not been present at the meeting, they had to rely on the unknown quantity of their fellow conspirator, Fuller, to neutralize this threat. As yet, there had been no report of any kind from SS headquarters.

Another phone rang, and Stauffenberg himself took the call. Shock registered plainly across his features as he reported the news:

"That was Karinhall. Göring has been killed—shot in his study!"

"What?" demanded Beck. He fixed an accusatory eye on the count. "That wasn't supposed to be part of the plan!"

Stauffenberg shook his head in confusion. "It wasn't." This was potentially bad news—very bad. Göring was an incompetent, and that would have made him easier to manage, easier to bring under the will of the conspirators.

"Any word on who killed him?" inquired Olbricht, his brows knitting in alarm.

"No. Lieutenant Haeften," the count said to his aide. "Take the car and get out there now—see what you can find out."

As the young officer departed, Stauffenberg rose to his feet and began to pace. He looked at the phones in irritation, and as if in response to his mute plea one of the instruments rang.

"War Ministry—Replacement Army Headquarters. Colonel von Stauffenberg here."

Again the count's shock was obvious to his coconspirators, as the color slowly drained from his face. The message was brief, the caller breaking the connection after barely half a minute.

"Well? What is it? News?" Beck pressed irritably.

"Yes—of a sort." Stauffenberg paused, looking so stricken that Beck wondered if he was going to be sick.

"That was Himmler," he finally reported, his voice dull. "He plans to broadcast a message of calm to the nation in a few minutes. He wanted to send us his best wishes, before he goes on the air—and to assure us that he is well. He told us not to worry—said that SS troops have secured the Broadcast House."

"Is that all?" breathed Olbricht, suddenly turning a sickly shade of pale.

"No—he requests the honor of our presence tomorrow at 1000 hours, in the Chancellery building. He plans to gather the general staff and make plans for the future conduct of the war."

At that moment Stauffenberg knew that encoding the messages had been a possibly fatal mistake. The loss of time had given Himmler a chance to react, and now the SS reichsführer had seized the initiative from the plotters. There was still a chance for the conspirators to win, to free Germany from the Nazis, but it was a small chance, and growing smaller every minute.

578 Squadron Base, Wendling, Norfolk, England

Staff Sgt. Frank "Digger" O'Dell
Wendling, Norfolk, England
July 22, 1944

Mrs. Lucy O'Dell
Roxboro, North Carolina

Dear Mama,

Well, it's not looking too good for your little boy fulfilling his plan of dropping a bomb down ol' Hitler's chimney, if the news we just heard is true.

As you can tell by opening this letter, we made it to England OK. When we left, it looked like the war would be going on long enough for me to get into it, and now it looks like it just might be over before I ever get a chance.

I was so happy that you came up to see me in Sioux Falls when I was in radio school. I told you I'd washed out of pilot training and that they wouldn't let me be a gunner on account of the fact that I was over six feet tall. That's why all the boys in the unit started calling me "Digger" O'Dell like the undertaker on the Life of Riley show.

Well, I fixed that. I forged a form that listed me as five feet ten inches, and that's how I got into gunnery school in Texas. I managed to pass, but just by the skin of my teeth. When the colonel pinned a set of wings on me I felt like snatching them out of his hand to be sure I had them.

We did our advanced training all over, and ended up in Casper, Wyoming, where we received our own airplane, a new B-24. There were only three crews out of forty to get a fly-away airplane. Those three crews were considered to be the best and we were one of those.

We finally flew across the Atlantic to England, where we'll be stationed. When we landed, they rode us from the airfield over to the barracks and all of the old hands were standing in the doorways of the barracks looking at us and yelling things like, "You'll be sorry," and saying if anyone wears a size 38 blouse or a 14-32 shirt, how 'bout moving into this barracks.

In spite of that, they turned out to be a good bunch of fellows. When we heard about ol' Hitler getting killed, we all went out to celebrate, though I felt pretty disappointed that I wasn't going to have much to do in the war. But the other fellows were happy that it looked like they'd live through it, so I guess it's okay for them. We went to an English pub and they taught me how to order an "arf and arf" which is two kinds of beer mixed together, though I thought they were pulling my leg and getting me to bark or something silly like that. But it's the way they talk.

Well, it's looking like it will be a quiet war after all, so I will probably write you real soon and be home before you know it. As Digger O'Dell says, "Cheerio! I'd better be shoveling off!"

Love,

Your Son

Staff Sergeant Frank "Digger" O'Dell

Headquarters, General Staff, Berlin, Germany, 1822 hours GMT

"It's very quiet right now," observed Colonel Wolfgang Müller, looking out the dirty window.

"Or perhaps it's merely the calm before the storm," said his friend, Colonel Günter von Reinhardt.

In the smudged glass, Müller looked with annoyance at the reflection of the tall, calm aristocrat. Reinhardt was always so composed, so calm—the antithesis to the overweight, balding, bespectacled figure that was Müller's reflection.

To Müller's frustration—and even with black-uniformed SS troops now surrounding the General Staff compound—his companion was lost in the mirror maze of history, consumed by events that had happened nearly two thousand years ago.

"It is the ancient problem of the Praetorian Guard," von Reinhardt explained in what Müller felt were maddeningly restrained and logical tones. "The Guard ultimately elects the new Caesar. Because they have the arms in the capitol, their votes count more than others. For example, when Cassius Chaerea assassinated Caligula, the Republic might have been restored. Instead, the Guards nominated and elected the cripple Claudius, preferring that the new dictator be loyal to them."

Colonel Wolfgang Müller shook his head. The tall, aquiline-nosed aristocrat was his best friend among the officers of the General Staff, but it was a friendship of opposites.

Müller's watery blue eyes focused through thin wire-rim spectacles at his companion. "All well and good, Günter, but outside are men with guns who will kill us if Himmler gives the order!" Müller wanted a firm, commanding voice, but his last few words came out with a squeak. Spiritually, Müller saw himself as a man of action whose physical body betrayed him. In his role of staff supply officer, he knew that he had helped to solve the logistics problems associated with the Vengeance Weapon project, but although he knew intellectually that that was a real contribution to the war effort, it fell well short of the Teutonic heroism to which he secretly aspired.

Reinhardt's brilliance had made him an officer much in demand; from intelligence to planning, senior officers enjoyed having his trained analytical mind at their disposal. Reinhardt was a member of the Nazi Party, but sometimes Müller thought he was a little too cynical in his humor to truly fit in.

The tall colonel joined Müller at the window. A high barbed-wire fence surrounded the compound, and within that barrier, facing out, a file of gray-uniformed Wehrmacht soldiers manfully stood guard in the hot July sun. Officially, everyone was still on the same side. Civil war might threaten, but it had not yet broken out.

Late in the night, a division of Himmler's SS troops had rumbled up to the General Staff compound. Hundreds of elite armed troops had piled out of their personnel carriers and surrounded the barbed-wire facility near Berlin.

General Horst Bücher, a fierce-eyed SS fanatic with dueling scars on each of his cheeks, had explained that on Himmler's orders, he was sent "only to provide security to the valuable military leaders of der Vaterland in this time of great national crisis." His cold, contemptuous stare had thoroughly contradicted the polite respect of his address.

"I know that man," Reinhardt said. "In fact, I gave him one of those scars myself." Absently, he fingered his own dueling scar, a thin line across his cheek that made him look, in Müller's opinion, even more distinguished.

It had suited the Wehrmacht to pretend that Bücher was there to help. Nobody failed to understand the real message: accept Himmler's rise to the führership or fall at the hands of the SS.

Reinhardt turned and sat calmly at his metal military-issue desk, which filled most of the tiny office. He was lucky to get a window office at all, even though his view was mostly of barbed wire and machinery. The room was neat and orderly, not a paper out of place—the complete opposite of Müller's own working space. He imagined that even Reinhardt's pencil drawer was neatly arranged with dividers.

Müller, too agitated to sit, paced nervously back and forth in the confined space, much like a monkey in a cage. He saw his sweaty brow reflected in the small mirror on the wall of Reinhardt's office and dabbed at it with a wrinkled handkerchief.

Again he peered out the grimy window at the military standoff outside. The Wehrmacht troops, so outnumbered, stood at crisp attention in their feld-grau uniforms, true German soldiers. The midnight-black SS troops laughed and gossiped among themselves, occasionally looking over at their Wehrmacht opposition with disparaging sneers. Finally Müller snatched his round glasses off his pudgy face, polished them furiously with a handkerchief, and put them back on, halfheartedly hoping that the surrounding forces had magically disappeared.

The General Staff office warren was a beehive of activity. In the narrow corridors, illuminated mostly by bare bulbs, officers and clerks moved rapidly, purposefully, carrying sheaves of paper in and out of meetings. The ranking generals were locked behind closed doors, arguing, exploring options, debating, forming and breaking alliances. The military high command of the world's mightiest fighting force had ground to a halt with the führer's assassination.

Müller's frustration built until he could take no more. "How can you just sit there?" he demanded of his friend, his voice rising uncontrollably at the question mark. "Great decisions are being made! Our lives and the very life of our nation is at stake! Why aren't you doing something?"

One thin eyebrow raised slightly, ironically. "What would you have me do, Wolfgang?" Reinhardt said. "We are soldiers. Our superiors make decisions, and we carry them out. Our superiors themselves are in the hands of world-historical forces. Our destiny is shaped by factors beyond our control, and we are merely the playthings of destiny. But I will give you this," he added, with the hint of his annoyingly superior smile playing at his lips, that smile that made Müller feel ignorant and angry, "As Hegel says, 'Amid the pressure of great events, a general principle gives no help.' Truth be told, I, too, feel somewhat anxious. But, 'what cannot be cured must be endured.' Come, my friend. Let me buy you a cup of the wretched stuff that passes for coffee in this place. And perhaps they will still have one of your favorite pastries."

Müller was only half placated, but he allowed von Reinhardt to lead him toward the canteen. His stomach was rumbling—it was fear, he knew, but fear made him hungry. Nervously, he wondered about the generals in closed conference, vividly imagining the chaos, the debate. What if the wrong decision was made? Would he go to his death bravely against the ferocity of the SS? His own boss, General Röwekamp, was a decent but ineffectual old fool, certainly no protection at all.

Reinhardt's hand on his shoulder was suddenly very reassuring.

General Franz Röwekamp, white-haired, long devoid of real power, a World War I leftover, had not wielded any meaningful authority among the General Staff since the war began. Supply, reserve affairs, staff support roles were all he'd been good for. Now, as the debate of the generals entered its third hour, he could sense that his peers recognized him as a leader. His moment had finally arrived.

The senior Wehrmacht officers had gathered quickly upon the news of

Hitler's death, traveling from the various fronts and headquarters to meet here. Keitel, the chief of staff, von Kluge and Mödel, the front commanders, all outranked Röwekamp, but they did not want the leadership of this meeting. There was too much at stake, too many ways to gain unwelcome visibility. Their silence made their collective will clear: Let Röwekamp have the floor.

Jodl, Hitler's lackey, sat by himself in a gloomy corner of the room, ostracized, but still a factor. Of the important officers, only the badly wounded field marshal Erwin Rommel was missing. There were even rumors that he was part of the conspiracy. Of course, there were rumors about nearly everybody right now.

The Reich's key generals sat around the long oak conference table. For security reasons, the conference room was below ground where nothing natural could penetrate. Cold artificial light reflected harsh shadows. Everyone looked older, more worn, defeated. Tension in the room was thick. The meeting was secret, but all knew that their respective positions, however they evolved, would inevitably leak. Until the factions resolved themselves, until winners and losers became apparent, any and every opinion might become fatal. Röwekamp was old. Let him take the risk.

Three hours earlier, long before the table became cluttered with half-drunk cups of vile ersatz coffee, before the stench of stale smoke and sweat made eyes water, before the harsh glare of the lights began to reflect the building madness, Röwekamp had made his key decision. *Consensus . . . we must avoid civil war, chaos for the Fatherland. I will lead gently, bring out all sides, and find the solution with which all can live.*

It had been a mission far more difficult than any he'd faced in a long, if undistinguished, career. But he had persevered, encouraging, listening, moderating.

At first only Stauffenberg, a mere colonel but the most visible of the conspirators and known to all present as the assassin of Adolf Hitler, had felt utterly free to proclaim his opinion.

"We are this close to peace! We cannot surrender all to that Nazi clown in a black costume! Our coup has been a success; Himmler cannot take power without your consent!" Stauffenberg pounded his remaining hand on the long, oaken conference table.

"Murderer!" Jodl hissed. "Traitor to the Reich! The führer's mission must be completed. None of you here have any right to gainsay the führer's orders. With Göring dead—at your hand, no doubt—Himmler is the highest-ranking party official; it is utterly right, legal, and moral that he assume leadership of party and nation." Left unstated was a likelihood obvious to all: Jodl would then become his chief of staff.

"We did not kill Göring, you irrelevant lackey," von Stauffenberg snarled.

"It was Himmler himself, don't you understand? You have sold out your people to kiss Hitler's rosy red rectum. Now you're only looking for another ass to kiss."

Jodl was on his feet in an instant; there was murder in his eyes. "Traitor!" he hissed. The look on his face made it clear he could not understand why the others at the meeting had not already executed Hitler's assassin. Stauffenberg looked at him with equal hatred, about to launch into another tirade.

"That is enough," Röwekamp interjected curtly. "Jodl, von Stauffenberg, this meeting is to discuss the issues at hand, not trade personal insults. In my day, we settled matters like yours on the field of honor. Colonel Count, do remember that Jodl is still your superior officer. Accord him the respect his rank warrants."

Sullenly, the one-armed colonel yielded to military discipline. "Jawohl, mein General." He saluted and slowly sat back down. Jodl did not salute, but also sat.

Field Marshal Mödel straightened up in his high-backed seat. "This matter must be discussed, of course, but it is the very height of insanity for us to consider the transition of power and the future of the State while looking down the barrels of Himmler's guns. Let us not forget that we command the armies of the Reich. Himmler knows that our deaths will not bring the armies under his control. There is a chain of command, and the other commanders are with their forces. Himmler has not won yet."

Murmurs of assent from the assembled generals at Mödel's assertion helped lower the combative temperature of the room.

Field Marshal Keitel put up his hand. His face was blistered and bandaged, and all knew that he had been very near to the bomb that had killed Hitler. Still, the wounding did not seem to have affected his aura of command. "Field Marshal, I utterly agree. We are soldiers. There is a chain of command. Our deaths may not matter to the destiny of the Reich. That is perfectly true. But our deaths do mean something to ourselves; at least that is true in my case. Perhaps today is the day when we must all fall on our swords like true German heroes. Then again, perhaps this is not the moment. I, myself, am not eager that it be thus."

Mödel laughed. "Field Marshal Keitel, I am not eager for it either."

The gallows humor had the desired effect. Keitel stood up to pour himself another cup of the awful brew that even the Reich's leaders were now forced to drink. No orderlies were allowed in this room; the matter was too important and the identities of all the conspirators still unknown. The fear of another bomb had everyone edgy. Even Keitel had suffered himself to be searched. Standing, clearly welcoming the relief from staying too long seated, the field marshal turned his eyes along the table.

Röwekamp too looked around, carefully studying the faces of his peers on the General Staff. He had known many of them for years, but he could not read them today. Too much uncertainty, too much at stake for people to reveal their true emotions.

"Perhaps I may summarize?" he ventured, looking from face to face and getting agreement. "Point one: Reichsführer Himmler's SS units occupy all of Berlin. It is more than possible that should we refuse to cooperate, we will die here.

"Point two: Since our deaths do not give command of the armies to Himmler, he has little to gain from killing us, and therefore we have some power to negotiate.

"Point three: Colonel Count von Stauffenberg's activities did not command unanimous support among our numbers. His opinions, while part of the discussion here, do not control.

"Point four: The fact that General Bücher has offered a meeting with Himmler suggests that Himmler also sees room for discussion. Perhaps a power-sharing arrangement, a coordination of goals, might be the best possible outcome. Gentlemen, do you agree with this summary?"

There was general assent except for Jodl and Stauffenberg. Jodl sat like a church mouse, clearly afraid to push Himmler's views too hard. For now, he seemed willing to remain quiet, though he would inevitably give a full report to the Reichsführer. His duty, his loyalty, and his self-interest remained together.

Stauffenberg tried one more protest. Standing, he looked down at his colleagues and superiors, his angular and ravaged form casting a dark shadow on the conference table, and contemptuously pronounced his position. "Very well. You remain Nazi puppy dogs. You will discuss and debate and eventually submit to the jackal's teeth. Understand this, however. I am not alone, and those who agree with me occupy positions of power. Not all of us are revealed. Himmler will have to contend with far more than he knows, as will you. There are no safe harbors, gentlemen. Everyone must take a stand or be swept away in the flood." He turned on his heel and stiffly marched from the room.

The arrogance of a mere colonel irritated several of the generals. Nobility or not, rank still mattered—though all ignored the bitter irony that they had been taking orders from a mere corporal—Hitler's World War I military rank—for years. Still, Stauffenberg represented power. Perhaps he even represented members of this table.

Röwekamp once more passed his calm gaze over the assembled officers, then concluded. "Perhaps it would be well to accept Himmler's offer of a meeting, a discussion of the future of the Reich. Then we can meet again and determine the appropriate course of action for our nation and our peoples."

There were nods from the other participants. Find out Himmler's plan. Gain more information. Postpone final decisions. Still shocked by the death of a man who, however mad, had represented the spirit of the German people and embodied their destiny, they struggled with a long-ingrained habit of subordinating their wills to a higher command.

The consensus was clear. "Then we agree. We will meet with Reichsführer Himmler and resume this discussion."

General Röwekamp pushed his chair back, rasping across the wooden floor, and stood up, his ancient body aching after sitting for so long. The other officers rose as well. It was a proud moment for the old man. *I may have saved my country,* he thought. Civil war was at least postponed, possibly foiled. He stood as the officers silently filed out the single wooden door, leaving him alone in the harshly lit room. Wisps of smoke visibly floated in the rays of light.

Suddenly he had a powerful need to piss.

Excerpt from *War's Final Fury,* by Professor Jared Gruenwald (Zurich: University of Zurich Press, 1955)

The assassination of Adolf Hitler had profound effects on the further conduct of the Second World War. It is ironic in the extreme that virtually none of them were among the objectives of the assassins.

While certainly one cannot fault the boldness of von Stauffenberg and his cohorts in terms of their military action, they were surprisingly timid in the follow through. A rational examination of the assassination plot reveals crucial weaknesses in organization and planning of the subsequent coup attempt—flaws that almost inevitably doomed the operation to failure. Also, the secrecy necessary to their survival in a totalitarian state was enough to ensure crucial delays in the activation of key elements of the coup attempt. The decision to announce the coup in coded messages broadcast to conspirators throughout Europe was a final, fatal blow—for by the time these messages were translated, the forces of the SS had already acted to fill in the vacuum of power.

And finally, the critical injuries to Rommel all but doomed the overthrow of the government to failure. Although the erstwhile field marshal was not an active participant in the plot, we now know that he wholeheartedly supported the conspirators' objectives. He had even consented to serve as the president of the new German government, intended for installation as soon as the conspirators had removed the Nazis from positions of control. Rommel's reputation as a capable field commander, and the respect he had earned from military and civilian quarters alike, had given him a status lacking in virtually any other potential leader. Furthermore, his powers of command and organization could have proven crucial in the key hours after Hitler's death.

There is also considerable doubt as to whether, during that summer of violence, the leaders of the Western Allies would have softened their announced position: that nothing less than the "unconditional surrender" of Germany could bring about an end to the war in Europe. Of course, if Rommel had offered an immediate armistice on the French front, he would have dangled tempting bait. . . . But such questions are mere grist for historians' debates, and we can never know the certain answer.

In any event, Heinrich Himmler inherited a situation that was dire in all respects. The enemies of the Reich were closing in from all directions (see Map 1), and nothing short of radical new policies could offer any hope whatsoever of triggering a reversal in history's grim tide.

Nineteenth Armored Division Mobile Headquarters, Normandy, France, 23 July 1944, 0618 hours GMT

There was a low rumble of thunder in the distance—real thunder, not an artillery barrage this time—as Colonel James Pulaski pulled open the flap of the headquarters tent and stepped inside. He blinked at the sudden darkness, and then his eyes adjusted to the dim light. For a moment he was reminded of the confessional booth, but then the connection vanished as he focused on the military tasks before him.

There was a long table spread with maps and papers, the staff officers and their aides clustered around, working on the immense business of siting and moving an armored division.

None of the officers—or many of the men, for that matter—had slept much over the past three weeks. While it was tough enough to move an armored division under any circumstances, bringing that division to a combat zone brought a myriad of unfamiliar problems.

"Jimmy!" General King motioned him to a conference area. The division CO was an exception to the staff's shared experience—King had been given command of the Nineteenth only three months earlier.

There were a few chairs for the senior officers. Henry Wakefield, the exec, was chewing on a cigar. Wakefield had been the acting CO until King had taken over, and he and Pulaski had always had an edgy relationship. The colonel wasn't sure what Wakefield thought of the new command structure. Wakefield's gruff manner didn't invite easy familiarity, though Bob Jackson, the CCB commander, didn't seem to have much trouble. But then Bob Jackson got along with everybody (his southern drawl and easy, almost aristocratic, manners were hard to dislike, though Pulaski admitted to himself that he was learning to do just that).

Pulaski sat down in the folding metal chair. "Afternoon," he said.

"How's CCA standing?" General King asked.

"Fine, sir," replied Pulaski. "We're ready to roll whenever you give the order."

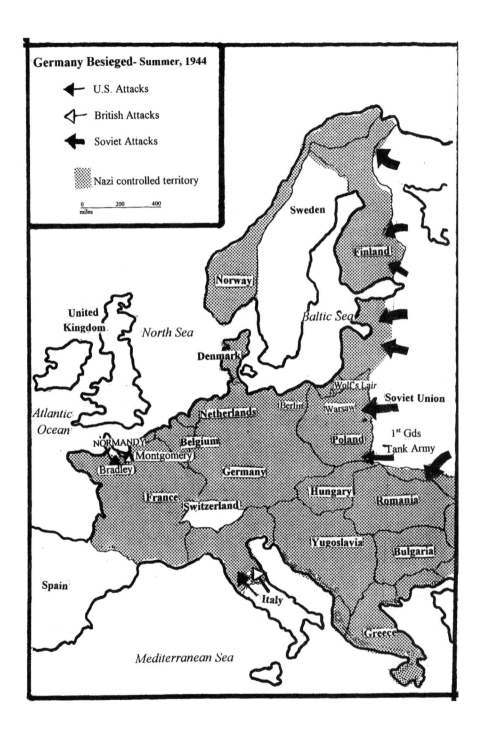

Germany Besieged- Summer, 1944

◄─── U.S. Attacks

◁─ British Attacks

◄ Soviet Attacks

▦ Nazi controlled territory

0   200   400
miles

Sweden

Finland

Norway

Baltic Sea

United Kingdom

North Sea

Denmark

Wolf's Lair

Soviet Union

Berlin

Warsaw

Atlantic Ocean

Netherlands

Poland

1ˢᵗ Gds Tank Army

NORMANDY

Belgium

Montgomery

Bradley

Germany

Hungary

Romania

France

Switzerland

Yugoslavia

Bulgaria

Spain

Italy

Greece

Mediterranean Sea

King's wide smile gleamed in the dimly lit tent. "Great, great!" he said. He looked up as Colonel Jackson came into the tent. "And Bob? You ready to go?"

"At a moment's notice, Gener'l," replied Jackson, with an easy smile and a nod to Pulaski."

"Good. And Henry, you've got the support battalions and logistics arranged?"

"They're shaking down pretty well, all things considered," Wakefield answered deliberately and precisely, speaking too slowly for the impatient Pulaski's taste.

King nodded in agreement as he lit his pipe. Puffing it slowly into flame, he looked around at the other officers, then nodded at his S2, the staff intelligence officer. "Colonel Grant will give us the best information we've got on the Kraut positions in front of us. Afterward we'll get the last word on the division battle plan. Colonel Clark will have your positions marked. Combat Command A will be leading the way. I want CCB no more than a mile behind CCA's tail."

The officers nodded. The entire division would create a road column more than ten miles long. The close proximity of the combat commands meant that their strength would be concentrated—but at the same time they would have to maintain discipline and organization in order to avoid a massive traffic jam.

"Now, Henry and I will be attending a meeting at First Army headquarters tomorrow at 0900. This is the big one, and when we get back I want the Nineteenth to jump on the ops orders and be ready to roll as soon as we hear the starting gun. We may be the new kids on the block, but I sure as hell don't want us to look like new kids. Once we get the word to attack, I want us to take off like sprinters—and keep moving until we get the word to stop. No excuses. Got it?"

A chorus of "yes sirs" responded. Pulaski was determined that his CCA would run like a well-oiled machine, though he was more than a little nervous. There were a thousand problems to solve and a thousand more too well hidden to discover until it was too late.

Still, he would be the best, or he would die trying.

SS Headquarters, Berlin, Germany, 0635 hours GMT

"You have come to report on the progress of Operation Reichsturm?" Himmler's quiet voice came out of the shadows as the new acting führer of the Third Reich—a role the reichsführer had taken on "with the greatest reluctance"— sat down at his desk, blinking up at the tall, handsome form of Horst Bücher as the general clicked his heels and saluted.

"Indeed, Herr Reichsführer," the SS general reported with pride. Himmler was—at least so far—refusing the honorific that had been so identified with

Adolf Hitler. There would be time enough for titles after the power itself was firmly in his hands. "The plan proceeds with remarkable success. Most significantly, the radio network and all broadcasting stations have all been seized. Your announcement this morning seems to have answered the needs of the public—the people mourn, quietly for now."

"As they should," Himmler agreed, with a tiny nod.

"The representatives of the General Staff will arrive within minutes—they've expressed a willingness to listen." He chuckled.

"Go on." Himmler's voice betrayed no amusement, no emotion.

Bücher focused his mind back to the present. "The conspirators have, for the most part, been identified. In accordance with your instructions, they have not been arrested—though, naturally, we keep them under careful observation.

"In the meantime the call-up of the Volkssturm has begun. Designated recruiting sergeants are summoning the remaining manpower reserves of the Reich—all men physically able to serve. The age eligibility bracket, for now, is fifteen to fifty years. The operation is careful and precise—for example, men who suffer from stomach ulcers will be gathered into special companies to simplify the dietary concerns of the field kitchens."

"Splendid. What is the anticipated increase in our strength?"

"We will create more than two dozen new divisions in the first month, Herr Reichsführer. However, I must caution that these formations will have little equipment or mobility. They'll be suited for barely more than static defense."

"Don't underestimate these men, my dear general—after all, they're Germans!" Himmler's tone carried a gentle hint of rebuke. "They will do as they are told, whether that be defend, attack, or die. Indeed, they can be replaced more easily than tanks. When the time comes to resume the offensive, they will doubtless serve as useful fodder for the enemy guns."

If Bücher felt any surprise at the notion of battered Germany going on the attack, his careful expression gave no clue. "All SS divisions have been placed on full alert," he continued. "We have no indications that any troops of the Wehrmacht intend to offer violent resistance."

"Is there any adverse reaction from the Gauleiters?" Both men understood that the approval of these key politicians, Nazi leaders for the various geographic regions of Germany, formed a crucial pillar of their ultimate success.

"It seems that Kramer, in Düsseldorf—also, I believe, Fitzmunde in Essen—refused to cooperate with the local SS authorities. Their replacements have proven more . . . reasonable."

"And the railroads?"

"The Gestapo has taken full control of all lines. Even should some aristocrat of a general take it into mind to move a division toward Berlin, he would find it quite impossible."

"The Special Transports continue?" Himmler asked the question nonchalantly.

Bücher allowed himself the shadow of a smile. "Yes, Herr Reichsführer! The number of trains has actually been increased—naturally, our Gestapo units are providing full cooperation. Your orders have been followed exactly, urgency added to the transports in light of the ominous developments on the military fronts."

"Yes, the war . . ." The new leader of Germany lowered his wire-rimmed spectacles onto his nose and looked up at Bücher in determination. "The war with the Allies we will consider soon—but first we must deal with the battle of Berlin. After all, 'Your objective, before all else, is to bring maximum concentration of force at the decisive point.'"

"Clausewitz, of course, sir," Bücher murmured. "The principle of the Schwerpunkt, and remarkably appropriate to our own circumstances. After all, we control the center of power—and this shall prove the point of our first victory!"

Himmler smiled his thin, tight smile. Now the generals were coming to him. The situation was dangerous—very dangerous. But, conversely, his position was strong indeed.

SHAEF, London, England, 0917 hours GMT

The situation in Germany had unraveled completely. Stauffenberg and the other conspirators had been outmaneuvered by Heinrich Himmler. Hitler was dead, but it was looking as if Germany had simply swapped one sociopathic tyrant for another. Or worse: had they swapped a dictator sinking into dementia for one who was still somewhat dangerously sane? The situation might now be worse than it had been before July 20.

Captain Reid Sanger felt his mind treading around in circles, like a hamster, revisiting each detail over and over again, not finding anything new but unable to stop. Along with several other members of the intelligence staff, they had spent hours in a small office that doubled as a conference room. The smell of stale tobacco had long since driven out any oxygen, and Sanger could feel a migraine coming on. He rubbed his temples.

"Do we actually know anything?" he asked.

"What is this—a philosophy class?" joked Captain Keegan, one of the numerous Yalies that tended to dominate the American intelligence community. "How do we know what we know? Can we know anything? Are we putting Descartes before the horse?" A chorus of groans followed by flying paper clips and rubber bands greeted the atrocious pun.

"My head is about to explode," complained Sanger. "Give me a break." He stood up, yawning, and stretched.

The other tired intelligence officers nodded wearily. They had been working for hours. Should the coup plotters be rescued now, or would Allied intervention deprive them of any legitimacy and hope in bringing down the Nazi regime? Could the plotters be rescued at all? If so, which ones? What about those who were left?

What about Himmler? Was his accession now certain? Were there moves that could yet pull out this abortive coup? Or would it be better to leave Himmler in place to hasten the fall of Germany? Or would it extend the war? Questions, questions, questions—all important, but all essentially unanswerable . . . except that answers—right answers—were being demanded upstairs.

"You still want a field intel assignment, Reid?" asked Lieutenant Foster. "Instead of doing all this fine work at headquarters?"

"Now more than ever," groaned Sanger. He wanted to be nearer the real war, not stuck in the rear, stuck in headquarters. Intelligence wasn't a combat specialty; he knew that going in. His German fluency was too useful to put him anywhere else. But he wanted more of the war than he was getting in London.

"All right," said Colonel Cook, calling the meeting back to some semblance of order. "We know we don't know much, but we've got to make a recommendation. Best guesses, gentlemen, and make them good."

The table went in order from junior to senior.

Foster started. "I think we try to rescue Stauffenberg and the key conspirators. It's the right thing to do; it gives hope to the others; we may get some propaganda mileage out of it. Himmler's won, and I don't think there's much we can do about it."

Keegan disagreed. "I don't think it's over, and letting the Germans work it out is best. Stauffenberg and company are doing this for their own reasons, not for ours. Support them if we can, arm them if possible, and figure that chaos is a benefit for our side."

Sanger was torn. Foster and Keegan had staked out the range of positions—do something, do nothing—and wearily the other officers weighed in more on one side than on the other. He could see both positions and it bothered him that there wasn't any clear-cut answer, at least not one that he could see. In his mind, he reviewed everything he knew, or suspected.

There had been various conspiracies over the years to assassinate Hitler, and Allied intelligence had assisted where possible, though most of the work and initiative was home grown. Stauffenberg and his crew had taken a shot at Hitler, after trying for some time to create an opportunity to remove both Hitler and Himmler simultaneously, which clearly would have been a superior option. Himmler had probably moved against the plotters, making Sanger suspect that he must have been at least generally aware of the plot in advance, though not knowing enough of the details or key players to enable him to stop it. *If indeed he wanted to stop it in the first place,* Sanger suddenly thought. But no, that was probably unlikely. If Himmler wanted to remove Hitler, it would have been done better, if for no other reason than that Himmler had better access, better resources.

No, this was game, set, and match for Himmler. As callous as it seemed, rescuing the conspirators was a bad idea. They weren't Allied agents, they were indigenous personnel with their own motives who understood the risks. And the Allies didn't even know all the players, making a rescue even more complicated. Better to let the situation play out, hope there were enough left in deep cover to make another move later.

"Sanger? Sanger?" The colonel's voice was sharp.

"Yes, sir?" he replied, mind coming back to the present. "Oh, yes, my recommendation is to let it play out. It's the best of a bad set of options."

The colonel nodded. "And that's the most definite remark I've heard today."

Reichstag Building, Berlin, Germany, 0930 hours GMT

The Wilhelmstrasse rumbled to a parade of long gray Mercedes staff cars—radiating an image of strength and control to the civilians, mostly very old or very young, or female, who gathered along the broad boulevard. Swastika banners draped in black bunting now lined the street, somber recognition of the national mourning over the führer's death as all Germany wore faces of shock and grief.

"I don't like this. I don't like it at all," Colonel Müller whispered to Reinhardt. They shared one of the cars with two other colonels. No doubt the other colonels had similar feelings, but they kept their opinions to themselves. "We could be walking into a trap. Himmler could kill us all. What does your vaunted history say about this?"

Reinhardt looked forward into the driver's compartment to catch Müller's reflection in the rearview mirror. "It is possible, of course, but remember that he could easily have leveled our headquarters. I am therefore fairly confident that we will not be killed—today, at least. Remember, this is a staff, not a single leader. If he kills us, military command authority automatically devolves on others, and those others are farther from Berlin. Himmler may prefer to keep those who control the armies under his physical influence. I rather suspect we will be allowed to live." He turned to look at the very agitated Müller and could not resist adding, "Most of us, anyway. Himmler may choose to make an example."

Müller shot him an angry and anxious look, then turned to stare out the window. Hordes of mourners wearing black armbands flocked the streets, an outpouring of spontaneous national grief—clearly Hitler still occupied an unshakable position in the hearts of the nation. The crowds had begun forming within minutes of the announcement of the führer's death, and there had been throngs throughout the city ever since.

Müller noticed one elderly woman wearing a black shawl. She knelt in the street, sobbing uncontrollably. On a piece of black velvet she had laid out military decorations. Obviously the mementos of a son or husband, now dead.

The cars rolled to a halt in front of the Reichstag, before the line of SS troops that ringed the building and stood with Schmeissers at the ready. Wehrmacht sergeants bearing their own submachine guns leaped out of the cars, opened the doors for the high-ranking officers, then snapped to attention.

The soldiers of the two rival armies, both German, regarded their brothers carefully, each watching for any hint of hostile action. The generals and their staff aides marched into the Reichstag for the meeting that would determine the destiny of the Reich.

Müller admired Reinhardt as he followed the taller man up the vast stone steps. Calm, distinguished, shiny black hair perfectly in place, uniform pressed and tailored, the man presented the very model of the New Germany. Absently, Müller patted his paunch and adjusted his glasses. As he approached the looming doorway he couldn't help checking to see if his shirttail had once again become untucked, acutely conscious of the Wehrmacht troops standing at impeccable Teutonic attention.

Within the massive conference room Himmler stood up from his seat at the foot of the immense, polished table, the very soul of friendliness and respect. The windows behind him let in the sunlight so that he appeared to be a shadow. The officers all had to blink and squint to see. It was an old meeting trick, but it was still effective.

"Gentlemen, thank you for graciously attending this meeting. This is a tragic day for all Germany, and we must take the right course for our people." He wore a black armband trimmed in red below the swastika insignia on his right arm. Walking over to greet the officers, he shook the hands of each general and marshal.

The elegantly formal Reichstag conference area was dominated by the huge table, but the richness of the carpet, the huge paintings, the vaulted ceiling scrolled like something from King Ludwig's reign, all spoke of the opulence and power of the Third Reich. Huge swastika banners, bold swaths of red and black, hung from floor to ceiling on each wall. The silver coffee service gleamed in the light of the July sun streaming through the huge, tall windows on the south wall. There were boxes of fine Cuban cigars, traditional German cakes dusted with powdered sugar, white-jacketed stewards, all the trappings of a formal military reception or government affair. Before the war, Müller remembered, this was the norm. Now, the sight of those cakes made his mouth water. And perhaps there was even real coffee!

He soon discovered that it was not only real coffee, but the cakes were made with real eggs and real sugar, and at that moment he decided that they were not going to die after all. Müller grabbed a large piece, then realized with embarrassment that the delicate cake was covering his uniform and the carpeted floor with crumbs and powdered sugar. He could see the distorted reflection of Reinhardt in the silver coffee urn as he sipped his coffee with casual elegance, not a crumb on him. How did he manage to stay so neat? No doubt it was an inherent trait, something ingrained into the Prussian nobility. Or maybe it was that he could resist the cake.

Himmler circulated quietly among the military leadership, a quiet word here and there, a reassuring pat on the back for the poor stricken Jodl, still bereft by the führer's death. Müller stood against the wall, staying just far enough from the refreshment table so that there was no chance anyone would notice him.

The Reichsführer SS—he had made it clear he did not want to be referred to as the "acting führer"—raised his hand and all eyes focused on him. "Gentlemen, let us attend to the Fatherland's business," he said quietly.

The room settled quickly, the generals seating themselves by rank; the colonels taking chairs along the wall. There was a slight clinking of china as the silent, efficient stewards freshened the cups of those sitting at the table with the real coffee. Müller desperately wanted another cup, but dared not fetch it himself.

Here were ranked the most famous and powerful military figures in all of Germany. Keitel, Jodl, Mödel, representing the Wehrmacht. General Adolf Galland, veteran fighter pilot and now the acting head of the Luftwaffe in the wake of Göring's death. Admiral Karl Doenitz, commander of the German navy, the Kriegsmarine.

Müller felt a nervous energy in the room, an extreme awareness of the importance and danger of the situation. He was witnessing history, a tale for his grandchildren if he ever lived that long, and the picture was burned into his mind. Himmler sat at the foot of the long conference table, facing at the far end the empty high-backed leather chair that had been Hitler's.

"Gentlemen, the future of our Reich rests on decisions in this room today," Himmler began. "We represent the German nation, and we must agree on the Reich's destiny."

One junior general, whom Müller decided must be one of the Stauffenberg conspirators, interrupted, "Our first order of business must be to appoint a new chancellor, and for that the Reichstag must be consulted. If we are to sit in judgment on the destiny of millions, we must act within the law. We have been ruled by a dictator long enough."

Himmler's brow creased almost unnoticeably as the genial smile he had used to woo the generals thinned. He collected himself and spoke calmly, deliberately. "Of course, General Bermel. I do not mean to suggest that we will override the law. However, this is wartime. Military necessities sometimes force compromises in the ways in which we must conduct our affairs. Our decisions will be ratified by the Reichstag in good time." He paused slightly.

Reading from the paper in front of him, Himmler returned to his prepared remarks. "Together we represent the military power of the Third Reich. Together we must first decide on the best course for the Reich. Together we must present a positive front to the great people who depend on us and whom we serve. Gentlemen, the National Socialist ideal cannot perish with the great visionary who has so transformed the nation and the world. The National Socialist ideal cannot go down to barren defeat. We will not return to the bankrupt and decadent Weimar days." His eyes gleamed with the passion of a true believer. "The Thousand Year Reich will yet fulfill its destiny."

General Bermel, with a furtive yet defiant look at the door behind which armed SS guards still lurked, interrupted again. "Yes, yes, yes. But what is now the reality of our situation? We have lost the war. We are being eaten up on two fronts. We are losing our allies, including the source of our oil reserves."

The general drew a breath, the only visible sign of his obviously profound emotion as he forged ahead. "The National Socialist ideal is kaput, finished. We must expunge the remainder of National Socialism from our government so that we can sue for an honorable peace. Herr Reichsführer, your day is done. You have brought us here under armed guard, you can kill us, you can struggle against fate all you like. Whether it is today or a year from today, you are defeated and the Reich lies in ruins. The only question is how many more German lives are you willing to throw away before you face the inevitable."

Even those who secretly agreed found the outburst shocking. Müller could see fear on the faces of several of the generals, fear that Bermel's outburst would lead to a mass execution. Himmler only smiled. There was no anger this time.

"General Bermel, I appreciate your desire for a frank and open debate on the issues. I welcome and encourage that. I would merely disagree on two points. First, there is no threat, no sinister force holding you here. You are free: free to stay, or free to go. My SS forces are simply acting as support for the national security. My goals are to prevent panic, despair, and sabotage, nothing more. The SS forces are here to protect you, not to hinder you, and above all not to harm you.

"Second, I pray we take proper consideration before we concede that doom is upon us. Certainly the war goes badly . . . mistakes, grave mistakes, have been made. But we have a chance now to make some corrections, significant improvements. I agree that our situation is serious, but I shall not yield the point that our struggle is doomed. If there is no objection, General Bermel, I would like to hear status reports on the military situation. From that, we can engage in a frank and free debate as to how we can all give our best to the German people we serve."

Even Bermel had to yield to such reasonableness. Himmler was being so polite, so conscientious, that Müller was suddenly, absolutely convinced that he was hiding something. Or was it that Himmler feared for his own power, and that the Wehrmacht had far more leverage than anyone suspected? For once, Müller wished he could hear Reinhardt's clear, logical historical perspective.

"Let us then begin with a brief status report. Field Marshal Mödel, what is the military situation that now faces us in the east?"

Mödel opened his leather-covered briefing book and proceeded like a man who had made up his mind to tell the unvarnished truth, a tactic that had been unwelcome in recent months at Wolfschanze. "We are facing utter disaster, Herr Reichsführer. Much of Army Group Center is destroyed, and our surviving units are forbidden to retreat. Thus they fall prey one after the other to Zhukov's tank armies. Where possible, they extricate themselves and fall back—against the standing orders of our late führer, I admit. Even so, they will barely reach the Vistula before the Mongol hordes."

The other Wehrmacht officers nodded; this was their shared opinion.

Himmler merely nodded gravely. "I think we are all agreed that the 'stand and die' order must be hereby rescinded," he announced.

Several of the Wehrmacht officers stared at each other. Himmler's right to give that order was not yet established, but it fit perfectly the decision they had known for months needed to be made. Now was not the time, nor was this the issue, on which to make a challenge.

"I concur, Herr Reichsführer," Mödel said curtly, choosing to take it as a suggestion rather than as an order. "That is an improvement, but it is not sufficient. We cannot halt the tide of the Soviet advance, but at least we will save a few of our divisions from the coming inundation."

"Thank you for your report, Field Marshal. Now, what is the situation in the west?" Himmler turned to Field Marshal von Kluge, appointed only a few days earlier as commander in chief—west, assuming operational control from the grievously wounded Rommel.

"I am afraid that the situation in France is nearly as bad as it is in Poland," von Kluge replied grimly. "For the time being, we hold the Western Allies within the Normandy peninsula, but the pressure is inexorable. Within a fortnight—a month at the most—they will have sufficient forces to break out. After that, I doubt we can stop them short of the Rhine."

"But for the present, you can hold in place?" Himmler inquired.

Von Kluge considered the question. "Yes, Herr Reichsführer—though I can give no assurances as to how long that will remain the case."

"And as to the state of the Reich's air forces," Himmler noted casually. "You have no doubt all heard that our esteemed Reichsminister Göring has fallen victim to the conspirators. I have taken the liberty of inviting the commander of fighters, General Galland, to speak of matters pertaining to the Luftwaffe."

General Adolf Galland, looking very much as though he would have liked nothing so much as to light up one of his trademark cigars, stood and looked at the Wehrmacht and SS officers with a frank expression on his lumpy, battered face—features that were not unhandsome but had been formed over a series of airplane crashes during the fighter pilot's adventurous career.

"You all know that the Allied air forces are pounding our country at an intolerable rate," he began. "Contrary to popular belief, the Luftwaffe is not devoid of fighters. And our finest weapon, a fighter that will revolutionize air combat, has been languishing under our late führer's decree that it be developed as a bomber."

"Is the situation hopeless?" asked Himmler.

"I would say not, Herr Reichsführer. However, there is little time to reverse the trend."

"Then perhaps we have been confronted with a historic opportunity." Himmler looked around the table with a confident smile. "I think we have heard enough about the tactical situation, at least for now. It seems that the basic problem we face is quite simple—we are waging a two-front war against powerful enemies and cannot bring sufficient force to bear against either of them. And our fighter forces have been hampered by . . . shall we say 'unrealistic' constraints. Is that a correct understanding of the information that has been presented to us?"

A few reluctant nods stirred the heads of the generals, as this was obvious even to Müller. What was Himmler's point? Did he fail to understand the magnitude of the disaster that loomed?

"That is all very true," began Keitel. "But it remains beyond our control."

"Perhaps," smiled Himmler, "but then perhaps not. Admittedly, the two fronts push us beyond the limits of our strength. But if one of them could be neutralized—held in check, as it were—would not the situation assume a very different light?"

Bermel shook his head angrily. "I defy you to make any plausible argument that victory could be seized from the jaws of our defeat. Hitler's directives have eviscerated the German forces, and led us to the edge of disaster. Nothing—nothing you can possibly say will change the reality of the bankruptcy of Nazism."

"Ah, General Bermel," Himmler said in a soothing, friendly voice, his narrowing eyes regarding his tormentor in a way that suddenly reminded Müller of a cat contemplating a mouse, "a dare. You wish a plausible argument of how Germany can yet win this war, to make the National Socialist dream a reality on the continent of Europe? Yes? Is this the challenge you wish met?"

Bermel glared at Himmler, then looked around at his fellows. Clearly they were happy for him to confront Himmler on their behalf, for no voice spoke in support of him. "All right, Reichsführer," Bermel said calmly. "That is my dare. I do not believe you can show us a credible plan."

"And if I succeed?"

"Then we must consider it." That was not too much of a concession, after all.

"Very well," Himmler said, giving a curt military nod. He signaled a steward, who opened the door to an adjoining parlor. An SS uniformed aide came in carrying a black leather attaché case. He gave a heel-clicking bow to the assembled officers, put the briefcase on the table and opened it with a crisp metallic snap. He removed a thick binder and presented it to Himmler, then began distributing a thin sheaf of mimeographed pages to each of the general officers. The colonels at the edge of the room, of course, received nothing.

"Gentlemen," declared the reichsführer, "Let me present Operation Carousel. . . ."

Normandy, France, U.S. First Army HQ, 1007 hours GMT

"Gentlemen, this is Operation Cobra: the attack that's going to get us out of these damned hedgerows for once and for all. First, we're going to plaster them with more bombs than have ever been dropped in one place before. Then we're hitting them with infantry, three divisions along a narrow front. This is gonna be the big one, men. Monty's had his chance—now we'll show him how it's done!"

General Omar Bradley was worked up, pacing with visible excitement as he spoke to the generals gathered in his HQ, a battered chateau situated in a grove of trees among the hedgerows of Normandy. The First Army commander was a small, scholarly looking man, almost bookish behind his wire-rimmed spectacles. But his voice barked with confidence and decision, and the four stars on his jacket confirmed the authority that was visible in his bearing, presence, and manner.

Listening to his commanding general, Henry Wakefield couldn't help but share his excitement. The Nineteenth Armored Division was ready to go, and now he—and the other division COs and XOs—were finding out where, and how, they would get into this war.

Bradley turned to Leland Hobbs, commanding general of the Thirtieth

Infantry division, the Virginia and Carolina Old Hickories of Andrew Jackson fame. "Think football: you footsloggers are my blockers. I expect you to hit them fast and hard, to open up the holes for the running backs."

Now Bradley turned his attention to Jack King, and to the commanders of his other two armored divisions. "When you get that ball, I want you to run with it—and run hard! Your objective is right here—"

With a snap, the general's pointer cracked against the map of Normandy that covered one wall of the room. Wakefield's heart beat a little faster as he and the other men identified Avranches, the historic city that lay far in the enemy's rear. All of them could see the potential, for beyond Avranches the roadways spread out to lead westward into Brittany, southward toward the heartland of France, and east, toward Paris and the Seine. He was going to war, at long last.

"Your S3s will have the details. I'll expect you want to talk to your men, tend to last minute details. But hear me on this: We have a chance here to bust this war wide open. Some of you are new to Normandy, others have been fighting and dying here for seven weeks. But if we give this attack all we've got, the days of fighting in the hedgerows are over. From here on we'll be looking to take Paris, cross the Seine . . . maybe move all the way to Germany!"

"One last thing," Bradley said. "There's been a lot of discussion about Hitler's death and what that means for the war. Right now, the answer is absolutely nothing. President Roosevelt and Prime Minister Churchill have both made speeches saying that the Allied aim is unchanged: unconditional surrender. Right now, the German political situation is in flux. Our intelligence reports are saying that with Göring dead, the most likely new führer is going to be Himmler. If anything, that means the Nazis will fight a little bit smarter now. Make sure this message gets out. The last thing we need is anybody slacking off figuring we've got this thing won already. Got it?" With a ragged chorus of "yes, sirs," the meeting broke up.

"Hank, I'd like to see you for a minute, if you don't mind," Omar Bradley said.

Once in his office, Bradley said, "Sit down, Hank. Coffee?"

"Thanks, General. Damn, it's good to be here at last."

"I know. It's good for all of us. I know you've been chafing at the bit for a long time. Let's see, the last time I saw you was . . ."

"Two years ago. At Fort Hood."

"Right. That was a wonderful show you put on for us that day."

"I had a good bunch of trainees."

"And they've been a damn fine crop of officers. You've been a real asset, even if you were stuck Stateside." Bradley paused and took a puff of his cigarette. "Hank—how are you and Jack King getting along?"

"Fine, General. He's a sharp man."

"Younger than you."

Wakefield nodded. "That's the way it goes sometimes. This is the army, after all."

Bradley smiled in return. "Hank, I know you want a combat command; and instead you've got the XO slot. More desk work."

"Somebody's got to do it, and I guess I've got more experience than most," Wakefield replied. He did want a combat command; he wanted it so bad he could taste it.

"Hank, you and Jack King go out and do your job, and it may not be over yet. Combat makes things change a lot faster than in the peacetime army."

"Yes, sir, I know that," replied Wakefield, the corner of his mouth turning up.

There was a pause, then Bradley said, "Hank—"

Wakefield waited. He suspected what was coming next.

"I wanted to talk to you about Georgie."

Wakefield continued to sit quietly. It was always good practice to let the other person do most of the talking.

"Hank, I've put the Nineteenth under First Army for now, but there's a good chance you'll get moved to Third Army. And for once the scuttlebutt's true. George Patton is going to command Third Army. He's been in the doghouse, but he's the best there is, and lack of diplomacy or no, he deserves the command and we need him to be in command."

"I've never disputed his competency, General," Wakefield said quietly. "In fact, I probably think of him as highly as you do—as a commander."

"I think a lot of you, too, Hank. Your style is about as different from Georgie's as night and day, but you get the job done. But there's nobody quite like him, and once Cobra gives us the breakout, Third Army's going to be racing like no other force on earth. Patton is going to be chewing up men, machines, and officers like gum, and I don't want to see you pushed out of the war just because you don't do things his way."

Wakefield nodded thoughtfully. He knew Patton thought of him as a World War I–era throwback and has-been, though that wasn't quite accurate, in Wakefield's judgment. Trouble was, Wakefield believed that you shouldn't throw out the baby with the bathwater and that a more deliberate style was better and safer in the long run. In the run-up to the Second World War, this had led to more than one head-butting contest between the two men.

Finally, he spoke up. "General, if I had my druthers, I'd druther stay part of First Army. But this is war. I'll do whatever you say or whatever my commander says, and if I work for Patton, I'll do my damnedest to do it his way. Hell, Jack King worships the ground he walks on, and he's my direct boss. I'll do my job and do it right."

Bradley nodded. "Hank, I know you will. I'd like to keep you in First Army myself, if it works out that way. Georgie thinks like a quarterback for one of those new-fangled passing teams. You're more of a fullback, ready to smash up the middle. But the team needs both. So, what did you think of Cobra?"

"I'll be ready when the center snaps the ball," he replied with confidence.

The sense of potential lingered in Wakefield's awareness as he and King left the conference and made their way by jeep to the forward outpost of the division. Everywhere the First Army tensed with an undercurrent of impending action. The MPs were extra vigilant at the numerous crossroads, and Wakefield saw men tinkering with weapons and communication equipment, striking encampments, and putting last minute fine-tunings onto the engines of tanks, trucks, and jeeps.

In the command group forward of the Nineteenth Armored, he found Jimmy Pulaski in the middle of one of the four fields where his Combat Command A had gathered. The colonel himself was supervising welders from the maintenance platoon who were blazing away at the fronts of several of Company I's Sherman tanks. Wakefield went over, put his hand on Pulaski's shoulder, and steered him away from the enlisted men. The sergeant moved forward, glad to do his job without an officer over his shoulder.

"Look at these things, General Wakefield!" Pulaski enthused. The metal glowed cherry red, and the general saw that a series of prongs were being fixed to the Sherman's transmission housings. "They call 'em Rhinos—and they're the best thing to happen to this army since we got bogged down in the hedgerows."

"I've heard about them—some sergeant worked them out. And the metal is coming from Rommel's Asparagus, right?" Wakefield recognized the iron girders as the same posts that had made such deadly beach obstacles along the Normandy shores on D-Day.

Pulaski nodded delightedly. "And we've already tried them—behind the lines, of course; we want the Germans to be surprised. You've heard about how many Shermans have been picked off going through the hedges, right?"

Wakefield nodded. Like all tanks, the M4 had only a thin plate of armor protecting its belly. When the stubby vehicles had tried to force their way through the mounds of the hedgerows, the tanks had been forced upward, and this vulnerable underside was inevitably exposed to the Germans who were always waiting just on the other side of the dense barrier. The defenders had destroyed far too many American tanks this way, which was one reason why the fighting in Normandy had dragged on so much longer than anyone had imagined. The hedgerows rendered each small field into a miniature fortress, and each position had to be reduced before the attackers could move on to the next.

"Well, with these Rhino tanks, the prongs dig into the hedgerow, and the tank can push right on through. We come out the other side with guns blazing, and only the frontal armor—the strongest plate on the whole tank—exposed to enemy fire."

"Let's hope it gives the Krauts a nasty shock. I think you'll get to try 'em out sooner than you think." The general went on to outline Bradley's attack plan, watching as Pulaski's eyes lit up at the prospect of battle.

"We'll be standing by," the colonel reported. "Just give me the word."

"It'll be a few days, I'm guessing, before the infantry chew you a hole. But when they do, I want you to move, and to move fast. This is the best chance we've had to win this war, and you'll be the one to get the job done. Pulaski— by the way—"

"Yes, sir?"

"You might want to let the sergeants run the welding. You'll have enough on your hands trying to run the combat."

Wakefield could see the embarrassment flit through the young colonel's face. "Sorry, General. I let my enthusiasm get out in front," he declared as the crimson sun shone in his blond hair.

"That's okay, son. Happens to all of us. Ready for some action?"

"Yes, sir! We've got what we've wanted—a chance. Just let me at 'em!"

Headquarters, General Staff, Berlin, Germany, 1434 hours GMT

"We got everything we wanted," Colonel Karl Schwartz grinned, leaning forward in the narrow jump seat as the crowded Mercedes limousine navigated the wide Berlin streets. "Operational control of the military, appointment of our own officers, everything! And a chance to win the war . . . if Operation Carousel succeeds."

"Everything—" Müller added dryly, "including the right to stay alive." The damp and spreading sweat stains on his clean uniform shirt threatened to bleed through onto his coat, the combination of summer heat and emotional tension. He leaned back in the seat, reminiscing on the powdered cakes—he had managed to snatch a second one as the conference was ending—and feeling a sense of contentment that reminded him of pleasant afternoons spent at his father's bakery.

"Oh, Himmler would never have had us shot," Schwartz retorted. "Tortured, perhaps, but shot, never."

Reinhardt lifted a slim finger to his lips and glanced at the driver's impassive face in the rearview mirror. Schwartz swiveled around to look, then laughed nervously, "Just kidding, Müller. You looked so scared."

"Scared, no," Müller shook his head. "But relieved, yes. It is a good arrangement, one that at least gives us a fighting chance."

"What do you know about fighting, Herr Supply Officer?" Schwartz questioned, eager for an argument to cover his own lapse.

Reinhardt interjected, "'An army marches on its stomach.' Napoleon."

Schwartz lapsed into silence. Then he started again. "What did you think of the plan?" he asked.

"Interesting," Colonel von Reinhardt stated, his eyebrow arching slightly. "Desperate, of course, but not without historical precedent."

"Naturally, you'd say that," Müller retorted. Müller's head was still spinning with Himmler's revelations. Would it really work? Was the war not lost, after all?

"No, no, Wolfgang, let us look at the situation. Himmler indeed has returned operational control of the military to the Wehrmacht. This is not only good for the nation, but it was Himmler's only historical option. Again, remember that he could have killed us easily were that his choice, but our deaths would not have given him power and might even have made powerful enemies."

"I'm glad you can consider your own death so dispassionately," Müller said sarcastically.

"I am merely a leaf floating in the stream of history," Reinhardt smiled. "We are all subject to fate's iron hand; I merely recognize and accept that reality."

"What about this power sharing?" Schwartz interjected.

The negotiation of the power-sharing relationship had followed the presentation of Himmler's Operation Carousel. Breathtaking in its scope, the actual arrangement was simple in details, just as Reinhardt had described. Himmler had the State, the Wehrmacht the military, with clear lines of demarcation, for the most part. The generals had supported it gladly; only Jodl, who had expected more for himself, was disappointed.

"Again, it conforms to the historical reality. Think about the Roman Senate faced with the death of Caligula. On the one hand, the Praetorian Guard is on the spot, close to the seat of power. On the other, the Roman legions can always return to Rome. Power sharing is in everyone's interest because civil war is in the interest of no one who has any power at all. Of course, power-sharing arrangements are always unstable, but someone will eventually win out. History will settle this; it always does."

Reinhardt was now in lecture mode, navigating in the mirror maze of history. Müller knew from experience that he could cheerfully continue in this vein for hours, so he interrupted. "I don't care what history decides; I want to know what to expect now."

"You, my friend, merely want to know where your next meal is coming from." Reinhardt reached over to pat Müller's ample belly as Schwartz roared with laughter.

When they arrived back at the headquarters, Müller followed Reinhardt back to his office and closed the door behind him. One issue in the Reichstag meeting had surprised Müller, something he felt a need to talk about. The suggestion had come from General Rick, who, like Röwekamp, was one of the old school.

"If we are to conclude a satisfactory arrangement to the war, one thing is critical," the old man had announced.

"And what is that?" Himmler had replied, in the oily friendliness that was beginning to grate on Müller, who believed none of it.

"We must stop the transportation of the Jews."

There was dead silence. Most of those at the table had long suspected some of the details of the "transportation to the east" that had been going on. However, a general conspiracy of silence, of willful ignorance, made this a forbidden topic to most. They didn't want to know, so they didn't know. They refused to know.

Himmler had smiled. "And your reasons for this extraordinary statement?" he had asked.

"World opinion," the old general had stated. "Even if Operation Carousel succeeds completely, we will need to negotiate a peace. The Jewish question is important to the West, and if we undercut the issue now, publicly, by stopping the excesses of previous policy, we will be in a better position."

Himmler had paused for a moment. "Hmm. Perhaps it is as you say. We must discuss this further. After all, a halt need not be permanent."

In response to Müller's question, Reinhardt's opinion was clear and straightforward. "Himmler's lying, of course. He has no intention of stopping the transportation," he said calmly. "In fact, he will probably speed it up."

"Why?" Müller asked.

"Because it is an SS and Gestapo operation and he is up to his neck in it. Stopping transportation may help those of us not directly involved in the event that we lose this war. But it will not help Himmler at all. His only hope is to finish what he has started and bury all evidence. If the entire story comes out—well, I think for once this is something quite unprecedented historically."

SHAEF, London, England, 1450 hours GMT

"This whole German situation is simply an example of shuffling deck chairs on the Titanic," pronounced Captain Keegan, his voice slipping into its annoying nasal register. "If the conspirators had succeeded in taking control of the government, perhaps the war would have ended sooner. With Himmler in control now, there will be few changes. Germany will inevitably be defeated, just as it would have been had the assassination not happened. No change."

"I'm not so sure," replied Reid Sanger, scratching his head thoughtfully.

"Right," drawled Keegan. "So, what improbable little scenario have you cooked up this time?"

Keegan was generally of the expressed opinion that anyone without the right school background was necessarily an idiot, which infuriated Sanger, but he'd figured out that the more successfully he ignored that supercilious tone of superiority, the easier his life was. On the other hand, Keegan had a point. Sanger liked to come at problems about ten degrees different from anyone else. He was often wrong, but occasionally he saw something that no one else could see. This time there was something nagging at him, something important. He was the sort of person who needed to think aloud, which was very hard to do when sniper fire was coming at him from his fellow intelligence analysts.

Fortunately, Colonel Cook intervened. "Right now, I want to listen to any idea, no matter how half-cocked, if there's even a slim chance of coming up with something useful. Keegan, put a sock in it. Sanger, if you have something to say, spit it out."

"Yes, sir," Sanger said, not looking directly at the colonel, but instead fastening his eyes on the ornately decorated ceiling in the small conference room. His fingers drummed nervously on the desk. "I was just thinking . . ."

Keegan snorted sarcastically, drawing an evil look from the colonel.

"I mean, Himmler had a countercoup plan in reserve, just in case someone managed to take out Hitler, which is logical. And Himmler doesn't seem to be quite as crazy as der führer, and he's got to have a more realistic view of his situation. . . ."

"Go on," the colonel said, encouragingly.

Sanger paused for a minute. "He probably did what most people would do, which is imagine what he'd do differently if he were top dog. . . ."

"Pay close attention," Keegan whispered to Lieutenant Foster. "You, too, can learn to be a top-flight intelligence officer."

"Shut up," said the colonel quietly, without rancor, but forcefully enough that Keegan retreated.

Sanger continued, not having registered the interruption. "So he's got to have some sort of plan he thinks will give him a chance to shine, because why bother taking over a country if you're going to lose shortly? Maybe it's just a plan to loot the treasury and skip town, but he's a true believer, so it's got to be some sort of big move he thinks will change the war and give him a chance to win. . . ."

"Interesting," said the colonel. "Keep going." He glared preemptively over at Keegan.

"So what kind of big move would he have up his sleeve? Germany has a two-front war and it's losing on both fronts—if he had some sort of time machine, he'd probably go back and keep Germany from getting into that situation in the first place, but he doesn't . . ."

"No shit," muttered Keegan, disgusted.

". . . so the only hope is to figure out how to cut this back to a one-front war . . ." His voice trailed off for a moment, his eyes unfocused. Then he blinked suddenly and looked down.

"Colonel, if I were Himmler, I think I'd try to cut a deal with Stalin. I think it's the only move open to him."

"Oh, cut the crap, Sanger!" burst out Keegan. "That's the stupidest idea I ever heard." This time the colonel let him run on. "First, it completely ignores the fact that the Soviets and the Germans hate each other's guts. Second, there's just no way Stalin would even listen to a proposal from the Germans. It's completely contrary to the man's personality, and it makes no geopolitical sense from the Soviets' perspective. They've got the victory, and Stalin knows it. The only possible motive for Stalin dealing with the Germans is believing that we were going to attack him, and if there's one thing we've made completely clear, it's that Stalin is on our team to stay.

"Third," he continued, barely drawing a breath, "Stalin agreeing to such a peace also totally abrogates the long-term Russian goal of weakening Germany so it doesn't pose a threat. Stalin isn't expansionistic; he wants protection and safety so he can work out his own problems. He didn't attack until provoked, but once he was, he defended himself, like Russia did against Napoleon. Fourth, there's nothing Germany can offer him that he can't take on his own. No reason to make a deal. I thought you said you didn't think Himmler was as crazy as Hitler. But this idea is crazier than anything Hitler ever thought of."

Sanger was still trying to work out his own thoughts. "I'm not so sure about that. I grant you it might be a tough sell to Stalin, but let's look at it this way. This is the end game, and Russians are chess players. Let's look at setting up the board for the next game. There's anti-Soviet sentiment in the west, and Stalin knows it."

"There is some ignorant paranoia, but it's not a big deal," pronounced Keegan. "We won't go Communist ourselves, of course, but that sort of paranoia is common only among the uneducated."

Sanger looked at Keegan directly. "Maybe, but I think you're wrong. In any event, even if you're right, Stalin will see it as more dangerous; he can't help it. He wants more Communist countries; that's the next goal after Germany is defeated. He's going to be looking at postwar positioning. He has to. So if there's a German proposal that makes sense on his terms, he'll listen."

"That assumes once again that the USSR is an expansionistic power, but there's no evidence whatsoever for that. They've minded their own business and kept the peace unless attacked. So why on earth would they even consider making peace with their historical enemies?"

"Because Himmler will make them an offer too good to refuse," said Sanger.

Colonel Cook leaned across the table and took the pipe out of his mouth. "Sanger, I'm afraid I have to agree with Keegan on this one. That's just too far-fetched."

Sanger shrugged. "I'm not sure I'm right either. I just can't think of another move for Himmler, and I know he's got some kind of move planned."

The colonel grinned. "Better be careful, son," he said. "If you keep talking like a crackpot, you'll never get that combat transfer you asked for."

Luftwaffe Airbase, West of Lublin, Poland, 2130 hours GMT

Paul Krueger lifted the bottle, let the clear liquid trickle into his glass. It was potato vodka, really vile stuff, but he tossed off the contents in a single, burning gulp, allowing the caustic liquor to sear its way down his throat, to rage like fire in his belly.

The pilot was already drunk, but nowhere near drunk enough. He didn't know if there was enough vodka in the world to deaden the impact of the event that had at first stunned, then horrified him, and ultimately left him grasping for any kind of meaning, of purpose, in his existence. His mind still reeled with the shocking news, the assassination that had pulled the rug out from under him.

At first he had refused to believe the radio reports, had turned furiously on those of his mates in the Jagdgruppe who had dared to ponder aloud the implications of Hitler's death. They were too afraid of him to argue. Then, when his colonel had finally received confirmation from Berlin, Krueger had wandered the airfield for hours, until finally he had found himself here, at the humble farmhouse that had been commandeered as a drinking hall for the pilots and officers of the fighter group.

"Mein führer!" He whispered the phrase, fought against the tears that stung his eyes, knowing that he could not reveal his sentiments here, when there were a dozen other pilots sitting quietly at the other tables. Even now, a few of them cast surreptitious stares at Krueger. Not that it was unusual to see him drinking alone—Hauptmann Paul Krueger had no friends—but it was strange to see the usually domineeering ace working so hard at impairing his awareness.

He could feel them looking at him, and he wanted to kill them for it. They couldn't know that it wasn't his mental acuity, his keen and nimble brain, that he tried to obscure. It was the anguish that threatened to shatter his heart.

Krueger sneered at a couple of majors sitting nearby, and the older officers quickly averted their looks, muttering quietly between themselves. They were fools, the pilot knew—they couldn't understand the impact of Hitler's death upon their future, upon the future of all der Vaterland. Then he had an even darker thought: perhaps they were not fools, but traitors!

It had come as no surprise to him that there were those among the Luftwaffe, no doubt throughout all Germany, who were relieved and gladdened when they heard the news of Colonel von Stauffenberg's treachery. Some of his own countrymen thought the man a hero, instead of the vilest kind of coward, one who turned against the flag, the uniform, the nation of his birth. But Krueger knew the truth. He was certain that the count would burn in hell for his betrayal of the Aryan ideal, of everything that had formed the high purpose of the German nation during the last eleven years.

Krueger lurched to his feet, sending the chair slamming backward to the floor and drawing looks from all across the dingy room. He raised his empty glass, ready to hurl it at one of the majors, and saw the man's eyes widen in fear. With a harsh bark of laughter, Krueger dropped the glass to the floor and staggered out the door.

He remembered, and relished, the terror that had flashed across the other man's face. He knew that many people found him frightening, and he cherished that sense of power. They should fear him—and they did.

How many people had he killed during this war? More than he could count, far more than the 150 pilots he had blasted from the sky. His face twisted into a tight smile as he recalled the long lines of refugees on the Polish highways five years ago, the way they had scattered before his bullets as his invincible fighter had roared along, stitching the roadway, the vehicles, the bodies with a lethal thread of gunfire. And before them there had been numberless Spanish peasants, members of a subrace every bit as low as the Slavs, who had felt the lash of his weaponry as he learned the potential of his splendid fighter, had exercised his marksmanship against the antlike creatures who fled the violence of the war that ripped at their country.

And finally there had been the fat Soviet columns, and the cities and the encampments, that had suffered under the righteous fire of his attacks. Sometimes his Me-109 had carried bombs, and Krueger knew of no greater thrill than to drop a lethal explosive into a fuel dump, to watch the hellish fireball billow into the sky, flames tickling the tail of his fighter as he raced away. Other times fusillades of bullets had speckled his aircraft, but never once had they nicked his skin . . . always the killing violence remained beyond him, burning and shattering his enemies while sparing his own life.

But it had not been enough. No matter how many he killed, in the end the Russians had been too many, and the rest of the Germans too weak, to achieve the victory that morality required—no, demanded.

He found himself in front of the operations building, and stumbled through the front door to find the clerks busily cramming papers into a metal stove. Flames crackled, hot and orange through the open door, and the office workers and a young lieutenant came to attention at the sight of the pilot.

"What're you doing?" demanded Krueger.

"The Russians," Leutnant Schimmer explained hastily. "They'll be here within a few days—the colonel told us to start burning the documents."

"The colonel is a coward and a fool!" snapped Krueger, infuriated at the defeatist attitude. He was about to lunge forward and push the clerks away from the stove when he was startled by a calm voice from the shadows in the far side of the office.

"Now, now, Paul . . . it's no doubt remarks like those that explain why you're still a lowly hauptmann, after all these years, all those kills." The speaker drew deeply on a big cigar, the end glowing like a cherry of fire, and the drunken pilot was stunned by an instant recognition.

"Galland . . . is that you?" he asked, gaping stupidly.

"General Galland, if you please," replied the other pilot, moving forward so that Krueger could get a good look at him. "My face has been rearranged a bit since the days of the Condor Legion, courtesy of a Messerschmidt instrument panel," added the commander of all the Luftwaffe's fighter forces, now acting head of the entire Luftwaffe following Göring's death. He offered the stunned and drunken Krueger a cigar. "Perhaps you'd take a walk with me?" He gestured to the still-open door, and together the two aces strolled into the night.

They paused for a moment while Krueger lit his cigar and drew a deep, satisfying draft. "It has been long since I've tasted anything like that . . . it is a pleasure," he admitted, vaguely aware that his foul mood had been whisked away like the smoke of the burning tobacco.

They resumed their measured strides, smoking companionably as they walked along the flight line, now the province of only a half dozen battered 109s.

"I came looking for you," Adolf Galland remarked, after a few minutes. "Though I'd hoped to find you in better condition."

"Why?" demanded Krueger, his old bitterness once again rising. "My plane is grounded, the engine useless. And now we have nothing left to fly for!"

"There I think you are wrong. Tell me, I remember from Spain that you were once a fine engineer . . . do you think you have retained your edge?"

The hauptmann shrugged. The fiery ember from his cigar cast an orange glow on his face. "I have been killing the enemies of the Reich for eight years. But yes, I think I still know how to use a slide rule."

"I have a job for you, if you are willing . . . and it is something that might actually make a difference, for Germany, for 'the Reich,'" Galland stated, allowing a trace of irony to bracket the last words. "I will need your engineering talents, but it is also a chance for you to fly—and to pilot an airplane the likes which neither you nor the rest of the world has ever seen."

"One of the führer's secret weapons?" asked Krueger. He knew about the Vengeance Weapon, the V-1 flying bomb that had just gone into operation. What else was in the arsenal? He felt immediately sobered, and his nearly broken heart was quickening in his breast.

"I will be visiting other bases on the eastern front," the general of fighters said evasively, "gathering the best men I can find. But I want you to come to Landsberg airbase by August first. There you will learn more, all you want to know."

"I will be there, mein General," replied Krueger. Impulsively he snapped out his arm. "*Heil Hitler!*"

"Yes," Galland replied, lifting his own cigar to the brim of his cap in a return salute. "Now finish smoking that, Paul . . . and try to get some sleep."

Wehrmacht Hospital, Vesinet, France, 2150 hours GMT

He couldn't sleep, not even with the drugs. He could feel everyone being quiet around him, but his mind kept circling in endless loops—the explosion, the roadside tree being blown apart, the car tumbling over and over. It was from the air, always from the air. And it was all his responsibility—his soldiers, his plans, his campaign failing, the forces of the Fatherland retreating, dying, defeated. He fought to concentrate, to focus his mind, and above all to keep himself from plunging down to utter despair.

The nurse in starched white, her voice barely a whisper, drew his attention to the door of the room.

"Herr Feldmarschall, Baron von Esebeck has been waiting outside for several hours . . . I told him that on doctor's orders you were not well enough to have visitors, but he was most—"

"Inform the doctor that I outrank him. And bring the baron in at once!"

Using his "general's voice" strained his reserves of energy, but he was pleased that the nurse responded with obedience—and von Esebeck came through the door moments later. By that time the wounded man had pushed himself to a sitting position and shifted his legs off the side of his bed. He felt a wave of dizziness and planted both hands firmly on the mattress. Slowly his thoughts cleared, at least somewhat. He felt as if his head were stuffed with cotton, that everything was distant and moving just out of his mental grasp.

"My Field Marshal!" The war correspondent approached with a look of concern. "It's splendid to see you so well—but surely you should lie down; I beg you not to exert yourself on my account!"

"I'm glad you came, my good man. Now, don't make me regret the welcome by sounding like my surgeons!" Rommel smiled, though the twisting of his wounded face immediately distorted the expression into a grimace. "Truly, they'd have me seek permission before I so much as twitch an eyebrow."

"They tell me it's a miracle—Professor Albrecht says he'll have to revise all his lectures, that you shouldn't be alive after such an attack."

"Nonsense. The Allies will not remove me so easily. Now listen: nobody will give me any news around here. How do we stand in Normandy?" It was an effort to sound normal. He wondered what was behind the baron's startled expression: *am I sounding slow, stupid, an invalid?*

Von Esebeck's eyes widened. "You have heard nothing, these last days?"

"Of consequence? No. Just that drivel about me having no right to be alive." Rommel remembered another question that had drifted through his mind these last days. "And Corporal Daniel, how is he doing?"

"I'm sorry, Field Marshal. Your driver was killed; regrettably, he died from his wounds the night after the attack."

"Blast it all." Another good man gone, and as always, no time for regret.

"Normandy . . . the line holds, as desperately as ever. We weathered a great attack from the British—they bombed a square mile of countryside into a waste, nothing but mounds of dirt. . . ." Von Esebeck was strangely hesitant. "That is, you have heard nothing about the führer?"

"What—no?" Rommel stiffened perceptibly, anticipating the news.

"Assassinated, by Colonel Claus von Stauffenberg. Three days ago."

Now the general leaned back onto the bed, enveloped in a wave of fatigue that was perhaps only shock in thin disguise. But truly, he was not shocked—he had known about Stauffenberg and some of the others, noble and honorable army officers who had considered and planned for this dire step. Now they had acted. *And I was in my bed,* he thought frustratingly.

Rommel had never been close to the führer. He had at one time admired and respected him, though he had little use for Nazis in general. Hitler had a magnetic personality, a remarkable memory for any book he'd ever read, and surprising physical courage. Rommel had commanded the escort battalion when the Germans entered Prague in 1938. He remembered that Hitler had asked him, "What would you do if you were in my place?" and Rommel replied, "I should get into an open car and drive through the streets without an escort." To everyone's surprise—especially his guards—Hitler had taken Rommel's advice.

It was after his return to Germany at the end of the North African campaign that his opinion of Hitler had turned increasingly negative. At first he'd believed Hitler to be a good man who inexplicably surrounded himself with sycophants, but his eyes slowly opened. He was one of the few who dared to argue with the führer directly, and when he saw that the führer himself was responsible for many of the decisions the Desert Fox thought were leading Germany to ruin and degradation, he was horrified.

Never a particularly political man, he had brooded over the matter for some months. He was aware that others shared his views, but he had made no effort to become involved with them. Instead, he'd turned himself back to his work, although with an increasing sense of futility and despair.

"Has the news been released—do the Allies know? Are talks under way toward an armistice?"

"Well . . . it has been announced to Germany and the world. Reichsführer Himmler made the declaration. The SS have backed him, of course, and the Wehrmacht . . . the Wehrmacht seems agreeable to the arrangement, for the time being."

Rommel shook his head, weary, fogged, but still able to see the overall picture from the correspondent's carefully chosen words. "You are unusually circumspect, my good reporter. When we were together in Africa you had a better way with the truth, at least to my face. Surely you mean to say that Himmler controls the government, that he is our Hitler's successor."

Von Esebeck blanched, then shook his head with a wry chuckle. "The field marshal is refreshingly direct, as ever. But you should take it for a fact that things are very much as they were before."

"Then the war is lost." Rommel made the statement in a plain voice, though inside he felt another wave of the debilitating depression. "Our tanks are better than the Allies', our soldiers more tenacious . . . but the war is lost because we lost the skies, and everything else lies under the skies. Well, what decisions have been taken? Perhaps with Hitler removed the ending may be brought about more swiftly."

"Now I must insist you be discreet!" urged von Esebeck, his voice dropping. "Give no one a reason to accuse you of disloyalty. There have been no arrests yet, but everyone knows it's only a matter of time. And when the Gestapo decides to act . . . well . . ."

"*Ach,* you're right. I shouldn't go looking for trouble when it will come and find me soon enough."

"Now, please, I have disturbed you too much. I must beg that you seek some rest."

"Surely, I will. But wait; I see you have your camera. Hand me my coat, there."

Rommel struggled into the jacket, his field marshal's tunic with medals and ribbons bright across the breast. He set his stiff-brimmed hat on his head and stood, trying desperately not to yield to a wave of nausea, waving away von Esebeck's outstretched hand. Instead, the field marshal leaned against the window, looking across a lawn dotted by lofty oaks. One tree, a giant that had been splintered by the impact of a lightning bolt, loomed close before him, and he focused on the blackened wood until his weakness passed. Finally he stood tall, turned back to the correspondent.

"Now, take my picture . . . here, of my right profile, so you can't see what happened to my face."

The baron obliged, the pop of the flash lingering in the view of Rommel's one good eye.

"Send that out as soon as you can," he said with real satisfaction. "Get it to all the wires. I want the Allies to see that once again I have eluded them." He sank wearily back into his bed.

Normandy, France, South of St.-Lô-Périers Road, 26 July 1944, 1214 hours GMT

Carl-Heinz Clausen inspected the long track of rubber cleats and steel pins, once again making sure that the whole assembly was laid in a perfectly straight line across the tops of the road wheels and the left drive sprocket of his Panther tank. He inserted the last replacement pin, tossing the worn original onto the pile of its fellows. Carefully squeezing a daub of grease into the sockets, he rotated the pin a couple of times to make sure it was well lubricated.

"All set—we're almost done!" he proclaimed, standing to admire the freshly repaired track.

"It's about time," grumbled Pfeiffer, groaning from the effort as he hoisted himself off of the grassy embankment that served to conceal the tank and its crew from the American troops poised barely a mile to the north. "Maybe then you'll let me finish my nap."

Carl-Heinz laughed. "You'll thank me when our tracks stay on during the next battle, Ulrich. Now, get ready with the block and tackle—we'll winch it tight. With any luck we'll be ready to roll by the time the lieutenant gets back."

As his crewmates pulled the track tight with the manual winch the stocky driver inserted the last shaft, then twisted the locking pin that turned the strip of track into a continuing loop around the Panther's left-side wheels.

"Ah, my baby," the driver said, giving the steel fender an affectionate pat. "How do you like your new shoes?"

Ulrich Pfeiffer snorted in amused disgust. "Did you treat your wife half as good as you treat your tank?"

"Always!" Carl-Heinz replied with a broad smile. "And she treated me well in return."

"Why do you think he has five kids?" Fritzi noted helpfully.

Leaning back against the hull, Carl-Heinz allowed his mind to drift back to Bavaria, to Yetta and the children he had seen only three times in the last five years. Ever since he had driven a Panzer Mark II into Poland during September of 1939, his life had been focused on these steel gray monsters of the Wehrmacht. He couldn't entirely suppress a twinge of melancholy, but as always he reminded himself that treating his tank well gave him his best chance of eventually getting home.

The tank's commander, Lieutenant Schroeder, came strolling back from the headquarters of the Panzer Lehr division, and Carl-Heinz joined his crewmates in greeting the young officer. Peltz, the loader, had been packing ordnance in the turret, and he scrambled out to gather with the others beside the tank.

"Did you see the general? Did you tell him about the noise that kept us up all night?" asked Fritzi.

"General Bayerlein has had reports of American armor all along the front, and he passed those reports along to Seventh Army HQ," said Schroeder, meeting the eyes of each crewman as if to assess their reaction to the lofty company he had been keeping. "He told his officers that no less a personage than Field Marshal von Kluge himself has assured him that the attack will come from the Tommies, over in the Caen sector."

"I'm glad we're out of there!" Peltz exclaimed. The others nodded in casual agreement. In the weeks after the Normandy landings, Panzer Lehr had fought against an endless onslaught of British armor, Sherman and Cromwell tanks that had rolled from beyond the far horizon in a limitless stream. Lieutenant Schroeder's tank had destroyed no less than fifteen of those, but the crew had all shared a feeling that their luck must inevitably run out. Thus, when the division had been transferred to the quieter American sector a few weeks earlier, they had all breathed a little easier.

"I still don't like it," Ulrich grumbled, after the lieutenant had gone to confer with the rest of the company's officers and NCOs. "I'm sure those were tanks we heard last night. They'll be coming this way any day now, mark my words."

"You never like anything," Carl-Heinz chided, clapping his friend on the shoulder. Sometimes the lugubrious crewmate was a real puzzle to him, for even now—when the weather was good and no battle lay in their immediate future—he seemed to spend his time worrying about bad things that were due to happen sooner or later. He was about to remark further on Ulrich's pessimism when he noticed that the other man had his head cocked to the side, clearly listening for something. Knowing that Pfeiffer, the radioman, had the best ears among all the crew, Carl-Heinz felt a shiver of alarm. "What is it?"

"Aircraft . . . lots of them."

"Jabos?" asked Fritzi, anxiously scanning the skies for a sign of the Allied single-engined fighters that had bombed and strafed the division so mercilessly for the last seven weeks.

"No." Ulrich shook his head with certainty. "Heavies."

By the time Lieutenant Schroeder had returned, all of them could hear the dull rumble of countless massive engines, a sound that merged into a droning basso that shivered the flesh in their bellies.

"Getting closer," the lieutenant observed, unnecessarily. The rumble had swelled into a growl and threatened to become a thunder. "I see them," Schroeder remarked calmly, inspecting the sky through his binoculars. "Let's get ready to button up, just in case."

In moments the men had picked up their few belongings—a teapot and cooking tins, a jug of water, and a few shirts that Peltz had washed that morning and left to dry in the sun—and stowed them in the Panther. They all stood on the hull, looking at the dots that now began to distinguish themselves as four-engined bombers, a whole stream of them, rumbling with stately dignity through the sky. And they were still advancing, on a bearing that would take them directly over the Panzer Lehr division.

"How many are there?" Fritzi asked, his voice unnaturally high. Carl-Heinz saw that all the color had drained from the young Saxon's face.

With a great display of unconcern, the lieutenant shrugged, though his hands shook slightly as he continued to press the binoculars to his eyes.

"Too many," Pfeiffer suggested, though by now his words were all but drowned out by the thunder of countless massive engines. Even as the leading bombers came almost directly overhead, the stream of aircraft extended to the far horizon, vanishing into tiny specks that continued to emerge from the distance.

Peltz crossed himself, and Carl-Heinz felt a cramp in the back of his neck as he craned to look upward. They were all watching for a telltale sign, a clue that they were desperately hoping not to see. "Please keep going," the driver muttered to himself, feeling the churning deep in his belly and groin.

"There!" snapped Ulrich, pointing toward a blue flare that suddenly sparked into view. The marker was off to the right, but almost immediately another brilliant speck of azure glowed to the left. The Pathfinders had marked the target zone—and they perfectly bracketed the Panzer Lehr division.

In seconds the five men had scrambled through the Panther's portals and snapped the hatches shut. Even within the shelter of their armored cocoon, the noise of the Allied air armada was a thunderous backdrop, an assault of sound that vibrated flesh and metal alike. Carl-Heinz drew a deep breath as his hands settled over the comfortable three-quarter circle of his steering wheel. With an effort of will he forced his fingers to relax, then almost immediately noticed that his knuckles had whitened again from the unconscious pressure of his grip.

Another noise began to seep through the all-encompassing rumble, a whistle that began deceptively soft, quickly swelled louder and louder as strings of bombs tumbled downward. And then came the first impacts, the sounds that made all the previous thunder vanish like remembered whispers. The ground shook, and the roar of explosions came from the right, the left, from behind and before them. Blasts crumped in the middle distance, then boomed with explosive pressure from terribly near. Dirt and stones showered onto the surface of the tank, a rattling tinkle that incongruously reminded Carl-Heinz of rain on his barn roof.

The ground heaved and the forty-ton tank lurched forward. The steering wheel became the only point of stability in his life, and Carl-Heinz clung to the steel arc as if it made the difference between life and death. For some seconds the sounds lightened, though explosions still came from all sides, and then the quaking pressure was right on top of them again. The Panther tilted sickeningly, and more debris thudded onto the roof, onto the hull and hatches.

Sneaking a glance to his right, Carl-Heinz saw that Pfeiffer still sat gloomily, bracing himself with hands extended to the grab bars on either side of his seat at the hull machine gun and radio. Ulrich looked back and shrugged his shoulders, then opened his mouth after something that was lost in the crushing reverberations of the explosive bombardment. The driver imagined him saying "I told you so," and for once he was forced to agree that his comrade's relentless pessimism had a certain grounding in fact.

A bomb smashed with a deafening roar and the Panther skidded hard to the side. Other sounds crumped in the distance, and then nearby again. Carl-Heinz lost all track of time—it seemed as though he had spent a lifetime in the midst of whistling death. He couldn't imagine anyone living through such an assault, and with a pang of regret he sensed that his own span of life must soon be ending. The sounds, the pressure and the violence of the bombing became a constant backdrop, and his regrets faded to a vague numbness as he awaited the imminent and inevitable blast that would mean his own death.

The destruction was endless, incredibly so, and it amazed him to think of so many bombs being dropped on a small patch of earth. And then, finally, it was over. The explosions ceased with a suddenness that nevertheless took a minute or two to sink in. Ulrich's lips moved, but though he was right beside him the driver heard no sounds, wondered if he had been permanently deafened by the onslaught. How long had they been bombed? Carl-Heinz didn't have the slightest idea.

Hesitantly, he pushed open his hatch, tentatively poking his head out of the Panther's hull. The grassy embankment before them was gone, replaced by a torn landscape of low hills, mounds of dirt that looked like nothing so much as the brown waters of a stormy sea. Jutting from one of these hillocks was the torn turret of a Panzer IV. In another place he saw the bogey wheel from another tank—or perhaps it was the same one.

Slowly he crept out of the hatch, then crawled up onto the Panther's turret where the ashen-faced Lieutenant Schroeder was shakily climbing through his own hatchway. Carl-Heinz joined him in standing atop the tank, looking across a landscape that was devoid of life, of men or machinery, even of trees or grass. Their own panzer was partially buried, with clods of dirt strewn across the hull. Somehow, miraculously, it seemed that the long barrel of the 75-mm cannon was undamaged.

Looking to the right and the left, or forward toward the line of roadway that led between St.-Lô and Périers, Carl-Heinz sought some sign of the rest of the division, of the five thousand men and hundred tanks that had composed their mighty outfit. Smoke rolled across the landscape, and he couldn't see very far, except when a swirl of wind momentarily clearing away the dirty smudge. But even then, in the full span of his view, there was nothing, nothing but the ruin and wrack of this bizarre moonscape. The conclusion was obvious, painful, inescapable:

The Panzer Lehr division had ceased to exist.

First Army Advance Observation Post, Normandy, France, 1215 hours GMT

General Wakefield accompanied Colonel Grant, the Nineteenth Armored's intelligence officer, in following Jack King up the hill. They found space among the many First Army brass who were already crowded between the trees. Everyone was talking about the ascension of the "new führer," though they all agreed that the German army would be just as tough as it had been last week, or last month. Conversation soon faded away, as the rumbling drone of many thousand aircraft engines drowned out any normal conversation. Most of the men had binoculars, and all had their attention fixed on the swath of green countryside visible for many miles to the south.

"That's the road, there . . . St.-Lô to Périers," Colonel Grant shouted helpfully. Wakefield nodded, though there was only one highway visible from their vantage.

"And the bombs are falling on the other side of it, right?" joked General King. The CO of the Nineteenth was in fine spirits, laughing at a private word shared with another division commander, then turning to urge his XO forward. "C'mon, Henry, you won't see anything from back there."

Wakefield mumbled his "thanks" and stepped into the gap between a couple of major generals. It seemed that most of the First Army Staff was here, though there was no sign of General Bradley himself. They were all gathered for a look at the first salvo of Operation Cobra, to be delivered by the heavy bombers of the Eighth Air Force now droning overhead.

"I thought they were supposed to be coming in from the west!" one of the generals barked, scowling at the river of bombers in the sky.

"That's what I heard, too—Brad insisted," shouted another, also angry.

Wakefield understood their displeasure, and he, too, was unhappy with the risk. If the bombers had come from either the east or the west, they could have made their whole bomb run over enemy positions. Any bombs falling short would still land on Germans, at least theoretically. With the current alignment of attack, however, shorts ran a danger of hitting the American troops who were supposed to lead off the attack. Had he been in charge, he would not have authorized this attack—better to have the infantry move a little more slowly, but be allowed to achieve their objectives without a threat from their own air force.

Far away the landscape was suddenly torn by explosions. Wakefield saw the debris and smoke fly, felt the concussions of the blasts through the soles of his boots, though it was long seconds before the first sounds reached them. As soon as it began the booming violence formed a steady background roar, a complement to thunderous engines as thousands of aircraft streamed down from England to pour their explosive cargoes onto the battlefield.

"The Old Hickories pulled back from the front, didn't they?" yelled a general.

"I heard a thousand yards," Colonel Grant replied. "This is their section of the front before us."

Wakefield remembered the briefing, knew that the Thirtieth Infantry Division was going to lead the way. He and General King had toured the Old Hickories' position, since the Nineteenth Armored was slated to move through them as soon as the dogfaces had punched a hole in the front.

"Les McNair himself came out to see this show open," King reported, drawing impressed nods from the neighboring generals. Leslie McNair was one of the highest ranking generals in the U.S. Army, one of the masterminds behind the Normandy campaign. For a time it had been whispered that he, not Ike, was going to command the whole operation. Now, knowing that he was in the vicinity, the men of First Army got some idea of the stakes the high command put on this operation.

"No hilltop for McNair," another general reported, clearly impressed. "I saw him heading out to the front—he's going to watch this from a foxhole."

"Brave man," Jack King cheerfully agreed.

But Wakefield wasn't thinking about army and front commanders any more. He was watching the cloud of dust raised by the bombardment, seeing it billow north, pushed by a slight breeze and the force of its own tumult. Already the road was obscured, and now the murk had enveloped the front of the Old Hickories' position. More bombs fell, a steady plastering that must certainly be eradicating every living being in the impact zone. The swath of destruction continued to expand, until it was obvious that the positions of the Thirtieth Division, even a thousand yards back from the front, were in grave danger.

"Goddamn flyboys!" one general cursed, while others started edging toward the back of the hill. "They're blasting our own men!"

And still the chaos rolled on, as subsequent bombers sighted not on the road but on the swirling dust cloud. The Old Hickory trenches, several unit headquarters, and the jumping-off positions for the attack, all vanished in the chaos. Furthermore, with the expanded impact zone moving far from its original boundaries, the destructive pounding kept moving northward. All the officers on the observation post ducked as a booming smash rose no more than three hundred yards from their hilltop.

"Christ! Let's get the hell out of here!"

Wakefield didn't know who made the suggestion, but it was the only sensible thing to do. With unseemly haste for a bunch of high brass, the officers beat a hasty retreat down the rear of the hill. The bombs were frighteningly close as the men milled about in the field where their command cars and drivers waited. As Wakefield and King hopped into their jeeps, other command vehicles were already racing away.

Before the generals of the Nineteenth started off, an armored car rolled into view, and a furious lieutenant jumped out. He was terrified and spitting mad, and he started shouting at the first general he saw—Jack King.

"They're killing our boys, General!" he cried. "A whole battalion of the Thirtieth is plastered to hell—and they even got that general, McNair, come here to see how we did. Damnit, General, get on the phone to someone—you've got to stop 'em!"

Only then did they realize that the thunder had ceased, reduced to the fading drone of aircraft engines rumbling into the distance. The bombardment had ended and, under a dark cloud of blood, debris, and tragic mistakes, Operation Cobra was under way.

Berlin, Germany, 1418 hours, GMT

Lieutenant Haeften could not sit still. He was not truly scared, not any more. He was beyond fear. He was dead already; his destiny was certain. It would merely take some indefinite amount of time to realize.

"We've failed, haven't we, sir," he said in a clear monotone to his superior officer and mentor, who rested in his office chair as if all was normal. It was not a question.

The one-eyed count, assassin of Adolf Hitler, looked up and grinned with a confidence that struck Haeften as nearly unfathomable. "Not the way I see it.

We may not have succeeded, but we did not fail. Hitler is dead, the Nazi high command is in turmoil, and the fate of the Third Reich is sealed. May the Fourth Reich yet to come be something that Germany can be proud of."

Haeften shook his head. "But Himmler as the new führer—isn't that worse? Haven't we simply made things worse by our actions?"

"No. Not at all." Stauffenberg spoke with calm assurance. "If we have done nothing else, we have demonstrated that there is some honor left in Germany, some courage, some revulsion at what Hitler and his bully boys have wrought. That will be part of the history, part of what is recorded. Werner, remember this, for as long as you have left: when you do the right thing, you win."

The lieutenant nodded. Surprisingly, the thought gave him some comfort in the face of his death. He was otherwise completely numb.

It was only afternoon, but with the blinds drawn and the room closed in, it could have been any time. The remnants of the conspirators, those who hadn't scurried for cover like mice into their holes, had been meeting around the clock. Telephone calls and surreptitious communications, coded phrases meant to activate this group and that—while many who subscribed to the conspiracy with their lips had failed to follow through with the rest of their bodies, especially when it became clear the momentum had moved to Himmler's SS, it was gratifying how many had stood up and struck their blows for a free Germany, free of Nazi tyranny and ready to rejoin the brotherhood of nations.

In spite of Himmler's preemptive takeover of Broadcast House in Berlin, made possible at least in part by Stauffenberg's fateful decision to send the notifications in code, the conspirators had not simply given up. The coup had been more successful in Paris and elsewhere, and the core plotters had moved more quickly after their initial slow start. But two problems bedeviled their effort: first, that Nazi loyalists were present everywhere, and second, that many fence-sitters were unwilling to commit themselves in the absence of clear victory.

There were moments. A room-to-room shootout in Wehrmacht headquarters in Paris between pro-Nazi and pro-coup forces left thirty dead and the coup forces officially in control of the military apparatus for a period of twelve hours. Then came a counterattack by an SS division—brave men armed with pistols were helpless against tanks and infantry. They had been brutally gunned down.

The last meeting of the core coup plotters had ended hours ago, with the only remaining issue concerning what would happen to the ringleaders. "I will not run," Stauffenberg had said. "Let them martyr me if they wish. A thousand more revolutionaries will grow from the soil." Haeften could see the conflicted, even scared, expressions on the faces of the other coup leaders: Beck,

Olbricht, von Quirnheim. They looked back and forth at each other; none could move.

Wolf Heinrich von Helldorf, the Berlin police president, and Dr. Hans Gisevius, the German vice consul for Switzerland, were the only two nonmilitary officers present. Gisevius, a member of the inner circle since the very beginning, had resolved to stay and face his fate with the generals, but von Helldorf was contemptuous. "Don't kid yourself, Gisevius," he had said. "For years the generals—yes, and the colonels, too—," he added, looking straight at Stauffenberg, "have shit all over us. They promised us everything; they haven't kept a single promise. What happened in this coup was right in line with the rest of what they've said—more of their shit."

Olbricht began to argue, but Stauffenberg interrupted. "Excuse me, my general, but the police president is correct. We are military officers, and there is no excuse for failing to meet one's objective. In fact, I highly recommend that you all follow Herr von Helldorf's suggestions. If you have not been officially implicated, return to cover. Hide. Flee to the west. Return to your duties if you can. Save your lives, and more importantly, prepare yourselves for another opportunity. It's not over. It will never be over while a single Nazi remains in power."

Von Helldorf looked triumphantly around. He leaned forward, hands on the conference table spread wide. Few of the military officers met his eyes. "See? Stauffenberg is right. We can hide, we can rebuild, we can try again. Gisevius, you understand, right? This isn't about some empty idea of military honor, this is about results, about winning the war even though we've lost this battle. Only a few of us are so exposed we can't just return to our duties, and those can flee to Switzerland or try to reach the Allies or the Resistance in France."

Gisevius shook his head. "Honor demands—"

Helldorf interrupted explosively. "*Germany* demands that we try to live to fight another day! Maybe you don't think your life means anything. Maybe it doesn't, but mine does, and while I'll lose it in the right cause I'll be goddamned if I plan to throw it away for 'honor.'" He spat the term. "You see where 'honor' got all those brave officers who spoke privately against Hitler but decided that it wasn't the right time to move their troops. I, for one, am not yet compromised, and I plan to stay that way. Who's with me?"

Reluctantly, Gisevius nodded. "I'll return to Switzerland and talk to the Allies." Haeften could see the shame on his face, even though he knew it was the right thing to do.

Beck said, "It matters not to me. I can't go back to my job. I'm known." Olbrich nodded in agreement. He was too visible as well.

"Then for God's sake, flee! Get out of Berlin; go to Switzerland. Go anywhere! But go! Stauffenberg, tell them. You're the most important of all."

The faces of the generals turned one by one in the direction of the one-eyed colonel. Suddenly Haeften was reminded of a nightmare image of his youth, a famous painting—the *Crucifixion,* by Matthias Grünewald. German crucifixion paintings were reputed to have therapeutic properties; the detailed and highly realistic wounds on the Christ figure were living evidence of Christ's promise to take all the sins of the world upon him, and miraculous cures resulted for those who beheld it.

Grünewald's *Crucifixion* had made a terrifying impression on Haeften at the age of ten. A majestic ten-foot representation of Golgotha, set in the dark of the night, with Jesus dead on the cross, the Romans and onlookers long since departed, four mourners—two Marys, the Blessed Mother and Mary Magdalene, and two Johns, the Evangelist and the Baptist— below. Each of the nail wounds and scourge marks suffered by the Savior was carefully placed, but then Grünewald had added many more wounds and open sores: all the sins of the world. Haeften had tried to run away at the horrfying sight, he had shrieked and cried and had nightmares for weeks.

But now, looking at Stauffenberg, he understood the painting at last. He was not surprised at Stauffenberg's next words.

"No. My position is somewhat different from that of the rest of you. I have one more role to play in this drama; you—as many as can survive—have another saga ahead of you."

They understood as well, and slowly, silently, they rose to leave, one by one, until they came to Lieutenant Haeften. "I'm afraid I must stay as well," he said.

Normandy, France, South of St.-Lô–Périers Road, 1627 hours GMT

The bleak landscape looked like hell on earth.

Carl-Heinz squeezed another drop of oil onto the rotor of his periscope sight, which was in danger of fouling from the grit and debris spattered about during the bombing. Meanwhile, the lieutenant had ascertained that their panzer was alone for at least two hundred meters to either side. The three other tanks that had remained of their original company were gone, the position battered so badly that they had been able to find the wreckage of only one of them. The nearby company of panzergrenadiers, infantrymen who worked in close concert with the German tanks, had also apparently been annihilated—even their slit trenches were gone, indistinguishable amid the barren moonscape of the cratered ground.

The lieutenant had found them a place of some shelter between two massive mounds of earth thrown up by the bombs. The crew spent a few minutes covering the tank with dirt and tree limbs, a hasty attempt at camouflage that did a remarkable job of blending the large machine into the landscape. After these minimal preparations they had settled down to wait, knowing that it wouldn't be for long.

Pfeiffer and Peltz were looking out from behind a low mound of earth, seeking signs of enemy activity, and now they came sliding down the dirt pile and hastened back to the tank.

"Time now for the really big guns to try and kill us," Ulrich said, with a sad shake of his head.

The whistling shells and subsequent explosions of the artillery barrage quickly drove Carl-Heinz and his crewmates into the shelter of the Panther. Hatches closed, teeth clenched, knuckles white around nearby handholds, the German tankers sat tight to wait out this next onslaught on their machine, their sanity, and their lives.

Ulrich was sure everyone was about to die, but then he glanced over at Carl-Heinz—the man was humming! How could any man remain as cheerful and self-possessed as Carl-Heinz under such terrible conditions? On the other hand, he was glad of Carl-Heinz's comforting presence. Lieutenant Schroeder might command the tank, but Carl-Heinz was the center of the crew, the stalwart rock from which everyone else drew comfort and protection.

For some reason, the tank acted like a pet dog under Carl-Heinz's hands. It did everything but sit up and beg. And Carl-Heinz was constantly tinkering with it, repairing it, tweaking it, modifying it. By now, Ulrich thought, it wasn't a panzer any more, it was a strange new beast of Carl-Heinz's own making. Carl-Heinz was simply the most capable and intuitive mechanic he'd ever met, and the work was all around him, even in the horrific noise.

Sometimes weeks had gone by without a single shot being fired. During that time Carl-Heinz was always busy. Their tent had a solar water collector for fresh water all the time. A carefully planned moat swept rain water away without ever touching a sleeping bag or duffel. An elegant stone cooking platform gave them fresh hot food far better than the normal campfire, with a windmill-powered spit for roasting. The creative use of netting landscaped their bivouac. Everything he touched turned into a work of mechanical art.

Not at all like Ulrich himself. Ulrich knew himself to be dour and pessimistic, but under the circumstances of this horrible war, he felt he was only realistic. Yet he envied Carl-Heinz in his fantasy, if that's what it was. He suspected that it wasn't fantasy, but rather that Carl-Heinz carved his own reality, his own elegantly crafted surroundings, wherever he went.

If only his luck rubs off on the rest of us, he half prayed as he hunched tighter under the thunder of guns.

578 Squadron Base, Wendling, Norfolk, England

Staff Sgt. Frank "Digger" O'Dell
Wendling, Norfolk, England
July 26, 1944

Mrs. Lucy O'Dell
Roxboro, North Carolina

Dear Mama,

Up until now, it was looking like all I was going to do in the war was go to school. I thought once we'd reached our airbase, we'd be going into combat, but instead we went to all sorts of briefings over about a week and a half. Most of the briefings were about how to escape and evade capture in case we got shot down. We now have escape kits with about five thousand dollars in different kinds of money, which we were told is some of the best counterfeit that was ever made.

Well, we've got our final crew together now, and our very own B-24. It doesn't have a name yet, like a lot of the planes such as *Memphis Belle*, which you've heard of, but there's a great big letter "P" in a circle on the tail with a bar over it, so we're calling it "P-Bar" for now.

Lieutenant Russ is our commander, and we did decide to call ourselves "Russ's Ruffians." Booker, our navigator is from California. The co-pilot is Lieutenant Webb. He's only a second lieutenant and Russ is a first lieutenant. Harry Glass and I are the waist gunners; he's got the left and I've got the right. Wagner is the flight engineer and upper turret gunner. There's a guy named Fry (he's from Georgia) in the nose turret, Kirby's the tail gunner. The bombardier is another lieutenant named Sollars. He's kind of fat. And there's Tony Hutt, who's the radio operator. He's my best friend in the crew so far. Part of the reason is that I am the backup radio operator. Tony's a short guy, real energetic, looks like he's spoiling for a fight. He's from North Philadelphia, which he says is a pretty tough neighborhood, so he's not worried about some Germans after growing up in North Philly, as he calls it.

Every night about five o'clock they post the battle order for the next day, if there's going to be a mission, and last week on July 24 we were on it for the first time. We got up real early for the mission briefing. Our target was a place called St.-Lô (those funny hooks over the 'o' is how the French write it). That's where the Americans were stuck.

The St.-Lô raid was going to be a two thousand plane raid. In our particular airplane, we carried twenty-pound frag bombs, which are really twenty-pound hand grenades in huge clusters held together with wire rope and wooden slats. As the bomb falls out, it has a propeller that spins counterclockwise so it will spin off and unloose all of the baling material holding the clusters together. Then, these hundreds of twenty-pound frag bombs would go raining down. Each of the airplanes in our squadron had hundreds and hundreds of these. And those frag bombs would then go right into the holes in all the apple orchards down there and rout out the Germans. That was the mission.

We went out to P-Bar in a jeep, opened the bomb hatch (the airplane doesn't have a real door; we go in where the bombs come out) and started the pre-flight procedures. We'd done it in training often enough, but it felt quite a lot different to do it for real for the first time. We all tried to do it by the book. A lot of the crews that had been there for a long time and flown lots of missions used a lot of shortcuts, but this was our first time and we didn't want to try any shortcuts, at least for now.

The B-24 is very noisy inside. I wore headphones so I could hear what the pilot said and also to protect my ears from the racket. We lumbered down the runway and took off. Now, the B-24 flies about 270 miles per hour, and I stand there with the window open pointing a fifty-caliber flexible machine gun. The IP, or the Initial Point, which is where the bomb run starts, was actually in England, and we flew right on across the channel to St.-Lô and dropped the bombs.

Well, I don't know exactly where we were in the two thousand airplanes, but by the time we got there all we could see was smoke. So we synchronized on the smoke and dropped our bombs. We didn't see any enemy fighters, so I didn't have much to do. But I carried a couple of empty ammunition boxes, wooden crates that held rounds for my gun, and I threw them out over the side hoping to hit some German over the head. I call them "Digger's Personal Bombs."

The raid went pretty smoothly, and we made it back home and landed. I read in *Stars and Stripes* a day or so after the raid that the German soldiers were stumbling around in the apple orchards, dazed with blood running out of their eyes and ears and noses, due to all the concussions.

But here's the bad part. Later that day, after I got back from the raid, I was going to the PX and the group navigator was there and he had not flown the raid that day. He asked me if I had, and I told him yes.

He replied, "Well, you know you plastered your own troops." And of course I didn't know that and there's still nothing official, but the scuttlebutt is that General Bradley was really against the raid coming in from north to south because he was afraid the bombs would drop short, which is evidently what happened, according to the rumors. So they agreed the raid would come in from the east side, but somehow the battle order got changed and

we came in from the north. I don't know but I think this may be a true
rumor.

Well, Lieutenant Russ took us to the pub that night in celebration of our
first mission. I ordered "arf and arf" and we had a big old time.

Your son is now a combat veteran and got to fight some Germans. What
with Hitler's death and the breakout from Normandy on schedule, it doesn't
look like this thing is going to last that much longer. I don't know if I'll be
home for Christmas, but not too long after that, it looks like.

Love,

Your Son

Digger

Normandy, France, South of St.-Lô–Périers Road, 1803 hours GMT

For nearly half an hour the 105- and 155-mm guns of the American army had
pounded the already blasted positions of the Panzer Lehr division survivors, a
thorough, crushing, and violent barrage. Even so, after the massive aerial bombardment the cannon fire was almost anticlimactic—except that the Germans
in the battered tank knew that the guns certainly presaged a ground offensive.

Exploding shells pounded near and far, sometimes showering the panzer
with debris, other times echoing dully in the distance. In the driver's seat, Carl-
Heinz felt a curious sense of calm, tempered by a growing impatience for the
actual attack. It was not that he wanted to kill Americans, but at least they
would be able to take some action against attacking troops instead of just sitting here wondering if they were about to take a direct hit.

He thought of the careful job he had done inspecting the linchpins on the
treads and was grateful that he had located and replaced several worn or bent
rods. At the same time, he worried about dirt clogging the air intake and wondered if a razor-sharp fragment of steel might already have cut into the tracks
or jammed one of the drive sprockets or road wheels. They could be sitting
here fully disabled, and he wouldn't know until it came time to start up the
tank and try to move.

Beside him, Ulrich sat glumly at his machine gun, while Fritzi and Peltz
waited in the turret, ready to fire the main gun. The lieutenant tapped his fingers
against his thigh, occasionally opening the hatch to stick his head out for a quick
look around. As the barrage moved on, the officer's inspections became more frequent, as they knew that the Ami—American—infantry would not be far behind.

Finally the shelling ceased altogether, and Carl-Heinz pressed his eye to the
periscope, seeking some sign of the attackers. He was startled by a thumping
against the side of the tank, followed by an unmistakably German voice.

"Panzermen? Hallo!"

With a swivel of the scope, the driver saw a panzergrenadier standing beside the Panther. The soldier, a *feldwebel,* was dirty, though the Schmeisser submachine gun slung from his shoulder was immaculate. Carl-Heinz suspected that he was with the infantry unit that had given their tank company flank protection.

Lieutenant Schroeder tossed open the turret hatch and looked down at the foot soldier.

"We have one machine gun left, over there." The sergeant gestured across the moonscape of the ground. "We've seen the Ami infantry on the way—just wanted you to know that we'll watch your flank. And ask you to keep your eyes peeled for tanks."

"Ja. And thanks."

The feldwebel had no sooner headed back to his own unit than the chatter of machine gun fire broke across the field. Carl-Heinz could see nothing moving through his periscope, so he settled down to wait, listening for the lieutenant's command and keeping his hand near the starter button. The small arms fire grew to a momentarily furious rattle, then died away. There was a flicker of movement in the viewing scope as human figures crossed the horizon of a dirt mound and vanished into a depression about a thousand yards away.

"Driver—start the engine. Loader—high explosive." Lieutenant Schroeder's voice barked the command through the intercom, and Carl-Heinz pressed the starter button, easing the motor into life as he heard Peltz jam a shell into the breech of the main gun. The turret whirred through a minor rotation, the long barrel depressing slightly.

"Fire!"

The gun spit a plume of smoke and bright fire, and almost immediately the distant mound of earth was torn by a violent explosion, a flash of flame in the midst of showering debris.

"Reload, fire!" Twice more the tank sent lethal bursts into the flank of the advancing infantry. Though they could see none of the effects of the shots, Carl-Heinz was certain that the surviving Ami infantry would take a long time to come out of those holes.

"Driver—reverse," came the next order.

Depressing the clutch sharply with his left foot, easing it out and then pressing downward again, Carl-Heinz started the tank backward. The Panther rolled smoothly out of the notch where it had found such scant shelter.

"Driver—stop. Left turn—forward—*schnell!"* The commands came in staccato cadence, the veteran driver reacting smoothly to each instruction. In seconds the tank was rolling along, perpendicular to the line of the enemy's advance.

"Driver—right turn. Forward, slow . . ." Lieutenant Schroeder's voice was hushed, the entire crew sharing the need for stealth. Through his scope Carl-Heinz tried to study the irregular ground, steering slightly to get around a deep bomb crater, bring the panzer forward until the tracks pressed against the ruins of an ancient hedgerow. The barrel stuck over the obstacle, and the driver pressed the clutch and pushed the gear lever into neutral. The engine idled smoothly as the crewmen scanned the ground before them.

In a few seconds the whistling sounds of artillery fire made them unconsciously shrink into their seats, and the ground shook as the barrage pummeled to the right—the position from which the Panther had fired just moments earlier. As always, Carl-Heinz was impressed by the accuracy and timeliness of the American artillery support—the Panther would have been pounded hard if it had stayed in position after shooting.

Before the shelling lifted, the driver saw another flash of movement in the distance, a spot marked by a flash of fire and the smoky residue of a big gun. He could barely make out the shape of a tracked vehicle and a squat turret distinguished by an unusually large gun.

"U.S. tank destroyer forward, twelve hundred yards," Fritzi remarked calmly, confirming Carl-Heinz's suspicions.

"Loader—AP. Gunner, train on target."

The Panther's long gun depressed slightly to bear on the creeping American vehicle as Peltz lifted an "AP," an armor-piercing round, into the breech. The tank destroyer crawled over the embankment of the Périers–St.-Lô road, and for a moment the armored vehicle was silhouetted above the landscape.

"Fire!" Fritzi had anticipated the lieutenant's command, and the gun spoke even as the order came over the intercom. The shot was true, the tank destroyer lurching to a halt as black smoke spilled out of the hull. In two seconds the entire vehicle vanished in a cloud of greasy flame, and Carl-Heinz couldn't help but wince at the gruesome fate of the crew. A fiery death in a burning shell of steel—it was a reality that every tanker tried not to think about.

"Jabo!"

Carl-Heinz didn't know who shouted the warning, but they all heard the scream of a diving single-engine aircraft. Reacting instinctively, backing up at high speed, the driver swiveled the tank around and drove across the rough ground, lurching through a crater, then cranking the wheel around to spin the tank through a desperate evasive maneuver.

A bomb blasted somewhere behind them, the concussion driving the Panther forward with brutal force. They skidded to the side teetering on the edge of a deep crater, but Carl-Heinz gingerly drove them forward onto level ground. He careened through a turn as another bomb exploded off to the side and then couldn't help ducking in his seat as a barrage of machine gun bullets rattled off the panzer's thick armor.

Ulrich sighed. "The next one will get us, I have a feeling."

Carl-Heinz ignored his comrade as he heard Schroeder's voice in the intercom. "Any damage?"

"She's driving well, sir," he replied, while Peltz, Fritzi, and Ulrich all confirmed that their own stations were still functional.

"Driver, reverse . . . back to our original position," ordered Schroeder.

Shifting smoothly, Carl-Heinz guided the massive vehicle over the rough ground, soon parking them between the mounds of dirt that in fact provided very little cover. They all saw the new craters, though no one commented on the accuracy of the American artillery.

Once more they heard the machine guns and knew that the panzergrenadiers were heavily engaged. For a long time they watched the flank, and once or twice Ulrich added the Panther's hull machine gun to the engagement. They saw some foot soldiers drawing closer, and again the main gun dropped high explosive shells into the advancing troops.

This time the panzer evaded by rolling to the right, again moving out just before the inevitable artillery barrage thundered down upon their firing position.

Carl-Heinz guided the tank by turning the big three-quarter round steering wheel. He brought them around another embankment, and they surprised dozens of American infantrymen who had taken shelter in the trenchlike depression of a lane. Ulrich pressed the trigger on the hull machine gun as the main cannon belched high explosive shells. Driving at full speed, Carl-Heinz raced the tank down the road as those of the enemy lucky enough to survive scrambled out of the lane.

A loud clang rocked the hull with deafening force, and the driver looked to the side to see an American infantryman scrambling backward, carrying the long tube of a bazooka. The turret machine gun chattered before the fellow could get to shelter, and the infantryman tumbled backward, torn by a fusillade of lead. Fortunately for the tankers, the rocket shell of the man's gun had caught the Panther near its thick frontal armor—weeks ago the Germans had learned of the lethal effectiveness of the bazooka against the side and rear armor of a tank.

Swiveling the periscope—once again operating smoothly, because of his quick grease job—Carl-Heinz saw American soldiers advancing past both sides of the tank. The troops were quick to throw themselves into craters as the turret wheeled in their direction. A look to the right showed that the panzergrenadier machine gun nest was overrun—or else the German infantry had retreated. In any event, the driver was glad to get the order to pull the Panther back to a position of greater security. Though he drove forward, Schroeder and Fritzi kept the turret turned toward the rear, using the machine gun and cannon to keep the enemy infantry from offering aggressive pursuit.

Soon they had found a new position, and were heartened by the sound of

Schmeisser fire off to the side, since that meant that at least some of the German infantry still survived. The tankers added their gun and their armor to the defense, and the GIs—though through no lack of courage—were unable to close in on the defenders.

By late afternoon, it was clear that the American attack had bogged down. Lieutenant Schroeder had brought the Panther to another sheltered firing position near the barely recognizable rubble of a stone farmhouse. The small arms fire had become desultory, and the weary tankers didn't have the energy to congratulate themselves. It was just another day for the German army in Normandy.

Nineteenth Armored Division Field Headquarters, Normandy, France, 27 July 1944, 0735 hours GMT

Lieutenant Colonel Frank Ballard looked at the long line of Sherman tanks with joy. He loved tanks, loved the way they sounded, loved the way they smelled, loved the way they felt as they rumbled over the ground. As commander of the Thirty-eighth Tank Battalion, Combat Command A, Nineteenth Division, VIII Corps, First Army—God, how he loved to recite the litany of command—he commanded his HQ platoon, a mortar platoon, a jeep recon platoon, and an M4 mortar half-track platoon, an assault gun platton, and three powerful armor companies and a light armor company.

It was a full battalion, an armored fist that formed half of the one-two punch of an American armored division. Ballard loved the boxing analogy, and he was confident that the Thirty-eighth was a match for any tank force in the world. Naturally, he had heard the reports: the German Panthers and Tigers had better guns, thicker armor. He supposed that that in part was true, but at the same time he had faith in his Shermans. They were fast, reliable, excellent at cross-country maneuver. And now each of his three M4 companies had four tanks with the 76-mm gun, with its long barrel and wicked-looking blast suppressor around the muzzle. And with his command tank, that made for a lucky thirteen, he realized with a chuckle. He would love to have a chance to put those up against anything a panzer division could throw at him.

All in all, it was a good day to be alive.

He strode down the long line of tanks—his tanks—returning salutes as he passed the enlisted men and noncoms who were not permitted to leave their tanks in a combat area. He had no immediate mission, just a desire to see his battalion arrayed in fighting trim, ready for action. A kind of eagerness possessed him, the same anticipation he had carried going into a boxing match. He had earned his boxing trophies at West Point by making it a point of refusing to accept that the other guy even had a chance.

"They're looking good, Frank," said a voice over his shoulder. He nearly jumped with surprise; he hadn't expected company.

He looked around to see his commander, Colonel Pulaski. "Yes, they do," he agreed. Both men looked at the line of vehicles.

"Ready to roll out soon?" Pulaski asked.

"You know it," Ballard replied. He looked at several of the tanks, those equipped with the ungainly prongs on the forehull, and laughed. "With the Rhino on the front, the damn things are even uglier than usual."

"Battalion in good shape?" probed Pulaski.

Ballard looked at his colonel. "As good as I can make it," he said. "Truthfully, I think we'll be fine, maybe a little shakedown stuff, but nothing we can't keep under control. This is a good bunch of men, and I know they'll do fine."

"I'd hate to disappoint General King," said Pulaski. "You wouldn't like it much, either."

"No, sir, I wouldn't," he replied. They stood for a moment.

"You served in North Africa, didn't you, Ski?" asked Ballard.

"Yep. I was a captain. Different place, Africa. And the Lees were antiques compared to these Shermans—the ones you say are so ugly."

Ballard only knew scuttlebutt about Pulaski; he knew about his Silver Star, of course, and he'd heard the rumor that there had been a lot of good luck involved. Still, he tended to think that might be sour grapes on the part of the gossipers. Pulaski was young, but then many of the officers were—including himself. Newness was the hallmark of the American army; it didn't take a lot of months for a man to be a veteran soldier.

"I was in Italy before the Nineteenth. Desk jockey, S4." S4, Administration, was responsible for supply, transport, maintenance, and personnel administration sections.

Ballard considered himself a good judge of people, and he decided he liked Pulaski. The man might need a little more seasoning, but so did a lot of people. Ballard liked General King, and respected General Wakefield. He was still getting to know the other officers.

"We just got the briefing on Operation Cobra," Pulaski said quietly.

Ballard grinned. It would be time for combat soon, time to see what his babies could do against the Wehrmacht. "So, what's the scoop?"

"Day after tomorrow," said Pulaski. "And we're leading the way. I want to see you and the other senior officers in two hours for a briefing."

Ballard looked at his colonel, eyes bright, smile wide. "Hell, what am I doing standing around talking to you, sir?" he said jokingly. "I've got to get things moving!"

Pulaski grinned at his eager tank leader. He hoped his other officers would turn out to be as good—and as pugnacious when it came to seeking out the enemy.

They seemed to be, but he knew that until CCA faced action, there was no way to be certain.

His next call was on his armored infantry commander, Lieutenant Colonel Dennis White. White was one of the "temporarily misassigned civilians" in this war, a professor of philosophy at a small liberal arts college in western Massachusetts, and looked the part, from horn-rimmed glasses to his ever-present pipe. Yet White's combat record was longer than Pulaski's own, and he had a reputation as a ferocious fighter.

White was in his tent, smoking his pipe while completing paperwork. "Good afternoon, colonel," he said in his mild voice. "I hear we're about to start moving."

"That's right," Pulaski replied. "Operation Cobra should get us off this peninsula and on into France."

"I spent a semester at the Sorbonne during my graduate years," White smiled. "Haven't been to Paris since. Don't suppose we'll get a chance to see the sights this trip."

Pulaski laughed. "No, I don't think so. Maybe when it's all over."

"Of course, by then the tourists will be back," White replied.

"On the other hand, maybe the war damage will be repaired."

"That's a point," said White. "Perhaps it isn't all bad news after all."

"So, Whitey—ready to roll?"

"Indeed I am, Colonel," replied White.

The tent flap moved aside suddenly. "There you are, Colonel!" It was Captain Smiggs, a short, energetic cavalry officer who commanded the CCA recon company. "I hear we're moving out tomorrow and I wanted to tell you that we're ready and eager to roll!"

"Good for you, Smiggy," replied Pulaski, grinning at his eagerness.

The captain was followed immediately by another lieutenant colonel, a friendly young man named Lorimar who commanded the combat command's artillery battalion. He greeted his colonel with a salute, a firm handshake, and an open and winning smile.

"Got your guns cleaned out?" Pulaski asked.

"My Priests are ready to hear some Kraut confessions," declared Lorimar, drawing a laugh from the other officers. The M7 self-propelled guns bore 105-mm howitzers in an open hull on the same chassis as a Sherman tank. These guns were called "Priests" because the antiaircraft machine gun mount on the front hull looked like a pulpit. Lorimar never missed a chance to make a joke on the name.

"I just hope you can get those things up to speed, Colonel," Smiggs interjected. "It'd be a shame to have to leave those big guns behind when we're racin' for the German border."

"Don't worry your pretty head about that, Smiggy. 'Big guns make fast tracks,' as my Cherokee grandpappy used to say," Lorimar retorted. "You just keep your head down when we start shootin', less you want a cheap haircut. Parted right down the middle, perhaps?"

Pulaski joined the rest of his staff in a hearty laugh, and in truth the colonel couldn't have been more pleased. His officers all had the right attitude; they had all done their work. Now only time and battle remained to prove the worth of Combat Command A.

Foreign Ministry Building, Wilhelmstrasse, Berlin, Germany, 28 July 1944, 0915 hours GMT

"Why do you think he wants to see me?" Müller asked the question as he and Reinhardt waited in the sumptuous anteroom outside of Foreign Minister Joachim von Ribbentrop's private office.

"Perhaps he'll ask you to ride one of those rockets of yours right into the Kremlin so you can personally ask for Stalin's forgiveness," Günter said with that thin, stoic face that left Müller unsure whether it was a joke or not.

Müller gulped nervously and pulled at the collar of his dress tunic, the uniform having suddenly grown too tight. He could feel his stomach begin to rumble with nervousness, as well as with appetite. The memory of those cakes at the meeting of the generals was still strong. Perhaps the foreign minister would offer them cakes made with real eggs. Or real coffee. Next to him, he noticed Reinhardt looking at himself in a mirror, making minor adjustments in his crisply tailored Wehrmacht uniform. *Why does he care?* thought Müller. *Doesn't he already know he looks perfect?*

He was spared any further fretting as the office door opened and a secretary ushered them into the famed diplomat's presence.

Müller was shocked. Von Ribbentrop was always reputed to be well dressed, elegant—even foppish. Secretly derided as "the champagne salesman" by Nazi insiders, von Ribbentrop was the class-conscious aristocrat that so many Nazis despised, and yet wanted to emulate. But what Müller saw was a broken man. His gray hair was unwashed, stringy, his eyes filled with shock and emptiness. His once-handsome face was saggy and slack on one side, his skin hanging limply on his cheekbones. His eyelids drooped. His famous toothy, radiant smile, part of so many photographs, was completely absent.

Müller and von Reinhardt stood at attention in front of Ribbentrop's large desk, waiting for the foreign minister to notice them. Finally, Ribbentrop waved limply at the chairs in front of his huge desk. "Sit down, sit down," he said. "You already know why you're here, of course?" The quaver in his uplifted voice showed it was a question, not the confident and commanding statement the minister originally had intended.

"Yes, in general, Herr Reichsaußenminister," said von Reinhardt in a careful voice, "We've been briefed on the outline of Operation Carousel, of course, but not on the specific roles we are to play, nor on how we may serve you." Müller could see Reinhardt's reflection in the glass that covered the desktop.

"What? What? No—well, perhaps. I don't know why you weren't informed . . . Nobody does his job any more. Well—you'll be accompanying me into the mouth of hell. Orders of our führer . . . our führer . . ." His voice trailed off.

Müller risked a sideways glance at Reinhardt, who sat at attention, calm and apparently relaxed as always. Even the buttons on his uniform gleamed with mirrored brightness. Ribbentrop was referring to Himmler, of course, not Hitler. Even though the succession was still not formalized, it was clear that Himmler would shortly become führer in name as well as fact. But Ribbentrop kept stumbling over the name.

Müller was aware of some of the background of the foreign minister, the sort of gossip and rumor that most officers or politically aware Germans knew. Ribbentrop and Himmler had once been close. On his desk he was known for having kept only two "party" portraits—one of Adolf Hitler, and one of Heinrich Himmler. But Ribbentrop had long been falling out of the courts of power, desperately clinging to his relationship with Hitler as the last threads of his authority and prestige steadily evaporated. And with Hitler dead, von Ribbentrop was obviously a shattered man.

Reinhardt waited patiently, and Müller steeled himself to do the same. Slowly, the Nazi foreign minister collected his thoughts, and the details of the mission came out.

Operation Carousel—an amazing plan to achieve peace with the Soviets, turning the course of the war from a two-front disaster to one in which the German forces would have only one opponent. There were many components to the plan—evidently Himmler had thought about this for a long time. Müller had raised the question with Reinhardt whether in fact Himmler had been behind the Stauffenberg conspiracy, but Reinhardt had dismissed it—Himmler was too loyal, too risk-averse. "An interesting hypothesis, however," Reinhardt had observed, smiling. "We'll make a historian out of you yet!" Reinhardt's opinion was that Himmler's plans were merely a contingency, because Carousel, for all its rich detail, was still a high-risk venture, suitable for a Germany in desperate condition, where few other options remained.

"Where was I?" the foreign minister asked. "Oh, yes—Moscow. You will be accompanying me to the Soviet Union for the secret talks. We will need military details, troops, numbers, that sort of thing. Effective diplomacy is about building personal relationships, trust, and grand strategies, but the treaties often come down to petty details. Petty details. That's you . . . what did you say your name was?"

"Von Reinhardt. Colonel Günter von Reinhardt."

"Von Reinhardt. Good name. Good family. Good to see fine young Germans of good family. Good. And you . . ."

"Müller, sir. Colonel Wolfgang Müller."

"Yes—Müller. Of course. Müller. And why did they send you to me, Müller?"

Müller didn't know what to say. In fact, he didn't know why he'd been sent. Fortunately, Reinhardt spoke up.

"Colonel Müller has been involved with the Peenemünde work, Herr Reichsaußenminister, and is knowledgeable about the Vengeance Weapons, but not so knowledgeable that his capture or torture would compromise Reich security."

Müller jerked in his chair. Capture? Torture? He stared at his friend.

"Yes, capture . . . torture . . . death . . ." Ribbentrop's mind was wandering again. *Damn you, Günter!* Müller thought. *Don't get him thinking like that!* "We must be prepared, of course. Dangerous mission. Very dangerous. Unsure of success. But what heroes we shall be—what fame we shall have—if we succeed."

Müller had no idea what he was talking about. He was in a room with an insane man talking about capture, torture, and death, and all he knew was that he wanted out—immediately.

"Then let me see if I understand you correctly," said Reinhardt, gently leading the foreign minister back to the objective. "As the Reich Foreign Minister, you, of course, are the sole person who can lead a diplomatic mission to the Soviet Union to negotiate the necessary treaty, which is a critical part—perhaps the critical part—of Operation Carousel."

Von Ribbentrop straightened a little bit at the flattery. The "champagne salesman" was a notorious fame seeker. "Yes . . . the only person . . . of course."

"If I understand the plan correctly, we are seeking to negotiate a peace in the east, so that we will only need to fight a one-front war. The military reality, unfortunately, is that the Soviet Union currently possesses the initiative on the front, so there is the obvious question of what Herr Stalin would have to gain from peace at this time. Am I understanding correctly so far, Herr Reichsaußenminister?"

Reinhardt's gentle prodding was having the desired effect. Ribbentrop was visibly calmer, more focused. Müller was deeply relieved. A dangerous mission with the possibility of torture or death was bad enough, but one led by a crazy man—well, of such stuff were nightmares made. His stomach growled loudly, embarrassingly. He hoped no one noticed, and it seemed that no one did.

Reinhardt had won over the foreign minister, and slowly, they laid out a strategy for the negotiations—what they had to offer Stalin that he could not win for himself on the field of battle, what they could not give up, how they would structure the negotiation process. Müller observed that Reinhardt seemed to be doing most of the work, inserting ideas into Ribbentrop's mouth so easily that Ribbentrop assumed the ideas were his own. *So that's the secret of being a successful staff officer,* he thought ruefully. It was a skill he found enormously difficult to master. Not that he was unwilling to butter up his betters; it was simply the skill itself he lacked.

"And our trump card," Reinhardt was saying, "is the one in Müller's possession."

Müller straightened up with a shock when he heard that. "T-trump card?" he said, a brief stammer robbing his voice of strength.

Reinhardt smiled. "The military secret of the Reich that Stalin needs most—our Vengeance Weapons."

"But surely—you can't mean giving that to the Russians!" Müller said.

It was Ribbentrop who replied with somewhat greater lucidity than before. He seemed to be going in and out of his fugue state. "I can see that you want to preserve the secrets of the State, young man. But don't worry. I, Joachim von Ribbentrop, will ensure those secrets are preserved. You see, it is only some of the technology we will give away. The V-1 is nearly obsolete already, right?"

"Oh!" Müller said. "You mean the new V-2? Yes—an amazing weapon. Amazing. But of course—the V-1 technology is not so secret, although it might set them on the path . . ."

"And there is even more technology in the research programs," Ribbentrop interrupted, a mysterious edge to his voice. "Secrets even you do not know." Müller wondered whether he really knew anything, or whether this was the sort of technology-as-magic thinking he'd encountered before. He knew that only a fraction of research projects ever brought forth useful results—the difficulty, of course, being that one never knew in advance which ones would pay.

"Of course, there are many issues yet to be decided. In 1943, when I last met Molotov, our sticking point was that we could not agree on an armistice border. We must plan . . . we must plan . . ."

He met with Molotov in 1943? Müller was shocked. That was a period in which Hitler was publicly certain that Germany would prevail, that there was no doubt. Now he was learning that there had been secret talks. *All this political work is too much for me,* he thought.

Reinhardt, on the other hand, was clearly eager to be part of this mission, and that made Müller feel somewhat relieved. Ribbentrop, in his estimation, needed a nursemaid as much as a military aide. Müller found himself being shunted aside as the two continued their planning, walking over to a table covered with maps. Müller, still seated, watched the two in a mirror. Two aristocrats, alike in some ways, worlds apart in others, but now lost in planning for their diplomatic objectives.

Müller, like many Wehrmacht officers, had nightmares about the Russian front. And now, all he could think about was he had only two days left before he'd not only reach the front, but penetrate it.

CCA (Nineteenth Division) HQ, Normandy, France, North of St.-Lô–Périers Road, 29 July 1944, 1005 hours GMT

Pulaski paced back and forth under the open sky. Flashes of red brightened the southern horizon, as they had all through the night. His command tent had been struck hours before, and all around him the olive-drab steel hulks of Sherman tanks waited in eerie silence. Nearby, his senior officers hovered around the command half-track in some semblance of patience, though the colonel himself was unable to contain his agitation.

Do I look like a command officer? Or do I just look nervous and untried? Pulaski knew he worried too much what other people thought of him, but damnit, he had so much to prove and so little time to prove it.

From the time he was six, he had understood his role in life: he was his family's golden boy, their hope for a bright American future. His parents had come to the United States shortly after the end of the First World War, saved their money and opened up a small grocery store in Milwaukee, where he was born. His parents didn't talk much about their Polish heritage. Jimmy was to be an American, and nothing else. He excelled in school and went on to the University of Wisconsin—and that was the first time he ever heard a Polish joke. Suddenly he wasn't an American, but a "dumb Polack," and it still infuriated him at the same time it shamed him. But he turned the fury and the shame into work, applying himself to his studies with diligence and passion.

While he was in Madison, going to school full time and working late nights as a bartender at Foamy Lohmy's, a well-known (some would say notorious) college hangout, he had signed up for the ROTC program—not out of any concern about Nazis, but because he could get a credit and exempt himself from the school's phys ed requirement. As a secondary benefit he'd been able to take showers in the old brick Armory—a luxury his Park Street boarding house was unable to offer.

His parents had in mind for him a career as a doctor or lawyer, but in 1933 he'd graduated at the top of his ROTC class and, as a result, had been offered a coveted commission in the army. He'd made first lieutenant shortly after the Nazis had rolled into Poland in 1939, and from then on he'd set his sights on one thing: war. By Pearl Harbor he was the XO of an armor company at Fort Hood.

His life, like everyone else's, had speeded up considerably after that. As a young major he got an assignment with Patton in North Africa, and in one blazing moment in combat, he'd won his Silver Star and a light colonel's rank—though, at some level, he wasn't sure he deserved either. He could only remember the terrible feeling of not knowing what to do, the feeling he'd doomed his men and himself—but somehow, he'd come through all right. When he took a round of German fire, he almost felt it was a payback for his earlier luck, but the wound was relatively slight, and after another period in a training command, he was back, a newly minted full-bird colonel. Now it was up to him to do the job.

"Damn it!" he snapped. "Where are those orders? It's time to move!"

"Maybe the Old Hickories are making some progress," suggested White, the lieutenant colonel commanding CCA's armored infantry battalion. He puffed reflectively on a pipe, looking every bit the part of the professor pondering some theory of philosophy. "They've been trying for two days."

"No thanks to the goddamned air force," snapped Ballard. "Those sons of bitches must have killed as many of our boys as they did Krauts!" The light colonel of armor smacked his fist with a loud clang against the fender of a nearby jeep.

Pulaski winced but saw that his tough tank leader's hand was apparently unhurt. And he knew that Ballard could well be speaking the truth. Three days earlier, the bombardment that was supposed to have opened the way for the infantry attack had also killed hundreds of GIs, most especially among the good soldiers of the Thirtieth Division, the Old Hickories. Now the survivors of that steadfast National Guard unit had worked their way forward into a meat grinder. Word was that many Germans—including a few tanks—had not only survived the bombardment but were able to muster an effective and deadly defense.

The other men—Lieutenant Colonel Lorimar of the self-propelled artillery battalion, the officers of the support units, and Captain Smiggs, whose reconnaissance company made up the final component of Combat Command A—stood mute. They no doubt shared the colonel's agitation but felt they could contribute little to the conversation. These were good men, Pulaski knew, well trained and supplied with fine equipment. That only made it all that much more vexing—why the hell didn't the brass give them orders to attack?

Pulaski's agitated musings were interrupted as a jeep raced between the parked Shermans and skidded to a stop before the CCA officers. The colonel first saw the two stars on the jeep's pennant, then recognized Jack King as the division commander bounced out of the vehicle while it was still rocking to a halt.

"General! Is it time?" demanded Pulaski.

"Yep, Ski, it is." The general's face was flushed, and he smiled grimly. "The infantry is still bogged down—so Bradley's given the order to send in the armor."

"Hot damn!" declared Ballard. "That is, hot damn, General!" he amended with a fierce grin.

"You move out right away. Follow the road to Avranches, like you've planned, as far as Sainte-la-Salle. And this is the key, Pulaski: if you come to a strongpoint, I want you to go around it. There'll be more dogfaces coming along behind to mop up. This is the time for you to make some tracks!"

"That's exactly what I was hoping you'd say."

King leaned in close and stared into his combat commander's eyes. "I know you can do this for me, Jimmy. This is modern armored warfare, and we both understand how important it is to move fast. Don't we?"

"Aye, aye, sir!" This idea was nothing more than Patton's own doctrine, as it had been the lifeblood of the Blitzkrieg in years gone by. Pulaski had done his best to learn those lessons and to make a goal of his own. He was determined to bring the art of fast maneuver to a new height, and CCA of the Nineteenth gave him the perfect tool for the job.

"One more thing, and it comes down from Army HQ: when you get to Sainte-la-Salle, you're to stop and hold. There's only one good road down to Avranches from there, and Third Armored has first dibs on it—they should get there before you anyways, since they don't have as far to go. The last thing General Bradley wants is a traffic jam. Understand?"

"What if there's no sign of Third Armored—I mean, if we get there first?" demanded the colonel.

"Those are the orders from Corps HQ—stop and wait. Is that understood?" King frowned, looking as though he wished he could say more.

"Understood, sir." Pulaski might have argued the point further, but his heart was already racing at the thought of prospective combat. And he knew the map: Sainte-la-Salle was a long way down the road, more miles than the American front had advanced in the last seven weeks. He saluted and turned to his officers. "You heard the general—move fast, and don't look back! Frank, Task Force Ballard will be leading the way."

"Gotcha, Colonel!" replied Ballard with a snappy salute. The men quickly separated to their various commands, and in moments the sounds of tank, half-track, and truck engines roared into a motorized symphony.

"Good luck," said King, shaking the younger man's hand. "And be careful."

"We'll be careful, but we'll be moving," replied Pulaski. "I want to kill some Krauts!"

"Just get Sainte-la-Salle—and try to get there in one piece," called the division CO as the colonel climbed into the cab of the command half-track. Sergeant Dawson, who would operate as radioman and machine gunner, stood just behind him at his weapon.

A few minutes later, Combat Command A was on the move. Spearheaded by several of the M4 tanks equipped with the hedgerow-busting Rhino apparatus, the motorized column started through the rear areas of the Thirtieth Division's jumping-off point. Task Force Ballard went first, and included Company B of the armored battalion and Company D of the armored infantry, as well as Pulaski's HQ company, and supporting platoons from the recon and assault gun companies. They would need two miles of road just for their tanks, jeeps, half-tracks, and guns. The rest of the command, with the half-tracks carrying the infantry and the rumbling fully tracked chassis of the turretless self-propelled artillery, slowly fell into line. Everything went smoothly as they started out, but even so Pulaski knew it would be a long time before the rear units would even get onto the road.

He rode near the front, the command half-track racing along behind the first dozen Shermans. The column of tanks quickly stretched far out of sight down the road, but in a few minutes the lead elements passed the front marking the Old Hickories' attack line. Pulaski's elation was tempered slightly as they passed between bomb craters and ruined jeeps and trucks, U.S. equipment that had been plastered by U.S. bombers. But now there was infantry on both sides of the road, battle-weary GIs who waved with reckless enthusiasm as the tanks rumbled by. The colonel waved back, and made a private vow to carry the front far beyond these battered troops.

Then they were into the bomb-scarred no-man's-land, and here they saw GIs as well—though these soldiers were more cautious as they waved at the advancing armor. They passed a cemetery, graves and headstones shattered by bombs. Pulaski crossed himself, strangely uneasy at this disturbance of the dead. A few minutes later a gun cracked loudly, and the shell from a concealed antitank gun cracked into the lead Sherman, blasting the turret right off the tank. A volley of return fire belched from the guns of the tank column, and the gun's camouflaged position vanished in a haze of smoke and debris.

"Who was that?" Pulaski asked, acid surging in his stomach at the knowledge that men under his command had just given their lives in this war.

"B Company, sir," Sergeant Dawson replied. The imperturbable NCO spoke without inflection. "I can't make out which tank."

They drove around the burning tank, and the colonel saw the number four on the back. With an irrational flicker of guilt he realized that he didn't know whose Sherman that was . . . he'd make a point to ask the B Company captain, Miller.

Soon the bomb-scarred terrain stretched to the horizon on all sides, and though the tanks and half-tracks had to crawl over piles of rubble and grind through the remnants of hedgerows, CCA barely slowed down in its steady southward advance. A few panzers took shots from the flanks, but these were quickly suppressed or destroyed by return fire—or hammered by the close air support provided by the Mustangs and Thunderbolts snarling in regular circles through the skies overhead. Tanks broke off the road, but the armored fist still advanced on a narrow front for maximum speed.

After an hour they ran into their first serious obstacle. A powerful antitank gun, one of the dreaded 88s, and a pair of tanks were dug in around a shattered crossroads. Three Shermans were knocked out in the first minute of the engagement, and the onrushing column of armor was forced to halt.

This was where the armored infantry went to work. Dismounting from their half-tracks, the GIs worked their way over the rough ground while, from several miles away, Lorimar's Priests hammered the German positions. One panzer, a Mark IV, was destroyed by a direct hit, and the foot soldiers picked off the crew of the AT gun.

Soon an M4 with the Rhino device ripped through a neighboring hedgerow and four more Shermans rumbled toward the second Kraut tank, a Panther. The panzer wheeled backward as several rounds from American tanks ricocheted off the thick frontal armor. In moments it was out of sight, and once again Combat Command A was rolling forward.

And then they were into fields of green, a region even beyond the initial bombardment. The road, still narrow and lined with hedgerows, rolled straight to the south over gently rolling country. There was no sign of any German defender.

"Give me the mike, Bill," Pulaski said, and Sergeant Dawson handed him the handset for the radio.

"We've got a clear road, men!" Pulaski barked into his radio. "I want everyone to move forward at full speed—understand that there is to be no delay! Let's make some tracks!"

Only then did he sit back in the turret of his half-track, letting the wind blow through his short-cropped hair. He'd be damned if he wasn't going to beat Third Armored into the little spot on the map that was Sainte-la-Salle.

Ukraine, Soviet Union, 1400 hours GMT

"Do you think we've crossed the front lines yet?" Müller asked, peering out the window of the Junkers transport. "Is that Poland down there—or the Soviet Union?"

In the seat beside him, von Reinhardt shrugged. "Borders are such tenuous things," he remarked. "What is Poland today was Germany yesterday, and will probably be part of Greater Russia tomorrow. As our late führer observed, 'The greater the amount of room a people has at its disposal, the greater is also its natural protection.' In that the Russian people and the German nation think alike. But to answer your question, judging from the evidence I'd say we've crossed the front."

He pointed out of the window, and Müller raised his eyes, then gasped at the sight of three fighter planes cruising just above and behind the lumbering Ju-52. Red stars on wing and fuselage gleamed like fresh blood in the sunlight.

"Th-they're Russians!" stammered the bespectacled colonel.

"MiGs, I think," Reinhardt agreed, with that maddening display of calm. "Though I confess that I'm not fully conversant with the machines of the Red Air Force."

This entire mission had already become a nightmare, and was only getting worse as far as Müller was concerned. He had asked Reinhardt about the foreign minister after their disastrous meeting. "Did you observe the slackening of the face on one side, the drooping of the eyes?" Reinhardt had asked.

"Why yes, but—" Müller started to reply.

"A minor stroke, I should think," Reinhardt said. "Brought on by shock at the führer's demise. Our foreign minister is, I'm afraid, in questionable health."

"But doesn't the new führer recognize it? Even a second's worth of observation is enough. I couldn't believe how disorganized his mind was. How on earth can the führer expect him to negotiate with the Soviets?"

"An interesting question. As the fictional detective Sherlock Holmes observed, 'When you have eliminated the impossible, whatever remains, however improbable, must be the truth.' If a man is obviously distraught, on the border of being nonfunctional, and is yet being sent on a mission labeled of critical importance to the Fatherland, one must assume either that those who send him are stupid or that there is no other choice, *hein?*"

"Damn it, Günter—don't play with me like that!" Müller said with unusual vehemence. "This is our lives—my life—we're talking about. If you know something, tell me. If not, tell me that."

Günter paused. "Müller, my friend, I'm sorry. I understand your concern, and quite between us, I share your worries. However, since there's nothing much we can do about our fate right now, I tend to make jokes. It helps keep me sane. But that's not fair to you. You need information. Let me tell you what I think . . ."

Ribbentrop was the highest-ranking official in the Reich with a background of dealing with Molotov and the Russians. At the same time, his power in the inner circle of the Nazi regime had been steadily slipping. Even Himmler, once his close friend and patron, had finally become disenchanted with the "champagne salesman."

Now, Himmler needed to open up new negotiations with the Soviet Union, Ribbentrop was the only man with the contacts and experience to make it happen, and yet there was substantially diminished respect on Himmler's part about Ribbentrop's competence—even before Ribbentrop's apparent stroke. It was unlikely that Himmler would put the fate of the Reich exclusively in that man's hands. Reinhardt assumed that this mission was only one front in

Himmler's wider plan, and that Ribbentrop—and the entire mission—could be anything from a key strategic piece to a mere sacrifice pawn in the larger chess game. Müller had sputtered with fear at the suggestion that they might all be put to death as soon as they landed; Reinhardt couldn't completely disabuse him of the idea because in his judgment, it was altogether possible.

"So what can we do about it?"

"Watch and see," Reinhardt said. "And wait for an opportunity."

The sharp-eyed officer closed his eyes, and nothing Müller said could get him to reopen them. He looked fretfully out of the window at the fighter escort, but he mostly saw his own and Reinhardt's reflections in the thick glass. Müller's stomach rumbled. He longed for pastry.

The Ju-52 began to descend, the fighter escort following. Müller got a brief glimpse of a bleak military field as the plane banked to align itself for final approach. As the aircraft descended through the gray sky, he noticed tanks lining the runway, their barrels trained inward. *Perhaps they'll shoot each other instead of us,* he thought, but he would never be so lucky.

After a smooth landing, the plane taxied to a stop before a large hangar. Soviet troops hauled the huge metal doors open. A tractor chugged and the transport was slowly eased into the hangar. In the dim light Müller could see hundreds of Soviet troops. They were all armed, rifles pointing at the aircraft. The doors rumbled shut behind them. They were trapped.

"Ah, the honor guard," said Reinhardt, leaning forward. Müller saw his face in the reflection from the window.

"Is that what you call it," said Müller dryly.

Müller could hear the clanking of the rear passenger door opening, and then loud, angry shouts in Russian as the enemy troops pushed into the transport. Although Müller didn't understand Russian, the meaning was clear. At gunpoint the guard relieved the Germans of their weapons, pulling them away angrily, threatening them. A huge, red-eyed giant of a man pulled Müller up from his seat. He was in a spitting, nearly homicidal rage, shouting angrily in Müller's face with what seemed to be beet breath. Müller was too overpowered to be scared, though none of his muscles responded to his command.

All the Germans—military officers and diplomats alike—were hauled off the plane, their weapons confiscated roughly with threats and shouting. Personal belongings were pulled away . . . including a few chocolates Müller had stashed in his pocket for a dietary emergency. The Russian who grabbed the chocolate immediately devoured them, wrapper and all, chewed them up, then spit out the waxed paper onto the dirt floor.

Müller noticed Ribbentrop, still dazed and seemingly unaware of his surroundings, being manhandled by the guards. *So this is how we die,* he thought, expecting bullets any moment, hoping that would be all, that he wouldn't be tortured first.

"Halt!" The shout echoed in the hangar. With a few remaining shoves and pushes, the guards backed off, although their weapons remained trained on the small German delegation. Müller turned to see a short, stocky man with a square face, thinning white hair and a white mustache, thin glasses under heavy eyebrows. He wore a civilian suit. *Viachislav Molotov, Commissar for Foreign Affairs,* thought Müller. He recognized him from newspaper photographs as well as from the briefing materials before the flight. *I'd bet a dozen strudels he planned this, and now he'll act as if nothing bad has happened.*

"Joachim, my good friend!" he said, heading for the German foreign minister who had fallen to the dirt floor. "How very good to see you!" He reached down to help the fallen Ribbentrop to his feet. Müller noticed a lack of surprise or concern on the Commissar's smiling face.

Ribbentrop looked up through dirt-smeared eyes. "Viachislav," he murmured. "Viachislav. He's dead, you know."

Molotov looked puzzled. "Who's dead?"

"The führer. The führer's dead." Ribbentrop's voice was wandering again.

Molotov seemed taken aback at von Ribbentrop's condition. This, obviously, had not been part of his briefing. Ribbentrop's deputy, State Secretary Baron Adolf Steengracht von Moyland, stepped up to present papers and to begin the diplomatic rituals. Müller tuned out most of the ceremonial portion, standing at attention and feeling like the guest of honor at a firing squad, surrounded by Russian troops. Finally, it was over, and he and the others were escorted from the hangar onto a waiting bus. Molotov, Ribbentrop, and Steengracht entered a long black staff car.

Müller stuck close to Reinhardt. If he was going to hell, he wanted company.

Replacement Army Headquarters, Berlin, Germany, 29 July 1944, 1600 hours GMT

A major of the SS, wearing a black leather trenchcoat with a swastika armband, leading a uniformed squad of six men with Schmeissers at the ready, marched down the narrow corridor. The rhythmic clatter of boots on the polished floor echoed in the confines of the building. Soldiers stopped their work as the armed patrol marched past. People moved out of the way, drew back with fear at the passing of the grim-faced troops.

The one-armed man at the map table looked up as the room around him fell silent.

"Colonel Count von Stauffenberg?" the major demanded.

The colonel drew himself stiffly to his full height. "You know I am von Stauffenberg," he confirmed.

"Very well. I place you under arrest for the assassination of Adolf Hitler."

Stauffenberg looked calmly at the SS squad. Slowly, deliberately, he stared around the room. Officer after officer dropped his eyes rather than make contact with him. Bermel held his gaze for a minute, then looked away.

"I have made no secret of my work. I am proud to have committed not murder, not assassination, but tyrannicide." His voice rang out clearly in the suddenly silent room.

The major's eyes narrowed in contempt. The soldiers were watching Stauffenberg, fingers tense at their triggers.

"Follow me," the major barked. Stauffenberg fell in line behind him. The SS troops formed an escort around the count.

The moment had finally come. Stauffenberg was ready to pay the price for his actions. He had imagined this scene many times since he'd first joined the conspiracy in the fall of 1943.

In his own mind and in the minds of his coconspirators, Stauffenberg represented the best of the old Germany. For nearly all of his career he had been a loyal servant of his country's government—indeed, his sacrifices had gone beyond what could have been asked of any man.

On the seventh of April, 1943, while commanding units of the German Tenth Armored Division in North Africa, he fought hard to cover Rommel's retreat. On that day his panzer column was strafed by a U.S. fighter plane, and von Stauffenberg lost his left eye, his right hand, and two fingers of his left hand in the attack. For months he worked to relearn how to dress himself, to write with his left hand, to function again as an officer. He wanted to return to the front lines, but instead he was assigned to the General Army Office under General Friedrich Olbricht, who was one of the conspirators.

It was Stauffenberg's uncle, Count Nikolaus von Uxkull, who had first recruited him into the conspiracy. Stauffenberg quickly became the pillar of strength that the conspirators so desperately needed. The brilliant but disfigured officer's natural leadership skills elevated him to the top of the plotters' ranks, but after the Allied landings at Normandy, he began to question whether it was still worthwhile to kill Hitler with the end of the war so obviously looming.

His mentor, General Henning von Tresckow, had given him a forceful argument that the assassination was still necessary. "What matters now is not the practical purpose of the coup," Tresckow had said, and Stauffenberg could still hear his voice clearly, "but to prove to the world and for the records of history that the men of the resistance movement dared to take the decisive step."

And so he had. Although the Nazis had retained control, although Germany had not changed, Stauffenberg could stand tall. He had pronounced the sentence of death on Adolf Hitler, and no one could undo his work. Now it was time for the end.

The count slid the fingers of his one remaining hand up his folded and pinned sleeve to pull out the thin knife hidden there. His death would come quickly, honorably, at his own hand, not through degrading tortures at the hands of the SS butchers.

Then there was a sudden yell, and the sharp explosive report of a Walther firing, followed by the soft thud of a bullet impacting flesh, and a scream of pain and shock from one of the guards. "Long live free Germany!" came a triumphant cry—it was Lieutenant Haeften. Bursting from his office, a Walther in each hand, looking like a caricature of the American cowboys whose images were as well known in Germany as in America itself, Haeften was firing rapidly at the assembled guards.

For a moment Stauffenberg watched his young protégé. It was clear that this was a hopeless attack, but then Stauffenberg remembered his own statement: "We have demonstrated that there is some honor left in Germany."

It was honorable to go down fighting, and quickly the old combat veteran joined the fight. With one rapid move he pulled out the knife he was saving for himself and stabbed it through the neck of the SS major, twisting the blade hard and feeling it slide between the vertebrae, killing the Nazi instantly. Gushes of red spurted from an opened artery, and the major's scream died in his throat, a gurgle of blood flooding the trachea. He looked over at the young lieutenant, who looked back.

Then the thunderclap of submachine guns echoed with ferocity in the confined room. The two members of the German aristocracy were no match for a squad of SS troops armed with Schmeissers. There were just too many to take out all at once. Screaming, men dove for cover as an avalanche of bullets ravaged the body of von Haeften. Ricochets blazed off metal desks and walls. Haeften collapsed backward, the last two shots from his pistols going wild. Stauffenberg tried to wrest the weapon from the hand of the dead major, then he, too, heard the noise and felt the impact of the machine gun slugs in his flesh. He recognized them; he'd felt them before.

The SS troops continued their fire long after both von Stauffenberg's and von Haeften's helpless bloody bodies stopped twitching, but finally the crashing din came to a stop, echoes dying like the end of an artillery bombardment. The soldiers watched the blood oozing from the two broken, shattered bodies. In the sudden silence, time seemed to stop for all the living.

Then the ranking enlisted man spoke up. "Get this mess cleaned up. We must file a report."

Even so, for a long time nobody moved.

Wehrmacht Hospital, Vesinet, France,
30 July 1944, 1520 hours GMT

"The Americans are hammering on the left flank . . . bombers, artillery, tanks. There's no question that they'll be through in a matter of days—if they're not already."

General Speidel's voice through the telephone was tinny and distant, but there was no mistaking the glum reality of the tones. Rommel knew his former chief of staff, now von Kluge's right hand man, was telling him the truth.

Normandy was lost.

"Thanks, my friend," he replied. "I have one favor to ask—can you patch me through to von Kluge?"

"I'll try—you know what the connections are like, even before the Allies started bombing everything in sight."

The Desert Fox hung up the phone in his hospital room while he waited for word of the connection. Stiffly, he pushed himself to his feet and limped to the window. Though he moved much more easily than he had even a few days earlier, he still chafed against the limitations caused by his sore leg. And the impairment of his vision was equally troubling—his left eye was covered by a thick patch, and as a result his eyesight had a flat quality, a lack of real depth or texture. A thick, almost stupefying, headache throbbed through his skull, the background of pain that was always simmering near the surface of his consciousness. Angrily he rubbed his neck and grimaced, knowing that these were things he could not control.

But where was there something, in truth, where he did have control? *Think, Rommel, think!* His mind had become a stuck tank, digging deeper and deeper ruts around the same dark pit.

He grimaced in frustration as he stared over the expanse of lawn and grove. As always, he found his attention drawn to the splintered oak, the blackened spire of trunk that had been shattered by some not-too-distant lightning strike.

"I know how you feel," he growled, aware that it was strange for him to be talking to a tree. "Both of us blasted from the sky . . ."

His bitter musings were interrupted by the jangling of the phone, and he ignored the pain to move to the instrument with a trace of his old alacrity. Snatching the receiver out of the cradle, he barked into the mouthpiece. "Rommel here."

"Herr Feldmarschall? I have Field Marshal von Kluge for you."

He waited for a few seconds, then heard the greeting in the clipped tones of the famed commander, widely known as the master of defensive warfare—a reputation he had earned on the eastern front.

Rommel remembered von Kluge's arrival in France, shortly after the invasion. Spurred by reports from Hitler's headquarters about Rommel's defeatist reports, the veteran of the Russian campaign had peremptorily informed the Desert Fox that "now you'll have to start following orders." It had taken exactly one day of touring the front for von Kluge to realize that Rommel's reports, regarded by the führer as almost treasonous, were nothing less than the truth.

"Hello, Hans," Rommel replied. "I understand that our difficulties in Normandy continue."

"Indeed . . ." He pictured von Kluge's reticence as the front commander considered how much he should communicate to the man he had replaced. Apparently he decided that Rommel deserved exactly what he had given—that is, the truth.

"The Americans have broken out on the left . . . I don't think we can stop this attack. We've identified no less than three armor divisions already through the breach—and as you know, once they pass the shell of our position, we have nothing in mobile reserve."

"It was inevitable, only a question of when," the Desert Fox declared sadly. "Tell me, are you making plans for a withdrawal—to the Seine, or farther if necessary?"

There was an awkward pause. "I have been given orders to stand for as long as possible," von Kluge admitted. "Orders that come from the highest source in the Fatherland."

"Blast!" Rommel snapped his harshest expletive. "I had thought that some good might have come out of that madman's death! Surely you can't stand by and let the whole Army Group be encircled?"

"Perhaps the situation is not so dire as that. After all, Montgomery still commands the British . . . as a result we have every reason to expect that they will move quite deliberately against our right flank. And Bradley is quite untested at this sort of warfare."

"But it won't be Bradley who closes the trap—trust me, they'll give Patton a command before much more time passes. And he is the one general over there who understands how to conduct armored operations!"

"Our intelligence suggests that Patton is too unpopular with the high command," von Kluge countered stubbornly. "And, in any event, I have my orders."

Rommel's temper surged, but he forced himself to hold his tongue. There was nothing to be gained by angering von Kluge, the man who had control over the situation. All Rommel could do was offer advice.

"The troops of General Wiese's Nineteenth Army, around Marseilles and Toulon, also in the Rhone valley?" he asked in carefully modulated tones. "Can you bring them north, a precautionary withdrawal?" Even with his mind thick and dull, he was smart enough to understand the necessary next move. Both field marshals understood that the campaign would be decided in northern France. An entire army, including at least one good panzer division, the Eleventh, was garrisoning a part of the country that had no strategic significance any more.

"It is a good idea," von Kluge conceded. "But, alas, such a withdrawal runs counter to my orders."

"But surely you can see what will happen if the Americans get around behind you—or drive on Lorraine, and cut you off from the Nineteenth?" He knew he needed to be slower, more subtle, in talking von Kluge around, but his emotions were slipping out of control. He was being too blunt, too forceful. *As dull as I feel right now, I can still see the obvious next step. Why can't he?*

"Of course!" von Kluge's answer was curt, letting Rommel know he'd pushed too far, too fast. "And do you know what has happened to officers, including generals, who have failed to carry out their orders?" Left unstated was von Kluge's concern that he, too, might be implicated in the conspiracy to kill Adolf Hitler. Rommel knew that von Kluge, like himself, had been approached by the conpirators, had even considered their proposal seriously, and that could easily become fatal.

"I see . . . well, I wish you the best of luck, Hans," Rommel concluded.

"Thank you . . . we both know that I'll need it."

Placing the telephone back on the table, the Desert Fox turned back to the window and its vista of greenery against the lightning scar. He knew that the war was lost, and he grieved for the fact that he was powerless to save even a single one of his brave men.

Sainte-la-Salle, Normandy, France, 1612 hours GMT

"Where the hell is Third Armored?" Pulaski was standing atop the turret of a Sherman, his field glasses trained along the road running northwest out of the tiny hamlet. He next studied the vista to the south, where the equally empty road vanished over the crest of a low elevation. A small church, steeple and cross silhouetted against the sky, commanded the height. Avranches, gateway to the rest of France, lay in that direction and so far as he could tell there was nothing to stand in his combat command's way.

Nothing except his orders.

"What should we do now, Colonel?" Dennis White, reflexively chewing on his pipe, squinted up at Pulaski.

The file of Combat Command A vehicles—tanks, half-tracks, jeeps, and tracked guns—was rolling to the right and left of the narrow lane they had followed to the village. The artillery batteries were taking positions behind a couple of low hills, while the men of the armored infantry battalion were busy digging foxholes and setting up machine gun nests atop the surrounding hills. But for now the preparations were cursory, since Pulaski had made it known that he hoped they weren't going to be here very long.

"Damned if I can tell you," Pulaski grunted. "I know what I want to do—get CCA onto this road, race down to Avranches. I'll bet dollars to doughnuts we could get there before sunset tomorrow!"

"Christ, Colonel—let's give 'em a knock-out punch!" declared Ballard. The ex-boxer's jaw was set, and he looked like he was ready for a match.

If he had been given a little more time, he might have decided to do just that, but even before the village was fully occupied his attention was drawn to a couple of jeeps racing down the lane in the wake of the fast-advancing armored spearhead. Presumably because he traveled through a combat zone, General Wakefield had wisely stowed away the one-star flags that had previously decorated his jeep, but even so Pulaski recognized the division executive officer when he was still a half mile from the village.

The colonel greeted the general as soon as the jeep pulled into the small square, a plaza between the church, mill, and inn that seemed to be about all there was to Sainte-la-Salle. A few local Frenchmen and women had hesitantly come forth from their homes, and now they gathered in front of the chapel, watching the Americans with considerable interest.

"General—welcome to Sainte-la-Salle!" Pulaski announced through a broad grin. "What you see is what you get."

"Good work," Wakefield agreed, looking around. "Not much of a social center, is it?" He didn't wait for an answer. "What kind of losses did you take getting here?"

Pulaski's ebullience faded a little. "Five tanks, sixteen men killed and another two dozen wounded, already evacuated. But we cut right through the damned Krauts, General! Blew up a couple of tanks and knocked out two of their eighty-eights." He shook his head at another memory. "Also, we learned that the reports about the Panther were right. Ballard saw two of his Shermans go toe to toe with one of the bastards. The Panther just took its time shooting one Sherman and then the next while the shells from those popgun 75s were just bouncing off the frontal armor. We did finally get the son of a bitch from the side, though."

"Now you're holding here?"

"Well, I was getting the men started on some positions . . . but listen, General—I'm glad you're here," Pulaski declared. "You can see we've beat Third Armored to the road! Hell, there's no sign of 'em as far as I can see. What say we get moving toward Avranches?"

Wakefield shook his head. "Nothing doing, Jimmy, sorry. General King's got his orders from Corps, and we're sticking to the plan."

"Where is General King, sir?" asked Pulaski, unable to hold his tongue against the borderline insolent question.

The general shrugged, his face a mask. "He had an urgent call from Army HQ—asked me to come out here and report on progress."

"What the hell happened to Third Armored, then?" The colonel knew that his tone revealed his exasperation. Wakefield frowned, but didn't make any direct rebuke.

Instead, the general merely shrugged. "Haven't heard, though I'd guess they ran into some stiff resistance somewhere up north of here. I've gotta say I'm impressed by the time you made, though. A nice piece of attacking, Jimmy."

Pulaski tried again. He pointed down the empty roadway. "But look— there's nothing down there! At least let me move past those hills, set up a position for the Third when they finally come through here . . . damnit, General, we've got the Germans reeling back on their asses! Let me get on with finishing the job."

"I told you, Jimmy, I can't let you do that. There's the plan, made by Bradley himself, and if CCA is on the road when a whole armored division tries to roll on through, there'll be chaos."

"But that's just the point—we'll be down the road and out of Third Armored's way! If we hit some resistance, we'll deploy, take out any roadblocks. Sending CCA down there will only let the next guys move that much faster!" Wakefield clenched his jaw and Pulaski saw that he was pushing too hard, especially with his own officers watching. *Slowly,* he thought to himself. He knew his own eagerness was starting to run away with him, and that was no way to get results.

Further debate was halted by the arrival of another jeep convoy, this one distinguished by a three-star general who wore two .45 automatics and swaggered up to the officers with a belligerent scowl. General George S. Patton cut a dashing swath on the battlefield, and there wasn't a man in the village square who didn't recognize him.

The officers of Nineteenth Armored saluted and stood straight as Patton marched right up to them.

"Henry, goddamn it, what the hell are you doing?" demanded the famous commander, in a voice that was almost incongruously high-pitched as it emerged from such a warlike visage. "Sitting on your ass here while the Krauts are getting away! D'you think you're on a goddamned picnic?"

Pulaski could see Wakefield's face harden.

"General, I'm following orders. Get to this town and hold," Wakefield shot back. "Orders from General Bradley and Jack King, my bosses."

"Get these goddamned tanks moving down this road, now!" snapped Patton. "Jesus Christ, don't you know you're out here to fight a war?"

"On what authority?" demanded Wakefield. "I'm under Eight Corps, First Army."

"Your division CO is getting the news right now—Third Army is activated, and I'm your *new* boss! And if you keep sitting here on your ass you're going to find yourself out of a job!"

The army commander stalked into the middle of the dirt street, spun around with both hands upraised. He kicked through the dust with his cavalry boots. "Damn it, Hank, look around you! This pissant little flea hole doesn't mean crap—it's Avranches that we need. And your boys here are at the front of the line—you need to get 'em rolling!"

Wakefield drew a deep breath, then turned to glare at the CCA commander. "Colonel Pulaski?" he roared.

"Yes, sir!" Pulaski snapped off a salute, made sure that no trace of his elation showed on his face.

"You heard the general." Wakefield's voice was a growl.

"We're ready to move out, sir!" Pulaski declared, turning to shout at his men. "Men of CCA—mount up! On the double! Colonel Ballard, get D Company rolling right away, have a look over those hills. The rest of us will be along the road in a minute—give us cover if you see any sign of the Krauts!"

Patton nodded with a smug grin. Wakefield's face was impassive, but Pulaski noticed his fists were clenched tight. He'd heard rumors that there was bad blood between his division exec and Old Blood and Guts Patton, and now he believed it. And he'd stepped in it, too, implicitly taking Patton's side against his own XO. He knew he shouldn't have done that, but it had been impossible to resist. He *knew* he was right, but he shouldn't have been so impatient.

Immediately the Stuart tanks that formed D Company, the light armor company, rolled forward. They rattled through the ditch and over stone walls, fanning out as they drove southward from Sainte-la-Salle. Soon the M5s were rolling up the first of the nearby hills, rumbling over the crests, spreading to protect both flanks of the long highway.

In and around the village more engines roared, and tracks clattered as the first Sherman tanks rumbled down the road within a minute of Pulaski's orders. The infantry, gunners lugging their heavy machine guns, lumbered down from the hilltop to scramble into their half-tracks and chase along behind the tanks. By this time Colonel Pulaski had scrambled into his half-track, and Keefer had started the command vehicle down the road in the wake of C Company's fourteen remaining tanks.

When he looked back, the last thing he saw was the two generals standing side by side.

Excerpt from *War's Final Fury,* by Professor Jared Gruenwald

At the moment of Hitler's assassination, the situation for Germany was bleak to the point of hopelessness. The Soviet Union's eventual victory was assured. Why, then, would Stalin consider making peace with his bitter enemy, someone who had double-crossed him scant years ago?

This was the genius of Operation Carousel. How can two sides consumed with mutual distrust, even hatred, negotiate a peace? The answer is in two parts: first, that each party gains through negotiated peace more and better than it could through military action, and second, that the terms of the peace make it difficult or impossible for either party to renege.

Stalin had growing distrust for the Western Allies, as is well known. The alliance between the Communist Soviet Union and the democratic West was one of convenience. As the war moved into its final phase, farsighted people on both sides were looking forward to an inevitable Third World War, involving the West versus International Communism, centered in the Soviet Union. Churchill, Patton, and even Rommel were among those who expressed grave concern about what would come next. Stalin could only assume that with the defeat of Germany, the unwelcome attention of the West would turn toward him.

By conquering as much as possible of Eastern Europe, as well as by supporting indigenous revolutionary movements throughout Western Europe, Stalin hoped to turn the postwar political environment to his favor. While his faith in the "historic inevitability" of Communism sustained his long-range vision, he knew that Marx did not predict instant or easy victory, or victory without some setbacks along the way. Operating on the principle that "Marxism helps those who help themselves," Stalin needed to look forward to securing his postwar base, for the "good will" of the Western Allies, he knew, would evaporate as soon as Germany fell.

Heinrich Himmler understood the *realpolitik* as well as Stalin. His problem was that Germany, trapped in an unwinnable two-front war, decimated by poor military decisions by the late führer, was hardly in a position to impose a unilateral peace. He couldn't merely offer what Stalin already had; that would not change Stalin's behavior. But he could offer Stalin several things of value. First was wider access to territory than Stalin would get from the Western Allies, including that *bête noir* of classic Russian foreign policy: a warm-water port on the Mediterranean. Second was a destabilized political environment that prevented the West from checkmating Stalin's moves. It is possible he believed that a tripartite rather than bipolar world would give Stalin additional maneuvering room. Finally, there was access to newer technology. Russia's classic need to modernize was unchanged under Communist rule. And Germany, even in ruins, possessed far more advanced technology than Stalin could get elsewhere.

One element that did not become known until well after the war was that Himmler, through his own back channels and independently of Minister von Ribbentrop, had been feeding Stalin a steady stream of "black propaganda," forged documents purporting to show a growing Allied intent to make the Soviet Union the next target. This had been done with a high degree of finesse and subtlety, with material having been slipped to Soviet agents through unrevealed German moles, over some time, more evidence that Himmler's Operation Reichsturm option was one of long planning. This propaganda effort may have played a crucial role in the diplomatic negotiations that were to follow.

It went without saying that the two men would double-cross each other at their earliest opportunity, but neither would double-cross until—or unless—it would redound to his advantage. This was an odd basis on which to build mutual trust, but definite knowledge, however base or distasteful, is a solid foundation on which to build effective diplomacy.

Himmler's moves, as we shall see, were therefore obvious. . . .

OPERATION COBRA

August 1944

**Rockefeller Center, New York, United States,
1 August 1944, 0800 hours GMT**

Chuck Porter stubbed out his cigarette and reached into his shirt pocket for another as he watched the chattering Teletype machine. Most of the AP Early team was clustered around as well; nobody moved. It was four o'clock in the morning, New York time; people were just starting work in England.

> FLASH/BULLETIN
> LONDON, 1 AUGUST, 0800 GMT
> COPY 01 HIMMLER NEW FÜHRER
> DISTRIBUTION: ALL STATIONS
>
> LONDON, 1 AUGUST (AP) BY EDWARD REED
> GERMAN RADIO BROADCAST TODAY THAT HEINRICH HIMMLER, HEAD OF THE
> NAZI SS AND GESTAPO SECURITY FORCES, HAS BEEN NAMED CHANCELLOR
> AND FÜHRER OF THE THIRD REICH BY THE NAZI GOVERNMENT MEETING AT
> THE REICHSTAG.
> IN HIS ACCEPTANCE SPEECH, HIMMLER PRAISED HITLER AND PLEDGED
> THAT "THE THOUSAND-YEAR REICH SHALL STILL FULFILL ITS DESTINY" AND
> THAT "THE FORCES ALLIED AGAINST US WILL SHORTLY KNOW TO THEIR SOR-
> ROW THAT THE GERMAN PEOPLE REMAIN STRONG EVEN WHEN THEIR
> SUPREME LEADER HAS BEEN MURDERED BY COWARDLY TRAITORS."
> WITHIN AN HOUR OF HIS ELECTION, UNDERGROUND SOURCES REPORT
> THAT A STRING OF ARRESTS AND EXECUTIONS HAS TAKEN PLACE, INCLUD-
> ING THE EXECUTION OF COLONEL STAUFFENBERG, REPUTED TO BE THE AS-
> SASSIN OF HITLER AND FAILED COUP LEADER. THIS IS DENIED BY THE
> GERMAN GOVERNMENT, WHO STILL BLAME THE ASSASSINATION ON "AMERI-
> CAN JEWISH SPIES."
> THE NEW NAZI LEADERSHIP INCLUDES GENERAL ADOLF GALLAND AS
> HEAD OF THE LUFTWAFFE. . . .

Chuck turned away from the Teletype as it continued to spew out a list of military and cabinet appointments. "Well, well, well," he said. "Looks like the Nazis have one last gasp in them after all. Still, nobody's as crazy as Hitler;

they've got to realize it's all over but the shouting, and I think you'll see some peace overtures coming soon."

"Suppose they do have some new secret weapon?" asked one of the night shift editors, a brown-haired, slightly cynical older reporter named Eaker. "Maybe they're going to put the war in extra innings."

"Bullshit," pronounced Porter with finality. "In fact, I want to alert the London bureau to start digging for early word on peace overtures. I know the phrase is 'unconditional surrender,' but with Hitler dead, my bet is we'll start talking with any halfway decent offer." He inspected the long line of faces and didn't see any opposition. "Good. Let's see if we can't get a decent scoop out of this."

Avranches, France, 1 August 1944, 1322 hours GMT

"It's a hell of an opportunity, Jack, Hank . . . just look at them go. The whole country's ours for the taking!" George Patton was in a great mood as he stood with Jack King and Henry Wakefield, looking across the bridges south of the city, gesturing at the columns of Shermans and half-tracks rolling across those spans and roaring into the French countryside.

"You're right, General. It's one helluva chance," King enthused. "I've got Pulaski and Jackson in a race to see who can get to the Seine first."

Patton chuckled. "Good men, there. I'll tell you, my money's on Pulaski." The general gave Wakefield a wink. "You too, Hank?"

The division XO nodded, forced himself to return a smile. "Jimmy's in a hurry, General, that he is." He was still stinging about the tongue-lashing Patton had given him at Sainte-la-Salle. It didn't help his mood to know that Pulaski had been right: CCA had raced all the way to Avranches before Third Armored appeared on the scene.

However, Wakefield was a practical enough man to admit to himself that the Third Army commander was correct about the combat commands' deployment, and about the situation in general. The U.S. Army, and particularly the armored divisions under Patton's command, had achieved a breakthrough of historic, even epic, proportions. The Nineteenth Armored, with Third and Fourth Armored Divisions hot on its heels, had rolled right through Avranches. In some places in the large city the enemy had fought hard to defend each block, while elsewhere the Americans had been slowed more by celebrating French than by fighting Germans.

But now they were through the city and had seized the key bridges over the Selune River south of the town. From here Old Blood and Guts was sending his spearheads racing across the countryside. Everywhere American tanks embarked on a surging offensive to liberate France, and to drive the Germans back to their own border and beyond. Patton had charged the Nineteenth with reaching the Seine, and crossing it if they could; King had subsequently informed both his combat commanders that they *would* make such a crossing, and that the only acceptable question was who would reach the east bank first.

The emphasis on speed still seemed vaguely reckless to Wakefield, not a proper way to run an advance. The division—hell, the whole of Third Army!—was attacking without flank protection, relying on the rapidity of movement to protect itself from counterattack. But the XO could not argue with success, so he could only pray that it continued.

"Well, Jack—keep 'em rolling," Patton said, accepting the salutes of his subordinate generals before climbing into his jeep. "Good luck to you and your boys!"

"Thanks, General! See you in Paris!" shouted King as the army CO roared away. The division commander raised his binoculars and stared at the file of tanks and half-tracks moving across the bridge. "There goes your lead combat command, Hank," he declared fiercely. "Ski's got 'em on the move."

"Yes, sir."

"General?"

King and Wakefield turned to see that Bob Jackson had joined them. Somehow the CCB commander had managed to keep his uniform neat, his face clean shaven, even in the midst of the campaign.

"Ready to move out, Bobby?"

"Right away, sir . . . I just wanted to check on the fuel priorities. Can we get the trucks on the Paris highway by tonight?"

Wakefield nodded. This was proper planning, an element of an armored campaign that deserved careful attention. Apparently his division CO had a different opinion, because King's voice was sharp.

"Christ, Bobby, let us worry about that. Get your tanks moving, and get word back to Army HQ when you've got a depot space cleared. We'll see that you get your gasoline."

"Of course, General! Very good, sir!" If Jackson was stung by the criticism he didn't show it, saluting smoothly and turning to march back to his jeep.

A second later Jack King turned to Wakefield. "What was that Patton said to you about Pulaski?" he asked.

Wakefield shrugged. "Our young colonel had some good luck at Sainte-la-Salle. He was trying to persuade me to let him advance, against orders, when Georgie rolled up. He chewed me a new asshole for trying to hold Ski back."

King chuckled wryly. "That's our boss, Hank. But you've got to hand it to him—he knows how to handle armor."

Wakefield could only agree, albeit reluctantly. He still thought the division could be advancing into terrible danger, and he didn't like the knowledge that their flanks were exposed, would be stretched by hundreds of miles before this was over. But if there was one lesson he'd learned in this man's army, it was when to keep his mouth shut.

"Let's get moving," King suggested, turning toward the division HQ vehicles. "I have a feeling our HQ is going to be set up wherever we stop for the night, and I'd like to get a few miles behind us by then."

"Yes, sir," Wakefield said, mentally preparing himself for an entirely unseemly measure of haste.

Just South of Roncey, Normandy, France, 2 August 1944, 0645 hours GMT

The camouflage-mottled Panther squatted in the farmyard, close against the concealment of a stone wall. The tank's long gun poked over the top of the barrier, trained down the long, empty road to the north.

In the driver's seat, Carl-Heinz Clausen switched off the engine to conserve fuel while the lieutenant climbed from the turret, announcing over the intercom that he intended to reconnoiter. From his position, Carl-Heinz couldn't see what lay behind them, so he popped open his own hatch and clambered down the sloping forehull of the big tank. The stone wall connected to a house, but the building stood on the other side of the wall—it didn't block the tank's line of withdrawal.

The driver saw a lower stone wall standing across the back of the yard about twenty meters away. The area around the farm was bare of trees, except for some brush fringing the nearby marsh. The only obstacle capable of stopping his tank, once he got rolling, was the house itself . . . and, of course, the muddy bog.

The road they had followed in the latest leg of their retreat from the St.-Lô position approached this farm in a straight line. Four days of running and fighting had brought them down this route, to this farm where they had elected to set up another ambush. For the nearest kilometer the road passed between the low swamp to the east and a forest of ancient oaks to the west; the American tanks, when they came, would be limited to that single lane, and the partially concealed Panther had a tight bead on the entire route.

Of course, a squad of infantry could slip through the forest and surprise them here—but the lieutenant was gambling that the Amis would be in too much of a hurry for such a tactic. Word was that their advance spearheads were already through Avranches. Now it was just a matter of falling back and making the enemy pay the highest possible price for each kilometer of France. No longer part of any coherent division, Schroeder's panzer fought on its own, always facing the forefront of the American advance.

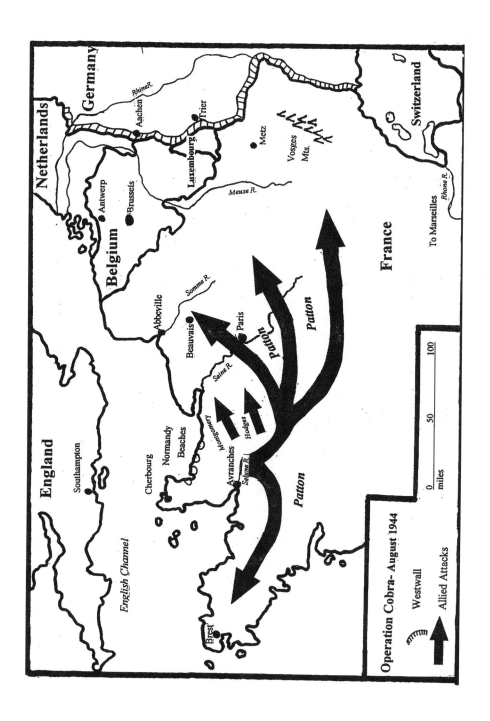

Carl-Heinz climbed back in as the lieutenant trotted back from scouting the other side of the house.

"Won't be long now—be ready to start at a word." The young officer scrambled up the turret with his usual efficiency of effort, settling onto the rim of his hatch so he could keep his eyes trained on that still empty road.

Carl-Heinz dropped into his own seat and clamped the metal hatch cover overhead. Ulrich Pfeiffer, at his radio and hull machine gun, sat in the adjacent position and shook his head lugubriously. The lean carpenter from Saxony remained convinced that the tank faced certain and imminent destruction here, as it had on many occasions since they had survived the cauldron of Kursk on the Russian front during the previous year. To Pfeiffer, today was simply another chance to die.

"Don't worry—the leutnant's got us tucked in snug," Carl-Heinz said, with a friendly nod. "We'll have the bastards cold as soon as they come into sight."

"Sure," Ulrich said sadly. "The first one . . . maybe the second. But what about the dozen after that?"

Clausen clapped his pessimistic comrade on the shoulder, humoring him but unwilling to agree. Sure, there were times when it felt as if the entire United States Army sought to destroy them, personally. Still, Carl-Heinz found that the thought of death didn't particularly affect him.

"Enemy observed." The lieutenant's voice came over the intercom, crisp and brief as always. Carl-Heinz instinctively placed his thumb over the starter button. "Driver—start the engine. Gunner, fire at 500 meters."

The Panther's gasoline engine roared into life. Carl-Heinz could see little through his driver's viewing hatch, and when he swiveled the periscope to look to the left he saw only the blocking presence of the stone wall. No matter—he'd grown quite used to driving the big vehicle exactly as the lieutenant ordered.

"Here they come—column of at least a half dozen tanks, maybe more—with some half-tracks bringing up the rear. They're moving fast and coming this way, so let's see if we can hold them up for a few minutes. Gunner, aim for the lead tank. Fire when you're sure of the target."

"I've got him, leutnant."

The crack of the long 75-mm gun rocked the Panther back and the first Sherman blew up in a spectacular fountain of flame. Immediately the American column dispersed off the road, but Fritzi put a round into a second tank moments later. The Shermans were not terribly well armored, but they were fast, and Carl-Heinz strained for a sight of the enemy tanks coming out of the woods before him.

"*Scheiss!* Behind us!" barked Lieutenant Schroeder. "Gunner, train forward—driver, back up—*schnell!*"

Double-clutching with his left foot, Carl-Heinz jammed the gear lever into reverse and floored the accelerator. The Panther jolted toward the rear, at the same time as Fritzi, the gunner, swiveled the long barrel to the front. The crew needed no prodding.

In moments the farmhouse concealed the tank completely from view up the road, the gun facing the thoroughfare at a perpendicular angle. "Driver— stop!" barked Schroeder, and Carl-Heinz immediately stomped on the clutch and knocked the tank out of gear.

"Swivel to the right—bring the turret around—full rear!"

The grinding of gears swiveled the barrel out of Carl-Heinz's line of sight and continued until he knew the long barrel was trained behind them, sighting over the compartment where the big engine rumbled and snorted.

Nerve wracking seconds dragged on—*Where are the damned Amis?* Carl-Heinz stared down the length of wall, watching the corner where at any instant tons of olive-drab steel could roll into view. He couldn't see to the rear but knew that Fritzi and the lieutenant were looking for targets to appear in that direction.

"Fire!" Fritzi, as usual, anticipated the lieutenant's order and the long gun instantly spit an armor-piercing shell.

"Got him! Driver—reverse! Gunner—train forward!"

Carl-Heinz smoothly backed the tank past the house as the turret once more swiveled toward the front. The driver stared through the periscope, startled as a Sherman appeared around the corner of the building. The American tank fired, the shell ricocheting off the Panther's frontal armor with a deafening clang. Fritzi shot back, hitting the base of the Sherman's turret. The resulting explosion blinded Carl-Heinz momentarily, but when his vision cleared he saw that the cannon of the M4 had bent back like an aluminum drainpipe.

The shell casing rattled into the turret as Peltz jammed another round into the breach. This time Fritzi didn't wait for the command, blasting his second point-blank shot into the forehull of another tank. Smoke belched from the hatches, and the gun stopped its frantic motion. The driver popped out of his escape hole but Schroeder quickly squeezed the trigger on the turret machine gun, dropping the helpless tanker halfway out of the hatch. The body collapsed forward, arms dangled off the front of the olive-drab tank.

"Driver—reverse!" snapped Lieutenant Schroeder. Again Carl-Heinz double-clutched and rocked backward. The Panther lurched as it struck the stone wall and then pitched up and over the broken barrier. Carl-Heinz saw the receding gap, a neat notch the size of the panzer, as he continued to back away from the house and farmyard.

"Driver—stop—forward—left turn; Gunner, train right!" Immediately Clausen repeated the gear-shifting process, the Panther responding with a grace worthy of its namesake. Quickly the German tank rolled past the back of the house. Risking a look through his periscope, Carl-Heinz saw the humpbacked silhouette of another Sherman rumbling off the road, straight toward the Panther. The American gun fired, but the fast-moving panzer had already darted past the gun trajectory—the shot was a clean miss.

"Driver—stop! Gunner—fire!" The Panther's cannon barked and Fritzi's shot caught the nearest M4 squarely in the forehull. Smoke instantly spewed from the ruined tank, secondary explosions continuing to rock the metal carcass. Another Sherman had darted off the other side of the road, racing toward the forest in a standard dispersal tactic in the face of ambush. Those tankers were obviously unaware that the German was now perched directly to their rear.

Fritzi settled into a careful shot, blasting the American tank in the back of the turret, where it was most vulnerable. The shell punched through the armor, and, while the Sherman showed no outward sign of damage, it stopped moving. Slowly, its gun settled toward the ground.

Meanwhile Carl-Heinz swung the periscope leftward to check the road. He saw half-tracks, white stars emblazoned on the doors, rolling into the ditch. Infantrymen scrambled out of the vehicles, ducking into the makeshift trench, racing toward the Panther.

He called over the intercom. "Leutnant! Up the road!"

"Loader—high explosive," Schroeder ordered, and Peltz smoothly replaced the antitank round in the breach as the turret swiveled to the left. Carl-Heinz pressed his eye against the periscope's rubber eyepiece, watching American infantry rush forward. They moved much more slowly than the steadily swinging tank gun. *They're doomed—why don't they run?*

"Fire!" The high explosive projectile struck the ground in front of the first half-track, concussion blasting the vehicle backward, killing the nearby soldiers in a flash of blast and shrapnel. Fritzi put the second round into the next half-track, which exploded in a spectacular fireball, the blaze popping off ammunition like stuttering bursts of gunfire.

"Driver—forward, right turn! Let's get down the road!" Carl-Heinz needed no coaxing. The Panther rumbled through its circuit around the farmhouse, rolled past smoking Shermans and then growled into high gear on the road. They raced at top speed, more than forty kilometers per hour, toward the south.

"Radioman—coordinates?"

"Three kilometers west of Mortain," Pfeiffer chattered into his microphone as the crew awaited a reply.

Carl-Heinz had heard the same rumors as the rest of the crew: that Avranches had already fallen, that they were all but surrounded here in Normandy as the American attack swept into the rest of France. But there was nothing he could do about that, so he concentrated on holding the rumbling Panther on the road, throttle wide open. A shell whizzed over the tank, and another exploded just beside them, but their luck held as the range between them and the enemy tanks lengthened. Within a kilometer, he had to drive through the ditch to avoid a pair of burned-out trucks, but he quickly regained the highway and rumbled over a low elevation.

At last they were out of sight of the American armored column, but the driver muttered a curse as he saw that the road before them was blocked with blazing tanks and trucks, all in the field gray of the German army. Marshes pressed close against either side of the road, and there seemed to be no way around the blocked road. Clearly this bottleneck had been a killing ground for the Allied air forces.

Lieutenant Schroeder threw open the turret hatch, rising for a look at the situation.

The fighter came seemingly from nowhere, machine guns spitting lethal bullets. The lieutenant's body was riddled before he could drop through the hatch. When Fritzi finally got him into the turret, Lieutenant Schroeder could only moan softly and die.

"More of the Jabo bastards!" shouted Peltz. "Looks like a bomb run!"

Carl-Heinz knew the Panther was a sitting duck, parked at the end of the file of wrecked vehicles. He turned the wheel violently, driving down the embankment and into the soft mud of the marsh. Gunning the engine, holding the throttle at top speed, he urged the big vehicle through the soft muck as bullets tore the earth around him.

"Come on, baby . . . you can do it . . . I know you can," he said encouragingly.

A bomb went off nearby, casting a sheet of muddy water across the periscope, and the desperate driver pushed open the hatch, sticking his head just far enough that he could see.

We're doomed—we're going to die here! He had the desperate thought as he felt the mud sucking at the treads, trying to pull the Panther down. Traction was all but gone, and the tank wallowed to the left, to the right, and back again as the tracks flailed at the too-soft ground. Gradually their headway slowed until they were barely crawling, and Carl-Heinz knew that if they stopped they would never get started again.

So he could not let them stop.

"Please, baby . . . do it for Papa," he whispered, vaguely aware that Ulrich was staring at him, wide-eyed, from the radioman's seat.

More bullets sprayed the muddy ground, but now the tracks were biting into solid dirt. The engine raced into an almost human scream, pushing them through water and mud. Sticky goo splashed up the forehull into his face, and Carl-Heinz spat it out, not taking the time to wipe his eyes.

Finally, with a groaning lurch, the huge tank found its footing, pushing to the edge of the marsh, then crawling up a bank. With his head still out of the driver's hatch, Carl-Heinz felt branches lash his face as he drove between two massive trees and straight into the cool shelter of a small woods.

Ukraine, Soviet Union, 2320 hours GMT

"I'm not cut out to be a diplomat," Müller said. "This waiting is driving me crazy!"

Reinhardt smiled. It was the third day of the negotiations between Ribbentrop and Molotov—or, more properly, between Ribbentrop's aides and Molotov. The work of the negotiations was taking place almost around the clock, with pots of awful coffee and stale bread sandwiches grabbed and eaten during the talks. Ribbentrop's collapse was now virtually complete; he was in bed with one guard while his staff tried valiantly to resolve difficult issues without the power or authority to do so. If they came back with a deal Himmler didn't like, Müller was sure they would be punished, probably killed. Alternately, Müller feared, Molotov could decide to have them all shot at any moment. The Russians were cold, unyielding, frustrating to talk to. It was just their traditional negotiating style, Reinhardt observed.

The meetings had stopped for an hour to allow people to shower and change clothes. Müller found the icy water terrible and jumped out in seconds, drying himself off and struggling back into his clothes. Reinhardt seemed to glory in the stoic torment, washing himself thoroughly. He studied his reflection in the small mirror, slicking his jet black hair down just so.

Müller hoped for a detailed briefing of the progress, but Reinhardt was not forthcoming. He suggested in vague terms that the situation was not quite hopeless, and that had to be enough for Müller. It wasn't. "They *hate* us, Günter," he said in a plaintive voice. "Or are you claiming that's just a negotiating ploy?"

Reinhardt smiled. "Those aren't mutually exclusive concepts, you know," he replied.

The conference was in a temporary barracks, surrounded by barbed wire and soldiers. Müller thought it looked more like a POW camp than the site of intergovernmental negotiations at the foreign minister level, but then any job on which he was assigned always turned out to be a lot less elegant than he expected.

What surprised him was Reinhardt. Günter had fast moved into a leadership position on the effectively headless team. Baron Steengracht was weak and inconsequential, a man fit primarily for embassy parties and occasions of show. He had been von Ribbentrop's "parrot" for years and was best known for his extremely beautiful wife, not for his intellect.

Reinhardt stepped up, first with whispered ideas, then with diffidently phrased suggestions that cut through complicated issues, and finally worked his way into the negotiations as nearly a full partner. Molotov regarded him suspiciously at first, then seemed to accept him as a man with whom he could do business.

"The Soviet Union is a peaceful nation," Molotov said with a grunt. "You had peace with us, but you lied. We cannot trust a nation of liars. This discussion is useless. We see no value in continuing." He began to stand up. Müller was panicked, then noticed that Steengracht seemed to be panicking as well.

"But Commisar," Steengracht said, rising rapidly to his feet in hopes of heading off the Russian. But it was Reinhardt who cut through Steengracht's empty protestations before they could get started. As Steengracht was saying, "We are prepared to commit the honor of the Third—" Reinhardt interrupted him.

"It's very simple, Commissar Molotov. You cannot trust us. Nor can we trust you."

"Eh?" said Molotov, taken aback by the nondiplomatic brusqueness.

"I beg your pardon!" said Steengracht with an icy stare, but Reinhardt ignored the clear hint to sit down and shut up.

"As Catullus says, 'Let none believe that a man's speeches be trustworthy.' If any part of our arrangement depends on mutual trust, we are doomed."

Molotov slowly settled back in his chair. His body language still radiated disinterest, but Müller thought he picked up some slight hint of amusement at the young German officer's efforts. "We agree with half that statement. We cannot trust you. You may explain further."

"Very well, Commissar. If there is no cessation of hostilities, the Soviet Union will eventually conquer at least the eastern portion of Germany. The only uncertainties are the exact number of casualties and the extent to which you will be able to penetrate before your allies stop you."

"Our allies have been reliable, unlike the German Reich," Molotov said dismissively.

"But that is not true. You worry about them constantly. You no longer worry about us, although you must still finish what has been started. But you must surely know that those allies have no more love for you than you have for us, and that once we are finished, you will surely be next."

Molotov grunted. "This does not interest us. You are merely trying to create distrust between us and our allies, an obvious tactic and unworthy. In any event, let Napoleon and Hitler serve as an object lesson for anyone who considers invading us. We have no fear."

"I suppose you must say that," Reinhardt said with a nod. "That's what diplomats must say. But as a military officer, I was trained to consider threat synonymous with ability, and therefore it is axiomatic that the Western Allies pose a threat to you. If nothing else, your allies surely are not eager to see the Marxist dream of the historic inevitability of Communism become fulfilled."

Müller was starting to get a sense of the real dialogue. This time Molotov's dismissive grunt was not accompanied by any attempt to stand and leave the negotiating table. *He must be interested in what Reinhardt is saying,* Müller thought.

"Then your goal must be to finish this war in the best position for the next one, for the next one will surely follow, and you will be its target."

"This is idle speculation and has no basis in fact," stated the commissar stolidly. But his eyes were interested.

Reinhardt took a deep breath. There was a mirror on the far wall, and Müller could see his face and the back of his head simultaneously. "We are not a threat to you as long as there is enough space between us for you to see a potential double-cross. If we can stalemate our enemies in the west, we can increase the buffer between you and them. You can use your military energies far better than crushing us by annexing better strategic territory. May I suggest Norway, for its Atlantic access, and Greece, for your long-awaited warm-water port?"

There was stunned silence on both sides of the negotiating table. This was an outrageous concession, far in excess of Reinhardt's authority, the sort of thing that normally would be broached over time. Molotov snorted, and Müller realized it was a stifled laugh. "So," the commissar said after taking a sip of tea with jam in it—which had become one of Müller's favorite Russian customs—and returned to his stoic Slavic demeanor. "You would trade away Norway and Greece for peace? You talk about a lack of trust. Why shouldn't we take Norway, Greece, and you?"

"Two reasons: First, you can't. If you double-cross your allies, you won't be able to go back, not with them. Certainly not without a peace offering at least as dramatic as what I'm suggesting. Second, you don't want to. You want a Germany with some significant military strength to tie the Allies down in the west. If we are able to throw them back into the Atlantic, all well and good. If we can only stalemate them, then they can hardly mobilize to go after you, at least for a long time." A glint of sunlight flashed into the mirror and onto his face. Müller could see a single bead of sweat, the only evidence of Reinhardt's tension as he spoke.

"And what about a German double-cross?"

"Commissar, even if you think we haven't learned our lesson, we would establish a demilitarized zone wide enough to make it impossible for us to achieve significant surprise. We can set up an observation system to help achieve this."

To the shock of everyone present, Molotov roared with laughter. "Young man, you astound me! I thought all initiative and creativity had been bred out of the Germans by Hitler! But perhaps it was only temporarily beaten down. You, Steengracht! Is this the outline of Himmler's proposal?"

Steengracht was clearly stunned by Reinhardt's presumption. He'd been kept mostly in the dark by Ribbentrop, and had not been expected to do much in the way of negotiation. But Reinhardt, Müller knew, was not privy to this sort of information either. He had simply figured it out on his own.

"Yes—yes, Commissar Molotov," the baron said. "I believe it is."

Molotov smiled. This time it wasn't the genuine impressed amusement that had been directed at Reinhardt. This was a cold smile. "And it is a good thing, for Comrade Stalin was not amused at a visit from the double-crossing Germans. Frankly, had there not been a worthwhile offer, we would have taken the opportunity for some revenge on the colossal damage you and yours have given us. But this time it looks as if you will be allowed to live."

Müller almost fainted at the words, and then he nearly fainted again as Molotov waved his hand. An aide left, and a few minutes later in came white-jacketed stewards bearing dinner on silver covered platters. "Just in case this was worthwhile," Molotov said, "I arranged for a meal to be provided. Eat hearty, for tomorrow we fly to Moscow!"

But Müller wasn't worried any more, for at least he would fly there on a decently full stomach.

First Army Headquarters, Normandy, France, 3 August 1944, 0910 hours GMT

Reid Sanger threw the duffel back over his shoulder and tried to straighten up. "I'm sorry about the extra cleanup," he said to the LST crewman as he disembarked.

The grizzled petty officer grunted. "You ain't the first, won't be the last," he said, tacking a "sir" onto the end after a noticeable pause. "Don't mind my saying so, it's a good thing you didn't join the Navy."

"You're telling me," said Sanger. He had been terribly seasick the entire Channel crossing, and the evidence would have to be cleaned up by someone else. His face was still somewhat green as he struggled his way off the boat and onto the Continent.

The port of Cherbourg wasn't designed for the amount of shipping currently surging onto its crowded docks, but evidently disembarking here was a world of improvement over the floating docks that turned the D-Day beaches into temporary ports in the days and weeks following the invasion. A huge crowd of milling soldiers, each trying to find his official destination, kept jostling him. Several sergeants standing on crates shouted directions, trying to sort order out of the chaos with only limited success, bellowing voices swallowed in the general din. As he moved away from dockside, he found a maze of jeeps, buses, and other vehicles, and began walking along the rows, saying "First Army HQ? First Army HQ?" over and over in a strange parody of a bird's mating call.

The bag had gotten quite heavy and his feet had grown unsteady by the time his call produced a response from a corporal standing by a jeep. "First Army HQ here, sir." The corporal looked at a sheet on a clipboard. "And you are?"

"Sanger, G-2."

"Oh, yes, sir. Major Sanger. Let me get that duffel, sir, and just have a seat. Got two more to collect before we roll, sir." The corporal took his duffel, to Sanger's relief.

There was one other man in the jeep already, a captain. "Hi. Reid Sanger, G-2 staff," he said, sticking out his hand.

The captain grinned. "Howdy, Major. I'm Sandy Morgenthaler, supply. First time in France."

"First time for me, too," replied Sanger. "Funny thing, though. Looks just like a U.S. Army base."

Morgenthaler laughed. "No shit," he replied. "I guess we won't sit in a café and sip wine while the mademoiselles walk by."

"Well, not until we finish whipping the Nazis, anyway," Sanger replied.

It took nearly an hour for the corporal to collect the rest of his charges, and finally the men were wedged tightly in the jeep, three uncomfortably in the back, and one next to the driver, a light colonel. It was too noisy to continue the conversation as the jeep made its way through the narrow and overcrowded streets of the town and into the countryside. Evidence of war was everywhere, from leftover pillboxes and barbed wire to shelled-out farmhouses.

The drive took several hours, passing through alternately pastoral and hellish landscapes. Sanger was touched by the sight of French children who extended stiff-armed gestures reminiscent of the Nazi salute—until they separated their fingers into the famous "V" for victory. One shouted *"Vive l'Amerique,"* and the cheer seemed to echo in his ears for a long time.

Finally they passed a small crossroads named Isigny, and it seemed appropriate that artillery bellowed in the near distance as they drove up to Bradley's First Army Headquarters, which had commandeered several buildings. Sanger started with the personnel office to get his billet, then tried to report to his superior officer, but had to settle for an adjutant. That was okay. He finally made it to his assigned sleeping quarters, considered briefly whether he wanted to find a mess hall, but the thought roiled his stomach enough that he gave up that idea immediately, then finally decided to call it a day and was asleep in minutes.

The next morning it took him a few minutes to remember where he was. Then he was up and dressing, ready to consider the possibility that a bite of breakfast might actually stay where it was supposed to. Breakfast was hot, if not good. Still, after months of what the British laughingly referred to as break-fast—cold toast, fatty sausage, and a rubbery egg topped with an absurd slice of cherry tomato—his taste buds were inured. He knew he shouldn't complain; he was doing a lot better than the civilians.

Nobody particularly had time for him when he returned to the office area; he got a quick minute with General Tony Flynn, the G-2, then he relied on one of the sergeants to show him around, help him commandeer an empty desk, and shoulder a load of reports requiring analysis and assessment. He already knew that the intelligence officers had been enormously embarrassed by their failure to realize the nature of the Normandy hedgerows and their consequence for military operations from the overhead photographs available to them, so when he saw a stack of photos and maps, he decided that would be a good place for him to start. He bent the desk lamp over to give him good illumina-tion, picked up a magnifying glass, and began to review.

Much of the photo recon information was from the bombing campaign. The photos reminded Sanger of pictures of the lunar surface he'd seen in an as-tronomy book from his adolescence. He started counting dead German tanks, one after another. It was hard to believe they had anything left.

He looked up, suddenly aware of another presence perched on the edge of his desk. "Hi—you must be the new guy. I'm Eades." Major Eades was tall and thin, with a shock of black hair falling over his eyes.

"Hi—Reid Sanger," he said, introducing himself in return.

"Going over the intel photos?"

"Yep."

"We pounded the hell out of them."

"Looks like it. I've counted four hundred dead tanks so far, and there are a lot of photos I haven't gotten to yet. I'm trying to put together some esti-mates."

"Good. The general wants us to put together an evaluation and a report. I've been putting together a first draft. Want to hear?"

"Sure. Let's have it." Sanger leaned back in his chair.

"'The battles of Operation Cobra have done it, and the enemy in the west has had it. The end of the war in Europe is within sight.' What do you think?"

Sanger considered it for a minute. "I dunno. I've always preferred to err on the side of caution."

Eades looked disgusted. "See those pictures? Take a good look. We can do it again if we have to. There's no way they can make a stand. In fact, my bet is on early surrender. What can they do? What on earth can they do to even make this a game any more?"

Sanger was still wincing over the humiliation he'd gotten for proposing that Himmler would make a move toward a separate peace with the Soviets, so he decided to keep that theory to himself, at least for the time being. "I don't know," he said. "But they're working right now to figure out something."

"Good luck," Eades snorted. "Mark my words, it's all over but the shouting."

Lager-Lechfeld Airbase, South of Augsburg, Germany, 7 August 1944, 1120 hours GMT

The roar of the Me-262 engines was a sound unlike anything Paul Krueger had ever heard before. He watched, slack-jawed, as the sleek airplane rocketed over the airfield in a blur of speed. Twin gouts of flame blasted from the jet engines, a shrieking whine that was music to the veteran fighter pilot's ears.

"How fast can it fly?" he asked General Galland, who grinned at him around his big black cigar.

"Seven hundred kilometers per hour or more," replied the new commander of the Luftwaffe. "I get the feeling we still haven't seen this aircraft's full potential."

"*Schwalbe* . . . she is aptly named. The Swallow is surely the quickest of birds."

As he spoke the jet screamed upward, vanishing into the heights like a rocket. Krueger felt a powerful envy for the pilot at the Swallow's controls. This was surely a machine that could make a difference!

"When can I take it up?" Krueger asked the next question with a sense of heart-pounding urgency.

"Right now, if you want." Galland pointed to a nearby hangar, where another one of the jets was being wheeled out, towed by a grunting Kettenkraftgrad, the ubiquitous tractor of the Luftwaffe.

"I do!" Krueger grinned with a sense of elation that he thought was gone forever.

Certainly, when he had left the airbase in Poland, flying to Berlin with the knowledge of Hitler's murder still a fresh wound in his psyche, he had felt as though all hope of victory, or even of a pretense of real fighting, was gone. When he had seen the damaged inflicted by Allied bombers upon the capital city of his Vaterland, his heart had nearly broken. How many buildings blasted, good German people killed, by the savage and barbaric onslaught from the skies?

And the train ride to Augsburg had provided further evidence of his country's shame. They had traveled at night, and he had learned that this was because the Allied aircraft had gained almost full control of the skies over Germany. Every city they passed had suffered some horrible damage from the air, and the big Messerschmidt factory in Augsburg—his final destination— looked as though it had been smashed beyond repair. He had been astonished, though not consoled, to learn that not only was the plant operational, but that it was producing aircraft at better than the prewar rate.

But the aircraft he had seen there had been Me-109s, capable fighters to be sure, but not machines that could have any lasting impact on the conduct of the war. He vividly remembered the performance of the Kingcobras he had fought over Poland, and of the tales he'd heard of the American P-51 Mustang. In the hands of well-trained pilots, the Mustang was supposedly as good as anything the Luftwaffe could put into the air. And that plane, though single-engined, reportedly had enough range to accompany the American bombers deep into Germany.

Even when a surprisingly cheerful Galland had met Krueger at the factory and brought him here by car, the veteran pilot had been unable to shake his sense of seething rage mixed with grim despair. He had looked at the rolling hills and green woods of Bavaria and had only pictured the cloud of war that was hanging over this area, the birthplace of Hitler's dream. Like the man, that dream of impeccable Aryan ascendancy had to all appearances died with the leader who had given it shape, form, and substance.

But then had come the sight of this beautiful airplane, and the bleak mood had vanished in the instant of this stunning demonstration, in his view of a machine that could far exceed the speed of anything else in the sky. He already could picture tactics: the Swallow could climb away from a battle that its pilot wished to avoid, and streak into a force of bombers at a speed that rendered useless the machine guns bristling from the vaunted Flying Fortresses and Liberators of the American bomber fleet.

A few minutes later Krueger was climbing into the cramped cockpit. The instruments were remarkably similar to the gauges in any other fighter. As the full bubble canopy was lowered, he was impressed by the excellent visibility in all directions. He watched as the maintenance crews worked at each of the two engines, strangely lacking in propellers, hanging sleek and smooth beneath the wings. Those wings were sheared back daringly, in a configuration that screamed raw speed.

It felt odd to be looking straight out the front of the fighter while it was sitting flat on the ground. The tricycle landing gear was unique to the Swallow among all German fighter aircraft. Galland had explained that the nose wheel greatly improved the safety of takeoffs—the original design had included just a wheel beneath each wing, but the craft had been tail heavy and hard to control.

Furthermore, it had shown a disturbing tendency to plant the nose into the runway.

The general had provided a few other pointers, and now he ran over them in his mind. . . . Don't change the throttle too quickly, either increase or decrease. The Jumo engines, for all their power and speed, are delicate, and a sudden infusion of fuel could cause them to flame out . . . while a decrease in the throttle would very likely cause a stall. Let them push me along . . . and they will carry me to the heavens.

He was startled by the loud rattle of a small gasoline engine on his right wing, even though Galland had told him that the two-cycle starter motor was needed in order to bring the powerful jet turbine up to speed. He listened to the sputtering of the little engine, then noticed that it was swiftly overwhelmed by the rising whine of the powerful turbine. Soon the port engine was powered up as well, and he was standing on the brakes, feeling the shuddering desire of this airplane to break away from the flight line and make its way into the sky.

The three wheels of the landing gear rolled easily across the smooth runway as the Swallow slowly increased its speed. He found the aircraft easy to steer, and he quickly aligned himself with the long stretch of pavement leading into the wind. When he released the brakes the plane shot forward, pressing him back into the seat with the force of acceleration. The runway blurred—the whole world faded to an indistinguishable haze—and he was aware of nothing but the roaring engines, the shivering pressure, and this tight cockpit.

Finally his speed was right, and Krueger pulled back on the geared stick, surprised by the ease of the elevator's movement. In another second all vibration had ceased, the twin Jumo turbines blasting the jet into the sky. Climbing gradually, mindful of Galland's advice, he retracted the landing gear and gently banked over the carpet of trees.

He was reminded of his earliest days of flying, in the soundless gliders that had wheeled and spiraled with such grace over the bluffs of Bohemia. Never since then—not until now, at least—had he known an aircraft with similar smooth flight characteristics.

Feeding more fuel into the powerful engines, he felt the force of acceleration press him even more tightly into the seat, recalled Galland's description: "as though an angel was pushing me through the sky." Now he pulled back hard on the stick, this time grateful for the mechanical advantage of the gearing that allowed him to so easily master the ailerons against phenomenal air pressure. He felt the aircraft soar upward without any appreciable loss of speed.

Conscious of the four cannon mounted in the nose, and mindful of the destruction he had witnessed in crossing Germany, he wished momentarily that an Allied bomber would stray into his sights.

But of course this was a test flight. He banked, again thrilled with the ease of the aircraft's handling, even at this almost unimaginable speed. Fiery exhaust streamed from the engines as he pushed the throttles to maximum thrust, racing past the field, barely aware of the antlike figures on the ground gawking upward at his fiery image.

An hour later he finally lowered his gear and settled back to the field, rolling toward the massive hangar, and to a future that, once again, gave him hope of victory.

Wehrmacht Hospital, Vesinet, France, 8 August 1944, 1520 hours GMT

The branches of the tree were stark and blackened, but the bark felt smooth against his back as he looked over the grassy lawn. His head still hurt, and the bandage over his left eye masked his vision in its vexing fashion . . . or perhaps it wasn't merely the bandage that masked his vision. Somehow, despite the doctors' assurances, he had trouble believing he would ever see from that eye again.

At least, after too long in the tiny room, Rommel had found the strength to walk outside. The weather was fine, the surroundings peaceful, and for some reason he had gravitated to this blasted oak that had first caught his eye from the window of his hospital room. Though the late summer sun felt good against his skin, and the light breeze was soothing, he found as he leaned against the tree that his thoughts were far away, his mood darkened by uncountable disturbing tangents.

In his hand was a letter from General Speidel, brought to him by von Esebeck as the correspondent had traveled back to Germany from the front. Because of the injury to his eye, it had taken Rommel a long time to read the words—and even then it seemed as if his mind was thickened, unnaturally slowed. Yet the gist of the message was clear.

The Normandy front had collapsed, succumbing to the disaster that every rational military mind had foreseen. The Americans had broken out along the coast at Avranches, and a new army—the Third—commanded by General George Patton was racing east, west, and south across France. Rommel had tried to get in touch with von Kluge, but that field marshal—no doubt overwhelmed by the unfolding disaster on his front—had been unable or unwilling to take any more phone calls from the man he had replaced.

News had reached him from several of his former subordinates during the African campaign, from his chief of staff Speidel and from Fritz Bayerlein, commander of the once-proud Panzer Lehr Division. Even some of the stubborn SS generals like Sepp Dietrich and Meyer, who had been so proud of his Twelfth Panzer, the Hitler Youth Division, were beginning to see the need for some strategic flexibility. The tactic was obvious—they should fall back, try to preserve as much of their men and matériel as possible. Rommel knew that even von Kluge saw this as the only practical alternative, but would he act in the face of Himmler's orders to the contrary?

It had been much the same in North Africa. Newly promoted to lieutenant general after commanding the Seventh Panzers, the Ghost Division, as it swept across France in an amazing blitzkrieg, Rommel was given command of the German forces in Africa. In a series of spectacular campaigns, the Afrika Korps entered into history. There, Rommel acquired the nickname of "the Desert Fox" for his brilliant tactics.

Among Rommel's favorite mementos was a copy of a memorandum from the British General Auchinleck about him. "There exists a real danger that our friend Rommel is becoming a kind of magician or bogeyman to our troops, who are talking far too much about him. He is by no means a superman. . . . Even if he were a superman, it would still be highly undesirable that our men should credit him with supernatural powers."

But in the end the Allies had swamped him with so many tanks, such utter control of the skies, that all the maneuvering and courage, all the resourcefulness and planning in the world, hadn't been enough to hold the field. Eventually his beloved warriors, in the end a full *panzerarmee,* had fallen prey to the inevitable victory of a stronger foe.

In that final defeat, as now, he felt a complete absence of supernatural powers. He didn't even have enough power to stand and walk unaided. He even felt his *fingerspitzengefühl,* his special "sixth sense" intuition for which he was famous, had deserted him.

A shadow fell across him, and the Desert Fox looked up, startled by the sight of a tall SS general. The man's face was marred by twin dueling scars, and he clicked his heels and raised his hand in a formal salute. He looked every bit the Aryan; in spite of himself, Rommel reacted to the sight of such a fine man. *If only he wore a Wehrmacht uniform rather than SS black,* Rommel thought.

"Heil Himmler!" the black-garbed officer declared. The greeting sounded odd. "Field Marshal Rommel?"

Rommel, capless, nodded in response and tried to appraise the man without squinting. Even in the sunlight his eyesight was not so good, though he was fairly certain this was a person he had never seen before.

"I am General Horst Bücher, SS General Staff, and aide to Führer Himmler. I wonder if I may have a moment of your time."

"Of course." Rommel was cautious, but curious as well. "Would you like to go inside?"

"If you are comfortable here, that is fine with me. To be truthful, I have had little opportunity to enjoy the sunshine, or a view such as this."

"I have nothing but time," came the bitter reply. "While my army is cut to pieces in France, I must sit here and languish under the orders of surgeons and nurses."

"I understand that you and the rest of the hospital will be evacuated shortly."

"Yes, before the Americans get here." The word had come down only a day before, yet another galling feature of his current, impotent circumstances.

"Your recovery is progressing well, I hope. Der führer himself asked me to inquire as to your health."

"Very well," Rommel replied. He didn't mention the constant pain in his head, his fear of loss of mental acuity, nor did he move, which would inevitably have revealed his stiff and awkward gait, disabilities that might cause this haughty, scarred general to regard him as a mere cripple.

"I take it that you do not approve of the way matters are being handled in the west?"

The Desert Fox shrugged. He was not about to blame a fellow Wehrmacht officer in front of this SS fellow. "It is not the handling of the army—it is the circumstances of the battle. Any fool can see that we have to pull back to a defensible position. The Seine, at the very least, or even the Siegfried Line and the Rhine. There we might stand against the Allies. In the open countryside of France, we will be cut to pieces."

"We still hold most of this country," Bücher observed.

"With what?" demanded Rommel bitterly. "Now that the Americans have a real tank general in charge, it is only a matter of time—and precious little of that—before Patton has made a wreck of the whole front."

"And you would recommend a full withdrawal?"

"Immediately," he snapped, growing irritated as a throbbing headache swelled between his temples. "First, pull Weise's Nineteenth Army out of southern France. It's only a matter of time before the Allies land there, and we have no hope of stopping that invasion. Then fall back, if possible faster than Patton can advance."

"And we can win?" asked the SS general.

"Win? No! The Russians will win, they will win everything." He was tired and irritated, and so he spoke his beliefs with uncharacteristic bluntness. "If you want to know what I think, we should surrender to the Americans now, invite them into Berlin as quickly as possible—before it is too late!"

"Interesting." Bücher did not seem disturbed by the forthright pronouncements. "But what if the USSR can be stopped?"

"Hah!" Rommel's laugh was bitter. "As well as that the sunshine be stopped, so that my tanks can move around without the accursed Jabos buzzing overhead, always ready to shoot them to pieces!"

"Thank you for your opinion," Bücher said, clicking his heels and saluting again. "I hope that your convalescence continues to proceed well." And he was gone.

And what exactly was that about? Rommel thought. He concentrated through his headache, and could think of only two possibilities. The first was that he was to be returned to his old command. *I've certainly ruined that,* he thought ruefully. He had never been comfortable with, nor much good at, politics. The second possibility was that the investigation of the conspiracy had fingered him as someone less than patriotic as a Nazi. *That, on the other hand, I think I've just confirmed.* Perhaps he'd sealed his death warrant just then. But better death than watching the slow annihilation of his troops.

Seine River, Fifty Kilometers Northwest of Paris, France, 10 August 1944, 1635 hours GMT

"Danke—but we'll walk for this part."

A dozen infantrymen jumped down from the Panther's hull, and Carl-Heinz didn't blame them. Looking at the long bridge with its litter of wrecked vehicles and bomb craters, he momentarily wished for a way that he could get the tank across the river without having to drive it.

This was a steel span of modern construction, and it seemed to be holding up well, though it was cratered from countless bomb hits. Now it was a key escape route, and the Germans would cross here until the Americans closed up behind them. Then the engineers would finish the work Allied bombers had started.

The troops stood aside as he drove the Panther slowly down the road and onto the bridge, knowing that the next minutes would be another very dangerous interval in these weeks that had borne all too many life-threatening moments. The river was broad here, and the bridge showed the effects of countless Allied bombs. He thanked God for the cloudy skies but knew from hard experience that the overcast restricted, but did not eliminate, the threat of Allied air power.

He came to a burned-out truck, engine still smoldering, and pushed it out of the way with the Panther's fender. Several dead men lay in the roadway, and though they were beyond any feeling he nevertheless carefully drove the tank around the stiff corpses.

His hands, stained with dirt and grease accumulated over weeks of desperate retreat, were steady on the big three-quarter round wheel as the battered tank rolled on across the paved span of metal girders. He couldn't help wondering: how many roads had they traveled down since Lieutenant Schroeder had been killed? They had crossed countless small bridges, but no barrier anywhere near as wide or as deep as this mighty river.

Fritzi and Peltz took turns watching the skies, as they had done during the long retreat across France. Sometimes they had wondered if theirs was the only tank left in the Wehrmacht. Of course, they had seen plenty of them on the sides of the road, inevitably wrecked by the bombs and guns of the dreaded Jabos.

"I'll get back to you, Yetta," he murmured, steering between still more burned hulks. "I will, someday." Odd, how much he had been talking to himself, or to his tank or his distant wife. It had become such a habit that Ulrich didn't even look up any more. His humming, however, had decreased.

It was the thought of home and family that had kept him going through this long retreat. The division was gone, and their army was coming to pieces around them . . . so it seemed only natural to think of loved ones back in Germany when he needed a reminder of why he was still fighting, why he must make sure that he stayed alive.

Finally they were off the bridge, climbing the road on the east bank of the mighty river. Another wrecked truck blocked the road, its bed blasted apart by a bomb, and Carl-Heinz used the tank to push it out of the way. More dead soldiers were lined up in a grassy meadow, proof that someone was taking charge of these remnants of a broken army, at least to give the fallen soldiers some semblance of a burial. A field artillery piece lay on its side in the ditch, and two dead horses—swollen grotesquely in the summer heat—lay in their traces where they had fallen.

Halfway up the hill Carl-Heinz pulled the Panther off the road, parking between several large oak trees while he and his crewmates emerged to stretch, to piss, and to take a last look toward western France.

"We'll have to find some fuel before too long," he remarked, unconsciously aware that the others had taken to looking to him for leadership.

"I'll see if I can siphon any from these wrecks," Peltz offered, taking a petrol can and a hose and starting down the road.

A line of shambling Germans on foot, with a fortunate few weaving among them on bicycles, still moved across the bridge, but there was no semblance of unit cohesion. These men were slumped with defeat and weariness, though on the exposed span they moved with some urgency, knowing that the great river at least placed a barrier between themselves and the relentless Americans.

"There—a general's car," remarked Ulrich dispassionately, pulling on a vile ersatz cigarette.

Carl-Heinz saw the trudging infantry move to the side as the big Mercedes rumbled onto the bridge and slowly made its way across, steering back and forth around the partially patched craters left by Allied bombs.

"Jabo," Ulrich murmured, flicking down his butt and squinting into the high, white overcast.

The droning of a single-engine plane was audible to them all in a few moments. Even though the tank was as well-screened as possible, Carl-Heinz felt his heart quicken, his stomach churn with the familiar fear.

The aircraft—an RAF Tempest or Typhoon, distinguished by the big air scoop beneath the cowling—screamed out of the clouds, approaching the river on a course directly above the road. With urgency borne of long experience, Germans sprang off the highway, scrambling into the ditches and trying to make their way into the hedges and woods to either side. Machine guns chattered, stitching a line of dusty strikes along the highway, blasting among the men who had thrown themselves flat in the undergrowth. Many soldiers tried to claw their way into the ground, while others twitched in the unmistakable pattern of men whose flesh was being torn by lethal bullets. Several, caught near the middle of the bridge, leaped into the water as the bullets raced onto the narrow span.

There was no such escape for the big staff car. Instead, the driver gunned the engine, jouncing across the rough pavement in a desperate bid to reach the far bank. He careened around the burning truck, scraping the fender along the bridge railing with a force that sent sparks flashing in the dull daylight. Before the car had covered even half of the distance, bullets slashed into the trunk and top of the vehicle. It veered crazily, smashing into the railing at the other side of the bridge. A blossom of fire boiled upward as the fuel tank ignited, and no one escaped from the battered vehicle.

A bomb fell away from the fighter's belly, and Carl-Heinz watched the missile fall. It tumbled just past the bridge to explode in the river, showering water over the smoking staff car while the concussion killed a dozen men who were floundering in the water.

Another plane roared in, shooting up the road—though by now the only soldiers who remained in range were well beyond sensation, much less further injury. All the surviving Germans had made their way off the road, huddling in impotent fury among whatever cover they could find. The second Jabo, however, proved more accurate in the bomb run, dropping the missile right in the middle of the span. It exploded with a shower of debris and pavement, though as the smoke cleared it was obvious that the structure of the bridge still stood.

As soon as the planes were gone, the soldiers on foot started shuffling across the bridge again, giving wide berth to the still-burning car. Peltz came back, boasting that he had recovered more than ten liters of precious gasoline.

When some of the shambling men had come up the hill far enough to pass the Panther's hiding place, Fritzi hailed them, "Hey—who was that down there in the car? Did you see?"

"Ja," replied a weary, limping Feldwebel. "That was Field Marshal von

Kluge, our front commander." He paused a moment to let that news sink in, then smiled crookedly, more like the leering grin of a skeleton than any real expression of humor.

Reichstag, Berlin, Germany, 2200 hours GMT

"You say von Kluge was killed in an air attack?" Himmler pursed his lips and frowned delicately at the SS hauptmann who held the radio report in his hand.

"Ja, mein Führer. Strafed by an American just after he had brought his HQ across the Seine."

"That is disappointing . . . he was performing rather well, I must say."

General Bücher, who stood on the other side of his leader's broad desk, cleared his throat gently.

"Yes, General?" Himmler's narrow eyebrows were raised in inquiry. He nodded in dismissal to the radioman, who left before Bücher began to speak.

"You may recall, mein Führer, that I spoke with Field Marshal Rommel a week ago. His convalescence seemed to be proceeding remarkably well. It may be that he will be able to assume his old command."

"Yes . . . that is indeed something to consider. But tell me, has there not been evidence against him regarding the plot against our late führer?"

Bücher kept his own scarred face expressionless but couldn't help noticing a touch of irony in the tone of Himmler's voice when he spoke about their former dictator. The SS general shrugged in response to the question. "One word, apparently spoken by a man in the depths of torture, that indicated our esteemed field marshal's name . . . I suggest that it need not preclude him from taking command in the field again."

"On its surface, no," Himmler agreed. He thought for several moments of profound silence. "Very well, send the message . . . Field Marshal Rommel is reappointed to Wehrmacht command in the west, as soon as his health allows. But Bücher . . ."

"Yes, mein Führer?"

"I think I shall assign you to his staff. As admirably fitted as our bold Desert Fox may be for military command, it seems that his politics demand that he will bear watching."

"As you wish, mein Führer." Bücher saluted crisply, maintaining his eyes on a spot above his leader's head. With a precise pivot, he turned and marched from the office. He was pleased. Rommel was a fine man, a good German, even if his political reliability was questionable. He would enjoy working with such a fine man . . . though that would not preclude him from taking other actions if necessary.

U.S. First Army HQ, Normandy, France,
11 August 1944, 0945 hours GMT

"Goddamn! Look at this!" Eades was nearly out of breath. "Von Kluge is dead! We got him!"

Sanger looked up eagerly. "No shit? Really? What happened?"

"Just a little north of Paris, evidently. His staff car was hit by a Typhoon, blown to bits."

"How do you know it's von Kluge?"

"Intercepted German transmissions. It was radioed in the clear by the field soldiers who found him. After that, there was a lot of code churning the air. Can't read it, but it's pretty easy to figure out what it says."

"Yeah," noted Sanger. "'Get us a confirmation. Are you sure? Details needed urgently. Are you really sure?'"

Eades laughed. For all his certainty about a quick German collapse, and his conviction that Sanger was far too pessimistic, he was a good guy and an able analyst. "Yep. Just like what our commanders would send. So, now what? It went from Rommel to Runstead to von Kluge, so who's next?"

"Rommel to Runstead to Kluge. Sounds like Tinker to Evans to Chase," observed Eades, referring to the famous Chicago Cubs baseball double play trio. Both men laughed.

"Then who's up next?" asked Sanger.

"Hell, I dunno. Does it make a difference?"

"It might. Guderian is available, I think." The noted panzer general had angered Hitler, and as a result had been placed in a more or less ceremonial position as inspector of panzers.

"Could be," said Eades. "Or maybe Himmler will put in some SS flunky who'll spend all his time trying to enforce 'stand and die' orders."

"That's possible too," said Sanger.

There was one name that did not come up in that discussion, or in the intelligence meetings that followed, because he was a man everyone knew to be too wounded for the job.

Rommel House, Herrlingen, Germany,
12 August 1944, 0900 hours GMT

"Herr Feldmarschall! You are there!" The voice on the telephone, tinny and distant as usual, was nevertheless filled with unaccountable relief. "It has been quite difficult to find you after you left the hospital."

"Yes, I've been here for the last few days. If I had stayed in Vesinet, I would be a guest of the Americans by now. And who is this?"

"Forgive me . . . this is Major Paulus, calling for Oberkommando der Wehrmacht. Here is Field Marshal Keitel."

For several minutes Rommel listened. His heart started to pound with a beat that he hadn't felt for weeks—for months, if he told the truth. Despite the fact that the situation in the west was terrible, that the Allies were advancing like an irresistible tide, he could not deny the allure that called him back to war.

"Of course," Keitel said in conclusion. "The führer was most clear that this appointment is contingent upon your health. But he wants you to know that, when you are feeling fit, the command in the west is yours once again."

"Thank you, Field Marshal," Rommel said, before carefully setting the telephone back into its cradle.

He took a few minutes to sit quietly and reflect upon this change of fortune. It was tragic, the fate that had met von Kluge—indeed, it was eerily similar to the death that had almost claimed the Desert Fox himself. *They don't understand—so long as the Allies control the skies, there is so very, very little that we can do on the ground!*

His head throbbed with the surging ache that was a constant part of his life, now. He felt the moistness under his eye patch, momentarily wondering if his left eye would ever see again, or if for the rest of his days his vision would consist of this curiously flat impression of the world. But then he remembered the tree that had been his inspiration outside of his hospital room . . . shortly before he had departed Vesinet, he had noticed sprigs of greenery sprouting from the blasted trunk.

And finally he shook his head, dismissing such concerns as unimportant. There was a battle raging to the west, and German soldiers were dying in great numbers. Now he had a chance to again play a role in that fighting. He couldn't win—no general could, given the constraints of Allied air superiority. Still, perhaps he could save some of those brave men. He remained too badly wounded to ride about in a car, to inspect and be seen by the troops as a proper general should. Yet perhaps there were some things he could do.

Finally he reached for the phone. "Get me General Weise, Nineteenth Army Headquarters."

It took just a few sentences to inform the man that he had a new commanding general.

"You are to commence a withdrawal north up the Rhone valley at the earliest possible moment," he began. "My intentions are to have you set up a line in the Vosges Mountains, west of Strasbourg and the Rhine. The Americans won't be there for several weeks, and when they arrive I want you to be ready for them."

"Jawohl, Herr Feldmarschall!" Weise hesitated for only a second. "That is, am I to understand that we are evacuating France?"

"Indeed, my General . . . the time has come to make our stand at the borders of the Fatherland."

Rommel didn't even put down the phone after breaking the connection. He spoke sternly to the operator, curtly informing her that he would accept no excuses for failure. He knew he asked her to perform a difficult task, to find a specific person amid the chaos of the disintegrating front in France. By the same token, it was something that had to be done.

While he waited, he pulled out some of the maps that he had had delivered to his rooms. Lacking proper desk space, he spread them across his bed. What he saw confirmed his memories, and his impressions.

Though his ear got sore from the waiting, he finally heard Speidel's voice.

"Hello, my General," he said to the man who had performed so well for him in Normandy. "I am glad they found you!"

"I don't know how . . . we have a temporary Army Command Post in a château overlooking the Seine, but we barely installed the phone lines an hour ago."

"I was lucky enough to get a good operator," Rommel observed.

"And no doubt you put the fear of the devil into the poor thing," Speidel added wryly. "But, to business: Surely you have heard about von Kluge?"

"Indeed . . . in fact, I am his replacement."

"That's the best news I've had all summer. But your health . . . ?"

"Is of no matter. Tell me, how much of the army has reached the east bank of the Seine?"

"Many men, though no one knows the exact number. Of course, we have left most of our guns and tanks behind . . . in a way it is like Dunkirk was for our British foes four years ago."

"An apt comparison," the Desert Fox agreed. "Does it look as though you will be able to hold at the river?"

"I am afraid we are already in full flight at least to the Somme," Speidel said. "And there are still American spearheads, Patton's men, who stand a chance of cutting off a good portion of our remaining strength."

"There must be an important crossing of the Somme," Rommel said, returning to his map. "Here, at Abbeville?"

"Two good bridges, yes, Field Marshal. It is perhaps the last bottleneck before we get into Belgium."

"And surely such panzers as remain to us are crossing there?"

"*Naturlich*—though nothing like an intact division made it out of Normandy."

"Tell me, is Bayerlein there?"

"Yes, right beside me."

"Put him on another line."

In moments, the former panzer leader of the Afrika Korps was speaking to his past, and now current, commander.

"Fritz, I want you to go to Abbeville . . . gather all the tanks you can, put together as much of a force as possible."

"It will be difficult, Herr Feldmarschall, but perhaps not impossible. I assume that I should assemble them west of the river, the Somme?"

"As always you understand me, Fritz. Jawohl, perhaps five miles west of the river. And a mile or two south of the main highway."

"I will assemble the panzers immediately. And I will be ready to move in twenty-four hours."

"Excellent, my General. And listen to me, for just another moment. I think it is again time for us to attack."

**Beauvais, France,
18 August 1944, 1855 hours GMT**

"More prisoners, sir," reported Captain Smiggs.

Pulaski looked over the ragged catch, a hundred or more unkempt, unarmed Germans, and he could only laugh. "Smiggy, I never thought that my recon company would be winning all of our battles."

"Sorry, Colonel . . . they just seem to want to turn themselves in to the first Americans they see."

"Don't apologize—we're all thankful, or we should be," the CO declared.

"I see we can't even refuel without filling our bag," observed Frank Ballard, coming up to join them. The CCA infantry had taken over from the recon company and were marching the Germans into a semienclosed barnyard.

"How long are we here?" Smiggs asked.

"We'll spend the night," Pulaski announced. "Smiggy, can you get the lay of the land around here, see where we'll need to put our pickets? It will take until dark to finish refueling, and we should try to get in touch with Army HQ, arrange to hand off the prisoners and set up our next depot."

"And if they can't get somebody here by morning, what about the prisoners?" asked Lieutenant Colonel White, cocking an eyebrow at the CO. "Are you going to want me to leave a company behind again?"

The colonel shook his head. "Then we just leave 'em here on the honor system and move on," Pulaski replied. "It won't be the first time—and I think we've got more important fish to fry."

"Couldn't agree more," replied White, whose mechanized infantry had sometimes been forced into unwelcome duty as jailers.

Pulaski looked around. Most of the half-tracks had already refueled, but all of Lieutenant Colonel Lorimar's self-propelled artillery battalion was still waiting to drive into the depot yard. In addition to the eighteen Priests, the M7 howitzers that were Lorimar's pride and joy, the battalion included a number of ammunition haulers, and numerous other trucks and bulldozers, all of which had a voracious appetite for fuel. As always, Pulaski found it frustrating to realize that his armor could drive a hundred miles in a matter of hours, but then needed to spend twice as much time just taking on gas and ammunition in preparation for the next headlong advance.

During the last two weeks, Combat Command A had carved a swath through France and the crumbling Wehrmacht. They had captured thousands of Germans, destroyed a hundred trucks and dozens of tanks. They encircled strongpoints, cut off enemy communications and transport, blasted through hastily formed defensive positions. They always kept moving, through days of long, fast attacks followed by brief intervals when the combat command regrouped, performed field repairs, and took on additional fuel and ammo. For the most part it was a heady time, a whirlwind of victories that stacked up one after the other, steadily increasing the Americans' levels of morale, experience, and skill.

Once the German line had cracked, George Patton's Third Army had been activated, with the Nineteenth Armored Division—and CCA in particular—as one of Patton's forward spearheads. Pulaski knew that some of Third Army had turned west, and now had enemy garrisons trapped in Brest, St. Nazaire, and several other key ports. Hopefully those cities and their harbors would be opened soon, for an advance like this was going to require solid bases of supply—and all those supplies had to come in over the waters of the English Channel or the Bay of Biscay. Other elements of Third Army had turned east and then curled north in an attempt to encircle the German line. And Pulaski's men, and their counterparts in Bob Jackson's CCB, had been turned loose to race eastward, and race they had done.

The aggressive combat command charged out of Normandy as a pure, tactical descendent of the dashing cavalry of yore. Along the way CCA liberated countless French hamlets, villages, and towns. In each, the now-veteran tankers had been feted with many bottles—calvados brandy in Normandy, numerous vintages of wines as they moved through different regions. They had been festooned with colorful garlands, cheered by delirious Frenchmen, and mobbed by women who were almost frantically eager to bestow kisses and other favors upon their American liberators. Priests had come from the churches, and Pulaski had been blessed under the shadow of more cross-topped steeples than he could count.

Pulaski had been briefed by General King as well as Colonel Grant, the division S-2. He knew that von Kluge's replacement, whoever he was, had at last persuaded Himmler to authorize a withdrawal, and the bulk of the enemy forces had wheeled away from their entrenchments and raced eastward.

Pulaski couldn't help but chuckle when he'd heard American officers grousing that this retreat never would have happened if Hitler had still been in charge—but there was a germ of truth to the complaint. After all, under their new leadership, the Nazis had shown more flexibility in their defense, and a willingness to give up a position so that troops could get away to fight another day. Now a great retreat was under way, Germans fleeing for home, struggling to cross the great rivers of France. Already most had passed the Seine, and now the bulk of the enemy was retreating toward the Somme River and Belgium.

Racing to the south of this massive movement, CCA had been the first American unit across the Seine, beating Jackson's CCB by a day and a half. A day later they had learned that Paris had been liberated, taken first by General Leclerc's Free French armored division under Patton's command. Now the Third Army was pulling up to the Seine along two hundred miles of its length, and many American spearheads had joined Nineteenth Armored in crossing the river and continuing eastward. It was not hard to believe that the war was practically won.

He remembered the festive party of just the previous night, when CCA rolled through another town only hours after the Germans had pulled up stakes. His men lingered for about an hour, accepting kisses and wine bottles from the populace in approximately equal numbers. But, as always, Pulaski had ordered them on, and his soldiers had responded with their usual alacrity. Being fast and first had become a matter of pride to the men of Combat Command A.

"My battalion should be into the fueling yard within the hour," Lorimar reported, breaking into Pulaski's reminiscing. "Are you going to try and move out tonight?"

"No . . . take your time about it, Lorri. We'll get on the road first thing in the morning."

"Good news, that," replied the genial artillery officer. "I got some thirsty Priests over there."

The others laughed. It was an old joke, but somehow the likable Lorimar made it funny every time he said it.

The colonel noticed a jeep working its way through the controlled chaos of the field depot, and then recognized the dashing figure of his division CO.

"General King!" he declared, joining his subordinates in saluting. "Welcome to our supply base—at least, it's been our home away from home for two hours and has a whole night to go before we move on."

"Really letting the moss grow this time, eh Ski?" replied the general with a chuckle, returning a casual salute.

"Just long enough to dig a swimming pool and roast a hog," Lorimar interjected.

"Good work, Ski, and all you men as well," declared King sincerely.

"Do we continue east, sir?" asked Pulaski.

"Slight change in orders, from Georgie himself," the general replied with a grim smile. "We've got another opportunity in front of us, and your boys, Ski, are in position to take advantage."

"Tell us what you need, General, and you've got it!" Pulaski was ready, and Lorimar, White, and Ballard leaned in as well.

"The Krauts are pulling two armies out of Normandy, and we've got 'em closed down to one main road." He gestured to the map on the hood of the jeep. "And it crosses the Somme River here, at Abbeville."

"That's no more than fifty, sixty miles north of here, sir." Pulaski grasped the possibilities immediately.

"Exactly. Now, I've got CCB coming up behind you, but they're a day away. You'll be on your own, Jimmy, but if you can get to Abbeville, shut down that bridge, your boys would go a long way toward putting the whole German western front into the bag."

The colonel's heart pounded at the prospect. Here it was, a chance to win the *real* prize, to shorten—hell, maybe to *win*—the war. "We can do it, sir!"

"Yessir, General!" Lorimar added.

"Good men. There's risk, but I think you can all see what we stand to gain."

"Say no more, General—we'll be on our way by the crack of dawn."

The Somme, South of Abbeville, France, 19 August 1944, 1115 hours GMT

As Pulaski saw the rippling waters of the river glittering before him, he felt a rising sense of disbelief and elation. He told Keefer to drive the command half-track off to the side of the road at the crest of the hill leading into the river valley. Leaning with an easy slouch, he watched Ballard's tanks roll past, racing along the rural lane above the river. The column halted when the lead tanks reached a hillside where the ground sloped steeply away before them. Colonel Pulaski pulled out the map.

"We're no more than ten miles south of the highway," he realized, speaking aloud. "What we need is a good track on this side of the river, running north. Keefer, move us up a bit."

The half-track rumbled through the field beside the lane, which was currently blocked by a column of Shermans. When the big vehicle reached the crest Pulaski looked in the direction he wanted to go and grimaced as he saw a wet valley, flat and slick like a bog, extending far inland from the riverbank.

For the last two days they had swept toward the northeast, leaving the rest of Third Army behind as they raced toward the Somme and the road that was key to the German retreat. General Wakefield had argued with General King and at first tried to put the brakes on his aggressive Combat Command, fearing they were getting too far ahead of themselves. Wakefield had wanted to wait long enough for three divisions to advance abreast, but in the end Pulaski had convinced Jack King of the opportunity that beckoned to them—and reminded them both of the Germans who were getting away every hour. Now they had an open flank before them, a chance to sweep deep into the enemy rear. By all accounts they were attacking a defeated foe, and it only made sense to keep him on the run.

There was one thing Pulaski learned about Henry Wakefield in that encounter. No matter what his initial feelings on a matter, when he made a decision, he stuck with it all the way, working to get his men all the air support and fuel that he could get his hands on. His respect for the man had increased—and for the first time, he found himself caring that he earned Wakefield's respect in turn.

Patton himself had heartily endorsed the intended encirclement. He had ordered the rest of the Nineteenth Armored, including the reserve combat command, as well as Third Armored and a couple of infantry divisions, to advance in support of CCA. Those troops remained some distance to the rear, and Pulaski knew that it was up to him to carry this attack as fast and as far as it could go.

An armored car came racing along a trail at the bottom of the hill, tires skidding on the dirt road, kicking up a small plume of dust from an excess of speed. Pulaski watched the racing vehicle with a thrill of pride—in some ways, these underarmed and weakly armored little combat cars reminded him most valiantly of the cavalry that was the inspiration for Patton's armored tactics. The recon patrols drove around the flanks of his command, often rushing into villages and strongpoints in advance of the first Shermans—just like the bold horsemen of an earlier century.

Now the M8 Greyhound raced up the hill, veering around the Shermans. The hatch on the armored car was open, and an officer was waving wildly as his driver steered toward the command half-track.

"Colonel! Colonel Pulaski!"

It was Captain Smiggs, the cocky young cavalryman who commanded the CCA recon company.

"Whatcha got, Smiggy?"

"Down there, around the shoulder of the hill. Sir, it's an old roadbed, probably Roman—made of stone. And Colonel, it looks dry, and seems to lead clear across the swamp. I've sent a platoon ahead to check it out, but there's tracks . . . farm stuff, and trucks, too. I'd guess it's good as gold!"

"Fine work, Smiggy. Keefer, you heard the man—let's get down there and have a look! Frank!" he shouted to Ballard, who was sitting on the rim of the hatch on his Sherman's turret. "Keep an eye on things here—but be ready to move!"

"Sure thing, Colonel."

His driver, by now well attuned to Pulaski's sense of speed, wasted no time in maneuvering the big half-track onto the narrow lane. They rumbled and lurched along at twenty miles an hour, chasing after the racing armored car.

In another few minutes he saw it, a narrow span across the marsh, clearly ancient, and apparently undamaged by the vagaries of twentieth-century warfare. A few lonely marble crosses marked a small cemetery on the near shore, but then the road extended over trackless greenery. In several places stone arches carried the road across swaths of open water.

"Will it hold a tank?" he wondered as Smiggs climbed out of his car and used his binoculars to scrutinize the far bank.

"Five armored cars and a Stuart drove across it with me, and it didn't seem to shake much," offered the captain. "But I guess there's no telling if it will hold a Sherman until we try it."

"How big is the marsh?"

"Goes several miles inland from here," Smiggs reported. "The combat command can get around it, but it might take an extra hour. I've got Lieutenant Mitchell up ahead, scouting the road to Abbeville. We found one route with the bridge blown, but he was on another track that looked promising."

"Good." Pulaski scrambled out of the half-track and spread out a map across the front of Smigg's Greyhound. Sergeant Dawson held the map down while the colonel next took out the folder of aerial recon photos he'd been given the day before. "That bridge?" he asked, indicating the span over a small tributary creek flowing into the Somme.

"That's the one, still intact here." Smiggs looked at the date and time on the photo. "They must have blown it in the last twenty-four hours."

Pulaski frowned in concern. "I wonder if they know we're coming . . . lots of woods over there. They could have a nasty surprise in our way."

Smiggy nodded. "It's possible . . . but Mitchell's been along this road near the river, and it was clear." He pointed to another swath of forest, a mile to the west. "Any concentration of force would have to be gathered here."

"And those guys will have their hands full with Task Force White, as soon as Whitey gets into position."

Pulaski thought of his orders, and the opportunity that lay before him. It would take several hours just to move his lead task force along that single-lane Roman road. And he knew that route through the marsh could lead Ballard flush into the flank of the retreating Germans, with a prime opportunity to sever the lifeline of the Abbeville bridge. Then, if Task Force White took the more circuitous route, they should arrive at the destination in perfect time to support the armor. They could make an attack first thing in the morning. The calculations took only a minute, and once his mind was made up there was no question about a decision. Conscious of seconds ticking by, Pulaski gave his orders. "Let's go for it."

"Sarge!"

"Here it is, Colonel." Dawson anticipating the order, had the radio warmed up and handed him the mike. "Low power."

"All Crimsons," he said, using the code name they had established, "this is Crimson Eight. Move forward, pronto . . . do not acknowledge."

Ballard's tanks started down the hillside immediately, and in a few minutes the first of them had reached the Roman road.

"Frank, I want your boys and Smiggs's company to head across this stone road, here . . . send one of your Shermans ahead to make sure it checks out as sturdy. Whitey and I will bring the rest of CCA around the marsh. We'll meet you south of the bridges—but when you get your battalion across, you should attack if the opportunity's right. We'll be up in support."

"You got it, sir!" replied the ex-boxer, his jaw locked in a scowl of determination.

The column of M4s started across the track, leaving fifty yards between tanks, while the rest of the command gathered at the base of the hill. By the time Lieutenant Colonel Lorimar came up with his self-propelled guns, CCA had received another visitor, and Pulaski clambered out of his half-track to greet General King.

"I had to ride hell-bent for leather to catch you, Ski," said the general with a broad grin. "Good work."

"I've got a chance here, Jack—looks like this track might take us all the way to the Abbeville bridges. I'm sending the tanks across here, and the rest of us are coming around the marsh."

"Excellent!" declared King, clapping one fist into the palm of his other hand. The division CO looked up at the half-track while the mechanized infantry battalion moved onto the Roman road. "I've got a fresh set of recon photos for you, taken this A.M. Looks like the Krauts still don't have any idea we're here. Make a little extra room in there, OK? I'd like to ride along."

Approaching the Somme River,
West of Abbeville, 1700 hours GMT

"Hey you, in the panzer!"

"Ja?" Carl-Heinz stuck his head out of the hatch.

"That's good—stay there while I get your picture."

"Why?" wondered the driver, though he obliged the aristocratic-looking photographer with a smile and a wave.

"Danke. It'll make a good shot for the folks back home."

Craning his head around, Carl-Heinz was not surprised to see something like two dozen German soldiers, mostly panzergrenadiers, perched on the tank's hull and turret, almost as if his tank had sprouted hair. It had been like that for many kilometers, all these footsore warriors willing to take advantage of one of the few vehicles rolling toward der Vaterland.

"Did you ride all the way from Normandy?" asked the photographer, speaking to a cocky *feldwebel* on the left fender.

"Better than walking—and this young fellow makes a fine chauffeur!"

"Say, you were with Panzer Lehr, weren't you?" asked the photographer, catching a glimpse of the division designation on the hull turret. "I know someone who's going to be glad to see you."

Ulrich, who had risen from the radioman's hatch, regarded the man warily. "Who are you?" he asked.

"Oh, forgive me . . . Baron von Esebeck, at your service. I am a correspondent for the German news service."

"And who will be glad to see us?" Carl-Heinz asked.

"There he is now." Von Esebeck turned and waved, shouting loudly. "General Bayerlein, I have found some of your lost souls!"

The commander of the Panzer Lehr division was standing at a crossroads just before them, but he hurried over to the tank and casually returned the crewmen's brisk salute. Ulrich was clearly embarrassed at being around generals and aristocrats; he slid back into the tank, letting Carl-Heinz do the talking. Carl-Heinz wasn't intimidated by anybody.

"You were with Schroeder's company, yes?" Bayerlein asked, clearly delighted to see a vehicle from his old division.

"Ja, mein General," Carl-Heinz replied. "I am sorry to say that the lieutenant was killed by an enemy aircraft."

Bayerlein shook his head. "Too many of my brave men fell that way . . . but listen, I need you. Follow that road, there. You'll see where to wait—and I will be along by this evening. And you panzergrenadiers, stay with the tank. I have work for you, as well."

Carl-Heinz guided the Panther into a narrow lane and soon saw a young hauptmann waving him over to the side of the road.

"Do you have an officer?"

"He's dead."

"These are your orders—take your tank down the road down to the landing on this bank of the Somme. You're to form up as part of a new *kampfgruppe*."

Carl-Heinz saluted, moderately grateful that there was some semblance of order returning to the German Army. A kampfgruppe was not a division, but it could be a formidable force of armor, and the name implied they were assembled for a specific combat task. He followed the directions and quickly found himself lining up in a camouflaged swath of relatively open woodland. Leafy nets were stretched overhead to conceal a large area, with lots of space between the trees.

Before long there were no less than fourteen Panthers, two dozen Panzer Mark IVs, and even six lumbering Tiger tanks all gathered here. The men emerged from their vehicles and gathered around a truck near the edge of the woods. They exchanged bits of news, all-too-similar tales of retreat and narrow escapes, especially when it came to dodging the bombs of the hated Jabos. Nor could they help speculating on whatever it was that had brought them together here.

Still, to judge from the elaborate extent of the camouflage, someone had put a lot of work into hiding a strong force here. Frequently Allied planes droned overhead, but none flew low enough to seriously inspect the grove. More tankers showed up, including a young captain, Schmitz, who strolled up to inform Carl-Heinz and the crew that he had been given command of their panzer and several others.

"A new company," he said with a wry smile. "We might have six Panthers before we're through."

An hour later General Bayerlein arrived in a command car, quickly emerging to move among the men with an easy familiarity that went a long way toward making them comfortable and reminding them that they were still soldiers in a proud army.

Carl-Heinz didn't know the man personally, but Bayerlein's reputation—earned at first under the Desert Fox in North Africa and solidified by his handling of Panzer Lehr in Normandy—was good. And in his stint as division CO he had never caused any unfair difficulties for his troops, which to most enlisted men was the best sign of a good commanding officer.

The tank crews began to gather in the center of the clearing, while officers separated them by the type of their vehicles.

"You are now one part of a new kampfgruppe—yours being the Panther Regiment," declared a Wehrmacht major, with no trace of irony.

"And that's the Tiger regiment, and the Panzer IV regiment," Fritzi whispered, amused at the grandiose title for this ragtag assemblage.

Ulrich laughed dryly, and Hauptmann Schmitz silenced him with a glare.

The major continued, taking no note of the interruption. "Field Marshal Rommel, the Desert Fox himself, is our new army commander. He has a job for us."

General Bayerlein climbed onto the back of a truck, and outlined the objective of this ad hoc formation. They would be attacking, for a change, and were promised supplies of fuel and ammunition, as well as replacements for all tanks who had lost crewmen. They listened to him earnestly, and Carl-Heinz couldn't help but feel a rush of enthusiasm as the plan was outlined.

"Where'd all these tanks come from?" wondered one officer, a lieutenant, speaking out loud.

"I don't know how much you know about Rommel," declared the general, with his first trace of humor. "But he ordered them to be here, and he doesn't take no for an answer. And another thing . . . our field marshal hates the Jabos as much as you do. Therefore, he has ordered rain for tomorrow."

That got a good laugh from all the men.

"You think I'm kidding?" smiled the general. "You all know the Desert Fox. He's got fingerspitzengefühl, intuition in his fingers. He knows these things."

And indeed, in a few minutes the tanks had been fueled from some trucks that had appeared, perhaps conjured by the same magic that had brought about this gathering of armor. Some of the Tigers were unable to top off their fuel tanks before all of the trucks had been drained, but Bayerlein explained that the big panzers wouldn't be driving far. "The Tigers will be the anvil," he explained, "while the rest of you will be the hammer, sweeping around the enemy's flank."

There was also a shortage of armor-piercing ammunition, but Hauptmann Schmitz made sure that Pelz stowed more than two dozen of the tank-killing rounds. Carl-Heinz learned that they were, in fact, the command tank for a "company" of five Panthers. All around men were checking equipment, cleaning and lubricating fittings, polishing gunsights, and checking radios.

By then night had fallen, and the clearing rumbled and roared to the sound of tank engines.

A few minutes later, the new kampfgruppe moved out.

**West Bank of the Somme, Abbeville, France,
20 August 1944, 0923 hours GMT**

Ballard's task force was in the lead, and that was how he liked it. The tank commander had met Smiggy on the north side of the marsh, and the captain and lieutenant colonel had both agreed that as they drew closer to the Germans, the Shermans should be at the front of the column.

"They've got a couple of A/T guns sighted on the track to the left, but the road along the river is clear all the way to the Abbeville highway."

"Is Task Force White up yet?" Ballard asked.

"Not yet . . . I've got a platoon back there to lead them in."

"How much farther do we have to go?"

"Two miles to the highway, no more," the captain of the recon company shouted upward. He was standing in the hull of his armored car, while Ballard leaned out of the hatch in his Sherman's turret. "I got a good look at it from the cover of some trees."

"What kind of traffic?" Ballard wondered.

"Mostly foot . . . I saw a few cars, trucks, horse-drawn carts. You name it, they're using it. But no sign of any unit cohesion. This ain't a march, Colonel— it's a rout."

"Not for long," the armored commander vowed. He twisted to look behind him, though the view of the road was blocked by the two trailing companies of his medium tanks. How long would it take for the rest of CCA to circle the marsh and join him? He knew he'd have to guess. Already some of the armored cars had made the trek—surely the rest of the Pulaski's men couldn't be that far behind.

He looked north, picturing the Germans getting away along the road to Abbeville. He knew what his colonel wanted, what his general wanted, and his general's general wanted. And it was what Ballard wanted, too.

Speed. It was the thing that had brought them this far, and it was the thing that would win the campaign for them. And he remembered a lesson from his boxing days at the Point: When you had your opponent on the ropes, never let him off, not even to draw a breath. The final connection was obvious, because right now the Germans were on the ropes, and CCA was an armored fist poised for a knockout.

"Leave that platoon to show Whitey the way," Ballard shouted down to Smiggs, making up his mind. "The rest of your boys fall in—we're going for the road!"

Immediately the tanks rolled, B company leading the way. Ballard remained outside his turret, where he could get a view in all directions. The terrain was partially blocked, with many copses of trees and small woods. Here and there a farmhouse dotted the landscape, which tended to be flat, with a few low irregularities that hardly qualified as hills.

"I followed that track through the woods," Smiggs reported, indicating a narrow lane through a small forest. "You might have to take your tanks down it and deploy on the far side of the trees."

Ballard was about to reply when the crack of an 88 shot across the field, and in the same moment one of B company's Shermans exploded into an inferno of flame and popping ammunition. There was no time for any of the crew even to open a hatch, much less have a chance at escape.

"Where the hell did that come from?" demanded Ballard, wincing at the knowledge that five of his men had just met an unthinkable death. He grabbed his microphone and spoke in a voice that was louder than he wanted. "Bruno Six to all Brunos—action front! Bruno One, engage in front. Bruno Two, refuse the left. Bruno Three and Four, deploy and move up in reserve. All Brunos, acknowledge."

The tanks of Task Force Ballard broke from the road at the first shot. A dozen Shermans were pushing through a field of mounded haystacks, while two more M4s were skidding around a farmhouse and others raced for the cover of the woods. Three were already burning, and then another cooked off with fiery violence. Shells zipped through the air, and he could tell that they were being attacked from in front, and on the left flank. They were taking a lot of fire, though he still couldn't see his attackers.

"Bruno Three, reinforce the left—move forward!" Ballard ordered.

More shots lashed out from guns hidden in the nearby trees. The flank attack was a powerful counterpunch, he realized with sickening awareness. Additional M4s went up in flames, and tufts of hay flew through the air following a near miss. Fires burned all over the clearing. Some of the pyres were merely hay, but all too many of them were wrecked tanks and dying Americans. Even though he had yet to catch sight of the enemy, Ballard knew from the volume of fire that this was the strongest opposition his battalion had yet encountered. His tanks were shooting back, but suffering in the face of serious resistance. At least a dozen Shermans were burning, and the shots coming from the nearby woods were frequent and accurate.

"Bruno Two!" he called to his infantry company. "Dismount—we need some flank protection!" Ballard clenched his radio mike, unmindful of armor piercing shells whizzing past his tank. "Crimson Eight, this is Bruno Six. Action front and left. Guns! I need some fire support!"

He was trying to get Colonel Pulaski on the horn, but he couldn't make the connection. He thought about demanding air support, but then he took note of the low overcast and drizzling skies, knew they would get no help from that quarter. "Jones, back us out of here!" he called to his driver on the intercom. "Get me someplace where I can see what's going on."

And then there were tanks of mottled tan to his left, rolling forward from concealment in the woods, blasting apart Task Force Ballard. More panzers rumbling into a head-on collision with his Shermans, and these newcomers were the biggest damned things Ballard had ever seen—Tigers, he knew. He had fought them before but now, somehow, the slab-sided behemoths seemed incomprehensibly huge. Vicious barrels of lethal 88-mm guns jutted from massive, angular turrets, belching death, punching armor-piercing shells through the relatively thin-skinned American tanks.

The Shermans fought valiantly, but even at close range their shells bounced right off the armored goliaths—Ballard's men might as well have been using peashooters, for all the damage they did. Everywhere, M4s were wrecked and burning.

More German tanks rolled from the flank now, Panthers and Mark IVs breaking out of the woods, and Ballard knew that his task force had been caught in a neat and very deadly ambush. They were trapped against the Somme, the river water glistening pastorally only a hundred yards away to his right. Many German tanks fired at close range, and Shermans, armored cars, and half-tracks exploded to either side. Jones maneuvered backward, the turret swiveling to line up a shot. The barrel spat smoke and fire, but the shell exploded with no apparent effect against the front of a Panther's turret.

The panzer fired back just as Jones popped the clutch and jolted the M4 into movement. Ballard felt the shot whistle past his ear and only then did he drop down into the turret and pull the hatch shut over his head.

He looked through the periscope and saw several armored cars bouncing through a field, turrets reversed to shoot at the pursuing Germans. One by one the light vehicles erupted, crushed like tin cans by the force of heavy German guns.

"Shit, Smiggy. . . . Goddamn . . . I'm sorry," he hissed through clenched teeth, a curse of regret and helpless fury.

A Tiger rolled past his position, intent on chasing down a retreating Sherman.

"Gunner—traverse right!" Ballard shouted. The turret spun and the 76-mm gun depressed, lined up on the rear of the big panzer. "Shoot the son of a bitch!"

The M4's gun spat smoke and fire. The shell hit the Tiger near the rear of the turret, the AP round punching a neat hole in the armor. Abruptly the German's hatch flew open to release a blistering gout of fire, as more flames spilled out the hole bored by the shell. No crewmen made it out of the big panzer.

Jones was still trying to get them out of there, skidding along a muddy track above the river, when a ringing explosion pounded through the hull. Smoke filled the turret and Ballard reacted by instinct and training, fueled by sheer panic. He pushed open the hatch over his head and tumbled out of the tank, slipping down the olive drab metal to sprawl in the muddy road. He looked up, vaguely aware that his tank was burning like a Roman candle. Machine guns chattered, and tufts of dirt flew up nearby. None of his crewmen were anywhere in sight.

And then he was running, blinking away tears of pain and smoke and profound, utter disbelief. A shell streaked past, ripping through the air with a shrill sound, and then the ground heaved and convulsed underfoot. Dirt and fire were everywhere, and Ballard felt himself to be weightless, tumbling, soaring in a strangely peaceful silence.

He was barely conscious as the waters of the Somme, surprisingly gentle and warm, closed over his head.

Excerpt from *War's Final Fury,* by Professor Jared Gruenwald

Field Marshal Erwin Rommel once wrote, "In the age of mobile warfare, the battle is fought and decided by the quartermasters before the shooting begins." This was a hard lesson for the Desert Fox to learn. In fact, it was a lesson he had decisively rejected only a few years previously, when he complained, "It has become the habit for quartermaster staffs to complain at every difficulty, instead of getting on with the job and using their powers of improvisation, which indeed are frequently nil." But as tanker ships were sunk in the ostensibly safe harbor at Tobruk during the North African campaign, he learned that there was a part of his military machine on whose proper functioning all else depended.

Adolf Hitler had seen the future of modern warfare much earlier. From 1932 onward, even before his election as Chancellor, he had supported the synthetic fuels effort to convert Germany's ample stocks of coal into the oil necessary to the war effort. He knew intimately how much fuel an aircraft needed, how much fuel a tank needed, and harangued his generals, often at great length.

Hitler appointed his personal architect, the famed Albert Speer, to run the mobilization of the synthetic fuels effort. By 1944, synthetic fuels were providing over half of the total fuel supply of Nazi Germany—and more than 90 percent of aviation gasoline! The extensive use of slave labor—going so far as to build one synthetic fuels site near Auschwitz for ease of staffing—was critical to the Nazi war machine.

Ultimately, both Hitler's decision to invade the Soviet Union and the strictures he placed on his generals in that campaign involved the economic and military issues surrounding oil. And when his campaign against the Soviet Union did not go according to his plans, Germany was forced to turn back to its own resources: the synthetic fuels effort.

It was not until early 1944 that the Allied strategic bombing campaign began to focus systematically on the German synthetic fuels factories. From raids on the mammoth I. G. Farben plant at Leuna to the famous attacks on the oil installations at Ploesti, Allied strategic bombing raids began to make greater and greater inroads on Nazi production of synthetic fuels. By autumn, the Luftwaffe was operating on only about ten percent of what it needed. This could have been fatal not only to the German air defense initiatives, but also to the Me-262 jet fighter program, except for certain special steps that were taken in the nick of time.

The Kremlin, Moscow, Soviet Union, 1430 hours GMT

Chairman of the Soviet Union Josef Stalin was a surprisingly short man, Müller thought—but that awareness in no way diminished the Communist dictator's fierce presence, nor Müller's desire to be someplace, anyplace, else.

Instead, he was supposed to stand at attention with the other members of Ribbentrop's embassy and put on a brave face. *And maybe it's a good thing we can do that—he's not our enemy, anymore. Is he?*

With one look at Stalin's affable face, at his easy grin as he clapped Molotov on the back and made some joke that Müller couldn't quite hear, the German colonel knew the answer. *He will always be our enemy.*

Müller had frequent nightmares about being trapped in combat, but after this taste of diplomacy, he was convinced that being shot at would be less stressful.

Ribbentrop's breakdown had grown during the negotiations. Like many of the Nazi hierarchy, he was a patient of the infamous Dr. Theo Morrell, although, unlike Göring, the diplomat had not taken advantage of the liberal use of morphine. Baron Steengracht had wanted to send for Morrell, not trusting the Soviet doctors, but that was impossible. Bed rest, injections of sedatives— that was all the treatment available.

Steengracht and Reinhardt had between them divided up responsibility for the mission: Reinhardt transacted the business; Steengracht handled protocol. Reinhardt deferred to Steengracht respectfully in public; Steengracht didn't interfere with Reinhardt as he negotiated with Molotov.

Müller was called in for a few sessions. Part of the negotiations involved the transfer of at least some of Germany's missile technology to the Soviet Union. Müller was deeply shocked, even reluctant to share the information, even at Reinhardt's urging. "We can't give it away, Günter! You don't understand—if the Russians get hold of this, they'll be able to dominate us forever!" It was unusual for him to quarrel with his friend, but Müller had been deeply impressed with Dr. Werner von Braun, the civilian scientist and engineer who ran the Peenemünde facility, and was totally convinced of the vital importance of the Vengeance Weapon technology—so convinced that he had accepted a commission in the SS in order to organize his slave labor force more effectively.

Reinhardt was patient and listened thoroughly. "Very well," he said finally. "But you've explained to me that there is a V-2 that will shortly make the V-1 obsolete, correct?"

"Yes," Müller replied. "Günter, you should see it. The new rocket will fly well over two hundred miles with a warhead twice the size of the V-1! You see, it can operate at high altitudes—and you can't even hear it coming because it travels faster than sound itself! And . . ."

Reinhardt laughed. "My friend," he said, "I have never seen you with such enthusiasm. This is indeed a powerful weapon. And you've given the necessary answer, you see. We can share the secret of the first weapon and hold for ourselves the second weapon. By the time we need to give our new friends the second weapon, presumably Dr. von Braun will be working on the third. Does that seem fair to you?"

Müller thought for a long time. "I suppose it does . . . but Günter, I truly hate to share any of this information. But I suppose that's why I'm on this mission, right?"

"I believe that's right. Only Minister von Ribbentrop knows for sure, and I'm afraid we won't be able to confirm this with him. But it is the only thing that makes sense."

When Müller actually had to make the presentation to Molotov, he found his knees trembling and an unnatural tightness clutching his chest. Still, he tried to present his facts in a coherent fashion, and as he warmed to his subject, he found himself enthusiastically selling the merits of the wonder weapon. Reinhardt observed later that it was his enthusiasm as much as the technical information itself that persuaded Molotov as to the value of the V-1. Müller wasn't sure whether he should be proud or not.

And now, after another uncomfortable plane ride, he and his fellow Germans were in Moscow, in the very Kremlin itself. Müller felt in a truly alien land, the onion-shaped domes altering his sense of what was normal in architecture. It was only the second time he'd left Germany; as a teenager he'd taken the train to Florence once, and that had been almost too exotic for words. While his friends marveled at the treasures of the Uffizi and the architecture of the Duomo, he found the best food he'd ever eaten in his life.

Müller was in danger of sweating through his best dress uniform; protocol was never his favorite setting. He far preferred a friendly German *biergarten*; better yet, the cold cellar beneath a *weinstube*. Caviar and champagne he could live without, especially when it came at such a price. Not that he would turn down food and drink when Stalin offered; at least there was a little consolation for him. He daydreamed through the obligatory speeches; his eyes wandered to a large, ornate mirror, a relic of the tsars. The mirror reflected into another mirror and so on; from where he was standing he saw a multitude of von Reinhardts glistening in dress uniforms, all from different perspectives trailing off into infinity.

The deal was done. Steengracht signed for the Third Reich, Molotov for the Soviet Union. There were numerous concessions—not only Norway and Greece, but a demilitarized and defenseless Sweden, assistance in installing Communist governments in Rumania and Bulgaria, German withdrawal from much of Poland, Hungary, and Yugoslavia to establish a demilitarized buffer—and worst of all from Müller's perspective, access to German rocket technology.

He was afraid they'd given away the store, but Reinhardt was reassuring, in his fashion.

"As Hans von Seeckt said at the Rapallo Conference, 'Whenever our policy in the west has run aground, it has always been wise to try something in the east.' Truly," he laughed, "it's in some respects almost irrelevant whether this is a good deal or not for Germany. The odds are against us. To do nothing means to die. The best thing to do in such a circumstance is to throw the dice, and as the English playwright Shakespeare put it, 'Cry "Havoc!" and let slip the dogs of war.' Remember, Germany has a new führer, and the rest of the world needs to learn to fear him as they did Adolf Hitler. An outrageous and unexpected treaty, even if in some respects less than ideal, will upset numerous calculations, and that is always good. Confusion to our enemies!" He lifted his champagne glass.

"Confusion to our enemies!" Müller returned the toast.

The Somme, France, 1442 hours GMT

Pulaski was confused. He was riding in the back of the half-track to get a better view, and he knew that Ballard had pushed ahead from the other side of the marsh—it was the only thing to do. But now he saw several Shermans coming toward him at high speed. Gunfire cracked and rumbled, and it sounded as though he was downrange of a good bit of the shooting.

"Where the hell is the general?" he muttered, frustrated. "Damn him anyway!" Sergeant Dawson, beside the colonel, raised an eyebrow and then quickly masked his expression behind his usually stoic facade.

Pulaski had good reason to be upset. General King had commandeered a jeep and driver from the CCA HQ company and had been racing up and down the column, exhorting his men to victory. But there was an awful lot of noise up ahead, a clear enough indication that Ballard had run into difficulty. And worrying about the location and safety of his division CO were two headaches that Pulaski could easily have done without.

"Keefer—get us up this little hill. I've gotta see what's going on!"

The half-track rolled onto a very small elevation, merely a high spot in a slightly rolling field. Even with the naked eye Pulaski could see fires and smoke—obviously a number of tanks were burning. A quick check with binoculars confirmed his worst fear: they were Shermans.

A shell crackled overhead, and another round exploded a few hundred yards away. Tanks were coming toward Pulaski and the rest of CCA, and most of these tanks were flat and wide tracked. Panzers.

More explosions ripped across the field. There were M4s amid the German tanks, engaged in a running gun battle, but there was no question who was getting the best of it. One after another the American tanks blew up or veered away from the crossfire to seek cover in the woods and ravines along the river. Nearby, Dennis White's infantry were advancing, but the dogfaces went to ground as shots whistled overhead.

Dawson had the radio powered and passed the handset to Pulaski as soon as the colonel realized he needed it.

"Lorri?" he called, urgency driving him to talk in the clear as he ordered rapid fire. "I need some arty support, right now! HE quick-charge fire!"

"Gotcha, Colonel. My Priests are just getting off that Roman road . . . I'll be set up to fire in a minute."

"Colonel—there he is," Dawson said curtly as Pulaski broke the connection. The sergeant, his face a blank mask, pointed across the field.

"Shit!" Pulaski was helpless to do anything but watch, and curse.

General King's jeep raced toward the rest of CCA. The vehicle careened onto two wheels as the driver skirted a rock, then floored the accelerator in a desperate attempt to reach the American position. The little car bounced over the ground as a massive tank rumbled on a converging course. "Hurry, damn it!" the colonel breathed, feeling sick to his stomach.

The panzer's gun spat fire, and a high explosive shell hit the jeep or perhaps the ground directly under it. In any event the car, the driver, and the general vanished in a curtain of oily flame, a yellow-white eruption that sent a single heavy shape tumbling out of the blast. Pulaski vaguely realized that he was watching the jeep's engine roll across the ground. Of the vehicle's frame or the two occupants there was no sign. The colonel crossed himself and found his hand lingering near the silver crucifix under his tunic.

All around him the guns of CCA were sending sporadic fire into the approaching Germans. Infantry had dismounted from their half-tracks, and small arms fire mixed with heavy machine guns and a few light antitank pieces. The tanks of Task Force White rolled forward, but far too many erupted from the strikes of deadly German fire. Together they made a lot of noise and threw a lot of lead, but the barrage was having very little effect on the lumbering panzers.

Artillery fire from Lorimar's battery began to whistle overhead, impacts sending fountains of dirt flying in the distant fields. But the German attack came on, panzers firing, Wehrmacht infantry scurrying forward in the wake of the tanks. The Shermans were gone, either wrecked or hidden, and the rest of CCA was scattered, men fighting wherever they first saw the enemy. And still the flank was enveloped, more panzers appearing on the left.

A Tiger tank rolled right through the wreckage of Jack King's jeep and Pulaski could only curse in outrage. The armored monster came on, muzzle spitting a shell that blew up a nearby half-track. Bullets whizzed around the colonel, pinging and knocking against the armor of his command truck. Explosions shook the air on all sides, and bits of dirt and spent shrapnel fell like rain on Pulaski's head.

It was at that moment he knew he had to issue a command he had never expected to say. "Retreat!" he called, gesturing with his hand, shouting the command into the radio.

The remaining components of Combat Command A wasted no time in racing backward, fleeing the onrushing Germans. A barrage of shells followed the withdrawal, a blaze of gunfire that raked the task force from two sides.

White's infantry pulled back, using the guns of Lorimar's battery as a defensive screen. The big 105-mm guns held the rim of the hill beside the marsh, using direct fire now, shooting at targets in plain sight before them. Some infantry scrambled into their transport, half-tracks that took off for the rear, while other dogfaces pressed into any cover they could find, using small arms to give cover and support for the bellowing Priests.

At least, for a few precious minutes, the thundering cannon halted the headlong rush of the panzers—even a Tiger could be destroyed by a single hit from one of the howitzers. Pulaski jumped down from his half-track and ran to a nearby hollow where a few GIs had set up an impromptu machine gun nest.

"They're coming fast, Colonel," reported a young sergeant, who popped open another ammo box even as he spoke. "Don't think we can hold them for long."

"You're right, Sergeant—we gotta move out. See if you can hold on for two more minutes, then haul ass outta here."

The howitzers continued to blast away, sounds of firing intermingled by roaring engines as the big vehicles twisted on their tracks so that the gunners could line up shots. Lacking turrets for their guns, the Priests could only be aligned by moving the whole vehicle, but they still managed to lay down deadly fire. A quick glance showed Pulaski several Tigers and Panthers wrecked and burning after hits from Lorimar's guns.

But the lumbering field artillery carriers were especially vulnerable to a flank attack, and when a trio of Panthers rolled out of the woods to their left, what remained of the CCA defensive line was immediately rendered untenable. One after another of the Priests exploded in booming fireworks, the guns sitting ducks for the panzers.

Now panic set in. Pulaski shouted orders to his men, urging them to withdraw. Lieutenant Colonel White, his pipe nowhere to be seen, cursed like a sailor as he tried to get his surviving half-tracks and infantry organized. The remnants hastily rolled back, but more accurate fire fell among them, and additional vehicles erupted in smoke, flame, and death.

"Colonel, I think you'll be wanting to mount up, sir," said Dawson, who remained calm in the midst of chaos.

The voice seemed somehow distant, almost irrelevant to him. Pulaski was rooted in the moment before him. He could not tear his eyes away from the growing carnage and chaos. But when Dawson tapped him on the shoulder, it broke the spell. He and the sergeant raced back to his half-track, which Keefer had wheeled around, ready for a flight to the rear. Just as the colonel prepared to climb up to the cab, a half-track blew up right in front of him. Burned men spilled out of the hull, and Pulaski and Dawson quickly dropped back to the ground and tried to help the wounded GIs.

The colonel found himself holding Lorimar. The artillery commander's legs were gone, and his face was an ashen white. His normally smiling features were sagging with an expression of dull disbelief. He managed to force out the words to a single question, words that came forth with a welter of foaming blood.

"What happened?"

Pulaski hadn't figured out an answer by the time Lorimar was dead.

Central Park West, New York, United States, 21 August 1944, 1230 hours GMT

The jangling of the telephone brought Chuck Porter out of a sound sleep. He thrashed, drawing a moan from the bed beside him. *Who is that?* He blearily struggled with the question even as his hand, operating by instinct, snatched up the phone and brought it to his ear. A look at the clock showed 9:30, and the sunlight streaming in the window added the "A.M." He had been asleep for about two hours.

"Porter here," he said—or tried to say, around the hacking cough that was a reminder of too many cigarettes and too little sleep. "This is Porter," he clarified.

He listened in growing horror to the frenzied voice on the other end of the line. He was slipping his legs into his pants even before he hung up, and by the time the call was finished he had completely forgotten the other person in his bed.

"Honey . . . what is it?"

Her voice brought him out of his daze as he was pulling on his shirt. Tricia, the AP receptionist from the night shift . . . they had gone to breakfast together after work, and found themselves back here.

"News flash—they're bringing in the whole staff," he said.

"Why?" Tricia demanded, sitting up in the bed, her sheet slipping down.

"Something's happened in Russia—it sounds like something big," Porter explained vaguely. And big trouble. He didn't voice his deepest concern, wanting to wait until he had more facts in front of him.

Two hours later he was looking over the story, and knew that he had been right.

FLASH/BULLETIN
LONDON, 21 AUGUST, 1200 GMT
COPY 01 RUSSIA DROPS OUT OF WAR
DISTRIBUTION: ALL STATIONS

LONDON, 21 AUGUST 1944 (AP), BY EDWARD REED
THE SOVIET UNION, IN A STUNNING DOUBLE-CROSS, HAS ANNOUNCED THAT
IT HAS SIGNED A SEPARATE PEACE TREATY WITH GERMANY AND HAS
DROPPED OUT OF THE WAR AGAINST THE AXIS.
   WINSTON CHURCHILL CALLED THE MOVE "A SHAME, A SHAM, A SIN, AND
A CRIME AGAINST ALL HUMANITY." NEGOTIATIONS BETWEEN THE SOVIETS
AND GERMANY HAD BEEN CONDUCTED UNDER CONDITIONS OF UTMOST
SECRECY; THE ANNOUNCEMENT CAUGHT THE BRITISH GOVERNMENT COM-
PLETELY BY SURPRISE.
   TOP ALLIED MILITARY AND CIVILIAN LEADERS ARE MEETING NONSTOP
TO COORDINATE RESPONSE. GENERAL EISENHOWER ANNOUNCED THAT THE
RUSSIAN DEFECTION "MEANS LITTLE IN THE INEVITABLE DEFEAT OF GER-
MANY." SOURCES HIGH IN THE ALLIED COMMAND ALL EMPHASIZE THAT THE
CURRENT GERMAN MILITARY SITUATION IS ALREADY SO WEAKENED THAT
THEIR DEFEAT IS STILL INEVITABLE.
   GEN. GEORGE PATTON, WHO HAD BEEN CRITICIZED FOR HIS REMARKS
AGAINST THE SOVIET UNION, WAS QUOTED AS SAYING, "WE DON'T NEED
THOSE SO-AND-SOS; WE'RE BETTER OFF WITHOUT THEM."
   OTHER GOVERNMENT AND INTERNATIONAL REACTIONS FOLLOW.

   MORE

AP LON 333898 JF/082144

"We've got White House quotes coming," Lambert said.

Porter nodded. "Damn. Wish I'd been a fly on the wall during those nego-tiations. Must have been some interesting deal making."

"You and the OSS," laughed Lambert.

It would be a long day, followed by a long night of work.

Later, he was looking through a stack of photographs just in from London. One showed a German tank festooned with soldiers during the rout from Nor-mandy.

"Credit to von Esebeck, huh?" he remarked to no one in particular. "That's the same photog that sent out the picture of Rommel a couple of weeks ago, just to show us we didn't get him."

Though some of the German soldiers were bandaged, and they were all filthy and unshaven, they waved at the camera enthusiastically. Porter knew that these Krauts had been running like crazy, ever since Patton had busted out in Normandy.

Sure they'd been retreating. But then why the hell did it look like they were on a goddamn victory parade?

The Teletype began to chatter again. In spite of the jangling alarm bells, hardly anyone ran to read it, figuring it was just a follow-up to the biggest story of the war.

Then he heard someone say, "Oh, my God!" He hurried over just in time to see the first news about the counterpunch in France that had just chewed up half an American division.

Kaufering, Bavaria, Germany, 1427 hours GMT

It was the single most astonishing sight Paul Krueger had ever seen in his life. General Galland's staff car had driven from the small village of Kaufering into the Eglinger Forest, then through wooden gates and under a vast network of camouflage. Hidden under the camouflage were literally hundreds of pieces of heavy machinery from bulldozers to cement mixers, trucks to cranes. The immense construction site was impressive enough, though not unprecedented, but what came next truly was unprecedented.

Krueger had heard rumors of the great underground factories the Reich was building in response to the Allied strategic bombing campaign, but he had never seen one in person. Most of those who did were slaves, an army of ten thousand Hungarian Jews, laboring until they died in support of the mighty Nazi war machine. Here, a railroad track ran through the construction area and into a mammoth hangar, and underneath was an immense manmade cavern, a concrete bunker whose far wall was lost to view in the dim light.

"It's three-quarters of a mile long and a quarter of a mile broad," said Galland with evident pride. "Never seen anything like it, eh?"

"No, mein General," Krueger said. He hadn't realized until that moment that he had been holding his breath.

"We're building a larger one at Landsberg. Once all this is done, we'll be able to produce nearly a thousand aircraft each month, all without needing to fear Allied bombing raids. Down here, we're invulnerable." Galland pointed to a large paved area. "The Me-262 is particularly vulnerable during takeoff. See that? It's an underground runway. The aircraft will never be exposed while on the ground, even when taxiing. Amazing, isn't it?"

"Amazing is too tame a word, sir," Krueger replied. He was filled with pride and awe at the majesty of the Third Reich.

"Come with me," ordered the Luftwaffe commander, and escorted Krueger on a tour he would never forget. Through immense passageways, a virtual underground road network, through an infrastructure of housing and construction sites that would eventually house ninety thousand people—the statistics made Krueger's head spin. Finally, they ended up in an engineering office. "Here's where you'll work. Some design work, mostly troubleshooting. Because, you see, everything you've been looking at is—so far—a huge waste of time and resources."

"Mein General!" said Krueger, shocked at what seemed nearly a blasphemous statement.

Galland shook his head sadly. "We can build the aircraft, though there are still some production kinks to iron out. What we can't do is fly them without fuel. You know already that we can't even supply the operating units. And with Romania going to the Soviets under the new treaty—ah, you didn't know that, did you? Well, it doesn't matter. We give it to them; they take it—it's all the same. Actually, it may be better this way; we might be able to buy some fuel from them."

"Well, if it's a waste, sir . . ." Krueger said with some hesitation. He didn't even like to think in such defeatist terms. There were problems, obstacles, to be sure, but they were there to be met and mastered, not to be the cause of surrender and despair.

Galland chuckled. "I said it's a waste so far. And unless we solve the fuel problem, then it will be a waste. Now, most of that work is being done at other levels. We'll have some role to play, I'm sure, but we're not the lead agency here. We have other problems. First and foremost, there's engine production. Airframes are no problem; we can produce them in quantity. But jet engines must be made to critical tolerances and they require some rare metals that limit our ability to produce them. Then there are problems with the workers. It's relatively easy to get our 'special labor forces' to do the sort of work we have around here. But the higher skill work . . . well, that requires some different motivational approaches. Brute force doesn't work quite as well."

"Perhaps the wrong sort of force is being used," said Krueger, his eyes blazing. This sort of thing he understood well. "The incentives of pain must sometimes be applied broadly, sometimes more specifically, and always with finesse." He smiled.

"Yes, yes, well . . ." Galland's voice trailed off.

Krueger had noticed that some people tended to be inappropriately squeamish about doing what was necessary to motivate workers. It was almost as if they confused the subhuman races with Germans, believing that they were capable of good performance without the incentive of the whip. Krueger knew better. He knew how to motivate workers to do the job.

Galland spoke again. "The engines are manufactured at the Jumo plant at Dessau."

"I will make sure production reaches appropriate levels at once, mein General."

Galland looked at him. "Yes, Paul, I believe you will."

South of the Somme, France, 2047 hours GMT

Henry Wakefield rode in silence, allowing his driver to guide the jeep along the maze of French roads. Sooner or later they would get to Combat Command A, or what was left of it. Pulaski's men had fallen back ten miles, chased by German armor the whole way. The aggressive young colonel had been handed a defeat that was already being whispered about in the same context as the famous American disaster at the Kasserine Pass in North Africa.

To Wakefield, the truth was much more personal: half the division had been wrecked, with a terrible cost in men. His division CO was dead, along with several senior headquarters officers. Lieutenant Colonel Lorimar was also killed in action and most of the command's tanks and self-propelled guns had been lost in the savage battle.

Wakefield was now the acting CO of the Nineteenth Armored Division. *Hell of a way to get a command,* he thought, though of course it was a traditional way to get promoted in wartime. He suspected that his position would be temporary indeed, considering Patton's poor opinion of him. But that was only a secondary, even trivial, worry right now.

The general's driver paused to squint at a map, then turned down a narrow farm lane. A pair of Shermans, tanks from Bob Jackson's Combat Command B, recently arrived on the scene, stood guard. Finally the new division CO located Pulaski's command post, set up in a small barn with three half-tracks parked outside. The vehicles were pocked and scarred, showing the effects of vigorous small arms fire. In the building canvas tarps had been draped across the doors and loft window to keep the lantern light from spilling into the night.

Wakefield didn't know what he was going to say. Pulaski had been going over a list, but when he looked up at the division commander his eyes were stark and red with grief and pain.

"I'm sorry, Jimmy," said the general.

"They came from nowhere, General . . . Tigers in the front. They shot my boys to pieces . . . General King's jeep took a direct hit. They blew him to pieces, sir! I should have died with them."

"You had no hint of the ambush? What about your recon?"

Pulaski's head slumped. "Smiggy was out in front, as usual, but we heard nothing from him. The Krauts were hidden in a woods to our left, let us get all the way past them before they moved out. It's like they knew we were coming, left us a good road. Shit, General, they suckered me! Smiggs is missing now . . . I guess the damned Krauts got him before we even got close. I've got a report for you here . . . it's almost done."

"It'll keep," Wakefield said. He drew a breath but didn't say anything else right then. Pulaski sure looked bad—didn't the man know he was lucky to be alive? On second thought, maybe he did know. Maybe the fact that he had survived while so many died was part of his misery.

The general cleared his throat. "I've got some good news for you . . . Ballard showed up. He's got a few dents, but he's getting the best care we have." He didn't add that the tank commander had been fished out of the Somme more dead than alive. "He'll be off his feet for awhile, but it looks like he's going to make it."

"Frank . . . alive? That's something," Pulaski allowed, but then his expression was wrenched by unspeakable pain. "Damn it, General, I sent him out there, sent them *all* out there!"

"He was doing his job, Ski, like you were doing yours."

And I'm doing mine, Wakefield reminded himself. He didn't know what else he could say, and that made him think that he wasn't doing his job very well, not very well at all. Suddenly the general was damn tired, and he knew the war was far from over.

Excerpt from *War's Final Fury,* by Professor Jared Gruenwald

In that period of August 1944, the Allies were handed a series of unpleasant surprises based on the creative and revitalized leadership of Nazi Germany.

Führer Heinrich Himmler's brilliant and unexpected move of negotiating an armistice with the USSR unquestionably gave Nazi Germany a stunning opportunity, a way out of a dilemma that would otherwise have swept the war to an inevitable close before the end of 1944. After all, once they had emerged from the Normandy quagmire, the Western Allied spearheads were able to roll across France without pause, and there is little reason to believe that they would have been held by the Siegfried Line or even the Rhine, without the revitalization provided by the treaty.

The return of Field Marshal Erwin Rommel to command also had an unquestionably invigorating effect. The Somme counterattack knocked back the American spearhead and bought enough time for many Germans to withdraw behind another river line. In a series of holding actions, Rommel was able to delay the Allied onslaught until his forces were safely behind the Siegfried Line in the homeland.

His evacuation of Southern France was a brilliant and timely maneuver, as well. When the Anvil landings swept ashore on August 15, the American and French troops found that their enemy had already withdrawn. General Truscott's spearheads raced up the valley of the Rhone with aggression and speed, but the Germans had too much of a start, and virtually all of them got away. Otherwise, nearly a hundred thousand German troops would have likely fallen or been captured—troops that could be employed to make a decisive difference later in the war. The classic photographs of the Panther tank carrying so many German troops to safety became one of the most famous images of the war, signaling a renewed German spirit.

At the same time, the energy of the Soviet advance was redirected—though not before the Red Army pulled up to the very gates of Warsaw.

By then, Russian troops were taking over for the withdrawing Germans across the continent from Norway to Greece. They wasted no time in establishing powerful airbases in Stavanger, a mere eight hundred kilometers from London.

It is perhaps well that, as yet, the Allies did not know that Stalin, in his deal with the devil, had also gained the initial capability that would lead to the development of powerful and deadly rockets.

From Norway, these rockets were just a short flight from the British Isles.

OPERATION CAROUSEL

September–October 1944

SHAEF Headquarters, France,
1 September 1944, 1030 hours GMT

"Goddamn it, Brad, it wasn't the boy's fault!" Patton's fist pounded on the table as he glared at his army group CO. Omar Bradley—Omar the Tent Maker, as Patton sometimes called him behind his back—had just made the suggestion that James Pulaski be relieved of his command, and the Third Army general's temper had flared into white heat. "Remember, I'm the one who pushed Jack King into sending the Nineteenth ahead of Third Armored, which set this up in the first place! He was doing his job—and I still think that bridge was worth the risk!"

"We've got a division shot to hell!" Bradley retorted. "They won't be fit to fight for another month, at least. And all this because you saw a chance—"

"That's enough," the supreme commander interjected, instantly silencing his subordinates. Eisenhower took a puff of his cigarette, extending the pause. Then he nodded to Patton. "All right, George, what do you want to do about this?"

Patton took a moment to collect his thoughts. The other two American generals, and the fourth man present—Field Marshal Montgomery, commander of all British forces in the theater—waited expectantly.

"We should keep 'em together, what's left of CCA and the whole Nineteenth Armored. They had a helluva run—they were the first of my boys out of Avranches! They deserve another chance. Pulaski needs to get back in the saddle. With replacements to fill out his command, I know he's going to be a fine officer."

Dwight Eisenhower leaned back in his desk chair, still smoking his cigarette as he pondered the recommendation. Field Marshal Montgomery, natty as always and wearing his jaunty beret, smiled a thin, superior smile at the sight of the American officers wrangling with their problem.

Bradley was the next to speak. "And Henry Wakefield should be given command of the Nineteenth." He glared at Patton in challenge but was surprised when the army general nodded in agreement.

"Yes, he should. He's a good man, steady—just what those boys need right now. And he's Third Army." Patton spoke sternly but left unsaid another key fact: Third Army looked after its own. Whether he liked the man or disliked him, he would only pull him out if he couldn't do his job.

Monty pursed his lips. "I realize this is a Yank matter, but surely that's an invitation to disaster?"

George Patton opened his mouth to reply, but Bradley spoke first and forcefully.

"The Nineteenth went up against Rommel without knowing it. It was a surprise, they got chewed up, and that's the way it goes sometimes. We can second-guess this thing to death, but frankly, we just need to realize that they slipped the varsity in on us when we weren't looking, and the Nineteenth took the brunt of it. No need to shoot the survivors. Henry Wakefield is overdue for his second star and a division command, and I, for one, think he's done and will do a fine job. We pull the Nineteenth back, rebuild it, then send it back into the game. That's my recommendation."

"And mine," growled Patton.

The supreme commander sighed and crushed out his cigarette. "Brad, we'll give Pulaski a chance for now, but I'm not completely sold on the man, understand? Let's keep continuity of command, Wakefield in charge and Pulaski still in charge of their CCA. We'll let the press know that we have confidence in our officers and this was nobody's fault. Got it? Henry is acting division commander and a brevet two-star as of now, paperwork to catch up. Everything stays provisional until the Nineteenth gets bloodied again and shows it can do the job. If so, then Pulaski's in permanently. If he screws up, he's history. Fair enough?"

"Fair enough," replied Patton with a nod. "He gets a chance, he'll do fine."

Eisenhower gave Patton a hard look. "I appreciate that Third Army takes care of its own. But George, for now I think he should be attached to First Army. I'm recommending that Brad puts him under Hodges."

Patton clearly wanted to keep arguing, but he growled, "That's okay with me."

Montgomery gave Patton a withering smile, as if to say how much he enjoyed his rival's discomfiture. Patton glared back, then stood up to leave.

Near Reims, France, 5 September 1944, 0910 hours GMT

Henry Wakefield held the communiqué in his hand, while Jimmy Pulaski waited quietly on the other side of the desk.

The message was brief, but the impact profound:

19TH ARMORED DETACHED VIII CORP, THIRD ARMY, EFFECTIVE 01/09/44.

NEW ASSIGNMENT TO RESERVE CORPS, FIRST ARMY, EFFECTIVE SAME. DIVISION IS TO BIVOUAC IN REIMS AREA AND AWAIT ORDERS.

AUTHORIZED: GENERAL GEORGE S. PATTON, CG THIRD ARMY.
CONFIRMED: GENERAL COURTNEY HODGES, CG FIRST ARMY,
GENERAL OMAR BRADLEY, CG TWENTY-FIRST ARMY GROUP

"Goddamn him," muttered the general under his breath, remembering the blistering tongue-lashing he'd received from Third Army's commanding general at Sainte-la-Salle. "That son of a bitch wanted speed, and when you gave it to him, you paid the price—and now this!"

Wakefield leaned back in his chair and rubbed his eyes, immediately regretting that his temper had led him to criticize a superior officer out loud. Besides, now that he thought about it, maybe a transfer to First Army wasn't intended as a punishment after all. But hell, it sure felt like one.

"I'm sorry, General," Pulaski said miserably. "Maybe you should just court-martial me, get me out of here. Hell, if it would bring any of those guys back, I'd just take myself out right now."

"Damn it, stop all that self-pity crap," growled Wakefield, his temper flaring as he found a more convenient target than the distant army general. "You know as well as I do that we can't change what's done. The problem now is what the hell do I do with you?"

They both knew the situation all too well: All the components of Combat Command A were shattered, reduced to mere cadres of their original battalions. Lorimar and Smiggs were dead, and Frank Ballard was in a Paris hospital, though he was expected to recover from the wounds he'd taken when a German shell had hurled him into the Somme.

Pulaski and Lieutenant Colonel White had done the best they could in getting the battered combat command to safety. Even so, half the men and nearly all the tanks and self-propelled guns had been lost before the survivors had reached Bob Jackson's combat command, which was coming up in support. Though CCB, the division's other main fighting element, had taken some losses in screening the retreat, the German pursuit had been halted—and now, with the addition of division reserves, CCB was already back up to strength. As to the men of Combat Command A, they had suffered the most thorough pounding of an American unit since Rommel's Afrika Korps had hammered another Combat Command A—that of the First Armored Division—at Kasserine Pass in Tunisia, a year and a half earlier.

"Does Intelligence know, yet, what happened at Abbeville?" Pulaski asked, shaking his head.

"I just got the summary this A.M. It seems that Rommel is back in command. Somehow he put an attack together, scraping up tanks here and there while the whole German army group was withdrawing from France. For what it's worth, you came damn close to cutting off two or three corps—Combat Command A of the Nineteenth Armored caused them some sleepless nights."

"And where do we go now?"

"First Army is just north of Third . . . and we're only a few miles from Reims, now. I guess we'll be staying put for a little while, licking our wounds. I don't have any orders from Hodges yet," Wakefield continued, wondering about his new army commander. An infantry general from way back, Hodges had none of Patton's fiery drive—but he was known to take good care of his men, and there was a lot to be said for that.

"In any event, we'll have a bunch of replacements coming in . . . though equipment, new vehicles, won't be here for two or three weeks. For now, I want to get the new men into their units, and start training them."

He sighed, shaking his head. "You did a lot of good while you were on the run, Jimmy . . . but you stuck your neck out too far, and we're all paying the price. I want you to take the lessons you've learned and try to instill them into the new guys."

"General—I—I know you opposed this operation, and I just wanted to say, sir—" Pulaski started, but Wakefield cut him off.

"If I thought you deserved an 'I told you so,' I'd give you one. Hell, I didn't know you were going to end up going up against Rommel. If I had, I'd of fought harder. It was a judgment call: you and General King—and General George S. Patton—" he pronounced the "S" like "Ass,"—"thought the risk was worth running, I was on the other side. If Rommel hadn't come back into command, chances are you would have turned out to be right. So you're not getting an 'I told you so' from me, not this time."

"Thanks, General," Pulaski said softly.

Wakefield's gruff voice softened. "Jimmy, there are some lessons you can learn here. Whenever you get your ass handed to you, there's always a lesson. We need to get more out of our intelligence staff, on the division level and in your own HQ. Recon was probably deficient, and we won't let that happen again. But part of the lesson is that lousy things happen sometimes, soldiers get defeated, and sometimes they get killed. Think about what happened, learn from it, but be careful this doesn't eat you up. Remember, you got pretty far before this happened."

Wakefield could see the strain on the young man's face. You could never tell which ones would break under this kind of pressure and which ones would grow into better officers. And he wasn't sure whether he could help Pulaski through it.

Right now, the boy looked like hell warmed over. But he stood at attention like a real soldier. "Yes, sir," he said. "Thank you, sir."

"Get going—you're dismissed!" Wakefield growled, glowering at the colonel's back as he turned around and left. He hoped the young man would recover from his defeat.

And why did the burden lay so heavily on this old general's shoulders?

Dessau, Germany, 6 September 1944, 1800 hours GMT

Paul Krueger looked out the window as the train crossed the bridge over the Elbe and pulled into the city of Dessau. On his shoulders were the twin bars and braided epaulet emblem that denoted his new rank, *Oberst,* or Colonel. He cared less about the rank than about what it would allow him to do: ramrod the production of Me-262s so their flaming jets would burn the skies clean of the enemy. At his side was his standard issue Luftwaffe Luger pistol, rarely used, but now, as always, fully loaded. He had plans, plans for making sure the Reich's new weapon would succeed. And if his pistol was needed to enforce his new authority, so be it. Whoever was not performing for the Reich was the enemy of the Reich. And Paul Krueger knew what to do with enemies.

He was anxious to proceed, knew that haste was a crucial part of his mission, but he was also aware that twilight was settling over this city. In order to perform his task in the manner he desired, he would wait until daybreak and then march into the Jumo factory with a full day before him, and the utter attention of the plant manager and his staff guaranteed.

Dessau, an industrial city on the Mulde River where it joined the Elbe about a hundred kilometers southwest of Berlin, was one of the few parts of the Reich where Allied bombers had yet to leave their brutal stamp. There were air raids here, of course, like everywhere, but they had been minor so far, and the damage was scant and well hidden.

It had been so long since Krueger had seen anything not scarred and burned by the war, that this place looked odd, almost alien to him. He felt a cold contempt for the softness he saw here. Perhaps it was his destiny to bring flames of strife here, flames that would purify weakness and rise up to incinerate the enemy.

With clanking wheels and a gush of steam, the locomotive trundled the train into the station. Krueger left the car carrying his small satchel, pushing his way through a meager crowd, over several sets of rails and then past an empty ticket booth. The civilians gave him a wide berth, he suspected not merely because of his rank or imposing appearance, but because of a certain icy mask he drew across his face. They knew that here was a dangerous man.

Galland had shared his plan and goals with Krueger. For the time being, the general had ordered a drastic reduction in the fighter resistance to the Allied bombing campaign. Krueger understood the necessity even while he raged against anything short of a full effort at all times. In the short term, more damage was inflicted upon the Fatherland, but conversely the Luftwaffe was no longer losing dozens of fighters—and, more importantly, their pilots—in the course of each day's operations. Instead, the weary and battle-worn Me-109s and Fw-190s were being stockpiled, repaired, and replaced, while the Me-262

Swallows were being built as rapidly as possible. Under Minister of Armaments Speer, the factories were being scattered across the countryside, and—though the aircraft industry remained the primary target of the enemy strategic bombing campaign—these smaller installations had proved an effective means of defeating the enemy raiders.

Likewise, airframes for the jets were being assembled at numerous plants dispersed around the Reich, and training of pilots was proceeding quickly. His mind was still filled with the stunning potential of the marvelous machine, the jet fighter that—if employed in sufficient numbers—could surely sweep the enemy from German skies. Krueger's own training, which had accompanied his promotion, had been fast but effective. The Swallow was superbly airworthy, and he had quickly mastered its performance traits. The main difficulties came from the engines, which, although powerful, were not as reliable as a rational pilot would have liked.

But the reliability of the engines was a secondary problem. The key problem was that the Luftwaffe simply lacked enough of them to put a sufficient number of the lethal jets into the skies.

The task before Krueger was unique in his experience, very different from the shooting down of enemy aircraft or the precise pulverizing of ground positions. He was to improve the efficiency and productivity of the Jumo Engine Werks, the key plant in the manufacture of the power plants. And he felt certain that the same tactics that had worked so well against Soviet aircraft in the skies would prove equally effective against plodding bureaucrats and recalcitrant factory workers.

He saw a line of cattle cars in the nearby freight yard, then stopped to watch as hundreds, eventually a thousand or more, people were prodded in a shuffling mass toward the waiting trains. These were the slave workers from the Jumo plant, he surmised, no doubt being returned to their barracks after their shift was completed. He looked at his watch . . . a little after 7:00 P.M. Already he had one idea for improving the production of engines. No doubt, after his tour on the morrow, he would have more of them.

Finding a Gasthaus near the station, he quickly settled into a room. There he took out the message once again, the piece of paper that would open the doors of the engine plant and gain the complete attention of everyone he addressed:

28 August 1944
Luftwaffe Special Operations Order

The bearer of this document, Oberst Paul Krueger, a combat ace of utmost capabilities, is hereby charged with an inspection of the Jumo Engine Works, Dessau. He is to be accorded every courtesy by the management of

the Jumo plant. His mission bears the full authority of Commander of the
Luftwaffe Adolf Galland, and Reichsminister of Armaments Albert Speer.
His recommendations are to be implemented with the utmost vigor.

The signatures of both Galland and Speer were affixed to the bottom of the order. Krueger was pleased to see that Galland's promotion, like his own, was
now official.

After a bath and a shave, Krueger left the hotel for a look at his destination. Again he felt the pedestrians part ways for him, and he relished the respect—and the fear—apparent in the citizens of this old Saxon city. Like so
many German industrial towns, it was a mixture of old buildings, especially
inns, hotels, and apartments, nestled tightly among large industrial installations—the train station, a bustling shipyard along the river, and of course the
great factory that was his reason for coming to Dessau.

The Jumo Engine Plant was near the train station, and for now he merely
walked past the silent yard and regarded the massive gray building with only
casual interest. He knew that jet engine production was the greatest bottleneck
in the production of the Me-262, and it angered him to know that, within those
impassive walls, men were not working as hard as they could to create what
could be the deliverance of Germany. He had the power to change that, and as
he passed the length of the massive edifice he felt the strength, the will, puls-
ing in his veins. It was hard to be patient. He needed a distraction from now
until the morning.

He passed a Rathskeller a block from the factory and decided to pass the
time over a few beers. The room at the bottom of the stairs was dark and small,
and there was only one customer—a stout old man who hunched protectively
over his stein. When the fellow looked up Krueger let the cold mask fall across
his face, knowing it would stop any unwelcome attempt at conversation.

The barmaid had been stirring a soup pot in the small kitchen alcove, but
when the pilot pulled back a chair she turned and quickly came to his table.
She was a perfect picture of Aryan pulchritude, from blond pigtails to plump
cheeks, blue eyes, and large, round breasts nicely revealed by her low-cut
blouse.

"And what will you be having?" she asked him.

He smiled tightly, conscious of the double entendre, wondering if she intended to suggest that she, herself, might be on the menu tonight.

"A Weiss, please," he said. He broadened his smile, though the expression
was still marked by nothing other than an upward curve of his lips.

She drew the beer herself, then lingered a little longer than strictly necessary at his table. He thanked her, giving her a frank, full-body gaze. She smiled.
"Please, sit down, if you can spare the time," he said, looking ostentatiously
around at the nearly empty bar. "What's your name, *fraulein?*"

"Gertrude Schmidt . . . call me Gerti, Herr General." She probably knew her military ranks, but he allowed her little flattery to go uncorrected.

"Ah, Gerti. My name is Paul. Paul Krueger." Krueger stared at her directly. She stared back, smiling. "Your talents are wasted in a quiet place like this."

She sighed. "It is a quiet night, Herr General—Paul. They're all quiet, now . . . most of our men are at war. And the people who are still here, they mostly stay home at nights. Fear of air raids, you know."

Krueger nodded. "Perhaps it will not be long before we Germans can walk about under our own skies again."

"Do you think it's possible? I mean . . ." She shook her head, obviously reluctant to sound defeatist.

He laughed. "I'm certain," he pledged expansively.

"Ah," she said, not wanting to argue. "You're here for the engine works, then?"

His eyes flared brightly. "Who told you I'm here for the engine works?" He grabbed her hand, held it to the table, hard. Shocked, scared, she tried to pull away, but she might as well have tugged at steel bands.

"No one—no one!" she gasped. "I only thought—"

"You're not here to think!" he barked harshly. "You're here to bring me another beer. Now!" As soon as he released her, she went quickly to the bar, drew another beer. When she returned to his table, his anger had passed, as quickly as it had come. He smiled. "Sorry, my dear," he said in his most charming voice. "But there are matters of security that aren't fit subjects for discussions, even by pretty barmaids."

She allowed herself to be mollified, to be coaxed into sitting back down. He reached for her hand, noticed the thin gold band on her finger. "Tell me, Gerti . . . is your man gone to war?"

She looked at him in appraisal, apparently deciding her loneliness was great enough that she would risk his company.

"*Ach, ja* . . . Fritz went in '41. I heard from him at first, but now . . . not for over a year." Not meaning to, she found her voice catching, tears beginning to pool.

"Now, now, *liebchen*. The Wehrmacht is a very efficient organization. They would have notified you if the worst had happened." He was lying, of course. Krueger knew that Fritz Schmidt was almost certainly rotting away in some forgotten swath of the Russian steppes . . . but there was always the slight chance that it was otherwise, and she was clearly willing to cling to the hope, no matter how false, no matter how manipulative.

More customers arrived, a pair of quiet German citizens. Krueger's eyes followed the swing of her ample hips as she refilled glasses and cleared a couple of tables. It occurred to him that it had been a very long time since he had had a woman.

He finished his third beer before her other chores were done and she once again sat at his table. Perhaps she was nervous because of his earlier anger. In any event, she chattered away, and he let her talk without paying much attention to the words.

The air raid sirens came as a rude surprise, piercing through the night, rising with a mournful wail until the keening sound seemed to penetrate every molecule, every fiber of her being.

The pilot leaped to his feet, his first thought that he should get to a plane, take to the air against the enemies of the Fatherland. Only with a shock of cold, piercing anger did he realize that there was no fighter for him here, that he would have to endure this affront just like any landbound citizen.

"Come—to the wine cellar!" Gerti urged, leading Krueger and the three other customers—elderly men who moved with the careful precision of experienced drunks—down the stairs into a small, stone-walled chamber.

Krueger wasn't used to being on this side of an air attack, and the feeling of helplessness frustrated and angered him. For a while he put his arm around the frightened barmaid while they sat in silence, listening for the sounds of the bombing. Instead, Krueger was startled to realize that they could feel the impact before they heard it, shivers of vibration that thudded through the ground. The impacts came closer, and bottles rattled on the shelves, while little cascades of dust trickled from the roughly hewn beams overhead. "This is a British raid," he said, knowing that the English practiced night bombing, while the Americans followed the more dangerous, and marginally more accurate, practice of bombing during the hours of daylight.

They huddled in the cellar, listening to the crump of countless bombs. Krueger knew that the target must certainly be the Jumo factory, and he feared that the confluence of Dessau's two rivers would make it easy to find even at night. He felt rage at the enemy airmen, an intensely personal hatred that flamed all the hotter as his own plans for the evening were disrupted.

Gerti shivered in the cold and dank cellar, and finally slid next to Krueger, taking his arm and draping it over her. Her head leaned against his shoulder. He looked down at her, and suddenly his mind was filled with cold contempt. She did not even know for certain her husband was dead, but she was working in a bar, flirting with patrons—even worse, coming on to them with red-painted lips and a blouse that flaunted her femininity.

Although the sirens still wailed, he could take it no longer—he stalked up the stairs, through the Rathskeller, and up onto the narrow street to see what was happening. He saw the searchlights stabbing through the night sky, watched the bright bursts of antiaircraft fire, and grinned fiercely as a British bomber vanished in a violent, vision-searing explosion. The bombardment continued, explosions booming a block away, but he felt no fear. Planes droned overhead, and more destructive loads thumped downward, sending fiery plumes shooting skyward from different parts of the city.

He knew that these bombs would not kill him. And as he watched, he felt something peculiarly exciting about the power of the bombing, even as he hated the men who flew the planes.

An hour later the last of the heavy aircraft droned away, and he returned to the Rathskeller. The three old men were sleeping in a corner of the wine cellar, but Gerti looked up wide-eyed as he came in.

"It's over . . . I don't think the idiots even came close to the factory."

"But—but the city? Are there fires?"

"Of course!" he snapped, suddenly irritated with her. He forced himself to grow calm. "Come here, I'll show you. And you three—wake up! It's time to go home!" He knew she would come with him.

He strode impatiently back to the street while Gerti locked up the bar. Krueger could see from the flames in the skyline that the bombers had completely missed the massive engine works. Instead, they had plastered a district of shipping docks and dilapidated apartment buildings near the Elbe, as well as a few blocks of residences just a street or two away.

Gerti gasped when she saw the nearby damage and looked at him in fright. "I live near there."

"I'll walk you home . . . we'll see how your place fared."

She nodded meekly, and he took her arm, leading her around the corner, standing back as several horse-drawn carts of the fire brigades trundled past. Flames rose just beyond the neighboring street, and everywhere there were weeping people, others shouting urgently, the sounds blending into a cacophony that had nothing to do with Paul Krueger.

"That's my building," she said, and he saw a three-story structure rising directly across the street from the swath of flattened houses. She took his hands, leaned into him, kissed him. With a shock, he realized he was aching with desire. It had been a long time since he'd had a woman. It was a lack he didn't notice most of the time, but now, after the air raid, he felt the yearning, mixed with hatred and contempt for this woman who would betray her own husband, a brave German soldier.

As he escorted the shaken woman up the stairs, and followed her through the door into her small apartment, he noticed her face, flushed with tears, was bright in the roaring flames.

"Thank you . . . I'll be all right now," she said hesitantly.

But the flames were roaring in his ears now, so loudly that he couldn't understand what she was saying, nor did he care. He pulled her close to him and wasn't surprised when she opened her mouth to receive his rough kiss. He kicked the door shut behind him and in the dim light began pushing her toward her bedroom. She kissed him back hungrily as they made their way toward her small bed. Then he slammed her back on her bed and tore away her blouse and brightly colored dress.

"Wait—stop, you're tearing it! No, let me—" she protested, but he was in no mood to listen. He slapped her, hard, so hard she fell backward, stunned.

"Whore! Slut!" he spat. "Making yourself available to every man while your husband suffers and dies on the Russian front!" She began to cry, to protest, and that gave him license to punish her, punish her for her unchastity, slapping her again and again, holding her hands tightly in his steely grip. She fought back, but he hit her harder and harder until her tears were mixed with blood, then he was ramming into her, his faced clenched in a snarl of hatred and disgust.

In the dark, afterward, the blood mixed with the shadows so that he could not see what he had done. She was moaning a little, still unconscious. He dressed quickly, his rage now spent, and left her, throwing a twenty-mark note on the bed.

When he returned to the street, the flames of the burning buildings cast blood-red shadows on his face and hands.

Jumo Engine Plant, Dessau, Germany, 7 September 1944, 0830 hours GMT

Oberst Paul Krueger strode into the factory like a conquering warrior. His Knight's Cross was prominently displayed at his throat, and the row of medals on his tunic gleamed like the treasures they were. Guards at the door— Gestapo thugs to a man—saluted instinctively, then eagerly pointed out the factory manager's office.

Krueger brushed past a flustered secretary, pushed open the door, marched up to the desk and glared down at the chubby man who regarded him with wide, startled eyes.

"I will be inspecting your plant immediately," he declared, crisply handing over the authorization paper signed by Speer and Galland.

"Of course, Herr Oberst! Allow me to make some arrangements." The man, whose desk bore a plaque with the name "Wilhelm Friedrich," quickly scanned the paper. His eyes widened, and he mopped at his suddenly damp brow with a silk handkerchief. Krueger was privately amused. His entrance had the desired effect, and he'd only been in the factory for minutes. This plant manager would be no problem: an overfed, balding bureaucrat who squinted at the world through his wire-rimmed glasses, more comfortable with abstract numbers than with the real machinery that carried pilots into the sky.

"C-can I arrange an escort? Or coffee—ersatz, I'm afraid."

"You will accompany me." *Never allow people like that a chance to recover. Dominate them by your every move.* It was a good plan, and it was working.

Friedrich made a gesture at his desk, which was covered with blueprints, requisition forms, and other detritus of the bureaucrat. "But, as you can see, Colonel, there are many things—"

"Now!" snapped Krueger.

"Of course . . . all of this, it can wait." Friedrich bustled out of the office, speaking to his secretary as he passed. "I will be unavailable for some time."

He turned to the airman as they stepped into the hot, noisy factory. "Shall we begin with the design and engineering section?"

"Very well . . . I intend to see it all," Krueger replied.

The opening of the tour did nothing to dispel the colonel's initial impressions. He took care to walk stiffly, to hold his face aloof from any expression of emotion as Friedrich led him through the vast engine works.

At first glance, he could see that much of the floor of the factory was devoted to the assembly of the elaborate compressor mechanisms that were the heart of the turbine engines. He had seen the blueprints and knew that many miniature fans were arrayed along a central axis, then contained in a housing that shaped the thrust of the jet exhaust—the expulsion that gave the Jumo 004 engine its uncanny power.

Friedrich led him down a catwalk, through the heat of the factory toward a series of glass walled rooms at the far end of the building. On the way he continued to prattle.

"Unfortunately, Herr Oberst, we have been delayed by raids from the American bombers. Part of our factory was destroyed this summer, and it took several days to rebuild. Furthermore, we are working on the dispersal of the assembly, especially the housings . . . these are being sent to smaller facilities hidden in the forests, more secure from bombing."

"Such dispersal has already been put in place for airframe assembly," Krueger noted coldly. "And that part of the work is proceeding on schedule. It is in the engines that the production of these jets is facing its most serious delays."

"I understand, Colonel." Friedrich mopped his pate with a handkerchief, and the pilot suspected it was not just because of the heat in the factory. "But you must realize that these engines are something totally new to the world. The assembly requires the complex facilities of a large factory, such as this. And really, the design should have had another half-year of testing before we began production—you see, there are difficulties in—"

"Perhaps you are the wrong man to solve them?" Krueger purred. "Shall I notify Berlin to appoint a replacement?"

"No—of course not, Herr Oberst. I was merely observing—" But the plant manager was talking to Krueger's back and had to rush to keep up.

The miserable manager led Krueger through the engineering labs, where men—Germans—in white coats pored over blueprints, models, and tests. They were diligent and apparently conscientious, working with slide rules and pencils, quietly discussing aspects of design and production, with only a few sideways glances at the manager and the Luftwaffe officer. The pilot observed everything but knew that he could not influence this work by his current set of techniques. Intimidation would not speed up the process. He itched to sit down and join the design work—he knew he could contribute there. But first things first.

It was a different story when they moved onto the factory floor. In most places the workers he saw were gaunt, skeletal creatures, men and women who—the manager explained—were brought by train to the factory every morning from camps in the forests beyond the city. They worked their long shifts and then were returned to the camps. Every morning there were new faces, because every night there were some who went to sleep and didn't wake up again.

"Where do they come from?" Krueger inquired coldly.

"Mostly Czechs and Poles," Friedrich explained, clucking his tongue. "Undesirable compared to good Germans, of course . . . but they have been provided for us, and we are grateful."

"And Jews?"

The factory manager nodded his head. "Yes, in fact . . . many of them are. We get the healthiest and the strongest of the wretches gathered for transport to the east. The others of my workers are political prisoners, or else were prominent leaders in their home communities. The stay in the camp is a means of breaking any unacceptable ideas and attitudes that they may have held."

Krueger paid particular attention to the assembly of the turbine compressors, where forty carefully machined blades were fixed to a central shaft. The engines were mounted on long racks, and the bright fires of welding torches cast an ice-blue light in the depths of the shadowy plant. Sparks dropped in long cascades, burning and curling across the concrete floor.

"We are having the most difficulty here," Friedrich admitted. "It is so hard to obtain the proper metals . . . if only we had another six months for development. But no, the ministry requires production immediately, and so we are learning as we work."

"What are your most serious problems?" asked Krueger in his icy voice, camouflaging the real interest he had in this technical work as he picked up one of the narrow, straight blades. He was surprised at its light weight.

"The turbine becomes extremely hot, as you can well imagine. Ideally, the blades should be coated with nickel or chrome—but these metals are unavailable. The engine derives some cooling from the actual flow of air over the parts, but we are experimenting with hollow cores on the blades. It makes them lighter, and also provides another avenue for cooling."

The pilot noticed that many of the technicians had slowed in their work as they watched the conversation.

"What are you gaping at?" he snapped. "The future of the Reich may depend on the work you do here—but you will have to do it quickly, and reliably! Do you understand?"

Immediately the workers returned to their assembly.

Next Krueger looked down into a long pit, where waves of heat rose up to wash across his face in a physical caress. He saw many of the slave workers tending the fires of a massive furnace, while others were spraying a thin film over the inside of the engine housing. Raising his eyebrows, he looked at Friedrich in silent question.

"This is a layer of aluminum that is placed over the base metal," the manager explained. "It is designed to prevent oxidation."

"Here, too, it seems as though your laborers are easily distracted," he suggested, as several hollow-eyed workers turned to look up at him, numb faces giving no hint as to the unabashed hatred that most certainly lurked in each heart.

"Those two—bring them up here!" he instructed, fixing his gaze upon a pair—a man and a woman—who were near to his end of the long pit.

In moments the workers were sent up the ladder, prodded by the clubs of several brutish overseers.

"You must work faster!" cried the pilot, in a voice that rang even through the din of the bustling factory. "Allow no distractions—take time for no delays!"

He gestured at the Gestapo guards who were following behind the manager. At his command, the man and woman were quickly lashed to one of the steel supports. He unsnapped his briefcase. It contained a very few papers—and a braided leather whip.

The Gestapo guards ripped the shirts from the victims, and to the horror of the plant manager, Krueger began to lash them. Their screams could be heard even over the loud machine sounds. The workers below paused, looked up. "Back to work!" Krueger shouted. "The next shirker will get twice as many!" Again and again he lashed, sweat beading on his forehead, the fire of the furnace reflecting in his skin. Soon the two were slumping in their bonds, nearly unconscious.

"Untie them. Throw some water on them and send them back to work," he ordered loudly. "If they can't keep up with production, have them shot." Wilhelm Friedrich's face had gone a pasty white, and he mopped at the sweat that was beading on his brow. *He will pay attention, that one.* Krueger had the thought with satisfaction as he followed the nervous manager back into his office.

In his tour of the factory, the pilot made note of a number of areas where he believed the production of the turbine engines could be streamlined. He wasted little time in addressing these issues to Friedrich, who remained awed and frightened by the presence of this horrible man, this decorated combat ace.

"The daily shift must be lengthened by an hour," he began. "The Reich cannot afford to let this plant remain idle for twelve hours a day."

Friedrich opened his mouth as if to protest, but then thought better of his reaction and clamped his jaw shut.

"I shall speak to General Galland and Minister Speer, and we will see that all available stockpiles of nickel and chrome are devoted to this program. You must understand, Herr Friedrich, that there is nothing—*nothing*—more important to the future of the Fatherland than the production of these engines!"

"I do, Herr Oberst—indeed I do!"

Krueger outlined several other areas where he had observed inefficient processes. Some workers had seemed exceptionally lethargic, and once he had seen a part dropped, precision components dented on the hard floor.

"But, Herr Oberst," Friedrich complained, after Krueger had presented his list. "The central problem is not procedures, it is the labor itself. My workers are conscripted from the camps, as you know, and there is an inevitable lack of proficiency and enthusiasm that attends such a source of recruitment."

"Surely working here is better than the alternative?" Krueger said calmly.

"Yes . . . but it is a universal problem. And in truth, some of these fools would rather die than help our great nation."

"Have them gathered in ranks at the train station tonight. I shall address them before they return to their camps. And I will need to speak to your captain of overseers before then . . . he is with the Gestapo, I presume?"

"Yes, Herr Oberst," declared Friedrich, breaking out in a fresh layer of sweat.

With a feeling of accomplishment, Krueger went into the sunny afternoon. He stopped at the Rathskeller, but the old Bohemian tending bar curtly informed him that Gerti hadn't come in to work that day. He had a beer anyway, but the brew seemed flat and tasteless. He could feel the bartender's eyes on him. He left an extra few marks for the girl.

Hours later, as Krueger was waiting to board his own train for the ride back to Augsburg, he faced more than a thousand frail-looking, cadaverous wrecks of human beings. He felt like a god, an Aryan god, as he stalked about on the platform, looking down at the sea of pathetic faces. The laborers were gathered in company-size blocks before each of the cattle cars that was awaiting, doors agape, on the siding.

"Your work here is important," he declared. "Far more important than the life of any one of you, or even your collective survival."

The pilot gestured, and a Gestapo man stepped up to each company. One person was pulled from the back rank of the group before each boxcar. The Gestapo repeated the flogging, ten hard lashes for each victim.

"You did not meet your quota today. As a mark of lenience, since this is the day those quotas are introduced, only one worker has been flogged from each car. Tomorrow, two will be flogged—unless your production improves. And if that doesn't do it, then one per car will be shot and replaced with someone more willing to do his duty."

Silent and sullen, the workers were marched onto the train. The Gestapo overseers were rough, willing to use their clubs and dogs, but even so the loading took a surprisingly long time. The pilot had thought that fear would compel even these subhuman slaves into some measure of haste.

"Surely, Herr Oberst, there is another way to get their attention!" Friedrich protested as the last cars were loaded at the doors slammed shut. The manager surprised Krueger with his boldness. "After all, these people—however pathetic—are needed in order to keep my plant functioning! If you start to kill them, I shall have to train replacements. This will inevitably cause delays."

"Delays are unacceptable," Krueger replied curtly. "And it would do you well to remember, Herr Friedrich, that a German who fails the war effort is essentially a traitor. And what happens to traitors can be worse than what we did to the animals on that train."

An hour later he was seated in a comfortable berth on the Augsburg train, secure in the knowledge that he had solved several problems. The jet engines would be coming more rapidly, now.

The red flames from the factory smokestacks illuminated the evening and he smiled.

Western Germany, 12 September 1944, 1350 hours GMT

Rommel's car trip from Herrlingen to Ulm was an uncomfortable affair, but nothing compared to the train ride from Ulm to Aachen. The journey was a nightmare of blinding headaches, throbbing pain in his left leg, and—most unsettling of all—deep-seated fear.

Would he be physically capable of handling a military command? Was his mind as clear as it needed to be, or would he show fatal hesitation at the moment of decision? Such flaws, he knew, would inevitably cost the lives of German soldiers, the very lives he was setting out to save.

The company of the SS general, Bücher, who looked so coldly at the world from his scarred face, was another unsettling aspect of the trip.

Of course, Rommel understood that, on some level, he owed this new appointment as western front commander to Bücher—the SS man's visit to the hospital had been some kind of test, and the Desert Fox had apparently passed. And he could take some comfort from the fact that two of his decisions had already borne fruit in lives saved and Germany's defensive position improved. Nineteenth Army had escaped from Southern France virtually intact, despite the Allied landings that had come only a few days after Rommel's withdrawal orders. And the counterattack at Abbeville had been a brutal setback to the American advance, buying enough time for the remnants of the Seventh and Fifteenth Armies to get across the Somme and continue their withdrawal to the German border.

There had been some suggestions, strong indications from Berlin that the retreating troops should try to form a line at one of the great French rivers, but Rommel had been adamant. He knew that the fortifications of the Westwall were empty, but they existed at least in part. They would give his men a place to stand, to defend, and—perhaps most importantly—to have some shelter from the deadly presence of the enemy air force. So he had defied the "suggestions," informing OKW and, indirectly, Himmler himself, that if the Desert Fox was to command, it would be under his own terms. Surprisingly enough, he had heard no more about making a stand in France.

They crossed the Rhine at Karlsruhe, traveling by day as much as possible. That industrial city had been smashed in many places by Allied bombers. Residences and factories had been reduced to ruins, and even a park had been smashed, a playground rendered into craters, a grove of trees reduced to skeletal sticks and splintered trunks. Traveling to Aachen first, they found another German city displaying many of the ravages of war. Here Rommel spoke to several division commanders, learned that the American First Army was drawing close.

"I need men, Herr Feldmarschall—and if you give them to me, I can hold here for a very long time!" reported the corps commander who was entrusted with the city's defense.

"I will do what I can," Rommel promised, before getting back on the train and for another night of traveling.

The field marshal felt himself drifting off, weakened by fatigue, and even then he was aware of Bücher sitting next to him, wide awake. Rommel had always been a man who needed very little sleep, but it seemed to him that the implacable SS general never slept.

In fact, Horst Bücher hardly slept during that long trip. He was too busy thinking about this man, this leader of men. He'd read in *Das Reich* that Rommel had been a member of the Free Corps along with Göring, Hess, Roehm, and Bormann, that he was one of the first Nazi storm troopers, but from the first moment he met the man he could see that was just Goebbel's propaganda machine at work.

It disturbed him that this fine man, an exemplar of the German spirit, was not a member of the Party, and that his loyalty was thus suspect. Although there was no evidence that Rommel had been involved in the assassination of Hitler and the planned coup, Bücher believed that the coup plotters had counted on Rommel's eventual support—and believed that support would help carry them to victory among the German people. *It wasn't a bad plan*, Bücher thought. Or, at least it wouldn't have been had the plotters been smart.

Bücher was here to evaluate Rommel for loyalty as well as fitness, to be Führer Himmler's eyes and ears, to take whatever action he deemed necessary. And he was deeply torn.

The fitness evaluation was only slightly troublesome. He could see the terrible wounds and even see some of the impact of those wounds on Rommel's spirit. The physical wounds would heal; Rommel's will was too strong for anyone to believe otherwise. The psychic wounds were tied up in Rommel's concerns about whether victory was possible, and this Bücher found difficult to understand. Victory for the Reich was its destiny, and to question that faith was not merely unpatriotic, but almost blasphemous.

But Bücher understood something about Rommel that perhaps Rommel did not even understand about himself: he was a tool of the Reich's eventual victory, and a tool must pass through fire and ice repeatedly to be tempered and strong. Rommel doubted the outcome now, but his temperament would force him to find a way to victory, for he could not bear to lose. This Bücher knew.

The political loyalty issue was far more troublesome, but Bücher believed he knew what to do there, as well. Rommel had little use for the Nazi Party and would likely have supported the coup, in Bücher's opinion. It pained Bücher to believe this from a man he had grown to respect so much in such a short time, but it was so. Very well. Rommel was a tool, a tool of the Reich, a tool of German victory. Afterward, he might pose a danger to the Party, and if so, Bücher knew what he would have to do. With regret, surely, but without hesitation. Absently, he touched the hilt of his Luger.

Rommel's scarred face leaned against the train window. Bücher reached up to touch his own scars. His were the evidence of dueling, but Rommel's were the sign of injury suffered in war. Bücher's father had a scar, too, a memento of the First World War. A bullet had shredded his cheek, barely missing his skull. Rommel's battle scars reminded him of his father. His father had something of Rommel in him—the love of Germany but the rejection of Adolf Hitler and the Nazi Party. Young Bücher had had no choice but to inform on him.

When the Nazis presented his father with a paper to sign, stating that he now realized his political views were in error, he had refused to sign, to his young son's shock and dismay. And three nights later the SA arrived, and he was taken away. His mother screamed and cried for a while, then grew silent and withdrawn, ignoring her son from that time on. Horst Bücher received a medal from the Hitler Youth for his bravery and courage, and he left his home for university the following year. He never went back.

If I can sacrifice my father to the good of the Party, I can certainly sacrifice this man if—no, when—the time comes, he thought, and a deep chill of emptiness opened inside him.

Moving along the border, the two German officers found increasing numbers of soldiers ready to defend their fatherland. The Westwall was an incomplete barrier, unlike the Maginot Line with which France had presumed to hold the Nazis at bay, but everywhere industrious engineers were busy creating new strongpoints, pillboxes, and trenches.

At Monschau, gateway to the key dams on the Roer River, the Desert Fox spoke with one of these officers, the colonel commanding an engineer battalion. "What do you need most?" was Rommel's key question.

"Concrete, Field Marshal. If you give me the material, I can build a line of fortifications that will hold up the Americans for years!"

"You will have as much of it as the Wehrmacht can provide," the Desert Fox declared.

Later he heard from an artillery major, desperately in need of ammunition, and a panzer division commander who declared that with twenty or thirty new Panther tanks he could stop any breakthrough that the allies dared to punch into the Westwall. The front commander's answers were always the same: he would do the best that he could, and he knew that the men could sense his sincerity.

Rommel took short walks along the front at these stops, keenly aware of his stiff gait—but also knowing that it was good for these troops to see their commanding general close to the enemy. Bücher, too, came along on these visits, but he seemed content to watch and made few comments—except to the SS components of the various installations, where he proved very useful in underlining the Desert Fox's authority.

Back on the train again, still rolling south, they passed through the thick forests and steeply wooded hills of the German Ardennes. Jolting awake from a nap as they emerged from a tunnel, Rommel noticed that Bücher was staring at him strangely.

"What is on your mind, General?"

"It's the effect you have on the men, Field Marshal . . . you bring them hope, and it is obvious that they will fight for you."

Rommel sighed and rubbed his forehead, behind which his skull still throbbed. With a grimace he leaned back in his seat. "If only it will do us some good. You know, of course, that our greatest enemy lies in the east?"

"Stalin?" Bücher looked puzzled. "He's a snake, I know . . . but I believe that he will stay out of the war as long as it serves his interests to do so."

"Precisely. For all we know, he needs this autumn to restore his armies anyway. They advanced hundreds of miles in the summer, and you know that the Red Army must gather its strength for a long time before it makes another attack."

"But surely if we can defeat the British and the Americans, we will be too strong for the Russians to attack alone!" Bücher insisted.

"I hope you're right," Rommel said wearily. He didn't voice another thought that continued to irritate the back of his mind: it was for just that reason that the Russians could not afford to let the Germans win this war in the west. Whenever Stalin chose to make his move—in Rommel's mind it was when, not if—it would create a very dangerous situation for the Fatherland.

Finally they reached the Army Group headquarters for the western front, the Hotel Continental in Trier that had been taken over by the Wehrmacht. Here Rommel and Bücher met Generals Bayerlein and Speidel, two of the field marshal's old compatriots from Afrika Korps days, as well as veterans of the Normandy campaigns and the withdrawal from France. Also here were SS Generals Dietrich and Meyer, who pledged full and apparently sincere support to their new Army Group commander. Both, however, found private time to talk with Bücher.

"It's good to see you, Herr Feldmarschall," declared Speidel, reappointed as chief of staff as the generals gathered for a conference.

"I admit, it's good to be seen," Rommel replied. "But now, on to business. What is the most recent intelligence? And what is our situation along the entire front?"

For two hours the officers briefed him, and despite his weariness the Desert Fox found that his attention was focused, his energy high. He learned that the British had been halted in Holland, short of the Rhine River at the barrier of the Waal. Knowing that Montgomery was in command there, Rommel felt certain that there would be no precipitous Allied actions on that section of the front.

The American First Army was drawing up to the border from Aachen south through the Ardennes, and though Courtney Hodges's men were making some aggressive probes—especially around the environs of that ancient city—the bulk of German reinforcements were being rushed into that sector of the line. With luck and determination, Aachen would hold.

"And Patton?" Rommel's eyes ranged south along the map.

"He is becoming embroiled at Metz, Field Marshal," Speidel explained. "Furthermore, Third Army seems to be plagued by serious supply shortages and has not yet drawn up to the Westwall."

"And to the south, in the Vosges?" Next, he turned his attention to the range of low mountains that stood between the bulk of France and the Rhine.

"The Americans, heavily supported by French troops, have attacked continuously, both from the Normandy front and aided by a new army that has come up from Southern France following the landings at Marseilles. But your orders to General Weise were prescient, if I may say so, Herr Feldmarschall. The Nineteenth Army made a successful withdrawal, and now our troops are holding in the mountains, and the enemy has not yet reached the river."

"What kind of train access do we have?" Rommel asked. "There are many troops that have been freed up from duties in the east—it is imperative that they be brought into line as soon as possible."

"The priorities of the Special Ministry have barred us from most of the Reich's rolling stock," Speidel explained.

Rommel turned to Bücher. "That is Himmler's province, is it not? We must convince him that the needs of the Westwall have priority."

"I must warn you that such an argument will be difficult to win, Herr Feldmarschall," Bücher answered frankly. "However, I have been ordered to return to Berlin as soon as you are established in your headquarters. I shall take the matter up with the führer personally and see what I can accomplish."

The Desert Fox nodded, his mind already moving on to other things. "Now let us analyze the enemy situation along the front?" he asked. "Where is he strong, where weak?"

It was Speidel who answered again. "We have little access to air reconnaissance, as you know. However, it seems obvious that the Americans of the First Army are the greatest threat to cross the border into the Reich, from the vicinity of Trier northward. The British are held up in the marshes downstream of Antwerp."

"And in the south?"

"Patton seems stymied by the fortifications of Metz . . . the Seventh Korps is defending heroically."

"Very good. Gentlemen, we will work with what we have . . . and we will work hard. I will be touring the front as soon as the headquarters is fully established. The rest of you all have jobs to do. General Bücher, I hope that your mission to Berlin is successful—and I will expect your return at the earliest opportunity." He was surprised to realize that he did, in fact, want the SS general back. Next he turned to one of the staff officers. "Make a note—I will need a good driver, someone of proven courage and skill. Though not for another week or so . . . I think there will be plenty to keep me busy around headquarters until then.

"That is all," he noted in conclusion. "We have work to do."

Reichstag, Berlin, Germany, 15 September 1944, 0900 hours GMT

Of course, Ribbentrop received adulatory press coverage for his "brilliant negotiations with the Soviet Union," while Reinhardt's name went completely unmentioned. This disturbed Müller far more than it apparently disturbed Reinhardt.

"I prefer to avoid excessive recognition. As Horace reminds us, 'Whoever cultivates the golden mean avoids both the poverty of a hovel and the envy of a palace.' The work is the important thing, and we have managed to deliver results."

Müller was unpersuaded. "Do you think we'll get a medal?" he whispered to Reinhardt, as they waited in the marble-floored anteroom outside Himmler's suite of offices—the "Throne Room," as the Wehrmacht officers had come to call it.

Reinhardt only laughed. He glanced in the mirror, made a slight tug on his jacket so that the fit was perfect. Müller quickly checked his imperfectly fitting tunic for food stains or crumbs. Then they were ushered into the Presence. Reinhardt clicked to attention, arm rigid and precise. "Heil Himmler!" he barked. Müller followed suit, though his salute was less perfect. Either way, Himmler didn't seem to notice.

"Please have a seat," the new führer said.

Behind Himmler, great banners draped the wall, black and red swastikas dropping all the way from the high ceiling. The window between the twin pennants allowed the brightness of the autumn day to illuminate the room, but the effect left the führer himself silhouetted in deep shadow. He seemed like a religious figure in his new majesty, even in the dim light.

Müller's stomach rumbled nervously. Even though he imagined that this would be a session of praise and recognition, he still wished he were anyplace else.

"I've read the reports on your mission. Excellent staff work. You are to be commended for your performance."

"Thank you," Reinhardt said calmly. He even sat at attention.

"Because of your exemplary performance, I have a new assignment for you."

This worried Müller. Normally, staff assignments would come through the normal chain of command. Any assignment the führer would give personally was likely to have serious drawbacks.

"Field Marshal Rommel, as you know, is once again in command of our western front. With Stalin neutralized, at least for the time being, nothing must stop his victory. I want him to have the finest possible staff. Colonel von Reinhardt, you are to be the field marshal's aide for plans and intelligence. You will have access to all Reich intelligence resources to assist in this role. Colonel

Müller, you will be responsible for supply and logistics, because of your excellent work with the Peenemünde program."

"And we will provide additional reports to you from time to time?" asked Reinhardt.

Himmler smiled slightly. "It is always appropriate for the führer to be aware of the actions of his senior officers," he said in his calm, quiet voice. "Field marshals, by the nature of their assignments, do not always have the time to provide a full accounting to the leaders of the State. You will take some of that burden off the field marshal's shoulders, and thereby be of service to the State."

"That is very clear, Führer," Reinhardt said.

It was about as clear as mud to Müller, but even he could tell that there was a big hidden agenda going on right in front of him. Fortunately, Reinhardt would explain it all later, hopefully over coffee and cakes. It was a good thing that Müller was not here by himself, he thought, for he would end up failing to understand what Himmler wanted and be shot for it or worse.

He watched Reinhardt for his cues, stood when he stood, clicked his heels and saluted, and left the room with all the military bearing his stout form could manage.

Müller was about to start asking questions as they emerged back into the light of the anteroom when he noticed Reinhardt stiffen slightly. One jet-black eyebrow raised slightly as a tall, scarred SS general entered the room. The general paused as well.

"Günter!" he said, his mouth spreading into a tight-lipped smile. "It's been a long time."

"Hello, Horst," Reinhardt said, his own mouth smiling as the rest of his face remained still. "And I see it's General now. Horst, this is Wolfgang Müller. Wolfgang, this is General Horst Bücher."

Müller gingerly shook hands with the SS officer. His grip was hard and wiry, his scarred face vulpine. "Glad to meet you, General."

"Horst and I went to Heidelberg together," Reinhardt said.

Bücher nodded. "Günter gave me one of these scars." He touched his cheek, traced the thin line.

"Though as I recall, you were generally a better fencer than I," Reinhardt noted.

"Indeed I was," Bücher said. Müller got the impression he was ready for a rematch at any time. The two men were superficially friendly, but cautious, aware of each other like two snakes poised to strike. "But that was then. I heard about your contributions to the Ribbentrop mission. Congratulations. Where to now?"

"Field Marshal Rommel's staff."

"Indeed?" Bücher replied with an ironic smile. "I'm attached to Rommel myself. I suppose then we'll be seeing a lot of each other in the months to come."

Reinhardt nodded. "I suppose we will. That will give us a chance to catch up on chess, perhaps."

"At which you do better than fencing," riposted Bücher.

Reinhardt merely glanced at the scar he'd placed on Bücher's cheek. "For the most part. And you've won a few games from time to time."

"Chess isn't a game of the real world," Bücher said. "It's an abstract of war, not war."

"'The chessboard is the world, the pieces are the phenomena of the universe, the rules of the game are what we call the laws of Nature.' Thomas Huxley."

"Ever the academician," Bücher laughed. It was not a friendly sound. "Perhaps you'll have the opportunity to get your hands dirty at the front."

Reinhardt nodded. "Perhaps."

Bücher entered the throne room and saluted. His heart filled with an honest thrill at the sight of Himmler's delicate features now creasing into a welcoming smile. *This man has true greatness . . . he may allow us to win, where our führer's weakness would have doomed us.*

"Ah, my dear general . . . please relax. And tell me, did you see our Desert Fox established in his new headquarters?" Himmler didn't rise, but gestured with a well-manicured hand.

The SS officer nodded, and allowed himself to sink into a chair. "He has some difficulty moving around—more than he would like anyone to know, and I suspect that he still suffers a great deal of pain. But his air of authority is real, and it was clear that the morale at headquarters improved merely from his presence. And he has a way with the men in the field . . . after talking with him, they truly *want* to fight."

Himmler nodded primly at the closed door. "Those two will be going west as soon as possible. They have demonstrated some capabilities, and I have assigned them to Rommel's staff."

"Indeed, Führer. I know one of them—Colonel von Reinhardt. We attended university together. In fact, he gave me one of my badges of honor." He touched his cheek lightly. "A smart man, and able, but an academician, not a warrior. In his proper place, he will be of use."

"And a staff officer role is his proper place?" Himmler asked.

"Yes, sir," replied Bücher.

"Before you return to the field marshal's staff, I have a more immediate assignment for you. I am afraid that I have intelligence from this city that indicates that trouble spots remain. That, in fact, is why I recalled you to Berlin."

"I am yours to command, of course."

"One of the problems is Fromm, commander of the Replacement Army.

We know that he was one of the original conspirators. He's a doddering old fool, but he still has influence with some of the defeatists."

"I will make arrangements immediately . . . the problem will be solved."

"And old Röwekamp, as well. It seems that he has begun to fancy himself a leader, merely because he was able to form some sort of consensus among the General Staff following the murder of our führer. He is another one that will serve as a good example."

"And there are more?"

"I have a list . . . a thoughtful list. There are those such as Guderian, even Keitel, who would make tempting targets, but they still have uses. So for now, alas, they will be allowed to live."

Bücher listened for several minutes, nodding in agreement with everything his leader said.

"It shall be as you wish, Führer. I can begin the task immediately. I presume that some are to be examples and others should appear more as accidents?"

"Correct. I shall want you to return to Army Group B as soon as possible, which you must do immediately when this delicate task is done. Now tell me, are there any other matters that require my attention in the west?"

Bücher briefed Himmler on the situation on the western front, feeling none of the reluctance to tell the truth that would have accompanied a similar order from Hitler. "Field Marshal Rommel expressed some concern over the availability of the trains . . . he feels that greater efforts must be made to carry the reinforcements from the eastern front into the Siegfried Line."

Himmler shook his head. "All available locomotives and rolling stock are required for the Special Transports. With our attendant withdrawal from Poland, several key areas—Auschwitz, Treblinka, Bergen-Belsen—are undergoing full evacuation. You must tell Rommel that the trains will be available to him only when the Reich's first priority has been sufficiently addressed."

"Of course, Führer."

"Now you must see to your accommodations, and your work," said Himmler, at last rising from his desk. His black SS jacket was impeccably tailored, Bücher noticed, and showed not a single wrinkle from his leader's chair.

**Nineteenth Division Headquarters, Reims, France,
16 September 1944, 1720 hours GMT**

Wakefield's face broke into a rare smile as he stood to greet his visitor. "Brad—good to see you," he said, sticking out his hand.

His commander, General Omar Bradley, shook the proffered hand warmly. "Good to see you, too, Henry. How's it going?"

Wakefield indicated the stacks of paperwork on his desk. "It's going, that's about it. Thank God for resupply. We're getting what we need, but it's like building a division from scratch once again. Same number, different team." He indicated a chair in front of his desk. "Coffee?"

"Sure," replied Bradley. Wakefield motioned at an orderly. The coffee was bitter and strong, the way Wakefield liked it, but Bradley winced slightly as he took a sip. "That stuff will put hair on your chest," he said.

"If we run out of gas, I pour it into the tanks," Wakefield joked. "What can I do for you?"

"Wanted to see you, see how things were going, when you are ready to get back into the war."

"I could start rolling now if you needed us," Wakefield replied. "Ideally, about four more weeks."

"Let's split the difference, call it two weeks. Okay with you?"

"Okay. Where to?"

"Luxembourg. You're still part of First Army, and you'll be on the right flank, starting the push into the German Westwall fortifications. In between Aachen and Metz."

These two cities, Wakefield well knew, were the most contested part of the war right now, and both were offering stiff resistance. General Hodges's First Army, which Bradley had given up when he took overall command, was engaged in the battle for Aachen. Wakefield also realized that the right flank of First Army was next to the left flank of Patton's Third Army, which was fighting to reduce Metz.

"That's good," Wakefield mused. "We'll be back in the line, but we'll still have some time to finish getting completely back up to speed."

"That's what I had in mind," Bradley said. "We'll move you back into the war, but right now we've got the time to move more slowly, so let's take advantage of it."

"Thanks," Wakefield nodded. "And Brad—"

"Yes?"

"Thanks for the command."

"Don't thank me," Bradley said. "You deserve it. By the way, how's the boy doing?"

"Pulaski?" Only officers of Bradley and Wakefield's generation would refer to a thirty-three year old as a "boy." "Hard to tell. He fell off a horse. Best thing to do is get right back on, but there hasn't been a horse for him to ride, if you know what I'm saying. The longer until the next time he gets some combat, the more time he has to fret about it. He's a good boy, but I'm worried a little bit."

"Should he be relieved?"

Wakefield shook his head slowly. He'd considered it a number of times and still wasn't completely sure he'd made the right decision. "No, I don't think so.

I think he needs another shot. He may need a little coaching to get through it, but once he does, I think he'll put himself back together."

"Maybe it's not a bad thing to get your men up into the line quickly," observed Bradley.

Wakefield nodded. "Yeah, I think you're right. The veterans need to get back into action, and the new ones need to see what it's like, not just hear horror stories."

"I know what you mean. By the way, Henry—"

"Yes?"

"I've got you under First right now, but it can go either way. Aachen or Metz. And Metz means working for George again."

Wakefield grimaced slightly. "Either way," he said, "we'll handle it." With some surprise, he realized that part of him wanted to rejoin Third Army, to be part of the action again. *Hell, Old Blood and Guts may be a son of a bitch, but he's a fighting son of a bitch,* he thought, though in front of Bradley, he kept his mouth shut.

"I knew I could count on you, Henry," Bradley replied.

Trier, Rhineland-Palatinate, Germany,
18 September 1944, 1045 hours GMT

"Mines—I need all the mines you can send me! When? Yesterday, of course! The Americans are bashing into Aachen, and brave Germans are dying because we can't lay a decent minefield! I'm not interested in excuses."

Rommel drew breath, listened to the agitated colonel on the other end of the line.

"That's better . . . I will expect the delivery by the day after tomorrow!"

He put down the telephone and called out the door of his office. "Loella?"

"Ja, Herr Feldmarschall?"

"Get me the figures on the concrete deliveries. I want to make sure those people in Berlin are doing all they can."

"Of course—and, sir, General Speidel is waiting to see you."

"Send him in, right away."

Rommel rose from his desk and limped to the window, fighting back the urge to wince against the constant pain. When would he be whole again? When would his body be able to match the speed and agility of his mind?

He shook off the thoughts, knowing that its attendant worry—when would his *mind* be restored to its earlier certainty and decisiveness?—was a pointless exercise in futile self-examination. He could not afford to waste time with self-pity and doubt. So much was riding on his shoulders, now, and he would have to do the best that he could.

But would it be enough?

His eyes wandered across the vista from his office window. The hotel was located high on a hill, and from here he could see the Porta Nigra, the ancient Roman gate that was a classic landmark of this city. Nearby was the ancient amphitheater, and not too far away rose the towers of the grand cathedral. Everywhere there were trees, mostly green and vibrant still, though a few showed the bright orange or brittle brown of approaching autumn. It was good to see a tree with signs of life. He missed the battle-scarred oak at the hospital at Vesinet. He hoped it was recovering as well as he was.

He was spared further maudlin dissembling by the arrival of Speidel.

Rommel gestured out the window. "We're fighting for our own homeland, our national treasures now. I wonder if that makes a difference."

"I think it does, Field Marshal—to officers and men alike," replied the chief of staff. "I know it does to me."

"And to me, as well," Rommel admitted. He wanted to sigh, to collapse into his chair and rest, but instead he turned to business. "What is the news about the manpower reserves? Has the transportation bottleneck eased?"

"Unfortunately, no, mein Feldmarschall. We have sent repeated messages to Berlin, but the word is always the same: the SS have the authority over all rail operations."

A more profane man might have made some harsh remark, but the Desert Fox merely shook his head and moved on. One consequence of his wounds seemed to have been a diminishing of his once-renowned temper. In a few minutes he and Speidel had finished the staff business, and by that time General Bayerlein was waiting to see him. The armored commander entered accompanied by another recent addition to the staff, Colonel von Reinhardt.

"Come in, Fritz. I hope you have some good news for me."

"I think so, Field Marshal. We have outfitted three panzer divisions with new Panthers . . . and each has an additional battalion of Tigers. They are currently being refitted north of here, in the area of the Ardennes."

"Good." Rommel turned to Reinhardt. "And what are your intelligence summaries of the enemies' intentions?"

The colonel stood at attention with that easy grace that marked so many of the aristocratic Prussians. Yet even so, Rommel found himself liking the man, gauging his comfort level as a mark of competence, not arrogance.

"We believe that the Americans will redouble their efforts at Aachen, Field Marshal. Patton remains tied up at Metz, not even adjacent to our border yet, and we suspect that the enemy has political reasons to conclude the early capture of a German city."

"Indeed. An interesting theory," the Desert Fox replied.

He found the young man to be thoughtful and intelligent, careful to distinguish between information he actually knew and his own suppositions and theories, a characteristic that had not been true of every intelligence officer he'd met. He enjoyed the strategic give-and-take, the discussion of options. He still felt his own mind was weaker, slower than usual, but he managed to keep up, though not without some effort.

An hour after the two men had left, Rommel remained busy at his desk. These days he found himself working as hard as he ever had, tending to a myriad of details in his headquarters, bringing order to the chaos that had resulted from the long withdrawal. Bayerlein and Speidel had proved themselves as able as ever, the former taking over the organization of panzer forces while the latter addressed matters of supply and reinforcement. Even the SS officers, Meyer and Dietrich, had submitted to the field marshal's commands with a minimum of resistance. Now, a week after establishing his headquarters, Rommel was feeling that things were beginning to come together. Many times during these long days the Desert Fox was afflicted by physical weakness brought on by his wounds, but his able lieutenants covered for him, and he felt fairly certain that his condition was not widely known among the troops. Though he had wanted to tour the front, he had remained in the headquarters since his arrival, finding that there were too many things here that required his direct attention.

Late in the day he was pleased to greet Baron von Esebeck, who as usual had been touring among the troops of the Wehrmacht, taking pictures and gathering news stories for dissemination throughout the Fatherland.

"I have to find a driver," Rommel mentioned. "It is time for me to get out and tour the front."

"I know just the man," von Esebeck informed him. "And I just learned that he is here, in Trier, and currently waiting for a new assignment."

Rommel liked Carl-Heinz Clausen at first glance. The tank driver was a square, blocky rock of a man. Although he'd taken time to put on a fresh tunic, his fingernails still betrayed a hint of the grease that the field marshal suspected was a permanent feature of his appearance. Clausen was smiling, revealing a gap between his two front teeth. Rommel remembered that this feature was supposed to be linked to sensuality. But then the man did have five children.

"You wanted to see me, Field Marshal?" the man said, saluting.

"Yes, yes. Tell me—you are the man who was photographed by von Esebeck just before Abbeville?"

"Jawohl, mein Feldmarschall!" Carl-Heinz Clausen replied. "At least, I was inside driving the tank—the other men were in the picture."

"Ah, you have an ear for detail. I like that," said the Desert Fox. "I also understand that you served under General Bayerlein, and distinguished yourself in the battle at Abbeville."

"Thank you, sir. I was fortunate enough to find a vulnerable flank. It was good to see the Americans turn about and run for a change." His wide-open, guileless smile was a treat for Rommel, who far preferred the company of enlisted soldiers to many of the officers and politicians who made up his daily lot.

"I am sorry to hear about the loss of your crewmates . . . though they tell me that the radioman—Pfeiffer, is it?—stands a good chance of making a recovery."

"That's what they tell me, Herr Feldmarschall." Carl-Heinz said. "We took a direct hit from a field artillery piece . . . destroyed the turret of our Panther. But by then, the battle was won."

"Good work. Now, to the reason I have called you here. I have need of a driver, and your reputation is very sound. I would like to attach you to my headquarters in that role. It will carry a promotion to feldwebel."

"I'd be honored," Carl-Heinz replied. "I'll take good care of the vehicle, sir—and the passengers, too, of course."

The Desert Fox laughed. "I need a good man, one who can offer me some help." He grimaced, touched the cheekbone that was still sore—though, thankfully, at last free of the eye patch that he once thought he'd have to wear for the rest of his life. "In truth, I do not move so well, but I believe it is important for a commander to see things—and to be seen by his troops. Therefore, your assignment will involve many hours on the road, as well as a high level of discretion regarding my infirmities."

He could see the honest sympathy on the man's face. "Certainly, Field Marshal. Sir—I'm pretty handy around a tool box, and I think I can whip up a few things that might make your life a little easier, if you'd like, sir."

"Well, Feldwebel Clausen, I certainly would like. I'm in your capable hands," replied Rommel, content with yet another command decision. This one, he thought, might turn out to be one of his best yet.

That night Carl-Heinz gathered his kit in the replacement barracks. *Personal driver to the Desert Fox—my, wouldn't Yetta and the kids be proud!* Events had started, of course, when he had bumped into the photographer on the street late in the morning of this same day. Von Esebeck had recognized him immediately and had asked him about events in his life since that now-famous photograph. Apparently the baron had been to see Rommel later in the afternoon.

Carl-Heinz had been idle for the last few weeks, as useless as a piston without an engine block. Of course, here in Trier he had been able to visit Ulrich Pfeiffer in the hospital, and he had written Yetta every day—and, even more miraculous, received her replies in a timely fashion. Waiting for his new assignment, he had watched new tanks arrive, including the massive Tigers—which seemed like clumsy behemoths to Clausen—and more Panthers than he had imagined Germany's factories could produce.

They were good tanks. He could remember his Panther rolling through the field full of burning Shermans, each marked with a white star in a crimson field he had later learned denoted them as one of Patton's spearhead units. Fritzi and Pelz in the turret, loading and firing round after round, watching the surviving American tanks flee in disorder . . . destroying them one after another as they raced for the shelter of the woods overlooking Abbeville.

The shell that had struck their Panther had come from nowhere, seemingly—though that wasn't possible, wasn't even conceivable for a force that had struck them with such profound and irrevocable power. Concussion had knocked the big panzer across the ground, and somehow, in the thickness of smoke and fire, Carl-Heinz had thrown open the driver's hatch and scrambled out. He remembered his shock as he looked back, realizing that the turret was completely gone. And with it had gone Fritzi and Pelz, two men who had lived and fought with Carl-Heinz for the last four years. Good men. Their loss saddened him.

And then he had noticed the faint movement, the vibration of the radioman's hatch. Pfeiffer, his chest torn by a shard of shrapnel, had pushed once, and then his strength had failed. Clausen had scrambled back onto the burning hull and torn the hatch back so hard that he had twisted a hinge. Ulrich was lying there, unconscious and covered in blood, and Carl-Heinz had somehow pulled him out and dragged him away before the Panther had been totally consumed by oily flame.

That evening he went to see Pfeiffer in the hospital, knowing that his new duties might put an end to these previously daily visits.

"Never mind about me," Ulrich had said, his voice firming up despite the bandages that still encircled his chest. "I guess I'm going to make it, one way or another. You know, I never thought I'd live through this war. I owe you my life, my friend."

"Don't worry about it," Carl-Heinz replied, "You'd have probably gotten yourself out anyway. If it bothers you, buy me a beer when you get out of this place—before you go back home, you lucky bastard."

The wounded man shook his head firmly. "Yeah, lucky, that's me. But you . . . be careful, Carl-Heinz. There's a lot of this war yet to be fought, and you've gotten yourself right back into the middle of it."

"Don't worry—I'll be driving the Desert Fox around. And we all know he leads a charmed life!"

"I hope you're right," Ulrich said, his eyes shining with melancholy. "You're too good a man to be killed."

"You're right about that," Carl-Heinz laughed. "Or is it the other way around? Only the good die young, so you and I, we're both safe as houses. Besides, I promised Yetta I'd come home; and if I don't, she'll kill me, you know."

"Seriously," Ulrich said. "Be careful."

"I'm always careful," replied Carl-Heinz with a toothy grin.

Broadcast House, Berlin, Germany,
22 September 1944, 2100 hours GMT

"This is Broadcast House, Berlin, interrupting our regularly scheduled program for a message from our führer."

The announcer in the booth pointed a finger at Heinrich Himmler, who sat on a stool, his speech displayed before him on a music stand.

"Men and women of Germany," he began. "Tonight I speak to you with a heavy heart, on a subject I had hoped to avoid. As you know, only a few short months ago, cowardly British spies assassinated our beloved führer, Adolf Hitler. Those responsible were arrested, given a fair trial, and subsequently executed." He adjusted his glasses over his watery eyes, and continued.

"I speak to you today so you might hear my voice and know that I am unhurt and well, in spite of the fact that I have only just escaped harm at the hands of the remnants of that small gang of criminal elements."

The elderly officer was alone, shuffling along the Wilhelmstrasse with the slight stoop of an old man, making his way on foot from the War Ministry to his apartment in the staff compound. He took no notice of the Mercedes that rumbled quietly along the street, then glided gently to the curb behind him.

"General!" Bücher stepped out of the car and spoke sharply, knowing that General Röwekamp would spin about indignantly.

When he did, Bücher shot him in the belly, and then again, in the throat. He stood over the man, watching him choke around his blood, straining for a last breath that would never come.

"You fancied yourself a leader, did you not?" he questioned the dying man. "Well, now it is your turn to lead many of your precious General Staff into death."

Röwekamp was not yet dead when Bücher reentered the car and gestured to his SS driver to pull away from the curb and turn at the next corner. Behind the car, the dying general's hand clutched at empty air, while in the backseat Bücher was already double-checking the next name on his list. He listened to the radio broadcast as the car drove on.

"It was clear at the time that the British assassins received aid from a small clique of ambitious, unscrupulous, criminal, and stupid officers, kin to those anonymous cowards who stabbed the German army in the back in 1918. Some of those officers were quickly identified and received the just and appropriate fate such treasonous activities so richly deserved."

"We knew there were others associated with that small clique, not directly involved in the assassination itself, but rather a few weak-minded, defeatist, envious second raters who were too incompetent to pose any threat to the German people and its leaders. Knowing full well that a thorough investigation would necessarily bring dishonor on the sterling reputation of our brave and gallant officers of the Wehrmacht, who have nothing in common with the black deeds of those small and stupid traitors, we elected to do nothing that might interfere with the war effort. We believed that these little ratlike cowards would scurry back into their holes and their incompetence would render them harmless."

"Tonight, unfortunately, we have discovered otherwise. Rats and cowards are not themselves dangerous, but when they become the tools and accomplices of enemy spies, they have the power to wreak untold harm. I have escaped, yes. But others have not been so fortunate."

General Friedrich Fromm, head of the Replacement Army and von Stauffenberg's commanding officer, was relieved that he had, so far, escaped any implication in the coup. As soon as he realized that the conspiracy was destined to fail, he had arrested all the plotters under his command and had them shot on his own initiative, then called on Himmler personally to pledge his loyalty. He knew that he could not escape all suspicion, since the assassin had been on his own senior staff, but he hoped by demonstrating his loyalty so aggressively, he could at least save his skin.

Tonight, he and several of his comrades, including Colonel General Erich Hoepner, were enjoying a rare evening out in a small biergarten located where one of the nastier Weimar cabarets once reigned. Still in a more-patriotic-than-thou move, he hoisted his stein and shouted, "To the führer!" for the fourth time that night. The crowd in the smoky bar cheered and drank with him.

Then the door suddenly burst open. Fromm looked up—*British* uniforms? That was his last thought before the commandos aimed their weapons, spraying his table with machine gun fire. He saw Hoepner go down before the bullets knocked him backward; his beer stein spilled over himself, and as his blood ran red on the sawdust floor the screams of the crowd echoed in his ears.

"An airdrop of British commandos landed in Berlin only two hours ago. They have all been killed by SS troops, but not before they managed to assassinate several German officers, including General Friedrich Fromm."

The use of the British uniforms was a good touch, Bücher thought. Himmler had a good mind for this sort of thing. And with numerous witnesses, the story would spread all over Germany. The time discrepancy could be easily ignored with good media control.

"Even now, officers of the Gestapo are arresting the remaining collaborators. These criminals and traitors will be punished for their crimes in a manner to which we National Socialists are well accustomed."

.   .   .

A knock came at the door of the home of the Berlin police president. Sleepily, the maid opened the door and three Gestapo officers pushed inside. "Wolf Heinrich von Helldorf?" they demanded.

"Up-upstairs," stammered the maid, pointing toward the staircase.

Up the stairs rushed the agents, pushed open the bedroom door, and ran inside.

"Wh-what is it?" mumbled the sleeping woman. Then she woke, and screamed.

Her husband opened his eyes. "Yes?" he asked, thinking it was his own police officers.

"You are under arrest for treason, Police President," the chief Gestapo officer said.

Von Helldorf took a deep sigh. His moment was here at last. He had hoped to live to fight another day, but that day would not come. "Just let me get my glasses," he said, and reached toward the nightstand. Instead of glasses he produced a Luger, and shot one officer through the heart. Three bullets slammed into him a moment later and his wife screamed as she watched his blood pour out onto the carpet.

For a moment, the Gestapo second in command contemplated shooting the wife as well, but decided not to. She would spread the story, and hopefully in the process flush out still more traitors.

"Shortly, I will report to you on the final fate of all those who fail our Fatherland in its moment of greatest need. In the meantime, let me assure you that the Reich remains strong, our soldiers valiant, our will unbreakable, and our destiny certain. With our enemy to the east having sued for peace, our enemy in the west will shortly be destroyed under the brilliant leadership of the German military, the finest the world has ever known. And our place in the sun will be forever secure.

"Thank you and good night."

Army Group B Headquarters, Trier, Germany, 23 September 1944, 0500 hours GMT

Carl-Heinz Clausen ignored politics, for the most part. People, in his opinion, made things unnecessarily complex, and he had trouble understanding why people would behave so badly when it was obviously unnecessary. Machinery he understood, systems he understood, so he confined himself to his job while all about him people buzzed about the Himmler speech and its aftermath. He couldn't avoid hearing all the rumors—Wehrmacht officers shot by the SS, another Nazi purge like the infamous "Night of the Long Knives." This person had been arrested, that person had been killed, this person was in the conspiracy, that person was not a conspirator, the British were behind it, the Americans were behind it, high party officials were behind it—how could anyone keep it straight?

There were rumors that Field Marshal Rommel himself had been incriminated, but that made no sense whatsoever. Still, Carl-Heinz had learned that many things involving politics made no sense whatsoever, so he kept a special eye out for his new commander.

He'd quickly grown into his role of driver, batman, protector, and even—Rommel joked—mother hen. It was obvious that the Desert Fox still hurt from his injuries, and that he was determined to overcome his pain and his limitations. That part Carl-Heinz understood, and he quickly assumed the role of valet and personal trainer in addition to official driver. He was the only person present when Rommel woke in the morning from a fitful night of pained sleep, having once again refused the pain medication the doctors had prescribed. Rommel would then get down on the floor for a rigorous set of push-ups and sit-ups that sent his body into spasms of agony, the sweat pouring down his face and chest, forcing himself to grow strong again, pushing himself past any human limits. Carl-Heinz was the only person other than the doctors who saw the still-red scars, the terrible evidence of his injuries. His rough, thick fingered hands, stained with grease, clenched in sympathetic pain, but Carl-Heinz understood the process of mending machinery, and knelt beside the field marshal to provide support.

Carl-Heinz spent his off-time scrounging materials to help his commander become more comfortable. He built a special chair to take the pressure off sensitive points, allowing Rommel to work more hours with greater comfort, he built a harness for the field telephone to keep the pressure off the field marshal's face, and constructed a sculpted and specially supported mattress to ease the pressures of sleeping. He did the same sorts of things for Pfeiffer in the hospital; he made no important distinction between the two men. He could help, therefore he did help.

The official duties of his job were few at the beginning. Rommel was primarily involved in affairs of headquarters, and needed little driving. But Carl-Heinz showed up early each morning before the Desert Fox awoke, got him ready for his day, then went to see Pfeiffer in the hospital, then spent the afternoon building his latest inspirations. A few hours off late in the day, then another visit to Pfeiffer and then to help the Desert Fox into bed for the few hours of sleep the man permitted himself.

About a week into his new duties, a staff captain greeted him as he entered Rommel's quarters. Everyone on Rommel's staff recognized the role Carl-Heinz had assumed, and was grateful for it. "Good morning, Feldwebel!"

"Morning, Captain," Clausen replied with a big smile.

"Better go back and pack a bag. You and the field marshal are going to Berlin today!"

Berlin. That was interesting. He'd never been to the capital, but then he had little use for cities under the best of circumstances. Still, it would be a long drive, and he'd made a few modifications to Rommel's seat in the back of the long Mercedes staff car, and he was eager to see how the field marshal would react.

He got back in less than fifteen minutes and went in to help the field marshal exercise and dress.

"We're going to visit the führer today," Rommel grunted as he struggled with his final push-up of the morning.

"Forty-nine . . . that's fifty! Up ten this week, Herr Feldmarschall," he said. "Good work!" If there was anything odd about a feldwebel praising a field marshal's performance, neither man noticed it. Clausen handed Rommel a towel to mop up the sweat. "By the way, sir, let me know what you think of your new seat today."

"Clausen, my man, you are a true miracle," laughed the field marshal through the pain of his sorely stretched muscles. "You're worth at least three divisions all by yourself."

Clausen waited just outside the open door of Rommel's office as the field marshal talked to two men Carl-Heinz recognized as Generals Speidel and Bayerlein.

"Do you think visiting Berlin is wise right now?" Speidel was asking

Rommel shrugged. "No, I don't. But it's necessary. Without the full use of those trains, the Allies are increasing their strength along the front faster than we are. Once again, it's a question of numbers—and the odds are already slanted because we have lost control of the skies."

"But you said last night that Aachen was holding out better than could be expected," the chief of staff noted.

"It can't last forever, and you know we've put every reinforcement there. What will happen when Patton gets through—or around—Metz? Or when Montgomery decides to act? You know as well as I do that we need men, and tanks, all along the line."

"Do you think you can do any better with Himmler than Bücher did?" Speidel continued. Carl-Heinz knew that the SS man had arrived back at the front HQ the night before.

"I have to try, and this is the best chance for me to get away, now that things have stabilized here for a short time."

"Here, perhaps. But in Berlin things seem far from stable," countered the chief of staff.

Rommel shook his head, a stubborn expression that reminded Carl-Heinz of a bulldog. "If I'm in danger, I'm in danger. Himmler knows where I am, after all, as do, I'm sure, the British and Americans. I can be arrested or shot almost anywhere. It's not as if I'm in shape to run very fast," he said ruefully.

"Do you plan to drive?" Bayerlein asked, inclining his head toward Carl-Heinz.

"Only as far as Köln—I want to inspect some of the positions in the Ardennes and around Aachen. From the Rhine, Clausen will accompany me on the train. The rest of you continue preparations for the Allied attack. It cannot be far away."

An hour later, Carl-Heinz was guiding the staff car along the highway north out of Trier. The field marshal had already drifted off to sleep in the newly engineered back seat, after praising Clausen's ingenuity lavishly. Clausen took care to accelerate gradually, even so.

Daylight came beneath a cloak of gray, and to Clausen—as to every other German soldier on the western front—this was just fine. He drove easily, allowing the big car to rumble over the bridge spanning a lofty gorge, then gently pressing down the accelerator as he began to climb into the steep hills of the Ardennes. He listened to the hum of the powerful engine, focusing his attention on a subtle squeak in the right front end. The bearings needed grease . . . he would take care of that in the motor pool at whichever unit they stopped, for what was sure to be a brief overnight rest.

They began descending the farside of the ridge when the driver's eyes, long attuned to roaming the skies, caught sight of a metallic flash sweeping underneath the cloud cover. At the same time, the Jabo banked, and Carl-Heinz knew that the car had been noticed. He stepped on the gas, felt the powerful vehicle lurch forward, careening down the narrow mountain road. A series of switchbacks lay just ahead, and he entered the first sharp curve with as much speed as he dared, skidding in a cloud of gravel and dust, careening perilously close to the edge.

But the wheels held, and he accelerated again, racing along a straight descent toward the next curve. He glanced in the mirror to see the plane diving closer, also that Rommel was awake and staring out the back window.

Carl-Heinz put the car into the next curve with reckless abandon, feeling the vehicle lurch sickeningly on the loose pavement—though at least this time they were skidding toward the uphill edge of the slope, not the precipitous drop beyond an outer curve. With a light step on the brakes, then a vigorous stomp on the accelerator, he pulled the machine through the turn without a loss of control. The stutter of machine gun fire sent a burst of adrenaline through his system, and he saw the dusty marks of the bullets striking the road a dozen meters behind them.

But now the curve worked to his advantage, for the aircraft had to pull up and wheel about before it could fire again. Clausen raced down the road, seeking some avenue of escape to either side. He saw it as they raced past—a tiny lane cut into the uphill side of the road, winding in between a thick growth of evergreens. Braking hard, he brought the car to a halt, then backed up in a spray of gravel and whirling tires.

In seconds he was adjacent to the lane, and he turned the car off the road, ignoring the branches that scraped along both sides of the big vehicle. They lurched over the rough surface and he winced at the thought of Rommel, undoubtedly still hampered by lingering pain, thrown so roughly about. But he didn't slow down, not even when the fender crashed into a tree trunk and crumpled back.

He finally came to a stop under a dense canopy of evergreens, and more bullets tore through the woods as the plane snarled past. But now the shots were random—clearly the pilot had seen where he had disappeared, but couldn't spot where exactly he had gone. Shutting the engine off, he listened, and a few minutes later the sounds of the aircraft engine droned away.

"I'm sorry about the rough ride, Herr Feldmarschall," he said apologetically, turning to see that Rommel was dusting himself off and leaning to look out the window.

"Well done, Carl-Heinz. This is much better than the last encounter I had with an airplane while in a car," said the great man with a laugh. "I heartily approve of your tactics. Once again, the Allies have failed to get me."

His expression turned wry. "Now let's see if we have the same kind of luck in Berlin. . . ."

Rockefeller Center, New York, United States, 0500 hours GMT

"Goddamn! At last!" Chuck Porter swiveled his chair around to look at the cavernous newsroom. In the middle of the night shift, most of the desks were deserted; a few cigarette-smoking reporters typed in a desultory fashion, three or four gossiped in the corner by the water cooler, one leaned across a desk reading a story as the other typed it. Heads looked toward him as his shout echoed on the floor.

Porter stood up, waving a memo over his head like a boxer self-congratulating his victory. "I'm outta here!" he shouted gleefully. "Next stop, jolly ol' England! My transfer was accepted!" He'd put in for the transfer four times in the past year and had been turned down each time. "Too valuable at the national desk" he heard over and over again.

"Son of a bitch," growled one of the night shift editors, half pleased, half in disgust. "Well, at least you'll be there for the last three or four weeks of the war."

"Yeah, and then I'll be heading into Berlin to cover the surrender," he replied smugly. "While you guys still play with blue pencils."

"We'll need them when your stuff comes in over the wire, Chuck," jibed Harry, the international desk editor, to the cynical laughter of the other reporters.

"Yeah—we'll keep up our proud motto: 'No reporter's word goes unchanged!'" Everyone laughed.

"So, Chuck, when are you leaving?" another editor asked.

"In a couple of weeks. Just as soon as they can arrange transport." He glanced over toward the switchboard, where Tricia's head was furiously turned away. *Hell,* he thought, but that was the way it went sometimes.

It was another quiet Thursday, and the newsroom had turned to gossip and some political chat. Nothing much was happening—until the four bell "Flash" signal began to ring. Porter beat everyone to the chattering Teletype.

FLASH/BULLETIN
LONDON, 25 SEPTEMBER, 0530 GMT
COPY 01 HIMMLER REPEATS NIGHT OF THE LONG KNIVES
DISTRIBUTION: ALL STATIONS

LONDON, 25 SEPTEMBER (AP) BY EDWARD REED
INTELLIGENCE SOURCES CONFIRM THAT A SERIES OF BRUTAL KILLINGS OF
GERMAN MILITARY AND POLITICAL LEADERS BELIEVED TO HAVE BEEN IN-
VOLVED IN THE COUP ATTEMPT THAT RESULTED IN THE DEATH OF ADOLF
HITLER IS TAKING PLACE IN AND AROUND BERLIN. ALLIED INTELLIGENCE BE-
LIEVES THAT THESE KILLINGS HAVE BEEN DIRECTLY ORDERED BY NAZI CHIEF
HIMMLER, ALTHOUGH BERLIN IS PUTTING OUT THE PROPAGANDA STORY
THAT THERE HAVE BEEN A FEW ARRESTS ONLY.

    IT IS UNCLEAR WHETHER ANY ALLIED DOUBLE AGENTS OR SPIES HAVE
BEEN ARRESTED OR KILLED IN THIS ATTEMPT.

    IN A RADIO SPEECH TODAY, HIMMLER CLAIMED TO HAVE JUST SURVIVED
AN ASSASSINATION ATTEMPT BY COUP PLOTTERS, WHOM HE DESCRIBED AS
"A SMALL GANG OF CRIMINAL ELEMENTS." HIMMLER ACCUSED "ENEMY
SPIES" AND "BRITISH COMMANDOS" OF HAVING SUPPORTED THE ATTEMPT.
THE KNOWN DEAD INCLUDE THE HEAD OF THE GERMAN REPLACEMENT
ARMY, GENERAL FROMM, WHO WAS THE COMMANDER OF COLONEL STAUF-
FENBERG, THE ASSASSIN OF ADOLF HITLER, AS WELL AS THE BERLIN CHIEF
OF POLICE.

    GENERAL EISENHOWER HAS DENIED ANY ALLIED ROLE IN ANY CURRENT
PLOT AGAINST HIMMLER, STATING, "THIS STRIKES US AS THE EVIL POSTURING
OF THE LATEST NAZI MADMAN TRYING TO CONSOLIDATE HIS POLITICAL

POWER IN A DYING GERMANY." HE STATED THAT NO CHANGE IN ALLIED WAR
PLANS WAS LIKELY TO RESULT FROM THIS SITUATION.

    CHURCHILL STATED, "WE ARE ALWAYS PLEASED TO SEE NAZIS KILLING
NAZIS, WHATEVER THE REASON," AND DENIED THAT BRITISH COMMANDOS
OR ANY OTHER BRITISH UNITS CARRIED OUT ANY ASSASSINATIONS IN OR
NEAR BERLIN.

MORE

AP-LON-333548-JF/092544

"I'll bet Ike and Churchill are lying on this one," Porter said, tipping a long ash into the metal ashtray perched precariously on the edge of the Teletype machine.

"Oh, yeah?" challenged Harry. "What makes you so damn sure?"

"The Himmler government is probably holding on by the skin of its teeth," explained Porter, taking a swallow of old coffee that had gone cold. "Churchill and Ike know it, see, and so they're going to give it a little push here and a little push there, and *bang!*"—he hit the table with his hand for emphasis—"no more Nazi government and the war's over by Christmas. I bet they're deep in negotiations with a shadow German government right now, ready to roll in and replace the Nazis as soon as the Himmler government collapses."

"I don't think so," said Harry flatly. "I think Himmler's got solid control of the government and the military. The SS is loyal to him personally, and this deal with Stalin made him look pretty good to the military as well. I think he's going to try to win one big battle with the Allies, then sue for peace on the grounds that Uncle Joe is worse than he is, and he might be right."

"Wrong!" replied Porter with complete conviction, using his index finger to punctuate his points. "One, there would never be a surrender deal. Churchill and Roosevelt won't permit it. Two, they aren't going to win a big battle. Three, Uncle Joe will be back in the war in a few months; he just needed a rest and now the German eastern front is empty. He owes them a double-cross, and he picks up a couple of extra countries on the way. Which, by the way, he'll have to give up. He needs our Lend Lease too much."

"Hey, that 'unconditional surrender' stuff was mostly designed to keep Joe happy. Now that he's out—and he's burned that bridge behind him once and for all—it's a new ball game. Himmler's an S.O.B., but he's not dumb, and I've gotta tell you, this one may surprise you."

"That's a load of baloney," Porter replied, "and when I get to London, I'll do a little digging around and I'll show you I'm right, and it'll come right over this Teletype. Count on it."

Reichstag, Berlin, Germany,
24 September 1944, 1030 hours GMT

"My dear field marshal!" Himmler got up from his chair and came around the desk to pump Rommel's hand. He moved with precision, his black uniform like a shadow on the man's pale skin. His teeth flashed, weird brightness above the shade. "It is splendid to see you moving around so well. All Germany must rejoice at the news that your health is so quickly restored!"

"Thank you, mein Führer. My doctors have been excellent, and I was fortunate that the wounds were not more serious."

"Nonsense! From what I hear, any other man would have been killed. You owe it to your own strength—as do we all. But again, I believe I speak for all our countrymen when I state that I am grateful you are making such as a successful recovery."

Rommel sized up the man who was the new dictator of Germany. He had no stomach for this small talk—and in fact, he felt considerably less hale than he looked. His head throbbed, and though he no longer had the patch on his eye, he was acutely sensitive to bright light. He walked without limping and stood straight, but the effort invariably made him tired and irritated.

Upon his arrival in Berlin he had confirmed the rumors that had reached the front headquarters. This man had just ordered the murder of at least a dozen senior Wehrmacht officers. Some had apparently been part of the von Stauffenberg conspiracy, while others—who could worry about poor old Röwekamp?—must have been merely slain as examples to the rest of the army. The Desert Fox couldn't help wondering if his own name would soon find its way onto that list.

Consequently, it was all that he could do to be civil to this Nazi, but he resolved to continue in that vein. Again he reminded himself that his job was the most important thing, for by holding it he could continue to save German lives.

"Please, make yourself comfortable," Himmler was saying, gesturing him to a soft armchair beside a grand marble fireplace. "As you know, I am not fond of spirits, but can I offer you some tea?"

"Yes, thank you." Rommel fidgeted, finding a comfortable position in the chair while the refreshments were brought by two black-clad SS stewards. When the servants had withdrawn, Himmler took a careful sip of his tea, then set the cup down with delicate, precise movements. He looked expectantly at the field marshal.

"Mein Führer—" the official title stuck in his throat, "I shall come right to the point. The armistice with the Soviet Union has created hope where, in all frankness, previously there was only room for despair. I do believe that the Allies can be held, at least for a time, at the Westwall. Though the fortifications are not complete, and our troops are lacking in material, their spirit is strong, and the terrain of our western border naturally lends itself to the defense."

"This is the analysis of myself, and the other experts I have consulted," Himmler agreed. "I believe that you were correct to withdraw from France as you did."

Rommel blinked, surprised by the words, but determined not to be put off from his point.

"You must realize that it is not enough merely to hold the line of the Westwall. Right now, the Americans are pulling up to the border in a series of spearheads, some of which are dangerously overextended. If I were to have a greater availability of offensive forces, particularly panzer divisions, it would be possible to deliver a sharp setback to these advances. The minor victory at Abbeville could be duplicated on a corps, perhaps even an army, scale!"

Himmler nodded, allowing a tiny smile to crease his lips. "You know, of course, that I have directed all the available armor forces from the east to be shifted to your command at the earliest possible moment."

"Indeed, Führer, I know of your orders. However, as usual, the devil is in the details. Given the current system of allocations, we lack the rail capacity to move more than a fraction of these troops at a time. I ask you to release the locomotives and rolling stock from the control of the Gestapo, and allow it to be used in this great transfer. I assure you that we could swiftly bring a powerful armor force, the equivalent of at least two panzerarmees, into the line on the western front."

"I understand your problem," Himmler began. "However, the trains allocated to the Gestapo are engaged in activities of great import to the future of the Fatherland. I am unable to release them for military purposes yet. Perhaps later, when their great task is done, they shall become available."

"But mein Führer, that will be too late! The opportunity for our attack is now, and the odds against us increase with every passing day. If we can make this transfer of troops with all haste, it might be possible to push back the spearheads closing on Aachen, even to reinforce the outposts at Metz, or in the Vosges Mountains!"

"There is nothing to be done about that," Himmler said, his tone ominously gentle. "I suggest we move the discussion to other aspects of the campaign."

"Such as?" Rommel knew his voice was cold, but he couldn't help it—or perhaps, he didn't want to help it.

"You mentioned Metz. I have heard that the Seven Korps is showing signs of weakening. Surely you can see that the city must be held at all costs!"

The Desert Fox was immediately, and forcefully, reminded of the previous dictator . . . this sounded exactly like a "Hitler edict." It was always "Stand and die"—at El Alamein, in Tunisia, in the hedgerows of Normandy, everywhere—and died they did.

"It is an impossible task!" he snapped, more sternly than he ever would have spoken to the previous führer. "Patton's men are pushing north and south of the city. If we don't withdraw, the entire Korps will be encircled—and captured. Do you want another Stalingrad?"

"Metz must hold!" Himmler retorted "It is key to my future plans on the front, to the activities that will commence when you *do* get your reinforcements—which, as I assured you, will be forthcoming."

Rommel wanted to insist that this was a ludicrous statement, that the city didn't stand a chance of holding out even for another month. But caution prevailed, and he bit his tongue, asking instead: "What plans are these you speak of?"

"The time will come where you will not be able to rest on the defensive. You will have to attack, and with such strength that the course of the campaign is reversed. For the time being, I want you to keep that thought in the back of your mind. Consider the possibilities, the objectives of an attack, if you were given sufficient forces to attack any realistic goal."

"It's not just the number of tanks on the ground that matters! There are two critical problems. The first is oil. While the armistice with the Soviet Union was clearly necessary, losing our supplies of Rumanian oil is a crippling handicap. It's true that we already had troubles in that area because of the Allied bombing campaign against the Ploesti oil fields, but now we're cut off completely. The second problem is equally serious. Surely you realize the effect of enemy air power? Even if we manage a breakthrough, a *Schwerpunkt,* our armor would be shattered by the Allied air forces!"

"Now please, my Field Marshal, I sense your frustration. But try to understand my position, which as you understand is also the position of your Fatherland," said the new master of Germany in a conciliatory tone, which surprised Rommel. He placed his fingertips together to form a steeple before continuing. "You've given me a thoughtful analysis, and I, too, share many of your concerns. Perhaps I can be of assistance with these two issues. First, the oil. I'm not sure that we are in fact cut off from oil supplies. Our new friends in the east have a need for hard currency and perhaps we can work something out. Let me see what I can accomplish on that front. What I would like from you is a sense of what you might accomplish given at least a single major influx of oil.

"Second, air power. It may be that I can offer you a morsel of hope. On your way back to the west, I would like you to go through Augsburg, to the airbase at Lager-Lechfeld, specifically. There, you should seek out General Galland of the Luftwaffe. I will inform him that you will be coming.

"I suspect that he can show you something that will change some of your most cherished opinions."

Lager-Lechfeld Luftwaffe Base, Bavaria, Germany, 1320 hours GMT

Krueger got out of the car and returned the salute of the guard outside of General Galland's headquarters. The pilot's step was light, for he knew that he brought good news . . . news that would ensure that the Luftwaffe would soon be in a position to strike the Allied Air Force a devastating blow.

"Ah, Colonel . . . how went your visit to Dessau?" asked the Luftwaffe commander, putting down his cigar and rising from behind his desk, which was strewn with blueprints, production figures, and maps.

"I can assure you that engine production should be undergoing a steady improvement," replied the fighter pilot.

"Splendid—I knew I could count on you!" Galland apparently decided not to inquire too closely about methods.

"And how fares the preparation of the *Geschwader?*" Krueger gestured out the window toward the row of jets he had seen on the field. He knew that here at Lager-Lechfeld, Galland was preparing the first all-jet fighter formation in the world.

"Coming together nicely," the general replied. "Here, let me show you."

An hour later, Krueger was standing in the great hangar, looking at an Me-262 that had been freshly delivered from the factory. The engines had been installed only the day before, and though they had been test-fired, the craft had not yet been airborne.

"How do you like her?" asked the general around a crooked grin.

"She's beautiful," Krueger acknowledged, struck as always by the clean lines of the fighter, the low-slung engines looking sleek and supernatural under the swept-back wings. The aircraft looked wickedly capable, and he felt again the almost unbearable compulsion to take it into the sky.

"She's the command craft of Geschwader 51," Galland said. "That is, your group, Kommodore."

"Thank you, General!" Krueger declared. He was genuinely pleased. This was more than he had expected. Unique to the Luftwaffe, the rank of kommodore meant that he was now master of three fighter Gruppe—nine *Staffeln,* or something like eighty aircraft. He looked at the row of jet fighters, more than a dozen for starters, lined up in the hangar and swore to himself that his unit would soon become a terror of the skies. "When will we be operational?"

"You already have the pilots, and these twelve planes. Additional aircraft are coming, several a day . . . though you're to complete training on the machines you have."

"And when do we move against the Americans?"

"Only when I give the word, not before. You can wait, I trust?"

"With difficulty," Krueger admitted, while his mind whirled with the prospects of the new post. A full Geschwader of fighters under his command!

"Perhaps you would like some marking, some notation to mark her as your own," suggested the general.

"I know just the thing," Krueger agreed.

Soon he was speaking to a young feldwebel, a man he had been assured was skilled with the paintbrush. "I want a flame motif here, along both sides of the nose," Colonel Krueger explained, marking the sweep of fiery tendrils with a gesture of his fingers. "I want this to be a visible symbol that is burned into the eyeballs of every bomber pilot who sees them."

"I understand, Herr Oberst."

By the time he had finished inspecting the other airplanes and meeting the pilots of his group, the artist was done. Krueger came back to his Schwalbe and admired the work.

"Yes, indeed," he mused. "This is an image suitable for escorting dying Americans all the way to hell."

Lager-Lechfeld Luftwaffe Base, Bavaria, Germany, 25 September 1944, 1525 hours GMT

"Pull around there," Rommel directed, and Carl-Heinz drove the big car up to the side of the big hangar. The mood of the meeting with Himmler, just the day before, was still a drain on the field marshal's spirits. He was frustrated, sour, and more than a little afraid—though not, of course, for himself. Instead, he was again suffering that old, familiar anxiety, the fear for the future of his country.

He couldn't shake his lingering sense of depression, the feeling that everything they did was hopeless, inevitably leading to death and defeat. Even the armistice with the USSR, which had seemed to offer such promise, now appeared little more than an opportunity for Stalin to grab all of Europe while the Germans and Anglo Allies—peoples who had more in common with each other than either did with the Slavic Communists—battered each other bloody in a pointless continuation of the war.

Still, at Himmler's urging he had agreed to take this detour on his return to the front. He didn't know why, didn't believe a Luftwaffe general could show him anything that would change his orders. Still, the new führer had been most insistent, and this base near Augsburg was more or less on the way back to Trier.

Now he got out of the car, grateful for Carl-Heinz's supporting arm. He took a moment to stretch and looked around at the huge airfield. There was evidence of new and hurried construction, the stumps of trees surrounding open fields.

"Ah, there you are, Field Marshall!" Accompanied by a waft of cigar smoke, a Luftwaffe general came around the corner of the building. "Our esteemed führer informed me that you would be paying us a visit."

Though the two men had never met, Rommel recognized Adolf Galland. He nodded pleasantly, then politely declined the cigar that the airman offered. "I hope you have not gone to any trouble. In truth, I do not fully understand why my visit here should be judged important."

"No trouble, no trouble at all. But come, allow me to get you seated."

Galland led the way past the front of the hangar to a small outdoor enclosure, a patio not unlike a Bavarian biergarten, where several tables, shaded by broad umbrellas, had been placed before the command building. Although he was a trifle surprised that they would not be meeting inside, the Desert Fox gratefully accepted a chair and a glass of iced tea. Enjoying the sense of mystery, Galland sat down beside him and took visible pleasure in snipping the tip off of another cigar.

"Now, I understand that the tactical situation of our ground forces is greatly hampered by the enemy's command of the air," began the commander of fighter forces.

"You might say that," Rommel agreed, voice heavy on the irony.

Galland laughed. "Forgive me," he said. "I don't mean to be flippant. In truth, it breaks my heart to see the way the German air forces have been driven from the sky over the battlefield. To think that we pioneered the use of close tactical support of our ground forces, only to have that strength preempted by our powerful enemy—and his almost unimaginable industrial capabilities."

"Indeed." Rommel liked Galland at once. This was another man who was not a politician, but rather a warrior at heart. He decided to speak frankly. "It is that capacity which has doomed our army to inevitable defeat. Try as we might, our panzers are helpless under the all-seeing eyes of the enemy air forces. That is why we cannot win this war."

"If we have no superiority in the air, you're completely correct, Field Marshal," Galland said breezily. "But what if things were to change? What if we were able to recapture, or at the very least, hotly contest our enemy's control of the skies?"

Rommel allowed himself a wry chuckle. "And if my panzers had wings, they, too, could fly."

It was Galland's turn to laugh. "Now there's an idea. But let me show you the next best thing. Wait just a few moments."

The Desert Fox heard a sound. It was a dull roaring, a distant wind that swiftly expanded to a growing howl. Observing Galland's calm smile, he felt certain that nothing was amiss but allowed his eyes to turn toward the southern sky, where the rolling green foothills of Bavaria formed a fairly close horizon. His eyes focused on a ridge line, where lofty pines waved against the sky.

Rommel's curiosity was piqued. This must be why Himmler had sent him here. Another of the Nazi "secret weapons"—but this man Galland thought he had something, and Galland did not seem the sort of man to be easily impressed.

The sound abruptly peaked at a piercing shriek, and at the same time a dozen streaking shapes exploded into view. These were aircraft, he knew, but like no other planes he had ever seen.

Holding a tight formation, flying at perhaps two hundred meters over the field, the twelve planes swept toward the airbase. In a blinding, deafening instant they were overhead, and then as quickly past, shrinking with impossible speed into the distance. Rommel watched in amazement as the formation scattered, four to left, four to the right, while the middle four to all appearances rocketed straight up into the air, shooting away from the ground in a gravity-defying ascent that seemed to defy all logic, everything the Desert Fox had come to understand about airplanes.

He looked more carefully as the formation reunited and made another pass, this time at more like six hundred meters of altitude. Now he could see that these were twin-engined craft, though there was none of the growling snarl that he associated with unmuffled gasoline engines and spinning propellers. Instead, there seemed to be trails of flame spilling from each engine, and these became visible as circles of incredible heat as the fighters gradually climbed into the sky.

"The world—and this includes the American Air Forces—has never seen anything like them before," Galland said, with no attempt to conceal his extreme pride. "And we are keeping them secret, but only for a little while longer."

"These are the Me-262 fighter aircraft," Rommel said, certain of his judgment. He was aware of the development program in general terms, though he'd never seen one of the craft before.

"Indeed."

"But will we have them in numbers, sufficient to make a difference?" he asked.

"That is part of my plan," Galland replied. "We are holding them back, gathering a number of Gruppen—including a full Geschwader right here—at Luftwaffe bases throughout Germany. Soon, the time will be right. The Americans will send their bombers into the heart of our country and be met with quite a surprise . . . and once again we will have a realistic chance of gaining control of the sky. At least for a period of time. A long enough period of time for the Desert Fox to change a few things on the ground, hein?"

An hour later Rommel was sitting in the back of his command car, with Carl-Heinz driving him out of the airbase and onto the road leading into the Bavarian hills. The Desert Fox leaned back in the seat, thinking.

He was not certain of victory—he was far too much of a pragmatist for that. But, for the first time in years, since his magnificent panzerarmee had been shattered in the dust of the African desert, he allowed himself to believe that his country once again had a chance.

578 Squadron Base, Wendling, Norfolk, England

Staff Sgt. Frank "Digger" O'Dell
Wendling, Norfolk, England
October 5, 1944

Mrs. Lucy O'Dell
Roxboro, North Carolina

Dear Mama,

I'm sorry that it's been a few weeks since I wrote last, but I'm well and everything is pretty good here. We've been flying a lot of missions lately, and in between we've been doing maintenance and other work. And—well, I've met someone.

We get some days off, because although there's maintenance, between raids we're really not all that busy, and Tony Hutt and I usually go into Wendling, and there's a pub we like to go to, and that's where I met Maura. She's from Ireland, though her daddy lives in London, and when she heard my last name she at first thought I was from Ireland, and I told her that my family was.

Now I wish I'd listened harder to some of the stories that Grandpa and Granny told about the Old Country, because it would have helped me make conversation with her. Anyway, Maura works in a local dairy, and she's a very nice girl. You'd like her, Mama.

The raids have been big business, and when a raid is on, there isn't a lot of time for anything else. The battle order normally comes out at five o'clock in the evening, and then you know that you're going to have to fly the next morning.

I usually don't have a lot to do until we're getting pretty deep into enemy territory, and then depending on the number of enemy fighters they send up sometimes I'm really busy and sometimes there isn't a target for me to shoot at.

We did fly one raid to a town called Schafhausen, and we were attacked by twenty to thirty Me-109s with light-colored bellies, dark on top. Several of them were camouflaged with white stripes so they looked kind of like P-51s. I fired at one fighter and he broke away right under us. He came in right under my waist window and he obviously didn't want to end up on the tail because the tail gunner has the best shot at any fighter because he doesn't have to worry about any kind of deflection. This fellow broke away so close that I could see the pilot sitting in the cockpit. I had my gun shooting straight down at the time he was breaking away under us, trying to hit him. I fired at another fighter that trailed black smoke but there were no flames. I didn't see any pieces flying off the aircraft but it was not unusual to see a German fighter trail black smoke even if you didn't hit him. The Germans are burning a synthetic fuel made from coal and God knows what else in their fighters.

When a fighter is coming in on you, you're closing pretty fast. What they're trying to do is get out about three or four thousand yards in front of you and a thousand feet above you and roll over and start firing. This way he flies what is called a Pursuit Curve and he always ends up on your tail unless he breaks away before he ends up back there.

Now when this fellow broke away under us, I could see him trailing black smoke. But when they start in on you, they throttle back so that they don't close so fast and then when they start to break away they almost invariably trail black smoke because they hit the throttles and give it all the power they've got to break away fast when they're in close.

That's why I'm pretty sure I hit that fellow but I'm not at all sure whether I hit him enough to shoot him down, because you'd probably see the black smoke either way. Now, Harry Glass, the other waist gunner, did shoot down one airplane because I saw it explode in midair.

The strange thing is, right after that mission, the enemy fighters seem to have pretty much disappeared from the sky. I guess the truth is they weren't hurting the raids that much, and even though it is hard to shoot them down, the Germans probably can't stand to lose as much as we can. But it's certainly made my job a little less exciting, although it is safer for everyone.

The Germans still have antiaircraft fire, though, so even though I don't always have a lot to do, we still have a little excitement every once in a while. We're getting a new airplane, because our old airplane P-Bar got pretty badly shot up over Kiel, which is in northern Germany on the Jutland Peninsula. The navigator, Booker, gave the heading to Sweden to our pilot, Lieutenant Russ, three or four times, but he didn't take it. We flew on over the target pretty badly crippled, dropped the bombs and came out, and by then the rest of the group was pulling away and leaving us behind.

We flew out over the North Sea above an island called Heligoland and this thing was nothing but a big, stationary antiaircraft battery with I don't know how many 88s and 105 and 155 millimeter guns on it. By the time we got over Heligoland, we were about twelve thousand feet and it looked to me like they were firing every gun on the island at us. We finally got away and flew on across the North Sea and landed at an emergency airfield in Scotland. Old P-Bar was in such bad shape I doubt it will ever fly again. They flew up from our group and picked us up and took us back the next day. When I last saw P-Bar they were just stripping the parts off it.

I hear we're getting another airplane shortly, and so we'll be going back to work in a few weeks. In the meantime, I'm getting to spend more time with Maura and I don't have too much to do at the base, so I think I'll enjoy it while I can. I'll write soon, and you do too.

Love,

Your Son

Frank "Digger" O'Dell

Army Group B Headquarters, Trier, Germany, 7 October 1944, 2330 hours GMT

"Colonel von Reinhardt, could you remain for a few moments, please?" Rommel asked. It was well after midnight, and a marathon staff meeting was just breaking up.

Reinhardt cocked a quizzical eyebrow. "Yes, of course, Field Marshal," he replied as he gathered the papers from the briefing he'd delivered earlier. Rommel was deep in conversation with General Bayerlein, and Reinhardt knew that it could be some time before that conversation was finished.

For an invalid, the Desert Fox kept amazing hours. Up at four and to bed after midnight, always alert and sharp. Reinhardt had detected a significant mood change since his return from Berlin by way of Augsburg, and that mood change was having its effect on the other members of Rommel's headquarters staff.

Müller was hungry, of course. It was their normal custom to find a midnight snack after the long meetings broke up; Rommel's late hours meant that the kitchen staff knew to leave out bread and coffee at all hours. Reinhardt could tell that Müller was eager to get out of the room and get at the food, but didn't want to seem unsympathetic to Reinhardt, who would be left behind.

"How did you know the Amis were going to make such a push at Aachen?" Müller asked. During the meeting, Rommel had congratulated his colonel of Intelligence on his accurate analysis of American intentions.

"Simple logic, really," said Reinhardt with Sherlockian dismissal, although he was secretly quite proud of an insight that had escaped even the Desert Fox—though admittedly Rommel's recent Berlin mission had kept him from focusing all his attention on the military situation. Nothing much escaped Rommel's eye; Reinhardt wasn't used to being around people whose analytical skills were as good or better than his own.

Reinhardt reviewed his analysis as much to confirm his own reasoning as to impress Müller. "One of the consequences of the so-called free press that the Americans pride themselves on is that military objectives must sometimes be subordinated to the need for propaganda, because the military and government cannot shape the propaganda message with full control. When there is little action or clear short-term gain, the press becomes anxious and wants to invent a story even if none exists. To gain significant morale and propaganda value, it was obvious that a good Allied move would be to capture a German city. As none of our other cities was even vulnerable at this stage of the war, the move against Aachen was therefore inevitable."

Müller shook his head. "Günter, I don't know how you keep all this stuff straight. It's like looking into echoing mirrors, the way you think. This is their point of view, therefore this would become our point of view, which modifies their point of view. . . . I have a headache that only a sandwich can cure."

Reinhardt laughed. "I'm a little hungry myself. Why don't you head for the mess hall, and I'll come join you as soon as I have a chance to talk with the field marshal."

That was all the encouragement Müller needed. "Okay, Günter. Don't worry—I'll save you some würst."

Reinhardt sat down at the long conference table, now littered with the detritus of a long meeting: paper, coffee cups, overflowing ashtrays. The dim electric bulbs had given him a headache. Now alone in the room, except for the Desert Fox and his general, he sat down, suddenly very tired. He looked at a long column of intelligence figures but couldn't quite focus on it.

"Sorry to keep you waiting, Colonel," said Rommel, suddenly appearing over his shoulder.

Reinhardt snapped back to consciousness. "No problem, sir. How can I help the field marshal?"

"Come, I just wanted to talk with you for a few minutes." Rommel led the way to his private office. Reinhardt noticed a slight limp, a slight droop of the shoulders. It was the first time he'd ever noticed any fatigue in the man, yet Rommel was still smiling, positive, cheerful.

"Here, sit down," Rommel said, gesturing toward a chair. He sat himself in the high-backed wooden chair behind his desk, which was filled with papers and reports, the evidence of true command responsibility. "Good job with the intelligence briefing today. I liked the way you combined political insight with military judgment in figuring out that the Allies would move against Aachen. A rare combination in an intelligence officer. Most are more narrowly focused. They think about the battlefield of the ground, when there are other battle-fields we must also consider."

"'War is the continuation of diplomacy by other means,'" said Reinhardt, paraphrasing Clausewitz. He sat at attention, curious why Rommel wanted to see him, alert because he didn't know everything that was going on around him.

"Of course, of course," laughed Rommel. "But while everyone says it, few take the time to remember what it means. In any event, I wanted you to know that I've noticed your work and I'm quite impressed."

"The field marshal is too kind," Reinhardt said, though he was aware that the Desert Fox was not the kind of man to give idle praise.

"Not at all, not at all," Rommel said. "Since you were assigned to me by Himmler's staff, I wanted to learn a little more about you. I got some of the background on von Ribbentrop's mission to Moscow. Evidently your political and military insight was quite useful to bringing back the treaty that took us at least temporarily from a two-front to a one-front war."

"Thank you, sir. As you say, however, any success on that front is tempo-rary."

"Oh?" said Rommel. "Your fellow members of the mission and Himmler himself tend to think Stalin's neutralized for good. In fact, General Bücher keeps reassuring me that I don't have to worry at all about the east, now or in the future."

"Highly unlikely, field marshal. We threw the wolf some food and that will keep him busy until he has time to digest it. Then he will look around for his next meal. The question is whether we will look like the most tempting entrée on the menu."

Rommel laughed. "A very good image. 'Most tempting entrée.' I like that. You have a way with words, Colonel."

"Our success—rather, your success—in the west will help determine Stalin's range of options. The big issue is whether the west will recognize the true threat to civilization in time to behave rationally. There is quite a lot of politi-cal pressure in favor of the 'unconditional surrender' goal, although perhaps that pressure is lessened since Stalin was one of its primary advocates."

"I see we think alike in some respects," Rommel mused. "I, too, worry more about the east than the west, at least in the long term. Though my com-mand responsibilities are exclusively concerned with the west. Are you a mem-ber of the Party, colonel, if you don't mind my asking?"

"'When one comes to a strange city, one should worship by all means the gods of the place,'" Reinhardt misquoted cautiously. He was a member of the Nazi Party, though not in fact a believer in much of Nazi ideology.

Rommel smiled slightly before replying. "On the other hand, 'No man is justified in doing evil on the grounds of expediency.' That was by Roosevelt. Not the current one, but the other. The one with the mustache. I always liked that sentiment."

Reinhardt was not used to being out-quoted by anybody. Like many smart and verbal people, he had grown to assume that other people tended to be ignorant. It embarrassed him to be caught short, and he very nearly blushed. Rommel, for all his military genius, was not known to be a scholarly man. In fact, rumor had it that he had never read a book outside the field of military arts. Reinhardt couldn't quite believe that, but it was true that Rommel's focus was in contrast to his own eclecticism.

"General Bücher is your friend, is he not?" asked Rommel.

"We went to university together," replied Reinhardt noncommittally. "He's a very talented swordsman."

"Though I understand you gave him one of those scars?"

"Yes, sir. But that was the only time I beat him at fencing. Chess, though, is another matter."

"Ah, chess," sighed Rommel. "I miss playing. We must have a game sometime."

"It would be my great pleasure, Field Marshal," said Reinhardt.

There was a long pause, then Rommel picked up a folder on his desk. "I took the liberty of reviewing your personnel file."

Reinhardt's arched eyebrow was the only answer he gave. He sat with utter rigidity.

Rommel tapped the folder. "You've had a quite distinguished staff career, Colonel von Reinhardt. You've impressed several senior officers, and reading between the lines I would assume that in some cases their action was essentially your advice. You've impressed me, and that is not the easiest thing to accomplish. But what is missing here is as interesting as what is present."

"Sir?"

"There is an absence of direct line experience. You seem to have avoided combat altogether." Rommel looked at Reinhardt directly, calmly.

The blush Reinhardt had been trying to suppress welled up in his face to his utter humiliation. Being shamed before this man he admired was a pain he would have done anything to avoid. "Sir—I have accepted every assignment and shirked no duty—I have not done anything to avoid danger—"

"Peace, peace," said Rommel. "I am not accusing you of cowardice directly or indirectly. I believe that you have not worked to avoid personal danger. I merely note that you have not sought it out, volunteered for combat as many of your peers have done."

"Sir—I believe I have served the Fatherland in the best way in which I am capable—"

Rommel waved his hand. "Please, I am not condemning you. I simply wanted to make an observation. Colonel von Reinhardt, you are a smart and capable man. I believe you are also a brave man, or at least that you will be when you face the time of trial. But you are a man who has built a wall of separation between you and the experience of life. You have developed the intellectual side of your inheritance, but that is not all there is in life. The problem with the other sides of life is that they are messy and imperfect, and I suspect that's difficult for you. You have enormous gifts, and I would like to see them developed to the fullest extent for your sake. No, I don't want to reassign you to a combat command right now. Frankly, I need you where you are. But I do want you to consider that your growth lies not in what you are already accomplished in, but in that which you have not yet pursued. Wasn't it Goethe who said, 'He only earns his freedom and existence who daily conquers them anew.'"

"Yes, it was, sir," replied Reinhardt, almost absently. Another quote. And Rommel not a reader. But the sentiment could easily have come from Rommel's own soul. Reinhardt wanted to respond, to defend himself somehow, but he felt exposed, vulnerable. He looked into the eyes of Rommel and saw his own reflection, but it was a shamed and small version of himself, not the sharp and distant intellectual he saw himself as being.

"Field Marshal, you have given me much food for thought. I will reflect on this. Thank you for your kind and thoughtful words, and for your consideration," he said, the formal words barely coming out of his mouth. He wanted to defend himself, argue, change the reflection he saw in the eyes looking at him. He was in the presence of a mind greater than his own, and it was a horrible feeling. In the compartment in his mind that always stood outside himself, he suddenly realized, *This is how others sometimes feel when they are around me.* The irony kept him moving, helped him stand and salute.

Then he paused, and said again, "Thank you, Field Marshal." This time it sounded completely different.

And Rommel smiled as he said, "You're welcome."

Dessau, Germany, 12 October 1944, 2000 hours GMT

Franz Steinberger was born in Germany, raised of German parents. He spoke German as his only language and had shared the misery and tragedy of 1918, and the resulting shame of Versailles, with the rest of the German people. He had attended a German *universitat,* and upon earning his degree in engineering had been determined to use that education for the betterment of Germany's industry, economy, and world power.

And then, in 1933, he had learned that he wasn't really a German after all.

He was merely a Jew.

Now, as he debarked from the crowded train, the packed compartment that always smelled of sweat, shit, and fear, he wondered how he could ever have considered himself a part of such a monstrous land. He looked around at this old Saxon city. With its homes and factories, gardens and parks, you wouldn't know it was a part of a darkness so all-consuming that it gave a meaning on earth to the Christian concept of Hell.

And maybe those Christians were right, he thought—for if there was such as thing as Hell, he was living it.

Yesterday the Gestapo had shot Model Zweiss, for no other reason than that the day's engine production had lagged slightly behind the ridiculous goals that had been established. Two more men had died during the train ride back to camp, from suffocation in the overcrowded cars, or perhaps merely from despair, and another had failed to awaken in the predawn hours of this morning, when the guards and their dogs had come to roust the slaves from their narrow, wooden bunks.

Now he shuffled in the crowded file from the train yard to the factory, eyes lowered in the long-practiced art of survival—you didn't want to give the guards a single reason to notice you, for that reason, however trivial, could mean a sentence of death. His body was broken, his limbs frail and skeletal, and his strength was a mere shadow of his former robust health.

His spirit, too, was grievously wounded. It had been gashed beyond repair when he had watched his beloved Annie loaded onto a different train, a crowded car that would roll toward the east, carrying Jews to a fate that none could speak of, for none had returned. But by now they all had their guesses, and with those suspicions had come an end to all hope.

But Franz Steinberger, bereft of health and hope, of spirit and of future, had one thing left. It was a thing that allowed him to crawl out of the bunk in the morning, that gave him the strength to board the train, to make the long walk to the factory, and to labor over the jet engines as if he really wanted to live.

Franz Steinberger had rage. It was a fire of fury that burned deep within the wellspring of his life. It was a hatred for Nazis, for all things German, that would not allow him to surrender, to lay down and die.

Because he had been trained as an engineer, he understood the significance of these mysterious engines. He had seen them tested in the factory, knew the lengths to which the designers worked to keep the powerful turbines cool. He could guess at the difference they would make in a war fought in the sky, in the effort to stop the bombers that periodically, and inaccurately, tried to bomb this plant into oblivion.

Many times in the past his rage had given him the strength to act, and today he would act again.

Steinberger was assigned the task of driving in the screws that completed the housing encircling each turbine. The housing was an aluminum-coated shell of hollow steel, through which air had to pass in order to maintain the cooling of the engine. He did his work conscientiously, for the guards were everywhere and he had no wish to throw his life away.

But each day there came a time when the overseers' attention was distracted—they were rebuking another worker, or laughing about some Jewess they had raped, or merely dull-eyed from fatigue and hangover. As he did each day, Franz waited for the right moment. He saw the guards look away.

And Steinberger took a strip of rag, the one accessory that the Gestapo did not inventory on a daily basis. He crumpled up the oily cloth, again looked to the guards—who were laughing, crowing like birds of prey he thought—and stuffed the rag into one small air passage. Quickly he dropped the last piece of the housing into place, and fastened the screws that meant that this engine was done.

The hooks came in, lifted the sleek turbine from the line, hauled it away for testing. It would fire, and it would run, and it would show no signs of malfunctions as the German engineers put it through its paces.

Only later, when it was run for a long time, hopefully when it was carrying a fighter plane and a Nazi pilot through the skies, would it begin to grow unusually hot.

Third Army HQ, West of Metz, France, 18 October 1944, 1723 hours GMT

"General, the Fifth Infantry has bogged down . . . they've been plastered all to hell, sir, and can't get around that castle." The operations colonel gave his report with just a hint of the exasperation that immediately welled up in the army commander.

"Son of a bitch!" Patton uttered the expletive out of a general sense of frustration. He knew that his boys were being killed on all sides of the well-fortified city of Metz, and it galled the hell out of him. Even worse, he didn't know what to do about it. He had to have that city before Third Army could advance to the German border, and yet he had been feeding his divisions into that meat grinder for weeks, now, with no perceptible progress.

He paced around the office, bit down on his cigar, and made up his mind.

"Get me Twelfth Army Group CG on the line."

Two minutes later he heard Omar Bradley's voice through the hiss of the telephone receiver. "Brad? I've got troubles."

"George, if you're going to ask for more fuel, you know—"

"Now just a damn minute, Brad—no, that's not the problem. But I need another division, something to give me a fresh punch against this goddamn Nazi rockpile."

"No can do," Bradley replied. "We're stretched too thin down there as it is."

Patton was looking at a map detailing the positions of Twelfth Army Group components, and he stabbed his finger at the icon for a tank unit. "What about Nineteenth Armored? They're right on my flank as it is—and I hear they're not on the front right now."

The hesitation on Bradley's end was palpable, but Patton utilized all of his patience to wait for his commander to talk. "Wakefield's boys, you mean? You're right, insofar as they haven't brought the whole division into line."

"Well, let me have 'em back, then!" Patton insisted. "They did good work for me in Normandy, and they need to get back into the field."

"You're all right with Hank, then?" Bradley sounded wary.

"Hell, Brad, like I told you before: he learned some things in Normandy, and maybe he's the kind of driver that Pulaski and Jackson need to hold onto their leashes. Sure, I'm all right with him!"

"Well, we can do that, then . . . I'll get in touch with Courtney Hodges at First Army, make sure the transfer won't cause him more problems than he can handle. I expect you'll have Nineteenth Armored under Third Army in another few days."

"Thanks, Brad. . . . I mean that," Patton said sincerely. The two generals broke the connection, and Patton's eyes once again fell on his map, onto the city of forts and trenches and castles, the great roadblock that stood to block his manifest advance to Germany. One more division, three hundred more tanks, fourteen thousand men to make more grist for the mill of battle.

He only wondered if they would be enough.

Excerpt from *War's Final Fury,* by Professor Jared Gruenwald

After the heady days of the breakout and the liberation of France, the stiffening German resistance of autumn struck the Allies as a cruel shock. The sweep out of Normandy had been a rush of speedy maneuver, highlighted by Patton's daring thrusts, at least until the setback suffered by the Nineteenth Armored Division at Abbeville. The rest of the Anglo-American forces followed more slowly, but still inexorably, and the enemy was driven all the way to the borders of his homeland.

The setback at Abbeville notwithstanding, the circumstance that brought the offensive to a halt initially was not Nazi defenders so much as a shortage of fuel. Though Montgomery's troops had swept through the great port of Antwerp in early September, the British field marshal's attention was focused on the great prizes of the Rhine and Germany. As a consequence, he neglected to immediately clean out the enemy strongholds along the Scheldt River estuary, positions that controlled access to that key deep-water harbor. By the time the importance of these islands and swampy lowlands was appreciated, the Germans had firmly entrenched. As happened so often, it was Monty's empire troops—in this case the doughty Canadians—who were left with the grim job of cleaning out the pockets of toughest resistance.

Meanwhile, Patton was insisting that, if Third Army was supplied with fuel, he could seize a long stretch of the Westwall before the Germans could fortify their border. History has shown his claims to be correct, but for a variety of reasons Eisenhower decided not to allocate the supplies to his volatile armor commander.

Instead, Ike determined that the Allies should approach Germany along a broad front, with the British in the north, and two American army groups pressing forward across the bulk of the approaches—General Patch's Seventh Army having come up from Marseilles to come into the line on Patton's right. Finally, the First Free French army, under General de Lattre, came into being and filled the southern part of the line, including the Vosges Mountains down to the border with Switzerland.

As desperately needed supplies were still being brought over the beaches in Normandy, Montgomery proposed a massive airborne attack, intended to carry his own army group across the Rhine and into Germany. Ike wisely declined to authorize this attack, which under Rommel's program of vigorous reinforcement would almost certainly have been a debacle. Instead, Monty's forces were charged with a vigorous campaign to open the approaches to Antwerp. They faced fanatical Nazi resistance, especially on Walcheren Island, at the mouth of the Scheldt, but slowly the key port was opened to the Allied supply fleets.

As a consequence, the major Allied attack was brought to bear against the German city of Aachen, a key link in the Westwall. Thousands of men gave their lives as First Army slowly, deliberately clawed its way through the fortifications, though throughout October Rommel's defenders managed to cling to the heart of the city itself.

Patton, meanwhile, had become embroiled in his own meat grinder, the heavily fortified medieval city of Metz. Division after division was fed into the gory maw of this rugged river town, and yet the Germans stubbornly refused to yield, or to allow themselves to become encircled.

At the same time, the Western Allies could only watch in impotence as Soviet forces rolled into Norway and Greece in the wake of retreating Nazis. Though the peoples of both countries resisted the new conquerors with the same determination with which they had faced the Germans, there was no stopping the implacable advance of Stalin's hordes. Lacking sea power, and now facing vigorous Allied naval interdiction, the Russians were nevertheless able to use their land armies to gain utter control of both countries. The incursion, of course, was aided—particularly in Greece—by Communist elements that had formed part of the resistance to the German occupation, and were now all too willing to welcome their Soviet benefactors.

In the meantime, the changing situation in Europe created some alterations in strategy in the Pacific War. The combined chiefs of staff in the US and UK both perceived the danger of a major setback in France, and as a consequence were reluctant to allocate any more resources to the effort against Japan. With some reluctance, however, the landings on Pelelieu, which were intended to secure a base for the subsequent invasion of the Philippines, were allowed to proceed on schedule.

The resultant, and horrifying, losses from this offensive were enough to convince the joint chiefs, supported by the president, to cancel the impending liberation of the Philippines. General MacArthur's objections to this change in strategy became so vociferous that President Roosevelt was left with no choice but to remove the controversial general from his theater command.

Finally, major naval resources were dispatched from the Pacific to the Atlantic. Admiral Halsey's Third Fleet was recalled from the western Pacific. After a brief stopover in Hawaii, this massive conglomeration of aircraft carriers and battleships made for the Panama Canal, intended to reinforce the US Army's efforts on the European mainland.

OPERATION BLOODY HELL

October–November 1944

Associated Press Bureau Offices, Fleet Street, London, England, 22 October 1944, 0800 hours GMT

For Chuck Porter, the worst thing about a late fall Atlantic Ocean voyage was neither the seasickness nor the fear of U-boats. It was being cut off from his continual news fix. He hated being out of touch, hated not having his finger on the pulse of the military and political worlds. There was the shipboard radio, of course, but the periodic static-filled news broadcasts were hardly a substitute for the bank of teletypes delivering raw news information in a constant stream.

His ship, the S.S. *America,* docked on Saturday. After debarkation and customs he caught a train to Victoria Station in London, checked into his hotel, and promptly fell asleep, the stillness of the bed perversely feeling like motion after the long days in the rolling Atlantic. He thought about playing tourist on Sunday and even went out, but the dreary wet weather drove him into the nearest pub, and he holed up for the rest of the day watching locals play darts. He wasn't much good at the game, but he held his own with beer.

Monday morning, his head ached from lager and travel; his mouth was dry and pasty. *A good way to start a new assignment,* he thought. He hailed a black London taxicab, not yet feeling stable enough to try navigating the Tube (though he was an expert on the New York subway system), and leaned back as the taxi threaded its way through increasingly narrow London streets toward the AP bureau office.

The office was located on the second floor of a nondescript building in Fleet Street, the heart of the newspaper district. The chattering of Teletypes and clouds of cigarette smoke told him he was in the right place even before he saw the name on the door. There was a small entryway guarded by an ancient-looking harridan with her hair in a severe bun and an overflowing ashtray on a desk piled with papers. A long ash dangled precariously from her current cigarette.

"Chuck Porter, from New York," he introduced himself.

She looked him up and down with critical eyes, as if he were some bum from the gutter—or some colonial refugee, he supposed.

"I'm the acting Paris bureau chief," he added after a pause.

She kept staring. Finally, she yelled, "Percy! Some gent from New York," then turned back to her typewriter, the ash grown longer.

From the din in the inner office emerged a short, balding man wearing an unbuttoned vest over a white shirt, necktie knot loose and collar gaping underneath. A stain of blue ink leaked through a shirt pocket with three fountain pens. "Porter? Name's Percy McCulley. Bureau chief, don't you know. So, you're to reopen the Paris office, eh? Fresh from New York, you say? Bad day to arrive, isn't it?" His talking speed was so fast and his British accent was so thick that Porter had trouble following it.

"Bad day?"

"Yes—but then you haven't heard, have you? Of course—no way you could have heard—goodness, Porter, it's busy enough without all this—guess you'll wish you were back in New York for this story!" McCulley was moving as he talked and Porter, his raincoat flapping, pushed his way through the crowded newsroom, straining to make out about every third word. *Big news?* he wondered, his mind racing through myriad possibilities.

A knot of reporters clustered around the Teletype, reading the news as it sputtered out line by line. *Just like home*, Porter thought. He picked up the clipboard that contained the Teletype material that had already come off the machine, skimming it to bring himself up to speed quickly. And then he slowed down as he saw the headline.

FLASH/BULLETIN
HAVANA, 22 OCTOBER, 0100 EST
COPY 01 ENTERPRISE SUNK IN U-BOAT AMBUSH
DISTRIBUTION: ALL STATIONS

HAVANA, 22 OCTOBER (AP) BY JAY WILLIS
A SHIFT IN MILITARY POSITIONING TO RESPOND TO THE SOVIET BETRAYAL TURNED INTO A MAJOR DISASTER LAST NIGHT. ADMIRAL HALSEY, BRINGING THE THIRD FLEET THROUGH THE PANAMA CANAL TO REINFORCE ALLIED NAVAL OPERATIONS IN THE ATLANTIC AND MEDITERRANEAN, WAS AMBUSHED BY A U-BOAT WOLF PACK IN THE CARIBBEAN SEA.

THE CARRIER ENTERPRISE WAS LOST WITH OVER 1,500 CREWMEN, INCLUDING ADMIRAL HALSEY. OTHER NAVAL LOSSES ARE REPORTED HEAVY, WITH INFORMATION STILL POURING IN.

THE NAVY REPORTS THAT SEVERAL U-BOATS HAVE BEEN SUNK BUT THAT AN UNKNOWN NUMBER OF ENEMY SUBMARINES ESCAPED.

"ALTHOUGH THIS IS A TERRIBLE TRAGEDY," REPORTED THE SECRETARY OF WAR, "IT IS ONLY A TEMPORARY SETBACK IN OUR CRUSADE TOWARD INEVITABLE VICTORY, FIRST IN EUROPE, AND THEN IN THE PACIFIC. . . ."

MORE

AP-HAV-387509-WQ/102244

"Goddamn," he breathed. This was big news, and for once New York would be busier than London. *And just after I transferred,* he thought, annoyed.

"Bloody hell goddamn," agreed McCulley. "Been a busy week, what?"

Porter shook his head. This was why he hated being away from the newsroom even for a day, much less weeks. What else was going on? He kept the clipboard as he followed McCulley back through the crowded newsroom.

The "Paris Bureau" would be in London for the next few weeks as he got everything organized before moving across the Channel. He needed to establish his team, get his sources straight, then move to Paris and up toward the front. He hadn't been in Europe for years. For the time being, he might even get to do some reporting again. The thought pleased him—bureau chief salary and reporter's work. An ideal combination.

He could tell which desk was his—it was the temporarily clean one. Old, battered, coffee rings and cigarette burns, God only knew what sort of gunk and mold lurked in the crevasses of the drawers, but it was his. He'd been a reporter long enough to check out the chair before he sat down. Sure enough, as soon as his predecessor had left, the other reporters had raided everything that worked. The chair was missing two casters. *You don't have to be a vulture to be a reporter, but it helps,* Porter mused.

"Here, I'll get you a chair that works," McCulley said, pulling the old chair away and stealing a working chair from a reporter who was out on assignment. "This'll do. I'll have the old one fixed as soon as I can. Of course, the Lord only knows how long that'll be. Here, now. Safe as houses. All comfy, just like home. Here, I'd better replace that typewriter as well. Besides, you'll be reading for a while, won't you, then? War moves whether you're available or not, don't it? Bloody inconvenient, what?"

"Bloody hell inconvenient," Porter agreed. He sat down to read.

He'd grabbed a few newspapers when he got off the ship, and a few more in Victoria Station, but the English press had a pretty poor reputation outside of the *Times* and the *Guardian,* plus what with censorship he didn't trust anything they reported anyway.

The wire service material was all fresh and uncensored, at least until it went through editorial before going out to the clients. He and the other editors played a constant game with military censorship, trying to slip good stories through while still staying on the good side of the government. And, he remembered, there wasn't a First Amendment in Great Britain. "Bloody hell inconvenient, what?" he murmured to himself in a phony English accent as he put his feet up on his semi-new desk.

There wasn't much new on the German-Soviet armistice story, though Porter suspected that there was still a tremendous amount going on behind the scenes. The American reds and pinks had made numerous excuses for the

Commie pull-out from the war, even suggesting that there had been a behind-the-scenes deal between Roosevelt and Churchill to invade the Soviet Union and tear down Communism. But anti-Communist feeling in the United States had raged forth. There had been a few riots where American Reds had been beaten by mobs. Even Eugene V. Debs had come out publicly to denounce the Soviet move. *Doesn't look good for World Communism,* Porter thought. Like a lot of urban Americans his age, he'd attended a party meeting or two, flirted with Marxism (and the freethinking girls at the meetings) a bit, but had put it aside.

The big story—at least until the Enterprise disaster—seemed to be Aachen and Metz. Rommel's counterpunch had slowed Patton's lightning march through France briefly, then it was hell for leather, with the Allies chasing the Nazis all the way back to the Westwall. General Hodges's First Army had nearly pushed the Germans out of Aachen, but then the news stories had been saying he'd "nearly" cleared out the city for over a month now.

And Patton was still bogged down in Metz, taking heavy losses in men. Porter followed the details of Patton's campaign much more closely, flipping through page after page of Teletype paper. While Hodges and the First Army might be strategically important, Patton always made the best copy, no matter what he was doing. His drive across France had restored some of the luster Patton had lost in Sicily in the famous "soldier-slapping" incident. Now, however, his reputation was being tarnished in Metz. There had been lots of casualties already, and new divisions were being assigned to the operation, including one that had served under Patton during the Cobra breakout. Metz was a meat grinder, no doubt, and Porter was sure that Rommel, the Desert Fox, was at work.

That was a great story: the ultimate rematch of the war. Patton vs. Rommel. It sounded like a title fight, the tough-but-tarnished good guy up against the noble villain for the heavyweight championship of the world. He liked a story with a clear dramatic thrust, and he was already rehearsing phrases and angles. It was only the morning of his first working day in London, and he was ready to go. He looked at the team of reporters, each working on his own stories. Time for an editorial conference, and then to work. He lit a cigarette in anticipation before calling his first meeting.

Reichstag, Berlin, Germany, 25 October 1944, 1550 hours GMT

"Come in, General Galland," purred Heinrich Himmler, leaning back in his chair so that his face was covered with shadow. "I've been reading your reports on the Me-262 program. Excellent work. Your group has been consistently ahead of schedule. One day I must come to see one of your hangars. Herr Speer tells me they are a sight to behold."

"Yes, Führer," replied the Luftwaffe commander, taking his cap and placing it under his arm. "It's always interesting to be there when someone sees the underground excavation for the first time. Even when you're told how big it is, it just doesn't penetrate until you see it for yourself."

"Well then, I shall certainly come at my very earliest opportunity," said Himmler. He looked down at the papers on his desk and picked up one sheet with a gesture that was oddly dainty. "But I gather that with all your successes, you continue to report one problem."

"Yes, Führer." Galland shook his head. "All the technology in the world means nothing without the fuels. We've been running on less than ten percent of the fuel we need—and that's the minimum level. It doesn't matter how brave our pilots or how superior our aircraft. Without fuel, all this is a waste."

Himmler nodded in return, then tilted his hands together under his chin. "Every day a line of people come to visit me, and the one thing they all plead for is more fuel, more fuel. Each need is real, of course, but priorities must be set."

Galland's shoulders drooped slightly. He expected yet another "no" answer; that's all he'd gotten for weeks and months, but without a "yes," he was helpless.

But then the Führer leaned forward. "Without recapturing air superiority, at least for a period of time, there is little chance of getting the fuel stocks we need. So I have decided that all the output of the synthetic fuels plants will be diverted to Luftwaffe needs. Your job is to plan a raid so huge, so utterly devastating, that you can shut down the Allied bombing campaign, at least for a time. Can you do it?"

"Can I?" Galland's eyes brightened. "With the new jet fighters, I can tear them apart as long as there is a supply of fuel." Then he paused. "You said, for a time?"

"Yes, for a time. Your mission will be to interdict the Allied bombing campaign. On the ground, the mission will be somewhat different. You see, I know where there is a virtually unlimited supply of fuel."

"Where?" asked Galland.

"In the stockpiles of the Allies," replied the Führer.

Nineteenth Armored Division Headquarters Building, Luxembourg City, Luxembourg, 30 October 1944, 1447 hours GMT

Colonel Frank Ballard was supposed to use a cane for the next month, but he could walk well without it. Besides, what he always liked best about tanks was that you didn't have to do a lot of walking. The jeep pulled up in front of the building in Luxembourg City that had been commandeered as division HQ, and he stepped out quite steadily, only using the cane for a moment to steady himself on the downward movement. "Here you are, sir," said the driver.

"Thanks, corporal," Ballard said, before striding confidently through the door. The last time he'd seen the Nineteenth, it had been dying around him, but now it looked almost back to normal. The staff was busy, but the men stopped working long enough to offer a hearty round of applause to their returning tank commander. The MP grinned and said, "Welcome back, Colonel. The general is in his office."

Ballard walked inside, conscious of his gait, wanting to look as healed as possible. Another lesson from his boxing days: don't let 'em know how much it hurts. He swung his cane jauntily, even though he could feel the lance of pain each time his leg came down on the concrete floor.

"Frank! I'm glad you're back!" Henry Wakefield roared in his deep voice, obviously delighted to see his returning officer. "How's the leg? More to the point, how were the Paris nurses?"

"The leg reaches all the way to the ground, General," replied the lieutenant colonel with a smile, then winced slightly at Wakefield's ham-handed grip. "And the nurses—well, *vive la France*, as they say." The men laughed together. In fact, the nurses had been all American and all business, but Ballard knew what he was supposed to say.

"Well, Frank, you've got your old command back." Wakefield nodded to Pulaski, who was standing off to the side. "Jimmy's been patching it up while you were gone, and I think you'll find it nearly as good as new."

"Thank you, General. It's good to be back." Ballard turned to Pulaski and saluted. "Jimmy, good to see you again."

"Welcome back, Frank," said Pulaski, with a voice empty of affect.

The wounded officer was shocked at the gaunt, hollow-eyed man who stood before him. After all, Ballard had been the one torn up and bloody at the end of the last battle. Why, then, did Pulaski look like the one who had been badly damaged? The colonel had escaped without a scratch physically, but he looked like too many of the horribly mangled soldiers who'd packed the Paris hospital. Surely Pulaski didn't think it was all his fault, Ballard thought. He'd seen men who looked like that in the hospital, men whose battlefield damage was inside, not outside.

Wakefield watched the two men closely. They had been the command team that had made Combat Command A work during that brief campaign that now seemed like such a long time ago. Would they be able to do it again? Pulaski, he was relieved to see, was steady as he met the gaze of this man who had been nearly killed under his command. Wakefield was still concerned, however, about Pulaski's morale. Instead of getting better, Pulaski seemed to be slipping deeper into depression. Would he ever again be willing to send Ballard and the rest of his men into harm's way?

The general remembered the sickening news of two months earlier, word that CCA was all but gone, ambushed south of the Abbeville bridge, destroyed by the shrewd counterattack of an enemy general who by all rights should have been dead. Now, the wrecked machinery had been replaced, and new men had arrived to operate it, but the general agonized over the constant question:

Would the result be the same?

When Ballard left, Wakefield turned to Pulaski and drew a deep breath. When he let it out, he spoke with what he hoped was confidence-building firmness. "Jimmy, you have command of CCA of the Nineteenth Armored, a combat unit in this man's army. You're activated as of today, and you'll get orders with the rest of the division in the briefing that's going to start right now."

There was no cheer, no protest, no reaction. Pulaski saluted, stood straight, and met his gaze. "Yes, sir," he said, and turned to leave.

"I'm sure you can handle it." Wakefield said, his tone intentionally harsh. "The orders came from higher up."

"General Hodges?" The colonel, who had had nothing to do with First Army command since he had been relegated to replacement training, was obviously puzzled.

"Not Hodges. You'll find out with the rest of the officers. And Jimmy—at least Ballard's okay. Had a vacation with nurses."

"The others aren't coming back from vacation," Pulaski said evenly. His face was devoid of expression.

Wakefield nodded curtly. He couldn't hope for anything else, not now.

The men left the office for the adjacent auditorium, where all the company-grade and higher officers of the Nineteenth Armored had gathered. The general noticed that Pulaski walked stiffly, avoiding any look at his superior officer. He did introduce Ballard to Diaz, and the two lieutenant colonels exchanged a cordial handshake.

"Ten-*shun!*" snapped the division sergeant-major, and with a shuffling of chairs the officers of the Nineteenth got to their feet. They were gathered, somewhat casually, into three groups: the seasoned men of Bob Jackson's Combat Command B, the fresh faces mixed with a few weathered veterans of Pulaski's CCA, and the division and support staff, the officers who handled the divisional artillery and engineering assets, as well as intelligence, supply, logistics, and all the other tasks that kept fourteen thousand men organized, fed, and supplied with the materials necessary to wage war.

"At ease," Wakefield said, striding to the podium. He looked over the men gathered before him, knowing they were rested and as well-trained as could be expected. They'd seen a little action under Hodges's First Army, and Bob Jackson's Combat Command B had known some successes. But now, once more, they were embarking into an unknown future.

"I'll get right to the point: We've been reassigned to Third Army."

Henry Wakefield kept his face impassive as he informed his officers. The staff and unit commanders of the Nineteenth Armored Division had gathered in the long barracks hall that had been training grounds and classroom for his recruits during the last month. Now they exchanged looks, a few wide-eyed stares or blinks of astonishment. But nobody vocalized a response.

"Patton needs us again, men. I guess he liked our work so much in Normandy that he decided he just couldn't win the war without us."

That provoked a few chuckles, though the officers, like their general, had a feel for the truth. The Nineteenth was being transferred because such a move was convenient for both armies. Wakefield's division was the southernmost unit of First Army and now would hold the northern flank of the Third. Wakefield had actually protested the move when it had first been proposed, but it was clear that Patton needed reinforcements if he was going to reduce Metz. Old Blood and Guts had been surprisingly enthusiastic about bringing Wakefield back, though Wakefield knew that the final decision had been made by Omar Bradley as commanding general of the Twelfth Army Group.

Now, Wakefield and Patton were stuck with each other, again. Maybe it would go as well this time as it did the last. He could hope. The general indicated his S-3, the staff operations officer.

"Colonel Clark will fill you in on the rest of the details."

Stepping to the side, Wakefield tried to suppress his emotions. He had learned that Hodges was a good man, careful and precise, one who cared about his troops. Of course, the Nineteenth Division's casualties had not been among the worst suffered by the army, since half the division—Combat Command A—had spent most of the time in rest and refurbishment. Wakefield knew that in Aachen, much of First Army had faced a bloodbath, and that was despite the general's care and concern for the welfare of his men.

Now, they were back under the firebrand, Patton. Perhaps the most surprising thing of all was that tank general's first words when he'd spoken to the Nineteenth CO. Patton had asked about Jimmy Pulaski by name and called him a "good man." This about the colonel who had led his unit into Third Army's biggest setback. Well, Patton was always a bit capricious, but for once he recognized when a man had done his best and gotten chewed up for reasons that weren't his fault. Too bad Pulaski hadn't heard it . . . or believed it.

Wakefield stole a surreptitious look at Pulaski as the wiry Clark spoke from the podium. Pulaski's eyes had blinked at the news, but then his empty face covered up everything else once again. Wakefield's fists closed. He felt frustrated, unable to do anything except make Pulaski get back up on the horse and pray that the man could ride.

"It seems that the Third needs our help to encircle and capture Metz," Clark declared, unrolling the big map against the wall. "Combat Command B, under Colonel Jackson, will lead the way. Combat Command A will be in ready reserve."

Pulaski was impassive but paid attention.

Clark went over the plan. He outlined a small bridgehead on the east bank of the Moselle River, where the 104th Infantry Division had established a perimeter but was unable to advance. "We're going to bust up this valley, here— more of a ravine, actually. Here, here, and here the Krauts have pillboxes. They'll be plastered by the air force, but it's going to be your job to clean them out. Once you do, this is good road here, all the way to the east side of Metz. And that's where you're to link up with the Fourth Armored, who're already coming up from the south."

The staff officer went on to calmly outline the scheduled air support, as well as the traffic patterns that would get the division's components smoothly over the lone bridge. He turned to Pulaski as he got specific. "Jimmy, your boys will wait here, around this town just north of the crossing. You'll have to be ready to move out at a moment's notice. Bob, you'll take CCB over the river at first light and draw up in these fields. You'll be sheltered from the Kraut artillery spotters, at least until you start moving up the ravine."

"Damn, that looks like a meat grinder down there," one man said.

"Yes, it is," Wakefield intervened with a grim smile. "But since we're talking about our meat, let's see that it's the Krauts who get ground."

578 Squadron Base, Wendling, Norfolk, England

Staff Sgt. Frank "Digger" O'Dell
Wendling, Norfolk, England
November 7, 1944

Mrs. Lucy O'Dell
Roxboro, North Carolina

Dear Mama,

Well, Russ's Ruffians have got ourselves a new airplane, and maybe even a chance to get home, but we've got some extra raids to go on first.

You've read in the newspapers about how lots of flight crews name their airplanes and usually paint Petty Girls on the nose and all. Well, we never could come up with a good name for our old airplane, so it was just P-Bar, because there was a big P with a bar over it in a big white circle on the tail, like it was a cattle brand or something.

This airplane has a name and some nose art already, but it's not a Petty Girl or anything. It's got a drawing of an old colored man driving a Model T Ford, and the name of the plane is Ford's Folly. Although Consolidated Aircraft designed the B-24, they didn't have enough factories to build all that we needed, so Ford Motor Company started building them as well. This plane is part of history because it's the first B-24 "H" model built by Ford, and that's why it's called Ford's Folly. Here's a picture of it.

There's something else special about it, and that's why we're all real happy with Lieutenant Russ for getting it. Ford's Folly has more raids on it than any other American bomber in the whole Army Air Force. Seventy-nine raids. That's an awful lot. And, if we can bring it up to a hundred raids, we'll get to bring the airplane back to the United States and go on a War Bond tour and maybe even to Hollywood, just like the Memphis Belle, which was the first American airplane to last twenty-five raids, even if it was a B-17.

But we've got to put twenty-one raids on the plane first, and right now, it's in no shape to fly. We got the airplane assigned to us on a Saturday. On Sunday morning, we went out and swung the compass and calibrated the instruments and a few things like that. Monday we checked out the guns and the turrets, and Tuesday and Wednesday we took it up to fly it a bit to find out all the things that were wrong, and the rest of the week was spent fixing it up.

Our first raid in Ford's Folly was to a town called Karlsruhe on the Rhine River. There was a railroad bridge across the river that was still intact, and the Germans were funneling materiel and men across the railroad bridge to fight off Patton, who was on a line between Nancy and Metz in France. We had strict orders not to hit the bridge; we were supposed to hit the marshaling yard (where the Germans get everything lined up and organized so they can send it out) only. On this particular raid, we got to fly deputy lead.

Our job was to synchronize on the lead bomber when the bombs were dropped. The lead and the deputy lead also carry smoke bombs, so when we drop them, it marks the spot where we want the other bombs to fall, so when the other airplanes pull up even with the smoke, the bombardiers would hit a toggle switch and drop their bombs on the smoke.

It's a strange thing being part of a large raid. Normally your own airplane is so loud you can't hear anything else, maybe a little shouting from the crew. When the raid is over, it takes a while for you to hear normally. But when the raid is large enough, you can hear the noise from the thousands of planes cutting through the noise of your own plane, plus the sound of *ack-*

ack and machine gun fire, and the whine of enemy fighters, not that there have been many of those lately.

Anyway, back to the Karlsruhe raid. Bombardiers are nicknamed "commissioned gunners" or "toggle-deers," because they have commission rank but all they really do is push the button. There's this big fancy Norden bombsight that's supposed to make bombing super-accurate, but in my experience it's really overrated. Now, Lieutenant Sollars, our bombardier, is pretty fat and the navigator, Booker, is taller than I am, and both of them together didn't fit too well in the nose of the airplane and even though we were flying deputy lead, my bombardier was not synchronized on the target. There is a tunnel under the flight deck to go back to the rest of the airplane, and Sollars was just lying in the tunnel with a flak suit wrapped around him. The flak was heavy over the target and we had lost three airplanes already from the flak.

Now, just before it was time for the bombs to be dropped, the lead airplane called on the radio and told Lieutenant Russ that it was time for him to drop, because the bombsight on the lead aircraft was frosted up. Lieutenant Sollars heard that and he called Russ and said, "I don't have time to synchronize! We'll have to go around again!"

Well, after losing three airplanes from flak, Lieutenant Russ just said, "Synchronize, hell! Salvo!"

So we dropped the bombs and as the other airplanes pulled up, they dropped their bombs on our smoke. Well, we missed the bridge, of course, but we also missed the marshaling yard, but at least two or three squadrons hit right in the middle of town and one squadron hit the north side of the town.

We have this German propaganda radio station in Calais that we can pick up and also one in Berlin that we listen to sometimes. Now, we know it's all propaganda and no matter what happens, the Nazis always exaggerate the numbers. But they called out airplane numbers, which they could tell from observing the fuselage markings on the airplane, and they could tell what group it was. And they said that day that the 392nd Bomb Group— which is us—had "indiscriminately bombed the town of Karlsruhe, killing or wounding 7,000 people." Well, I'm sure those numbers are awfully high, but if they say it was 7,000, it was probably at least 700.

Everybody's still talking about the fact that there are hardly any enemy fighters up against us any more. I can't imagine the Germans are fresh out of them just yet, so I can't shake the feeling that there's a Nazi surprise coming up soon. We'll handle it, because I sure do want to go on a war bond tour. I'm sure we'd visit Charlotte, at least.

I'll miss you for Thanksgiving this year, but the base claims we'll be having turkey and cranberry sauce. Did you know the English don't celebrate Thanksgiving? It was an American holiday the Pilgrims started. Maura has never eaten turkey, if you can imagine! Well, this year she will.

Sorry it took so long between letters. The word is that we'll be flying a big mission next week, a very long penetration raid, so I'll be busy, but I'll write just as soon as I can.

Love,

Your Son

Digger

North of Metz, France, 10 November 1944, 1620 hours GMT

Rommel's staff car had been running well, but out of habit Carl-Heinz opened the hood and checked the dipstick to gauge the level and clarity of the engine oil. It was dark, dirtier than he liked to see, but supplies were scarce enough that even the field marshal's car had to make do with longer than usual intervals between oil changes. Well, they'd be back in Trier in a few days, and the driver made a mental note to be sure and change it then even if he had to get up at 0200 to have the car ready for his vigorous commander's next early morning start.

Slamming the engine compartment closed, Carl-Heinz leaned against the fender and looked around. Lush pines rose on all sides, climbing the steep slopes that bordered this narrow cut between a couple of high ridges. The sky was clear, but even as the hour approached midday the light of the sun was filtered down in this ravine. He could see the brightness on the branches of trees up the hillside, but here beside the splashing brook he was surrounded by murk and cool mist.

"Hey, sergeant? Want a cup of tea?" Carl-Heinz Clausen looked up to see another feldwebel gesturing to him from the mouth of a nearby bunker.

"Jawohl! Thanks!" Carl-Heinz left the staff car and sauntered over, ducking low to enter the dark, concrete-walled compartment. He knew Rommel would be a long time yet, meeting with staff officers, reviewing plans, and being seen by the soldiers, and after all, he could see the car clearly. A little light seeped in through the door and the narrowed slits of machine-gun ports, but a small stove glowed with a friendly red light, and the smell of fresh-brewed tea cut through the underlying scents of sweat, grease, and gunpowder. The feldwebel handed him a tin cup and Carl-Heinz wrapped his hands thankfully around the warm surface. *"Danke schön,"* he said, his large, toothy grin flashing in the dim light. "November is getting a little chilly, don't you know."

"Ah, *bitte schön,"* the feldwebel replied. "Don't mention it. It certainly has gotten nippy in the past few weeks. Much cooler than the last place I visited courtesy of the Desert Fox." Carl-Heinz noticed that his companion looked much older than he. His face was haggard, outlined with a bristle of gray whiskers, and his eyes were sunk into dark wells on his face.

Looking closer, at the sallow skin and thin, bony hands of the other sergeant, Carl-Heinz made a guess. "You were in Africa with him, then?"

"Ah, yes," the grizzled sergeant replied, taking a sip of tea. "The Ninetieth Light Division, from Tripoli to Alamein . . . and all the way back to Tunisia. It would have ended for me there," the sergeant's tone was wry, "but I was lucky enough to come down with a two-month case of the runs, so they sent me back to hospital."

"Luck," Carl-Heinz observed. "It's odd what one considers lucky after some time in the army."

The two men laughed; the grizzled sergeant's laugh turned into a cough, and he took another sip of tea. Carl-Heinz let his own tea warm his hands and let a comfortable pause develop. He looked at the man's hands and realized that they looked young. The sergeant was probably no older than he.

"Alamein . . . that must have been a bitch," Carl-Heinz said.

"Ach, ja. Monty had eight hundred tanks . . . we had about a hundred. And even so we held that bastard up for damn near a month." He coughed again. "And you—been Rommel's chauffeur for long?" He grinned, showing an absence of malice as well as a few missing teeth.

"Only since the retreat from Normandy."

"Hey—I recognize you! You're the tank driver from that picture!"

"Yep," Carl-Heinz said. "That's me, speaking of luck. Odd to be recognized just for bugging out."

"Hell of a drive, I read."

"It had a few moments of excitement," he replied, grinning widely so the gap between his front teeth shone in the dimness.

"So that's why you get to drive the Desert Fox. Good choice."

"I've got a reputation for dodging well," Carl-Heinz said, laughing. He took his own first sip from the teacup. There was no sugar, of course, and the leaves had been steeped more than once, but the heat was welcome.

"You're a lucky man, Sergeant," said the sergeant. Carl-Heinz dimly saw other men, a pair beside each of the guns, but they watched through the vision slits and let the two noncoms enjoy their tea in relative privacy. "That's a great man you're driving around . . . I hope you're careful with him."

Carl-Heinz nodded. "I take care of him like he was my own mother." And it was true. The Desert Fox was a strong man and recovering at a speed that amazed the doctors. Ever since his trip to Augsburg and seeing the jet fighters—Carl-Heinz wished he'd had a chance to open one up and get a look at its innards—he seemed a changed man, a reborn man, a man with hope. But Carl-Heinz still saw him each morning, sweating painfully through push-ups, sometimes needing to be helped from his staff car (unless, of course, someone else was around who might see him), showing the effects of his terrible wounds.

Carl-Heinz was still the main one who took care of him, made sure he took time to eat and to sleep, modified his car seat and office to reduce his pain. He was forceful enough that Rommel had jokingly taken to calling him *Mutti,* or mother.

The infantry commander had been extremely nervous at first, but Rommel's sure touch with people had put him at his ease. General Bücher never ceased to be amazed at how people fell under the spell of the Desert Fox.

If the man chose to be political, he would be formidable. Yet he doesn't know, or perhaps just doesn't care, he thought. *And a good thing, too. Otherwise he would be a threat to the Party and then I would be forced to act.*

Bücher suspected he would inevitably be forced to act anyway and arrange an "accident" for the field marshal, but he pushed that thought back deep in his mind.

Look at me, he thought wryly. *I'm falling under the Desert Fox's spell myself.* If he could convince Himmler that the Desert Fox was completely content in the military sphere, then that would be the best thing for all concerned. That was a big if, unfortunately.

Bücher brought his attention back to the conference table, where Rommel was patiently reviewing lists of material and supplies, marking maps with contingency plans, and gently building up the morale and self-confidence of the commander for the battle to come.

"You won't be expected to hold forever, just for a while longer. I know it seems that we've been pushed into a slow and inevitable retreat, but in fact there will be a counterattack such as the Allies have never seen. Remember, there are the Russian front troops arriving daily, the reassigned veterans of the Normandy campaign, and many others. And there's more—some things I can't speak about yet." Rommel patted the commander on the shoulder. "Be of good hope, mein Oberst, for we shall yet prevail."

Bücher followed the two men as the Desert Fox set out on his inspection, more to be seen than to actually see. Smiling, confident, strong, his scars receding, the Desert Fox was the model military officer. Soldiers clustered around— *to touch the hem of his garment,* thought Bücher, in a flashback to catechism class back in second grade in the *kinderschule.* He hadn't thought about religion for a very long time, but there was something about Rommel, something special indeed. . . .

The tour of fortifications and men ended, they headed back toward the car. Bücher noticed that Mutti, for once, was not bent over the engine, but instead was scurrying out of one of the bunkers, snapping off a salute as he opened the door. Rommel settled down into his seat, carefully modified for maximum support, while Bücher opened his own door and sat in an ordinary seat. He didn't begrudge his superior officer any comforts, especially after the wounds he'd suffered, but he was amused. *What is it about this man that calls forth such loyalty?* he thought again. Rommel and the führer were such different people, yet they both had this special effect on others. Himmler was a good leader, but he was missing that quality. Bücher realized that he was missing it too.

The finely tuned engine roared and the staff car pulled away, heading for the next fortification.

The trees around him moved from blazing color to the stark bare limbs of winter, but they were healthy trees, not sick, not damaged. And the evergreens were as majestic as ever. Rommel was tired, but satisfied with his visit. In the past month, he'd spent more and more time on his expeditions to the front lines, inspecting the fortifications of the Westwall and here in France, lending the authority of his presence to the units who were preparing to face what everyone assumed as an inevitable onrush of American and British arms. He talked to officers and men, saw to preparations, issued orders, heard complaints, even listened to suggestions. He knew the importance of an effective response, encouragement, a promise of support, or merely a presence to let the troops know that they were important, that their problems mattered.

He at last began to feel like his old self again, rising early, eating simply, maintaining long hours and a schedule that often left his staff and assistants gasping for breath as they tried to keep up. Carl-Heinz—"Mutti"—was as fresh as ever, in fact, he was humming to himself as he drove the staff car. The scarred SS general beside him was obviously worn from the day's travel. *But he is a man of combat, of action. These meetings and inspections aren't what he's used to,* Rommel thought. *He is a good soldier, even if he is SS.*

Rommel's troops were not beaten. He now saw grit and determination where before he had observed only fear and hopelessness. The fortifications of the Westwall were strong, but more and more the men spoke of coming out from their defensive positions, of taking the war to the Americans. They took pride in knowing that they were frustrating Patton's advance, disrupting the pace of the entire Allied offensive. There was even some cheerfulness. Rommel was far too modest to realize all the contribution he himself was making to the change in attitude.

As important as the improving morale, he was at last beginning to assemble a strategic reserve. Fresh tanks were continually arriving, swelling the ranks of the dozen panzer divisions under his command. Operation Carousel, the rotating of forces from east to west, was nearing completion, and many veterans—and equipment—of the Russian front were finding their way into the army of the west.

Nineteenth Division Mobile Headquarters, Luxembourg, 14 November 1944, 1221 hours GMT

Lieutenant Colonel Reid Sanger. He rolled the new title around in his mind yet again. *Lieutenant Colonel Reid Sanger.* It sounded good—hell, it sounded great.

"Congratulations, Reid," said General Flynn, shaking his hand.

"Thanks, sir," he replied. He was still a little dizzy; he hadn't expected a promotion.

"There's a note from your old boss, Colonel Cook. Says this is your payoff for predicting the German-Soviet deal. Did you really do that?"

"I'm afraid it was just a lucky guess, sir," Sanger replied.

"Hell of a guess," said Flynn. "You've got a good gift for this sort of work—you know how to put yourself in the other guy's place. The biggest problem in this work is the temptation to think the other side is stupid or ill informed. It's always best to figure they're smarter than you are; if you turn out to be wrong, at least you're wrong on the right side."

Sanger nodded. "That's how I feel, sir," he said. "I know I'm wrong more than I'm right, but overestimating the enemy is better than the reverse."

"You kill fewer of our guys that way," Flynn said. "I'm going to be sorry to see you go."

"Thanks; me, too," said Sanger. "It'll be interesting to be closer to the front, though."

"Yeah, but look out for the Nineteenth. They've had a bad time of it. Got their ass caught in a crack when Rommel came out of nowhere. Their previous S-2 was killed, and they've been rebuilding for the past few months. Right now, things are pretty quiet for them, but I expect they'll heat up pretty soon. They need good eyes and ears to keep them out of trouble. That'll be you."

"I'll do my best, sir."

"I've met Henry Wakefield, the CO. Smart guy. Doesn't suffer fools gladly, but he likes people who stand up to him. My advice is don't mince words with him. Tell it straight and stick to your guns."

"Thanks for the heads-up, General."

"Sanger, we'll miss you around the zoo. Good luck."

Wakefield was as gruff as General Flynn said he was. "So you're my new S-2," he growled. "Says you've never worked at the division level, all army level and above. Right?"

"Yes, sir, but—"

"Used to being part of a staff, reaching consensus by majority vote, right?"

"Sir, I—"

"You'll find out pretty quickly things don't work like that at the division level. You're in charge, you make the call, and if you're wrong, men die— understand?"

"Yes, s—"

Wakefield continued like an unstoppable tank, rolling over everything Sanger tried to say. "Says here that you've made some good calls on the grand strategic situation."

"Well, I—"

"I don't give a damn. That's not division-level intelligence, understand? I need tactical information and I need it on time to the best of your ability, which had damn well better be good enough. You take the grand strategic crap that comes from higher headquarters and break it down into something useful to the Nineteenth. You'll send information back up the chain, too, but you do that *after* you've supplied my intelligence needs. Got it?"

"Got it, sir." He was pleased to get a complete sentence, even a short one, complete before Wakefield was able to continue.

"You speak fluent German, it says."

"Native, sir," he interjected.

Wakefield's eyebrows lifted. Sanger hurried on. "Parents taught me; I spent a summer in Germany with family before the war."

That stopped Wakefield. "So, this is like the Civil War for you. Choosing sides, fighting your own relatives?"

Sanger hadn't thought of it that way before, but he nodded. "Guess so, sir, in a way, but I'm an American. Always was. And I hate Hitler and the Nazis even more than most, because I know what he's done."

"Killed your relatives?"

"Indirectly, sir. Turned them into Nazis themselves."

Wakefield chewed on that for a few minutes. "We're going to do our goddamnedest to kill as many of them as we can here."

"I'll help, sir. I can think like them."

Wakefield stuck out his hand. "You'll do, son," he said, more warmly than he'd said anything else. "Welcome to the Nineteenth."

"Thank you, sir," Sanger replied. "Happy to be here."

Clark, the S-3 operations officer, got him settled in. "We've just been reassigned to Third Army," he said. "Our target is Metz." Sanger got busy with the intelligence data, then got on the horn to corps and army group headquarters to start getting more. He was determined that the Nineteenth would have the right information on the right schedule on his watch.

Lager-Lechfeld Luftwaffe Base, Bavaria, Germany, 19 November 1944, 1008 hours GMT

He snatched up the jangling telephone before it had finished the first ring.

"Oberst Krueger here," he said.

"This is the one, Kommodore!"

The tinny soundpiece could not mask the taut excitement in Galland's voice. Krueger knew that the Luftwaffe head was calling from Berlin, the center where the rudimentary German radar system was tracking the incursion of enemy bombers. Receiving input from air division headquarters located all over the country, the central command station gave Galland the unprecedented ability to control the launch and deployment of all the fighter forces in the Fatherland. It was a technique first employed by the RAF during the Battle of Britain. Now it would send a force of fighters against an armada of bombers that would make the air battles of 1940 look like mere skirmishes.

"We've tracked a huge stream of bombers over Belgium, making for northern Bavaria or perhaps Czechoslovakia. I'm sending up every Geschwader in Germany and your boys will be leading the way."

"Jawohl, mein General!" snapped Krueger, unconsciously sitting up straight as he listened to the disembodied voice. He barely heard the click as the connection was broken.

In another second he had shouted the orders sending the great airbase into a controlled frenzy of activity. He knew his jets were ready, and that the pilots, as they had been through weeks of training, remained taut with barely contained tension. And there was fuel, blessed fuel, for once enough to do the job the way it should be done.

The Klaxon brayed, and pilots raced from their barracks and briefing rooms. Krueger ran too, but even as he moved he took in the fierce grins on the faces of his pilots, sensed the elation buzzing in the air. For weeks they had trained, learning the new aircraft, all the time sitting on their hands when the Allied bombers came over. But, with the sounding of the battle horn, that frustrating interval came to an end. These fighters would finally take to the air, winging after real targets, and the pilots of Geschwader 51 would at last have the chance to avenge themselves against the bombers that were raining such misery onto their homeland.

The Kommodore stopped at the door of his office, for just a moment watching the pilots racing across the flight line. Not one of these young men thought he would die today, and each was eager to take his magnificent aircraft into action. Krueger, of course, knew that this sense of invulnerability was misguided, that some of these soldiers would in fact lose their lives. He didn't much care, as long as they took enough Amis with them. He knew that these young pilots, none of whom had a background including the hours, the kills, that he himself had amassed, would certainly make mistakes. Sometimes those errors would be fatal, but at the same time they had the chance to make the enemy pay an even higher price.

Outside, massive hangar doors were trundling open, while tractors chugged with basso force. One after another the sleek jets were rolled forward, with Krueger's Schwalbe marked with the distinctive pattern of red flames, leading the way.

The three Gruppen of his Geschwader, all based at this massive airfield, totaled sixty of the jets, the largest concentration of Me-262s in Germany. At many other bases, there were individual Gruppen, or in some places even a single nine-plane Staffel, of jets attached to formations of piston-powered aircraft. And, like his men, the pilots of the 109s and the Fw-190s were also eager to make this flight of vengeance.

Before him, the jets rolled forward, lining up in takeoff position, but for the time being the powerful engines remained silent. Due to their massive rate of fuel consumption, the high-performance aircraft had a very limited range. Kommodore Krueger had given strict orders that they not fire the engines until the last possible minute. But this didn't hold back the pilots. Exultant and jaunty, even flippant, they scrambled into the cockpits. With bubble canopies raised, they waved cheerfully to the ground crewmen who raced back and forth below.

Feldwebel Willi Schmidt, the crew chief and mechanic who had been with Krueger since Poland, helped him to strap in and pull the canopy closed. Schmidt then went to the starboard engine and stood, the pull cord for the two-cycle starter motor in his hand. He was ready to activate on the pilot's command.

In the meantime the kommodore of Geschwader 51 listened to his helmet radio, as a low power transmission from the field tower kept him appraised of the course of the bomber stream. He knew that, though the enemy aircraft might be on course to several different targets, the Americans would maintain their concentration of force for as long as possible. He also understood that Galland's tactic called for a huge force of fighters to intercept this bomber stream. It occurred to him that if they succeeded they would trigger an air battle unprecedented in the history of the world.

"Enemy bombers advancing toward Regensburg/Prague axis. Range to target, one hundred twenty kilometers."

The words crackled in his earphones, and he decided it was time to act. With a chop of his hand, he signaled the ground crews, and immediately the gasoline starter engines rattled from his starboard, and moments later his port, wing. All across the flight line, the similar high-pitched snarls indicated the little motors being started. Soon the jet engines began to catch, and the now-familiar howl grew to a commanding whine as the mechanics hustled away from the planes.

He looked across the Geschwader, saw that at least a dozen of the jets were still being worked on by their crews. Unfortunate, but not surprising—these high-powered engines were still temperamental and touchy, and of his sixty brand-new aircraft Krueger would today be happy to get a mere fifty into the air.

But there was no longer time to wait. He released the brakes, his flame-painted fighter leading the procession of jets onto the runway. Two wingmen lined up at his flanks, for on this wide runway the fighters would take off in threes. Opening the throttle, he let the acceleration press him into the seat, and angled his powerful aircraft toward the enemy in the sky. The jets to the right and left kept pace, and the trio of deadly planes lifted smoothly, banking in unison to angle away from the field.

Behind him the young men who were the hope of Germany took to the air, a formation propelled by fire, roaring upward on a mission of death.

Army Group B HQ, Trier, Germany, 1305 hours GMT

It was after his latest expedition, a jaunt that had carried him as far north as Holland and back in a week, that Rommel returned to his headquarters in Trier. After driving all night, his staff car pulled into the city during the mid-morning. Rommel—with, it must be added, Mutti's advice—had selected a small combat car, protected with a little bit of armor but capable of high speed travel, as his new command vehicle.

Mutti drove the car along muddy tracks, even fording streams and rivulets that were now frequently swollen by the increasingly heavy autumn rains. When an early snowstorm had caught them in the Ardennes Forest, the driver once more proved his skill, negotiating narrow and winding roads without an appreciable loss of speed. Now Carl-Heinz stopped the car in front of the hotel, and immediately the field marshal went to the situation room where his staff, alerted by reports of his return, had gathered.

Günter von Reinhardt, now chief of intelligence for Army Group B, was responsible for conducting the briefing. He hadn't quite gotten over his unaccustomed embarrassment when confronted with the field marshal, but he was determined to win the man's unvarnished respect. The brief smile on Rommel's face as he sank into his chair at the head of the table and the slight nod that told him to begin was enormously reassuring. He had not yet disgraced himself, only not proved himself. He didn't reflect how seldom he found any need to prove himself to anyone else.

"What is the latest news?" asked the Desert Fox.

"We have an American movement, spearheaded by armor, coming around the north of Metz," reported Reinhardt, indicating troop movements and positions on the large map. "You will need to decide whether to try and reinforce."

Reinhardt had already made up his mind about the proper course of action. He knew that the dynamic in the room was fairly balanced, with General Speidel, his chief of staff, and others holding out for reinforcement, himself on the other side. There was also a Himmler directive—a "stand and die" order—to take into account. But this was not a democracy, after all. Only one vote counted.

Normally, Reinhardt would use this as a test of the intelligence of the commander, but this time he found himself holding his breath, waiting to see if his own judgment would be validated by one of the few men he'd ever met whom he judged his true superior.

Rommel looked at the map, unaware of the mental challenge he was posing to his subordinate. It was an interesting strategic puzzle. The massive network of fortifications, including twenty ancient castles and strong points, had held up Patton's army for a month and a half, but he could see that the end was at hand. Already the U.S. infantry had pushed south of the city, crossing the Moselle River and swinging northward to cut Metz off from the Rhine. Now, with an armored spearhead racing to meet them, the time had come, he decided, to cut his losses.

There was a complication. Führer Himmler had commanded him to hold Metz at all costs, but in his mind that was only another datum, not at all conclusive. As far as he was concerned, the days when German generals followed militarily foolish directives merely because they came from a higher-ranking source were over. He was the commander and would make decisions up until the moment someone chose to remove him.

"No . . . no more troops to Metz." This kind of decision, no matter how necessary, no matter how justified, was always painful to make.

"Is it your order, then, that they will hold with what they have?" Bücher asked. The room was looking expectantly at the Desert Fox, waiting for him to cut the Gordian knot, for they were fully aware of Himmler's order, and too aware of the fate of past generals who ignored the commands of Adolf Hitler.

Rommel shook his head. "Too impractical. The Americans will just have the chance to put the whole garrison in POW camps. Instead, send orders to General Schmidt they are to withdraw as soon as they can, under the cover of darkness tonight, if possible. Tell him that he is to bring out all the men and matériel that he can."

"Mein Feldmarschall!" Bücher's scarred cheeks flamed red with protest. "This is in direct contradiction to the orders of the führer. I must protest!"

Careful, thought Rommel. He had no intention of changing his mind, but there was no need to cause unnecessary strife. "I can understand how you might see it that way, General, but the key order I received from Führer Himmler is to win the war in the west. I think he would agree that is my highest responsibility, and I'm sure you would agree with that yourself."

Rommel's mildness took the edge off Bücher's rage. "Of course, mein Feldmarschall, that would be the führer's highest command. But—"

Smoothly, Rommel took the first point and moved on. "And therefore, I must make certain tactical decisions that, while they may go against the führer's first preference—and my own, I might add—are necessary given the situation. Did not our late führer himself say, 'Strength lies not in defense but in attack'? Very well, let us follow the words of our late leader and prepare for an attack. In the meantime, we should not waste resources on defense. Colonel, would you see to the orders?"

"Yes, Field Marshal," saluted Reinhardt. He was obviously having a hard time concealing his grin.

He had not convinced Bücher, but he had brought the room to his side. So be it, the Desert Fox reflected. The days of German soldiers dying in pointless lost causes were over, so far as he was concerned.

Not all of Himmler's orders, fortunately, had been foolish or wrong. Just yesterday, he'd received a Himmler directive that was quite unlike the "stand and die" orders for Metz. In fact, this latest directive followed very closely Rommel's own feeling on the conduct of the campaign. It was time, as he'd suggested to Bücher, to think about going on the offensive. Trains were rolling, finally, bringing reinforcements into the Westwall. His armored divisions were rested, well-equipped with new tanks and personnel. The weather, too, was getting worse every day, and this greatly limited the Allies' ability to dominate the front through air power. Today's clear skies notwithstanding, the field marshal knew that it was time to think about an attack.

Even as he was internally ticking off these reasons, a dull rumble began to penetrate the walls, the foundation of the Continental Hotel. A chandelier rattled slightly, and Rommel felt an unmistakable sensation in the pit of his stomach.

"Bombers." Speidel, the chief of staff, was the first to speak.

"Coming here?" asked the supply officer, Müller, his voice squeaking comically. At first, Rommel had wondered about the fat little supply officer but had discovered that the man was competent and detail driven in his work, which was the most important element of the job.

"Let's go have a look," Rommel said coolly. The droning of thousands of engines, in any event, would bring a postponement to the rest of the meeting.

Indeed, the thunder of Allied aircraft all but drowned out further attempts at conversation. The officers looked grimly around the room, each of them knowing they heard another great bomber raid, a veritable river of bombers moving on the Reich. Rommel led his staff out onto the hotel's highest balcony to witness the event.

Tiny specks in the distance, the American bombers formed a swath that stretched from the right to the left horizon. The massive formation of four-engined aircraft was passing north of the city, obviously destined for a target farther to the east. The leading elements had already crossed into Germany, but there was no sign of antiaircraft fire, or harassment from the Luftwaffe. The aircraft rumbled on, toward whatever targets the enemy, with utter impunity, elected to bomb. The great airplanes formed an implacable testimony to the might of Allied air power.

"How many of them are there?" Bayerlein asked softly.

No one answered. There was no obvious response, except that they could all see thousands of individual specks.

"Like stars in the night sky," Rommel finally mused.

"If we could only strike at them, hurt them the way they hurt the Fatherland," growled Speidel, "then we might just have a chance."

"Maybe we do have a chance," Rommel suggested. He recalled those marvelous fighters and wondered if this was the raid that would draw them into action. "It will be interesting to see what develops."

For once he was without fear, contemplating the aerial might of his enemies. Without further explanation he led the group back to the conference
room.

After the meeting, Rommel assumed that Bücher would call Berlin; what surprised him is that he asked permission first. "Mein Feldmarschall, because of
your decision to abandon Metz in contradiction to der Führer's orders, I'm
afraid that I am required to contact Berlin in this matter. I regret the necessity,
but I must follow my orders." Bücher stood at rigid attention in Rommel's office, his scarred cheeks still blazing red, as if he was afraid to be reprimanded.

Rommel nodded. "Of course, General Bücher. You must follow your orders, and I took for granted that you would. You're a good soldier. And as for
me, I do not lightly disregard these directives, but you see, my superiors are
the General Staff. Führer Himmler can make suggestions, but ultimately his
only power is to remove me from this position. As the field commander, I
must make tactical decisions as I see them." He spoke mildly, his eyes fixed on
Bücher all the while.

Bücher kept at attention. "Mein Feldmarschall, I believe you are correct in
theory about the chain of command, but in practice that is not the way it is.
Please take my advice, sir, and reconsider your orders regarding Metz. You cannot go against our führer. You simply cannot."

"I know you mean well, General, and I understand your concerns. But I am
a soldier, like you. And I am a German as well. I cannot and will not abandon
my fellow Germans to needless destruction, nor will I sacrifice unnecessarily
soldiers who can be used more productively from a military perspective. If
there is personal risk to me in my decisions, so be it. I make others risk their
lives each and every day; it is only fair that I assume the same risks for myself.
Call Berlin, General Bücher, and say what you must. We are all soldiers, and we
must all do our duty as we see it."

The SS general paused for a long moment before saluting Nazi-style. "Yes,
sir," he said, clicking his heels before pivoting to march out of Rommel's office.
The Desert Fox watched him go and wondered whether he had just signed his
own death warrant. He hoped that it would not have to be Bücher's duty to kill
him. He respected the man and knew that following those orders would hurt
Bücher deeply.

Skies Over Augsburg, Germany, 1300 hours GMT

Colonel Krueger scanned the skies before him, seeing a virtual landscape of enemy bombers. He had never in his life seen so many aircraft gathered in one
place. As the forty-three airworthy jets of his Geschwader raced closer to the

leading heavies, he could not help yielding to a momentary doubt. Could they possibly have any impact on this huge force? But then the fiery rage leaped up into his heart and he howled with glee. For they were sheep and he led the wolves, and before the day was over everyone would know who was who.

He knew that other Gruppen, more jets and hundreds of Me-109s and Fw-190s, were sweeping against this massive force from all directions. In the distance he saw dogfights between Luftwaffe fighters and the P-51 Mustangs of the bombers' escorts, angry specks wheeling through the skies, snarling into combat, here and there trailing plumes of smoke or bright fingers of flame.

Others of the speedy American fighters were above him, and they dove like buzzing bees, anxious to give combat. A quick glance showed him at least sixty, maybe even eighty or more Mustangs, all diving toward Geschwader 51. With a tight smile, the Oberst in the jet with the painted nose knew that he could ignore these pests. His throttle fully open, he felt his powerful fighter pull away from the enemy escorts, and he laughed out loud at the thought of the enemy fighter pilots' consternation.

His Me-262 raced in the lead, diving toward a B-17, closing at an impossible velocity, a combined speed that must have exceeded one thousand kph. Together with all the rest of his pilots, he had practiced this head-on approach. At these speeds, they had to aim quickly. At the same time, the hope was that the speeding jets would be virtually impossible to target by the U.S. gunners.

The American formation was flying directly into the heart of the Reich, and Krueger led his wing of fighters to stop them, a storm of defending interceptors breaking on the massive bulwark of heavy bombers. He was acutely conscious of this epic confrontation indeed, surely God Himself would have held His breath, except that it all happened too fast. Tracers from the bombers' turrets and nose guns flared outward, falling short or veering wide of Krueger's shrieking aircraft.

Swiftly aligning his gunsight, the kommodore drew a bead on the leading bomber and released a short burst from the four cannons mounted in the Schwalbe's nose. His aim was true, and he saw the B-17's cockpit glass shatter in a series of small explosions. Immediately the Flying Fortress lurched out of formation, canting to the side and tumbling earthward in a spiral of doom.

By then, Krueger was into the midst of the formation. He snapped off a shot at another bomber above him, and the massive aircraft disappeared in a blossom of smoke and flame as its bomb load ignited. Unconsciously yelling in his exultation, the German pilot flew his jet through the fireball and found himself racing away from the bomber formation. Around him the other jets of the Geschwader were also breaking into the open, leaving a number of burning, smoking, and lumbering B-17s in their wake. Once more those tracers reached, like striking, venomous snakes, for the fighters . . . but again they fell short.

Krueger led the jets through a long arc, still ignoring the fighters that dove toward them only to vanish in the rear as the Me-262s curled around for their next attack. He looked to the right, to the left, and behind . . . good, most of his men were still with him. Acutely conscious of the fuel burning up in his tanks, he banked, dove toward the bombers again, knowing that they had to attack quickly.

This time they came against the bombers from the starboard quarter, and the closer relative speeds of the two formations allowed him to take a more deliberate aim. He fixed his sights on the base of a Fortress's wing, and sent an extended burst into the joint with deadly accuracy. He saw the wing crumple away, and the aircraft plummeted from the skies, twisting in a spiral so tight that the centrifugal force held the crew in place. There would be no parachutes from this one.

More of the big bombers were blowing up on all sides, as they were beset by a greater number of fighters than they had ever before encountered. Nearby Me-109s screamed past, with Mustangs in close pursuit. Elsewhere, Fw-190s pulverized the four-engined American aircraft with their lethal cannon. Here and there a German fighter spiraled downward, trailing flame and smoke, but for the first time in a long time, perhaps forever, the invading bombers were suffering appalling losses. Equally important, their escorts were overmatched in their desperate efforts to protect their charges.

Krueger found himself coming up behind a formation of B-24 Liberators. Ugly planes, he thought, as he blasted the twin-ruddered stern of the nearest, leaving the plane to cartwheel chaotically, spinning downward in its last descent. He noticed that his fuel was low, and though he snapped off another salvo he couldn't stay to determine the effects of his rounds. Instead, he arced away, leading his pilots toward the replenishment offered by their giant airbase.

Minutes later, on a course for home, he flew through a wheeling dogfight between Mustangs and Me-109s, and though he took a quick shot at one of the Americans his speed was so great that he knew he had little chance of scoring a hit. He saw another jet fly clear of the combat, but then a blossom of flame trickled along the wing of the Me-262 as the engine overheated and caught fire. Immediately the fighter tucked into a dive, but before the pilot could open the cockpit the inferno had spread to the fuselage. Krueger shook his head, imagining the sheet of flame covering the pilot, consuming him in fire, and shuddered. He couldn't think of a worse way to die.

And finally his guns were empty, and his fuel tanks nearly the same. Only with the greatest reluctance did he lead his fighters back toward Lager-Lechfeld, and when he looked behind he saw, for as far as his vision could carry, a sky that was filled with blotches of smoke, bursts of violent explosion, the detritus of dying bombers, and everywhere glorious plumes of fire.

Finally, the broad runway beckoned, and as he nursed his jet through a low-power landing he saw ground crewmen running forth, fuel carts rumbling and ammunition wagons already in place. They would refuel, rearm, and once again take this fight to the American bombers. With luck, the Geschwader could hit the attackers perhaps twice more before the battered survivors finally made it to the safety of their bases back in England.

578 Squadron Base, Wendling, Norfolk, England

UNSENT LETTER FOUND IN "DIGGER" O'DELL'S FOOTLOCKER

November 20, 1944

Dear Mama,

You won't get to read this letter until after the war is over or earlier if I don't make it home. I don't want to send it now because it would just make you worry even more and there's nothing I can do about it anyway. But I need to write down what happened today and then put it away.

Harry Glass, the other waist gunner, is dead, and I saw him get shot and killed. *Ford's Folly* is full of holes; Lieutenant Sollars, the bombardier, and Sergeant Wagner, the upper turret gunner, and I are all in the hospital, and I'm lucky to be alive and I'm not hurt too badly. A lot of other B-24 crews aren't so lucky. Over 700 bombers, B-24s and B-17s, are down. Planes have gone down in our bomb group before, but never so many. It's so bad that for the time being, there won't be any more raids. Can't say that bothers me a whole lot, to tell the truth.

I want to write down all the details of the raid while it's still fresh in my mind.

Fry, our nose turret gunner, had washed out of navigation school, so he was the assistant navigator on our crew in case our navigator was hit or killed, and he always went to the navigation briefings. So one of my duties was to go to the gun shack and clean and oil his guns as well as my gun and it was also my duty to pre-flight his turret to make sure everything was in working order. But we had all gotten away from that sort of thing, which was really stupid because in large measure our lives depend on how well we do every part of our job. I guess part of it is laziness and another is just being fateful and maybe showing how brave and nonchalant you are when you really aren't that brave at all, you're just being stupid.

In any event, I put his guns in the turret and didn't turn on any electricity and didn't check anything at all. As a matter of fact, I took me a blanket and went out and laid it in a wheat field that grew right up to the edge of the runway and laid down and took a nap.

It was finally time to take off, and Lieutenant Russ said, "All right boys, let's go!" I always get on board through the camera hatch, which is about a three-by-five hole in the bottom of the airplane with a door over it that a camera can fit in and take pictures. For some reason, I dropped back out of the camera hatch and scrubbed my feet on the ground once or twice before going back in. So we took off.

While we were forming the group, Fry got into his turret and started checking it out. He called me and asked if I had pre-flighted his turret, and I, of course, said I had, because the lieutenant could hear everything on the interphone. He said, "Well, the reticule in the sight doesn't work. The bulb doesn't light." I told him to take the bulb out of the trouble light, which is a light on a flexible kind of fixture that you could shine and move around like a portable flashlight in the turret. He said there was no bulb in the trouble light. So he had no sight whatever in his guns, which could have been real trouble, but I don't remember any attacks coming from the nose, in any event. See, that's the trouble with flying an airplane that had got washed out on a raid; there was lots of stuff wrong with it and we're still finding it all out.

While Fry was telling me what kind of bad shape his gun was in, I began getting my gun ready. The ammo box, which carried five hundred rounds, was on the side of the airplane and a flexible metal chute came up from the box and hooked onto the side of the fifty-caliber machine gun that I fire. There was no hook on the metal chute, but I had a roll of safety wire in my parachute bag and I wired the ammo chute to my gun and got it firing. Harry Glass's ammo chute fit onto his gun, but the apparatus that holds the gun steady while it's firing came off in his hand. Now, I'd managed to scrounge me the first spool of very strong nylon cord I ever had, and it was on a wooden spool. I took my knife and I cut the nylon cord off the spool and we jammed it in the apparatus that held his gun out the window so it would fire. But I lost my nylon cord.

Anyway, we had taken off and formed the group and hit the enemy coast and crossed into Germany up in the Ardennes on our way to Dummer Lake, which is a rather prominent landmark in northern Germany, and was used for an IP, that is an Initial Point, from which to start a bomb run. Our target was Regensburg.

We had some flak after a while. I put on my flak helmet while that was going on and just stood there and watched it. After a few minutes, the flak stopped. I took the helmet off and laid it on the ammo chute and was just sitting on the ammo box on the floor looking out the window at the scenery when all of a sudden I could hear guns firing.

We were in the low left squadron, and the only thing we were leading was Tail-End Charlie, which is the farthest man from the front of the group and we were just in front of him. I looked up when the firing started and about the same moment someone in our airplane—and I don't know who it was—yelled "Fighters!" and I looked up and it looked as though the sky was black with them.

I know how to recognize most German fighters, especially Me-109s, but these were different. Swept-back wings, kind of shark-line . . . and no propellers! They were actual jet fighters. I had heard about them but never seen them and I didn't know the Nazis had any and I think that the generals on our side probably didn't know either, or if they did they sure didn't know how many. There must have been forty to fifty of them, and they were moving faster than anything I'd ever seen before in my life. I just stood there for a minute looking at them as they were closing on the group.

"Digger! They're coming up on your side!" yelled Harry Glass, who was looking around over my shoulder, and that broke my concentration and I started firing at one fighter and he broke away right under us. He came in right under my waist window and he obviously didn't want to end up on the tail because the tail gunner had the best shot at any fighter. He just lays the sight on the nose and fires away. So fighters usually try to break away under you before they end up on the tail. This fellow broke away so close I could see the pilot sitting in the cockpit. Of course the fighter pilot didn't know that the tail turret was out of commission. I fired at another fighter that trailed black smoke but there were no flames except from that jet exhaust, so I have no idea if I hit him or not.

Harry Glass was now shooting on his side, because the jet fighters had to throttle back as they got near so they wouldn't close too fast on us, and then after they shot they'd break away and give it all the power they had so they could break away fast. I saw one of the fighters explode in midair, and Harry got him.

Now the next fighter I fired at, I thought I had really hit him, because he was burning in the nose, but as he got in closer, I could see that the fire I was looking at was the flames from his guns. This fighter had designs painted all up the sides, and I'm guessing he was some sort of group leader. A 20-mm shell hit my gun and it exploded. One piece hit me squarely between my eyes and cut my goggle frame in two. A couple of other pieces hit me in the chest. I started bleeding and had trouble seeing but I never went totally unconscious. I do remember Harry Glass saying, "Digger's been hit!" I must have looked a lot worse off than I really was. Booker, the navigator, yelled, "Glass, get off the damn interphone, there's a lot cooking up here."

I could hear Sollars telling Lieutenant Russ that he'd better salvo the bombs to lighten the aircraft, and I heard that number-three engine was windmilling and burning, and then I heard the command to abort the mission, we were hit and going home.

I was able to wipe some of the blood out of my eyes and saw Glass explode another fighter but the fighter was firing too and then I saw Harry fall back and then slump down. I was able to crawl over to him and I tried to get out a bandage over a very large hole in his head but he never said anything or even opened his eyes, so I think the chances are he never knew what hit him.

In the meantime, with number three burning and windmilling, I was afraid the airplane was going to explode, so I started taking off my flak suit and put on my parachute. But finally the fire went out and they feathered the prop, and we were on the way home. I crawled back over to Harry Glass but he was dead. I found out later that the lieutenant thought I was dead, too, and he was surprised when we landed and they found me alive. I ended up in the hospital, of course, and with a few pieces of flak picked out of me, but all in all my damage was pretty light and I'll be back in action in a couple of weeks. I'm getting a Purple Heart for this, though that was the one medal I never did particularly care to see.

The lieutenant came to see me. Harry Glass was dead, Wagner, the upper turret gunner, was badly wounded and probably wouldn't return to action, and Lieutenant Sollars had been hit but not too badly. Number-three engine would have to be replaced, but otherwise *Ford's Folly* was fine except for some guns and electrical work needing replacement. "We'll make that war bond tour yet," he said. I told him only twenty to go and number thirteen was behind us now, and he laughed a little bit.

He told me that this was the worst raid we'd ever had. Those jet fighters were everywhere, backed up by the usual Me-109s and Fw-190s that the Germans normally flew. The jets were Me-262s, which the Germans had had for a while but never put into action. "Hitler didn't want them," Russ said.

"Then for once I'm sorry the old S.O.B. got killed," I said.

The Germans shot down nearly a third of what we'd sent up, and that's not counting the planes like ours that got shot up but didn't go down. We were lucky.

The word is that we won't be flying any raids for a while, until they figure out what to do about the jets. Also, because it's getting into winter and the weather is turning bad, there was going to be some falloff in raids anyway, so we'll have time to recover and patch everything up. The men are starting to call the mission Operation Bloody Hell, which in my opinion it was.

But I have to tell you, Mama, it looks kind of bad right now. As I wrote, you won't see this letter until after the war except if I don't come home, so I want you to know I love you and I miss you and I'm all right at the moment.

Love,

Your Son

Digger

Fortress Metz, France, 21 November 1944, 1101 hours GMT

Combat Command A made its camp in a series of narrow valleys on the west bank of the Moselle. The battalions were broken into task forces for the upcoming assault. Task Force White would lead the way, so Dennis White's tank company, armored infantry company, and supporting platoons occupied a town and several farms right on the riverbank. Task Force Ballard was in a nearby valley, while Task Force Miller—commanded by the senior company commander in CCA—filled the clearings around a village another mile away up the river. The headquarters company and Diaz's artillery battalion were downriver, but within easy distance of the bridge.

The men slept close to their vehicles, knowing that orders to move could come at any time. Colonel Pulaski took over a small farmhouse as a temporary headquarters, and Sergeant Dawson established a radio room in the kitchen. Pulaski and Lieutenant Colonel Ballard paced anxiously around the yard. Occasionally they rushed into the house when they heard the crackle of the radio. On those instances, Pulaski was pleased to note that his tank commander, who still limped on his wounded leg, was able to move with considerable alacrity when the situation demanded. Dennis White, meanwhile, was as imperturbable as ever, puffing on his pipe, finally drawing Diaz into a game of chess.

Pulaski stayed close to his command post, following the developing battle through the radio reports. The weather was overcast, with fog and occasional drizzle. Though air support was available and the clouds broke apart every once in a while, for the most part this would be a ground battle.

The first news was encouraging, as Bob Jackson's Combat Command B pushed through the initial ring of German fortifications and raced out of the compacted bridgehead. The fight was savage—Pulaski learned that in the early going eight tanks were destroyed assaulting a single pillbox. Eventually the strongpoint was reduced by a plastering of artillery, and the armored spearhead moved on.

Listening to disjointed reports, hearing from messengers that periodically passed through the HQ, Pulaski tried to form a picture of the action. In a few minutes Jackson's tanks encountered a lone Tiger blocking a crossroads. The crackling voices over the radio reported a window in the clouds and called for air support, but the overcast closed in before the tactical bombers got to the scene—and in any event, the panzer was taking advantage of an overhanging ridge wall as protection from the ground support aircraft. Accurate artillery fire flushed the leviathan out of its lair, and then cheers erupted from many American throats when a pair of Shermans equipped with the high-powered 76-mm gun blew up the Tiger with a series of flank and rear shots. In the CCA headquarters, Sergeant Dawson broke into a broad grin, then settled back to his stoic vigil.

"Hope they leave some Krauts for us," blurted one of the green second lieutenants, betraying his nervousness by the quaver in his voice.

Dawson's expression turned to scorn, and Pulaski felt a chill of ice in his stomach. It wasn't the same . . . having been there himself, it could never be the same.

At sunset, Ballard, White, Miller, and Diaz returned to their individual commands, all suspecting they'd be moving out by the next day. Overnight, the men got a little sleep. It wasn't easy, but they all knew they'd need to be well rested when they went into battle. Pulaski stretched out on a narrow cot in the back of his half-track, but every few minutes he jolted awake, listening to the sounds of distant artillery fire or droning aircraft engines.

Midmorning the next day they heard the new reports: CCB had come up against a tougher position, a medieval fortress commanding a view a long way down the constricted valley. Dawson relayed the news when Pulaski was pacing outside, reporting more calls for artillery and air support, and that further radio traffic betrayed the consternation of the advance elements. Frustration built in Jackson and his subordinates as more and more casualties were taken, and finally a sense of despair prevailed as the CCB spearhead was forced to go to ground.

The clouds glowered and pressed low, soon releasing a freezing chill that dampened hopes as well as men, for the weather put an end to all hope of air support.

An hour later General Wakefield came through Pulaski's HQ, his command jeep skidding to a quick stop.

"It looks like we're going to need you, Jimmy," he announced around a tin cup of steaming coffee.

Pulaski took a deep breath. "We're ready, General," he replied.

And he was, he finally realized. The demons from the debacle at Abbeville were still there, but today he and his men were facing a fresh challenge, a new obstacle here. He was not yet whole, but he could function.

Pulaski watched the general head for the front to get a close view of the situation, knowing that when he returned CCA of the Nineteenth Armored would once more hurl itself into the war. The knowledge left him with a bizarre kind of eagerness, as if now that the event was inevitable he wanted nothing more than to get it over with.

Two hours later the division CO returned and led Pulaski into a small command office in the house he had commandeered for an HQ. The colonel sensed Wakefield's consternation and tried not to let his own emotion show as he waited for the general to speak.

"Jimmy, it's your turn."

Pulaski's heart pounded as he stood before the desk and listened to his general. On the surface before him was a map of the Metz region, with tiny flags marking the efforts of Nineteenth Armored to sweep around and cut the city off from the Rhine.

"Yessir, General. We can get going right away." Suddenly his hands felt cold, and even in the crisp air he felt as if he'd moved into a slow motion state. He knew that Wakefield's orders meant trouble in CCB's attack, probably heavy casualties, but right now he didn't care. Wakefield's explanation confirmed his suspicions.

"Jackson's boys have been chewed up pretty bad. They're bogged down around these forts." The general thumped his fist on the map. "You're to take CCA into action. Go around this strongpoint to the south, and hit the damn Krauts hard."

"Yessir!" the colonel replied, saluting.

"And Jimmy . . . ?"

Pulaski paused, waiting.

"I wish I could tell you to bring 'em all back alive . . . but we know that's not going to happen. You've got to make this breakthrough—understand?"

The pause grew longer, before Pulaski finally replied, "I do, General."

"Good luck."

By the time the last words were spoken, the commander of Combat Command A was already headed out the door.

Three hours later, Pulaski was standing on a bluff overlooking the bridgehead on the east bank of the Moselle River. A shattered bridge lay below him, with a pontoon span constructed by U.S. Army Engineers in place immediately beside the wreckage. The weather was still socked in. They could hear planes droning over the clouds, but they would be of little help. A column of Sherman tanks was rumbling across the river, and though he could not make out the patch at the base of each turret, he knew that these were his men, his tanks. Dennis White was there, riding in one of the lead half-tracks, ready to command the spearhead as CCA went into action. Ballard's men would follow, though for now the long column of tanks and half-tracks was still waiting to get onto the bridge. Still farther away, Task Force Miller wasn't even in sight of the crossing yet, while nearby the eighteen Priests with their support vehicles were ready to bring up the rear.

Pulaski scrambled into the back of the command half-track and took his place beside Sergeant Dawson at the machine gun. Keefer eased in the clutch, and the big vehicle rumbled away from the river, following the road that twisted up the face of these looming highlands. Joining the middle of the armored file, the half-track rolled along at a satisfactory speed.

To the colonel's right was a sprawling expanse of concrete, turrets, and balustrades, the entire surface pocked by explosions, with a smell of death lingering in the air. The burial details hadn't had a chance to clean out the bodies, and the men of Combat Command B had only paused here long enough to catch their breath.

Next they passed a series of burned-out Shermans, and Pulaski touched his crucifix in honor of the new dead. Finally they found Bob Jackson. The usually dapper colonel was dirty and plenty discouraged.

"They're dug in deep, Ski," he reported. "Y'all might want to wait until we can get some air support."

Pulaski shook his head. "I've got orders to go in."

"Then good luck to you," offered Jackson.

"Say, Bob?" Pulaski suddenly had an idea. He indicated the rising ground before them. "Is your artillery sighted onto those heights?"

"Yes—Colonel Zimpel has the ranges down pat by now."

"Can you have him give me some cover until Diaz gets sighted in?"

"Sure thing."

Pulaski radioed back to his artillery commander, ordering him to bring up the guns and get situated. In the meantime, the colonel, as well as Ballard, White, and Captain Miller, were briefed by CCB's weary officers. An hour later the combat command once again started forward. Minutes later a chatter of machine guns drew the colonel's attention up the road. He heard the thump of artillery, the whistling of passing shells. He didn't flinch as explosions rocked the ravine, a quarter mile behind him. He could see the outlines of another pillbox farther up the slope, and knew that his GIs were already closing in on the obstacle. Several Shermans, concealed as much as possible amid the rocks of the rising slope, fired high-explosive shells at the concrete fortifications, shots that sent dust, rock, and debris crashing outward from the mountainous facade.

Scrutiny through binoculars revealed one antitank gun, firmly emplaced in a fold of rocky ground, screened by an overhang of the upper cliff as it fired down the road. Fortunately, the ruggedness of the terrain helped the Americans as well since the Shermans pulled close to the upper slope and were able to partially mask themselves from the deadly eighty-eight.

For several minutes the stalemate held, high-explosive rounds from the tanks blasting against the cliff while the German gun spat its lethal shots along the road, several shells just skimming over the tops of the American formation. One ricocheted off the top of a turret, and Pulaski watched as the tank hastily reversed, tracks crunching over gravel and rock until it skidded around the shoulder of an embankment. Immediately the antitank gun found another target, spitting shells into the rocks before another Sherman, sending showers of fragments exploding in smoke and flame.

Pulaski snatched the radio, barked into the mike.

"This is Polish Eight to Willie One and Willie Two! Damn it, move up there! Get some dismounted infantry after the son of a bitch!"

Before the dogfaces could move out, however, one of the tanks got lucky. A shell careened into the hollow sheltering the A/T gun, and a blossom of flame erupted, meteoric blasts of shrapnel coursing outward, tumbling down the slope, marking the grave of the eighty-eight with a fiery pyre.

The column rolled forward again, pushing upward, making good time. Shells tumbled downward from the heights, plumes of smoke marking the concrete and stone face of a strong fortification. The tanks rolled forward as fast as they could, all but careening around the tight corners of the twisting roads.

More shots whistled into the column, and another Sherman, the lead tank, went up in a blossom of flame. The column skidded to a halt again, tanks returning fire while infantry raced forward, helping the driver and hull gunner from the burning M4. They couldn't do anything for the rest of the crew, as the turret was already charred black, spuming a cloud of thick smoke.

American infantry crept up the defile, seeking to take out the gun with small arms fire, but they were quickly pinned down by a machine gun that chattered from the heights.

"Polish Eight to Decker?" Pulaski made the radio connection, using the day's code name for his artillery commander. He studied the map, then reported the coordinates of the stubborn emplacement. In another minute the mobile artillery found the range and the facade of the fortress disappeared behind a cloud of smoke, fire, and debris. A tremendous volume of shells—no doubt CCB's guns were joining in—pummeled the position, and when the dust settled there was only wreckage and rubble to be seen. Meanwhile, ignoring the shrapnel and machine guns, troops hooked chains to the disabled tank, and soon the wreck was pulled out of the way by the following M4.

Inching forward following the artillery barrage, squads of infantry overwhelmed some German positions, swarming over one machine gun nest after another in a burst of small arms and hand grenades. Other emplacements were plastered by direct tank fire and artillery. The gray clouds parted for a moment and tactical fighters swept in, guns winking from their wings, and at last a whole series of strongpoints was reduced to shattered stone and broken, bleeding bodies.

Again the column rolled forward. Sergeant Dawson, beside Pulaski in the turret, kept up a steady volume of suppressing fire from the heavy fifty-caliber machine gun. From before and behind, the guns of CCA pounded the enemy positions, raking the heights and giving cover to their own advance. More fighters droned overhead, but already the skies had clouded over again. Under the screen of thickening mist Ballard sent his tanks hell-bent for leather between two pillboxes. They ran the gauntlet without loss, then turned to plaster the emplacements from behind.

The road began to level out as it reached the upper level of the bluff that had dominated its lower course. The tank drivers kicked in their clutches, moving into second and third gear, rolling forward at a speed that started to feel exhilarating. More pillboxes came into view, and these were deluged with fire while the column stayed on the move. Mobile artillery, now rolling quickly at the tail of the column, paused to deploy long enough to smash one or two of the strongest obstacles. Pulaski was pleased to see that Diaz's battalion performed like veterans, firing with speed and accuracy, then quickly advancing to set up in a new battery position. In other places, the infantry spilled out of their half-tracks, ducking through ditches, crawling in the fields, blasting with small arms fire and satchel charges to knock out machine gun nests and more antitank guns.

And then the tanks rushed forward again, finally able to disperse off the narrow road. They rolled through fields of dried wheat, following the curve of a small stream. Some of the Shermans plunged recklessly through a small grove of saplings, and the radio burst into exultant cries as the crew of one M4, a tank armed with the lethal 76-mm gun, put killing shots into a Panther tank and two Panzer IVs.

"There'll be a medal for those boys," Pulaski promised, clapping Dawson on the shoulder.

"Yes sir!" agreed the sergeant, white teeth standing out against the smoke-smudged stain of his face.

"Do I look as bad as you?" the colonel asked with a laugh, the first laugh he'd had in weeks.

"Worse, colonel," replied Dawson, without missing a beat. "But not as bad as them."

The sergeant pointed, and Pulaski saw a file of ragged, unshaven Germans emerging from the woods with their hands held high over their heads. Immediately a squad of infantry converged to take charge of the prisoners, while the rest of CCA moved on.

The tanks were advancing faster now, rolling at top speed through good country, driving an armored wedge into the German lines. All of Pulaski's frustrations, his memories of death and defeat, the lingering nightmares of Abbeville fell away, at least for now, as his men pressed the attack in a storm of cordite, gasoline, smoke, and fire. The misty rain did nothing to slow them down, and the colonel reflected—not without some pride—that for once they had carried a major attack forward without air support.

Finally they were through, and the road to the Rhine beckoned them beyond.

Rumania, 22 November 1944, 1820 hours GMT

Rudolph Zeitzman was furious. "What do you mean by this new demand? We had an agreement, and I insist you honor it!"

His Russian counterpart sat stolidly as the thin-faced German diplomat raged. "This is the new agreement," he said in a thick Russian accent, utterly unmoved.

Zeitzman took a deep breath, willed himself to calm down. These Soviet negotiators had no honor, no sense of proportion. First, they'd negotiate for hour after hour over something essentially irrelevant, then adjourn and postpone the key issues, and whenever he thought he had a deal, the next day there would be "minor" changes that upset everything.

The Russian bastards knew the German peace offering had been a sign of their weakness, and clearly intended to wring every last advantage from it. And for all he knew, then they would invade again, unless Germany was so successful in the west that it could negotiate once again from a position of strength. Right now, the issue was oil. Germany would have never surrendered the rich oil fields of Rumania in any peace agreement, except the Soviets were going to take them anyway. Now Zeitzman's mission was to negotiate for a supply of oil for the German military, and he wondered, not for the first time, whether he would be successful, or whether these Slavic scum would just make him dance like a puppet and then go home empty-handed. The latter option was unacceptable; the führer's representatives had made it clear that failure was unacceptable. The German tanks needed fuel, enough fuel to defend the Fatherland.

He looked at the agreement again. "This is twice the agreed-upon price for only three-fourths of the oil we requested."

The Russian held his hands wide. Zeitzman noticed with distaste that his thick, calloused fingers had their nails bitten to the quick. "The oil fields and refineries are heavily damaged, as you know. We did not receive them in good shape. We are only now learning the extent of the damage."

"Comrade Stalin ordered you to cooperate fully with us!" Zeitzman argued, trying a new tack. Führer Himmler, knowing that oil resupply was the critical military issue, had personally called Stalin, who had agreed that the Soviet Union would sell oil to the beleaguered Germans. Himmler had advised Zeitzman that the Russians would dodge and weave and change their minds a hundred times, but added, "We *need* the oil. Make sure you get it." Zeitzman shuddered at the definiteness of the order. He fully understood the consequences of failure.

The Russians were still sitting at the narrow conference table like fat potatoes with no necks. He hated them. They didn't respond to the Stalin sally, they just sat silently. *We can wait you out,* their body language said. Zeitzman knew they were right.

He caved in. "Very well. We accept the revised terms. But these are the final set of changes."

"Of course," the smug commisar said, and Zeitzman knew he was lying through his decaying teeth.

Berlin, Germany, 24 November 1944, 1200 hours GMT

"You tried to convince him otherwise?" said the führer of the Third Reich to his agent on the other end of the telephone.

"Yes, mein Führer," replied Horst Bücher. "I went to him privately after the meeting to discuss the political ramifications of retreating from Metz, but he has decided that the military issues are the only ones with which he is concerned. I informed him that I would have to report this situation to you."

That was interesting. Bücher had informed Rommel of his intent to report his disobediance to the führer. How unlike the SS General. Heinrich Himmler wondered whether Bücher was going soft. Rommel had that effect on people sometimes, though Himmler would have thought Bücher was immune.

"You did correctly," purred Himmler in a soothing tone. No need to provoke the man, at least not now. He was confident he could win Bücher back, and for now perhaps Bücher's attitude could be useful.

"Thank you, mein Führer. But for now, what should I do?"

"For now, you've done enough," Himmler replied. The German Führer already had a response in mind, one he would otherwise have assigned to Bücher. Now he would have to find someone else to carry out a very special mission.

Army Group B HQ, Trier, Germany, 2020 hours GMT

"A very pretty puzzle, indeed," observed Günter von Reinhardt.

"What do you mean, a puzzle?" argued Müller. "We beat them! We swept them from the air!" He was as excited about the air battle as if he'd personally fought in it. His arms spread wide and swooped over the bar stool. Günter laughed. The two men were enjoying a late repast at a local pub that had become the unofficial officer's club for Army Group B headquarters.

The two had adapted well as members of Rommel's staff. Reinhardt's intelligence responsibilities continued to expand as Rommel learned that Reinhardt would not shade the truth, even when it involved admitting that he did not know a particular answer. Müller's supply skills were stretched to the limit with the immense logistics planning of troop movements from east to west. Yet he had thrown himself into the work with enthusiasm, and been rewarded with notable success.

"Ah, my good friend, you confuse military success with strategic success, as so many do. Victory in the air is not victory; at most it sets the conditions for victory. This undoubted triumph, however glorious, only changes our situation from utterly hopeless to merely bleak. Our opponents outnumber us and we have our backs to the Westwall."

"But our soldiers are better than theirs, and so are our generals!" Müller replied, unwilling for once to surrender to the sardonic and cynical jibes of his friend.

"Regardless, Lanchester's Law is against us."

"Who?"

"Frederick Lanchester. The strength of one's forces is measured by the square of the number of units. Therefore, the relative strength of one force against another is measured by the differences in the squares. Outnumbering one's opponent is the only strategic advantage that matters. And we are outnumbered."

"But Günter—that just doesn't make sense! If so, all we ever have to do is count up the forces in a battle and then we know who will win! History is full of examples where generalship or good soldiering or weapons or position made all the difference! You should know that better than anyone." He took another swig of beer.

Günter smiled. "You know, tonight I'm wondering if everyone isn't smarter than I am. You're right, of course, but Lanchester's Law still applies."

"But—but," Müller stuttered. The alcohol was starting to befuddle him.

"Clausewitz again. It's the schwerpunkt. You don't have to count all the forces on either side, just those at the decision point. If the Allies outnumber us overall, but we outnumber them at the critical point of the battle, then Lanchester's Law operates in our favor. Weapons and position and other military tools can leverage one's forces, start the squaring at a higher number—that's why they are sometimes called 'force multipliers'—but soldiers, generals, and politicians alike tend to value those elements at a far higher value than they're worth. Ego, mostly, and an unwillingness to accept that one is in a disadvantageous position."

"So you're saying we aren't doomed after all?"

"No, of course not. The key question for our Desert Fox is how to find a critical decision point where Lanchester's Law can operate for us, rather than against us, then work out the strategy to get us there. If anyone can do it, Rommel can."

"Now there I agree with you," said Müller definitely, taking a deep swallow, then stuffing a bite of a thick würst sandwich into his mouth. Arguing was thirsty work.

"So," he said around a mouthful, "tell me—what's with you and our field marshal?"

Günter was silent for a moment. He regarded his own reflection in the mirror behind the bar. "He's a very smart man."

Müller nodded. "I know. But hearing you say so—well, that's the first time I've ever heard you say something like that."

"You're right. I don't often have occasion to say so. But perhaps that shows a lack of wisdom on my part."

Müller looked at him, puzzled.

Lager-Lechfeld Luftwaffe Base, Bavaria, Germany, 25 November 1944, 0817 hours GMT

Adolf Galland personally flew to the airbase to congratulate and commend the kommodore of Geschwader 51.

"We hurt them, and badly . . . I wouldn't be surprised if we don't see any more daylight raids, at least for a while," declared the Luftwaffe commander, chewing on his cigar and looking out the window of Krueger's office.

The kommodore shook his head, irritated and restless as he gestured at the steady rain. "Maybe it's just the damned weather," he snapped. "Nobody can fly in this shit!"

Galland laughed, exhaling a big cloud of smoke. "Trust me, it will be a long time before they send their whole air force over the Vaterland again. That's why I want to order you out of here."

"What?" Krueger looked at his commander in astonishment.

"Relax . . . I'm bringing your Geschwader forward, closer to the front."

The pilot felt his pulse quickening, subject to memories of battles four and five years earlier. "You mean in the west, of course?"

The general nodded. "We're moving hundreds of fighters to bases on the border, close to the Westwall. You'll be flying close support for our ground operations again. Think of it, Paul! With a chance to compete again for air superiority over the battle!"

"No Stukas, this time," Krueger replied grimly. Like all fighter pilots, he had regarded the lumbering dive bombers as little more than deathtraps.

"This time the bombing will be done by Messerschmidts . . . 109s, and the 110s we have left. The jets and the Focke-Wulfs will be flying cover, going toe to toe with the Allied fighters."

The fighter pilot smiled. "We'll send the bastards down in flames."

"How many of your Stormbirds are operational?"

Krueger shrugged, scowling at the reminder of the Me-262's biggest problem: reliability. "I have fifty-five machines on the base. On any given day, I can put somewhere between forty and fifty of them into the air. My ground crews are replacing engines as soon as we can get them in. Of course, fuel is becoming a problem once again. . . ."

"That will have to do." Galland shrugged with remarkable nonchalance. It wasn't nearly good enough, but he knew better than to push the point. "I've marked you for three fields near Bitburg, not far from Rommel's headquarters, as a matter of fact. How long will it take you to get ready for the transfer?"

"We can move as soon as the weather clears," Krueger replied.

"Good. I've arranged for ground transport for your equipment and crews. Get them started right away, so that your bases can be up and running as soon as you fly in."

With that, Galland was gone, leaving a lingering memory of his casual salute and the wafting cloud of his cigar smoke.

Before that odor dissipated, Krueger had gone to work. He sent clerks after maps, informed his unit commanders, and sent the base into a frenzy of activity. It seemed as if the gods of war were smiling upon him, for the very next day dawned clear and windless. Before noon, his fighters were taking to the air. Forty-nine of them proved airworthy, though several limped along on single engines for the westward flight.

But the distance was not far, and barely ninety minutes later the first jets were touching down on the landing strips at their new bases. These were smaller facilities, of course, so the Geschwader would be dispersed into its three Gruppen.

More importantly, Krueger knew that they were now based almost in the shadows of the Westwall.

East of Metz, France, 26 November 1944, 1351 hours GMT

"There they are, Colonel—a full retreat back to the Westwall."

Frank Ballard handed Pulaski his binoculars, and the commander of CCA looked into the valley, watched the file of German vehicles and men heading eastward with visible speed. The clouds had broken during the early morning today, but by now the low overcast had rolled back in. A chilly mist was falling, though it frequently parted enough to offer visibility of two or three miles.

The highway twisted through a broad, forested valley, and in most places it was concealed by trees from direct observation. But where they could see it, the road was packed with men. Metz was being evacuated, and these were the defenders, now heading toward the safety of Germany with all possible speed.

"Should we get down there . . . break that column right in two?" Ballard asked. "Recon has found a few tracks down this bluff. With luck, we should be able to get the Shermans down one or two of them."

Pulaski considered the opportunity. The terrain was bad, but his armored battalion commander was right . . . the doughty M4s could undoubtedly pick and choose a few routes down into that narrow valley.

But what would happen then?

There were thousands of Germans, and hundreds of enemy vehicles, within view of just this one vantage. How many more of them were down there? And were they anticipating just such a flank attack?

On the other hand, if Combat Command A stayed up here, on the safety of the high ridge, they could make the lives of those retreating Krauts very uncomfortable indeed. Diaz could bring his guns up, and artillery fire could hammer the road. Though the range was long, even the tanks' main guns could provide a threat to the enemy vehicles on that tiny ribbon of roadway, the retreating troops' only link to their homeland.

The memory of his last incorrect guess haunted him. This was Rommel he was up against. "No, Frank . . . we'll stay up here. Get your tanks deployed for some long-distance shooting. I want to call in every piece of artillery we have, get those shells smashing down onto the road."

"That's all?" Ballard asked. His tone was bland, but Pulaski felt his tank commander's eyes boring into him. The colonel blinked, then continued.

"Also, we'll let the air corps know if this weather clears, a couple dozen fighter-bombers will make a real mess out of that."

"Yes, sir," Ballard replied, his tone quiet and unemotional. Pulaski couldn't tell if he was disappointed—or relieved.

"Are you saying you want to charge down there?" the colonel snapped.

"Not at all," Frank replied. "Not at all." When Ballard turned to look into the valley, Pulaski tried once more to read the emotion on his subordinate's face.

And once more he failed.

Approaching Westwall, Saarbrucken, Germany, 2200 hours GMT

In the moonless night, SS General Erich Höffner recalled the comments by Heinrich Himmler, führer of the Third Reich, about the retreat from Metz. "If German troops get the idea that retreat is an option, their will to fight will be shattered. If they believe that the Allies will accept ordinary surrenders and not insist on the 'unconditional surrender' terms, they will be inclined to surrender. And above all, if Wehrmacht field marshals believe that their tactical issues outweigh the larger strategic concerns of the Reich, then the Reich is doomed. It is necessary, therefore, to provide a clear and incontrovertible lesson to all concerned, while at the same time striking a particularly powerful blow at the West."

"But what about the field marshal?" Höffner had asked.

"All in good time, all in good time," the führer had replied. "Our Desert Fox has one more hunt before he is ridden down. For now, this lesson should be sufficient to keep him focused for his remaining task."

And now it was up to Erich Höffner to carry out his own task. He had completed many such tasks for Adolf Hitler. As a protégé of the famed commando leader Otto Skorzeny, Höffner had carried out a variety of special missions, all of extreme danger and extreme importance. Although his target this night would be Germans, even this was not unusual for the SS commando. Enemies of the Reich could be anywhere, and sometimes examples must be made for the cause.

His handpicked commandos were dressed in American military uniforms, insignia forged by SS specialists—they were Combat Command A of the Nineteenth Division besieging Metz. Intelligence sources revealed that the colonel in charge of that command was reputed to be unstable and revenge seeking—or could be portrayed that way by the German propaganda apparatus.

Who better to take the blame?

The commandos slid through the dark night. General Weitz, commander of the retreating Metz garrison, was retreating by the book, leaving appropriate covering fire, withdrawing in stages, slowing up the enemy advance to allow his forces to escape and move to the new positions Rommel had chosen for them. Behind, the Allies were advancing inexorably. The dark night was punctuated with flashes of light and the dull crunch of munitions. The earth shook slightly underneath him, the sure sign that combat was near.

He moved into position. There, below, was the column of retreating infantry, edgy and on guard and yet oh so relieved to be pulling back. Weitz was not covering his flanks sufficiently, but then he had every reason to be sure that the Americans had not broken through his lines. This was a bugout, and the only thing he had to worry about—he assumed—was a too-rapid American advance into his rear.

But, my general, you are now going to enter the history books, the tragic victim of an American maniac, he thought. Erich Höffner knew how to follow orders and understood fully how the greater good sometimes required sacrifices.

He gave the signal for attack.

The massed firepower of multiple machine guns illuminated the night as it cut a swath through the retreating Germans. For a long moment, the soldiers were paralyzed, unable to determine from what direction the fire was coming. Then came hurtling grenades—the Allied style, which Höffner found awkward to handle—and then came panic. Soldiers ran in all directions at once, colliding with one another, crouching behind tanks and trucks, diving into the ground in a futile attempt to hide.

In English came the cry, "Surrender! Throw down your weapons!" repeated in German. Slowly, the remaining soldiers dropped their guns and stood, shaking with fear, as the German commandos came down from the hill in their American uniforms. The remaining Germans were marched into a nearby farmyard, disarmed, their weapons piled neatly outside the fence. The scene was carefully staged to show that a surrender had taken place.

When they were all lined up, hands tied behind them, Höffner gave the order. Lifting their captured American machine guns, the commandos sprayed bullets at the disarmed and helpless captives. And the captives died screaming, horrible bullet wounds gushing blood. They died with arms and legs ripped from their bodies by the explosion of grenades. They died suddenly as bullets or shrapnel penetrated brains and hearts. They died of other bloody wounds as well, some quickly, others slowly.

In moments there was silence once again, punctuated by the crackling of fires set by explosions and by gasoline, by a few remaining screams from the nearly dead, and incongruously by the ordinary sounds of the winter night.

"Quickly!" ordered Höffner, and the commandos planted the killing field with evidence, dog tags and insignia, stripped a few of the more mutilated and unidentifiable corpses from the initial attack and placed them in soiled and bloody American uniforms marked with the Nineteenth Division's insignia. A white star in crimson uniform patch shone dully in the reflected light from a truck headlight not yet dead. The scene would not fool a criminal investigative team, but any such team would be made of the SS, and they would not be distracted by irrelevant details. This looked like a callous massacre of helpless prisoners—which it had been—but one committed by American troops—which it had not.

Höffner could hear motors. The troops ahead were returning. He and his commandos could easily kill them as well, but the goal of the evening's work was achieved. Rommel was correct, there was no need to waste any more German lives than necessary. This lesson would travel rapidly among the troops. Surrender and retreat were truly no option. The barbarian Allies would massacre them. Only victory or death on the front.

The SS commandos slid back into the darkness to hear the first cries of horror as the comrades of the dead discovered the bloody hell that had consumed their fellows.

Army Group B HQ, Trier, Germany, 27 November 1944, 1121 hours GMT

"It's General Weitz, Herr Feldmarschall," said Rommel's secretary, and he went into his office to take the call.

"Yes, General. How goes the retreat?" Rommel asked.

"They've been massacred! Shot after they were captured, helpless, tied up! My God, Field Marshal, it's unbelievable!"

"Massacred? Shot after being captured? Slowly, slowly. Exactly what happened?"

As the general spoke, Rommel's face grew steadily more pale. An entire company of men captured and then horribly massacred in what should have been a relatively safe retreat. Losses were to be expected, but not this. With a sudden and sickening feeling, Rommel realized that this massacre was ultimately his fault.

"And the evidence, you say, points to the American Nineteenth Division?" he asked, his fingers numb as they held the telephone.

"Yes, yes! Our men shot at least a few of the attackers; we have uniforms, dog tags, other evidence. The investigative teams from the SS have been ransacking the site, although they haven't been able to do much because of the advancing Allies. Shall I bring you the evidence?"

"Never mind, General," Rommel said, stunned but thoughtful. "I think that your call is all the evidence I need." He tried to be as reassuring as he could, and finally hung up. His mind raced furiously. He knew that soldiers could be guilty of atrocities in the heat of battle, soldiers of any side. All commanders knew that. It was possible that it was an American atrocity, but it was too convenient, too targeted. No, far more likely this was an SS operation. A message, primarily aimed at him. *I told you not to retreat,* was Himmler's message. *Follow my orders or suffer the consequences.*

"Very well," Rommel said, answering aloud. He opened the door to his office. To his secretary, he barked. "Staff meeting. At once. There are developments." Then he strode down the hall, barely using his cane, to Bücher's office.

"Yes, mein Feldmarschall?" said Bücher, curiously.

"Retreating German forces were attacked, captured, and then massacred, ostensibly by the Nineteenth American Division last night." His words and tone were blunt, harsh. He waited and watched as Bücher processed the information, and immediately—Rommel could see it on his face—found himself reaching the same conclusion that he had.

"Mein Feldmarschall—I want you to know that I know absolutely nothing of this. I cannot believe—"

That was what Rommel wanted to know. This was not Bücher, at least not personally. If it had been . . . Rommel could still feel his temper boiling up. But instead he held up his hand. "We are all soldiers. We do our duty. What others do is frequently not up to us." Bücher's reaction pleased him. SS or no, the man had something salvageable in him. Let him study this issue on his own and reach the conclusions that seemed right to him.

The Desert Fox realized that he had to do the same.

Broadcast House, Berlin, Germany, 28 November 1944, 0800 hours GMT

The AP office in London never missed an Axis Sally broadcast. "It's mostly lies, and the rest is exaggeration," said Percy McCulley, the London AP bureau chief, "but there's often a kernel or two of truth buried inside. Useful way to get some unofficial information." He turned the radio knobs slowly, trying to bring in the static-filled signal.

The concluding sounds of the Glenn Miller Orchestra faded into the sultry voice of Axis Sally's propaganda program. "That was 'In the Mood,' and I'm in the mood tonight, just like your wives and girlfriends back in America who are so very lonely that right now they're finding comfort in the arms of the 4-Fs you left behind." She chuckled in a low, sensual voice. "This is your friend Sally, coming to you from Berlin, with music, news, and personal messages. Tonight we have a sad message for all our listeners. The Nineteenth Armored Division, facing the heroic defenders of Metz, massacred over a thousand German prisoners after they surrendered. Using machine guns on the helpless prisoners, many of whom still carried white flags, the savages of the Nineteenth, led by Colonel James Pulaski, carried out an atrocity."

"What the hell?" shouted a shocked Pulaski when he heard his name. "A massacre? What is she talking about?"

Frank Ballard put a hand on his colonel's shoulder. "Just Nazi bullshit," he said. "Don't worry about it."

"You may remember that Colonel James Pulaski is the careless young hothead whose Combat Command A blundered into a brilliant German counteroffensive in Abbeville a few months ago, giving the Allies their worst defeat of the war. Why he wasn't court-martialed, we don't know. It may be because Pulaski arranged for the death of his CO, General Jack King. That was a career-advancing move for General Henry Wakefield, a man George Patton once called 'a fat slug posing as a tank commander,' and who now commands the Nineteenth."

In the Ardennes Forest, Private Billy Cooper rubbed his cold hands as his fellows clustered around the tinny radio. "Goddamn," breathed one of the other privates. "I'm glad I'm not in the Nineteenth."

"You and me both, brother," said another.

"Do you know what I think?" purred Axis Sally. "I think Colonel Pulaski has gone crazy. First he kills his CO in collusion with his exec and leads his own men into a trap. The exec keeps him from getting court-martialed because your officers only care about each other—they don't care whether you live or die—and don't worry that he's gone around the bend. His own officers have been reporting that Pulaski was falling apart, and now he massacres German soldiers who had surrendered, in direct violation of the rules of war."

Colonel Sanger always felt he had a professional obligation to listen to Axis Sally. But when he heard the Nineteenth being mentioned, he immediately sent an orderly to get Wakefield. The burly general came within minutes and listened in silence until she finished. "Goddamn Nazi bitch," he swore under his breath.

"Men of the Nineteenth Division, your own Combat Command A has disgraced you with this cowardly and despicable massacre. Worse, watch as your own officers cover it up with lies and more lies. And if your commander is Colonel Jimmy Pulaski, the Panicky Polack of CCA, watch out before that maniac leads you all to your deaths. Now, back to music, with the Andrews Sisters singing, 'Don't Sit Under the Apple Tree with Anyone Else But Me.' Of course, you know your wives and girlfriends have worn out that old apple tree by now. . . ."

"Turn it off," said Wakefield. "Get me Pulaski." The boy was just recovering from Abbeville. Now to be tarred with a prisoner massacre—and that awful nickname—Wakefield was worried about a relapse.

Luftwaffe Advance Airbase, Bitburg, Germany, 30 November 1944, 1320 hours GMT

Krueger carefully controlled his rudder, guiding the jet through a shallow turn, back toward the runway he had departed only minutes before. The starboard engine gave him plenty of thrust, but still the Stormbird was difficult to steer in a straight line.

Angrily he cursed the dead weight slung under the port wing, the engine that had burned out as the Me-262 was climbing from the airbase, leading two Gruppen on a hunt-and-kill mission in search of Allied fighters. The malfunction had forced him to send his wingman in command of the two dozen jets, while he made this awkward return, infuriated by the failure of the delicate machinery.

Despite the obstinate handling of the plane, he was able to line up on the runway and make a nearly flawless three-point landing. Rumbling up to the hangar, he popped the canopy and jumped out as the jet rolled to a halt.

"I need a new engine, Willi!" he shouted angrily to his chief mechanic. "And I want it mounted by tomorrow morning!"

"Jawohl, Herr Kommodore!" replied the enlisted man, turning to shout the orders to his crew.

Krueger knew that they had several new engines in the maintenance shed, and that Willi would have no difficulty making the installation. But still, the loss of today's mission was galling in this winter weather. Chances to fly had become increasingly uncommon. Today was a rare cloudless day, with perfect visibility and light winds, an ideal chance to make life difficult for the

American and British Jabos that so relentlessly savaged the German positions on the Westwall. His rage mounted. On the one hand, he knew that the temperamental engines tended to malfunction, but on the other hand, that was the purpose of having a mechanic. His fists clenched as his temper rose.

Though the strategic bombing campaign had been suspended, the enemy air forces were still making life dangerous for the brave soldiers in the front lines. The Luftwaffe fighters had been moved to advance bases such as this one, all along the border, and whenever possible tried to harrass the Allied ground support aircraft. Krueger himself had shot down two Thunderbolts and a Mustang on his last mission, but that had been more than a week ago.

Eight days of foul weather had kept the air forces on both sides grounded, and now it was exceptionally aggravating to have this opportunity canceled by mechanical failure. The engines were still the weak link of this magnificent aircraft; it was inevitable that, on one of these days, his own airplane would be one of the offending laggards.

Why did it have to be today? he thought. *Someone will pay.*

He advanced into the hangar, his temper flaring. He picked up a wrench and strode toward his hapless mechanic.

Excerpt from *War's Final Fury,* by Professor Jared Gruenwald

The two key events of November 1944, Galland's Gambit and the Metz Massacre, had a dramatic effect on the military campaign to follow.

The devastating losses suffered by Eighth Air Force on the ill-fated raid of 12 November inevitably had a chilling effect on the entire strategic bombing campaign. Of 2,576 bombers launched on that fateful mission, more than seven hundred were shot down, and an equal number landed with serious damage and casualties. This was a loss rate higher than any other mission, and was clearly unacceptable to USAAF command. Flyer morale crumbled, and bitter recriminations flew among the American generals. Although reports were muffled, news of the debacle even leaked into the press at home.

Galland's Gambit, as the attack came to be known, thus paid off in an immediate cessation of daylight bombing raids. The Me-262, still plagued by engine design flaws, production difficulties, and worker sabotage, was a machine that nevertheless gave the Allied air forces serious problems. Its appearance in the skies during 12 November took the Americans by surprise; though the British had had some inkling that the machine was in the works, their warnings to the U.S. airmen had been ignored.

Responsibility for the Metz Massacre was assigned variously to the American Nineteenth Division's Combat Command A and to the Nazi SS, each side furiously blaming the other. The propaganda target, however, was not the American forces, who were affected relatively slightly, but rather the German regular troops, who, like all soldiers on the battlefield, tended to be a powerful conduit for rumors of all stripes. Dramatic and lurid rumors, such as this was, tended to have a strong effect. Whether the Germans believed that the Allies would in fact massacre their prisoners wholesale, as opposed to the occasional atrocity committed by both sides, or whether (as even some contemporary rumors had it) the SS would do it instead, made little behavioral difference. Feeling they had no option but to stand and die, they stood, and often they died. This behavioral change stiffened the resistance the Allies faced as they continued to push their way slowly through the Westwall.

The American naval reinforcements proved of little use in the European Theater, as by now the Germans had lost all control of the seas. Even their U-boat campaigns were stifled by the loss of the French and Norwegian ports. Though some vessels, equipped with the revolutionary snorkel devices that for the first time allowed the subs to perform their entire missions while submerged, were able to leak through the Allied blockade into the Atlantic, most of these subs were intercepted and destroyed before they could reach the sea lanes. The remainder of Halsey's fleet was most useful, perhaps, as it went into patrol off the coast of Norway and proved somewhat of a deterrent to Russian ambitions.

For their part, during November, the Soviets made use of their skills at winter operations. They moved huge air assets and many ground troops into Scandinavia, projecting their air power far beyond the Norwegian coastline. The Soviet fleet, bottled up in Leningrad for nearly the entire war, moved forward to Oslo, and set up a base there just a short sortie from the waters of the North Sea.

At the same time, on the ground the battles had degenerated into bloody campaigns in the autumn mud and rain. The successful but costly offensive at Aachen had ripped apart a great portion of First Army. Subsequently, in an attempt to move south of the city, Courtney Hodges's men found themselves trapped in a grueling campaign in the Huertgen Forest. Here the offensive was measured in dozens of lives for every yard gained. And though the harbor of Antwerp had finally been opened to Allied shipping, even that mighty seaport was barely able to slake the supply needs of the insatiable armies. A steady bombardment of V-1 rockets was not successful in closing the port.

Generals such as Patton and Montgomery continued to dispute the course of the war, which Eisenhower was necessarily managing in light of an increasingly difficult political environment as well as military concerns.

Concurrently, the German position in the Westwall was growing more solid by the day. Reinforcements from the Russian front made some contribution, though it wasn't to be an overwhelming force; OKW decided to maintain nearly 80 percent of the eastern front troops in readiness for the eventual Soviet attack that all thinking Germans suspected to be inevitable. Still, the treaty bought some time, and some desperately needed increase in Wehrmacht strength.

Rommel had garrisoned his fortified line from Switzerland to the English Channel, and still had enough troops to gather twelve panzer divisions as a strategic reserve. The respite from strategic bombing did not extend to the tactical air support for the ground war, but now, fortunately for the Germans, the weather became problematical. Cloudy skies, rain, blustery winds, and early snowstorms proved a great equalizer, removing the Allies' greatest advantage, and giving the defenders a chance to strike back.

Rommel was keenly aware of the Allies' supply difficulties and knew that he might be able to launch a single, devastating attack. He, like Eisenhower, faced strong political pressure to act, but this time the pressure coincided with his own military aims. He saw a chance to launch an offensive, the first major German attack since Kursk in 1943.

It was an opportunity the Desert Fox was ready to grasp.

OPERATION FUCHS AM RHEIN

December 1944

**Associated Press Bureau Office, Paris, France,
1 December 1944, 0946 hours GMT**

Chuck Porter shook his head as he inspected what had once been the Paris AP bureau office. Under the occupation, the Gestapo had used it as a command post because of the already-installed communications lines; on their retreat, they had savagely ripped out every bit of useful equipment and every file cabinet and left the office looking pretty much like a war zone.

"It's better than it looks, boys," he said to the three reporters who had accompanied him across the Channel and into liberated France. There'd been a fair amount of competition for the initial slots: Donald Lester, originally from South Carolina, who'd progressed up through the Havana bureau, Steve Denning, an ex-army brat whose father had fought with Pershing in Mexico, and Troy Winter, who'd moved from southeastern Wisconsin to the Chicago office and then international from there. They'd worked on city papers before joining AP, and the youngest had more than ten years with the organization.

"Let's get busy." Chuck pointed at some push brooms in the corner. "Now you see what reporting is really all about."

In spite of the inevitable grumbling, inside of an hour, they'd created the semblance of an office. There was no wire equipment, though, and at the normal rate for civilian service restoration it would take weeks to get back on line. The office had two couriers to carry stories back to London, with military censors waiting for them in Antwerp, where the primary transportation was. Troy had complained about that. "This is 1944, for God's sake! Two to three days to file a story—hell, that's like we're back in the nineteenth century!"

"Nah, look at it this way," Porter said, leaning back dangerously in an office chair and putting his feet up on the desk, "being cut off means that they can't send stuff to us, either. Think of it—no orders for filler stories, demands from client papers to find out what happened to their local boys or to get the East Palooka, Indiana, slant on things. . . ."

"No memos!" added Steve.

"And from my point of view, the very best thing is that we don't have a single client paper!" smiled Porter. One of the primary duties of a bureau chief was liaison with local client papers. "I'm officially demoting myself back down to reporter for the duration!"

"You mean *pro*moting," said Don.

"Somebody's got to teach you boys how to spell and write a decent head-line," grinned Porter.

This was the life, Porter thought. His treasured portable Underwood in its leather case, a notebook and a pen, and a war to cover. "Boys, let's go cover some news," he said. "Troy, you've got SHAEF headquarters. Don, you get Monty and the Tommies."

There was an immediate complaint. "Hell, Chuck, Monty's already got an army of reporters around him. He collects them. What am I going to find up there?"

"Something newsworthy," Porter snapped back. "Steve, how about some local human interest stuff?"

"Parisienne women after liberation!" Steve replied. "I'll have to do some in-depth digging!"

"No fair," complained Don. "He gets French women, I get Monty and a few Canadians. Where's the justice in that?"

"Justice? You expect justice?" shot back Troy. "I get to sit through briefings and get shuffled from officer to officer."

"So, Chuck, what are you getting?" probed Steve.

"The Metz story and the Third Army," he said smiling, putting his hands behind his head.

He held up his hand to stifle the chorus of complaints. "Hey, rank hath its privileges, you know. Besides, I'll be chained to this desk within a month. This is my last chance in the field, and I'm going to make it count."

War resembled a huge construction site with occasional smears of blood, thought Porter as the jeep bumped along the damaged road. He pulled the top buttons of his jacket as tightly as he could to protect himself against the cold, but it did little good. The only warmth was the glowing end of his cigarette. He wished he had brought an extra pair of long underwear. December was gray and turning harsh.

On the other hand, he was finally in the war, and even more importantly, a reporter again, if only for a little while. That made up for almost any amount of cold, drear, and rubble.

His few weeks in London had turned into a blur of camping out in one SHAEF office after another, soliciting the web of permits and documents enabling him to cross the Channel to begin a new AP France bureau. After SHAEF came dealings with the French provisional government and a memo-rable meeting with Charles deGaulle, who evidently assumed the sole purpose of the AP was to serve as his personal press office, and virtually dictated a se-ries of stories on his own glorious return to *la belle France*. Porter had met the type before: they weren't real if they didn't see their name in the paper. He had flattered and taken ostentatious notes, and finally ended up with a series of elegant documents topped off with the signature of deGaulle in all the key places.

Paris was relatively undamaged, except for places where Nazi insignia had been torn down. Dictatorships liked advertising, evidently, Porter mused, but swastika billboards grew boring in a hurry. When Porter pulled into Paris, dusty in fatigues and helmet, he was mistaken for an American soldier and nearly hugged to death by young Parisienne *filles*—not that he objected.

He'd had the experience of being cut off from his daily news fix again. The disaster in the air with the new German secret "jet" fighter was still on everybody's minds; the U-boat menace that had resurfaced with the sinking of the *Enterprise* seemed to be subsiding once again. Neither situation, he was assured by everyone in the command structure, was enough to change the ultimate course of the war, and his sources seemed sincere enough, so that's what he had reported.

The nearly universal opinion was that the Germans were finished, with the proviso that cornered rats were still able to bite. Porter hoped he wasn't too late to at least see a little bit of action.

Headquarters, Nineteenth Armored Division, Luxembourg, 0955 hours GMT

"You know, Hank, the papers are going to say 'Patton took Metz.' But you and I both understand that's not true. It was men like yours, and the whole rest of Third Army. Goddamn it, how I love those boys—what a magnificent collection of warriors!"

Henry Wakefield agreed politely with his army commander, but at the same time he felt himself growing tense. How much of Patton's words were just bombast, and how much did Old Blood and Guts really mean? He suspected that was a question that wiser men than himself would be debating for decades, possibly centuries.

Still, he had to admit that George S. Patton had a way of getting things done on the battlefield, and in the army, that Wakefield could only admire. "It was a tough nut to crack, General . . . but it's been a fine week since then!"

Indeed, following the capture of Metz, Third Army had lunged toward the Saar region of Germany with its typical aggressive speed. In a series of brilliant advances, units such as the Fourth and Nineteenth Armored Divisions had raced toward the border, bagging thousands of prisoners, striking close to the very Rhine itself.

"But that's not why I came by, Hank," explained the army general. "Good news, for once. I've got a few companies of tank destroyers available . . . I'd like to attach one of them to you."

"We can always use the help, General," replied Wakefield enthusiastically. Tank destroyers were not as effectively armored as tanks—their turrets were open to the sky, for one thing, making the crews very vulnerable to enemy snipers—but they had better guns than even the 76-mm Shermans and could provide a useful punch against German armor. A company of the big-gunned vehicles would make a big difference in his division's striking power.

"I thought you'd feel that way. Captain Zimmerman's a good man—I've had my eye on him since Cobra, back in Normandy. He'll report to you in the morning."

"Thank you, General."

"And Hank, why don't you attach him to CCA? I like knowing we've got an outfit there with aggressive command and a little extra punch."

Patton phrased the idea as a question, but Wakefield recognized it for the order that it was. At the same time, he was rather surprised to realize that he would have made the same decision himself.

Army Group B HQ, Trier, Germany, 2334 hours GMT

"The great German military genius," observed Günter von Reinhardt, "is in good staff work." He stretched one arm and then the other, then shook his head from side to side, clearing his mind from the intense focus of the last several days.

Müller looked up from his own maze of paper. "I wish you'd make up your mind about the placement of the last two panzer divisions," he complained. "It's hard enough planning POL resupply with the limited stocks we have without adding in the complication that we don't know where the trucks will be going."

"Ultimately, my friend, the decision isn't mine to make," Reinhardt said, standing up. "But I will get you the decision as soon as possible. For now, let me buy you a cup of fine gourmet coffee before we return to this fascinating exercise." He glanced down at the maps laid out on the long conference table, held down with a variety of objects, numerous pencil and pen marks showing the complex strategic discussions that had taken place over the last three days. "We must finish this work, but I, for one, need to clear my head a little bit, or I'm liable to begin to confuse our troops with theirs."

The canteen was on around-the-clock status in Rommel's field headquarters. The coffee was ersatz, but it was hot and it was available even though it was past midnight. Tonight there were also sandwiches and some stale cake. Müller piled his plate high.

"Do you think this will work?" Müller asked.

"Do you know, I really believe it might," Reinhardt said thoughtfully. "It's an audacious plan, and one with a degree of unavoidable risk, not even mentioning the well-known adage about first contact with the enemy. Still, this type of plan has certainly worked before, and that without our Desert Fox in command. I'd say we have a good chance of victory, and I can't imagine any plan better. And after all, *ce n'est pas victoire, si elle ne met fin à la guerre.* Montaigne. It's not victory if it doesn't end the war. Of course, the current definition of victory is survival."

"But we're still outnumbered," Müller said through a mouthful of cake. "And according to your law . . . what was it, Langer's Law? . . . aren't we already doomed?"

"Lanchester's Law. Remember, the force difference is critical, but the force at the decisive point is what ultimately counts." Reinhardt paused. The situation was far more complex and had far more variables; he had an innate distaste for oversimplification. On the other hand, Müller looked more cheerful, and perhaps that was an outcome worth achieving, even at the cost of semantic exactitude. "A lot depends on our work. It is amazing, is it not, how much paperwork is involved in taking a plan that originates as a few sweeping arrows on a large map and turning it into the operational orders that make units and men move on the battlefield?"

"And how much more effort it takes to move them around during the battle than it does to push counters across the headquarters map," interjected a deeper voice.

Reinhardt looked up to see Rommel's scarred face smiling down. He shot to attention. "Field Marshal! We were sharing a cup of coffee—may I fetch you some?"

"I would be eternally indebted for a cup of coffee. I would even be indebted for a cup of what they serve here. May I join you?"

"Of course, Field Marshal. We would be honored." Reinhardt pulled out a chair for his commander, then quickly got a cup of coffee and piled a few of the stale brown-bread sandwiches on a blue metal plate.

"Thank you, colonel. Gentlemen, how goes the planning?"

Reinhardt immediately answered for the two of them. "Very well, sir. We should finish the order lists by morning and have detailed guidance ready for dissemination."

"And the most important part of the campaign—how goes the supply planning, Colonel Müller? I think you have the harder job this time, with no disrespect to your colleague. You have to spin straw into gold, or preferably into gasoline."

"Just call me Rumpelstilskin," Müller said. "I mean—" Reinhardt raised his eyebrows at the unaccustomed witticism from Müller. It must have been his fatigue; he knew how much Rommel intimidated the pudgy supply officer.

Rommel laughed. "Good for you, Rumpelstilskin. You see, I am very easy to please. Only deliver miracles on a regular basis, and everything will be just fine. So tell me about your miracles."

Müller took a deep breath. Reinhardt could see some anxiety forming on his round face; he hated to do briefings, far preferring the meticulously prepared memorandum. But he was on the spot. "Sir, even with the Rumanian fuel influx, the key to the supply situation is our ability to capture Allied depots and resupply on the move. I've been coordinating with Günter, and there have been some deviations from the initial sweep to make sure we are able to keep up supply. But it makes me very uncomfortable, because I can't predict capturing enemy supplies with the same accuracy with which I can predict our trucks moving up behind the tanks. Worse, the intelligence information—sorry, Günter—can't tell me exactly where the Allied supplies are located. There must be a major depot somewhere between here and Antwerp, but where exactly it is, I cannot tell."

"Of course not," murmured Rommel. He knew that was a point of vulnerability in any attack. "So your orders are, Colonel, that I must make sure to locate and capture a certain minimum level of enemy supplies?"

Müller always had trouble knowing when his leg was being pulled. His eyes grew wider. "Orders? No, sir, not orders. . . ."

Rommel laughed along with Reinhardt. "I must disagree, Colonel. In fact, those are orders, because I must follow them, mustn't I?"

Sweat actually sprung out on Müller's face. Finally, he seemed to realize that he was being toyed with, took another deep breath, and said, "Well, Field Marshal, if you put it that way, I suppose they are orders."

Rommel saluted. "Very well, Colonel Müller. I shall follow them. I presume, Colonel Reinhardt, that the colonel's orders have been properly implemented?"

"Of course, Herr Feldmarschall," replied Reinhardt, a slight smile playing over his lips. "All Colonel Müller's orders are implemented with top priority and at once."

"Good," nodded the Desert Fox. "I always appreciate decisiveness in the orders I receive." He smiled as he took a sip of coffee. "I've read the first set of planning documents," he said.

Again, Reinhardt was amazed at the stamina and focus of his commanding officer. He knew that Rommel had not only read them, but marked them with detailed comments that missed nothing. He was able to keep the whole complex endeavor in his head, which Reinhardt found remarkable in anyone, and especially in one who had suffered such wounds.

Rommel's health had made an astounding recovery; the rumor mill ensured that every bit of medical information made the rounds of the senior officers. Personally, Reinhardt watched Carl-Heinz, the stocky driver and personal aide. When Carl-Heinz fussed over Rommel, Reinhardt suspected poor health; when Carl-Heinz seemed more relaxed and devoted to his engines, Reinhardt suspected Rommel was doing well.

Still, the scars and damage from the attack were permanent. Rommel carried a cane, though he used it seldom. He had given up the black eye patch he had worn for several months, though Reinhardt had seen Rommel on more than one occasion moving a piece of paper back and forth to bring it into focus. There were moments of sitting and standing where there was obvious pain and discomfort.

Nevertheless, no matter how many late nights Reinhardt worked, he had never known Rommel to go to bed before he did or to wake up any later than 0500. While there was a little evidence of fatigue in the face, there was clearly none in the intellect. Reinhardt wished that were always true of himself.

"I see, Colonel Reinhardt, that you have assigned yourself some forward duties in this operation. You'll be with the . . . First SS Panzers, if I recall?"

"Yes, sir," replied Reinhardt. He felt vulnerable under Rommel's calm stare. "At first I saw my primary role as necessarily being at headquarters to process intelligence updates, but there will be a particularly tough 'fog of war' situation in the opening moves of this campaign. By reducing the lag time of information and being able to make some on-the-spot analysis of the opening moves, I believe I can reduce some of the inevitable uncertainties."

Rommel regarded him quietly. Reinhardt had thought a lot about this. He wanted to do the right thing for the campaign and not be inappropriately influenced by Rommel's suggestion that he take a more active role, and when it became clear to him that this would be strategically useful, he kept checking to see if his decision was flawed and personal. But it was too complex; he couldn't be certain. Rommel, on the other hand, would be certain, and Reinhardt waited for the response.

"While intelligence officers normally should remain at headquarters," Rommel said thoughtfully, "I think this is one of the special situations where a forward perspective will be useful and appropriate. I look forward to your reports, Colonel. And now, gentlemen," he said as he stood up, "I believe that well-rested officers make better decisions. I plan to follow my own advice, and I suggest you do the same. We will be briefing the senior officers at 0800, and I will see you then."

Reinhardt looked at Müller. The supply officer removed his glasses and polished them with his napkin. "You know," Müller said, "that's the most intense coffee break I've ever experienced in my life."

Carl-Heinz pulled the cloth over the boot one last time, ensuring that the leather was polished to a black, mirrorlike sheen.

"All finished, Herr Feldmarschall," he said, straightening and regarding Rommel with a critical eye. "Everything is in place. But are you sure you won't eat more breakfast? You've only had four hours of sleep."

"No . . . thank you, Carl-Heinz. I am well rested, and as well fed as I can be, and I am, as always, grateful for your thoughtfulness and care." The stocky feldwebel understood the dismissal and nodded. Rommel knew his cheerful aide would find another way to ensure his charge was well fed and rested. Eggs would appear on a plate before him in his office, a coffee cup would magically remain warm and filled. Carl-Heinz had enlisted all of the staff and most of the officers in a conspiracy to take care of the Desert Fox. The man had enormous natural leadership gifts; he was a man people wanted to please. *He would make an outstanding commander,* Rommel thought.

The commander of the German army in the west drew a deep breath and studied himself in the small mirror, the one concession to vanity he allowed in his office. The glass was framed by a branch of oak that had been struck by lightning, and ancient superstition proclaimed this as a portent of good luck. Idle superstition, he knew . . . but then, he would take all the luck that he could get.

"The generals are assembling in the hall," his driver added. "The mood is good. General Dietrich is in the anteroom as you requested. He, on the other hand, seems rather annoyed and nervous, according to the orderly."

"And he doesn't even know why I want to see him, yet." Rommel muttered ironically to himself. "Well, I mustn't allow the esteemed panzer general of the SS to fall even more out of sorts . . . thank you, Carl-Heinz. That will be all for now."

This was another minor thorn in Rommel's side. How he hated having to deal with office politics! General Sepp Dietrich had arrived late last night with a letter from Himmler assigning him as commander of the newly formed Sixth SS Panzer Army. Rommel, however, had other plans for the Sixth Panzer Army, and those didn't include having it under the command of men in black uniforms if he could help it. Dietrich posed quite a delicate personnel problem. A man whose route to military command came from being a friend (and personal bodyguard) to Adolf Hitler back in the Beer Hall days, the kindest thing one could say about him was that he was a capable division CO.

Rommel did not dislike him personally but felt certain that command of an entire panzerarmee was well beyond the man's abilities. Dietrich owed his newest assignment to Himmler's mistrust of the Army—and of Rommel. Rommel was learning to understand Himmler's messages; now it was time to send one of his own in return.

Dietrich was pacing back and forth. "Heil Himmler!" he said with enthusiasm as Rommel entered. Dietrich looked like what he was: an old man fond of the bottle, a tough man, a bully boy gone to seed in a position beyond his skills. He would be overwhelmed by responsibilities, and his failures would end up costing the lives of good German soldiers. Rommel put a smile on his face and reached out to shake his hand.

"Good to see you, Sepp," he said. "I have an important job for you."

The SS general was momentarily taken off guard. "But Field Marshal, I have a job—after working with you in Normandy, the führer said—"

Rommel cut him off with a hand on his shoulder. "I know. But I can't spare you on a minor field job. I need someone I can trust."

"A minor field job?" Dietrich asked, puzzled.

Rommel smiled. "I need for you to serve as my executive liaison between Führer Himmler and my own headquarters during the upcoming campaign. I need a man I can trust, someone who knows the complexities of Berlin . . ."

"But Herr Feldmarschall!" Dietrich's objection was immediate, and was reflected by his interruption. "I am a fighting soldier! Besides, my assignment was given to me directly by the führer himself. My loyalty and service is unquestioned!"

"That's exactly why I need you in Berlin. This is the most important campaign in the war, and the führer deserves the best coordination and liaison possible. No one else can do that role. It has to be you."

Flattered in spite of himself, Dietrich wavered only slightly before returning to the offensive. "But I have fought in Russia, in France, for years! All my life's work has brought me to this point!" He was moving into pleading now. Time for Rommel to administer the coup de grâce.

"There is something else, Sepp. Something that has to remain between you and me for now."

Dietrich paused, suspicious. Rommel lowered his voice almost to a whisper. "Upon victory, I have a special assignment for you."

Another pause. "What—what is it?" asked Dietrich in a tremulous voice. Rommel let the suspense build. The fish was chasing the bait now.

"I need a military governor for Antwerp, someone who can crush the resistance and hold the port for me against all comers. I believe only you can do this."

Dietrich's rheumy eyes looked at Rommel. "But why can't I command the panzerarmee and then transfer to be military governor?" he objected.

"While you are in Berlin, you need to gather your own forces to come in and begin the new occupation," Rommel said in a conspiratorial voice. "The Sixth will be moving out almost immediately, and you have to be ready to move in right behind us. There won't be time otherwise. Of course, if you feel being military governor is too low of an assignment for you . . ."

"No, no, of course not!" said Dietrich hastily. "So you want me to maintain liaison and at the same time arrange for an SS occupation force?"

"Exactly!" said Rommel. "Can you do it for me?"

"Of course I can," said Dietrich proudly. The men shook hands. "By the way, have you decided who gets the Sixth?"

This was a delicate moment. "I think so. A panzer general who was shuffled aside after Moscow, '41."

"Guderian?" Dietrich's face registered surprise and, perhaps, a hint of understanding. After all, Colonel General "Hurrying Heinz" Guderian was the godfather of German Blitzkrieg operations and had commanded some of the most brilliant dashes through Poland, France, and Russia during the early years of the war. He had fallen from favor with Hitler because of his failure to capture Moscow at the end of 1941, but military men understood that the real fault for that failure lay with the conflicting orders issued by Hitler himself.

Eventually Guderian had been appointed as the inspector general of panzer troops for the Third Reich, a mostly honorary job. He might have become chief of the General Staff, but Hitler's death had frozen the senior command structure, and so Guderian had been forced to sit out the rest of the war, until now. Even Dietrich could see that there was no man better suited to the current task. His face betrayed his feeling that he had been conned, but still— military governor of Antwerp . . .

Rommel continued, "You'll need to stay for the initial planning work and then return to do the briefings. You'll stay in constant contact with my headquarters and be on the move with your new units as soon as Antwerp falls."

Dietrich was smart enough to realize he'd been outmaneuvered, but a military governorship would be more than acceptable as a consolation prize. "Very well, Herr Feldmarschall," he said with a salute.

"Good man," said the Desert Fox, as he left his office and walked toward the conference room—the former dining room of the converted hotel that served as his headquarters—where his officers awaited. He was relieved things had gone that easily with Dietrich; it could have been messy, especially if the SS panzers refused to accept his choice of leader. He had put a lot of thought into the right choice of bribe. *Perhaps I will learn to play politics eventually,* he thought ruefully.

Rommel was well satisfied with his choice of replacements for Dietrich. Guderian's presence at the conference table had excited the other officers. Rommel had kept Guderian's appointment a secret until this moment, because he suspected that Himmler would have opposed it. *It is better to seek forgiveness than permission,* he thought, wondering what military man had first realized that concept. Sometimes Rommel thought he'd run his entire career on that well-worn principle. The relationship between Himmler and his SS forces, which were personally loyal to the Führer, and the regular Wehrmacht forces, always delicate, were particularly fragile at this critical juncture in the war because Himmler, no matter how hard he had tried, had not quite gotten the same level of control that was held by his predecessor. Rommel knew he did not actually possess the authority to reassign Dietrich and appoint Guderian in his place, much less to preappoint Dietrich as military governor of Antwerp, but by the time the lines of command sorted themselves out, the campaign would be over, for better or worse.

The other reason for keeping Guderian's appointment secret was for just the reaction he was getting now. His plan would only work if all of these generals, and through them all the colonels and captains, all the sergeants and soldaten, believed that it would work. And for that to happen, the Desert Fox had to appear utterly confident, supremely capable, and completely in command. A few well-timed surprises, such as the return of the highly respected Guderian, would do a lot toward getting the attitude he required from his team.

The officers rose in unison as Rommel entered. He returned their salute, dipped his head in a slight, gracious gesture of acknowledgment. "Please, be seated," he said.

He looked over the group as the high-ranking officers quickly settled into their chairs. The attending officers included generals commanding more than a dozen panzer divisions, and twice that many infantry formations. General Fritz Bayerlein, commander of the Panzer Lehr division, and longtime friend and ex-chief of staff to Rommel in Africa, and General Hanz Speidel, Rommel's current chief of staff, were with Rommel on the stage, while the rest of the men were gathered in the hotel's former dining room. Crystal chandeliers illuminated the room with an incongruously pastoral glow. He noted with satisfaction that General Guderian had taken a seat in the front, and that a parade of officers had come forward in turn to shake his hand. Under other circumstances Guderian would have been on the podium with Bayerlein and Speidel, but the surprise and morale value of his presence in the audience made that a better location.

"Good morning, gentlemen," Rommel said, moving to the lectern. "As you know, our strategy for the past several months has been first, to retreat to the fortified positions in the Westwall; second, to reinforce the line with the Russian Front units; third, to defend firmly against the advancing enemy. Meanwhile, the Luftwaffe has managed to stop the strategic bombing campaign against the Fatherland with its new jet fighters, at least for the time being. We have been highly successful in achieving our strategic goals. We can now delay the enemy's advance for quite a long time to come. In the final analysis, however, we cannot stop them forever."

This was no more than the officers—and the Allies, for that matter—already knew. A few of the hardcore SS officers wore shocked looks, for any defeatist talk, no matter how rational or justified, seemed on the edge of treason to them. General Bücher, Rommel noticed, did not look shocked. The senior SS liaison had seen the same things Rommel had in their extensive tours of the Westwall fortifications.

"Having stabilized the front as much as possible, it is time to return to offensive operations," Rommel continued. A slight whispering buzz greeted that statement. Although German field strength was substantially higher with the Russian Front troops than it would have been had Germany continued to fight a two-front war, and the remarkable Me-262s had neutralized Allied air superiority at least for the present, the German supply situation was still precarious, and offense carried higher inherent risks than defense.

"Our critical vulnerability, as you all understand, is in supply, especially fuel. But ultimately, our enemy's vulnerability is in the same place." Rommel moved to the large map. "While the Allied resources far exceed our own, fuel does no good unless it is delivered to the tanks and other vehicles that require it. And a tank without fuel is merely a target. Because France does not make its own supplies, fuel is brought in by the means of ports controlled by the Allies. The key resupply point is here." Rommel snapped the tip of the pointer against Antwerp.

"We have been trying to disrupt the Antwerp supply process primarily by the use of V-1 rockets, but that has been largely unsuccessful. Gentlemen, we will take Antwerp, disrupting Allied resupply operations, and not incidentally taking those supplies for our own use, and from there we will be able to move southward, cutting off the gasoline spigot from enemy tanks that will quickly exhaust their own fuel reserves. Properly executed, this campaign will result in nothing less than the destruction of the Allied armies in the west.

"Gentlemen, this is Operation Wacht am Rhein."

The whispered buzz grew louder with excitement. This was a daring, amazing plan, and, although dangerous, one with a real chance of ultimate success. A few voices began to sing the famous patriotic song, *"Lieb' Vaterland, magst ruhig sein/Fest steht und treu die Wacht am Rhein!"* Other voices joined in, filling the room with the sound of martial music. Rommel smiled. This was the reaction he hoped for.

Colonel von Reinhardt stood up. "Herr Feldmarschall, I propose a different name for this operation. To strike fear into the enemy heart and to remind them that we are led by the Desert Fox, I propose this operation be known as Operation *Fuchs* am Rhein—the Fox on the Rhine!" A loud cheer broke out among the officers. Rommel could only bow his head and accept the recognition. His heart was full. He would lead these soldiers to victory.

As the cheers continued, Rommel finally held up his hand for silence. "For this effort, we have the use of two reinforced panzer armies . . . the Fifth, under the command of General Hasso von Manteuffel, and the Sixth, which is as of today under the command of General Guderian. General Guderian, I want to apologize to you for your demotion from inspector of panzers back to a mere combat command."

The apology drew sharp bark of laughter from Guderian as well as the other officers. It was well known that the noted panzer leader had been "kicked upstairs" and that a combat command was what Guderian wanted. From the momentary scowl that passed over the man's features, Rommel suspected that what he really wanted was in fact Rommel's own job, to be up here leading this whole offensive. In a different war that might have been the case, but the Desert Fox smiled tightly at the knowledge that, for now, the onetime student would remain the new schoolmaster.

Manteuffel and Guderian both stood, accepting the applause and congratulations of the officers. The Wehrmacht officers applauded loudly and generously; there was notably less enthusiasm among the SS, who had expected to be under the command of one of their own. *Well,* thought Rommel, *if I lose, it matters not; if I win, it matters not.*

When they seated themselves again, Rommel felt the full attention of his men. He drew a deep breath, ready now to explain the plan in more detail.

"I propose to strike the Allies here, in the Ardennes Forest. We will revisit the Blitzkrieg that served us so well in 1940, striking to the Meuse River. Once we have forced a bridgehead, our armored spearheads will turn north, clearing through Belgium, retaking Antwerp. The British armies will be surrounded, and the Americans will be left without their primary source of supply."

He continued talking about operational details, speaking for more than an hour, then answered questions for another hour. The interrogatories were detailed and often challenging, since Rommel did not require "yes men" in his service. Everyone present recognized that the plan was ambitious and risky, and they probed for weaknesses. There would be numerous small-group meetings and breakouts, detailed analysis of the planning documents, necessary adjustments to be made, but it would not be long before they were ready to strike.

As Rommel turned the briefing over to Speidel, he could let his mind wander for a while. He looked out over the officers. Even the SS were interested and enthusiastic, in spite of the increasingly dour expression on the face of Sepp Dietrich. He knew the man would be complaining to Himmler within the hour and perhaps would return with papers placing him back in formal command, although Rommel would make sure those papers never made it to his desk. This was a risky game, but no more risky than others he had played. Perhaps Himmler would have him shot—win or lose—but then soldiers always acted at risk to their lives. Or perhaps, Rommel thought, the orders for his death had already been given. He looked at Bücher for a long moment and wondered, not for the first time, if he was staring into the face of his own death.

Luftwaffe Advance Airbase, Bitburg, Germany, 9 December 1944, 0817 hours GMT

Willi Schmidt cowered slightly as Colonel Krueger came out of the hut into the chill air of the flight line. The bruises along the right side of his face had changed from purple to yellow, but the fear of another pistol-whipping was strong. He had seen Krueger's temper flare dramatically before, but it had never been directed at him until the day the engine on his Schwalbe had died.

"The new engine is installed, Kommodore," he declared, saluting. "Would you care to inspect your machine?"

"Yes, of course, Willi," said Krueger with a smile. Since the beating, Krueger's temper had receded, to be replaced first with embarrassment and withdrawal, then with excessive friendliness. Willi tried to relax, but he couldn't help tightening up whenever the kommodore drew near.

The two men crossed the tarmac toward one of the small hangars that had been hastily erected under the protection of the ubiquitous evergreens. Most of the jets remained outside, sheltered only in earthen revetments screened by camouflage netting, but the kommodore's aircraft had been moved inside for the repair job.

It was strange to work in this small airfield after the broad installation of Lager-Lechfeld and the steppes of Russia. Here, the dark hills pressed close, and tall trees grew between the barracks and briefing huts, helping to conceal the installation from Allied aircraft. To enhance the claustrophobic effect, the seemingly eternal overcast pressed low in the leaden skies, concealing the rounded summits and extending tendrils of mist down the ravines and gullies of the steep slopes.

In neighboring valleys, the two other Gruppen of the kommodore's Geschwader were quartered in similar facilities. They were connected by dedicated telephone lines, and the kommodore spoke constantly to them, trying to control them as closely as if they were physically present. It was the price for moving closer to the front. From Bitburg, and the other bases like it, Krueger declaimed regularly, the Luftwaffe would once again rise to challenge Allied air superiority over the battlefield.

Within the hangar, the flame-draped Me-262 looked as good as new. The entire jet had been repainted to match the immaculate gray green paint over the new engine, and the artist had taken great care to restore the distinctive nose to its bright, fiery insignia.

"We test fired it for ten minutes . . . it runs well," added the mechanic, praying that he was correct. The temperamental jet engines weren't nearly as predictable as the piston engines that drove propeller aircraft.

"Good. Now, if only this *verdammt* weather would clear, I could find out for myself," said Krueger, patting Schmidt on the back in a friendly gesture that only made Willi more nervous.

The gloomy weather was all the more frustrating for the kommodore, Willi knew, because tomorrow the entire force of Army Group B would hurl itself against the Americans in the attack named Operation Fuchs am Rhein. Krueger, drunk on too many snifters of cognac last night, had laughed at what he considered the Desert Fox's naked ego, but Willi Schmidt had heard that his own officers had insisted on the operation's name in spite of Rommel's own reluctance. Willi thoroughly approved.

The Geschwader was perfectly positioned to fly over the front and contest the Allied air superiority, but the raging winter weather showed every sign of lasting for another week or more. That meant no aircraft on either side. He knew that the ground troops welcomed the absence of aircraft, but all the fighter pilots chafed against the conditions that prevented them from proving their mettle. Willi assumed the American fighter pilots felt the same, though he would never have suggested it.

"We've got the whole Gruppe in as good a shape as possible," the mechanic offered in a sympathetic voice that turned into a whine.

Krueger didn't notice. "Well, keep up the work, Willi . . . sooner or later the sun will come out again," he said cheerfully.

"Jawohl, Herr Kommodore!" The mechanic snapped off a salute as Krueger, impatiently stalked out of the hangar and glared up at the sky as if he were willing the heat of his gaze to tear through the mist, to dissolve the clouds and open up the sky for his aircraft.

But instead, the overcast seemed to press closer, and as if to flaunt its superiority, it began to send flakes of snow drifting downward.

Army Group B HQ, Trier, Germany, 15 December 1944, 2207 hours GMT

"Ready for a drive tonight, Carl-Heinz?" said the Desert Fox with a broad smile that indicated unusually good spirits.

"Certainly am, sir! Nice weather for a drive, isn't it?" replied the driver as he opened the door to the rear seat and made sure that his field marshal was comfortably seated. Rommel's chief of staff, General Speidel, joined him, and Carl-Heinz thought that the second officer seemed tense, thin faced, compared to the easygoing cheerfulness of the army commander.

"Where to, sir?" he asked, as he slid into the driver's seat and put his hands on the big steering wheel.

"Start out west and keep going," Rommel said with a chuckle.

This was the night, Carl-Heinz knew as they passed out of the city. The word had been kept close, but it was impossible to conceal a major action from the troops who had to carry it out. He knew more than most because of his proximity to the field marshal, but the rumor mill was unstoppable, better than the Gestapo itself in finding out whatever there was to find out—and making it up if there wasn't anything good to know.

The hour was approaching midnight, but there was activity everywhere. Guards were posted at all crossroads, though after a brief word with the soldiers on duty the field marshal's car sailed through each checkpoint.

Soon they were following a column of tanks, the hooded headlights barely illuminating the engine housing of a growling Panther. The night was black, heavy overcast blocking any potential light from the moon or stars. The driver remembered the many campaigns where he had been at the wheel of one of the armored behemoths. Now he felt no envy for the men in the panzers, though a sense of kinship still nagged at him, suggested that he should really be driving a tank right now.

The launch of the huge battle was imminent. He fixed every part of his vigilance on the task before him, knowing that the German army's chances of success depended on the health of the man in the backseat of the car. Carl-Heinz could sense it in the attitude of the guards at the checkpoints, in the looks that followed the command vehicle as it wove its way between the massed formations of the Wehrmacht.

They rolled down a slope and through a broad valley. Though the road signs had been removed, Carl-Heinz remembered this place, knew that they were crossing into Luxembourg. To the right and left the gaunt, white "Dragon's Teeth" of the Westwall rose from the darkness and then faded away behind them. The road meandered into a grove of shattered evergreens, the scene of battle a few weeks earlier. German artillery had fired long and hard in the desperate effort to halt the American advance before the borders of the Reich.

From the distance, now, he could hear the blasting of heavy gunfire. Flashes lit the horizon to the north and west, and there were still tanks everywhere, rumbling toward the enemy, breaking from the road into companies and platoons. Even when he could no longer see them, the driver heard the rumbling of engines in the night, felt the quivering of the frozen earth under the crunching tracks of Panthers and Tigers.

They crossed the next ridge and abruptly the night sky was illuminated by the glare of massive searchlights, whole batteries of them, all directed toward the layer of low clouds. The effect was startling as the light reflected down before them, brightening a vast swath of landscape. Carl-Heinz could see individual trees and farmhouses on the rising ground two or three kilometers before them.

"Impressive, don't you think?" Rommel suggested from the backseat.

"Indeed it is, Field Marshal!" the driver replied. "Very clever." He admired mechanical creativity. It was the sort of idea that he had from time to time, though he'd never worked on a scale such as this.

"It was suggested by some of the men who had fought on the Russian front . . . 'artificial moonlight,' they called it. It seems to turn a dark night into something much more visible."

Carl-Heinz agreed. He picked up speed with the rest of the column, finding that most of the tanks had now moved off of the road. They were rumbling forward, climbing the far slope of the ridge.

"That's the Schnee Eiffel," Rommel explained helpfully. Carl-Heinz knew the Desert Fox sometimes liked a fresh audience to explain things to, as much to focus his own thoughts as to enlighten the listener. "There are Americans up there, all along the front."

"But not for long," Speidel added, trying unsuccessfully for a light tone. It was clear to Carl-Heinz that the chief of staff preferred his charge to be back at headquarters.

The artillery fire was closer now. Soon, they drove past the fortified revetments around a battery of heavy guns. For a few minutes the firing of the big cannon was deafening, crumps echoing through the air, followed by the tearing sound of shells blasting upward and out, toward distant and unseen targets.

The lights continued to brighten the night, eerie and ghostly against the white sky. The fields of snow stood out in stark brilliance, and even the forests were arrayed in visible details, individual trees jutting from soft groves. Flashes of fire sparked here and there, marking the strikes of artillery shells.

And they were still driving west.

First Army Front Lines, Ardennes, France,
16 December 1944, 0130 hours GMT

Private Billy Cooper was cold . . . more than that, he was damned cold. It made him feel a little better to use that word, even in the privacy of his own thoughts. It was a word that would have gotten him a whipping from his father as recently as a year ago, had he dared to use it on the family's Iowa farm. He amplified his feelings by letting himself wish for a cigarette. Damn that sergeant, anyway, telling him he couldn't smoke while he was on sentry duty. It wasn't as though the Germans were going to be doing any attacking.

Of course, he had heard the stories, always meant to scare newcomers like Billy. Some poor sap was stuck in the foxholes on the front lines, and when the relieving sentry had come the guy was found with his throat slit, grinning blood from a whole new mouth. In fact, the stories worked—they were scary. But that did nothing to ease his longing for a cigarette.

Instead, all he could do was listen to the wind. It was wintertime, and the winter wind in these European woods sounded pretty much like the winter wind in an Iowa woods. He crunched his feet on the snow, and that, too, sounded a lot like footsteps in a Midwestern winter.

Come to think of it, though, this sound was a little different. There was more of a moan to it, a faint rumble that was more suggestive of distant thunder than a winter wind. Of course, he knew there couldn't be any thunder in winter, but still . . .

The longing for a cigarette was forgotten as Billy strained to hear. That was thunder, but it wasn't coming from any cloud.

And then the night turned to day. At least, that was his first impression. The whole forest was illuminated by impressive brightness, soft, white light that outlined the nearby pine trees down to their individual needles and drooping, snow-laden limbs. Blinking in astonishment, Billy looked upward and saw that the layer of overcast was shining with the circles of bright lights—searchlights, he guessed, directed upward so that the light bounced back down across the snowy woods.

The noise was even louder now, clearly mechanical in nature. The young private pushed through the fringe of evergreens that sheltered his foxhole, getting a look down the open slope into a floor of the snow-swept valley. The Germans were on the other side, he knew, and there shouldn't be anything moving out in the open.

But contrary to his expectations, there was movement out there, a lot of movement. He stared, wondering what he should do. There were machines crawling across the fields, rumbling from the forest on the other ridge through the valley bottom, crawling up the hill straight toward him. He saw great, armored monsters everywhere, tanks with wicked gun barrels pointed forward, lethally fixed on the American lines, many drawing a precise bead on Billy Cooper's foxhole!

And then he was running, tripping through his foxhole, scrambling along the path the sentries had trampled in the snowy woods, leading back to the company CP.

"Halt! Who goes there?" The harsh voice broke from a thicket, and he knew he was almost there. There was a password, some phrase that was about as far from his mind right now as those fields in Iowa. Instead, he just shouted.

"Sarge! There's tanks out there! German tanks! More fuckin' tanks than you've ever seen in your life!"

Command Vehicle, First SS Panzer Division, Belgium, 0411 hours GMT

Colonel Günter von Reinhardt did not expect such a close correlation between war and skiing. He did not care for either activity.

The December weather had turned to freezing drizzle for Operation Fuchs am Rhein, which was good on the one hand because it completely shut down air operations, but bad on the other hand for anyone who had to be exposed to the elements in a fast-moving vehicle.

Another *thump* as the speeding half-track moved over a hillock and trundled across the field. His forehead cracked against the window, and his shoulder was bruised by a hard jolt on the armored door. "Watch it, Colonel!" shouted the driver above the roaring engine. "A man can get hurt all too easily in here!"

"Here I am, wounded already, without ever coming under enemy fire," Reinhardt chuckled ruefully, rubbing his shoulder.

The driver was too busy trying to keep control of the half-track. Freezing drizzle, Reinhardt had learned all too quickly, made traveling in armored vehicles an interesting experience. When he stood up to search the scene with binoculars, it coated the front of his field jacket with ice, numbed his fingers, and windburned his face—*just like skiing,* he thought. Sitting down again, the half-track lurched and the driver spun the wheel wildly; even on a field there was little or no traction because of the ice. Worse than the ice was the mud; in some places the ground was so bad Reinhardt had seen panzers mired in it, the crew cursing and digging to free it; once he had seen a panzer towing another out of the muck. In the past, these vehicles had been counters moving across a flat surface, and the greatest environmental hazard had been the headache he got from the cigarette smoke in the headquarters building.

The beginning of the morning run had been spectacularly beautiful. The freezing rain had coated the trees in a jacket of ice, icicles frosted every surface from trees to houses to cliffs, hiding all the damage tanks and war had done to the European countryside. The headlights caught them in odd reflections, and Reinhardt wished he had time and a camera to record the beauty.

Now gray muck illuminated the battlefield. The half-track lurched up out of the field and onto a road; another dizzying turn and then more speed, sliding alongside a column of panzers, rushing to the fore. And then a sound: *crump! crump!*—a flat-sounding noise, a muffled bass note, growing louder, then more in an irregular rhythm. Nearing a crossroads, Reinhardt got a glimpse of a sign: Bastogne, 8 km.

That vital road junction was an early key to the success of Operation Fuchs am Rhein. It needed to be taken quickly and completely, a mere eyeblink in the campaign. And that was the sound ahead.

Reinhardt tried to unfold his map on the bumping, swerving seat with only moderate success. His eyes were sharp, but the map became a shaking blur. He found St. Vith, key to Guderian's advance and already captured by the German spearheads. But south of there, Manteuffel had hit a tough nut . . . there, in Bastogne. It was only a small dot on the map, but Bastogne was a place where several key roads came together. That could be a curse for a sleepy little town during a war.

He glanced out the window. Beside the road he saw a column of disarmed, demoralized American soldiers marching toward a POW stockade under the watchful eyes of a *volksgrenadier* company. It was good duty for those men; useful without being too deadly . . . although in this weather simply being outside was the same as being in combat.

The noise grew louder as the First SS Panzer Division advanced. They were nearing Bastogne, now. Reinhardt had learned from advance reports that many GIs had gathered there, infantry and armor and tank destroyers. They were proving stubborn and had already repulsed several attacks. If Rommel's offensive was to have a chance of succeeding, Bastogne must be taken, and quickly—but at what cost and at what speed would yet be determined.

His heart pounded with excitement, a different excitement than the intellectual challenge of pushing markers along a board. He was riding to the sound of the guns, moving into real combat rather than seeing the overview and sometimes the aftermath. It was confusing; he could not form a complete strategic overview of the situation. He was frustrated by the limitations of his senses, daunted by the physical discomfort. It would be easier to think, to understand, if he were looking down on a table, his map illuminated by good light and colorful markers.

But these were real men and those were real cannon and Reinhardt's planning effort had sentenced numerous men on both sides to death this day. He thought of the famous statement by the American general Robert E. Lee: "It is well that war is so terrible—we should grow too fond of it."

And in truth it *was* thrilling, exciting, terrifying, a rush of emotion, an exhilarating flood of feeling. He wanted to pound on the dash of the half-track, to shout "Faster! Faster!" to speed into the fray, into the very jaws of death. *How unlike me,* he thought, but that was a distant realization, for he was swallowed up in the feeling, in the moment, in the absence of perspective and strategic vision.

Now there were flashes of light in the gray sky and the noise was louder, so loud and deep he could feel it as much as hear it. He was nearing the leading edge of the battle.

Malmedy, Belgium, 17 December 1944, 0917 hours GMT

"Schnell! Schnell!" The sharp-faced SS colonel fired several shots from his Luger into the air. His American prisoners, dirty and unshaved, moved faster, carrying the freshly captured jerry cans toward the waiting panzers.

It had been a good morning for Colonel Jochem Peiper. Top priority for all leading-edge units was fuel—the Allied fuel depots were known to be in this area. And early in the morning his SS panzer unit had stumbled upon this depot, overruning it easily. The American soldiers never knew what hit them, and within minutes they had surrendered.

"It's good to have fuel, Colonel," said his driver as yet another five-gallon can was poured into the tank. The huge beasts got only half a mile to the gallon; refueling was a constant problem.

"*Doch,*" replied Peiper with a laugh. "And these new manservants—why, they're better than Jews! Look at them run! They'll make good slave workers when this campaign is finished."

"Colonel!" shouted one of his forward scouts as a fast car motored into the captured depot. "Americans on the move!"

All the fuel had not yet been consumed, but his panzers had enough to keep going. The information about the dump had already been radioed to Army Group B headquarters; the rest of the fuel would be put to good use.

"Who will take charge of the prisoners, Colonel?" asked a lieutenant who had been overseeing the refueling operation?

It took Peiper only a moment to decide. "We have no time for prisoners and cannot spare the men. Kill them."

The roar of the panzer engines coming to life nearly drowned out the sound of bullets and screams as the prisoners were gunned down.

Stavelot Fuel Depot, Belgium, 1117 hours GMT

Chuck Porter's reporter's notebook was filled with crabbed writing. "Stavelot . . . largest filling station in Europe . . . over two and a half million gallons of gas, all in five-gallon cans . . . two million road maps of Europe . . . nobody to wash your windshields . . ."

This was the sort of sight that made a good human-interest story. The roads in every direction were lined with can after can of fuel. All sorts of military vehicles, from tanks to trucks, from jeeps to ambulances, pulled up along the road, emptied cans into thirsty engines, tipped the cans on their sides, then drove off. Other soldiers picked up the empties and left full ones in their place. It was a zoo, a mammoth near traffic jam, and Porter couldn't see for the life of him how people could get in or out in all the confusion.

His jeep was moving toward the Ansleve River bridge, when suddenly he heard the sound of cannon fire, and then return fire. His driver, a corporal, said, "I think we'd better turn back, sir," and started to do so.

"Turn back? Hell, no—at least not yet. Let's get over there. Now, corporal—I'm here for a story, and that looks like a story."

The corporal shrugged. "It's your funeral," he said.

Porter patted his shoulder. "Hell, we're not going there to fight, just to take a look. Then we'll both bug out. I don't have any intention of either of us getting killed. Okay?"

The corporal smiled and sped up toward the sound of gunfire. "You got it, sir."

As they neared their objective, Porter saw a sheet of flame in front of the bridge, and to his horror, huge panzers emerging through waves of heat and oily smoke.

"Goddamn!" shouted the corporal. "The Nazis are across the Ansleve River!" He slammed on the brakes.

There were trucks filled with men—American soldiers—moving toward him, away from the bridge. Without waiting for orders, the corporal swung the jeep around and joined the retreating column.

"What the hell is going on out there?" Chuck Porter demanded, shouting the question at one truckload of men after another. There was a story here, but he couldn't find out enough to write it and he didn't have a way to file it. Few of the vehicles were going slow enough for the passengers even to hear the question, but finally he got his answer.

"It's an SS panzer unit, coming up from Malmedy! They overran a smaller fuel dump this morning, killed everyone. We filled a ditch with gas and set it on fire to try to slow them up, but those fucking panzers rolled right through! We don't have much defense here—looks like the Nazis are gonna get themselves a gas station!"

The reporter could see that this was a retreat and a big one—and a disaster for the Americans. The evidence was undeniable, in the wide stares of the drivers, the hunched, defeated posture of the men clustered in the backs of the crowded vehicles. The jeep sped around the line of trucks. Here and there a truck had broken down, and invariably the disabled vehicle was unceremoniously pushed into the ditch to clear the road for the rest of the disorganized column. When he looked closely, Porter saw the insignias of several divisions, most notably the 99th and 106th. These were intermingled without any pattern, further proof that this was a general rout.

The corporal pulled up at the farmhouse that had been his bivouac, an artillery regiment CP, or command post. Porter got out, and the corporal sped off. The officers and staff were madly gathering maps and papers, burning some, jamming others into satchels, which were hastily tossed into jeeps and trucks.

Of course, there had been the rumors last night: the Germans were attacking with tanks; the unit would be going into action in the next few days; this was a serious raid intended to break up First Army's imminent drive through the Westwall and on to the Rhine. The artillery officers had laughed about the futility of the Nazi maneuvers as if anyone could stop this inexorable Allied advance.

No one, Porter noticed, was laughing now.

"Hey, where are the Krauts?" an American officer shouted as Porter entered the CP.

"Comin' fast!" he replied. "Tiger tanks in the lead! They've crossed the Ansleve Bridge and are heading this way."

"Porter!" It was the regimental CO, shouting to him as the driver over-revved his jeep. The other officers of the CP started scrambling into their vehicles, and engines were roaring into life all around. "Get in! We're falling back before Jerry gets here!"

Porter piled into the back of the jeep as the driver popped the clutch and tore away from the inn in a skidding frenzy of churning slush. Behind him, the German army was pulling into the biggest gas station in Europe.

SHAEF Headquarters, Paris, France, 1540 hours GMT

"What's the word, Brad?" General Eisenhower asked, fixing his subordinate army group commander with a frank stare. "This isn't any spoiling attack, is it?"

"No, sir, it doesn't seem so. But I'm confident First Army will be able to stop the Krauts before they do any real damage."

"Monty doesn't think so."

"What does he have to say about it?" George Patton, uncharacteristically silent until now, spoke up with a belligerent glare.

"He thinks this is a major offensive, and I happen to agree with him."

"What's their objective?" challenged Patton. "Besides knocking First Army around and delaying the move against the Rhine? It's not like they think they can kick us out of France any more! This is a desperation move. Rommel's out of options, so he's drawing to the inside straight."

"Nevertheless, the potential is serious. Intelligence has ID'd what? Some eight panzer divisions? Two panzer armies?" Ike retorted. "That's one helluva punch, and if they cross the Meuse, they could do some real damage."

"They'll never get that far!" Bradley insisted, though his voice lacked an element of conviction. "If nothing else, they don't have the fuel." Patton nodded in emphatic agreement, his cigar held tightly between his teeth.

"You've got to remember, the British have been here before," Eisenhower countered, in his ever-rational, patient delivery. "In 1940, to be precise. The

Krauts came through the Ardennes, and the next thing you know the British Expeditionary Force was scrambling into fishing boats on the beaches at Dunkirk."

"But the U.S. Army is here now!" Patton roared. "And damn it, Ike, I'm not about to let some goddamn goose-stepping Nazis push me back from the Siegfried Line."

Eisenhower nodded. "I know, George . . . and I agree with you. But that doesn't change basic facts. And one fact is this: Rommel cannot be allowed to cross the Meuse."

"We can stop him!" Bradley interjected.

"I hope so—but I've made a decision that will help. I'm transferring First Army to Monty until this mess is over. He'll take charge of the northern flank of this bulge in our lines. You, Brad, with Third Army, are to shut them down on the south."

Eisenhower held up his hand as both generals started to protest. "We'll argue about it later. For now, Monty's got the word. He's drawing his Tommies down to the river, and will hold a line from Namur eastward. If the Germans get that far, they'll be stopped."

"And what about us?" demanded the red-faced Patton.

"You'll have to get yourself into the attack as soon as possible. Drive north, try to reach this road junction here—Bastogne, the name is. It's almost surrounded, and it's a key to travel through the Ardennes. I'm trying to get the 101st Airborne—truck-mounted for now—into there to try and hold the line, but it seems like the Krauts are moving too fast."

"I already have plans drawn up for a turn north," said Patton confidently. "Fourth Armored will be on the way by this evening."

"This evening?" the supreme commander replied, startled.

Patton grinned.

"And just to be on the safe side," Eisenhower continued, "I want you to send somebody as far west as the Meuse. Tanks, a whole armored division if possible. Someone that can drive northward, in case Rommel reaches Dinant, here in Belgium." Eisenhower indicated a little dot on the map. "Do you have anybody in position?"

"It's pretty goddamn unlikely Rommel will make it to Dinant. If so, though, I can get someone in position," Patton answered. "It's the Nineteenth Armored—that's Henry Wakefield's boys. They're refitting after Metz, farthest west of any of my units."

"Well, George, think they can handle it?" asked the Supreme Commander.

"They're Third Army now," growled Patton. "And they did okay in Metz."

"Then give them the job."

Near Stavelot, Belgium, 18 December 1944, 1718 hours GMT

Chuck Porter stopped, put his hands on his knees, and took several great, heaving breaths. In spite of the snow and cold, he was sweating. Behind him, he could hear the crackling of breaking twigs and the crumping sound of boots against snow. In the dim gray light nothing much was visible past about three feet. Porter had no idea where he was—except that he was trapped, cut off, and probably about to die.

The end had come upon him suddenly. Out of the trees came a line of panzers; noises of screams mixed with gunfire and the booming of great cannon, flashes of blinding light mixed with swirling smoke, the sensation of his jeep swerving suddenly, leaving the road, upending in a ditch. He had been thrown out onto a snowbank, bruised and cut but not seriously injured.

Scrambling up and into the trees, heart pounding, he had virtually no memory of the brief battle; it was a blur, a mental block. When he caught his breath and looked back from the shelter of the trees, he saw the surviving American soldiers with hands up, surrendering to rifle-wielding Germans wearing gray uniforms.

He turned to run, rustling the bushes, making too much noise. He heard *"Dort! In den Büschen! Erhalten Sie ihn!"* His college German, rusty at best, helped him decipher the shouts: "There! In the bushes! Get him!" He did not stop to think whether surrender would be the best choice; he simply ran, hearing the growing sounds of footsteps behind him. He was out of shape, terribly out of shape. Tree branches slashed at his face, he was tangled, trapped.

He stopped, gasped, pushed through, ran again. Then his foot twisted in a gnarled tree root and he went face down in the snow. And they were upon him. *"Kamerad! Bitte schießen Sie nicht! Ich übergebe!"* he called out, begging them not to shoot; he surrendered. *"Ich bin ein amerikanischer Zeitungsreporter."* He had no idea if it would help by telling him he was an American newspaperman, but he would say anything, anything to avoid the sound he feared would be next, the point-blank sound of a rifle firing, ending his life.

He could barely understand the soldier's barked command. *"Stehen Sie oben! Setzen Sie Ihr überreicht Ihren Kopf!"* Awkwardly, he stood up and put his hands over his head, trying to keep his hands in plain view. He hoped he was translating properly. This was not the sort of German phrase he had studied in his long-ago classes. *They never teach you anything practical,* he thought.

The soldier yelled out new commands: *"Bewegung! Schneller! Erhalten Sie zurück mit den anderen Soldaten!"* He couldn't move any faster, not with his hands over his head, but he struggled through the snow at his best possible speed, crossing through the ditch and up into the knot of shivering American prisoners. He noticed the wrecked jeep; the sergeant who had been driving was dead, crushed in the wreckage, one arm hanging into the snow. He shivered in fear and guilt.

The soldier who had captured him was talking to an officer, a tall, thin-faced colonel, if his reading of Wehrmacht insignia was correct. *"Er sagt, daß er ein amerikanischer Zeitungsreporter ist,"* he was saying.

"Ein amerikanischer Zeitungsreporter? Sehr interessant. Trug er eine Waffe?" replied the colonel. Porter strained to hear, to make out the language. They were clearly talking about him. "He says he's an American reporter." "An American newspaper reporter? Very interesting. Was he carrying a weapon?"

"Nicht daß ich beachtete. Er trägt eine Karte irgendeiner Sortierung, aber ich kann nicht lesen, was es sagt," replied the soldier. Porter listened intently, pointing eagerly to the press card the soldier mentioned.

"Lassen Sie mich mit ihm sprechen." The colonel came over to him, gestured to one of the guards, who grabbed the reporter by the shoulder and shoved him forward. The guard escorted him to a command half-track to talk privately.

"Sprechen Sie Deutsch?" asked the officer.

His reply was halting as he grasped for the words. *"Ein wenig. Ich studierte es in der Hochschule."* He spoke only college-level German, just a little bit at that.

The German officer smiled, then switched to a formal English, somewhat accented. "I speak a little English; I studied your language in the college as well. I am Colonel Günter von Reinhardt, intelligence officer for Army Group B. And you would be?"

"Porter. Chuck Porter. Associated Press, Paris bureau chief." He gave a deep sigh of relief. His heart was still pounding with fear, but he realized he had just drawn a royal flush.

"Bureau chief?" He looked skeptically at the press pass Porter wore around his neck. "And you would normally find an Associated Press bureau chief in the front edge of a combat zone, rather than in an office many kilometers away?"

"When the bureau chief can get away with it, yes," Porter said with a tentative smile. "The same way you might find an intelligence officer in combat rather than in headquarters." He held his breath, wondering if a smart remark like that could get him shot.

Reinhardt laughed. "When he can get away with it. Indeed. And you are seeing somewhat more of combat than you had wagered, correct?"

"I am, colonel. This isn't exactly what I had in mind." Irony and humor seemed to be the right tone to take with this particular Wehrmacht officer. Porter knew he'd be spending the rest of the war in a POW camp. *Well, maybe I can turn this into a book when it's all over,* he thought.

"And as a reporter, you are always looking for interesting news stories, a unique angle?"

"Of course I am," Porter laughed. "Got any good leads?"

Reinhardt looked at the newspaper reporter with calculating eyes. "I understand that while you are an American, and presumably patriotic, you are also a reporter and believe in accurate news. Is that correct?"

"Yes, on both counts."

The German officer reached a decision. "Very well. I am thinking that you might prove useful as a communications channel as well as a neutral reporting source on the events of today and the next few days."

"Colonel, I'd like to do my job as a reporter even under these circumstances. But I want you to know that I'm neither a propagandist nor a traitor," Porter said.

"Of course not," said the colonel seriously. "That is not my purpose. I will ask you only to be an honest channel of information. If you are interested, there will be only one requirement, and that is your parole. No attempts to escape, no attempts to go into areas we set as off-limits. Do you agree?"

Porter thought for a moment, inspecting the offer for hidden traps. "If I decide I can't go along with what you want, I can elect to become a regular prisoner of war. Agreed?"

"Agreed." Reinhardt turned to the guard. *"Dieser Mann kann vom Gebrauch zum Feldmarschall sein. Ich werde ihn mit mir nehmen. Er hat sein Wort, um gegeben nicht zu versuchen zu entgehen."* Porter translated in his head. "This man may be of use to the field marshal. I am going to take him with me. He has given his word not to try to escape."

"Jawohl, Herr Oberst," the soldier said, saluting. He took a long, mean look at his prisoner, as if to send the message that Porter had better not try anything.

Porter had no intention whatsoever of doing so.

Mobile Command Post, Army Group B, St. Vith, Belgium, 19 December 1944, 1757 hours GMT

"Pull in here," Rommel said, and Carl-Heinz obediently turned off the road to park between a pair of half-tracks. The whitewashed vehicles clustered like suckling piglets around the shambling ruin of what had once been a sprawling inn. A small banner beside the doorway identified the building as the forward army headquarters.

"Get a cup of tea and a bite of bread," the field marshal suggested. "I'm going to get an update on the situation, but be ready to move again within the hour."

Before Carl-Heinz could acknowledge the order, Rommel was out the door, striding purposefully into the makeshift headquarters. Only as he returned the salutes of the guards at the door did he realize that he had left his cane behind in the car. He should be exhausted, he told himself. He'd been on the road for more than seventy-two hours, never napping for more than a few minutes in the lurching car. Yet instead, he was more energized than he had been since getting wounded. In fact, he realized in surprise, he hadn't felt this much vigor since the heyday of his campaign in Africa!

He found Speidel and Reinhardt poring over a map in the gas-lamp brightness of the inn's great room. Without ceremony the Desert Fox made his way to the table for an impromptu briefing.

"Great news, Herr Feldmarschall! We've captured a major Allied fuel dump, here, at Stavelot. Well over a million gallons, possibly even two, of fuel. We've sent word that all synthetic fuel stocks can be diverted to the Luftwaffe; we won't need them any more. We're loading up front line units with all they can hold and shipping the rest back to bring up reinforcements." One of Rommel's biggest concerns had been whether he would have the ability to bring up the forces in the rear. He had the troops, and now he had the fuel. This changed everything.

"Overall, the first three days of the rest of the campaign have gone as well as we could have hoped," Speidel continued. "The Americans have shown some resistance here, and here. . . ." he slapped the map, highlighting a rugged elevation known as the Elsenborn Ridge, "but we've isolated these pockets. Guderian's spearheads are closing on Spa from the north. They've already captured St. Vith and are moving on the Meuse."

"And Manteuffel?"

"He's almost surrounded Bastogne. You remember, the town that controls the road network for the whole region. It's being held by a few Americans, but they're trying to get more reinforcements in. Our infantry have attacked for more than a day, but haven't made any progress."

Aside from Bastogne, it was success everywhere, Rommel noted. The initial spearheads of the attack cut through the stunned Americans with more speed than the Desert Fox could have possibly hoped. The field marshal had driven along in the wake of the lead panzer divisions. Several times he had passed hastily constructed POW compounds, where stunned Americans looked out from behind fences of barbed wire.

He had stopped at various unit headquarters, and everywhere learned that the attack was proceeding at a good clip. On the northern shoulder, the enemy had shown some initial resistance, but Guderian had hastily committed an extra panzer division, and finally the Tiger tanks had rumbled over the American trenches.

More prisoners . . . more headlong advances. Everywhere it seemed that the Americans were falling back where they weren't surrendering. The Ardennes had in fact been held only by a thin screen of units, and once the German armor had punctured that screen, they had found great opportunities for advance.

Best of all, the weather stayed bad. When it wasn't snowing, there were heavy clouds pressing close to the ground, shrouding these already dark hills in a gloom that prevented even the most rudimentary air activity.

Rommel hardly noticed when a thick piece of bread found its way into his hand—Mutti taking care of him again. He was surprised how good it felt to take a big bite; he was hungrier than he thought.

"Get a message to Guderian," Rommel said, ready to head back to his car. "I want him to get his spearheads to the Meuse with all speed, then to throw a bridgehead across. And remind Manteuffel to watch the southern flank. Patton's down there, and he's sure to take an interest in what's going on." The field marshal took one more look at the map. "I am going to Bastogne myself. We need those roads—that's where the battle will be decided!"

"Yes, field marshal!" Speidel promised.

As Rommel turned to leave, he paused. "Colonel von Reinhardt—will you walk me to my car?"

"Of course, sir," said the young colonel.

As they walked back into the cold, Rommel asked, "And how does the battlefield look from a speeding half-track?"

"Very big, sir, and more than a bit confusing," replied Reinhardt a bit ruefully.

Rommel laughed, and patted him on the back. "That was my first impression, too. And you know, it hasn't changed much over the years."

Reinhardt nodded. "Field Marshal, I kept one of the prisoners that we captured."

"Oh?" said Rommel, quizzically.

"Yes, sir. It seems that the Paris bureau chief of the American Associated Press decided to get his own personal look at the front lines, and got a somewhat closer look than he expected. I asked him for his parole, because I thought that an American reporter's perspective on this campaign might have a good impact on their public sentiment, making it more likely to achieve decent terms."

"Interesting idea," mused Rommel. "Colonel, you have a good grasp of the relationship of military operations to politics, and now you demonstrate an understanding of propaganda as well."

"And," continued Reinhardt, nodding an acknowledgment of the compliment, "I thought it might prove useful to have a German-speaking American who was not of the military."

"It might, indeed," said Rommel. "Do keep a close eye on this man," he added. "Even supposed noncombatants have been known to give surprises."

"Yes, sir," replied Reinhardt. "I plan to take that very seriously."

Carl-Heinz had the car door open. "I'll see you at headquarters," Rommel said, and then he was gone.

Bastogne, Belgium, 20 December 1944, 1017 hours GMT

"They can't get through—the verdammt Americans have blown up six Tigers!"

The colonel of the panzer battalion could not keep the tremor out of his voice—perhaps because he accurately anticipated General Horst Bücher's displeasure with his report.

"Then you will send in twelve, twenty, a hundred more—do you understand? You must keep attacking! And if you cannot follow these orders, you will be replaced with someone who can!" declared the general, fighting to hold his voice steady. All his nerves jangled, and frustration threatened to explode out of his every pore.

"Jawohl, Herr General!" declared the colonel, snapping his arm upward. "Heil Himmler!"

The officer spun on his heel and stalked out of the farmhouse where Bücher had set up his temporary command post. Climbing into his armored car, the colonel roared off through the slush and the thickening night.

The SS general found that he was still trembling. *These idiots—can't they see? Bastogne* must *fall!*

He stared at the map, wishing that his task was as easy as he had made it sound to the battalion colonel. In truth, however, this Belgian city was proving to be a remarkably stubborn nut to crack. Thus far the city had been attacked by elements of First and Second SS Panzer Divisions, as well as Panzer Lehr, and all these offensives had been repulsed in the wooded hills that bordered Bastogne on all sides. Too, the Americans had managed to hold open the road from the west, and German intelligence had confirmed that several reinforcements—including the crack 101st Airborne Division—were now fighting their way to Bastogne. Panzer Lehr had moved to bypass the city, but was finding tough going in the rugged terrain. The two SS panzer divisions, meanwhile, were regrouping to the north and south of the key crossroads, preparatory to commencing another series of attacks.

"We need that city—that road!" Bücher declared. At the same time, a voice of reason in the back of his mind suggested that he would never get it merely by bashing his tanks into a brick wall of defenses.

But he didn't know what else to do, so he waited through the hours of the night, listening to the reports about the next offensive . . . more losses, tanks destroyed, men—including the colonel he had sent back into the fray—killed.

Each fresh piece of information confirmed that the Americans were holding the city's perimeter with determination and courage, while the reinforcements were drawing ever closer to the western edge of Bastogne.

And he didn't know what to do about it. The sense of impotence, of failure, was nearly intolerable to Bücher. Rommel and Manteuffel had sent him here to speed up the offensive, to see that a key crossroads in the Wehrmacht's path was seized and held. But it seemed that he could do nothing to break through the armored shell of American resistance.

The car that rumbled up to the building sounded no different from the myriad of machines that constantly arrived here—until the guard at the door snapped to attention.

"Herr Feldmarschall!"

Bücher heard the feldwebel announce Rommel's arrival, and the SS general immediately stood ramrod straight.

The Desert Fox, his scarred face a match for Bücher's own, strode easily into the headquarters, his cane virtually ignored except as a pointer. He nodded smilingly to Bücher as the staff made way for him at the map table.

"Still outside the city, eh, Horst?" The army commander's tone was calm, even friendly—further gouges into Bücher's sense of pride.

"Yes, field marshal. I am sorry to report that each of three panzer divisions has been repulsed outside Bastogne." The general's shame urged him to beg for forgiveness, to offer his abject apology, but the discipline instilled in a lifetime of service held him silent.

"Yes . . . I think something needs to be done."

The SS general stood at attention and waited.

"We have three different efforts under way, and this is clearly dispersal of our strength. General Bücher . . . I would like you to take the leading elements of all three divisions and command an attack against the city."

"Of course, sir!"

"You understand my needs?"

"Yes—Bastogne must be taken, and quickly."

"Correct. You will take such elements of the panzer divisions as you can gather to form Kampfgruppe Bücher. Then, I suggest that you attack from the west."

"Yes, field marshal!" Bücher hesitated, then voiced his concern. "But from the west . . . isn't that exceptionally risky? That's where the American relief forces are approaching."

"Precisely. And that's where the city defenses are likely to be the weakest. Concentrate all the artillery from three panzer divisions against your target zone, and then strike on a very narrow front. And, General Bücher, good luck to you. The success of our attack now rests upon your shoulders."

·   ·   ·

SS General Horst Bücher had learned the arts of warfare from the famed commando Otto Skorzeny and had quickly advanced through SS ranks because of his Aryan heritage, his quick and ruthless mind, and his total loyalty to the party. And now he had a combat command and a military objective: Bastogne, thanks to the trust placed in him by Field Marshal Erwin Rommel.

He sat upright in the hatch of a Tiger tank's turret, surrounded by a cacophony of artillery fire, shells exploding everywhere, splintering trees and scarring the landscape. Around him were dozens more of the armored behemoths, mottled white in winter camouflage. The Americans were dug in on the heights before him, and he imagined them cringing under the tumultuous onslaught. He knew that just beyond this hill ran the road to the west, and the city limits of Bastogne. And he knew that, as soon as this barrage was lifted, he would lead these tanks through the pulverized forest and into the key crossroads.

Bücher didn't stop to wonder about the source of his confidence, but he was utterly certain that he would win. He had sought out many role models and mentors in his career, beginning with the Hitler Youth leader who counseled him to turn in his father so many years ago, and onward and upward. Virtually every man he had put his trust in had disappointed him, as had his father. This one was weak in his dedication to the Party, that one was a drunken whoremonger, the other one was not pure in his Aryan genotype. Only two men—Adolf Hitler, who was nearly a god, and Heinrich Himmler, his earthly apostle—had not disappointed him in his dedication, and neither of them was quite mortal in Bücher's eyes.

Now there was a third: the Desert Fox, a man who represented all that was good and noble about the German race. And this great man trusted him—him, Horst Bücher!—and today he had the chance to prove it by leveling this pocket of American resistance.

Yet there was a deeper challenge underlying Bücher's concern, and he was not sure what to do about it. For the first time the purity of his Nazi faith had begun to weaken, to show signs of inner tarnish.

After the Metz Massacre, he had received his long-expected order from Führer Himmler: He was to kill the Desert Fox at the conclusion of this battle, once victory was certain or defeat inevitable, and to make it look like a combat death. That would be easy for a man of Horst Bücher's skills, but he had reached a decision, a momentous one for him. Führer Himmler's massacre at Metz—for Bücher had instantly known the truth about who had arranged it— had sickened him, not because of the deaths, but because of the dishonor, especially when he knew Rommel was right.

Therefore, Bücher would disobey the orders to kill Rommel, the first time in his life he had ever disobeyed a Party directive, the first time in his life he had ever condoned behavior his leadership believed to be treasonous, or even mildly anti-Party. For once, Bücher saw Himmler's directive about Rommel as being self-serving, motivated by envy, not by Party. Surely, he thought, Adolf Hitler would never have done anything like that. The Metz Massacre would have been justified had the retreat been cowardly or unneeded, but Himmler was simply wrong about the military situation. He wished he could argue the point, but he knew that would be futile.

What does it matter? he thought. *I am planning to disobey my orders, and I know the penalty for disobedience. It is I, not the Desert Fox, who will not survive this campaign.*

His mind snapped back to the present, to the awareness that the artillery fire was slackening. Now he could hear tank engines rumble into life. He dropped through the hatch as the massive panzer began to inch slowly up the artillery-scarred hillside.

Somehow American solders had survived, and gunfire pinged off German armor. But the panzers replied with cannons and machine guns, and the huge treads crushed right over the crude trenches. Here was an enemy machine gun nest, quickly obliterated by fire from the tanks' main guns. There an American tank destroyer took a few bold shots, until the crew in the open turret was killed by swarming panzergrenadiers. At the hilltop there was no pause as direct hits on two Shermans knocked out the last barrier before the city.

Soon the German tanks were rolling down the hill, some of them racing onto the road, others driving right around the houses and fields that formed the city's fringe. The barrage had reduced many buildings to rubble, but these were still defended, infantry shooting rifles, automatic weapons, and bazookas amid the mounds of shattered stone.

Three Tiger tanks formed the leading edge of the sally along the main road, while five Panthers rumbled behind. Bücher's command tank followed the Panthers; while companies of panzergrenadier infantry spread out to either side. Guns firing constantly, the panzers growling slowly, inexorably into the city. The sound of BAR and rifle fire sputtered in the tight confines. Smoke grew, confusing the landscape, combining with the ice and freezing rain in a way to give the phrase "as cold as hell" a very special meaning. Americans held sniper positions in every tall structure, and their own tanks returned fire. But whenever a Sherman fired, a position could be marked and fire returned, the heavier fire of the Tiger tanks invariably destroyed the undergunned, underarmored enemy.

The joy and passion of deadly combat swelled within Bücher, and he rose to sit atop the turret, signaling for the infantry and the rest of the armor to move up. The combat spilled through the streets of Bastogne. House by house and street by street the enemy was forced back.

Bullets filleted the air around him as Bücher shouted furiously, dismounting from the tank and drawing his pistol. He rushed among the infantry, waving them forward. It was unwise, stupid, but death was not something Bücher feared, it was something he welcomed. And the presence of an SS general risking enemy fire like a common soldier was something that soldiers noticed, remarked on. Victory must be certain if a general officer would risk himself so!

Now tanks and infantry pushed into the city square. A feldwebel raced up to Bücher, saluting over the silly grin on his face.

"Good news, Herr General! We've captured the fuel depot before the Amis could destroy it!"

Bücher threw back his head and laughed, exultant at this final triumph, the reserves needed to carry Rommel's offensive over the Meuse and beyond. He lifted his pistol, firing the weapon into the murk of a burning building, a place where the Americans had refused to surrender.

A Sherman was backing down a side street, muzzle pointed forward. A shell from an eighty-eight made a direct hit, shattering the turret and barrel. The cheers and yells of his soldiers showed the battle was moving forward; Americans were retreating and his men were fighting, shooting.

"Rache für Metz!" he heard one man shout. He was surprised that there were common soldiers who did believe the propaganda message about the American atrocity at Metz. Revenge was a good message.

So he, too, shouted "Rache für Metz!" Soon other soldiers picked up the cry, and Bücher saw another American fall, shot in the back in the growing rout.

Nineteenth Division Mobile Headquarters, Sedan, France, 1524 hours GMT

Sergeant Johnson brought Wakefield a steady stream of reports as the battle developed through those overcast December days. At first the general had thought that the initial messages must be some kind of overreaction, but as he huddled in his headquarters tent, his big hands wrapped around a hot mug of coffee it was pretty obvious that the situation was deteriorating quickly. The German capture of the Stavelot fuel dump had been a stunning reversal. In moments, the campaign had changed from one in which the Allies had ample fuel resupply and the Germans little or none into one in which the situation was in dire danger of reversal.

"Even with the loss of Stavelot, we've still got some fuel reserves," Colonel Sanger began, answering the unspoken question that was first in everyone's mind. The S-2 was holding an impromptu intelligence briefing on the fourth day of the battle. All the commanders of the Nineteenth had gathered around, sharing Wakefield's certainty that they would soon be thrown into the fight.

"That being said, there's a lot of news that's less pleasant. First Army's getting ripped up all along the Seven Corps front," Colonel Sanger explained. "It seems like a lot of units aren't even responding. Like they've been overrun or cut off already."

"The whole corps?" Pulaski demanded, blinking in astonishment.

"That's what it seems like."

"Damn." It occurred to Wakefield that, a few weeks earlier, Nineteenth Armored had been a part of that corps. "It looks like being assigned to Third Army might just have pulled our fat out of the fire." *For the time being, anyway,* he privately amended.

"Any word from Patton?" the colonel asked, directing his question to the division CO.

"No, but I heard that Ike got all the top brass together to try and figure out what's going on."

"Well, we're ready to move."

"You got those tank destroyers OK?"

"Yes sir," Pulaski replied. "That Zimmerman is sharp . . . I've put one platoon with each of my task forces."

"Good. You'll be out in front. Bob?"

"CCB is ready too," pledged Bob Jackson in a Virginia drawl. "Give my boys half a minute to kiss their girlfriends good-bye, and they'll be ready to attack hell itself."

The jangling of the general's telephone interrupted the conference, and Wakefield moved with alacrity to take the instrument at Sergeant Johnson's summons. He listened for a minute to the familiar, high-pitched voice of his army commander. When he hung up, it was with a sense of resolve mingled with relief. At least now they could do something.

"Jimmy, how soon can you have CCA rolling?" Wakefield's voice was tense, and the colonel obviously shared his emotion.

"Within the hour, General. Where do you want us?"

"You're on the left flank of Third Army . . . in the best position to get up to Dinant. The Krauts are crossing the river there, and after they do they're sure to turn north, toward Antwerp. You're to move against Dinant, with CCB coming right behind. You'll have enemy panzer divisions on both sides of you when you get there, but that's the only crossing Rommel has. You take out those two bridges, and his army is cut in half. I want you to see if you can't cut their supply line right there."

"You got it, General. We're ready to go!" Both colonels acknowledged the orders, and Wakefield was already heading toward the door.

"All right, then. Move out!"

The Kremlin, Moscow, Soviet Union, 21 December 1944, 1922 hours GMT

Intelligence briefings continued in another quarter as well. The GKO, the State Defense Committee of the Presidium of the Supreme Soviet, followed the military situation with great interest.

"And what do you think of the chances of the Desert Fox?" asked Stalin, sipping a cup of tea.

It was always difficult for a briefing officer to determine what kind of answer Stalin wanted, whether an honest answer or one that fit his own preconceived notions. The deceptively calm, even casual delivery with which Stalin asked the question was an unreliable gauge.

Sweating even in the cold Kremlin conference room, the briefing officer collected his thoughts to give the best answer he knew. "Because of the oil we sold Germany, Rommel has sufficient reserves to launch a solid attack, and can continue to move if he captures Allied reserves on the way. It's a difficult situation for him at best, but if he reaches Antwerp, the course of the war will alter in serious ways. Ultimately, the Allies will advance through Italy and attack from the south, but that is a slower campaign."

"And if he does not take Antwerp?"

"Then he will return to the Westwall and continue to fight a holding action, trying to wear the Allies down. But whether he wins or loses, he has now stretched the war out for at least one additional year. We can adjust that amount of time either way by selling or by withholding oil from the Germans."

"Very good," said Stalin. "That gives us the time we need to build up a massive offensive that will capture all of Germany to the banks of the Rhine in one single march. Molotov, what would your young friend think of that?" Molotov had been very impressed by the German military attaché von Reinhardt.

"I suspect he knows. Germany's trouble is that they have too few options. They must smash the Allies, negotiate a quick peace that is not too painful, then move back against us, and that is highly improbable. The Allies will still exact an enormous price for peace, because with few exceptions their leaders are unable to see the long-range consequences. All that reinforces our long-range plan."

"I would prefer greater certainty. Let us discuss ways to interfere with any temporary successes the Germans might achieve."

Excerpt from *War's Final Fury,* by Professor Jared Gruenwald

The spearheads of the great Fuchs Am Rhein offensive cut through the lightly held First Army front with stunning force. For the first time, the American army experienced the full might of the Blitzkrieg. Rommel attacked with fif-teen panzer divisions, a half-dozen top-line infantry divisions, and nearly thirty divisions of the *Volksgrenadier*, the under-equipped formations made up of older men and youths drafted during the last year of the war. The tanks led the way, driving fast and hard while the foot soldiers came forward in waves to overwhelm bypassed strongpoints.

Though in many places surprised formations—mostly infantry, with a few artillery elements in support—recovered quickly to offer serious resistance, the tide of the attacking Wehrmacht was too powerful to halt. The practice of Blitzkrieg—lightning war—conceived by Guderian and perfected by Rommel, worked as well as it had in 1940 and 1941. The armored spearheads plunged deep into the American rear, while those bypassed defenders who were not quickly captured were at least surrounded and effectively cut off from rein-forcement or retreat. The capture of the Stavelot fuel dump, in particular, was a huge success for the Germans and a disaster for the Americans.

Rommel's plan involved the use of two great armies on the attack. On his right flank, the Sixth Panzerarmee under Guderian was to drive for the Meuse, cross that river barrier, and sweep all the way to Antwerp. This was the direct route to victory. On the left, the Fifth Panzerarmee under Manteuffel was to thrust westward, securing the open flank of the attack to reach the Meuse and, if possible, cross.

In the north Guderian's panzer forces bypassed the areas of initial resis-tance, most notably along the crest of Elsenborn ridge. Leaving these zones for the infantry to mop up, several armored divisions seized key road junctions at Monschau, Malmedy, Stoumont, and finally Spa. With the capture of that last town, the road to the Meuse lay open, and "Hurrying Heinz" Guderian wasted no time in sending his lead Kampfgruppe racing toward that great river. His goals included the propaganda prizes of Liege and Brussels, and, of critical im-portance to Rommel's master plan, the key Allied supply port of Antwerp be-yond.

South of the Sixth Panzerarmee, the Fifth made even more dramatic progress, although it, of course, had farther to go. Charged with protecting Guderian's long flank, General Hasso-Ecard von Manteuffel, a classically trained cavalry officer who had attained notable success on the Russian Front, sent his panzers in an all-out dash through rugged country in a race to reach the Meuse at Dinant. The force ran into serious resistance at the key cross-roads of Bastogne, and only Rommel's arrival on the scene and inspirational plan of attack allowed the Germans to seize that town before the arrival of American relief forces. At the same time the Wehrmacht troops captured enough petrol to send their spearheads forward with renewed determination. Capturing interim Allied supply dumps on the way to Antwerp was also an es-sential part of Rommel's plan. Not only was his own supply of petrol limited, capturing Allied supplies achieved two additional goals: first, it allowed his spearheads to race ahead of his own necessarily slower resupply efforts, and second, it deprived Allied troops of their own opportunity for refueling, taking at least some American tanks out of the battle as effectively as if they had been destroyed in battle.

Although SHAEF intelligence officers recognized within the first two days that this was a major attack, by then the initial line of the front had been ruptured. Eisenhower was receiving conflicting reports from a variety of sources. Before any of his subordinate generals grasped the full potential of this attack, he saw the threat to Antwerp and acted to protect that port. With First Army effectively cut in two, he divided command between Bradley on the south and British field marshal Montgomery to the north.

With his controversial decision to give Monty full control over the northern flank of the Bulge, Ike angered his American generals. However, there is no denying the fact that, as Guderian's panzers approached Liege, Bradley had few troops in position to stop this prong of the attack. Field Marshal Montgomery dispatched British troops as well as reserves drawn from the U.S. Ninth Army to establish a solid line on the north side of the Meuse from Namur through Liege. He effectively ceded the territory south of the river to the Germans but was able to establish a strong defensive position behind the natural barrier of the river. Guderian's tanks reached the Meuse along a fifty-mile front, but here they found all bridges blown and a powerful defensive force waiting on the far bank. The weather stayed bad, effectively grounding all air support, but there was no way for the Germans to force a crossing.

To the south of the Bulge, Patton made haste to extricate his army from a planned series of operations in the Saar region. He then commenced vigorous counterattacks against Manteuffel's flank. His primary objective became the recapture of Bastogne, which was rapidly becoming a German fortress. However, it grew increasingly clear that, with First Army fully punctured, SHAEF had insufficient reserves to block Manteuffel's westward lunge. And so it was at Dinant, not Liege, that the Wehrmacht reached, and crossed, the Meuse. An initial defensive line established by elements of the 101st Airborne Division was overwhelmed by the attack of no less than three panzer divisions.

Nevertheless, stiff resistance on the west bank of the river limited the German crossing to this single city. Rommel wasted no time pushing his tanks through Dinant, from where they immediately swept northward. Although his supply line was limited to two bridges in Dinant itself, the field marshal pressed deep into the Allied rear; in effect, he accepted the narrow supply line in an effort to send the great body of his mobile force driving toward the coast. Passing to the west of Namur, these panzer divisions outflanked Montgomery's river line. British forces moved to block, with Montgomery himself accompanying his main armored formation, XXX Corps, in an attempt to get in front of the German advance.

But the enemy was moving too quickly. As he had in Africa, the Desert Fox again used captured fuel to resupply his panzer divisions—fuel that, like the panzers, could only cross the river and reach the German leading elements by traversing those precious Dinant bridges. From the British flank the German armor swept north, ready to close a trap upon the Allies that would shatter American supply capability and cut off Montgomery's entire army group.

All these efforts converged beyond the small Belgian city. Dinant, however, remained the vulnerable flank in Rommel's dramatic advance. Like Waterloo in an earlier war, Dinant would become the critical point on which everything depended.

Nineteenth Division Mobile Headquarters, Sedan, France, 23 December 1944, 1022 hours GMT

Reid Sanger drew a deep breath. This was not the first division intelligence briefing he had run, but he knew that it was the most important. General Wakefield and Colonels Pulaski and Jackson were right in front of the small room, while the rest of the ranking combat command officers and division staff were crowded in wherever they could find room.

"There is no doubt that we're facing the biggest German attack in the west since 1940," he began, pleased to see that he had the men's attention. "In fact, in numbers of our troops and enemy troops engaged, this is undoubtedly the largest battle ever fought by the U.S. Army. And we of the Nineteenth Armored have been given a key role to play."

He turned to the large map which occupied most of the wall behind him.

"We've identified two panzerarmees attacking side by side through the First Army sector. The enemy's objective is audacious—it seems he wants to cross the Meuse and take out our base of supply here, at Antwerp. This, of course, would surround Monty and the Tommies in the north and leave us high and dry, without enough gas to drive our tanks out of harm's way.

"To the north we have Guderian, and the Sixth Panzerarmee. He had the direct route, but it seems that he's been halted at the Meuse. The Tommies, with help from a couple of American armies, have held a line from Namur eastward, and it doesn't look like the Krauts are getting across the river.

"But the Fifth Panzerarmee, under Manteuffel, is making one hell of an end run. They've punctured First Army and crossed the Meuse here, at Dinant. So far we've been able to limit them to that one bridgehead, but Rommel has pushed a lot of tanks across there—at least four panzer divisions. To put it

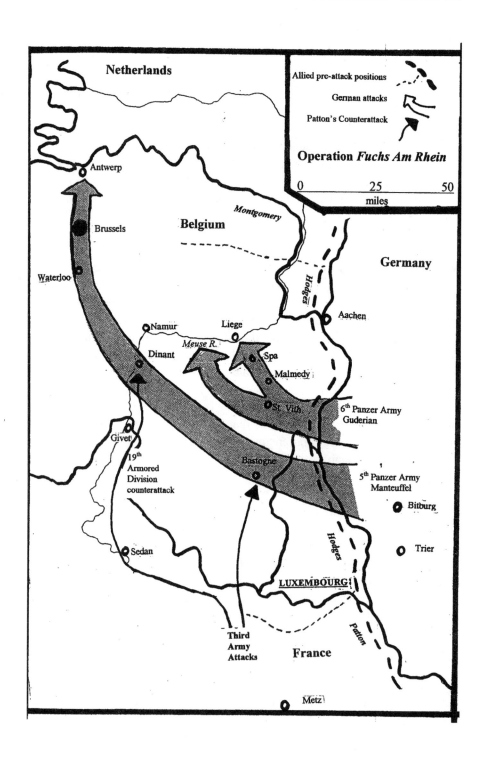

Netherlands

Allied pre-attack positions
German attacks
Patton's Counterattack

Operation Fuchs Am Rhein

0   25   50
miles

Antwerp

Brussels

Belgium

Montgomery

Germany

Waterloo

Hodges

Namur

Liege

Aachen

Meuse R.

Dinant

Spa

Malmedy

St. Vith

6th Panzer Army
Guderian

Givet

19th
Armored
Division
counterattack

Bastogne

5th Panzer Army
Manteuffel

Bitburg

Hodges

Sedan

Trier

LUXEMBOURG

Third
Army
Attacks

Patton

France

Metz

bluntly, he's loose in our backfield, he has the ball, and he's racing for the end zone."

Sanger paused as the door at the back of the room opened. When he saw the glowering visage, the big frame with the two pistols holstered in his belt, he reflexively snapped to attention and saluted. "General Patton, sir!"

Immediately the officers of the Nineteenth scrambled to their feet.

"Carry on," declared the Third Army CO, nodding to the men, then indicating Sanger with his swagger stick.

"Yes, of course General . . . that is . . ." Suddenly the S-2 found himself at a loss for words.

"And what does this mean for us, Ed?" asked Wakefield pointedly. Sanger was grateful for the question; it helped his mind get back on track.

"Third Army has got to hit Manteuffel in the flank and break up his attack. Some of our divisions are fighting into the Ardennes, trying to take Bastogne back. For us, in the Nineteenth, we've been given the chance to go for the jugular—here, at Dinant. It's the only weak spot—he's got half an army already across the river, and every can of fuel, every round of ammo for those guys is being carried forward across those bridges."

"So if we get to Dinant we'll have Germans on both sides of the river?" Jackson asked.

"Yes." Sanger didn't pull any punches. "You'll have to worry about several divisions of tanks and infantry in the Ardennes, here, within a day or two's march of the city. And I noted he's got four panzer divisions across the river. One of these, Ninth Panzer, is just moving onto the west bank in our latest recon photos. No doubt, if we make a nuisance out of ourselves, Rommel will have them try to cross back and get into the fight."

"How do we get there?" inquired Wakefield.

"Our jump-off point is here—Givet, France, a border town on the Meuse. We'll go up the east side of the river, the same side as Dinant. Roads are rough, but early recon says they don't have a lot between Givet and Dinant, at least not now. But of course, speed is very, very important."

"Damn right!" growled Patton, striding through the crowd of officers along a path that seemed to appear magically before him. In five steps the general had joined Sanger on the small stage, and the S-2 wisely stepped aside.

"You men are in a position to win this battle at a stroke," Patton declared. "And if you don't do it, no one else is going to." He glared around the room, as if daring anyone to challenge him. Instead, he received only undivided attention as he turned to Wakefield.

"Hank, you're going to have to send your boys fast and hard into harm's way." Patton fixed his glare onto James Pulaski, whose eyes flashed bright at the prospect before him. "Don't waste time with prisoners, don't get slowed down by enemy strong points. Just get to those bridges and knock 'em out, understand?"

"Yes, sir!"

"All right, men," Patton said with the hint of a feral smile. "Let's go to war."

Army Group B HQ, Dinant, Belgium, on the Meuse, 0736 hours GMT

"Tomorrow is Christmas Eve, Herr Feldmarschall," Carl-Heinz pointed out while maneuvering the car around a series of shell craters on the outskirts of Dinant. In the gray light of the predawn hour, buildings rose from the mist, the skeletal facade of a city ravaged by war. Gaunt, leafless trees seemed to grope through the murk with claws extended, and the Desert Fox shook off a shiver of foreboding.

"You're right. I had forgotten," replied Rommel.

"Ach, it doesn't mean so much I guess, not in the midst of this," said Carl-Heinz, gesturing at the ruined city. Here and there Rommel saw a glowering Frenchman, eyes expressing all the hatred evoked by the second German conquest in five years.

"It was just south of here that I crossed the Meuse with the Seventh Armored Division," the field marshal mused as the car moved along paths that had been cleared through the city's rubble. "Of course, that was back in 1940."

"I was with Guderian's corps, then," the sturdy feldwebel replied. "I remember when the Stukas came wailing down at Sedan . . . and then we rode across the bridge, and it was all over for the French."

"And now it comes to this, new tanks with the same old men, attacking the same river against a new enemy. . . ." Once again Rommel felt the twinge of melancholy. He wondered if the world would ever be finished with war. So many men dead, so much beauty destroyed.

"There's the river, Field Marshal," Carl-Heinz said, pulling the car to a stop near the crest of the bluff that led down to the Meuse. The bridges had been blown by retreating Americans, but Wehrmacht engineers, for once able to work without constant interference by Allied air forces, had quickly created two crossings. Now those precious spans, the tenuous links between Rommel and the panzers spearheading his attack, were gray with troops and tanks. Already four panzer divisions had crossed the river, and he knew that he was watching the fifth, just below.

At least he had fuel for this phase. Bastogne was now safely in German hands, and his panzers had been refueled with American fuel. The campaign so far had captured nearly forty thousand American and British soldiers. His volksgrenadier units had been decimated by the need to guard makeshift POW camps, with thousands of his soldiers no longer available for his use. *Well, that is good duty for those brave men,* he thought. Still, he needed every body he could get.

At the same time, he felt an icy twinge to the breeze coming from the west. Of course it had been cold since the attack had been launched eight days ago, but that had been a damp, chilly murk that had penetrated every fiber of every man's being. This was different, colder and, more ominously, drier.

The Desert Fox looked across the city his forces had just captured. Speidel and Bayerlein found him here, as their own car made its way along the crowded road. Rommel pointed to the city's dominating feature, the great citadel perched high on its limestone bluff.

"Bring all the antiaircraft guns you can get your hands on. I want that castle to bristle with them."

"Of course, Herr Feldmarschall," Speidel answered. "Will you make your headquarters there, as well?"

Rommel shook his head. "No sense in making it easy for our enemies to find us. Instead, I'll make my field headquarters in there," he declared, pointing to a château that stood on a bluff several hundred feet above the deep river but was a mile removed from the dominating fortress.

Again he looked west, watching the panzers roll into the distance, vanishing into the forests and countryside as they dispersed for advance and battle. Beyond that horizon, he saw patches of blue sky through the overcast, the first clear air since the attack had been launched eight days ago. It was a bad sign, he knew, but there was no turning back now.

"As soon as you have a land-line established, get me Luftwaffe headquarters, Galland himself, if you please, on the telephone. I have a feeling the weather is going to change, and we're going to need some fighter protection for those bridges."

Luftwaffe Advance Airbase, Bitburg, Germany, 24 December 1944, 1118 hours GMT

Even from the field at Bitburg, the jets had to expend precious fuel in the flight to Dinant. Still, Kommodore Krueger had been able to cycle his Me-262s through a rotation insuring that a dozen or more of the lethal fighters were circling the bridgehead during all the hours of daylight. With the assistance of a few other jet Gruppen located near the front, as well as the constant presence of several hundred Me-109s and Fw-190s, the Luftwaffe ensured that Allied air interference with Rommel's advance was minimized.

Naturally, a few of the hated Jabos made it through the fighter screen to make bomb runs, but the constant harassment had thus far prevented a hit that closed even one of the two bridges. The Allies had allocated most of their air power to this point, and for the three days since the weather cleared, a series of epic battles had torn through the skies over the city on the Meuse. Krueger himself added ten Allied planes, including seven fighters, to his list of kills, and though he lost a number of men from his Geschwader he was satisfied with the way the battle had developed.

Now he squinted through the cockpit glass, nearly blinded by the reflection of sunlight off the fields of snow. The ribbon of river, unfrozen and now an iridescent azure in the sparkling daylight, marked the line of advance. The gray sprawl of Dinant jutted in irregular chaos from the near shoreline. High upon its limestone cliff, the gray mass of the citadel dominated the Belgian city and surrounding countryside. The spire from the Church of Notre Dame had somehow resisted the best efforts of ground and air forces and remained as a lofty observation point high above the southernmost of the two bridges.

Krueger's eyes quickly rose to scan the clear sky, and he didn't have to wait long to see his targets: a squadron of American Thunderbolts angling down for a dive-bombing attack. A hundred Mustangs swarmed overhead, but for now the German ace ignored the fighters. His two wingmen remained tight to either side as the sleek jets screamed through the air, blasting past the P-51s as they rocketed toward the ground support aircraft.

The fat Thunderbolts—"Jugs," as they were called by pilots of both sides—maintained their bomb runs. Krueger allowed his sights to fasten on the first enemy plane and fired a burst of cannon shells into the engine compartment. Black smoke belched, and the P-47 banked away. The second tactical aircraft flinched as the lethal projectiles shattered the bubble canopy, and the kommodore was vaguely aware of his wingmen's tracers raking the rest of the formation.

In the next seconds the jets were past and Krueger pulled up, leading the flight into the heavens with a speed that the pursuing Mustangs couldn't hope to match. He cast a look behind, saw the dark waters of the Meuse rocked by surging explosions. He was far above by the time the spray and smoke had settled, but even from here he could see that the two bridges remained intact.

With a quick glance at his fuel gauge, he saw that the dial had dropped to the halfway point. He couldn't see any more bombers for the time being, but below and behind him were plenty of Mustangs growling for a fight. With a push on the stick he brought the Stormbird over, knowing he had time for one more pass before he had to head back to base and refuel.

It wasn't until the flight back to Bitburg that he noticed his temperature gauge. The starboard engine was beginning to run a little hot, but still within the tolerance range. He shrugged it off. There were certainly more Allied aircraft to come, and he had important work to do.

578 Squadron Base, Wendling, Norfolk, England

Staff Sgt. Frank "Digger" O'Dell
Wendling, Norfolk, England
December 25, 1944

Mrs. Lucy O'Dell
Roxboro, North Carolina

Dear Mama,

Merry Christmas! I am out of the hospital and feeling fine right now.
The weather has been very bad, so there haven't been any missions, but it
looks like that's going to change.

We've got some new crewmen, but I haven't really gotten to know them
yet. The new battle orders have been posted and they call for "maximum effort." We've been working on repairs, and the old bird's in pretty good shape
now, I think. So it's time to put another mission on her so we can run her up
to a hundred missions and come home on that War Bond tour, if the war
lasts that long.

We're heading for a place called Dinant, in Belgium. You've probably
heard that the Germans have tried to break through the line where we've
pushed them back almost to the Rhine. Word is that the top brass aren't too
worried; they think it's just a counterthrust to take some of the pressure off,
but they're also taking it real cautiously. Rommel and the Germans are
across the Meuse, which could actually be some trouble, but we've blown
most of the bridges except for this one town called Dinant, where there isn't
anything much except some bridges. Well, if we can tear up those bridges,
then the German tanks will be trapped on our side of the river, and then it's
just mopping them up. I don't mean to make light of that; it is still a lot of
work to mop them up and some good boys will get killed, but it's not like it
would make us lose or anything like that.

We would have already done this mission, except the weather has been
too bad for flying, which has been an advantage for the Germans, but our
weathermen tell us that the skies are starting to clear up and when they do,
then we will fly. Actually, we've already started flying, but not the heavy
bombers. There are some small fighter-bombers—the P-47 Thunderbolts,
which everybody calls "Jugs" because that's what they look like, and while
you wouldn't want to fly them all the way on a deep penetration raid, they're
good for things like damaging bridges and low-altitude work. If the Jugs take
out the bridges, it'll all be over, but if they can't, then we'll go to work and
take them out once and for all.

Of course, we're all just a little bit nervous about the Nazi jet fighters, but Dinant is close enough to England that we'll be able to put up just about every fighter escort we've got. Their jets might be better than our fighters, but we've got a lot more fighters, so the odds are going to be on our side. One way or another, those bridges are going to go down.

I wish I could be there for Christmas, but I will be home by next Christmas, either because the war will be over or because we will be flying back on our War Bond Victory Tour. So I will see you very soon.

Love,

Digger

South of Dinant, East Bank of the Meuse River, Belgium, 25 December 1944, 1140 hours GMT

The column of Shermans was rumbling along at more than twenty miles per hour. They were still in friendly territory, but Pulaski knew they had crossed the border from France into Belgium a few miles back. At any minute they might encounter the initial screen guarding Rommel's southern flank, the lethal crack of a hidden gun that would signal the opening round of battle. His recon spearhead under the apparently teenage Captain Holland were racing ahead. Those brave men sped along in Greyhounds and jeeps, but the rest of the combat command was close behind.

This was no time for caution. For two days the division had raced across country. It was Christmas Day, now, and the holiday had brought a wonderful present: The skies were clear, and the cold temperatures were actually a benefit to the movement of tanks and trucks. Roads that had been quagmires a few weeks before were now frozen hard, and once the unit had formed up—and Pulaski had located a priest to say a very quick mass—CCA had been off and running. Captain Zimmerman and his first platoon of tank destroyers were rolling right behind, with Task Force Ballard. White and Miller's men, each with its own platoon of TDs—tank destroyers—came along directly behind.

The improved traveling weather was a fine development, especially because the main highway ran on the far side of the river. Since CCA of the Nineteenth Armored had rumbled through the border town of Givet, the American tanks had been making their way along a succession of country roads and winding lanes. A series of deep gorges plunged like defensive trenchworks perpendicular to the convoluted bank of the winding river, and these made for slow, even painstaking progress. But Pulaski was reluctant to take his men too far to the east. Their objective, after all, spanned that very flowage. Still, as the rumbling tanks, half-tracks, and trucks worked their way on a narrow road through the woods of another stone-cored ridge, he began to wonder if they weren't wasting time in this rough terrain.

His musings were interrupted as the column ground to a halt. In his command half-track ten tanks behind the leader, Pulaski rose to stand in the turret and realized that the first Sherman must have reached the horizon of this next ridge. In another moment he saw Frank Ballard making his way stiffly down the steep trail, a route that was barely wide enough to let the tank commander squeeze between his hulking charges and the enclosing trees.

"There's a Kraut A/T gun, an eighty-eight, with a look over the road," Frank reported from the front of Pulaski's half-track. "They let the recon boys slip past, hoping for big game. Lieutenant Pinnow caught a look at it and signaled back. It's a good spot for an ambush, Ski—I'm thinking we should send some infantry across the valley to take it out."

"How long to get 'em over there?"

"An hour at least, maybe longer. It's more than a mile away, steep terrain."

James Pulaski jumped down from his vehicle. "I'd hate to lose the time," he said, following Ballard back up the trail. "Let me get a look at the lay of the land."

A minute later, binoculars pressed to his eyes, he lay beside the lieutenant colonel in the brush next to the road. The dirt track, frozen hard as steel and dusted lightly with snow, crested through a narrow pass and then twisted down the far side of the ridge. A pasture ensured that no trees obscured the view of the road from the opposite elevation. Though both men scoured the far rise, Pulaski knew that an antitank gun would be well camouflaged, all but invisible to observers until it began to fire.

"Pinnow put it there, near the crest, below that stone outcrop."

Pulaski stared, but the emplacement was very effectively camouflaged and remained invisible to his eyes.

"They've got a good, clean shot for the first hundred yards," Ballard pointed out.

"But afterward we'll be into the woods down there, pretty safe from shelling," Pulaski countered.

"True, if there's just the one. If they have a battery of guns, it won't make any difference. We'll never cross that first gap."

Pulaski looked through the powerful lenses again, ignoring the eyestrain that started to give him a headache. How many guns could there be? Certainly not many; this rugged ground was not an obvious route for a counterattack against Dinant. He made his decision.

"We don't have time for a dismounted attack. Bring a tank destroyer up here, park it in these trees next to the road. Then have your lead boys make a break for it, guns tracked on the far bluff." That last suggestion was merely for psychological effect. A moving Sherman stood little chance of scoring a hit with its main gun. "We'll have the M10 keep an eye out, ready for counter-battery fire."

Ballard hesitated only a moment before nodding. "I'm going in the lead tank," he informed Pulaski, his jaw set.

The colonel was on the point of denying permission, but he understood what Ballard was doing, and he couldn't argue with it. So he nodded, and a minute later the M10 tank destroyer was rumbling into position, flattening several saplings in order to clear a shot at the opposite ridge. The lumbering vehicle looked very much like a Sherman tank, except for the fact that the turret was open to the sky. This exposed the crew to considerable danger but allowed the vehicle to accommodate a much larger gun than even the 76-mm Sherman's armament. In this case, the M10 had a three-inch gun that, while it would have difficulty with the armor of a Panther or Tiger tank, would be lethal against lesser panzers or any antitank gun emplacement.

"Good luck, Frank," Pulaski said.

"Thanks, Jimmy." With that, Ballard climbed back into the turret of the first Sherman in line. Expanding on one of the lessons of Abbeville, Frank had taken his upgunned M4s and formed them into a single company, and he determined that his own vehicle would ride at the lead of this potent formation. Buttoning down the hatch, he vanished into the armored monster as it immediately snorted into life.

Pulaski stayed at the ridge crest as the column started forward. His binoculars dangled on his chest as he squinted at the far side, trying to will any Germans hidden there to reveal themselves. White patches of snow marked many meadows in his field of view, but the landscape was broken by countless patches of gray-and-brown rock, small houses, many stone fences, and lots of wooded groves. There were a thousand hiding places, any one of which could conceal another lethal gun position.

With a lurching jolt, the M4 rumbled over the crest, quickly skidding through a turn to race down the narrow, exposed road. Abruptly the tank accelerated, taking off like a sprinter as it rumbled toward the shelter of the trees. The next tanks rolled forward, all the tankers sensing the menace in this speedy deployment.

The colonel saw the muzzle flash of the eighty-eight and felt the impact of the shell through the soles of his feet before he heard the sound of the gun. It was right there draped in white camouflage in the shade below the cluster of rock. How could he have missed it? A violent explosion jolted the air, sending dirt cascading. Pulaski cried out in relief as he saw that the shell had missed the racing Shermans. By then Ballard was halfway down the slope. The other M4s were racing behind without slowing down.

And then the tank destroyer spoke, roaring out a response with a flash of flame and smoke. The crew was good. Their shot smashed into the German gun emplacement in a violent eruption of flame and debris. Pulaski got a glimpse of a barrel pointing skyward and then swept his eyes across the rest of the ridge, looking for another gun.

But there was no other resistance. By the time Ballard's tank had vanished into the woods at the base of the slope, the whole column was rolling forward. Pulaski swung onto the door of his half-track as it crawled by.

"Only one gun," Sergeant Dawson observed laconically. "They must be thin down here."

Pulaski mumbled an agreement, relieved that their first encounter hadn't been bloody—at least, not for the men of CCA.

At the same time, his mind once again rekindled the smell of burning tanks and the wreckage-strewn fields of Abbeville. Just when he thought the memories were gone they seemed to surge back, as strong and oppressive as ever.

Temporary Supply Depot, Dinant, Belgium, 1211 hours GMT

"Baron von Esebeck? You took the photograph of that tank, right?" said Chuck Porter, offering his hand.

"Yes, I did," von Esebeck smiled.

"Good work. After this is over, drop me a line. AP is always in the market for good stringers."

Esebeck laughed. "The German News Agency will be able to use American stringers as well, if you'd like to do some stories for us."

"Maybe we can talk about some contracts later on," Porter said. "When this current story is over."

His newsman's itch was going full blast, especially after seven days as a prisoner of war. There were a bunch of stories here, and he was ready to interview everybody in sight. He didn't know how or when he'd be able to file the stories, but he was imagining the byline: "Somewhere Behind Enemy Lines, by Chuck Porter." This was a Pulitzer-making situation; somehow he'd get the most out of the opportunity.

Dinant was a good-size burg in Belgium, as nearly as he could make out, and to hear the Germans talk, it was now German property.

Colonel von Reinhardt had introduced him to the baron, a real nobleman! Porter was impressed, though also disappointed the man didn't wear a monocle; he looked just like a normal person. Esebeck was more of a military man than Porter, but Porter had managed to gather that the Germans were across the Meuse River in force, with two bridges nearby so that more tanks as well as convoys of fuel could continuously reinforce the advance. Apparently, American resistance had, so far, kept them from bridging the river in more places.

"The key, you see—as I suspect your generals have by now figured out themselves—is here, in Antwerp."

"Antwerp? I don't get it," said Porter.

Esebeck smiled a superior smile. "What do tanks run on?"

"Gasoline, I guess. Maybe diesel fuel."

"And can they just pull up at a station and yell, as you Americans say, 'Fill 'er up and check the oil!'?"

"Guess not," Porter said. He was starting to figure it out, but it never hurt for the interviewee to underestimate your intelligence.

"And therefore, this fuel has to be brought in, then taken on trucks to the tanks."

"Makes sense."

"And would you care to guess where most of the fuel for your army arrives?"

Porter looked up at the baron. "I guess that would be Antwerp."

"That's right. And when Antwerp falls, shortly thereafter, all your tanks will become fixed-gun emplacements."

"Shit," Porter said. That would shut down the war in Europe completely. The best the Allies could hope for would be stalemate.

"I would say that's the appropriate American response," Esebeck said.

"And what stands between you and Antwerp?" Porter asked.

"The bridges of Dinant," Esebeck replied.

Waterloo, Belgium, 1621 hours GMT

Field Marshal Bernard Montgomery, beret tilted rakishly, strode back and forth in the small temporary headquarters of the British Twenty-First Army Group. "It's up to us to pull the Americans' fat out of the fire once again," he said with a shake of his head. Artillery fire thundered, the sound booming from the distant south.

"Excuse me, sir?" said a staff general hesitantly. "But is it wise to have yourself, the entire headquarters, here, so far ahead of our main body?"

"We must see the ground in order to make a plan," replied the field marshal. "For it is here, tomorrow or the next day, that the issue will be decided." He frowned, looked at a large map on what had once been a dining room table. "We've held at Namur, all the way to Liege. And still that crafty Desert Fox gets across the river, in the Yank's sector of course."

"Yes sir," agreed an aide, opening a folder and laying out a series of aerial reconnaissance photos.

"Are these the most recent pictures?" Monty clucked in displeasure. "They were taken yesterday noon!"

"I'm afraid the blasted rocket-planes have cleared our fellows out of the sky, at least for the time being," reported the RAF liaison officer. "We hope to get something fresh later today."

The field marshal studied the pictures. "These show better than three divisions already across the Meuse, and turning this way. We know that Rommel can move quickly. . . ." He stroked his chin pensively, toying with his thin mustache as he concentrated. "Yet there have been no reports from Charleroi. Can you ring them again?"

"The phone is still out," replied the aide. "We're working on restoring the line. Our radio calls have not been able to raise any reply."

"Surely they're not within twenty miles of here, not yet," suggested another staff officer, an older colonel.

"Surely." Montgomery nodded decisively. Taking a deep, invigorating breath he turned to the window. "What an auspicious omen!" he declared, sweeping his hand over the vista of gentle green hills and small orchards. "A British army to gather once again on the fields of Waterloo—my opportunity to defeat Rommel for good, this time as decisively as Wellington did Napoleon!"

He stroked his long, thin nose thoughtfully. He still smarted at the criticism of his defeat of the Desert Fox in the Battle of El Alamein in Egypt. Claims that his pursuit of a broken enemy had been too slow, that a preponderance of Allied equipment and air power had made his victory inevitable. Rubbish! He had won a great victory, blast it all! Well, this time there would be no doubt. No doubt at all who was the supreme military genius of the war.

"When is General Horrocks going to get here?" he asked, checking his watch.

"Advance elements of Thirty Corps are less than an hour away, Field Marshal," replied the aide. "And until then we have First Armored, now on the scene."

"Splendid." The field marshal nodded at the line of Sherman tanks rumbling through the valley road, a few hundred yards away. "I don't see how the Jerries can get here before that!"

The fresh crump of gunfire, surprisingly close, broke through his reverie. Explosions burst among the British tanks on the road, while other blasts ripped through a nearby orchard. "What the devil is that?" he demanded, staring to the south. "How did they get here so fast?"

Montgomery did not panic—it was not in his nature. Instead, he turned to give orders that would start to set things right, that would stop the enemy breakthrough in its tracks. He frowned, wishing he had a little more time. He saw racing vehicles coming over the horizon, British recon elements in a disorderly retreat from an enemy that must certainly be close behind.

He did not hear the whistling sound of the next artillery barrage, was not aware of the shell that tore through the roof of his headquarters. He would never know of the two panzer divisions that had raced north faster than any soldier had a right to expect, that even now commenced a surprise attack against a hastily raised British position.

And the explosion that tore through his body happened so quickly he never heard the sound.

Army Group B Field Headquarters, Dinant, Belgium, 26 December 1944, 0621 hours GMT

"Good news, Herr Feldmarschall." Reinhardt maintained his even tone, but his eyes sparked with the portent. "Both the Second and the Twelfth panzer divisions are into Brussels."

Müller added his own positive tidings. "The one hundred sixteenth is regrouping in the city. Unfortunately, we did not capture the fuel reserves there that we hoped to find. Still, we have that great depot in Stavelot as well as the reserves in Bastogne—so long as we hold the bridges here in Dinant, we have easily enough petrol to carry three divisions and more all the way to the coast."

"Splendid. It would seem that Montgomery is no Wellington, eh?"

The staff officers shared a hearty laugh. It was Speidel who raised his coffee cup in a toast. "Rather, perhaps, Napoleon could have learned a thing or two from our Desert Fox."

With a dry chuckle, Rommel turned his attention back to the map. He pictured the fields at Waterloo, now littered with the wrecked hulls of British armor. Like every European professional military man, he had visited them in his youth. Monty had tried to make his stand there, but the spearhead advancing from Dinant had made him too thoroughly outflanked. The lone British armored division on the scene had been overwhelmed at the crossroads north of La Belle Alliance, and the stone walls of Hougomont farm had given little pause to the guns of Rommel's Tigers. Reinforcements, American armor and British infantry, had arrived at the field too late, for by then the road to the Belgian capital was firmly in German hands.

And now that Brussels had been taken, there remained no real obstacles between the panzer spearheads and the great Allied supply center at Antwerp. Rommel began to believe, to really believe, that the attack would succeed.

"What is the word from the south?" he asked Bücher, who had just been in contact with Manteuffel.

"Patton is bogged down south of Bastogne," said the SS officer. "It does not look like he will get into the city, or even within artillery range of the key roads."

"Excellent." Rommel paused to reflect, still studying the map. "Any threats from farther to the west?"

"It seems the Americans are stretched very thin there," the SS officer continued. "We have several volksgrenadier divisions holding that front, and they report very little offensive pressure."

"And we have room to fall back there," the field marshal noted, thinking of the old men and youths making up the volksgrenadier, the "People's Soldiers" who had recently been recruited from the Third Reich's thin manpower reserves. Of course, many of these troops had fought for him at Normandy, and he knew they made staunch warriors—as, indeed, did all German men—but for now it would be enough for them to give ground slowly if pressed.

"Closer to home?" wondered Rommel, following the serpentine line of the Meuse south of Dinant. He stabbed at the city of Givet, just south of the place where the river flowed from France. "American armor was reported here, this morning . . . correct?"

"Yes, Herr Feldmarschall," Bücher noted. "But there is no good road on this side of the river. And if they try to come up on the west, Ninth SS Panzer Division is in position to block them."

"And of course the enemy would know that Ninth Panzer has been bombed for two days. So perhaps they'll try to come at us through the woods."

"Perhaps." Bücher nodded. "Though it's unlikely they could get here before tomorrow."

"Too close for comfort," Rommel said, shaking his head. Again he studied the map, looking at the road leading into Dinant from the southeast. "Panzer Lehr is in convoy here, scheduled to reach the bridges by this evening, correct?" Though he made the remark as a question, he took no notice of his staff officers nodding their heads; he already knew the answer.

"When they cross they will give you six panzer divisions west of the river," Speidel offered. "And we have captured fuel enough for all of them."

"I don't want them to cross," the Desert Fox stated. "We are vulnerable in only one place, along the river, and we know that enemy tanks might be moving in that direction. I want Panzer Lehr diverted off the highway. I need a screen of armor south of Dinant."

Bücher turned to the switchboard to get the new order on the way to Manteuffel when the field telephone jangled in the background. The lieutenant at the microphone listened for a moment and then turned to Rommel.

"Herr Feldmarschall, we have reports of an American armored attack approaching Dinant from the south. They are five kilometers out, coming through the woods along the river."

Southern Outskirts of Dinant, Belgium, 0642 hours GMT

Pulaski put his head down, clapped a hand over his helmet, and sprinted across the road toward the shelter of the low stone wall. He crawled and scraped across the hard-frozen ground with Sergeant Dawson right behind, and he felt his heart hammering as he leaned against the frost-limned rocks of the barrier. He noticed that he was in a cemetery, and hunched lower, using the granite bulk of an ornate cross for cover.

"No shooting that time," he remarked, trying to sound droll.

"Yes, sir," Dawson replied, checking over the radio. "But don't you think you should get back into the half-track?"

Pulaski chuckled wryly. "Sounds good to me, but not until I see what's holding Frank up."

Crawling like men who knew that a mistake could get them killed, the two Americans made their way out of the cemetery and around a battered tavern. Beyond, the country road straightened to become a city street, but there were no Sherman tanks rolling down that beckoning avenue. Four or five of the M4s, however, were wrecked and burning at the near end of the road.

He found the commander of Task Force Ballard huddled with some of his officers in the shattered shell of a mill. Captain Zimmerman of the tank destroyer company was there as well, in this field headquarters of pockmarked walls and blasted, gaping roof. The officers had been trying unsuccessfully to get through to the Air Forces liaison, to call in a tactical bomber strike against the crossroads directly ahead of them.

"What's the hold-up?" Pulaski asked.

"We count four Tigers, hull down, really well concealed on the far side of the street. Two have direct fire down the road, and one has a good enfilade from each side. They cooked off four Shermans inside of a minute," Ballard reported tersely.

"Shit!" Pulaski kicked a shard of rock out of his way. He turned to Dawson. "Sarge, see if you can get through on your set."

While the sergeant ran up his battery and tried the call, the colonel went to the front of the mill and, crouching, looked out the empty socket of the front door. Smoke from the burning Shermans wafted past, and, while he couldn't see the Tigers, he had a pretty good idea of where they must be hiding.

"What about flanking them?" he asked as Ballard joined him.

"They picked their place well. To our left there's a little ravine with a stream at the bottom, too deep for tanks. To the right there's a park, acres of open ground exposed to direct fire. The only way around is to back out of here and try to come into Dinant from a different road."

"We don't have time!" snapped the frustrated Pulaski, angry with himself. He turned to the sergeant, who was still repeating the call sign through the radio. "Any luck?" he asked unnecessarily.

Dawson only shook his head.

"I can hear the damn planes overhead. Why the hell can't we get in touch with them?" demanded the colonel, as the steady droning of engines rose to a high-pitched whine. In the near distance, bombs—lots of them—crumped into the ground, reverberating through the pavement with tremors that brought trickles of dust from the sagging ceiling timbers of the ancient mill. Perhaps the bridges that were his objective were getting pasted by the air forces, but he couldn't afford to take that chance. Combat Command A of the Nineteenth Armored had its own job to do.

Tensely he paced back to the door and looked down the street. Shifting his gaze, he could see the open field of parkland between the two shattered buildings across the way, then followed the view to the south where his men bunched in the fringe of rural woodlands.

"Can you get through to Bob Jackson?" he asked the sergeant.

Dawson nodded. A few moments later he had the commander of the Nineteenth Armored's Combat Command B on the radiophone.

"How far south of town are you?" Pulaski asked. "We're up against a nut here."

"Ten klicks . . . just passing the spot where you took out the first eighty-eight," Jackson replied. "Call it two hours at the most."

"Bring it on, then. I have a feeling we might be needing you," Pulaski said. He signed off, then looked at Frank Ballard. "We'll spread 'em out here, start a strong flank attack across the park, with the tank destroyers in support. A minute later we'll send a swarm of Shermans down the road, and take the damn Krauts out with sheer numbers."

The lieutenant colonel nodded. "I'd been thinking something like the same thing," he admitted. "It'll be tough at first, but it's our best chance."

"How many M4s with the 76-mm do you have?" Pulaski asked, again studying the cramped narrow, littered approach up the street.

"A good dozen," Ballard answered. "They're in the lead."

"They'll have to try for shots at the Tigers as they show," the colonel ordered.

"And in the park?"

"We'll put the rest of the armor there." Pulaski turned to Zimmerman. "You have a few of the M36 Tank Destroyers, don't you?"

"Three, still operational. Now that's a tank killer."

Pulaski nodded, even as he grimaced at the awareness that there were all too few of the lethal vehicles. The M36 carried a much more deadly weapon than the M10s that made up the majority of his tank division. It had a 90-mm gun, and it had proved to be the only American armored vehicle that could take out a Tiger with a single shot. Of course, they had the typical vulnerability of the tank destroyer: no roof on the turret. It would have been suicide to send the TDs between the wrecked buildings on the street, since German snipers could have picked off the gun crews with a few well-placed shots.

"Put them on the far right, screened by a few Shermans on the outside.

They might be able to get a shot at that dug-in Tiger." He left unspoken his second concern, that his own right flank was totally exposed as he made this rash attack. Once before Rommel had struck him in a vulnerable flank, breaking up an attack and shattering the combat command. The tank destroyers wouldn't protect them against a serious threat, but they might give pause to any panzers leading the enemy attack. "I want Task Force Miller to follow Frank's men up the street. Whitey, your boys will guard our right—but you'll need to reinforce our progress once we make our way into the city."

He would have liked to have a strong force to post here, to guard their line of communication and retreat. But the bridges were the main objective, and he was determined to reach that goal as soon as possible. Furthermore, he knew that Bob Jackson and CCB were not too many miles away. Pulaski could only hope that his men could hold out for that long.

Fortunately, a lane provided a route of dispersal inside the shelter of the woods, and it took only twenty minutes to deploy CCA for the attack. Infantry dismounted from trucks and half-tracks, ready to rush forward in the wake of the tanks. The eighteen guns of Diaz's artillery battalion were deployed a half mile back from the edge of the woods, and they took a few ranging shots along the buildings and ruins where the Tigers were hull down.

"When I give the word, I want smoke—as much as you can deliver," the colonel ordered. Lieutenant Colonel Diaz nodded enthusiastically, and Pulaski once more remembered Lorimar at Abbeville, and his cheerful wave before the predecessors of these guns had been overwhelmed by attacking panzers. But he couldn't waste any more time with this kind of worry.

"You take the left, the street attack," Pulaski told Ballard. "I'll come across the field with the right flank. Remember, give us a minute or two before you move out."

The lieutenant colonel agreed and took his position in the lead Sherman, rightly observing that his gunner had proved to be as steady and accurate as any tanker in the division. "Make that first shot count," was the only suggestion Pulaski could offer.

He and Dawson, in the half-track, would follow in the second wave across the field. He didn't take time to pep talk his men. They knew the stakes as well as he, and all recognized the desperation that had driven them to such a risky onslaught.

Finally the tanks had rolled into position, taking advantage of the last screen of saplings before they rumbled into the open. Dawson, who had been keeping the radio channel open, passed the instrument to the colonel who used the daily code to issue orders to his artillery.

"Ducky Six—this is Popcorn Ten. Give me everything you've got, established coordinates," he ordered.

The crack of the guns thudded through the woods, and moments later shells whistled overhead to explode in the clearing and among the wrecked structures of Dinant. After the blasts, white smoke billowed through the air, and seconds later the next volley of projectiles rocketed past, and then the next, and still another.

In a few minutes the fringe of the city was obscured by a thick cloud of pale, foggy smoke, and Pulaski knew the opportunity had come. With the radio open to all commanders he barked the "Go!" order.

Immediately the tanks rolled. Small trees bent and snapped as forty Shermans and eighteen tank destroyers rolled from the woods and trundled onto the vast park. Pulaski saw a few cagelike soccer goals, realizing with an odd sense of incongruity that they were charging across a series of playing fields. More smoke shells crashed into the German position, and now the leading elements of the attack wave were half-obscured by smoke, ghostly shapes that rumbled and clanked and roaring with monstrous presence.

A shell from an eighty-eight screamed out of the cloud, torching an M4 in the front rank. There was no way to tell if the shot had come from a Tiger or an emplaced AT gun. The tank gunners didn't wait to find out: dozens of Shermans spat high explosive shells into the murk, a barrage that flashed and smoldered, discoloring the smoke cloud with alternating swaths of fire and darkness.

To his left Pulaski could see Ballard's upgunned Shermans waiting in line. Abruptly those tanks, too, rolled forward, driving steadily into the smoke that drifted through the street. Another M4 went up in flames, but now the leading tanks were rumbling between buildings, cannon and machine guns raking the stunned Germans in their foxholes and strongpoints.

A half-dozen Shermans came upon the hidden Tiger, and at the cost of two of their own they plastered it with enough fire to disable the turret and blast both tracks off. Sappers rushed forward with satchel charges while the surviving armor rumbled on, spreading out through the streets of the medieval city. Seeing their fate, the German tankers popped through the hatches to make a run for it. Bullets cut them down before the last of them had taken two steps from the wrecked Tiger.

Flames seared the street before him and another Tiger went up. And then Ballard's column rolled into sight. The lead tank halted so that the gunner could draw a bead, and the 76-mm gun drilled an armor-piercing shell into the side armor of yet one more of the Nazi behemoths. That panzer crackled into blistering flames, and none of the crew appeared.

Ballard popped open his hatch as the half-track rolled into the town. Fierce gunfire marked infantry battles in the nearby buildings, but the noise was moving away as CCA infantry knocked the Germans out of one building after another. The lieutenant colonel raised his thumb in a salute.

"We're in!" shouted Pulaski, feeling the emotion himself. "Now let's get to those damn bridges!"

Aboard B-24 "Darling Debbie," Nearing the Meuse, Belgium, 0935 hours GMT

"Fighters! Fighters!" Lieutenant Lester "Sky" King heard the intercom call from his nose turret gunner just about the time he noticed a series of small white puffs ahead of the lumbering B-24. At first he'd thought it was strange-looking flak, then he realized that he was seeing exploding 20-mm shells. The heavy Liberator shook from end to end as the gunners began firing 50-caliber machine guns at the shrieking Me-262s swooping out of the gray winter sky.

From the flight deck, the aircraft commander could only see ahead and slightly to each side as he concentrated on staying in formation, moving toward the bridges of Dinant, the target. Soon it would be up to the bombardier to fly the plane through its bombing run, then it would be time to get the hell out of there—if it wasn't already. Radio chatter among the gunners as they traded information about the positions of attacking fighters kept him up-to-date on the engagement. "On your six! Coming in fast! Charlie, look out—he's underneath you!"

The plane lurched as flak exploded. He noticed an Me-262 pull up under his left wing, as if he was joining the formation, and begin pouring 20-mm shells into the B-24 ahead of him in the formation—it was *Ford's Folly*. "Jesus," he said to his copilot. "That's Russ's plane." The pilot was a good friend.

Suddenly, the number-three engine burst into flame. "Abort, goddamn it—abort!" he yelled, as if Russ could hear him. "Get the hell out of there!" But he could see the bomb bay grinding slowly open, preparing to drop its load, possibly short of the destination, but at least somewhere they might kill some Krauts.

Now number four was on fire, and the plane looked like a flying blowtorch. The bombs were dropping. "Bail out, Russ," he shouted helplessly. He looked over at the attacking Me-262, an aircraft distinguished by bright flames painted on the nose. It was so close he could see the pilot grinning at him. He wished he had a gun of his own so he could wipe the goddamn smile off the bastard's face, but all he could do was keep his aircraft steady.

Skies Over the Meuse, Belgium, 0941 hours GMT

Krueger tightened his finger on the trigger, directing a stream of cannon shells into the swollen belly of the lumbering Liberator.

"Burn, you bastard! Go down!" he hissed through his clenched teeth.

Despite the flaming engines, the stubborn bomber refused to go down. The Me-262 roared past, close enough for the pilot to read the vulgar Americanism *Ford's Folly* scribed onto the huge aircraft's bulbous nose.

The black blossoms of antiaircraft fire shivered in the air, and rattles of shrapnel tickled the skin of the jet fighter. The German ace ignored the distraction, picking another target from the sea of heavy bombers.

The Stormbird's gun ripped into this new target with shocking effect as the bomber exploded in a blinding flash of light. *That's one who won't be dropping his bombs,* Krueger thought with a warm flash of satisfaction.

Then he was through the formation, and though his starboard engine was again running a little hot, he raced back around, determined to find the plane he had first targeted.

There it was, at the front of the squadron, smoke pouring from number-three engine, but still flying. It was a doomed plane, but the bomb bay doors remained open as Krueger swept closer. He wanted to prevent the bomber from dropping its load.

But before he could press the finger, his jet lurched hard, shearing to starboard. With shock he saw flames pouring from the housing of his engine, a white-hot fire that was melting away his precious jet before his eyes. He would never learn of the small rag inside, a memento of his long-ago visit to the Jumo factory in Dessau.

Krueger shrieked as flames surged upward from the deck, licking the inside of his thighs, teasing his groin. The Stormbird lurched and skidded through the sky, utterly lacking the nearly angelic grace and speed of its true flight. The right engine still burned, melting away before his horrified eyes. He sensed the hunger of the flames, and again he screamed.

The blaze had started within the turbine, an incendiary cancer devouring metal and air. From there, flames had sucked through the fuel lines, engulfing the fuselage in a hellish grip. Hydraulic lines had melted away, and the aluminum skin of the aircraft flaked into vapor.

The pilot's world spun in disequilibrium. The Liberator, *Ford's Folly,* was upside down . . . no, it was he himself who was inverted. The fighter tumbled closer, but Krueger's guns were forgotten as he wrestled with the stick, fought for some semblance of control over the dying aircraft. Pieces of his beautiful plane broke away, and the controls flopped loosely in his clutching hands.

Pain seared his skin, cruelly melting his flight suit, consuming his flesh. Heat and agony and stinking fumes threatened to overwhelm him. Struggling for mastery of his senses, of his tortured body, Krueger kicked at the floorboards, pushed at the unyielding glass of his canopy, and screamed.

Now the massive American plane was huge before him, and he saw the bombs tumbling from the swollen belly. A great sheet of metal stretched before him like a wall, rising beyond the fires that framed his field of view.

Fully out of control, the dying Me-262 tore through the twin rudders of the Liberator, but now Krueger was only aware that tongues of fire were groping for his face. He kicked his legs, but those limbs were charred into blackened coal, and it seemed as though his life had dissolved into sound, shrieks of unspeakable pain.

And then the fire reached his eyes, and glowed there for a long, satisfied moment.

From Mission Narratives, 392nd Bomb Group, December 26, 1944 (Dinant Raid)

Mission Narrative Summary

On the morning of 26 December 1944, we were alerted for an attack on the bridges of Dinant, Belgium. Twenty-four squadron aircraft took off. Nearing the Meuse River, the formation was attacked by twenty or more Me-262 jet fighters for about five minutes. Several of the enemy aircraft were camouflaged with white stripes to simulate P-51s. One aircraft had a flame pattern painted on its nose. The enemy aircraft attack was pressed home vigorously, coming in singly . . . most of the attacking planes were firing 20-mm time-fused shells, some of which were noticed to explode before hitting our planes. . . . The enemy fighters were themselves heavily engaged by many P-51s, and after several minutes the German aircraft were destroyed or driven off, but not before they inflicted damage on the bomber group. As a result of this attack, four of our ships are missing, including Aircraft 466 (*Ford's Folly*), which was last seen at 11:58 A.M. near Dinant when hit by enemy aircraft. Fire broke out in nos. three and four engines, and one of the Me-262 crashed into the tail structure; both airplanes burst into flames, peeled over, spun in, and crashed. No chutes were seen.

Additional Narrative Report

Takeoffs began at 0730 hours and were accomplished without incident. We went through the usual assembly and headed toward the target. Just as we neared the Meuse River, a flak barrage began to come up from the town below. We were caught by surprise, and the gunners immediately began shoving chaff out the chutes. It was nearly noon.

I was concentrating on keeping my element in position when my copilot said, "Look at the funny-looking flak." I glanced out and saw numerous small white explosions just below us. I saw *Ford's Folly* (Aircraft 466) in tight formation and all engines running, blazing fiercely from the top of the wing in the number three and number four engine area. The flames were so intense that they were trailing far behind the tail assembly. I realized then that the "funny flak" was exploding 20-mm cannon shells, being fired by an Me-262 with flames painted on the cowling. I turned my attention to pulling up closer to the lead box. When I looked again, *Ford's Folly* was gone.

Army Group B Field Headquarters, Dinant, Belgium, 1020 hours GMT

For long minutes the violent onslaught of bombs rocked Dinant, crushing buildings, shaking the ground, churning the river water into mud and terrifying the German soldiers and Belgian civilians who sought shelter wherever it could be found.

The thunderous bomber assault had driven the headquarters staff into the château's wine cellar. Though several of the German officers undoubtedly would have soothed their fears with one of the many vintages lining the walls of the chamber, the presence of their stern field marshal made teetotalers out of them all. The noise overwhelmed any attempts at conversation, so the men sat in stoic silence. Rommel watched them exchange sidelong glances, eyeing each other for some outward sign of fear.

Waves of explosions rocked the city, and though all of these men had experienced Allied bombardment, the field marshal suspected that for most it was the severest pounding of their lives. Certainly he had never felt such a massive, crushing blanket of explosions. Rommel took care to keep his expression aloof, though he flinched and then chuckled when a near strike brought several bottles crashing down from their racks. Dust trickled down from the rafters, so that by the time the violence began to fade every officer was coated in a fine layer of grime.

"It seems to be ending," Rommel declared finally, as the explosions thudded into the distance. He looked at his pocket watch. "About thirty-seven minutes' worth. Quite a few bombs in one little place. Well, it's time for us to get back to work and to see how much damage our enemies have inflicted."

They climbed the rickety stairs toward the kitchen, Carl-Heinz insisting on going first, checking beyond the door for danger. "It's safe," he reported after a moment, and the rest of the officers followed Rommel back into the realm of daylight.

The droning of aircraft engines was still thunderous, albeit fading, as the field marshal led his staff through the inn to the balcony overlooking the river valley. He saw immediately that one wing of the château had suffered some serious damage, and the gate house had been smashed to pieces, but the bulk of the building was intact, including this broad vantage that gave them a clear view to the west and south. At the same time, he recognized that Allied fighters and dive bombers were swooping, unimpeded by the Luftwaffe, over the entire area—apparently the enemy had regained control of the skies.

Smoke billowed throughout the city, concealing the bridges and much of the near bank. The steeple of the Church of Notre Dame still jutted from the murk, while overhead the citadel was a scene of ruin and rubble. Even so, many AA guns still barked from the edifice, hurling their shells after the departing stream of bombers.

Again Rommel looked below, but thick smoke seethed everywhere. Here and there a black oily plume arose, marking the place where an aircraft had gone down. The murk was complete, masking the entire course of the river.

The whine of a motorcycle engine rose above the fading aircraft noise, and a courier emerged into view, climbing the hill from the waterfront, racing his two-wheeled machine toward the château. Rommel, barely limping, hurried across the courtyard to meet the rider at the gate.

"How are the bridges?"

"One of them is ruptured, Herr Feldmarschall. I was told that it will require at least a day for repairs."

"And the other?"

"The engineers are completing their inspection. It still spans the river . . . it was wrenched around a bit but took no direct hits. They said to report that it should be ready for transport in less than an hour."

Nodding his thanks, Rommel returned with his staff to the map tables in the conference room. "Are the telephones working?" he called to his operator.

"The lines to the bridges are out, Herr Feldmarschall. However, I have a wire to the citadel, and to our emplacement on the roads leading into the city."

"What word from the Americans to our south? And from Panzer Lehr?" The Desert Fox impatiently studied the map while the man relayed the questions. He could sense the cusp of battle. They were so close to victory, to a victory that would far outshadow anything he had done in Africa or Normandy, a triumph that would outshine even the great Blitzkrieg of 1940. With one bridge, the supplies to the leading elements of his army would be restricted, but he knew they could still advance. Antwerp—and with it the Allied army in Europe— was still vulnerable.

As long as they held Dinant.

"The Panzer Lehr division is three kilometers from the city, field marshal," reported the lieutenant at the switchboard. "As to the Americans, we lost contact with them after they moved through the initial defensive outposts south of the city. I am trying to contact our forward positions now."

"I want the Ninth SS Panzer Division to send a Kampfgruppe back to this side of the river." Rommel gave the order with confident certainty. "They should have full priority as soon as the bridge is cleared for traffic."

"Bring them back?" Speidel asked.

"Yes . . . I think we might need them in the city. This is where the battle will be won or lost."

Rommel acutely felt the vulnerability of his bridge, and he wanted more tanks in place to protect it. Panzer Lehr would be here soon, but they were coming from the east. The Ninth SS Panzer had crossed the river yesterday but was still near, just on the other bank as a matter of fact. He could bring them back, and with Panzer Lehr coming out of the Ardennes the Americans could be caught in a deadly vise.

The next words from the switchboard confirmed his fears, even as they warned him that he might be too late.

"Herr Feldmarschall!" The radio operator blurted out the interruption. "The Americans are in the city attacking from the south! And they are advancing toward the bridge!"

Dinant, Belgium, 1045 hours GMT

The men of CCA of the Nineteenth Armored found shelter in their tanks and in the cellars and basements of Dinant as hundreds of heavy aircraft rumbled overhead, pounding the city with a lethal bombardment. It turned out to be fortunate that Pulaski's attack had been held up at the southern fringe of the place, for most of the bombs fell to the north and west. Obviously the Air Forces were targeting the bridges across the Meuse, though there was no way for Pulaski or his men to judge the success or failure of the mission.

From the narrow mouth of a cellar door the colonel did see the barrage of antiaircraft raised by guns arrayed around the lofty citadel that was the city's dominant feature. Conversely, that castle received a great deal of the bombers' attention, until the fortress and its surrounding knoll were completely masked by the smoke and dust raised by countless explosions.

The cessation of the bombing was sudden, a brief dwindling of noise and then only the sounds of droning engines as the stream of aircraft turned back toward England. That sound was still a resonant thunder as the tanks and infantry of Combat Command A rolled forward. The men of the Nineteenth quickly found that the upper city had not been too badly shattered by the aerial onslaught. At least the major streets were more or less open, passable to tanks, half-tracks, and jeeps.

Pulaski gathered with Ballard, Diaz, Miller, and White, and Captains Zimmerman of the tank destroyer company and Holland of the recon unit, in a square overlooking the river valley. There he spread out a map of the city on the hood of a jeep. The stuttering chatter of small arms fire echoed from nearby streets, occasionally punctuated by the blast of a tank gun or grenade.

He pointed to a tall steeple rising from the rubble of the riverfront. "The bridges are down there, past the church. Whitey, Miller, take everything you can get—bring the bridges under direct fire, and then get some men down there with demolitions."

Dennis White nodded. "How many of the tanks do I get?"

"Most of our Shermans." Pulaski turned to Ballard. "Frank, you've still got a company of seventy-sixes, right?"

The armored commander nodded, and the colonel pointed along the street leading into the square from the east. "That's the road to Bastogne . . . Kraut reinforcements might be coming that way. I want your company in position to enfilade any move along that route. Diaz, get the range, and be ready to give him supporting fire. Until then, put some fire onto the bridges and the riverfront—but be listening for Frank's word."

The lieutenant colonel of artillery nodded, and Pulaski took another moment to stare at the map.

"Holland, get some outposts along that road, ready to give us advance word of any threat. You can move out now."

In moments the Greyhounds and jeeps of the recon company were roaring out of town, while Pulaski tried to think, to plan. His mind flashed with the vivid memory of Rommel's tanks hitting CCA in the flank at Abbeville, breaking up the combat command just when victory seemed within reach. He remembered Lorimar and Jack King, Frank Ballard shot to hell in his tank. He vowed to himself that he wouldn't let that happen again, and then he looked at Zimmerman.

"Captain—you'll be our reserve. Park your tank destroyers around this square, and be ready to move where we need you."

"Yessir, Colonel!" Zimmerman's dark eyes blazed with determination. Pulaski almost felt sorry for any hapless Germans that came under the guns of the M10s and M36s.

"All right, men—our objective is right there, less than a mile away. We all know how important this is, so I'm not going to explain it to you. But I know you'll do your jobs." He pointed overhead, to a turreted attic that rose high above the square, with windows opening onto three directions. "That'll be my CP . . . Frank, I want to string a wire to your tanks, and Diaz too, so we've got secure communications. I'll talk to you as soon as you're in place. Now, move out!"

More engines roared into life as the colonel, accompanied by Sergeant Dawson, entered the nearby house and quickly found the stairs leading up. The colonel and the sergeant—with the NCO carrying the radio as always—found a good vantage in the turreted attic to establish his command post. He looked out the window across the city and tried to make sure he was doing the right thing.

The combat command was spread out below, advancing through the wartorn city. Pulaski took a look at the citadel, saw that it was now under attack by tactical aircraft. Colonel Diaz and the self-propelled guns of his artillery battery took up position in the park on the south side of the city, the 105s in easy support range of the entire combat command. The rest of Combat Command A, the tanks and supporting infantry, moved against moderate resistance. Only Zimmerman's tank destroyers remained undeployed—this small company was now parked in the plaza just below the colonel's vantage.

From here Pulaski could see the street leading east, including the tall trees and square houses, most of them gaunt and battle scarred, on the hillside beyond. Ballard's tanks, concealed by low walls, rubble, and buildings, were invisible even from this lofty attic. Through the lingering dust of the bombing, however, the colonel could see just far enough to make out the road to the Ardennes and Bastogne. Sooner or later Germans would be coming from that direction.

As if in response to his observation, the phone buzzed.

"German armor—Tigers in the lead!—coming into the city on the highway. Moving fast, considerable numbers. More than I can count right now."

Frank Ballard's voice on the field telephone betrayed his tension in his clipped, sharp enunciation. Still he was precise and careful, and if he sounded excited he avoided any suggestion of fear.

Pulaski clutched the receiver to his ear, trying to mask the trembling that wanted to jar his hands. It was happening again . . . panzers coming out of the murk of battle, eager to smash his combat command. He drew a deep breath and turned away from Sergeant Dawson, hoping that his apprehension hadn't shown on his face. After all, he had expected this attack, had planned for it. He was as ready as he could possibly be.

Binoculars to his eyes, he studied the road. Massive Tigers, clearly identifiable even from three kilometers away, led the procession, and he could see that in a few minutes they would come under the guns of Ballard's Shermans.

Pulaski took up the phone again. "What's your position?" he asked Frank, managing to keep his voice steady.

"We're hull down, on some high ground south of the street. Holding my fire now . . . I gotta tell you, Ski—this looks like it could be a whole division."

"You have contact with Diaz, right?"

"Yes—he was getting his coordinates squared away a few minutes ago."

Pulaski tried to keep the tension out of his voice when he answered. "He has the range on the road, but he'll wait for your signal to open fire. Make your move when the time seems right. Don't forget you can fall back to the south—even if the Krauts pursue, Jackson and CCB are coming up fast in support. And Diaz is back there to give you direct fire support."

Pulaski and Ballard had already discussed an added benefit of a southerly withdrawal: if the Germans took the bait, a pursuit would pull them away from CCA's advance to the bridge.

Closer to home, Pulaski had a clear view down several streets where most of his Shermans, flanked by hustling squads of infantry, fought their way down the steep incline toward the lower city and the riverbank. One tank shot point-blank into a stone house, blasting a German strongpoint into rubble, while American infantry fired into doors and windows of a nearby inn. Grenades flew in, and seconds after the resulting explosions GIs piled in, attacking through every opening. At the same time the tanks moved on, still firing, gaining position for the assault on the next block.

Beyond that descending slope, past a tantalizingly narrow section of riverfront warehouses and docks, a single span of engineering barges stretched across the chill waters of the Meuse. This was the only place that mattered, the jugular for Rommel's advancing panzers. Now the surface of that bridge was smooth and free of debris. Pulaski could see a convoy of trucks parked in a waterfront lot on the near side of the river, and wondered why they didn't start across. Then, with his binoculars pressed to his eyes, he saw the reason: on the far bank a column of vehicles was moving onto the crossing, rolling toward the embattled city. He focused his glasses tightly and cursed; here, too, massive Tigers were in the lead.

Just below, parked in the intersection dominated by this house, Pulaski looked into the open-topped turrets of his battle reserve. The ten tank destroyers parked there included seven M10s and three of the M36s with their lethal 90-mm guns. He had gathered these as a last-ditch defense against the attack from the east, but now there was a new need.

In less than a minute he made his way down from the tower and into the street. He found Captain Zimmerman smoking a cigarette in the turret of an M36. The men who drove and fought in these tank destroyers were gathered around a couple of small fires they had built in emptied fuel drums, and now they watched the colonel and their captain with interest.

"It's hunting season," Pulaski shouted. Immediately drivers scrambled into their vehicles. One after another the throaty engines growled to life.

"Where d'you want us?" asked the young captain.

"On the edge of the bluff," came the reply. "We've got unwelcome company coming across the bridge. See what you can do to hold 'em off."

"You got it, Colonel!" declared Zimmerman, flashing a grin. "We got some places picked out for just such a shootin' gallery."

By the time the tank destroyers had rumbled away—most of them only going a block or two to get a good view of the bridge—Pulaski could hear shooting from the east. He and Dawson scrambled back to their lookout to see blazing panzers blocking the highway under Ballard's position. Flame and smoke spat from the hidden Shermans and one after another German tanks torched into fire. Even the huge Tigers were vulnerable to flank shots from the upgunned Shermans, and with his glasses Pulaski saw that several of the great turrets had been charred by armor-piercing hits. Diaz's artillery, too, was brutally accurate, as shells from his guns rapidly and relentlessly marched up and down the road.

But the attack inevitably revealed the positions of the American tanks, and now the panzers were starting to find the range. Dozens of German guns shot upward from the street, while a few Tigers turned off the road and climbed toward the dug-in Americans. In one place a point-blank gun battle raged, and the hulking German vehicle inevitably got the best of it, destroying a Sherman in an oily blast of fire. Growling on, the Tiger lurched around the wrecked M4, then jolted to a halt as another U.S. tank scored a direct hit on its track.

More shots erupted from the west, and Pulaski saw that his tank destroyers had occupied commanding positions overlooking the river valley. Explosions flashed on the bridge, and several tanks on the long span began to burn. He raised his binoculars again and watched with whispered cheers as the M36 Tank Destroyers lived up to their billing, the big guns combining to pick off four Tigers in the first minute of the engagement.

But many more panzers were rolling onto the bridge, nimble Panthers skirting the wrecks, one rolling recklessly right across a burning armored car, then racing for the near bank. Several tank destroyers shot at it, but the tank seemed blessed with arcane protection as every shell went wide. On the road beyond, the procession of enemy tanks rolling toward the bridge seemed endless, a tight column bunched on the opposite riverbank as it slowly crept onto the floating span.

The next explosion was huge and accurate, the blast sending the lead Panther skidding off the bridge to disappear into the icy water. As if on aerial parade, a squadron of aircraft, white stars painted on their wings, swooped down the river valley, strafing and bombing the panzer column caught on the exposed bridge. More planes dove from above, wreaking terrible havoc among the vehicles waiting to cross. Thunderbolts and Tempests snarled past, machine guns, cannons and bombs—in concert with the barrage from the tank destroyers—finally halting the advancing column. Mustangs and Spitfires, even twin-engined medium bombers, roared overhead in great formations and then wheeled back to attack in proud evidence of their regained mastery of the skies. Scores of panzers burned, and the few operational vehicles on the span were trapped in the midst of blazing wreckage.

At the same time, the first of the Shermans rumbled into the wharves along the river. High-explosive shells blasted trucks that were laden with fuel intended for Rommel's advancing panzers. Everywhere the thin-skinned transports ignited into spectacular fireballs.

"Get the engineers moving down there—I want that bridge blown to hell!" Pulaski shouted into the microphone. Already he saw men darting onto the end of the bridge, M1 rifles popping off, then joined by a chattering BAR as GIs picked off German tankers who had escaped their vehicles.

Pulaski looked again to the east. The Tigers had made their way farther up the hill. Though many had been halted by the narrow alleys or the effects of crippling hits, several had rolled right through Ballard's position. Pulaski saw a Sherman rumble out of a small alley in the command position on the left flank. The long barrel was extended toward the cross street. The colonel's binoculars confirmed the identity: on the rear of the turret were the twin red shields marking Frank Ballard's vehicle.

A great Tiger was trapped before the American tank, unable to traverse its gun because of stone buildings to either side. The M4 fired once, and the panzer spumed smoke and fire as its on-board ammunition cooked off. A man scrambled out of the driver's hatch, and a second later the entire tank was consumed by flames.

Ballard's tank started to back away—but then there was a flash from nearby. A rocket burst from the alley and exploded against the turret of the Sherman. The tank lurched, and smoke billowed from the stricken vehicle.

"Goddamn panzerfaust!" cursed Dawson as Wehrmacht infantry swarmed over the wrecked tank. The stubby, bazookalike tank killer was wielded by a large soldier who led the squad into the next street, while other German soldiers plastered the disabled vehicle with grenades.

"Frank—goddamn it . . ." whispered Pulaski, first appalled, then drained by a wave of melancholy. He shook himself violently, teeth clenched as the tide of battle moved closer—he would mourn for his friend later.

"They're coming through," the colonel observed grimly as more of the German armor poured around the roadblock and rumbled into the city. Three Panthers were in the lead, rolling fast toward the crest above the river. The main road would lead them into the plaza just below, and from there they would have access to many streets leading down to the waterfront.

How long till Jackson would get here with Combat Command B? He didn't even have time to call.

"Come on, Sarge," Pulaski said. Once again the two men pounded down the narrow stairway to the street. Keefer had the half-track idling, and as soon as they jumped in he started to roll.

A few blocks later they came upon three Shermans guarding an intersection that apparently widened into a small, now abandoned, marketplace. Lieutenant Allen, the executive officer of C Company, signaled from the open hatch of his turret as the half-track rolled up.

"Where's the rest of your company?" asked the colonel.

"Along these few blocks, sir. We were shooting at the trucks on the wharf, but we kind of run out of targets."

"New orders—and new targets, I bet. Get yourself headed to the big square at the top of the hill. I'm going to round up the rest of your boys."

"Yes, sir!"

The young officer wasted no time in leading the three tanks up the street. A few minutes later Pulaski had gathered a company of Shermans, pulling the tanks back from the now-successful attack on the docks. He took a last look at the valley and saw that his infantry had advanced halfway across the bridge, that the men of his engineering company were busy placing charges along the floating pontoons that supported the span. The counterattack from across the river had been utterly shattered, blocked by the wreckage of its own first wave, scattered and broken by roaring aircraft that still pounced on any suggestion of a target.

Lieutenant Allen's three tanks and an equal number of Zimmerman's tank destroyers were straddling the middle of the square when Pulaski arrived with eight more Shermans, together with a few trucks and a couple of jeeps hauling light antitank guns. The colonel's half-track led the rest of the ad hoc battle group out of the narrow, ascending streets. They rolled into the square atop the hill, the plaza underneath the turret where Pulaski had his lookout post.

"Spread out here!" he shouted. "Get shots lined up on the main road, and watch the side streets, too—we can't let ourselves get outflanked!"

The M4s started to move again, but simultaneously the first panzers rolled into view from the opposite direction. Shermans and Panthers blasted each other at point-blank range, a cacophony of shuddering booms, violent explosions, and whining shrapnel. Pulaski forced himself to stand behind the cab while Keefer guided the half-track along the road behind the tanks. Dawson manned the fifty-caliber machine gun, and the colonel found himself unholstering his sidearm in a reflexive gesture.

That chaos of noise was suddenly overwhelmed by the thunderous boom that shook the valley, vibration jolting even the heavy iron vehicles. Dirty water and smoke billowed above the waterfront, mixed with pieces of planking and barges—enough debris to confirm that the bridge was blown.

Nearby a building collapsed, bricks and stones rattling off the hull of the half-track. A burning Sherman jolted past, skidded sideways, to crash into the stone fountain on the square. Lieutenant Allen jumped out of the hatch and was followed by a billow of smoke as he ran for the shelter of a nearby doorway.

Loud shots cracked through the neighboring streets, and Pulaski realized that more tank destroyers had joined the fight, lengthening the American position to the left and right as the panzers tried to find a way around this roadblock. More and more tanks were burning—a sickening number of them Shermans— but now the rest of CCA was coming up from the riverbank, added fresh guns, iron, and blood to the raging fight.

Then Dawson was handing Pulaski the radio, saying something that the colonel couldn't understand through the din.

"Ski . . . are you there, Ski?" The flat voice, even through the static, conjured up the square block of the man who was speaking.

"General?" It was indeed Henry Wakefield.

"Jackson is in the city, Ski . . . he's joined up with Diaz, hitting the Krauts in the flank. He'll have that highway cut in no time! But what's your progress down there?"

A German shell blasted through the door of the half-track. The vehicle lurched, and Pulaski felt a slicing pain coupled with a gentle tug against his legs.

"We did it, Hank . . . we got the bridge!" he said, the words coming out in a rush.

And then the detonation came. Some vague time later he was lying on the ground in a spreading pool of blood. He fumbled for his crucifix. His pain was distant, like his thoughts, which continued to move even farther away, until they were nowhere at all.

Nineteenth Division Mobile Headquarters, Givet, France, 1421 hours GMT

Wakefield put down the radio. He unclenched his big hands, trying to shake off the chill that had come over him with the broken connection.

"He did it," he said to Colonel Sanger. "Jimmy got the bridge. CCA has cut Rommel in two. Get me Third Army on the horn. Hell, let's tell SHAEF and everybody."

"Yes, sir. But, General, about Ski . . . what happened to him?"

"I don't know." Wakefield looked at the silent radio set, trying to muster some sensation of triumph. "Let's try and get some more help in there and pray that it's not too late."

Army Group B Field Headquarters, Dinant, Belgium, 1455 hours GMT

"Both bridges are gone, Herr Feldmarschall . . . and Panzer Lehr is bogged down by enemy resistance, taking serious damage from a flank attack. I encourage you to leave here—you must not be taken prisoner." Speidel did not try to put any pleasant gloss on the news. Instead, he reached forward, as if he would take his commander by the arm and physically lead him to safety.

Rommel simply stood, thinking. The situation was grim, the facts incontrovertible. Rommel could see the maps, he could look out the window, he could examine his own mind and judgment. All his knowledge pointed toward the same conclusion: at the decisive point, the place where the result of the battle would be determined, the Americans had won.

Speidel tried again. "I tell you, the Yankees have cut off our bridgehead.

But all is not lost, Field Marshal . . . we can fall back to the Westwall, pull out with much of the army. We must start by saving you!"

"There will be no saving my five panzer divisions already across the river," Rommel chided gently, almost absently.

"No, of course not. But we have to make of this what we can." General Speidel spoke reasonably, with patient logic. His whole manner projected a calmness that matched his commander.

Surprising himself, Rommel felt the same way, though he couldn't understand why. After all, the loss of the bridges could have only one effect on the overall battle.

"Our attack has failed . . . we'll never get enough fuel to the panzers, and they won't be able to get to Antwerp." His mind followed that conclusion to the inevitable results . . . the great armored arm of the Wehrmacht was finished. And the surviving infantry, mostly volksgrenadier, would trudge back to the Westwall, frostbitten and demoralized. What kind of treatment would Himmler afford the men who had failed to achieve his magnificent victory? "Yes . . . we have to make of this what we can."

Far across Germany, the country's eastern border had been thinned of troops, so much of the army dedicated to this one great gamble. His gamble. The gamble that had failed. Stalin's Red Army was there in the east, in great numbers, and the Soviet dictator would see only opportunity in German disaster.

"But we can still save that army—most of it, anyway!" Speidel insisted. "The key is for you, my Field Marshal, to get away!"

"And get away to what? To see the Red Army parade into Berlin, to sweep all the way to the Rhine? While the remnants of the German Army die in the Westwall, holding the Americans and British at bay for a few desperate weeks of hell?" He looked up, almost preternaturally calm. In his heart, in his mind, he could see only one way out. As Alexander the Great had shown, the only way to deal with the Gordian knot was to cut it, to change the game from one that was rigged into one that was still winnable. He had to save the German army and counterbalance the threat from the east. Therefore, there was only a single solution.

He looked around the conference room. Speidel was here, of course, as were his staff officers Reinhardt and Müller. Carl-Heinz Clausen stood unobtrusively in the corner, stationed at the door to Rommel's inner office. Horst Bücher, the SS general, back from his reduction of Bastogne, looking at him with calm assurance, waiting for him to solve the insoluble. A young lieutenant operated the telephone switchboard.

The Desert Fox thought about the Metz Massacre, the slaughter of innocent prisoners, the propaganda killings masquerading as the work of American butchers. It had been Himmler's message to him, of course, and clear enough even for an apolitical Swabian soldier to understand. He smiled, his mind racing around his new solution. It had, it seemed, the additional virtue of frustrating the führer.

"Günter," Rommel addressed Reinhardt informally. "Please be good enough to bring us a new set of maps from storage. I wish to see the entire front in the west."

"Of course, Herr Feldmarschall." With a click of his heels, the tall intelligence officer departed.

The Desert Fox drew a deep breath and spoke to no one in particular. "Bring me the telephone. I would like to speak to Baron von Esebeck." Müller brought him the handset and Rommel paused for a minute, waiting for the operator to make the connection. He looked at Müller and spoke with genuine affection. "Wolfgang, go out to the courtyard and have a look. I'd like to know how close the Americans are getting to my headquarters."

"Of course, Field Marshal!" Müller saluted and hurried away, but Rommel was already speaking into the phone.

"Baron? Hello. Can you come up here, to my headquarters. Right away, please. I need the help of someone who speaks good English."

Rommel looked over the maps Reinhardt brought, contemplating, examining his plan for potential flaws, concerns. A moment later he heard the arrival of Baron von Esebeck, accompanied by a short, balding fellow wearing American combat fatigues. The newspaper reporter Reinhardt had captured.

"Herr . . . Porter, is it?" the Desert Fox asked politely.

"Yes, sir," the reporter replied in his halting German, confused and quizzical. Rommel smiled again.

"Herr Porter, I believe we can do each other a mutual service. I need the assistance of an honest translator, and as a reporter, I'm sure you would like access to a newsworthy story."

Rommel could see the eagerness on the reporter's face. "Sir, I'd be honored to help, but I'm still an American, sir. I won't betray my country."

"Of course not," murmured Rommel. "Nor will I ask you to. I merely want you to provide honest translation. Nothing more."

He noticed the raised eyebrow on Reinhardt's face. The intelligence officer had figured out the situation, at last. Now it was time for the others to know. He cleared his throat, for once in his life at a loss for words, unsure where to begin.

"Gentlemen, I have reached what I believe is a decision of unavoidable necessity. This operation is over. We can fight on, of course, but only by throwing away German lives with no benefit to the Fatherland. We can retreat, but in my military judgment that will only postpone the day of reckoning, and not by long. Again, we will lose many German lives for no appreciable gain. The danger in the east I cannot dismiss as lightly as others do, with no disrespect to the diplomatic efforts of our own Colonel von Reinhardt."

"Sir, I guaranteed that Stalin would refrain from attacking us only as long as it was in his self-interest to do so," interjected the colonel. "With the current situation, I believe it is only a matter of a short time before Stalin's self-interest argues for another choice."

"As do I, Günter," Rommel said, nodding acknowledgment.

The field marshal could see the growing awareness on Horst Bücher's scarred face. "Sir—" the SS general interrupted. "This discussion is most inappropriate. Political decisions are taken in Berlin, not by field officers, regardless of their rank, with no disrespect intended, sir."

Speidel, Müller, and von Esebeck were still obviously puzzled by the direction of the conversation. Rommel held up his hand.

"This is now a military decision, and as the field commander I am the only person in a position to make it. I understand there are political consequences, but the decision necessarily still rests with me. Gentlemen—" he paused, took a deep breath, "I plan to surrender Army Group B to the Allies."

If an Allied bomb had crashed through the window at that very moment, it could hardly have set off a greater explosion. "What?!" "No!" "Field Marshal, what are you saying?" "Surrender? Never!"

Rommel stood under the buffeting of competing opinions, remembering his view of the scarred, broken oak tree from his hospital window as the winds of debate and opposition swirled around him. Like that tree he would stand in the tempest, hold firm until the fury stormed past.

Finally he held up his hand to still the room. "I see no other alternative. I believe General Patton sees the Soviet threat as clearly as I do; I can only hope our surrender will be in time to save the Fatherland from a worse fate and a worse tyranny than it has suffered these past years."

"You can't do this—you can't!" shrieked Bücher, his scars glowing redly as his passion rushed to his face. "Field Marshal—" he was pleading now, nearly in tears, "think about this! You're betraying the Fatherland to its enemies! You'll go down in history as the worst sort of traitor! Look—there's still hope! Where there are Germans, there is still hope. We are the Aryan people; we will succeed—we have to succeed! Fall back, let us regroup. We will attack again and again and again . . . and if we have to go down, let us go down like men, not like cowards! Sir, you're a wounded man; you've been under enormous pressure. Today is a grim day, but there's no call, no justification for such an enormity of a response! Surrender? How can you even think of it? You're the Desert Fox! You're an inspiration to your men! Tell them to fight and they will fight! One of us is better than any ten, any twenty of the enemy! Don't you see?"

Rommel walked toward Bücher, tried to place his hand on the man's shoulder, but the SS general tore himself away. "Field Marshal, you cannot do this. Tell us now that you have changed your mind, that this was simply a momentary lapse. . . ."

The Desert Fox slowly shook his head. "Horst, I must do this thing, although you must believe me that it is truly the most painful and difficult choice I have faced in my life. I would do almost anything else . . . but the truth is, I see no other hope for the Fatherland. Look—you have been a good soldier torn between two masters. I know you must now call Berlin, and Berlin will take what action it can. Like all soldiers, you must do what you must. As must I."

He turned back toward the others. Speidel was unable to conceal his elation and remained utterly obedient to Rommel. Reinhardt was on his side. Müller would follow Reinhardt. Von Esebeck and the reporter would play their roles. He wondered briefly about Guderian and Manteuffel. No, they were good military men, they would understand the situation the same way as he did. There were some subordinate SS commanders to deal with, but with care, that could be managed. This was a campaign once again, and Rommel could manage it well.

"Gentlemen, I have listened carefully, but my decision is firm. Surrender is our only viable option. Baron, you and Herr Porter will make contact with the Allied general whose division was opposing us in Dinant. Use the radio and speak in the clear. Explain that I want to negotiate the terms of a surrender. Hans—" he looked at Speidel, "I want you to contact the Fifth and Sixth Panzerarmee headquarters and explain the situation to Manteuffel and Guderian." Speidel bowed his head in acknowledgment. "Colonel von Reinhardt, you'll provide tactical support to this process. I need a list of units and commanders, current positions, and other information necessary to support the stand-down. Colonel Müller, assist him, please."

He was pleased to see his officers snap to and attack this new problem with the professionalism they had shown in planning the overall campaign. It was then he noticed that General Bücher had silently left the room.

Nineteenth Division Mobile Headquarters, Givet, France, 1644 hours GMT

"General Wakefield . . . we're getting a radio call." Sergeant Johnson was unusually hesitant. "It's . . . well, it's someone named Chuck Porter—an AP correspondent captured by the Krauts. He says he's got a message for us—a message from someone who claims he's Field Marshal Rommel of the German army."

"Hello?" Wakefield snatched up the microphone, in no mood for word games. "Who the hell is this?"

"General Wakefield . . . of the Nineteenth? My name is Porter. I'm here, in Dinant . . . in the German HQ, as a matter of fact. With Rommel and a couple of his staff officers. The field marshal wants to talk to you about the terms of a surrender."

"Surrender? There's no way in hell I'm going to surrender!" the American general growled.

"No—no, General. It's Rommel. He wants to surrender . . . to you."

Wakefield froze, unable to believe his ears. His teeth clamped down on the unlit cigar. "Is this some kind of fucking joke?"

Another voice came on. "General," it said in German-accented British English, "I am Baron von Esebeck. I can assure you this is not a joke at all. Feldmarschall Rommel wishes to discuss the terms of a surrender of the German forces."

Wakefield cupped a hand over the mouthpiece and spoke to Johnson. "Put me through to General Patton—pronto!"

"I . . . er, I was just about to tell you, sir. He's here."

And there he was, Old Blood and Guts himself, all three stars gleaming on his shiny helmet. "Hello, Hank," Patton said with unaccustomed mildness.

Wakefield put up his hand. "Quiet!" he barked.

Patton's face showed he was unused to being given orders by his subordinates. Johnson quietly spoke up, "General Patton, sir—"

"What is it, sergeant?"

"That's Rommel's headquarters on the phone—they're calling to surrender."

The look on Patton's face would be remembered forever by everyone in the room.

Army Group B Field Headquarters, Dinant, Belgium, 1732 hours GMT

Horst Bücher pulled the Luger automatic from his holster, checked the gun to make sure that the action was smooth, and rose from his desk. He had done his duty to the Fatherland; he had explained the situation to the führer, who had—not surprisingly—exploded at the news. "Stop it!" hissed the voice through the telephone. "Stop the surrender at all costs! I feared something like this; that's why you were given the earlier orders concerning the fate of the Desert Fox. It is a serious mistake that those orders were not carried out earlier. Do it now. It is no longer important whether it looks like Allied action or not."

Bücher put down the telephone. He felt his world crumble around him. Erwin Rommel was a traitor, and yet Bücher admired him as he had admired no other man.

Was it only a day or two ago that the SS general had resolved to disobey his orders to kill Rommel? After everything that had happened to him in his life, he should have known better than to put his trust in any man. The Party was his real father, his only father. Hadn't that been proved to him, time and time again? Humans were weak; the Party was strong. And the party leaders were always right.

Perhaps, Bücher thought, some good might come out of this after all. For Rommel would have to arrange an in-person meeting with someone very senior on the American side, perhaps Patton or Bradley . . . or even Eisenhower. And wouldn't it redeem everything if at the same time the Desert Fox died, Patton died as well . . . at the hand of the SS? His scarred face broke into a bitter and twisted smile.

His first stop was the SS communications feldwebel. That man would be loyal to Germany, to the Party. "Where has the field marshal gone?" he demanded.

"There is a truce in Dinant," the feldwebel replied, nearly stuttering in his fear. "The field marshal's staff car is flying a white flag; they will meet Allied generals in the Church of Notre Dame in the center of the city."

"Very good," he said, and strode away, eyes blazing, scars furiously red. It was late afternoon and already dark. There were wide stone steps in front of the headquarters château. At the bottom were several staff cars, one of which he commandeered.

"Horst," called a calm, clear voice behind him. He looked up. There was Colonel Günter von Reinhardt standing on the top of the steps. "Stand where you are. I can't let you leave the headquarters."

Bücher's eyes narrowed. His smile was cold. "I am your superior officer, Günter. Don't give me orders."

"I know where you are planning to go, Horst. Give it up. He's right, you know. Himmler is wrong. Only Rommel's move has a chance of saving Germany."

"No, Günter. If we surrender, Germany is not saved. Some men live, but Germany—the glorious Fatherland—is lost. As Hitler said, 'The world is not intended for cowardly nations.' Or cowardly field marshals, either."

"It's not cowardice. Our Desert Fox is brave and calculating. This surrender defends us against a far worse evil from the east. Watch and see—Germany will be stronger for this."

Bücher shook his head. "No. I'm going now."

"No," Reinhardt said, lifting his own pistol, a Walther. "I can't let you."

"I'd just as soon not kill you, Günter, but I will. Count on it."

"*Aut tuam mortem aut meam.* Your life or mine."

Another quote, Bücher thought. *How like the man.* "*Tuam,* then," replied Bücher, whipping out his concealed Luger and firing. The more experienced warrior's bullet slammed into the intelligence officer's chest. Reinhardt fell backward, red welling up over the gray of his uniform.

"Good-bye, Günter," Bücher said, sliding into the driver's seat of his commandeered staff car and turning on the engine.

Wolfgang Müller stepped out into the cold, dark air and shivered. "Günter," he called, "where are you? The field telephone lines have been cut! One of the communications officers is dead—they need you inside!" There was no answer. Again he called, "Günter? Where are you?"

In the weak light of an exposed bulb next to the main château door, he saw a horrifying sight: his friend sprawled, bleeding blackly from a chest wound, blood leaking from the side of his mouth as well. "Günter! Günter! I'll get some help! What happened?" he gasped, babbling in near panic.

Reinhardt's weak voice gasped back, "Wolfgang—wait! There's something more important. . . ."

Müller knelt beside his friend, "I can't hear you, Günter. Let me get some help. You're going to be all right."

"Horst Bücher . . . he's gone to kill the Field Marshal . . . to stop the surrender. You've got to stop him."

"I can't stop him—the phones are dead!"

"You've got to drive . . . stop Bücher . . . Wolfgang, Germany depends on this."

The thought of Germany's fate resting on Müller's round and pudgy shoulders was ludicrous, but Reinhardt's weak hand reached up to grab Müller by the arm. "I'm serious, Wolfgang. It all depends on you now. You must stop Bücher. I believe in you. You can." The effort was too much; the wounded colonel sank back, coughed up more blood, and closed his eyes.

"Günter! Günter! Speak to me!" Wolfgang Müller was near tears, but his friend and protector had sunk into unconsciousness. "Help! Help!" he cried out to the darkness. As other officers boiled out of the building, Müller straightened up. Slowly, carefully, he made his way toward the line of staff cars.

Givet, France, 2200 hours GMT

The enclosed jeep sped along the road to Dinant, three-star flag whipping in the wind. It was part of a small, fast convoy, including several armored cars and a half dozen of the reliable Willies, traveling with dimmed headlights along a winding riverside thoroughfare. The winter night was cold and dark, and a startling array of stars winked across the heavens.

In the command jeep the two generals sat in silence, knowing the size of the gamble they took. Patton was right, Wakefield knew. There was no time to wait for orders from higher headquarters, but they understood this could be a trap.

"It's my opinion that Rommel's honorable," growled Patton. "At least as honorable as any Nazi son of a bitch can be. But he's got some SS divisions under him. I don't know if he can make them surrender."

"If he gets most of his divisions to stand down, we can handle the rest," replied Wakefield. "Hell, we've got him beat whether he surrenders or not. The question is how long and how much."

"And how fast the goddamn Russians are going to move while they wait for Ike and the politicians to make up their minds."

Wakefield knew that his army general had sent a message to SHAEF detailing Rommel's proposed surrender. However, Patton had also made sure that he was out of his HQ before the communication was sent. By the time he got a reply and instructions, events would have moved far forward.

"Faster, man!" Patton snapped to the driver. That sergeant, who was already racing along as fast as safety allowed, nodded tersely but Wakefield noticed that he made no move to accelerate further.

The three-star general paid no attention. "Could be an SS trap, though."

Wakefield grunted. He'd thought of that, too. "Jackson's boys are still attacking. They hit Panzer Lehr in the flank and busted the Krauts up pretty good. Together with CCA they're keeping the pressure on. At least half of Dinant is in our hands, and the Krauts have no way to cross the river."

"Any word yet about the boy?" Patton asked gruffly.

Wakefield could only grunt a negative, thinking about Pulaski. "Frank Ballard turned up . . . his tank got hit again, but he's going to make it."

"He, Pulaski . . . all those men. They're heroes," Patton said, his voice thick with emotion. "By God, they deserve every medal this man's army can award!"

Wakefield nodded, but his thoughts were cold. Again, as the Belgian countryside sprawled dark in all directions, the night seemed to close in—except for those sparkling stars. It was a view haunting and dangerous yet, at the same time, strangely peaceful.

Church of Notre Dame, Dinant, Belgium, 27 December 1944, 0111 hours GMT

The cathedral was the dominant feature of Dinant. It had suffered battle damage, but was still standing. Carl-Heinz had maneuvered Rommel's staff car through the wreckage in the dark, the headlights turning the battle scene into a shadowy nightmare.

A crew of enlisted men set up a quick conference room, moved additional lights into position, set up white flags for the surrender conference. Rommel got out of the staff car, feeling suddenly vulnerable because he could not see into the darkness past the narrow ring of lights.

"Let me know when the Americans arrive," he said to his driver. He strode into the chancel to stand in the pews, looking up at the altar. Carl-Heinz stood quietly in the back after crossing himself. It had been far too long since he'd been in a church, Rommel thought. He had a lot to pray about, to atone for. He had led his armies to defeat, and now he was about to surrender, always a difficult act for a military man, regardless of the circumstances.

He was suddenly very tired, drained of all emotion and feeling, ready to collapse into one of the pews. He studied the Jesus on the cross, saw glimpses of the Passion in the stained glass windows as they flashed into sudden brilliance when they were hit by a headlight. His own cross was heavy on his shoulders, he thought, though perhaps not as heavy as the one borne by the man at the front of that church.

He heard a noise behind him and turned slowly around. "I had asked not to be disturbed—" he began, then stopped. "General Bücher," he said. "Somehow I am not surprised."

Carl-Heinz noticed the gun in the SS general's hand and reached for his own pistol, but without taking his attention away from the Desert Fox, Bücher fired. The shot echoed in the empty church, but Rommel realized that the noise elsewhere was so loud it was unlikely that anyone had heard. The driver grabbed his stomach, moaned in pain.

Rommel stared at Bücher coldly. "He was a good man . . . better than either of us, I'd warrant. You didn't have to kill him."

"Isn't there a different life you would do well to concern yourself with?"

"You're going to have your way with me . . . but whether I live or die, the war is lost."

"We will win!"

"The Russians will win, you fool. I was merely trying to prevent that."

"You're wrong, Field Marshal, and you're a traitor. I finally saw your weakness, though the führer saw it first and better. The Reich will win, the Party will win. I know this to be true." Bücher stood straight and tall. "In the meantime, it is the duty of every good German to execute traitors. But don't worry; you won't die just yet. With any luck, you'll die alongside an American general or two; perhaps Patton himself!"

Rommel's tiredness was overwhelming, his loss was now total. He sat down in one of the pews.

"Stand up!" growled Bücher. "Keep your hands where I can see them."

"No, Horst. Go ahead and shoot. I'm tired; it will be a relief."

"You're a coward as well as a traitor," said Bücher as he lifted his Luger to point it directly at Rommel's head.

Squinting through his glasses, Müller was afraid he would become lost or stuck navigating the narrow and rubble-filled streets of Dinant. His only saving fortune was that the church was so large he could not miss it, and there were headlights and vehicles all around.

His heart pounded in his chest, his stomach growled, he was afraid he was going to be sick. Him against an SS commando general? It was ludicrous. This was not his skill. And Günter dead . . . no, he wasn't ready to face that. Germany rode on his shoulders, his weak and pitiful shoulders. That's what Günter's dying words had said. *No matter. In a little while I'll be dead, too,* he thought, knowing there was only one possible outcome for a gun battle between himself and Bücher.

There—there was the church! "Where's the field marshal?" he gasped as he piled out of the car.

"In the church," said a feldwebel. "He's not to be disturbed."

Müller looked at him wild-eyed. "Message from Berlin," he gasped. "Urgent!"

"Oh, all right. You may pass. But if the message isn't urgent enough, let the field marshal's wrath fall on you!"

Müller opened the outer wooden door gingerly and slipped into the small anteroom. Another set of wooden doors opened into the cathedral itself. Heart pounding so loud he knew it could be heard even through the thick wood, he slowly pulled open the door, praying that it would not squeak. There—the sound of voices—Rommel and . . . yes, Bücher. A good marksman could easily have stopped the SS general from here, but Müller was not a good marksman. He slipped into the church as quietly as he could, fearful that at any second Bücher would turn around.

His foot slipped; he nearly fell. He dropped to his knees into something warm and sticky. It was Mutti—Carl-Heinz—bleeding from a stomach wound, unconscious, possibly dying. Müller nearly vomited. He crawled forward, sliding from pew to pew, hoping that he was quiet enough in the echoing vault of the church. He was closer, close enough to hear the conversation. Bücher was arguing, explaining himself. It wasn't enough to kill the Desert Fox, he had to make the Desert Fox understand first.

Müller's holster had a snap closure on it; he pried it loose as quietly as he could, pulled the gun out. He had never fired it in anger; he suddenly worried that the gun would not work. He raised it, pointed squarely at Bücher's back. There must have been some noise, some clue, because he suddenly saw Bücher begin to turn toward him, his gun coming up, and the supply officer closed his eyes tightly and fired. The recoil knocked him backward as the noise echoed on and on.

Then he did vomit, then looked up to see the Desert Fox place his hand on Müller's shoulder. "Thank you, colonel. That was a brave thing you did." Müller could see only the legs of the SS general; the rest of the body was hidden by the pews.

Müller was tongue-tied in the presence of Rommel. He could only mumble, "He killed Günter," his eyes watering more than usual behind the wire-rimmed spectacles.

"I'm sorry," whispered the field marshal.

Rommel stood, opened the church door, and called to the guards waiting outside. As soon as one of the guards got a look at the carnage inside, he blew his whistle loudly, and within seconds the church was full of guards. A lieutenant, nearly incoherent with panic, managed to stutter out, "Are you all right, Field Marshal?"

"Yes, I'm fine," he said. "Get a medic for Carl-Heinz—now!" His driver was still alive, but in need of immediate attention.

Dinant, Belgium, 0442 hours GMT

Three jeeps rolled forward into the square before the lofty steeple. The flag with three stars marked the second jeep as the transport of an army general. Four armored cars had taken up positions in the surrounding intersections, and GIs still darted from building to building, insuring that each was clear of Germans.

Wakefield looked up at the lofty church and wondered how the spire had survived the battles that had raged in this city during the last five years . . . and then it occurred to him that it had probably also survived wars predating his life by many centuries.

Around the church were several German command cars flying white flags. From the church doors came a stocky man, limping slightly. He wore the peaked cap and leather jacket of a German officer, and as the Americans got closer Wakefield recognized the man from the multitude of pictures that had reached the Allied lines during the war.

This was Erwin Rommel, the Desert Fox.

Behind him was a balding, pudgy colonel and an equally balding but non-descript man in army fatigues.

The plain-looking man startled the general by holding out his hand instead of saluting. After a moment's hesitation Wakefield shook, then turned his eyes to Rommel as the other fellow spoke. "General . . . I'm Chuck Porter. Originally with the Associated Press, lately a prisoner of the Germans. This is Baron von Esebeck; he's a German reporter. We're the semiofficial translators, I guess."

Patton, in the meantime, was looking the German field marshal up and down with a look of bemused curiosity. Rommel saluted crisply, a gesture that Patton returned. Then, with Porter and a German staff officer translating, they began to discuss the surrender.

Berlin, Germany, 0631 hours GMT

The führer sat in the dark room, chin propped on folded hands, and thought. Then he spoke. "We must assume that General Bücher has failed in his mission. Send word to all SS units that they are to ignore any orders from Rommel or anyone at Army Group B—anyone on the General Staff, for that matter. From this moment on, all military matters are under my personal jurisdiction. Second, send word—supported by troops—to the General Staff to that effect, and make sure you tell them why. They harbored a traitor and elevated him to supreme command; there is no reason they should complain about their loss of independence now.

"Third, send notification to all Wehrmacht units that any commander moving toward surrender is an enemy of the Reich, and the penalty is immediate execution. Send it on open channels, no codes. Fourth, place a reward for one hundred thousand Reichsmarks for the capture or death of Rommel." Heinrich Himmler paused for a long time.

"Now to long-range plans. Russian front troops and equipment can be shifted into the Westwall to stiffen those defenses. Trains will run at night to limit casualties; the jet fighter gruppen will make protecting train movements top priority. Remaining Russian front troops will fortify as much as possible where they are; our erstwhile friend and ally to the east will certainly attack us the moment he is able. Were the V-1 documents altered as I asked?"

"Yes, führer," said one of the three aides busily taking notes. "Dr. von Braun's staff assure me that the adjustments are subtle enough that there is no way to tell that their V-1 will not work until they reach the test stage. While they eventually will be able to fix the problems, it should take between four and six extra months of development before they will have a working version. By then, Dr. von Braun assures us, the V-3 will be operational."

"Good. At least someone has behaved competently. Dr. von Braun certainly has earned his SS commission. If his prediction proves correct, we will see about an additional reward."

He leaned back, the darkness shadowing his face. He took off his glasses, rubbed the bridge of his nose, then put them back on. "If the Allies believe they will simply stroll into Berlin now, they will have a major surprise in store for them."

The aides stood, saluted, and left. In the darkness, the Führer smiled. It was not over yet.

The Kremlin, Moscow, Soviet Union, 0935 hours GMT

When the intelligence report came in, Colonel Sergei Aschev looked at it for a long moment. The chairman would have to be notified, but people who brought bad news were often never heard from again. He looked around at the bustling staff in the Kremlin communications room and picked out his victim. "Lieutenant Stamovitch! Come here, please," he barked.

"Yes, sir?"

"This report must be taken to Comrade Stalin at once!"

Stamovitch paused. He knew the rules of the game, and he knew that messengers who brought back bad news were sometimes never heard from again. "But comrade, I have already been assigned . . ."

"I am countermanding any other orders you have. Take this report to the chairman; it has precedence over everything!"

Stamovitch knew there was no way out. "Yes, sir," he said morosely. He saluted and left, the message almost burning in his hand.

Feeling like a man on his way to the gallows, he walked slowly, steadily, methodically through the corridors of the Kremlin. Then he brightened, for he saw a victim of his own, Lieutenant Krigoff, junior to him, but handsome and strong and destined for great things. Stamovitch hated him.

"Ah, Krigoff," he said with a nasty smile. "Just the man I was looking for. Here. Take this message to the chairman, at once. It's top priority from the radio room. Critical intelligence from the front."

Krigoff looked at Stamovitch. But instead of the expected reaction as the hot potato was passed, Krigoff smiled back. "At once, sir!" he said, saluted smartly, and swiveled on one foot to march briskly in the direction of the chairman's office. Stamovitch was left with the feeling that, somehow, he had been outmaneuvered.

"Yes?" said the chairman. "What is it?"

"We have just received word that confirms the brilliance of your diplomatic strategies, Comrade Stalin!" the lieutenant said brightly.

"What is it?"

"Rommel has surrendered Army Group B to the Americans!"

"*What?*" roared Stalin. "Let me see that!" He tore the report from the young lieutenant's hand, and skimmed it. Then he looked up at Aschev, eyes blazing in anger. "What do you mean, confirms my strategy?"

"Certainly you foresaw that there would be a collapse of the German initiative in the West, as well as increasing conflict between the German military and Himmler's SS. Himmler will have little option but to further strip his eastern front troops to shore up the Westwall, and you have the option either to scoop up Germany like the inside of a soft-boiled egg, leaving only the western shell to frustrate the Americans and British, or help Himmler stalemate the west, tying up the forces on either side so that the Soviet Union is free to operate."

"Hmm, yes," replied Stalin thoughtfully. "That is what I had planned. Very astute of you to realize it so clearly. It is, I must admit, somewhat more rapid and more total than I had expected, but with rapid response it will all play out in accordance with our objectives. Historical inevitability is a great thing, is it not, *Major* Krigoff?"

"Yes, sir!" he replied. "Although it is not so good for capitalists and facists."

The great man laughed. "You'll make a fine addition to the planning staff, major."

Roxboro, North Carolina, United States, 30 December 1944, 1521 hours GMT

She tore open the telegram with trembling fingers. She already knew what it said.

> THE SECRETARY OF WAR DESIRES ME TO EXPRESS HIS DEEP REGRET THAT YOUR SON, STAFF SERGEANT FRANKLIN O'DELL, HAS BEEN REPORTED MISSING IN ACTION SINCE DECEMBER 26, OVER BELGIUM. IF FURTHER DETAILS OR OTHER INFORMATION ARE RECEIVED, YOU WILL BE PROMPTLY NOTIFIED.

Missing in action. She clung to the small hope remaining, but in her heart, she knew her son was dead.

Givet, France, 1620 hours GMT

Chuck Porter pulled the last sheet of paper from his Underwood portable and gave it to the Teletype operator he'd managed to scrounge from the military. *This is Pulitzer stuff for sure,* he thought. For an over-the-hill editor, he had been given an opportunity to have a front-row seat at the defining moment of the Second World War, and it was an exclusive AP story. *It might even mean a raise.* He smiled.

FLASH/BULLETIN
PARIS BUREAU, 30 DECEMBER, 1030 EST
COPY 01 ROMMEL SURRENDERS
DISTRIBUTION: ALL STATIONS

GIVET, FRANCE, 30 DECEMBER 1944 (AP) BY CHUCK PORTER
FACED WITH THE FAILURE OF A DESPERATE PLAN TO BREAK THE ALLIED AD-
VANCE AND COUNTERATTACK, GERMAN FIELD MARSHAL ERWIN ROMMEL,
ALSO KNOWN AS THE DESERT FOX, SURRENDERED THE ENTIRE GERMAN
ARMY ON THE WESTERN FRONT TODAY.

THE SURRENDER ATTEMPT NEARLY FAILED ON THE GERMAN SIDE WHEN
A DISSIDENT SS GENERAL ATTEMPTED TO ASSASSINATE ROMMEL AS WELL AS
GENERAL GEORGE PATTON, WHO HAD COME PERSONALLY TO DISCUSS SUR-
RENDER TERMS.

THE ROMMEL ATTACK HAD BEEN AIMED AT THE KEY ALLIED SUPPLY DE-
POT OF ANTWERP IN BELGIUM, WHERE ROMMEL HAD HOPED TO CUT ALLIED
SUPPLIES, PRIMARILY FUEL. THE ATTACK WAS STOPPED IN THE TOWN OF DI-
NANT, BELGIUM, BY FORWARD ELEMENTS OF THE US NINETEENTH ARMORED
DIVISION, WHICH WERE NEARLY WIPED OUT IN THE PROCESS.

THE DIFFICULT AND DANGEROUS LIAISON BETWEEN GERMAN AND AL-
LIED COMMANDERS WAS HANDLED BY A CAPTURED AP REPORTER, CHUCK
PORTER. . . .

MORE

AP-PAR-387199-WQ/123044

Excerpt from *War's Final Fury,* by Professor Jared Gruenwald

The ultimate collapse of Nazi Germany came quickly on the heels of Eisenhower's great victory at Dinant. Although Rommel's audacious attack had
come close to reversing the tide of war, the bold offensive could not survive
the fatal severing of its supply line. Indeed, the gamble had required the use of
every available scrap of Nazi power, and the final result was an end to all the
Third Reich's prospects for victory.

When Dinant was retaken by U.S. troops, Operation Fuchs Am Rhein was
over. From there, Rommel's decisions were pragmatic. He was confronted with
a clear choice, though he was rare among high-ranking Germans in that he saw
the choice for what it was: In truth, his country had lost the war. Now, should
postwar Germany be dominated by the Soviets, or by the Western Allies?

There were immediate difficulties following Rommel's surrender. His key
generals, seeing the situation as the Desert Fox saw it, followed his surrender.

Individual units, however, especially those commanded by the SS, often continued their resistance. A few withdrew into Germany; a small percentage actually fought and died continuing the battle their commander had given up.

The Americans and British were quick to seize upon the opportunity, accepting the wholesale surrender of German divisions. Led by the fiery Patton, American and British armored columns rushed to the Rhine and crossed with the full assistance of defeated Germany. From there the autobahns to the country's heartland stretched wide, inviting, and undefended.

Hailed as a hero and the savior of Germany by some, reviled as an unparalleled traitor by others, Rommel is indisputably the man who redefined the European landscape permanently. The repercussions of his bold decision to surrender are still with us.

EPILOGUE

New Year's Day 1945

Dinant, Belgium,
1 January 1945, 0930 hours GMT

A dusting of snow attempted to render the battle-scarred city a uniform white, but the lingering heat of warfare defied the wintry blanket in too many places. Flames licked upward from the hulk of a Tiger tank, the wreck angled sideways in the street between two burned out buildings. The fire consuming the panzer was hot enough to melt a surrounding circle of snow-covered ground. Everywhere sprawled the bodies of men killed violently, though somehow this grotesque proof of war was gentled by the fresh white powder.

Wakefield walked alone, leaving the division HQ which had been set up in the building that had served as Rommel's own command post. Patton had taken control there, sending out word of the surrender while that newsman worked on his report. A Big Story, the general admitted, allowing himself a little flush of pleasure. The biggest in . . . God only knew how long.

At last, out of breath and sweating in the chill air, the burly general reached the plaza overlooking the Meuse. Less than a kilometer to the west stretched the river, and he could clearly see the broken remains of two bridges.

He also saw blackened tanks and twisted truck frames, dozens of them—more than he could easily count. This was only part of the cost—the toll in machines—exacted by the severing of Rommel's lifeline.

Now the place seemed insignificant, no more than a small, cluttered square in a city that happened to have arisen on a long river. Before him he saw the road into the Ardennes, the route of approach for the Panzer Lehr division's counterattack. That was the highway leading eastward, to Bastogne and to Germany beyond. And right here was the square, a convergence of that highway, city streets, and the river below that had for a few hours mattered more than anyplace else in the world. Armored monsters, Shermans and Panthers, had roared at each other here. And in the end the Americans had died and the Germans had been stopped.

On the far side of the square, underneath the shot-scarred turret of a half-ruined house, he found the wreck of a half-track. The body of the truck was canted at an odd angle from the chassis. The death wound was a gaping hole in the port-side door. The vehicle had burned, but the colonel's eagle and the CCA's crimson badge and white star were still visible on the twisted steel plate.

He turned his back to the half-track, reconstructing Pulaski's final moments on earth. He saw tracks through the rubble where the Panthers, desperate to reach the bridge, had come around the side of the plaza, driving through a once-walled garden. One of the panzers must have come upon Pulaski's half-track from the flank, probably unnoticed by the Americans—after all, Pulaski had been intent on the radio message to his division commander. A single well-aimed high-explosive shell had removed this impediment, and the Panther had rolled on.

Wakefield stayed beside the vehicle long enough to smoke a cigarette, lingering over the butt until the acrid taste stung his lips. He dropped the smoking stub next to the half-track, pausing for a last look at the wreck.

When he finally started toward his headquarters he noticed that it had once again begun to snow.

Wehrmacht Field Hospital, Trier, Germany, 1030 hours GMT

Staff Sgt. Frank "Digger" O'Dell
Trier, Germany
January 1, 1945

Mrs. Lucy O'Dell
Roxboro, North Carolina

Dear Mama,

By the time you get this, you should already have learned that I'm alive. I'm in a German hospital, and I'm going to be okay. I'll be coming home very soon, they tell me, now that the war is over.

As they probably told you, *Ford's Folly* got shot down over Dinant, and only Tony Hutt and I made it. I got hit again, this time in the leg, so I had to crawl to the camera hatch and bail out. I bailed out kind of low, which is generally not a good idea, but this time it meant that I got out below the flak, which may have saved my life. I got captured by farmers pretty much as soon as I landed, and now here I am.

It's kind of noisy here in the hospital right now. We had a visit from Rommel himself. He was here to visit his driver, who got wounded, and then made the rounds. He even came to visit us Americans, and I got to shake his hand. He even speaks American. Funny thing, though. You know, he's the only general I ever met, and he's on the other side.

I'll write more real soon.

Love . . .

He paused, wondering if he should add on a P.S. He remembered the moment a few days previous, after his shoot-down and capture, when the senior Allied POW came by for a visit. "Friend, you're the luckiest bastard that ever walked the face of the earth," he said.

Digger O'Dell looked down at his bandaged body. "How do you figure, Captain?" he said.

"Why, haven't you heard? No, I guess you haven't, not speaking German and all. But the war's over, at least here!"

Digger could hardly believe it. "Over?"

"Yep. We knocked out the bridges in Dinant, stopped Rommel's spearhead, and the Desert Fox surrendered."

"Son of a bitch!" breathed Digger.

"No kidding. Son, looks like you'll be going home. How's that for a happy new year?"

The aviator put his hands behind his head and smiled. Now if he could only find a smoke . . .

GLOSSARY

Ami German slang for "American."

AP Armor-piercing ammunition, fired by tanks, as opposed to HE, or high explosive ammunition.

biergarten A bar.

blitzkrieg "Lightning war," a German-developed technique for rapid offensive warfare using armored forces with air support; first used against Poland in 1939.

bocage Thick foliage or woodland, often used to describe the Normandy countryside before the breakout in August 1944.

CCA (CCB) A U.S. armored division's primary aggressive forces were organized into combat commands. They were normally called Combat Command A (CCA) and Combat Command B (CCB). There was also a Combat Command Reserve (CCR), not addressed in this book. (For more detail, see the Appendix, Nineteenth Armored Division.)

CP Command post.

Desert Fox Famous nickname for Field Marshal Erwin Rommel, earned in Germany's North Africa campaign.

dog robber Slang term for a personal aide (to a high-ranking official) who is responsible for obtaining scarce supplies, from steaks to nylons, by "robbing dogs," if necessary.

feldgrau Field gray, the standard color for the German army, much as olive drab is for the U.S. military.

feldmarschall German military rank of field marshal.

feldwebel German military rank, equivalent to U.S. sergeant.

fingerspitzengefühl An intuition in one's fingers; a kind of sixth sense. Often used to describe Rommel's ability to carry out plans and operations that others would never have thought of in the first place.

Focke-Wulf Fw-190 A German military fighter.

gasthaus Literally "guest house," or inn, normally with a restaurant or bar as well as some guest rooms.

Gauleiters The regional Nazi Party boss in each Gau (the main territorial unit of the Nazi Party; there were forty-two Gaue in all), responsible for all political and economic activity, as well as for the mobilization of labor and civil defense. There was constant tension between the Gauleiters and the central government and Nazi establishment, usually resolved by Hitler in favor of the Gauleiters.

Geschwader A fighter air squadron consisting of three fighter Gruppe, each of three Staffeln, or approximately eighty aircraft total. Commanded by a kommodore.

Gestapo *Geheime Staatspolizei,* or State Secret Police. Originally created in 1933 under Hermann Göring, the Gestapo was slowly integrated into the SS and gained wider responsibility for criminal police and spy work. The Gestapo's Section IV B4, headed by Adolf Eichmann, organized the "final solution of the Jewish question."

Gruppe A fighter air group consisting of three fighter Staffeln, or approximately twenty-six aircraft total.

hauptmann German military rank, equivalent to a U.S. Army captain.

Hitlerjugend The Hitler Youth was a perverse Nazi equivalent to the Boy Scouts, offering Scouting-type activities combined with military training and political indoctrination. Most German males were members during the Nazi years, up until the war's end. In 1935, Rommel, then an instructor at the War Academy, was attached to the Hitlerjugend for the purpose of improving their discipline but had a falling-out with the head of the organization, Baldur von Schirach, because he felt von Schirach was focusing too much on sports and military training and not enough on education and character development. As a result, Rommel was removed from his position shortly thereafter.

Jabo German military slang for single-engine fighters (Mustangs, Hurricanes, Thunderbolts, Typhoons, Spitfires, and the like) used by the Americans and British in ground-attack missions.

Jagdgruppe A German fighter squadron.

Kettenkraftgrad A small Luftwaffe tractor used to tow aircraft.

Kriegsmarine The German navy, commanded by Admiral Karl Doenitz.

leutnant German military rank, equivalent to a U.S. lieutenant.

Luftwaffe The German air force, built up and commanded by Hermann Göring, with General Adolf Galland as commander of the Fighter Arm.

Messerschmidt Me-109 A German military fighter.

Messerschmidt Me-262 Schwalbe/Sturmvogel This high-performance jet fighter was more than one hundred miles per hour faster than the fastest Allied fighter but was held back from full production by Hitler's thirst for vengeance on the RAF rather than to fight on the Continent. Hitler did not finally approve mass production until January 1945. The military value of this aircraft might have been substantial. Of 1,433 Me-262s built, only about 200 were allowed into action, but in March 1945, six of them shot down fourteen B-17s in a single fight. The fighter version was known as the *Schwalbe,* or Swallow, the proposed bomber version was known as the *Sturmvogel,* or Stormbird.

Night of the Long Knives A program of executions and liquidations carried out against the left-wing socialist elements of the Nazi Brownshirts, or *Sturmabteilung* (SA) in June 1934. This temporarily reassured the German middle class about Nazi "extremism" and also consolidated Hitler's control over the party and Germany itself.

oberst German military rank, equivalent to a U.S. colonel.

OKW *Oberkommando der Wehrmacht,* the high command of the German armed forces.

Operation Valkyrie The July 20, 1944, bomb plot to kill Adolf Hitler and the coup plans that were to have followed, involving the neutralization of all SS and Gestapo installations within the Third Reich, and the takeover of all communications facilities, particularly public radio stations.

Panzer A German tank.

panzerarmee A full German tank army.

panzerfaust An antitank weapon similar to the American bazooka, with less range but able to be operated by a single soldier. It was a simpler weapon, launching a bigger bomb with greater penetrating power.

panzergrenadiers Infantrymen who worked in close concert with German tanks.

rathskeller A bar.

Reichsaußenminister The Reich foreign minister. Reichsminister is simply Reich minister, or head of any state ministry, such as Finance or SS. *Außen* means "outside," as opposed to, say, the Minister of the Interior. The ß, or "ess-zet," is a combination of "s" and "z." It is pronounced as "ss" and is often spelled that way in English transliteration of German (außen=aussen). Similarly, an "umlaut" vowel (ä, ë, ï, ö, ü) is spelled with an extra "e" (Göring=Goering).

Replacement Army A reserve force of walking wounded, trainees, military school cadets, workers who could be taken from their jobs, and soldiers on sick leave. It was commanded by General Friedrich Fromm, who was a fence sitter with regard to the coup. Stauffenberg was the chief of staff to Fromm.

scheiss German expletive "shit."

schnell German for "quickly."

schwalbe See Messerschmidt Me-262.

Schwerpunkt The "decisive point," a strategic concept identified by military theorist Carl von Clausewitz.

SHAEF Supreme Headquarters Allied Expeditionary Force, the coordinated United States/British military command headed by General Dwight D. Eisenhower.

SNAFU Officially an acronym for "Situation Normal: All Fouled Up," but another "F" word was more commonly used.

Special Transports The transportation of Jews and others to the death camps as part of the "final solution."

SS The *Schutzstaffel* was the elite striking arm of the Nazi Party, a virtually separate armed force with wide-ranging and independent authority, from protection of Nazi leaders, antisubversion activities, political enforcement, certain military operations, and the administration of "race and population resettlement," which included the concentration and death camps. SS troops had their own uniform and their own ranks. Heinrich Himmler was the *Reichsführer SS,* reporting only to Hitler, and a man of enormous power and evil.

staffel A fighter group of approximately eight aircraft.

sturmvogel See Messerschmidt Me-262.

Tommies Slang term for the British.

universitat German university.

Vengeance Weapons The *Vergeltung* ("Reprisal") weapons, popularly known as the V-1 and V-2 flying bombs, were developed by Dr. Werner von Braun's engineering team at the Peenemünde plants. The V-1 offensive against London began six days after the Normandy invasion, followed by the V-2 in September. Eisenhower later observed that if the Germans had been able to use the V-1 and V-2 against the Allied landing points, they would have posed a formidable obstacle. The rockets were also used extensively against the port of Antwerp, both before and during the historical Battle of the Bulge, but were not successful in disrupting the Antwerp docks or the landing of Allied troops.

volksgrenadier The "people's soldiers," units of the Replacement Army (*q.v.*).

volkssturm The "people's attack," or *volkssturm,* involved the mobilization of every German between the ages of sixteen and sixty capable of bearing arms to defend the Fatherland "with all available means."

Waffen SS The military arm of the SS grew to parallel the regular army, with its own panzer units; it actually outnumbered the regular army in some military districts. At its height, there were thirty-eight SS divisions with nine hundred thousand men.

Wehrmacht The German military establishment.

Weimar Republic The German government between the fall of the kaiser at the end of World War I and the takeover of the Nazi Party in 1933. Best known for high inflation and social decadence, as illustrated in the movie *Cabaret,* based on the stories of Christopher Isherwood.

Westwall A line of German fortifications along the France-Germany border. Incomplete at the time of the Normandy invasion, the fortifications were built up quickly to create a barrier between the advancing Allies and the German homeland.

Wolfschanze "Wolf's Lair," Hitler's command headquarters for the eastern front. It was located in East Prussia, far from any city, surrounded by woods, heavily guarded, and accessible by only a single road.

APPENDIXES

The Plot to Kill Hitler

There were several plots to assassinate Adolf Hitler. The final and best known of these was the Bomb Plot.

On July 20, 1944, German conspirators led by Colonel Count Claus Schenk von Stauffenberg carried out what became known as the Bomb Plot against Adolf Hitler. Stauffenberg carried a briefcase containing a bomb into Hitler's conference room at Wolfschanze, Hitler's field headquarters. He placed the briefcase on the floor under a massive oak table as close to Hitler as he could get it, then left "to make an urgent call to Berlin."

Lieutenant General Heusinger was briefing Hitler on the situation on the eastern front. Colonel Brandt, Heusinger's aide, moved to the table into the spot where Stauffenberg had stood, where his foot brushed against the briefcase. He tried to move the briefcase with his foot, but it fell over on its side. So he reached down and moved the case to the other side of a thick concrete support holding up the table, away from Hitler.

At 12:42 P.M. the bomb exploded. Although several people, including Colonel Brandt, lost their lives in the explosion, Hitler received only superficial wounds.

Believing that Hitler was dead, the conspirators attempted a military coup in Germany, but their own indecision as well as the later information that Hitler had survived, doomed the plot. The Gestapo took a bloody revenge against everyone who was even remotely suspected of being in the plot. Between six hundred and one thousand Germans lost their lives, many under the cruelest tortures.

The name of Field Marshal Erwin Rommel, the Desert Fox, who had been gravely wounded on July 17 when his staff car was machine gunned on a Normandy road by an Allied fighter plane, appeared on a conspirator's list as a candidate to be president of the Reich. Other conspirators, under torture, denounced Rommel. Rommel denied these charges, and there is no evidence that Rommel was directly implicated in the Bomb Plot. It is possible he was aware of some portions of the conspiracy, but that is far from certain.

Because of Rommel's military and popular reputation, he was not arrested immediately but was offered instead the chance to commit suicide to avoid arrest. On October 14, 1944, Rommel took poison and died instantly. He was given a state funeral. He never returned to command the German forces on the western front.

All because a foot bumped a briefcase. . . .

On Alternate History

Isaac Asimov, in his seminal time travel novel *The End of Eternity*, articulated the key principle that should govern "alternate history" or "what-if" novels such as this: the concept of the "minimum necessary change" (MNC) that produces the "maximum desired result" (MDR). From seemingly trivial incidents can great transformations occur, as shown in stories from Ward Moore's classic *Bring the Jubilee* to the recent Gwyneth Paltrow movie *Sliding Doors.*

The Bomb Plot against Adolf Hitler on July 20, 1944, really happened as described in this book up until the moment when Colonel Brandt attempts to move the bomb-containing briefcase under the table. In reality, Brandt slid the briefcase farther under the table and behind a concrete stanchion, a barrier heavy enough that the blast failed to kill Hitler. Our MNC (minimum necessary change) was to have Brandt stifle a sneeze at that moment, and therefore not to move the fateful briefcase. This results in the successful assassination of Hitler, the MDR (maximum desired result) that drives the rest of this story.

The bomb plotters, in spite of their undoubted heroism and idealism, were evidently the original "gang that couldn't shoot straight." It's highly unlikely their intended coup would have succeeded even if the bomb plot had come off as originally planned.

There is no evidence for Himmler's countercoup described in the book as Operation Reichsturm, but we believe it not to be inconsistent with his character, especially considering Göring's weakness as a potential führer. Likewise, the idea that Himmler concludes a separate peace with Stalin is our invention, but it seemed to us to be a logical move, one of the few ways to give Nazi Germany any chance whatsoever, even a slim one, and also the only way to bring real suspense to the final moments of our alternate World War II in Europe.

Our real historical figures are described accurately to the extent possible; their actions and words in the post-assassination story are of necessity invented but are to the best of our abilities faithful to the personalities involved.

The Nineteenth Armored Division

The U.S. Nineteenth Armored Division is an imaginary unit, but it is structured and manned as if it were a real division, and placed into the existing Allied military structure. It was not unusual for a division to be moved from

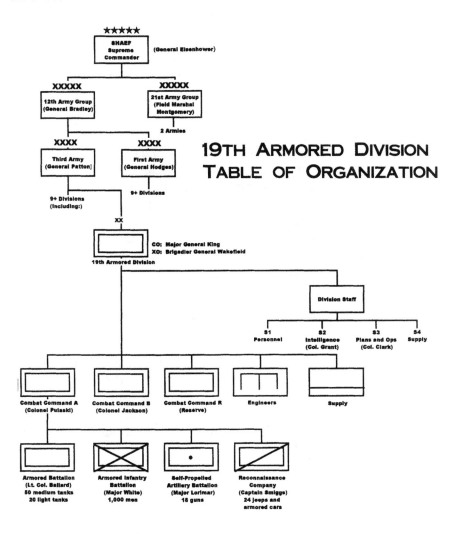

19TH ARMORED DIVISION
TABLE OF ORGANIZATION

control of one army to another, as happens to the Nineteenth in this book. Manning and equipment levels described in the text represent initial levels.

It should be noted that the corps level of command, existing between division and army headquarters, exerted a great deal of operational influence in U.S. Army operations during WWII. For the sake of our story and characters we have for the most part ignored this level of military organization. For the same reason the third combat command of a typical U.S. armored division (Combat Command R, or reserve) has been omitted from our tale.

Consolidated/Ford B-24H *Ford's Folly*

While less well known in the popular imagination than the Boeing B-17 Flying Fortress, the Consolidated B-24 Liberator was a powerful heavy bomber that was critical to the Allied strategic bombing efforts in World War II. The B-24H cruised at 290 miles per hour, with a 2,100-mile range carrying 5,000 pounds of bombs.

To maximize production of the aircraft, it was built not only by Consolidated Aircraft, but by Ford Motor Company as well, in their Willow Run plant.

There was a real airplane named *Ford's Folly.* It was the first B-24H put into service from Ford's Willow Run plant, served in the 392nd Bomb Group, 578th Squadron, 8th Air Force, and was flown on its final mission by "Rudd's Ruffians," Odell F. Dobson (coauthor Michael Dobson's father) serving as waist gunner. At the time it was shot down near Koblenz on September 11, 1944, it had flown seventy-nine missions—more than any other American bomber in the European theater. Only two members of the crew survived: Dobson and Roger Clapp, the radio operator; they completed the final months of World War II at Stalag Luft IV and, later, on a forced march through much of what is now Poland. The amazing true story is told in Bruce Lewis's *Four Men Went to War,* published by Leo G. Cooper in the United Kingdom and by St. Martin's Press in the United States. We also drew on original source material, consisting not only of Odell Dobson's oral history tapes but also of eyewitness accounts from Don Scharf and Bob Tuchel (who were in the plane directly behind *Ford's Folly* when it was shot down) for real information on the final moments of a doomed airplane.

Messerschmitt Me-262 Jet Fighter

The Messerschmitt Me-262 was an amazing technological achievement. The world's first operational turbojet fighter, the most technologically advanced fighter interceptor of the war—the superlatives go on for this amazing airplane.

In spite of its technological prowess, the Me-262 had little impact on the conduct of the war. First, and possibly most telling, Adolf Hitler wanted the plane developed as a "blitz bomber" rather than as a fighter interceptor. Second, the perennial fuel shortages made it nearly impossible to build and fly the airplane in quantity. Although more than 1,400 Me-262s were manufactured, no more than 300 ever saw combat, and according to General Adolf Galland himself, no more than 50 or 60 were ever operational at the same time.

It was Galland's opinion that if the Me-262 had become operational even eighteen months earlier, the course of the air war in Europe would have changed. He writes, "I am of the opinion that with only three hundred Messerschmitt Me-262 jet fighters we could have on any day shot down a minimum of two hundred bombers. If this would have continued for a week or two, then the day bombing would have had to be stopped."

ACKNOWLEDGMENTS

Success has many fathers, and failure is an orphan. In this book, those elements that are successful have many fathers, and any failures or mistakes are the sole responsibility of the authors.

Many people provided advice, counsel, support, and hard work on our behalf in the creation of this book. First, we thank our editor, Brian Thomsen, for his tireless work and advocacy in getting this manuscript accepted as well as whipped into shape, and our agent, Elizabeth Pomada, not only for business support but for advice and counsel in every aspect of the project. Jim Mintz, Tor's project editor for this book, provided exemplary leadership. Copyeditor Juli Barbato's eagle eye was invaluable.

Special thanks to Barbara K. Dobson for her work in drawing together all the information about the real *Ford's Folly* and for transcribing Odell Dobson's wartime oral history tapes. Patrick Dobson, Donald Niles Sr., Don Perrin, and Kevin Rose provided extensive technical support on the details of military operations. The amazing Frank Chadwick sent us a very detailed critique of the book and caught many of our technical errors; those that remain are through no fault of his. Edward R. Smith created the background and original character of Reid Sanger for an unpublished juvenile novel. Allison Niles prepared the maps.

Many readers, advisers, and helpers critiqued and supported us in so many ways, from technical advice to literary criticism, from research support to advocacy, from key information to material loans, including (in alphabetical order): Rosemary Althoff, John Ardington, Fred Baxter, Walter J. Boyne, Tim Brown, Charles Clancy, Troy Denning, Odell F. Dobson, Samuel Freeman, Scott Gemberling, Rosina Harter, Mickey Johnson, Hal King, Rob King, Michael Larsen, Chuck Leffler, Brian Librandi, Walter Mason, Joel Mumma, Warren Phinney, Charlotte Porter, Janet Rasmussen, Jim Runtz, Mary Seghers, Patrick Seghers, Jim Singer, Phyllis Singer, Lester Smith, Robert Van Der Linden, and Steve Winter. If we've forgotten anyone, we most sincerely apologize.

Our manuscript reviewers were drawn from numerous sources, including our "Fox on the Rhine" seminar at the 1998 GENCON® Game Fair; the Alliterates literary society (http:\\www.alliterates.com—of which Doug Niles is by far the most handsome member; members of Usenet discussion groups on alternate history and World War II; as well as friends, colleagues, and coworkers who volunteered their time, help, and moral support.

And, of course, we thank our families, especially our wives, Christine Niles and Deborah Dobson, for their patience, love, and support throughout this project.

Visit Michael's website at http:\\www.dobsonbooks.com for additional information, bibliographic citations, comments, game scenarios for Douglas Niles's SPI/TSR boardgames ONSLAUGHT: D-DAY TO THE RHINE™ and WORLD WAR II: EUROPEAN THEATER OF OPERATIONS™, as well as the original transcribed oral history of Odell Dobson's last flight aboard *Ford's Folly* and subsequent experiences in a German POW camp.

—Douglas Niles and Michael Dobson, July 1999